THE MIRROR GAME

C A S S I D Y   C L A R K E

Website : cassidyclarkewriting.com
Cover Designed by : HILLARY BARDIN (@reebardin)
ISBN: 9781957993065
First Edition: December 2025

10 9 8 7 6 5 4 3 2 1

~Dedication~

To the girl who thought she'd never be able to write something she loved this much again.

This one is for me.

Content Warnings

THE MIRROR GAME includes content that may be triggering to some
readers, including:

Death

Amnesia

Blood/Gore/Body horror

Religious terminology/rituals

Grief

Possession

Illness

Food descriptions

Mild language

Violence

Misogyny

Physical and emotional abuse

Hallucinations

Manipulation

Drowning

Panic attacks

Harm and death of animals

Light spice (fade-to-black only)

Please read safely.

PROLOGUE

TEMPEST

There were sharks in these waters.

And, to his amusement, it seemed he'd been cast in the role of chum today.

Tempest, God of Nature, lowered his head to sip at his drink as they circled him, one after the other—fishers by trade and by stench, two men and a woman, rugged and seething and sore in the mind.

He did not need to see them. He need only gaze down at the tavern's seaglass-tiled bar counter and let voiceless whispers interrupt his intention to bore himself through his final night on the road.

He had chosen this tavern, so small it barely counted as more than a merchant's stand, for two reasons:

Firstly, it was cheap, which meant more drink for less coin. And less coin was certainly what he needed, seeing as the former resident of his body hadn't had much left by the time Tempest came into possession of it.

Secondly, its windows were propped open, inviting the elements in to visit.

He and the elements happened to be quite friendly.

The wind warned him of the fishers forming a triumvirate around him, each a point of a triangle meant to prevent him from running. As they shifted into position, floorboards creaking and chatter quieting, he picked up his mead and finished it off with a toss of his head.

He was not Cassi. He would need every bit of its honeyed flavor to sweeten his tongue if he intended to get out of this confrontation smoothly.

If.

"You need to leave," said the fisherman closest to him—his breath smelled of honey, too, but none of it carried into his words.

Tempest frowned down at his tankard.

This wasn't going to go prettily.

"Have I done something to cause trouble?" he asked, leaning forward a bit, running his fingers over chips in some of the seaglass. The turquoise bits had always been his favorite—they were rarer, more beautiful, a hint of green and blue twined to create something new.

This host used to have sea glass in his eyes. Which would have been helpful, he was sure, had he allowed himself to disguise the proof of his godhood.

It would have helped him blend in better. It would have probably stopped him from getting ousted from every town he'd stopped in, often before he even had the chance to lay his head down for an hour or two.

But he'd had enough of illusions. If honesty ruined his welcome, so be it.

"We know what those eyes mean," rasped the woman to his right. "Word has spread across the kingdom. Those with golden eyes are not to find safe harbor here."

"You're not welcome here, Ship-Breaker," said the man directly behind him—his cigar-laced breath hit Tempest's neck before curling up to his ear, tattling on the lungs that bore it, mocking the fear that roiled beneath the man's robust form.

Ship-Breaker.

How quickly they forgot his other titles.

He raised his hand, signaling the bartender, who hovered at the other end of the bar. Caution hung heavy on the man's withered, weather-beaten face, but the wind had whispered of his bravery when Tempest first walked in—a long service in Atlas's navy, a stint spent in their crew of shipwreck trackers…and a coin bearing Tempest's crest buried in his shirt pocket.

"A shot," he said.

"What sort?" asked the bartender.

A rumbling emotion he couldn't quite name—or maybe didn't want to—hooked his mouth into a smirk. "Dealer's choice."

A favorite game of his middle sister's.

"Are you daft?" hissed the man to his left. "We told you to leave!"

He cocked a brow at the fisherman. "Do you own this tavern?"

"He might as well, how much drink he buys," muttered a man at one of the two long tables behind Tempest—the wind giggled as the man's wife smacked him in the arm, hissing a warning not to get involved.

The fisherman leaned in, his burly dark beard clumped with seawater tangles and bits of flung fish guts he hadn't quite managed to comb out after cleaning his catch. "As my friend said," he growled, Atlas accent thick and slow and salted with a drawl, "you're not welcome here, Ship-Breaker. Take your liquor and get out of our town."

Gladly. Though he mourned the lost chance to have a night of sleep on a real bed.

The bartender set the shot glass in front of him before retreating back to his place of safety, pretending to polish glasses at the end of the counter. The liquid in the glass sloshed a bit as he set it down, a droplet or two spilling over the lip and landing on the seaglass, brightening its color.

He swiped his finger over the droplet…and satisfaction rumbled deep inside, a thundercloud purring in anticipation of the coming storm.

He plucked the glass up from the counter, dangling it between his thumb and forefinger, giving it an experimental sniff just to be sure.

Salt and rain and the feral, keening cry to be freed.

Seawater.

"Ship-Breaker," he mused softly, teasing the lip of the glass with his tongue. "Do you know my other names, friend?"

If the fisherman gave an answer, Tempest did not hear it. As his tongue tasted the ocean, his blood churned like a storm-tossed sea, cold thrill chasing the last bit of heat from his body.

Ship-Breaker. Storm-Wielder. Ice-Spitter.

Sea-Singer.

"It's all right," he said when the fisherman didn't speak. "You'll learn them."

Sailors of unsavory ilk always did, right before Nature swallowed them whole.

He placed the glass to his lips. Met the bartender's gaze—a silent apology.

He tossed it back, brine washing away the honey.

The tavern blew apart behind him.

Wind sang in harmony with the fishers' screams as it tore the tavern apart board by board, sending the patrons—and the tables—scattering in every direction.

A wave, sourceless and alive and *hungry,* swept in beneath the doorframe, through the open windows, through every crack and cranny of this half-wrecked shell. It surged forward as the fishers staggered away from Tempest, shouting, desperately trying to keep their footing in what had suddenly become storm-tossed waters.

The wave crested upward—paused, as if looking at him, as if waiting.

So there were sharks in the water. That was all right.

He was not the chum.

He was the rotting *water.*

With a tip of his head, tired, temper-torn, he signed away his right to mercy.

The wave consumed his hecklers in one fell swoop. And when it washed them away, still screaming, Tempest set the shot glass back on the bar counter with a heavy sigh.

"Another, please," he said. "For the road."

He was waging a war against sea-beasts of a different caliber. His siblings were another kind of monster with another kind of teeth, and he could not tame them with a wave and a breeze and half a thought.

He didn't have the energy to waste on misguided guppies in this particular pond.

The bartender did as he was asked, his hand steady as sea legs. Tempest took his shot, then took his leave, not sparing a glance back at the sundered tavern...nor at the paltry pouch of gold he abandoned on the soaked bartop. All the coin he had left to pay for the damage he'd caused.

He wouldn't be needing it where he was going.

CHAPTER 1

FINN

Madness carved the facets of the world into fractals.

Every groove in his glazed wooden armrest. Every fleck of glitter winking at the edges of his eyelashes. Even the fibers buried in the violet sleeve of his stiff, well-tailored jacket had edges sharp enough to cut.

Scraps of eternity hidden in plain sight. Mind-boggling. Mind-breaking.

But his mind had already been broken—broken and built back better.

Finnick Atlas, Trickster God, sipped blithely at his wine as he watched Tenebrae hold court in the Atlas throne room.

Of course, to the false queen who thankfully ruled outside the ironclad gates of his skull, Finnick Atlas was long dead. In his place ruled Occassio,

Goddess of Time, second-in-command to the Chaos God who sat on his mother's throne.

Rage crested and fell just as quickly, cooled with a long draw of his wine and a reminder to himself to look bored.

Long game, long game. The longest game he'd ever played.

That was all right. A victory on this scale could not be rushed.

He'd learned that lesson the first time he'd tested his mettle against deities. And he made it a point to never need a second warning.

So he sat in the plush, padded throne that ordinarily belonged to his father, one ankle propped on his knee and his head held at a haughty angle, glitter-glazed eyes taking in the trembling man kneeling at the foot of the dais. The once-gleaming golden floors, embellished with etchings of artful celestial bodies curling in patterns around a giant sunburst in the center, were dull and grimy beneath the man's knees…mostly because of the dried blood. Tenebrae didn't seem too anxious to scrub away the evidence of the fate that befell most people who crossed the threshold of the grand doors.

"Please," the man was begging, as so many before him had begged. "My family and I, we don't want any trouble, we don't mean any harm. My infant daughter, she's ill, and every healer left in the city has told us we need to take her to Arborius for any hope of a cure. If you could just give us special permission to—"

"Neither entry to nor exit from Port Atlas is permitted." Tenebrae's voice, *Jericho's* voice, rang deceivingly sympathetic—the way these meetings always began. Starting with sweetness and sorrow…ending with blood and exposed bone. "Surely you've heard."

The man's eyes hollowed out in desolate plea. "We have. But she'll *die*."

"Yes, so we assumed," Finn drawled, swirling his wine and offering the man the pretty little pout he was so used to Occassio leveraging against him. "But this is not a sanction put in place idly. The war threatening to break past our borders intensifies. Artem has joined the Nyxian cause, and rumors suggest Lapis and Tallis could be considering the same. Crossing into any other kingdom is far too dangerous."

This was their little game, Occassio and Tenebrae's—Tenebrae playing the part of a grief-stricken new Queen inexperienced with war, Finn playing the part of Occassio playing the part of a power-hungry prince rumored to have killed his brother and sister to ascend to his current rank as Heir.

Thanks to his well-oiled gossip mill, the Chaos-cloistered Atlas people knew him now as the assassin of their beloved First Prince and their lost-and-found Heir. Tenebrae's idea—he hadn't wanted the people getting any ideas of rebellion in their heads, and if they knew there were spare royals wandering the other kingdoms…well. Hope could find root in even the most sparing of soil.

For many who lived in the lower levels of Port Atlas, they wouldn't have had to suspend much disbelief. The lie of his ambition matched the truth of his power well enough that most of his contacts wouldn't have been surprised to hear he'd finally snapped.

Queen Adriata and King Ramses, dead by the hands of Nyxian assassins. First Prince Kallias and Princess Soleil's blood drenched his own hands. And Prince-Consort Vaughn had finally succumbed to his wasting sickness, his funeral held privately to allow his newly crowned widow to grieve in peace.

A well-pruned garden of vehement, violent lies. One he'd been tasked to maintain with *great* prejudice.

No weeds; no whispers of the truth.

That his parents were alive, sequestered in the driest portion of their drowning dungeon. That Nyx had neither assassins nor alliances left to their name after Tenebrae's brutal assault on their capital and queen.

That Soren—as she now preferred to be called—and Elias, if all had gone well on their voyage, should be arriving on Arborian shores any day now. That Kallias's fate had been guided by his own hand, not Finn's, and Vaughn…

There had been neither glimpse nor gossip of his brother-in-law yet, dead or alive. He had yet to decide whether that was a disappointment or a relief.

The man ignored him, pleading with Tenebrae. "Princess—"

"Queen." The correction from Tenebrae fell like a snowflake—cotton-soft, but composed of bone-chilling cold.

The man paled. Finn could see the bob of his throat even from the top of the dais. "Please," he whispered, but hopelessness had already left its mark. If the man pushed further, his blood would join the sanguine splash of nauseating color on the floor.

"As the Queen said, the answer is no." Finn stood swiftly, gesturing to the doors at the back; one of the guards broke from her post and approached the dais, bruise-blue braid swinging with metronomic precision. "Officer Angelov, if you'd please escort this man out."

Raquel Angelov bowed her head in silent acknowledgement, her complete lack of expression sending spidery discomfort crawling across his back. Even if it was an act—one he'd directed himself—it still struck him all kinds of wrong, seeing the passionate Nyxian warrior reduced to a blank-faced effigy of broken will.

Another casualty credited to him.

Tenebrae believed Occassio had cracked open Raquel's memories to withdraw information about Tempest, Anima, Elias, Vaughn, and Soren—then had warped them, rearranging her very personhood until she became pliable as wet clay on a potter's wheel. A different breed of madness than the one that had taken him; one that scared him far more.

There had been talk of killing her anyway. But he'd managed to tip Tenebrae in favor of keeping her in their service, ready to become either bait or a bargaining chip depending on what the situation called for.

So they'd fooled everyone into thinking. And as long as Raquel was good enough not to get herself caught, that ruse would continue until the proper time came to move forward.

In the meantime, Raquel would find a way to smuggle this man and his family out of Atlas. So long as he—

"You *witch*," spat the father, still on his knees, hanging his whole weight over to keep Raquel from pulling him to his feet. Spittle sparkled in the lights of the ballroom as it flew from his lips and landed on the rusty glaze across the floor, turning dried brown to damp scarlet. "You're sentencing a child to death for what? Your own cowardice?"

Ah, fool. Finn drowned a wince, a groan, in his next gulp of chilled wine, wishing the musty notes of citrus and grapefruit could truly blunt the edges of what would come next.

He'd never been fond of the stuff, but Occassio was, so her preference was now his performance. It didn't matter, anyway. His mind stayed clear no matter how many drinks he had, no matter what was in the pipes he smoked, no matter how desperately he wished he could drown out the horrors he witnessed residing over the Chaos God's court.

With that insult, the man had sealed his own fate, snatching it right back out of Finn's hands.

It was over before Raquel even removed her hand from the man's shoulder; the blood that spurted from his severed neck spattered her knuckles like rings of ruby. The corrupted vine that had neatly garroted the man's head from his shoulders writhed and roiled as it retracted to the base of Tenebrae's throne, slurping the blood into its stalk like water.

"Clean that up," said Jericho's voice from Tenebrae's lips, bored cruelty curling the mouth that used to read him bedtime stories in silly voices and sing him songs when Adriata was too busy to offer a lullaby. "And make sure his family understands that any further defiance will be met with the same punishment."

Raquel's lashes hardly fluttered as she bowed, a testament to the strength of her stomach, the steel that bore up her spine. "Yes, Majesty."

Finn looked away, the wine souring in his stomach, a taste like iron in his mouth. A taste like the blood that still hadn't realized its job was done, pumping out of the man's body in great, frantic gushes as if it might still save him—as if it could reach across the gap from neck to head and pull the whole body back together.

Long game, long game. Small losses won bigger battles.

So he finished his wine while lounging in his throne, watching them drag the body away and take a mop to the layers of lifeblood on the floor.

Small losses. Bigger battles.

It didn't make the sting of defeat any easier to bear.

CHAPTER 2

RAQUEL

While Raquel Angelov had occasionally imagined herself trapped inside an Atlas dungeon, she'd never imagined that it would be by choice…or that she would be walking the cells as warden, not prisoner.

And even that wasn't the strangest part of all this. No, the strangest part was that she now held the fate of her kingdom's greatest enemy in her bloodied hands…and chose every day to keep her alive.

She could hardly remember a time when she hadn't hungered for Adriata Atlas's death. The only demise she'd craved more had been that of Adriata's son…First Prince Kallias Atlas, the murderer of Raquel's sister.

The forget-me-not bracelet brushed against her wrist as she reached down to fiddle with the keyring on her belt, and she squeezed her eyes shut, trying to drown out the image of that prince the last time she'd seen him.

Golden-eyed. Short-haired. The wind wrapped around him like a shield, like armor.

"I said I would give you the chance to claim your debt. You did not take it."

Somehow, by refusing to take the death that was hers by blood-right, by war-right, she had sentenced him to a worse fate: a quiet, unseen death. A last word unheard, a last breath unwitnessed.

He had died all alone.

No. She dug her nails into that thought and tore it apart strip by strip, letting it fall to her feet in ribbons of refusal. He was not dead. Soren was not dead, Finn was not dead. Kallias would not be dead either.

She would accept nothing less than his whole and entire survival.

She left the tatters of fear behind her, wishing they didn't trail on her heels as she made her rounds through the dungeon. Just as when she and Finn had first arrived in the city, all but one cell was empty; Tenebrae's rule did not make use of prisoners. Dissenters were made either examples or unwilling recruits.

All but two.

The cell at the far end of the block was the only one occupied, the only one not strung with spiderwebs and dusted with mold. The taste of salt-infused mildew reached in and dragged chipped, earthy nails up the column of her throat as she drew in her usual bracing breath before stopping in front of this cell—in front of the pair of prisoners within, who looked up at her with utterly opposite eyes.

King Ramses, with a calm gaze and a thin smile; Queen Adriata, with burning irises and cracked lips that bent into a sneer.

In these royals, she saw each of their sons…and their youngest daughter. Finn gleamed in the King's composed expression, the diplomatic mask that covered a cunning mind; Kallias's smile was an exact portrait of his father's. And Adriata's glowering countenance was inch-for-inch as intimidating and riled as Soren's in her most feral moments.

Raquel did not bow; she never did. That wasn't part of the role Finn had cast her in, and she wouldn't have bent before this queen even if it was. But she nodded, at least. "Your Majesties."

"Officer Angelov." Ramses pulled himself to his feet, the hitch in his movement catching her concern—from what she understood, he'd taken a bad blow attempting to fight his way out of the palace beside his wife. His clothes were ragged and bloodied, silk torn to scarlet strips over his ribcage, and behind his bent-framed glasses, he wore two black eyes. "What do you bring from the throne today? Threats? Reminders of our place?"

"Food." She held up the sack in her hand. "And some truth, if you'll hear it."

They'd bided their time, Finn insisting that they wait to make sure nothing had been done to tamper with his parents' minds during the brief time Occassio held his body as her own. But it had been weeks now, and her repeated visits to this cell had always reaped the same results. None of the marks Finn had told her to watch for had made themselves known.

"We will hear no truth from you," spat Adriata. "Not from a Nyxian mouth, nor from the mouth of one serving whatever *thing* has taken over my daughter—"

"And what if it came from your son?"

Finn's voice injected cold adrenaline into her veins, but her slight startle was nothing compared to the reaction from Adriata, from Ramses; the King sagged, eyes widening in horror as his son parted the shadows, eyes glowing gold behind his glasses. His eyelids were painted with purple shimmer and lined in plum-tinted kohl, a smoky accentuation of his gilded irises.

While the King only stared, the Queen was quicker, angrier—she surged up and slammed her hands against the bars like she might break right through them, the rage she'd directed toward Raquel tripling in strength as her gaze devoured her youngest son's godly countenance.

"You," she spat. "Whatever you are, whoever you are, you are *not* my son, I know what those eyes mean, I *know*—"

"Adriata, stop." Ramses put out a shaking hand to catch her blows, his gaze riveted on Finn, his mouth taut and trembling. "Finnick? Talk to me, boy."

Finn's chin quivered—only for a moment, and it stilled so quickly she might have imagined it. "It's me, Papa. I know what it looks like, but it's me."

"Prove it," hissed Adriata. Hanks of sweat-and-dirt-clumped hair swung into her face, her skirt was torn diagonally from left hip to right ankle, and every inch of her was painted in bruise and betrayal, but still she held her spine straight as a lightning rod, ready to take whatever the storm threw at her.

It was…hard, not to admire that. Hard to behold the strength of queens without marveling.

Kallias carried that same strength, that same might in the face of something that should have humbled him. It drove her to distraction.

Had. It *had* driven her to distraction. And now it drove her to rage.

"I can't prove it, Mama," Finn admitted. "Not in any way these gods couldn't imitate. And honestly, I'd prefer you spit in my face rather than fall for one of Tenebrae's tricks, so if you don't believe me…that's all right. Don't believe me. Just listen."

"We're listening," Ramses said, gazing intently at his son. "Tell us everything."

Raquel turned away, keeping her back to the cell as Finn approached it, her eyes trained on the staircase and her fingers hovering near his wrist in case she needed to warn him of approaching intruders. No one besides her usually came down here, but they couldn't rule out a surprise visit from Tenebrae.

The god thrived on chaos. If he wasn't getting his fill upstairs, he might just descend to siphon it from Adriata's near-manic rage.

Or Raquel's.

She hated the queen in that cage more than she hated anyone—at least, anyone mortal enough to succumb to her blade. But every time that hatred tried to stir the storm in her chest into a frenzy, she clamped her fingers down over her bracelet and breathed.

And breathed.

And breathed.

For Kallias, she would put that anger to bed. It would see its day, but not until this was over.

So she listened as Finn told them the story of Soren sacrificing herself to Anima to save her battlemate's life. The story of Occassio coming to him in the guise of a harmless Lapisian Mirror, stringing him along until it was too late for him to turn back. The story of Skyhaven and the relic and the whipping. The story of sailing to Sirena on the *Starsinger*.

The story of Kallias surrendering himself to Tempest against all their pleas and all his promises. The story of salt-crusted letters bound up in spare twine.

The crinkle of paper broke the stunned, grieving silence between them all—perhaps the one commonality that connected them to each other. It drew Raquel's gaze back to the cell against her better judgement.

"This is for you, Mama," said Finn. "Kallias wrote it before…before."

The tips of the Queen's fingers did not tremble as she reached out and took the folded letter, but her lower lip did, the faintest quiver of emotion as her eyes swept across Kallias's handwriting on the front—a delicate, clipped address simply to *Mama*.

Raquel turned away again as the Queen unfolded the paper.

She had seen throats torn open, bones broken, and heads severed in the throne room above, and had not once turned her head from it. But she could not watch yet another of Kallias's goodbyes; could not see the echoes of his tears in the salt and sand that flaked from the paper. Even that single glimpse of his handwriting fanned the flame of a wild, reckless jealousy, an urge to rip that letter from the Queen's hands and devour Kallias's words herself. Whatever it took to hear *something* from him that she had not already memorized, that she could not recite in her sleep.

My greatest love was you.

The creak of her leather gloves pinned beneath her curled fists muffled the sound of Adriata's skirts brushing against the floor—it was only when Ramses hissed his queen's name in alarm that she turned to find Adriata on her knees, the letter held loosely in her limp hand. Her expression stayed fixed, stoic as stone… belied only by the constant well of tears dribbling from cheek to chin.

Without warning, those storm-gray eyes snapped up to Raquel's.

It was not accusation in the Queen's eyes, not really—but still, something there suggested Raquel was being scrutinized. Reassessed.

"My son is dead?" The lilt of her voice made it a question.

Ramses utterly paled. "No," he said—then, when they both held their silence, he repeated it as a plea. "*No.*"

Raquel could not say it, and Finn didn't force her. "We did everything we could, Mama."

"Soleil lived." The Queen's storm turned its eye to Finn now. "You lived. Why not Kallias?"

"It's different." Finn's throat bobbed. "Soleil was tricked. I…it was different. Kallias gave in willingly. I don't know what that means for him."

"My son is dead." No question this time—barely any words, any *breath*, at all.

A groan wrenched from the King's chest, and pity touched her for the first time as the battered man collapsed against the wall, sliding to his seat, agony indescribable twisting his features. Another groan, guttural and grief-thick and only just forming words—"My boy, my *boy*—" and he bent near to the floor, tearing at his hair and kicking his heel into the dirt as if a second pain might drown out the first.

Had her father taken the news of her disappearance from her company so terribly, moaning and weeping and beating the floor, kicking like he intended to dig a grave of his own? Had her mother shed a tear for her elder daughter, her failed prodigy?

Had they even noticed she was gone at all?

"Soleil?" Adriata's voice had taken on the quality of a dreamer…something she'd heard before in soldiers who had yet to shake off battle-shock. "Soleil is still alive."

Not a question. Not a statement. A demand for it to be the truth—and if it was not, for it to become so with great haste.

"Yes," Finn said quickly. "I saw her before I came here…she and her battlemate are sheltering in Arborius with Aunt Gen."

A considerable downplay of the dire situation Soren currently found herself in; even if Arborius had not been a safe haven, even if it had not been ruled by Soren's extended family, the princess would have had no choice but to chase the far-flung hope of Anima's relic being able to separate her and her own divine infiltrator.

But at least they *had* hope, far-off or not. Raquel would have preferred that over having true futility shoved in her face like an ether-soaked rag.

Adriata lowered her head, a half-nod that failed before its final rise. "Why didn't you go with her?"

Finn's shoulders dipped. "I chased Kal when he left, and it gave Tenebrae everything he needed to get rid of you. To take Jericho in truth. I'm not running this time. Atlas needs a defender, and…" A pause, and when he spoke next, there was a rasp of emotion he so rarely wore. "That position is newly abandoned. Someone had to step up."

Abandoned. A small, soft piece of Raquel's heart cried out in harmony with that word, matching it pain for pain, grief for grief, rage for rage. *Abandoned.*

Abandoned on foreign shores, her only farewell a salt-crusted letter and ink streaked with fallen tears.

Abandoned with nothing but whip scars on her back, lightning blistering her bones, and a silly bracelet to tell her it had ever been otherwise. That once upon a time, Raquel Angelov had been loved.

None of this made itself known in her face, her eyes, her hands—she made sure of it. Had *been* making sure of it, every day since she'd first crawled her way beneath a broken, neglected section of what had once been Port Atlas's first checkpoint…a gate that now sat abandoned.

Tenebrae, it seemed, did not fear any enemies that could be deterred by a guarded gate.

"You."

It took a moment for her to realize Adriata was speaking to her; the Queen's furious gaze fastened to her as a sailor lashed their ship before a squall.

Not on her face—on her hand, which had slid into her pocket, thumb brushing over the hidden letter.

She hadn't dared leave it in her quarters, though it could be just as much of a risk to keep it on her person. Old habits, hammered into her by life in the barracks—if you didn't want something taken in the name of hazing, you kept it with you.

Adriata's expression crashed closed, hiding whatever emotion had once peeked through. "You have one, too?"

Some territorial instinct snarled at the demanding tone—an instinct that tugged her back one step, as if the Queen might reach out and try to steal the letter straight from her pocket.

As if she felt the same crushing need to take in every one of Kallias's myriad last words.

"Yes." The single, harsh syllable scraped every ridge of her tongue, dropping from her mouth with all the inflection of a stone.

She did not like the way the Queen was looking at her. She did not like the way the Queen said, "Hm," as if Raquel had answered a hundred questions with that one word.

"We did everything we could," Raquel said, echoing Finn's words—to Ramses, who had yet to recover from his wave of grief, his palms crushed into his eyes as he wept silently. For him, she could offer a hint of her sorrow…for him, whom Kallias had never spoken ill about, who clearly held love equal and unconditional for each of his children. "I did everything I could to…I tried…"

Her voice failed her.

In the end, what did it matter? What did words like *we did everything we could* and *I tried, I tried* have to offer a grieving father?

She had failed. Nothing before or beyond that mattered.

Footsteps thudded somewhere above their heads.

"Time to go," she hissed to Finn, whose mannerisms altered immediately…and by *immediately*, she meant he'd already shifted shape by the time she turned to face him. He no longer slouched, exhausted and heartsick—instead, he practically preened against the backdrop of shadowed stone, his chin tipped up catch the gleam of torchlight in his mocking smile, his eyes glossed over gold once again.

She tried not to shiver.

On rare occasions, when she was still small, her parents would take her and Jira to the Andromeda Theater to see one of their acclaimed performances. As a little girl, such things had terrified her—she'd been too young to understand the concept of acting, too young to realize that the villains sweeping their way across the stage were not monsters in truth. They committed themselves so very well to their roles that even when she got older, she silently feared they had forgotten themselves in the glamour, lost in the illusion, fully believing themselves to be the ghouls whose costumes they wore.

Finnick played his part much the same. And though she was grown now, far beyond such whimsical things as believing actors had lost their true selves to the deceitful magic of the stage, that old foolish fear crept back into her heart as he stepped away from the cell, rolling his shoulders and lightly bouncing on his heels.

"Pleasure chatting," he said smoothly, and turned to make his way back up the moaning, mildewed stairs without even a parting glance.

Raquel turned to follow him, but the Queen's voice hooked the heels of her boots, yanking her back: "Officer Angelov."

Reluctance aching in the hinge of her neck, she turned her head just enough to catch the Queen in the periphery of her good eye.

"Protect my son," Adriata said.

Fury splintered the knucklebones in her clenched fist, but she held its leash with all her might—made sure that when she replied, not one bit of that compromising heat bled through. "With my life."

The Queen's posture failed her, easing her against the bars. "Thank—"

"For Kallias," she interrupted. "*Not* for you."

And with that, she followed Finnick up to the palace's ground floor, ignoring the guards who'd come to take their shift.

CHAPTER 3

FINN

The Trickster God did not spend his nights on sheet and satin, though he'd longed for exactly those things while Occassio's power—his power, now—had cost him most of his sleep these past few weeks.

Since that selfsame magic bent the knee to him, sleep no longer held the appeal it once did.

Instead, he spent his nights in one of two places…in halls built from shattered glass, practicing his ability to travel through mirrors, or stalking the familiar shadows of Port Atlas's streets.

Tonight, he forced his feet to take on the latter venture, though the former called to him with siren-like sweetness. And if he was being honest, that temptation was steeped in necessity—that mirrored maze held secrets he needed up his sleeve if his ruse was to continue.

He had done well avoiding Tenebrae's direct focus thus far, but that wouldn't last long—and when those rapt, ruinous attentions found their way at last to him, his sparse knowledge of Occassio's true self would not save him from being found out as a fraud.

The part of a liar was the hardest to learn—you never knew which pieces were fabricated and which were not.

As his soles touched the street—so familiar he could have walked it blind, so utterly *his* that in five paces, he should encounter a cobblestone with a chip in its corner, and in eight more paces, there would be a gap with no stone at all— hatred bubbled up inside him.

Not for his streets, which he had missed so fiercely he'd had to remove his sandals just to properly feel the fact that he was home.

Not for his people, most of whom cowered in their homes tonight, some just brave enough to peek through their curtains and watch him pass.

No. This hatred, more sacred than any he'd held before, burned against what Tenebrae had twisted his kingdom into.

He hated how silent these streets were. He hated the *Closed* signs hanging from the doors of the most popular—and now, entirely abandoned—taverns. Hated the fearful looks, the click of locks being fastened as he walked by, the occasional sight of a body too limp to be living cast aside in nearby alleys.

Mostly, he hated the new abundance of broken cobblestones, shattered and left to cut into sandals and bare soles alike. Tenebrae couldn't be bothered to pay attention to what the city actually needed from its ruler; after all, this was nothing but another puppet show to him, the throne merely the stage he forced his marionette to dance upon. If his loftiest desire was to wear a crown on his head, he'd already accomplished that.

To the people of Port Atlas, their royals were all dead…save two. One so lost in her grief, so similar to Adriata, that she would allow no one to venture outside the "safety" of Port Atlas's walls…and the other a blood-betraying murderer.

Small losses. Bigger battles. It was all part of the plan.

If it kept his parents alive until Soren brought the numbers they needed, it would all be worth it.

Even so, outrage soaked his tongue in a bitter brew, far worse than any concoction he'd been forced to choke down under various guises these past few weeks.

Speaking of guises…he'd walked too long without donning one.

When he passed the next alley, he ducked in and out of it in a flash—anyone watching would never guess the same person had come and gone so quickly.

Partly because he was no longer the same person.

In his place now walked a taller, bolder man, dull brown hair coiffed in a style not unlike a cresting wave, wearing the plain clothes demanded of a man walking dangerous ground…but boasting riches in subtle, shifty ways. Gold cuffs lined the shells of his ears in triads, ending with a shimmering diamond pinned to each lobe; matching chainmail covered the exposed portion of his chest, so delicate it could have been gossamer rather than gold; and the cape swishing behind him, while black as the rest of his clothing, was sewn from the finest velvet money could buy, the sort no one could get ahold of anymore thanks to the war with Nyx.

His Jaskier disguise had become much more convincing now that he had the advantage of auramancy.

"I thought I told you," said a voice to his right, another cloaked form falling into step with him, "to tone it *down.*"

Finn rolled his eyes and stuffed his hands into his pockets, ignoring the burning sensation of Raquel's signature glare boring into his temple. He was slowly but surely growing used to being its sole recipient; though it still scorched, he no longer worried she'd set his hair on fire with her eyes alone. "And I told *you,* the best way to be ignored is to act like you belong out here. People think twice about confronting someone who'll walk these streets with his gold out in the open."

"You're a walking target."

"No, I'm a walking warning sign." He tweaked the chainmail at the hollow of his throat as if adjusting a cravat. "Anyone with the stones to flash their riches here has the steel to back them up."

Her expression didn't soften. "You don't have the steel."

"Sure I do." He gestured to her, a sweep of his hand that began at the crown of her head and ended at the toes of her boots. "Why do you think I asked you to come along?"

A low growl—then a sigh. "So who is this character of yours, anyway?"

"My real father," he said. "Utter scoundrel, from what I hear. Dropped me on the steps of the palace as a baby and—"

"Be serious."

"Fine." He muttered some derogatory words about Nyxians and their stifled senses of humor before adding, just a smidge louder, "Some prick lordling who lives in the country with his inherited riches and a flock of roughly thirty-eight peacocks."

Just a *hmm* this time, no accusations of foolishness—he didn't like that she'd already learned how to tell his lies from his truths, even now that he was back in top form. "He has a very punchable face."

Despite the Trickster God title he'd placed on his own shoulders, he was still quite human underneath; human enough to enjoy the intense swell of satisfaction that only came with long-awaited validation. "*Thank* you. I wholeheartedly agree."

"What are we doing out here, Finnick?" He knew that tone by now, too—the tired, heart-worn mutter of a soldier forced to defend the home of her enemies due to promises she'd made to a dead man.

Dead.

He had to force himself to use the word—to face it, to understand the exact depth and breadth of the hurdle he would need to scale in order to make everything right again.

"There's someone I need to see," he said. "Someone I need you to get out of the city."

"An ally?"

"An enemy."

Raquel's eyes narrowed. "If they're an enemy, why aren't we killing them?"

For all Raquel's more irritating qualities, he did have to appreciate her inclination toward efficiency. "Because before she was an enemy, she was a good enough friend to earn one chance at mercy."

"And if she doesn't take it?"

No hesitation—in his heart or in his reply. "Then I won't offer it a second time."

Silence took over after that, walking alongside them as they made their way through Port Atlas, Finn's shoulders loosening the closer they got to the lower city.

Here, it felt easier to breathe—here, Tenebrae's fist hadn't yet fully closed, allowing bits and pieces of normalcy to drip through his stifling fingers.

Normalcy that included Finn snatching back the first piece of his kingdom he'd ever laid claim to, rebuilding the crown he'd fashioned from city shadows and tavern tunes and the occasional cheat at a game of cards.

It wasn't long before they found the alley he needed—an exact dupe for the other hundreds of alleys in Port Atlas, but for the loose brick one could slide away to reveal a certain seer's shop.

He paused at the mouth of the alley, memories flooding in…memories clear as cut crystal, unsmeared by madness or magic.

Memories of coming here with Fidget, her skipping steps halting abruptly at the sight of the façade…a sheer curtain of nerves falling over her cheerful face, her ankle rotating oddly as she stared.

"Your seers have to hide here?" she'd asked him, favoring that ankle like the idea made it ache.

Knowing what he knew now—knowing her history of manacles and cages and demands for visions at another man's whim—he could guess that reaction hadn't been part of Occassio's well-wrought ruse.

Something about that thought soured his stomach.

Unfortunately, what he was about to do wouldn't sweeten it any.

With Raquel guarding his back, his fingers flew through the motions of revealing Luisa's door. The twinkling sign above had once been a comforting thing, a reprieve from the false faces he wore all day long, a reassurance he would get some good information and better company from one of the very, very few people he'd handed a kernel of his trust.

Before she'd betrayed him in favor of the goddess who'd tried to rob him of both mind and body.

Even so, this was not about anger. This was not about hurt. Those were the sorts of things mortals indulged in, and he wasn't playing mortal today.

First, to make her sweat.

He rapped on the door with one knuckle—a formality he didn't normally waste time on.

Not today. Today, he wanted her to come to him.

The door did not open right away, but it didn't have to—he could see her in his mind's eye well enough.

The path she would take from her desk to her door. The caution with which she would peer through the peephole. The knife she would grab when she didn't recognize his borrowed face. And the slowness with which she would turn the knob before—

The door swung open, silent on what had to be freshly oiled hinges, halting after revealing only a sliver of the shop beyond. He dismissed the fizzing pink light surrounding the edges of his vision with a simple blink, putting on a guileless smile as Luisa peeked around the edge of her door.

His greedy, shrewd friend bore the same changes all other Port Atlas citizens seemed to don these days; tired eyes, pinched mouths, and hollow cheeks had all come into fashion under Tenebrae's rule. She leaned in such a way that he couldn't see the state of the shop itself, nor the knife in her hand…but that was all right. He had already *seen* both.

The shop, empty and dark and void of most of her usual stock; the knife, cheap and small and not nearly enough to prevent him from forcing his way in if he so chose.

Now that he knew how to wield it, divinimancy was making great strides toward becoming his favorite new toy.

"Evening," he greeted, his accent rising into the dialect of the northern shores. "I'm seeking a seer, and I'm told you're the best this side of the Vela."

"You were told wrong," she retorted. "This shop is closed."

"I'm also told," he said, holding out the hidden weapon in his hand: a bulging bag of coin that jingled conspicuously with the movement, "that your time is precious, but worth the price one pays for the privilege."

Honestly, if one had to pick a weakness, money was the worst choice—the easiest to exploit, the hardest to eradicate, and the most readily available to anyone powerful enough to be a true threat.

Because Luisa took one look at that hefty canvas bag and, without even asking for a name, moved aside to let them in.

Finn stepped into the shop—then stepped aside, making room for Raquel to pounce.

He kicked the door closed with a quick snap of his heel, giving the lock a deft twist as Raquel bodily shoved Luisa back from the doorway, drawing her blade without so much as a grunt or gasp of effort.

While the two women clashed—Raquel with her freshly sharpened sword poached from the royal treasury, Luisa with her silly little knife—Finn made his way to the counter where Luisa did her readings, dropping into her chair and kicking his feet up, his heels pinning down a couple tarot cards. He reached for the little notebook she kept beside her covered crystal ball, flipped it in the air once, and caught it already open.

A crash, a curse—a shelf falling over, Luisa tumbling after it. Raquel swung downward, but a flash of lavender cut across Luisa's front, deflecting the blade. Auramancy—the powerful sort that could take illusions and turn them into something tangible.

Finn idly licked the pad of his thumb, turning page after page, searching for whatever Luisa had written down last. Gods, her handwriting was atrocious. Probably on purpose, so no one could snoop around—exactly like he was doing now.

"Need any help, Angelov?" he called without looking up.

"Use that tone with me again, and you're next," Raquel snapped.

"I'm shaking in my sandals." He flipped to the next page, a thin slice of pain cutting across his finger as the edge of the paper nipped him—he muttered a curse of his own, sticking his finger in his mouth.

A wrathful growl, and suddenly the desk jolted beneath his heels—he looked up to find Raquel twisting Luisa's arms behind her back, silver lightning flickering in her eye, static inspiring strands of her hair to stand tall against gravity's tyranny. Luisa's hair stood on end, too—her chest heaved up and down as she looked between him and Raquel, fear staking its claim on her features.

"Please," she gasped, struggling against Raquel's hold, failing to move the staunch Nyxian warrior even an inch. "Whatever you want with me, just—"

"Oh, stop," he grumbled around his bleeding finger, popping it out of his mouth and shaking it out. "Honestly, Lu, you're better than begging."

Her gaze fastened to his, terror dampening to suspicion. "No one calls me that."

He offered her a grim smile. "One person does."

With a snap of his fingers, he felt his own auramancy shimmer away, dissolving from the soles of his feet to the crown of his head...a slow, taunting reveal that allowed him to enjoy the satisfaction of watching her face drop in horror.

In shame.

Too little, too late, if he said so himself. But he couldn't pretend it wasn't gratifying.

"Finn," she breathed. "But I thought—"

"That your goddess had her way with me?" He spread his arms out to their full span, never dropping his smile. "Should've known better, honestly. Every seasoned gambler knows to throw a coin or two on the underdog...and never to bet your whole purse in one place."

He wriggled his fingers, coaxing a spectral coin to tumble between them, watching carefully as her face dropped in realization.

"What..." She swallowed so hard he could hear her throat constrict. "What did you do?"

"What *I* did is not important." He pushed the chair back with the groaning scrape of wood against wood, letting his heels drop to the ground as he leaned forward, steepling his fingers beneath his chin. "What's important is what *you* did...and what I'm going to do with you now."

Luisa swallowed. "I had no—"

"Angelov," he interrupted, "my neck's a bit sore. I'd rather not look up just now. Would you mind terribly—"

Before he could finish, Raquel flipped Luisa to face her before shoving her down across the desk, the back of the seer's head cracking against the wood. Luisa's face contorted in pain, mouth opening...

Her yelp of pain choked off as Finn set the point of a glimmering dagger in the hollow between her clavicles, dancing the tip across her throat until it came to rest on the pulse fluttering in the crook of her neck. Not drawing blood, not dealing pain—just the featherlight kiss of spectral steel to skin.

The simplest of threats. But sometimes simple was best.

"If you try to tell me," he murmured, "that you had no choice but to betray my seldom-given trust, I will happily ensure you have no choice in this matter, as well."

Luisa's throat bobbed. She did not speak; she only stared.

"Try again," he prompted, never breaking eye contact.

Luisa kept staring. He watched, patient, as her gaze glazed over with pink light...then faded almost as quickly as it had flared. "I can't see what you're going to do to me."

"That's because it's entirely up to you." He stood up, never changing the pressure he so carefully applied to the dagger's point. "Now, here in Atlas, traitors to the crown are executed. I assume you're aware of that policy."

Another bob of her throat. Her skin shimmered in the dim lights of the shop—the result of a lotion she wore that came infused with fine-ground sparkle. "Yes."

"However, my Nyxian friend here—oh, forgive me, my manners. Officer Angelov, meet Luisa. Luisa, meet Officer Angelov."

"Pleasure," Raquel said flatly.

"My Nyxian friend here," Finn continued, "told me something very interesting. In her kingdom, even if someone betrays crown and kin, their prior loyalty is taken into consideration when deciding the severity of their punishment. Good deeds, military accolades, services rendered to the crown, testimony by their neighbors…all that fun stuff. Nyxian mercy is a thing to behold, it seems."

"Get to the point," Raquel ground out.

"I'm *making* my point."

"You're showing off."

Maybe, but he so rarely got the chance, he could hardly pass it up. "So, Luisa, in honor of Officer Angelov's customs, I'm willing to offer you a choice. Something you claim your dear goddess never gave you."

Now he flexed his hand, forcing the tip of the dagger beneath the first layer of skin. Still no blood, barely any pain. Simple threats to grow that simple fear in his old friend's eyes.

"Choice number one," he said. "I lean just a little bit harder on this dagger."

The seer-shimmer in Luisa's eyes blazed and died once more—checking his conviction, perhaps. Her nostrils flared as she dragged in a shallow breath and whispered, "And choice number two?"

"You take that bag of coin I brought here. You follow Officer Angelov out of this city. You leave, and you never come back." Simple threats, simple fear…simple choices. The last of the simple things left in his life.

Now confusion clouded Luisa's gaze instead of magic. "You would actually let me go?"

"I've never tried this the Nyxian way. Good to try everything out at least once." Finn shrugged. "You were a great help to me for a long time, Lu…right up until our last bit of business, I might've even called you a friend. You can imagine I don't have many of those."

Her mouth pinched with guilt. But she didn't offer an apology—and that was fine. He might've lost his patience if she'd tried.

"After today," he continued, "mercy will no longer be something I can afford to experiment with. You understand, I'm sure, exactly what it means that I am offering my last portion to you."

Now Luisa's lips thinned. "Which is the mercy? The dagger or the escape?"

Gods, he'd miss that cutting insight. "To be honest, I'm not entirely sure."

"I'll take my chances on the escape."

"I thought you would."

She waited, expectant; he gazed back, hand steady, not letting up on the dagger.

"Is there more?" she prompted.

"There is a catch."

"There always is with you."

Now he removed the dagger. He nodded to Raquel, and she allowed Luisa to stand, though she kept her hands fastened firmly around the seer's wrists; one wrong move, and the leashed lightning riding through Raquel's veins would strike more than twice.

He slipped his fingers into his pocket, removing a piece of paper sealed with wax...sort of. The seal didn't seem content to remain stationary; instead, though it stayed within the boundaries of its diamond-shaped border, the center undulated as a mercurial puddle, a lesser mimicry of the mirror relic Occassio had been so eager to get her hands on.

"This seal is enchanted," he said, laying the letter on the desk and tapping a finger on the paper. "If anyone but my younger sister opens it, their minds will be broken before they can read a single word...and so will yours."

Luisa tipped her chin upward. "You're bluffing. No Occassio-blessed wielder can set a trap using magic like—"

"Except I'm not Occassio-blessed," he interrupted. "I'm something brand new. If you want to test it, please, be my guest. It won't bother me any. But if you choose sense over stupidity, seeing as we both know you're nowhere close to good enough to catch a bluff from me, you'll see that this finds its way into my sister's hands and no one else's."

Luisa's jaw flexed, her expression curdling like spoiled milk as she chewed on the unpleasant truth: he had her well and truly cornered. She had no way out but the one he'd offered.

"Where is she?" Luisa finally muttered.

"Arborius. And if that information finds its way into any ears or out of any mouths that aren't present in this room...well, I'm out of clever threats for the day, but I'll let you imagine." He settled back in her chair, doing his best to affect a dismissal in his posture. "Go gather your things. You have five minutes."

Once she stiffly nodded her understanding, Raquel released Luisa, her eyes tracing the seer's path all the way to the door at the back of the shop. The instant it closed, Raquel turned back to him, glancing down at the envelope.

"You really think that will keep her from opening it?" she muttered.

"Gods know." He shrugged again. "Don't worry about it. I have other precautions in place if that fails."

"You're risking everything by trusting a woman who's already betrayed you once."

"Like I said, I have precautions in place." He raised an eyebrow at her. "Have I failed you yet?"

Her mouth bent at an unhappy angle, her hands flexing into fists. "Not yet."

"Well, if I ever do, I give you full permission to say *I told you so*. Until then, let me do what I'm best at."

At exactly the five-minute mark, not a second sooner or later, Luisa emerged from her quarters with a bag…a bag mostly filled with coin, judging by the way its contents strained against the bottom of the bag.

Greed. It would get her killed; not tonight, but it would. He didn't need divinimancy to tell him the end of that story.

Luisa gave him a long, long look—in the end, all she said was, "Good luck, Finn."

He held out the envelope; when she took it, he said, "Luck's got even less of my trust than you do."

With one last shake of her head and a sweep of her cloak, she followed Raquel out, the door swinging shut silently behind them.

He glanced to the belongings Luisa had left behind…most notably, the crystal ball covered at the corner of her desk.

One errand done for today.

One more to go.

CHAPTER 4

RAQUEL

The rain began the moment the seer's silhouette vanished past Port Atlas's frontmost abandoned guardhouse.

Drops that tasted more of salt than petrichor traced the curve of Raquel's lips and gathered in the corners of her eyes, mimicking the tears she'd run out of weeks ago.

They stung. She liked it.

She tipped her head back, letting her hood crumple around her shoulders; the stormwater soaked through her hair in mere moments, settling a chill deep beneath her skin.

Still, she couldn't bring herself to banish the storm; not when the rumble of thunder reverberated through her hollow chest like a welcoming purr.

Not when her lungs opened up for the first deep breath she'd taken since finding her way to Finn's quarters a handful of weeks back and being greeted with a quick, "Glad you got my note. We have work to do."

Dawn drew near as she drifted down the path back to the palace; she could only tell because the clouds had lightened from pitch to ash, washing this silent city in varying hues of black and gray and white. To hear Finn tell it, Port Atlas had once been a city of beautiful buildings and cheerful people; now, chaos had leeched away all its color and character.

To see it this way would have broken Kallias's heart.

Something pinched the base of her throat. She batted it away.

No. More. Damned. Tears.

Her feet knew these streets now—well enough that even though she'd tipped her head back to let her skin drink in the rain, she knew when the cobblestones beneath her boots flattened into paving stones…when the grit beneath her soles shifted from stone to sand.

Without looking, without thinking, she had veered off course…and ended at the beach.

She'd passed by a dozen times, on a dozen nights just like this, and every time she stopped. Every time she stared.

Every time she walked away.

But this time, lead seeped into her soles when she tried to turn aside, anchoring her to the boundary between city and sea.

Another prickle, this time at the back of her neck. She rubbed it away.

Grief. Even with her magic back, even with her kinship to the sky restored, her damned useless heart seemed determined to bind her to the land.

Somewhere out there, sheathed in shadow, the ocean called to her. Roared to her. Demanded an audience with the one who'd failed to protect its beloved prince.

She would grant it what it wanted…soon. Not tonight.

A third sting dug beneath her skin, this one at her wrist, just below the bracelet that prince had given her…along with an unkeepable promise.

Say the word, and you have me.

Throat closing up, she forced her leaden feet forward.

Then buckled to her knees.

She barely caught herself before crashing facefirst into the cobblestones, skinning the heels of her hands. As she blinked hard, trying to focus on her fingers, they refused to still—they wavered before her in blurry streaks of watercolor paint, blending and bleeding, darkness curling over the edges of her vision no matter how wide she forced her eye open.

Not grief.

Not grief that had stolen her strength and smothered her breath. Not grief that drew her throat tightly shut now, refusing to let air in or out. Not grief churning her thoughts into storm-tossed waves, each dissolving back into the surf before she could ride one back to shore.

She laid her heavy head on the cobblestones.

The path vibrated beneath her ear at a crisp one-two, one-two beat—footsteps. Coming closer. Coming fast.

Just before her eye failed her entirely, she managed one entire thought: *Poison.*

The world came back in shades of pain.

The darkest shade painted a necklace around the base of her throat, a swollen sort of discomfort that thinned every breath. Next was her head, a low pounding in her temples that struck her eardrums until they rang. Then came the burning in her knees and hands, telling her she'd lost a layer or two of skin from the caps and palms.

The mildest of all—and the most difficult to bear—was the bruising now mottling her pride.

Finnick would get gods-damned *giddy* with condescension over this.

If she survived whatever *this* was.

"Look who's decided to join us," said a voice somewhere above her head. Boots shuffled, leather creaked, and then the voice came again, now directly in front of her: "Do me a favor and open your eyes, beautiful."

Feminine. Young enough that it surprised her. Most of Tenebrae's disciples—at least, the ones she'd encountered—were older, having worshipped him in secret for some time.

Gods knew how they'd discovered her duplicity. Maybe someone had followed her and Luisa from the shop. She'd been as careful as always, but—

"Hey." Fingers snapped in front of her face—this voice was male, still young, but decidedly less friendly than the former. "Your respite is over, Officer Angelov. We have questions."

Reluctantly, she dragged her eyelids open, blinking away the blur until streaks of color and shadow melded into discernible faces.

And then she blinked again—and again, and again, because the colors and shadows had drawn out two faces of remarkably similar features.

Sienna skin. Dark sable hair. Sharp cheekbones. The only true difference was that one leaned more feminine, her mouth cut in a smirk and her brown eyes gleaming with anticipation, while the other scowled, his features decidedly masculine and his eyes entirely emotionless.

Both her captors wore belts—the man's laden with weapons, the woman's lined with vials and a quiver of darts.

"Poison," she croaked—the word still lingering in her mind.

The woman's eyebrow quirked. "Three poisons, actually. You're a hard one to drop."

One of the few blessings Skyhaven had given her: each member of the community underwent the process of building poison immunity when they reached adulthood. Raquel had taken to it exceptionally well, allowing her to build immunity to an unprecedented number of poisons: seventy-two in total.

She'd told Kallias twenty-seven. She'd told her company eighteen, then had "confessed" to Jakob that the true number was thirty-three. Jira had cornered her one evening and informed her that it had to be at least forty, because she'd been slipping common toxins into her drinks for some time and hadn't noticed Raquel suffering any ill effects.

She stopped accepting food and drink from her sister—and Soren—after that.

If this woman had managed to find one that worked so rapidly, she was a skilled poisoner, indeed.

Raquel swallowed hard, the sides of her throat gritting against each other like she'd coated her esophagus in sand. "What do you want."

The twins—she had to assume they were twins—exchanged glances, an entire conversation flickering between their blinks and eye-shifts and twitching lips.

The twins in her company communicated much the same way. It drove everyone a bit crazy, especially Jakob, who often snapped at them to stop being such gossips…even though they hadn't said a single word.

"Firstly," said the man, plucking a stiletto blade from his belt and flipping it artfully between his fingers, "I want to know what could have persuaded a Nyxian officer to come all the way to the heart of Atlas just to bend the knee before the Chaos God."

"Secondly," said the woman, planting her hands on the arms of the chair they'd chained Raquel to, her nose mere inches from Raquel's, "I want to know everything you know about Finnick Atlas's ascension to Heir…and how much of his mind remains intact."

Raquel's suspicions began to take a different shape.

Not Tenebrae's people—not unless they were especially good at falsifying honest anger. This woman's smirk had fallen away, replaced with a vengeful scowl that suggested grief hid behind it. She'd said his name with a familiarity no other member of this city's underbelly dared to…not even Luisa, whom he'd once called a friend.

Finnick had mentioned allies that might yet linger in the city—allies even he had a hard time tracking down. But could luck really have smiled on her that kindly?

Her record with luck lately suggested the answer was no. Better to tread carefully—let them give away as much as they would before she started revealing anything herself.

"What do you care for the prince's fate?" she rasped.

It was still strange, the protective instinct that now reared its head in matters related to Finnick Atlas. A feeling so familiar it kept Jira, her long-dead sister, constantly at the forefront of her mind and heart.

Maybe it was because Kallias's last wish had been for her to protect his brother, who hardly seemed to need it. Maybe it was because Finnick's sharp wit and keen sense for risks worth taking might as well have been a portrait-perfect copy of Jira's. Maybe it was because, against all common sense, she'd grown almost fond of the absolute menace that was Atlas's Second Prince turned false Heir.

Whatever the reason, she had resigned herself at the start of all this to the knowledge that if it came to protecting herself or protecting Finnick, it wouldn't be much of a choice.

Just like it hadn't been a choice for Kallias.

"We care nothing for it, if the rumors ring true," the man said gruffly. A better liar than his sister, whose struggle to hide her emotions played out plainly across her face. "Kin-killers don't belong on the throne of Atlas. But we suspect that's not the truth of the matter, is it?"

She knocked her head back, bracing her tired neck against the chair, pretending to ponder her answer while examining the room she sat in.

Empty—and not just of other people. The walls were barren, mildew and rat-holes the only décor plastered across their peeling-paint surfaces. The only furniture to speak of was the metal chair beneath her. No windows, and only one door…only one route for escape, and her captors guarded it with the promise of poisoned blood or a pierced heart if she made any move toward it.

Nowhere to call forth a storm.

Static rippled over the surface of her skin—her magic sighing in frustration.

Soon, she thought—another ripple followed, stronger, and she growled to herself. *Soon.*

"If you know I work closely with the Heir," she said, not meeting their gazes, "and you know enough about him to ask after the state of his sanity, then you know I won't give you your answers."

Finnick's reputation here, to those who were unlucky enough to know his true name, held enough weight that these people—whether friend or foe—had to know he didn't choose his inner circle without care and cause.

Easily broken people made poor bedfellows for scoundrels.

The woman sighed, her fingers sliding into one of the pockets hanging from her belt, withdrawing a vial filled to the cork with cloudy green liquid.

Raquel didn't recognize it.

That didn't bode well.

"Disappointing," said the woman, not sounding particularly disappointed at all. "We were so hoping to do this nicely. Manners don't cover half the distance they used to these days."

Panic burned low in her throat, but she swallowed hard to stop its ascent. Instead, she let it seep into her blood—fear stoking the swill of adrenaline pumping through her, struggling to make headway against whatever they'd used to subdue her.

She pressed her back flush to the chair. Braced her heels against the floor. Dug her fingertips into the steel arms. "Can I ask who I have the pleasure of being hosted by?"

"You can ask," said the man. And said nothing else after.

She'd expected that answer. Still, she'd hoped for a slightly longer version, one that would give the energy buzzing through her veins time to properly channel itself into the chair.

Beggars couldn't be choosers. If they refused to be stalled, she'd work with what she had.

Heat swarmed into the infinitesimal gap between muscle and skin as she concentrated, her arms and hands stinging as if she'd plunged them elbow-deep into a beehive. But this pain didn't repel her—instead, she stoked it fiercely, agitating that trapped energy until even her clothes began to prickle and shift, the cloth held aloft by the electric current shivering over every inch of her.

No place to call in a storm—so she would become one herself.

The woman approached, uncorking the vial with a careless clamp of teeth and a jerk of her head, a single drop of overspill landing in the dip of her chin. She licked it away as she leaned over Raquel.

"You're not the only one whose blood has a taste for poison," the woman murmured. As she leaned over Raquel, she gripped the back of the chair to brace herself—

And as her body stiffened, folding at the waist and knees and every other joint as lightning barreled into her muscles and bones, Raquel dropped her head, thrust her weight forward, and head-butted the woman square in the forehead.

Winded and dazed, twitching and shivering, the woman collapsed in a senseless pile—her eyes open but unseeing, her spasming fingers still splayed out, seeking the vial she'd dropped. All the vials on her belt had shattered beneath the lightning's caress, poisons of various colors and viscosity staining her leathers.

A couple of those stains smoked—one even bubbled, slowly melting through the leather, eating toward her skin.

All this Raquel noted in the span of a moment—and a moment was all she got, because the man shot forward the second the poisoner dropped, hissing threats as he yanked a knife from his belt and threw.

Steel glinted, thought stopped, and her body snatched the reins from her mind.

Raquel crashed to the floor, flipping halfway through a backwards somersault, the top of her head flat to the floor—the screech of metal on metal told her the back of the chair had taken the blow meant for her. Without pausing to breathe, she rolled forward, undoing the somersault and surging back to her feet…or, at least, she tried to.

Instead, her quivering knees gave out, forcing her to kneel, the chair still strapped to her by her wrists and waist.

Fine. She didn't have to stand.

Instead of tugging against the chains, she gripped them tightly, channeling her magic into each and every link.

Already, that surge of power had begun to recede…thrill trading places with exhaustion, a pervasive fatigue that clouded her veins and blocked the lightning's path.

Weakness.

She'd gone too long without magic, and she hadn't practiced enough since it had been given—begrudgingly—back to her. It was a muscle untrained, and it would only handle so much strain before it tore.

So at first, when a sound like a cracking stick exploded in the center of her skull, she thought she'd channeled too much, too fast.

Then the ringing in her ears.

Then the floor pressed against her throbbing cheek.

Then the blood painting her tongue with the unmistakable tang of iron.

After several seconds too long, her mind caught up to what had happened to her body:

The man had kicked her beneath the chin, driving her teeth into her tongue and throwing her from her knees to her side, prone on the cold wooden floor.

Wood didn't hold lightning half as well as metal.

"Vidia!" The man's barking voice spun in twirling-top circles, bouncing off the sides of her skull until it shuddered into the form of a name—*Vidia*. The poisoner?

"Vash," came the answering mumble—slurred and shivering, as if her tongue wasn't quite under her own control.

Vash and Vidia—those were the names Finn had muttered at the tail end of his (upsettingly but expectedly) short list of allies, the names he'd told her to keep an ear out for, always spoken in tandem. He never uttered one without the other close behind.

The Fangs of the Vipers.

Thank the stars he'd only kicked her, not cut her—gods knew what coated that array of beautiful blades sheathed in his belt.

A cough dammed up the slick of blood coating her throat; she swallowed it, bracing against the wave of nausea that came with her own blood dribbling down into her stomach. Better that then to draw his attention back to her.

Panic to adrenaline to strength. She turned her attention back to her chains.

Bit by bit, she fed her lightning into the metal—though her vision blurred and spun, she kept her eyes glued to the steel links keeping her wrists secured to the arms of the chair.

And bit by bit, those chains began to sting, to quiver…to heat. To melt.

A sharp breath. A flex of her arms. A prayer to…well, to no one, really, but old habits died hard.

And with a single surge of strength—strength, to combat the weakness she had fed into her restraints—she broke the chains at their molten links.

She forced herself onto board-stiff legs, the room dipping her more gracefully than a trained dancer…more gracefully than a prince turned pirate, his freckles mimicking the spread of the stars, his grin capturing their shine…

And at the same time her half-numb hand collided with the door, it opened outward, her support flying away from her before she could stop it. The shadowy corridor beyond offered no help as she swayed, the floor rushing up to meet her—

Until two hands, ghostly and bloodless and startling in the dark, caught her by the shoulders.

"Vash? Vidia? What happened?" demanded a man's voice…barely a voice. The air seemed reluctant to carry it, each word so heavy with fatigue—with something worse, maybe—that each syllable dropped to the floor before they could do more than brush past Raquel's ringing ears.

"She's *Tempest-blessed*, that's what happened," snapped the other man…Vash. "Are you wearing anything metal?"

"No." Again, that *no*…it carried more than it ought to, for such a small word. "What should I…"

He trailed off. Stiffened. His fingers tightened on her arms before one released to palm the side of her head instead, holding on when she flinched away.

"Where did you get this?" A real question this time, not a demand—each word stank of desperation as he tapped the third mourning braid pinned along the scarred side of her head. The one she'd plaited with a strip of the shirt she'd stolen from Kallias long ago.

After a burning tavern, broken ribs, and a grin like the breaking dawn had changed everything between them.

When she finally blinked her vision clear, her instincts sent her rearing back from this stranger; his grip tightened again, arresting her in place. His features screamed of illness: sunken, pallid cheeks that nearly matched his dove-gray eyes; limbs that may have once been strong, judging by the broad span of his shoulders, but now trembled even from the effort of holding a half-conscious woman still; and worst of all, the death-rattle rasp that accompanied every heaving breath, each exhale smelling sharply of rot and fear.

"This," he repeated, tapping again—not the cloth in her mourning braid, but the leather band that kept it secured. "Where did you get it? Who gave it to you?"

"What does it matter?" she asked, each word scabbed over, coarse with the blood drying on her lips. She twisted her head to spit some out.

"Tell me." The sick man shook her—not roughly, but with enough urgency that it hurt. *"Tell me his name."*

She was too tired; too confused, too hurt, and it didn't matter enough to keep that name hidden beneath her bleeding tongue. It didn't matter, because he was already gone, smothered by the overbearing hand of a god, and what worse could this half-dead man really do?

Blood bubbling from her lips, grief bubbling from the wound deeper inside, she whispered, "Kallias."

All remaining color drained from the man's face.

Before she could make sense of the devastation churning in his eyes, he dropped both hands to her shoulders, so close to the base of her neck that she instinctively dragged in a deep breath, bracing for an attempt at strangulation. He shook her again, harder this time, but his voice came out weaker, shakier: "How did you get it? Where is he? What did you do to him? *Tell me what you did to my brother!"*

Brother?

"Kallias Atlas has one brother," she spat. "And you're not him."

The wildness in the man's eyes whipped into a frenzy. "Finn. You've seen them both? You have to—"

"Easy," Vash cautioned, approaching from behind Raquel, carrying his sister; Vidia's body still twitched and jerked, her eyes closed, her hands bloodied and her limp fingers shimmering with shattered glass. "I told you to let us handle this."

"What did she tell you?"

"Not much of anything before she shocked Vidia half dead." Vash slipped around the gaunt man, jerking his chin toward the chair. "Don't put her back in that. Sit her on the floor. I'll be right back."

The man holding her by the shoulders forced her down to her seat. She peered up at him, trying to place his features…seeking any Atlas traits in his countenance.

Nothing—no resemblance at all. No trace of red in his ebony hair, no freckles, no biting smiles or kind eyes.

Just pain. Just pallor.

"Who are you?" she demanded, doing her best to whittle the wooziness out of her voice. "I know the faces of both Atlas sons, and yours has nothing in common."

The man's brows pulled together, a battle beginning and ending in his eyes before she could make sense of it.

"I am Prince-Consort Vaughn Drakos-Atlas," he said, "and you are going to tell me what happened to my brothers."

CHAPTER 5

FINN

He found her trying to break a mirror.

The dull, repetitive *thud, thud, thud* of various bits of her body—fist, foot, elbow, other elbow—followed by a filthy, shrill curse actually brought a smile to his face.

"Darling, I'm home," he called, glazing his voice in pleasantry, sweeping off his cloak and hanging it up on its hook. He ruffled the last of the illusion magic out of his hair, sparkles twirling like snowflakes in his periphery before vanishing into thin air. "How was your day?"

"Welcome back, love," she crooned, meeting and exceeding his singsong. She dropped her forehead against the mirror, a duller thump that spoke of accepted defeat…for now. "I see you didn't fall into a vat of acid."

"Alas, despite your unceasing prayers to the contrary, I encountered nothing so dire on my journey."

After tossing his satchel onto the bed, he plopped down on the foot of it, sitting cross-legged and rubbing his sore soles as he observed his deific prisoner.

Occassio seemed intent on maintaining her illusion, despite her current position…despite him knowing the truth of what lay beneath. She clung to her goddess face with utter tenacity, the sharp cheekbones and multicolored eyes hiding softer features and a gilded glare. Her see-through chiffon gown drifted in airy folds around her like magician's smoke, but the seamless violet garment beneath clung dutifully to her skin; its sweetheart neckline and high-hipped holes for her legs reminded him of a popular style of wetsuit here in Atlas.

She leaned against the mirror's glass, her elbow propped above her head as she peered out at him—chips of reflective glass and precious gems cuffed her sheer, shimmering lavender sleeve, complementing the belt of bejeweled violet silk fastened snugly around her waist. Finery upon finery upon finery.

If he tried, he could see straight through the false splendor to the real girl hiding beneath. But for now, he let her have her costume. No harm in it.

"I don't suppose my brother's discovered your little trick yet," she said.

"Nothing little about it. But no." He shrugged. "Honestly, I've hardly seen him."

"Hm." Her glimmering gaze wandered away, taking in the cloak he'd hung up. "No blood. Luisa took your offer?"

"One of them." Only time would tell if she'd chosen well.

Occassio tapped her fingertips against the glass, each nail clinking a different note. During the first week they'd shared quarters, she'd done her damnedest to drive him mad—for the second time—with those nails. She'd dragged them down the glass, scratching like a caged wildcat; she'd plinked out horribly discordant tunes, using the mirror as her pianoforte; she'd screamed loud enough to shiver the glass in its panes, whittling her voice to a stiletto-sharp pitch.

When he'd taken to working at his desk with earplugs in, humming bawdy bar tunes that shifted into more obnoxious keys every time she tested something new, she'd tired quickly of that strategy.

He unfolded his legs, pushing himself to standing and walking to the mirror—Occassio's stance didn't change at his approach, but he appreciated the small alterations he did see.

A deepening of her double dimples on one side. A faint curling to her fingers, an instinctive shift toward a fist. The faintest undulation across her skin, the disruption revealing a heap more freckles, circles under her eyes so dark he almost thought they were bruised, and a shadow over those deceptive doe eyes that might have been fear.

All gone between one blink and the next. A brief blurring that tried to reveal her true face…and failed.

Good that it did. He didn't want to see it…didn't want the memories that came with it.

Even those glimpses were enough to spill champagne bubbles across the tip of his tongue.

He bit down on it until he tasted blood instead, crossing his arms over his chest, regarding the caged goddess with a tip of his chin. "Now I have an offer for you."

"I'll save you the time." She pressed her lips to the glass, a whisper disguised as a blown kiss: "Take your offer, shove it back down your honeyed throat, and let it *rot*."

He flashed a grin, tracing his thumb over the glass—over the divot in her chin. "You're too sweet to me."

She grinned back. A baring of teeth that flashed sharp and serrated, the illusion of a shark's maw hidden behind a pretty girl's lips. "If you let me out, I'll be happy to show you just how sweet I can be."

From what he could tell, her auramancy was all she'd kept ahold of, and of that, only the flashy bits—nothing concrete. Otherwise, he had to assume she would have tried breaking the glass with something more than her own hands.

Unless she was biding her time, hoping to lull him back into underestimation. But that was a game he knew the rules to. If she began to play her cards in that direction, he'd be there to deal a different hand.

He rapped on the glass. She covered her ears, groaning as he said, "Tempting. But I think I'll pass."

"Can you at *least* keep your hands to yourself?"

"Not really." As a child, he'd once kept a small glass tank in his room with a handful of fish as pets. His mother had eventually given it to Kallias because he couldn't be trusted not to disturb them with constant tapping. "Well, if you don't want to hear my offer, I guess I'll pick for you."

"Pick what?"

He cracked his knuckles before placing his palms flat against the mirror's surface; with a murmur of sweet nothings against its pane, solid glass eased itself into rippling liquid, Occassio's face distorting nightmarishly beneath the surface.

He trailed his fingers through the fluid glass; warm on the surface, but approaching frigid beneath. Not the most inviting mystery.

But the Trickster God needed no invitation; and even if he did, he couldn't afford to wait for one. Tenebrae grew increasingly impatient with his excuses and avoidance every day, and he didn't have a gods-damned prayer of holding up this ruse if he didn't exchange the lie of Fidget in his head for the truth of Occassio.

"Where I search for you first," he said. "Guess I'll let your magic make the choice for me."

Her face fell so far and fast, he almost expected to hear something shatter. "What?"

Another thing he'd learned over years of this trickster work—the satisfaction of explaining one's genius was never worth the time one wasted on monologuing.

So instead, he parted the surface of the mirror, throwing it open like a set of curtains, and told it to take him someplace else.

Some*time* else.

CHAPTER 6

FINN

Even after wresting godhood into his own body, fortifying his bones with scaffolding of otherworldly, immense, eternal power…chronomancy hurt like the *depths*.

His foot jammed down into solid stone, bruising the sole and stabbing a lance of pain up his leg; his hand flew to his mouth to muffle the bark of pain and the likely-anachronistic curses that followed.

"Occassio's sparkling *spit*," he groaned into his palm, reaching down with the other hand to rub his aching shin. "Ow, *ow*, Tempest's barnacled *balls*—"

It better not be broken. So help him, if he'd broken his first bone in his entire life because of this, he was going to have to start believing in higher powers;

real ones, not the group of false idols trying to stake their claim over his kingdom and kin. The type of higher power that paid people back for right and wrong in the measure due to them.

Gingerly, he took a step, cautiously pressing his weight onto his leg; it held. Ached, too, but held.

Good. He'd make an awful man of faith.

Once that blinding pain dropped its broken-bone bluff, fading into a dim second pulse beating in his leg, he forced himself to take in his surroundings.

The smell of incense caught his attention first—thick and smoke-choked, spicy in a way that turned his stomach rather than tempted it. It came from a cart sitting across the stone-paved road from him: a cart decked in gold and silver silks, its wares hanging from gold-painted hooks or artfully arranged on glass display shelves.

On a handful of those shelves rested incense holders crafted from various materials: stained glass, unrefined gemstones…even sea glass, though he couldn't smell any brine past the smoke smothering everything in its holier-than-thou perfume. Gold and silver strings dangled from the hooks, strung full of beautiful blown-glass beads.

Something about them tickled the back of his brain. A flicker of Elias's hand clasped at the hollow of his throat, his lips moving in silent but fervent prayer.

Those beads had been far humbler in composition, though similar in shape. However, rather than a rose-eyed skull dangling from the bottom, these necklaces boasted a…

He squinted, silently cursing himself for not bringing his glasses.

A lamp? A lantern? It looked like a lantern, no larger than a thumbnail, made from finely crafted gold.

Well…finely crafted *fool's* gold, if he had to guess. False silver, too. No street vendor he'd ever met actually carried precious metals. Anything that valuable would be kept behind lock and key in the jewelers' shops.

He glanced behind him, meeting his own eyes in the reflective surface of a window: behind that glass, past his own face, he could see dresses and other garments arranged on mannequins…all styled in ways he didn't recognize.

Oh, depths. His face.

He wasn't exactly sure what would happen if he wore his true face around the past—he'd done it the first and only time he'd messed with chronomancy before, but that had been using Occassio's mirror relic. And seeing as Soren hadn't made mention of it, he couldn't be sure if that jaunt to the past had even been *real*.

Better not to risk it. Gods knew what kind of damage he could cause.

He shielded his eyes to peer deeper into the tailor's shop; no workers, no customers. A quick glance at the sign hanging from the door confirmed it was closed for the day.

He turned back to the window, covering his whole face with his hands this time. When he pulled them away, Jaskier's face smirked back.

Gods, it really was a punchable face. At least he'd made enough adjustments to make it passably handsome.

His hair was mostly his own, its waves carefully styled; however, he'd tamed it down to a sun-bleached blond, washing away any tint of red. His freckles were gone, which admittedly, he didn't love. The beard was a nice touch, though. He'd never been able to grow one well himself.

After another stolen glance through the tailor's window, he quickly adjusted his clothes: pale trousers stuffed into dark boots with a greenish tint to the leather, a billowing cream shirt with cuffs at the wrist—the most familiar garment he could see—and a sea-green tailcoat embroidered with mist-colored thread and outfitted with pearlescent buttons. The tailcoat had a cloak sewn into the shoulders: one made with supple, heavy material that matched the boots, capped with leather epaulets that jutted out rather than up.

More suited to his actual hair and complexion than the fake one, but that was all right. He wasn't here to show off his fashion sense.

Not subtle, surely—it wasn't the sort of ensemble one would wear to stay invisible. But it would make him look important, and important people weren't often stopped on the street, even if they seemed out of place…and more importantly, they weren't asked many questions.

He pressed his palms flat to the storefront's glass window, setting his forehead against it, soaking in its cool touch as he opened his mind. Opened his eyes.

Magic blushed at his periphery, pulsing inward until his vision narrowed to a pinpoint.

In that shimmer of pink, the future opened a tentative hand, holding a shy offering to its new master: a vision.

A vision of this city square from above, streets fanning out around it in spokes—one of those streets gleamed a bit brighter, and when he focused on it, the world swooped downward like he rode on the back of a diving bird, leading him to the image of an abandoned, dilapidated cottage…

Leading him to rustled pockets and bouncing curls and wide eyes that stirred memories of sweet tabs of chocolate melting in his fingers, melting on his tongue, coating a pile of pristine strawberries nestled in a picnic basket destined for a lighthouse—

He bit his tongue again, and the vision shattered, the future closing its fist around it.

Divinimancy. Despite its former attempts to drag him down into the kind of madness people couldn't come back from, now that he'd leashed and collared it, it seemed content to follow his leading.

For the most part, anyhow.

It was a shot in the dark. But at least his magic had offered him an approximation of a torch.

He turned out from the shop's window, taking quick stock of the area: he stood at the edge of the city square's bottommost curve, its several branching streets paved in gleaming silver stone. In the center of the square stood a fountain, empty of water and wishing coins—only piles of old mildewed leaves remained, drying in rotting piles atop a multitude of colorful stones set into the fountain's floor.

The fountain itself towered over the people milling beneath it; a figure wearing robes, their features carved in a vague mimicry of a face. Their arms extended out to either side, their palms tipped at an angle—Finn guessed that during the warmer seasons, water poured from those palms to fill the fountain's shallow basin.

The street he needed was past that fountain. But he wasted a moment on curiosity, on the scholarly intrigue he had cast aside in his youth in favor of darker, dangerous pursuits.

Around the statue's neck hung another lantern—this one large enough to recognize without the help of his glasses. Carved from stone, not gold, its once-sharp edges warped by time and touch; finger-shaped divots dented its surface, as if hundreds and hundreds of hands had sought comfort from the imaginary flame burning in its stone center.

Somewhere above, the sun broke through the clouds. The light spilled in a careless current across the empty fountain, lighting up the stones in brilliant rainbow…

Lighting up the silver trim along the edge of his pocket.

Lighting up the lithe-fingered hand creeping its way past that trim from behind, barely dipping its fingertips into the silken lining before he seized it.

Lighting up the muddied sole of the boot that jammed itself soundly into the seam between his knee and his calf, driving him down with a bark of pain.

By the time he forced himself up, ears ringing with fury and knee ringing with lingering pain, that boot was several steps ahead of him, its owner darting around the nearest shadowed corner in a flicker of roughspun brown cloth.

Well, at least he hadn't lost his touch—they wouldn't have had time to take anything valuable before he grabbed them, if he'd even had anything valuable in his pockets to start with. In fact, the only thing he'd kept on his person for this venture was—

A stone fell into his stomach, blood draining from his face as he patted his pocket.

You have got to be kidding me.

He shoved his hand wrist-deep into the pocket even as his feet started off in the direction the thief had gone, his mind refusing to accept the empty space; he even tugged the lining out entirely to be sure.

That pickpocket had stolen his depths-damned note from Kallias.

He'd grabbed them fast enough to stop them from grabbing anything valuable; anything *heavy*.

But paper? You only needed two gods-damned fingertips to steal a piece of paper.

"Occassio's crooked *teeth*," he hissed, though this was one mistake that couldn't be blamed on her middle-fingered manipulation. He shouldn't have brought the note, but even though his madness had abated considerably, paranoia remained; he didn't trust it anywhere except on his person.

It had worked fine up until now.

When he rounded the corner, the thief was already rounding the next one. With a brief glance left and right, he launched himself onto the half-rotted ladder leaning against the left wall, thrusting himself upward; each rung he set foot on snapped half a second later, but they provided just enough leverage for him to reach the roof.

His bones jarred up into his elbow joints as he landed on palm and knee, but his usual routine of cursing and blowing on his scraped skin would have to wait; though he couldn't see the hooded thief from this angle, he could *see* them in his mind's eye, a glowing ember whose path through the future glowed brighter than the enchanted stones they lit the streets with during the Saltwater Festival.

Every slap of his boot on the thin metal roof elicited an atrocious tinny *clap*; stealth was out of the question on rooftops like this, so speed would have to do.

Unfortunately, this thief was so fast that they were almost keeping up with the map his foresight drew of their intended path.

Almost.

With a quick twist of the clasp, he shed his conjured coat and cloak, leaving them to dissolve into wasted magic behind him. This was going to require a jump, and the last thing he needed was to get tangled up in his own outfit upon landing—or for his cloak to snag on some jagged bit of debris on the way down, snapping his neck faster than a holy soldier picking the wrong time to propose.

The lip of the roof gave way to empty air. Rushing wind. A thrill of heady adrenaline he hadn't realized he'd missed this much.

Kallias had the sea. Jericho had the gardens.

He had rooftops and alleyways and the giddy terror that only came with falling.

He landed on bent legs, rolled, then leapt back to his feet just in time to snatch the wrist of the fleeing thief, pinning them to the alley wall with their hand above their head.

Sun beamed down on them, a thin blade cutting through the alley shadows—lighting up the note still clutched in their fist.

Lighting up the inky freckles scattered in firework sprays across their rich brown skin.

Lighting up the cacao-dark eyes that peered at him beneath a dusty cloak, doe-like, dangerous in their youth. Dangerous in the way they drank him in.

Dangerous in the way that his heart stuttered in recognition.

"You know," he said, "once upon a time, they broke the fingers of pickpockets."

A rapid double blink. A catch in their breath…*her* breath.

Fear.

He caught her other hand when it swung around to try and punch him in the jaw, a frantic blow that never had any chance of landing.

He brought that hand to his lips. Kissed it.

"A pleasure to meet you," he purred to Cassandra Medeis, who trembled in his grip…frightened and frustrated and, fortunately, entirely mortal.

Her eyes narrowed, but her smile widened. Guileless. Innocent. So damned *young*—barely younger than him, maybe eighteen or nineteen, but eons younger than her jaded, jeering future. "Likewise."

He silently praised himself for having the forethought to study up on Old Sanctan. They didn't have many texts on the language in their library, as its use had died off just about everywhere, but it hadn't mattered. Between his memory and his magic, he'd been near-fluent by the end of the night.

Mostly his magic. Even he wasn't smart enough to memorize an entire language overnight.

"I'd like my paper back, please," he said. Or thought he said. His heart was pounding too loudly for him to hear his own voice.

Depths. *Depths.* This wasn't the plan. What good was gods-damned soothsaying if it didn't warn him about the *important* things?

Maybe, despite his hostile takeover of her divination and her deity, luck still answered to only one mistress.

But not *this* mistress. This girl had not yet tasted goddesshood; the heavy cloak she wore seemed to be in the best repair of all her clothes. Her plain shirt was two sizes too large, dyed a dull shade of oatmeal and done up with buttons— or rather, done up with two buttons and an assortment of hodgepodge replacements. A knobby shell, a fake shard of crystal, and two smooth pebbles had been sewn on instead, and the pebbles seemed close to falling out as well. Her ill-fitting trousers had been tailored for a taller, broader body; they were cuffed at least three times at the ankles, and even the extra material of her shirt shoved into the waistband couldn't hide how badly it gaped. Gods knew when she'd last had a solid meal.

Emotion tried to worm its way past sense. He firmly shut it out.

Pity was not part of the game.

Her gaze flickered to her captured wrist, then back to him, eyes pleading for mercy. "Can't give anything back if you don't let go."

He gave her a look.

A sheepish grin. She shrugged one shoulder. "Had to try."

Her accent caught him off guard—a lilt like lemonade, sweet and tart, sugar and citrus. Not much like modern Lapisian dialects. "Does that really work?"

"You'd be surprised."

"I am surprised—surprised that you thought that would work." He twirled her with a ballroom-worthy maneuver, capturing her arms in a cross over her chest; as she struggled and spluttered, he pinned them with one of his arms while plucking the paper from her splayed fingers with his other hand.

A tactic that would not have worked on the version of her he knew currently; but this girl, while quick as a frightened cat, had none of the razor-sharp killing instinct—or the pretty knives.

"There's no need to be *rude,*" she said primly—followed by a decidedly rude attempt to bite his wrist.

"Relax." He spun her once more, this time away from him, taking a few steps back while she got her bearings. He held up the note between two fingers, raising his brow. "Big market for personal letters in this city?"

She huffed as she wobbled to a dizzy halt, planting her hands on her hips. "It was a *mistake*, all right? I thought you had a pocket full of notes."

He blinked. "It is a note."

"Not that kind." At his maintained blank stare, her other brow came up to join its twin. "I hit you in the knee, not the head, right? *Empiric* notes?"

"Oh," he said. "Right. Of course."

She frowned at him. "Are you actually pretending you're a stranger to *money*? Wearing that outfit?"

Money? What kind of backwater kingdom used *paper* as money?

"Honestly, I don't handle much myself," he lied. "I have people who do that for me."

"Oooh, Mister Fancy has *people* who spend his money for him, hm?"

"I prefer *Lord* Fancy, actually."

Her giggle did a somersault—loud, then quiet, then loud again, like it had surprised her by coming out and she had to decide whether it was worth trying to suppress it again. "Of course. My deepest and most sincere apologies, *my lord.*"

What was he doing? Making her *laugh?* Making stupid *jokes?* Gods, this had gone too far already. He had to get out of here. He'd have to come back at a different time, in a different guise.

"Well, misunderstanding aside, it was lovely meeting you, Thief." He took another step back, offering a nod and a bow, keeping his eyes fixed on her face. After all, taking one's eyes off a pickpocket was the worst mistake one could make. "Better luck with your next endeavor."

She cocked her head at him, amusement slipping into curiosity. With a graceful spread of her arms, fingers posed just so, she offered him a curtsy worthy of a queen. "You as well, my lord."

Bile burned the base of his throat, bitterness washing in with the dip of her curtsy and washing back out as she stood, flashing him a smile that bent in ways both achingly familiar and utterly new.

Truth. So strange, to see the truth of this girl, this goddess—to look at her and see no trace of menace or manipulation.

But this was the past. It might as well have been another hallucination for all the bearing it held on the reality of why he was here.

"You!"

The bark of another voice—gritty with anger, feminine in timbre—turned both of their heads.

At the other end of the alley stood two uniformed figures—at least, what he had to assume was a uniform. They weren't exactly military, all robes and beaded necklaces and velvet slippers instead of stiff brocade and shining buttons and sheathed weapons, but the way they held themselves screamed power of some sort.

As did the strangled, near-silent gasp that hooked Cassandra's breath behind him.

As did the gleam of gods-damned *gold* in their narrowed eyes.

Again, honest fear showed itself off in the quiver of her hands as she threw her hood back over her head, donning a mask of flimsy shadow.

"Let me guess," he said as the robed figures approached, controlling his own trepidation as he met their golden gazes, "I'm not your first target today?"

"Please," was all she said in return—such a ragged, desperate thing that emotion almost slipped its leash. Almost made him remember when mercy was a thing he had any interest in. "Please, lie to them, I'll give you everything I've got—"

Ice clotted his veins. "Stop. Begging."

Her mouth immediately shut, but her eyes…those kept pleading.

His voice could carry truth, too, when it served him. And the cold contempt in those words, the same hate that implored him to use one of his spectral weapons to put an end to her life centuries before their paths ever crossed…that was the truest thing he'd felt in some time.

But he'd learn nothing to help his own godly performance if he let her get caught now.

Besides…had he not chased her down this particular alley on this particular day, gods knew if she would have landed in the path of these people at all. And if this somehow changed the way her future unfolded, gods knew what it could do to *his* future.

Revenge shook hands with resignation, making a deal to wait its turn as he said, "Get behind me and don't say a word."

Another whoosh of breath, this one tainted with relief—and soured by terror. She followed his order, ducking behind him just as the robed figures crossed from the sunlight soaking the cobblestones to the shadows swathing this alley in a false dusk.

"Son," said the one in front—a woman just barely older than his mother, her stern features lined with crags that spoke of frequent scowls, her salt-and-pepper hair pulled back with two gilded clips shaped like the rays of a rising sun, "is this boy causing you trouble?"

Now that they'd drawn closer, he could take in the details of their vestments: long, shin-length tunics in metallic silver, damask patterns wrought throughout the fabric in shimmering gold. Each of them wore shining breastplates strapped over their chests; a burnished-gold etching of a lantern shone in the center of each breastplate, the heavy layers of prayer necklaces around their necks rattling unpleasantly over the metal.

At the end of each of those necklaces, golden charms resembling that same lantern gathered in clusters; not street-caliber gold, but the real stuff. Weighty. Valuable. Some kind of status symbol.

And as if that wasn't enough, in the heart of those lanterns—the "wick" where a flame would normally burn—diamonds the size of his smallest fingernail practically begged to be plucked from their gilded prisons.

Yet, despite the fact that they wore enough jewelry to buy a pickpocket a palace…they wore no weapons. That, he didn't like.

"I apologize for the commotion," he said, smoothly slipping into an accent that mimicked theirs. It was unlike any he'd heard before—vaguely Tallisian, maybe, but softer. "Everything is fine. My brother here—" he looped his arm around Cassandra's neck, giving her a quick shake as he grinned, "was just pulling a bit of a dirty trick on me. You know how kids are."

The woman did not look convinced. "This is your brother?"

Cassandra's throat bobbed beneath his arm.

"I understand the skepticism, believe me. But alas, no matter how many times I beg my mother for the truth, she continues to claim so." A shrug. A chuckle. A flash of auramancy-whitened teeth. He strode forward with confidence, tugging Cassandra along with him, ignoring her stumbling feet and ragged breaths. "I'll get him home. Thank you for—"

Both figures extended their arms, blocking his way.

"Your *brother* here is a thief," said the woman, her lip curling in distaste.

"Yes, well, seeing as he only stole from me, and I'm feeling generous today—"

"He stole from the church," spoke the woman's partner for the first time. He was younger, lighter of hair and complexion; his gaze roiled with more excitement than anger. "A parcel of sacrifices dedicated to Sancta."

Smile fixed, Finn hissed from the corner of his mouth: "Scale of one to ten, how bad—"

"Nine," the girl hidden inside the hood peeped.

Fantastic. "Change of plans. Follow my lead."

She might have asked another question—the robed officials might have said something, too—but Finn didn't hear them. He was already gone.

Back up the wall he went, hauling himself onto the roof—without pausing to take in the strained muscles or sweat gathering beneath his clothes, he whipped back around and dropped to one knee, reaching his arm down. "Grab on!"

The robed figures shouted, advancing in one swift rush—Cassandra wasted a moment gazing up at him in stark shock, her mouth rounded into an O shape. "*What?*"

"Trust me!" he snapped.

No time to ponder the irony there.

"Oh, you *better* not be double-crossing me," she groaned, gripping his wrist tightly.

"That's rich, coming from you."

"Huh?"

"Nothing. Hold on!" And with a swift tug that took surprisingly little of his strength, he dragged her onto the roof with him.

Or rather, he got her halfway up. Instead of landing on her feet, something jerked at her from below, slamming her ribs-first into the roof. As she sucked in a cry of pain, Finn craned his neck to peer over the edge.

The woman had a tight grip on Cassandra's boot, tugging her back toward the alley floor—but luckily, those boots just happened to be suited for a dockworker's feet, and Cassandra was built more like a dancer. When she kicked, the boot slid right off, baring a foot covered in bruises and blisters.

Not ideal. Not when they were about to run for their lives. But somehow, he had a feeling this mortal version of a prissy goddess was well-acquainted with unideal situations.

They were sprinting before the figures below even had time to shout; he shoved Cassandra in front of him, huffing, "How well do you know this city?"

"Better than a carriage driver knows the backside of his horse," she panted, and gods, he hated that it got a laugh out of him.

"Good. Then you lead!"

Loud thuds behind them told him the figures had made their way to the rooftop themselves, but now that she was no longer cornered, confidence carried the girl before him like a gust of wind beneath the wings of a gliding bird. She shook off her other boot and sprinted on her tiptoes, fingers laced through his…

And for the second time that day, he found himself chasing a would-be goddess through a city long since lost to time.

CHAPTER 7

RAQUEL

She had forgotten there was a third Atlas prince.

Not by blood, but by marriage—the man who now sat across from her on this cold wooden floor, holding a steaming cup that stank of medicinal herbs between his trembling hands, was royalty only in name. Princess Jericho's husband.

Kallias and Finn's brother-in-law, who they claimed wielded necromantic power.

Who Elias had told her, in hushed tones while the Atlas siblings reunited in Sirena, was likely dead. Either due to his illness or due to Tenebrae tying up loose ends.

Who wore no metal…not even a wedding band.

Vaughn finally met her gaze, and she held it—refusing to flinch away from his sunken-socket eyes, his colorless lips, his protruding cheekbones.

Not dead after all, but that meant very little; he looked worse off than some of the corpses she'd helped drag to their pyres.

She had not been returned to the chair, but she'd been bound again…this time with leather straps, which wouldn't absorb the electricity coating her skin. So here they were, at a stalemate, both kneeling on the dirty wooden floor and doing their best to ignore the pacing footsteps outside the door.

"Tell me where my brothers are," he said…not for the first time since Vash and Vidia had left them.

And, not for the first time, she held her silence.

"That leather band in your hair, that's Kallias's—I had a set made for him two winters ago. He never takes them off his person; he's too afraid to lose them. So either he gave that to you, or you stole it, and either way, you have to have some idea of where he is now."

She spat blood on the floor between them. Didn't bother to follow it up with words.

He would have no answers from her—none but what she'd given up in a dizzy fit of despair.

Finn had named Vidia and Vash as allies. But if they were here, sharing space with the disgraced prince whose illness had been the catalyst for this entire war…they may have been persuaded to pledge allegiance to the other side.

And until she knew for certain, she would give them nothing.

Vaughn glanced at the blood, then back up at her…perhaps with a shadow of guilt darkening his eyes. "I'm sorry for that. Vash and Vidia…they have their methods. Especially when it comes to Nyxian soldiers found on the wrong side of the border."

"I'm familiar with their *methods*." Acid stung the tip of her tongue. "They've done nothing to me I didn't expect." *Nothing I have not endured before.*

He gazed at her for so long without blinking that she almost wondered if his heart had finally given out.

"Please," he whispered…that breathless plea so weighed down with fatigue that she almost felt sorry for him. "If they're dead, tell me they're dead. Whether you or Tenebrae or some other god did it, I don't care. Just tell me they're dead so I can get on with grieving. The hope is so much worse."

"Dead?" She tipped her head back, never looking away from him. "Like your wife?"

The pain that crashed over his features…it could only be named *annihilation*. His breath caught and held; his shaking hand abandoned his mug to press over his heart, kneading it with stark desperation. As if it would not continue beating without some sort of force behind it.

She hated the familiarity of it. Hated the pain in her own chest that tried to claw its way out to meet its twin.

"Yes," he whispered. "Like my wife."

Abject misery. Undiluted grief.

My greatest love was you.

"You could have stopped this," she rasped. "All of it."

His laugh came out dry and brittle, rattling like a toss of sun-bleached bones. "I *tried.*"

And there was no blow she could level against him worse than that—than the blow she had already taken herself.

That they had tried, and it had not been nearly enough.

So she took a deep breath, dust and despair tickling her nose, both threatening to make her eyes water. But tears were for another place. Another time.

She would not answer his questions. But maybe he would answer hers.

"How many of you are there?"

The grief in his gaze slunk away, replaced by caution. Tension flickered in his jaw, fluttering muscles pacing from one side to the other and back again, like he was chewing on something tough and tasteless. "Enough."

"What are you all doing out here?"

"You are the prisoner here, not me. I owe you no answers."

"Nor I you." She shifted back on her haunches, taking some of the pressure off the small of her back. "Yet you ask for them. So let's play a game of debts…one answer buys you one answer in kind."

He studied her closely. "You could lie to me."

"An advantage you share." Though she didn't think a lie would disguise itself well on his face. She'd just begun to learn Finnick's tells—she greatly doubted this man's would be more difficult to catch. "Even risk, even reward, Prince-Consort Vaughn."

Vaughn looked away, strands of his hair falling over his eyes like strokes of inked calligraphy, sweat and oil reflecting what little light struggled to brighten the room.

Then, without looking back: "Are my brothers dead?"

This, at least, she could answer with some truth. "Not physically, no."

"You know what I mean."

"You asked a question, and I answered it. Your brothers are breathing. Their hearts are beating. In body, they are every bit as alive as you and I." She gestured between her bloodied face and his haggard one with a clumsy jerk of her chin. "Probably more alive, actually."

He released a long breath. "Fine. Ask your question, Officer."

"Do we serve the same master?" Gods, it nearly gagged her, referring to that twisted creature as her *master*. But this was the part Finn had given her—this was the act she'd agreed to.

So she swallowed her sick and waited.

Vaughn's expression did not change, but his body betrayed what his face would not—a quaking shudder shook him from shoulders to toes, and when he leaned forward, he looked her dead in the eyes. "I would drive a white-hot blade through one ear and out the other before I *ever* bowed to the monster who destroyed my family. Us before all."

Us before all. She hadn't heard that phrase before…not from Finn or Kallias or any Atlas she'd met in the weeks since she'd arrived. But he said it like an oath, like a creed…like it proved something. Like it *mattered*.

Or would have mattered, if the right ears were present to hear it.

Unfortunately, strange mantra aside, she believed him. Which meant it was time for a gamble of her own…and she wasn't half as steady at the betting table as Finnick.

But that only meant that when she gambled, she gambled carefully. And she rarely found herself in possession of anything but a winning hand.

"And if I told you," she said, each word handed tenderly to the slight breeze that always wound around her body, who carried it to Vaughn's ear like a loyal courier, "that I would flay my fingers to the bone with my teeth before I served the god who stormed my kingdom, killed my queen, and orchestrated the possession of one member of my company and the deaths of many others…what would you tell me then?"

His nose wrinkled delicately. "I would tell you that you certainly know how to paint a picture with your words, Officer Angelov. And that I would be a fool to believe a woman who was recently overheard ordering fishers to chum the waters with what remained of Tenebrae's latest *examples*."

All part of the show. Those fishers had gone sallow-faced and quiver-handed at the bloody bags she'd handed them…full of rats she'd hunted herself in the upper dungeon level, bisecting each before dropping them into the burlap sacks, allowing their innards to seep through and stain the cloth.

If they had opened the bags before tossing them into the sea, it would have caused problems quickly. Finnick hadn't cared for the risk, but he'd acknowledged their lack of options. She'd seen him cross lines before—would probably see it again soon—but at least he was still human enough to shudder at the grisly fate Tenebrae had demanded for the bodies of those he executed on a whim.

The fishers, thankfully, had been too afraid of what they'd see to peek inside the tied-off sacks.

"We've all done revolting things in the name of survival," she said stiffly. "Haven't we, *necromancer*?"

His fists clenched so tightly within the cross of his arms that she heard his knuckles crack. "Some of us have more choice in the matter than others."

Before she could rip into him for *that* flimsy bit of reasoning, the door opened behind him, admitting Vash—no sign of Vidia.

He leaned against the wall, his daggers shifting on his belt, the sheathes jangling together like a host of windchimes. Her aching jaw pulsed when he propped his boot up behind him, eyeing her without fear. "Well?"

"She doesn't seem to be magically corrupted," Vaughn muttered—he didn't sound particularly pleased. "She's calm. Able to sit in silence without breaking it herself."

"So. In Tenebrae's service, but not swayed by his song." Vash tipped his chin downward. "Another point in favor of my theory, Officer."

She let her gaze shift out of focus…let the fatigue wash over her mind and blur her vision. Let it cloud the pain.

Rage against anything that would see you to ruin.

Guilt weighed down her empty stomach…but some sour, vicious satisfaction followed it.

Why should she rage when he had not? Why should she shy away from ruin when he had embraced it so utterly?

He had not considered her wishes before laying his life at someone else's feet. Why should she follow his?

"If you're going to torture me," she slurred around her swollen, bleeding tongue, "then torture me. If you're going to kill me, then kill me. If you're considering a ransom, we both know that no one in that palace—prince or god— would pay even a scrap of copper for my life. If you believe I serve Tenebrae, you know I will tell you nothing…and if you believe I serve Finnick Atlas, you know I will tell you even less. Stop wasting both of our time."

"Despite what you might think, Officer, I don't relish causing pain." Vash's lip curled. "Even for those who saw fit to kidnap a little girl and raise her to despise her blood family. But this is a different kind of war, and I can't afford to wait for answers. I will give you one last chance: tell me whether Finnick Atlas is in possession of his own mind and body, or I will bleed the answer from you."

Raquel let her head loll, her sore chin settling against her chest. And she said nothing more.

Rage. Ruin.

Oh, she had plenty of rage. All of it for him, because it was *him* who had seen her to ruin, even before she'd read that ink-and-paper order.

They could cut her flesh and taint her blood and taunt her spirit all they liked. It changed nothing.

So she said nothing when Vash dismissed Vaughn from the room.

She said nothing when he undid his belt and laid out his weapons like a peddler displaying his wares to a half-interested party, testing the weight of each until he found one to his liking.

And she said nothing when that blade found its way beneath her skin, a pick working its way into a lock…a tool meant to extract what would not be shared willingly.

CHAPTER 8

FINN

They ran long enough that Finn had time to thoroughly educate himself on all the reasons this was the worst decision he'd ever made in his life.

And as short as that life had been thus far, it had contained a *shocking* amount of bad decisions, so for this to top the tally…

Cassandra's hand fit just so in his, her crooked fingers bending where his dipped, her callouses scraping against his the same way daggers bumped against each other on a blade belt—weapons crafted in different forges, beaten by different tools and bearing different costs, but created to serve the same purpose.

Thieves alike. Yet her leaps across these rooftops suggested less unsavory skills; he'd been dragged to many a performance of a traveling Lapisian ballet troupe his parents favored, and the girl he trailed now took those jumps twice as gracefully as their prima.

Barefoot and all.

"I think that's far enough," he panted, after they'd circled and zigzagged and doubled back so many times even his perfect memory was starting to lose the thread of their path.

"Why?" Panting, Cassandra came to a spinning halt, flipping back her hood and beaming at him; her flyaway curls stood on end, coaxed to new heights by static and wind, casting dark spirals against the backdrop of the peekaboo-blue sky. "Out of breath already, Your Lordship?"

"*Yes*, and considering your lungs have to be half the size of mine, I'm shocked you're still standing."

"Breathing's overrated." She beat back her escaping curls with a huff; she removed two loops of linen from around her wrist, trapped the curls in her fingers, then folded them into two buns at the top of her head. The sun shyly peered out, cutting across her brown skin, drawing her slightly darker freckles out of hiding. "You're more than welcome to clamber down if you like, but I'm not setting foot to floor until I know that I know that I *know* those clerics are gone."

The unfamiliar word buzzed in his ears. "Clerics?"

"Sancta's smelly *soles*, you really aren't getting enough air to your brain, are you? *Yes*, clerics—the Emperor's faithful enforcers? Gifted with magic by Sancta? The golden eyes usually give it away."

"I know that," he protested. "I didn't say it like a question." He absolutely had. Slip of the tongue.

"You have a funny way of making *everything* sound like a question."

"It's this damned accent. Confuses a lot of people."

"Hm." Cassandra put her hands on her hips, tipping her head back to regard him closely—too closely for his comfort. "And what accent would that be, anyway?"

He flashed a grin. "Drop-dead gorgeous, if you believe the whispers."

She snorted. "I will shove you off this roof."

"I'm sure you'll try your best."

"Who are you?" Now that suspicious purse of her lips gentled into curiosity…and confusion. "No nobleman I know could jump roofs with me leg for leg…wouldn't save a pickpocket from getting her fingers snapped, either."

He couldn't help glancing at those crooked fingers of hers again, hooked in her pockets.

When he'd taunted her about broken fingers, it hadn't occurred to him that *once upon a time* for him could be *today* for her.

Enough, Finn. This girl's long-dead. And as for the version of her that lived on, he'd done far worse than break her fingers for what she'd tried to steal from him.

"I'm a fool," he answered honestly. "That's really all you need to know."

"And does the fool have a name?"

"Does the thief?"

Her lips twitched. A poor attempt to hide a smile. "If I told you that, then we'd both be fools indeed."

"Well, we can't have that." He jerked his chin upward. "Only room for one fool on this roof, if you ask me."

"Duel me for the privilege?"

"Actually, considering those clerics aren't looking for me—" and considering he'd finally gotten a grip on his senses, "—I may just yield the spot to you."

He strode to the edge of the roof, prying up his soles despite the conflict that stuck them to the shingles. Logic pled to run, instinct begged to stay, and the mire of indecision between the two pooled gritty dissatisfaction in his stomach.

Just over logic and instinct's squabbling, cleverness raised its hand, offering him a dice he hadn't yet considered rolling.

The plan had been to spy from a distance—to gather truth as an invisible ear, then retreat back to his own time and method-act his ass off until he could get his parents safely out of the kingdom.

But if he was honest…it wasn't the most efficient plan. It wasn't the plan that would get him the *real* answers he needed: the tiny intimacies and hidden quirks that came with knowing someone in truth, not watching them interact with others.

He muttered a curse, rubbing his hand over his auramancied beard.

Finnick Atlas, shying away from committing to a con. He never thought he'd see the day.

He couldn't fool Occassio—the goddess had lived too long, seen too much, played enough chess games to have memorized every possible move. Thief to thief, con to con, she would outthink and outcheck him every time.

But not if he flipped the board before she ever moved a piece.

So instead of jumping down to seek out the nearest reflective surface, he closed his eyes. Dug up his courage.

She'd done the impossible once—had tricked him into feeling something for her, into offering his friendship, revealing far too much before he recognized her for what she was.

And once the impossible had been done, it could no longer be called impossible. Which meant he could return the favor.

He knew this con inside and out, as both conman and mark. He had befriended Fidget— Occassio's sequined, sweethearted, sweet-toothed disguise— with exactly this motivation. And though he'd lost that game, it had mapped out his weaknesses in bright ink, dyeing them the same shameful red as a failing score on an arithmetic test.

He could play that game better now. Could play it perfectly, if he dared.

He turned back to her, calm stilling the flow of his blood as he shoved his hands in his pockets—a habit developed from the tremors he'd suffered under assault from her wretched magic.

Those hands did not even twitch as he said, "Of course, I'd be a terrible gentleman if I didn't at least walk you somewhere safe."

"But you've already walked me here." If there was one lock he'd always been able to pick on this girl, it was the latch to her smile—it swung open freely for him, a mischievous grin clean of manipulation.

The same could not be said of his as he grinned shyly, scratching the back of his neck. "I know, I know. But I figure if we get rid of your cloak, find you some shoes—"

"You want to do *more stealing*?"

"—And with the help of those poufies—"

"*Poufies?*"

He reached up above his head, miming out her two knots of curls. "Sure. I don't know what they're called."

"They're…" She paused. Frowned. "Huh. Y'know, I'm actually not sure."

"Whatever they are, they don't exactly scream *thief*. That'll help us."

She reached up and squeezed the poufs herself. "What *do* they scream?"

He pitched his voice up, cupping one hand around his ear. "*Help, please, we're attached to a madwoman who keeps shoving us under this smelly hood!*"

She gasped, gripping the front of her cloak. "I beg your pardon!"

He put his hands up in mock surrender. "I didn't say it. The poufies did."

"Maybe you don't want to walk me home, then, lest you end up downwind of my *smelly hood*."

He chuckled, holding out his hand. "I'm joking. Come on, let's get you home before that storm rolls all the way in, huh?"

She set her hand in his. "Fine. But no stolen shoes—I don't need more of the Emperor's lapdogs sniffing at my ankles."

By the time they reached Cassandra's street, his body had started to realize they were in the wrong time.

His back felt close to splintering down the center, like it carried the full weight of sustaining his presence here. A familiar coppery tang soured the back of his tongue, suggesting blood in places it ought not be, and though eye-strain was to be expected without the help of his glasses…well, they didn't usually burn quite so badly, the pressure behind them like a hand trying to shove them out through their sockets.

He didn't have long.

Preoccupied by pain, he didn't notice Cassandra had stopped until he collided with her, her fingers splayed out, palm pressed to his chest.

"I don't let people follow me home without knowing their name," she said primly.

He glanced at the house—well, more like a hovel—behind her. "But I've already followed you."

Her lips pursed. "Then I don't let people *in* without knowing their names."

"Wasn't planning on coming in."

She groaned. "I'm trying to thank you with the proper manners, Your Lordship."

He probably should've put some thought into this. *Jaskier Lionett* leapt to the tip of his tongue, a long-learned reflex—but it soured there, curdled by the memory of their past and future heist.

"Alexandros," he said instead, and it almost hurt as badly as the memory of that auction did. "Alexandros Ryder."

A scoff. "That's the most ridiculous made-up name I've ever heard."

"It's not made up!" Not his, certainly, but not made up, either. It belonged to his youngest uncle on his father's side, though he'd reversed the order—Alexandros had been his father's surname before marrying Adriata, and when they bestowed it upon Kallias as his middle name, word had it that the uncles had all argued for a solid day and a half over which of them Ramses had named the boy after…before Ramses reminded them that it was once *his* surname, as well.

Though, if his Uncle Ryder was to be believed, Ramses had pulled him aside after the others had left and assured him he was the true namesake.

Cassandra's shoulders eased, as if having something to hold against him made her feel better—probably it did. "Well, then, thank you, Lord Alexandros Ryder."

"You can call me Alex." This con was going to be hard enough without having to answer to his brother's name—one of them, at least. "No *Lord* necessary."

Her lips twitched. "Might be too familiar for someone I just met."

"Well, then, let's hope we meet again, Miss…?"

"Cassandra Medeis," she said. Finally. "But if you insist on getting familiar, my friends call me Cassi."

Hot and cold collided in his chest—a calamitous meeting of blistering anger and sinister satisfaction.

"When we meet again, Cassi." He bowed, took her pickpocket's hand, and kissed it—memorizing the path beneath her bare feet, the color of the bricks, the creeping vines that nearly obscured the peeling white door behind her.

He could find his way here again when he needed to. But for now, the silver shimmers beginning to waver before his eyes—and the runny-nose rush of heat in his sinuses that suggested a nosebleed was fast approaching—told him it was time to go.

"Take care of yourself," he added. "And maybe consider retiring from mail theft."

She rolled her eyes. "Trust me, it won't happen again."

Even without looking into the future, he somehow doubted that.

CHAPTER 9

RAQUEL

For days, Raquel Angelov held her silence.

Days of bloodletting tools working their way around her important veins and organs, causing the most agony while doing the least harm. Days of her praying to anyone, *anyone* who might be listening that none of those blades were coated in Atlas's notorious Viper venom. Days of only her growling stomach and the clink of metal and glass breaking the silence. Days of bottles containing liquids of various viscosities, colors, and effects pressed to her lips, Vidia expertly forcing the poisons down her throat.

Some of them didn't do a thing. Those, Vidia jotted down in a small journal, and Raquel never tasted them again.

Others ignited the second they touched her throat, burning her insides for what felt like hours.

Others made her wretchedly sick, muscle-twisting cramps contorting her body and forcing her to vomit up what little food and water they'd given her.

Others caused hallucinations more tangible than her waking reality; so real she could have counted every freckle on Kallias's face before his eyes melted from his sockets, dripping down his cheeks in molten gold tears, the letter in his hand still extended toward her.

So real she could feel Jira's heart stop as she clutched her sister close, hands pressed against the mortal wound in Jira's back, screaming for her to *stay awake, stay awake.*

The most dangerous were the ones that caused no pain, physical or otherwise. These lulled her into a state so close to sleeping, nothing felt quite real…so close to sleeping she often found herself speaking without meaning to, her thoughts spilling from her lips unbidden.

When she came to from those softer horrors, she often found her lips and tongue bitten bloody from her half-conscious effort to keep herself from answering questions she couldn't remember being asked.

Only one thing reassured her after those spans of lost time: that even when she came back to her senses, the other tortures continued on…which meant they hadn't gotten the answers they needed.

Which left her here: curled on her side, blood seeping from her newest wounds, scabs from previous ones itching badly enough to count as pain. Her cheek had gone numb, pressed so hard into the wood that every line of the grain imprinted on her skin.

Her throat tingled painfully. The taste of blood and bile and some kind of sour herb had fermented on her tongue; by now, she could probably wield her breath as some kind of weapon.

She rolled onto her side with monumental effort, swallowing down a groan as her abused muscles and skin begged for mercy. Once her itching scabs touched the rough flooring, she writhed desperately, using the wood to scratch the barely-closed wounds.

Bad practice, to pick off scabs before healing was done. But if there was one gods-damned torture she couldn't withstand, it was *itching.*

Best not to let them find that out. She had to imagine Vidia had an itching powder somewhere in her arsenal.

Only when stinging pain and thick, warm droplets of blood replaced the itching dryness did she fall limp again, letting her head settle against the floor, closing her eyes to the smudged, colorless room.

Ringing ears. Feverish heat. So many injuries that they'd ceased to hurt her individually; instead, they melded together, accosting her with single-minded suffering.

When the door creaked open, she didn't look up—but she recognized the soft curse, followed by painfully slow footsteps that found their way to her side.

"You reopened your wounds," said Vaughn.

She kept her head down. Maybe if she feigned unconsciousness well enough, he would leave her to the only scrap of rest she'd managed to get since Vash and Vidia had started their work.

Cold fingers touched her ankle, featherlight and frigid.

Her body reacted without direction from her mind; her feet flailed, kicking with all her strength at any part of him she could reach, hate stoking itself into fury as she—

"Whoa, whoa! Sorry—I'm sorry, I thought you were—Officer Angelov!" Vaughn skidded away from her feet only to lean in front of her face, showing her what he held in those ice-cold hands.

Bandages. Salve. And what appeared to be a canteen hanging from a strap over his shoulder.

"I'm here to help," he said slowly. "That's all."

That fast, what little fight had risen up within her fizzled out. She let her legs drop, panting, nearly gagging at the smell of her own rancid breath.

It made sense…some, anyway. They couldn't keep torturing her if she got an infection and died on them.

He slid his hand around her bicep, every movement cautious, his dove-gray eyes probing her carefully for any signs of violence as he gently hauled her up and set her against the wall.

"Here." He pushed the canteen into her lap; she stared at it, absently noting the sky and sea design etched into the metal.

"What's in this?" Gods, her *voice*—so ragged from all the poisons she'd swallowed, she could have passed for an angry mountain cat if she'd had the inclination to growl.

"Water. Nothing else." He paused, then took the canteen back—he unscrewed the lid, gave it a cursory sniff, then put it back. "Well, a couple lemon slices, too."

She looked down at it, then back up at him. He gazed at her expectantly, an apologetic smile fixed on his pale lips.

"I don't know how you expect me to drink this," she muttered.

His face fell. "I swear, it's just—"

She leaned forward to draw attention to her bound arms. "My *hands*, Prince Vaughn."

She could have sworn his cheeks flushed—from bloodless gray to almost-pink. "Ah. Right."

He reached his arms around her and felt for her hands, nearly pushing her nose into his chest—the smell of herbs embedded in the fabric of his shirt turned her stomach, and she turned away, swallowing hard.

With a muttered *sorry* under his breath, he cut away the bindings digging into her wrists; she leashed a groan of pain as blood rushed back into her hands, pins and needles stabbing her fingers and palms.

One blow dealt in her favor.

Even with her hands free, it took several minutes for her to regain feeling and motion; once she did, she scooped up the canteen and *guzzled,* rinsing her mouth and spitting out the water three times before actually daring to swallow any.

While she drank, Vaughn stood up, pacing a couple strides here and there—judging by the way he kept craning his neck, pretending to study the walls or ceiling, he was trying to avoid awkwardly staring at her.

Maybe he and Kallias had some traits in common, after all.

All at once, her stomach turned again. She capped the canteen, setting it aside…but keeping it within her reach. "Why did you cut me loose?"

Vaughn shrugged, fiddling with the cuffs of his sleeves. "You couldn't drink the—"

"You could have helped me drink. It would have been smarter. Why unbind me now?"

He hesitated, his gaze sliding away from her…then back, settling on the side of her head.

Mouth going dry, she instinctively reached up to touch the leather band in her hair.

"What did I say?" she rasped.

No answer.

She slammed one palm against the wall, forcing herself up—she barely made it to a wobbly crouch before collapsing back to her seat, panting, panicked. *"What did I give them?"*

"Nothing," Vaughn said quietly. "Nothing—"

"Then why are you looking at me like I *broke?*"

She knew the look—had seen it on Aeris's face the day his father whipped her within an inch of her life, and again on Finnick's face after Aeris had done the same.

She had seen it on Kallias's face too, wavering and fogged by fever, when she came to on Patch's ship and heard herself muttering without real consciousness behind it.

"I am Raquel Corentine Angelov. When I pass on, you will…you will reach out to Tobias and Ramira Angelov, and you will see my body remanded to them, as is honorable practice."

"I am Kallias Alexandros Atlas. You are not dying today, because I will not allow it. Do you hear me? You are not dying today. *That is an order, Officer Angelov."*

"Tell me what I gave them." Her voice rasped against the lump in her throat; a whetstone cut against steel.

"You gave them nothing," he promised. "It was me—I came in to check on you this morning. You weren't really awake, I don't think…you were still sleeping off Vidia's poison, but…"

"But?" Gods, she couldn't breathe. The pain, the illness, all of it faded, drowned by the pounding of blood in her head, the need to know how much she'd given away.

Her late battlemate had told her once that she tended to ramble in the midst of fevers and herb-induced hazes. It hadn't surprised her, not after a lifetime of Jira—and, for a time, Aeris—teasing her about talking in her sleep.

But this…more than Finn's wretched schemes, more than her own hidden loyalties, this secret was *hers* to keep. *Hers* to hide. Because if those who knew Kallias here also knew that he'd kissed a Nyxian soldier…that he'd shared her bed, saved her life, made her *promises*…she didn't know if they'd forgive him for that.

Her and Kallias…whatever they'd been, whatever they'd had, it belonged to no one but them.

To no one but her.

"You were holding this," Vaughn said, lifting his hand, something pinched between his thumb and forefinger.

Paper. Paper dappled with damage and tied with twine. Paper that riled a *panic* so pure that she forgot pain entirely. Forgot dignity. Forgot silence.

She threw herself at it, both hands grasping; that left her nothing with which to halt her fall, but a few bruises were a small ransom to pay for the irreplaceable. *"Give that back."*

Vaughn didn't step aside or stop her; he let her snatch the paper, the same way he let her fall, her elbow and knee ringing with pain as they jammed into the floor.

She folded it against her chest, over her thudding heart.

When she said nothing more, Vaughn knelt in front of her; his jaw quivered a moment before clenching. "You've been speaking to him in your sleep. Asking why he left you."

She steeled her own jaw. Smoothed her features. "Delirium makes a mess of the mind. Gods know what I was babbling about."

He regarded her with solemn eyes. Crossed arms. His veins stood out starkly against the pale sheath of his skin, ropey and dark. "Was he delirious when he wrote that he loved you? Can a pen babble when commanded by a steady hand?"

She said nothing.

To lie would not convince him. To tell the truth would be a betrayal—of herself, of Kallias, and of the vows she'd sworn to herself after Skyhaven.

Never again would she break.

Never again would she give what had not been earned.

Never again would she allow what was hers to be taken.

"You don't have to tell me anything," he said at last. "But I told Vash and Vidia they're done."

She blinked. "You…told them?"

He smiled, so sheepish she could almost forget he was halfway a monster himself. "I *am* still Prince-Consort…legally, anyhow. If they disobey my orders, I can have them court-martialed when this is all over."

Not true. When this was over, he would either be dead—along with the rest of them—or known to his entire kingdom as a traitor.

If his current state was anything to judge by, she doubted he'd survive to see the end of the month, let alone the war.

Regardless, if Vash and Vidia were still following their known chain of command, she was hardly going to argue with them.

"Why would you have them stop?" she demanded.

Vaughn shuffled his feet, glancing down at his boots. Not fond of eye contact, this prince. "You don't have to tell me anything," he said again, "but I know what I heard; I know what I read. And I believe this is what Kallias would want me to do."

No, Kallias would have wanted something far worse if he'd found her like this. As did she. But he was gone, and Finn couldn't afford any fewer allies.

And even if he could, she was in no state to avenge herself on the poisoner and the assassin in question.

Instead, she asked, "So what now?"

"Now, either you can treat your wounds—" he raised the bandages and waved them, "or you can let me do it, if you prefer. I was a physician once upon a time—my mentor, he was actually Nyxian, if you can believe it. And then…well, I suppose we'll all have to sit down and decide what to do with you next."

She squinted, suspicious. "What do you mean, *all?*"

CHAPTER 10

RAQUEL

Her captors were not the only people in this building.

What had seemed like an abandoned shack turned out to be a much larger structure that, while it certainly seemed to have been abandoned for some time, only had the one room in such a severe state of disrepair.

It made sense that they'd kept her there—always smart to isolate a prisoner, to give them the sense that they were being kept far from anyone who might show them mercy or kindness.

Though Vaughn had proven himself to be a rather poor captor.

In any case, this was not merely a building set aside for the holding and torturing of prisoners.

This was a safe house.

An infant's wails greeted her when she stepped out after Vaughn; a hum of chatter pulsed beneath that piercing cry, many voices mingling in quiet discussion. The scent of herbs both smoked and fresh embittered the air, pungent enough to bite into her broken nose; beyond that, a spicier, savory scent that made her mouth water.

Medicine. Food. People. *Children.*

"This is a hideout," she said.

Not working with Tenebrae after all—sheltering innocents from him and his, doing their best to escape his eye without fully fleeing the city.

Or at least, she guessed they hadn't taken her outside Port Atlas. Only the lightest whiff of brine still lingering in this drafty hall supported that, but it was enough.

Vaughn tightened his grip on her arm—then loosened it again when she tensed. "Sorry. Yes—everyone here has a reason to stay out of Tenebrae's sight. But they fear trying to escape, too."

Her toes—some broken, some bruised, and all bare—protested mightily as she started walking again, the chilled floor numbing her soles. Odd, for Atlas to be cold enough to pierce into her Nyx-hardened skin. "And your reason for staying?"

"My reason is my business."

"And what about your reason for betraying the brothers you claim to love so dearly?"

He halted like he'd run face-first into a wall. "I *never*—"

"That's not what I heard."

"They don't know what happened—not the whole of it."

"Does that help you sleep soundly at night?"

A miserable smile. "I haven't slept soundly in over a decade, Officer Angelov."

He stopped before a door with a puddle of light leaking out beneath it— when he flung it open with a long whistle, most of the bustle halted. Only the wailing infant, some giggling children, and a few whispers here and there continued on.

"Everyone," Vaughn said, "sorry to intrude, but I have a guest who needs food—and a medimancer. Is Briar awake?"

Raquel peered beyond his shoulder to get a look at the room and the people inside.

The *refugees.*

Everywhere she looked, tired eyes rose to meet hers, sleepless bruises struck deep beneath their eyes. Some held babies or shepherded children close to their sides; others wore blue-tinted armor that flashed in the light of the hearth, calling all her muscles to arms, her hand fumbling at her waist for a belt of knives that had been taken from her days ago.

But these Atlas soldiers weren't the same ones she'd met on battlefield after battlefield, bloodlust in their eyes and war cries on their lips. These soldiers looked like they'd lost a different kind of war—like they could barely fight to drag their next breath in or keep their eyelids open, let alone try to put down a Nyxian warrior with no weapon or war-wear of her own.

When Vaughn called again for *Briar*, a woman stood up in the back of the room, a towheaded little girl propped up on her hip; she navigated the room with murmured *excuse mes*, not flinching as the little girl tugged at her knotted brown hair. "Yes?"

"I know you just got here, and I know you're sapped trying to help Sarah. But my friend here needs healing that I can't offer."

Briar looked to her with a kind smile—but after looking longer than a second, that smile twisted. "Wait. I know your face."

"Briar," Vaughn warned.

"No, I know her." Briar bundled her daughter against her and stumbled back. "She works in the palace, Vaughn, she works for *him*!"

"She doesn't—she *doesn't*," Vaughn said again, louder, as the room erupted into alarmed mutters. "Vash and Vidia did their due diligence, as did I. There's more going on here than meets the eye."

That much was clear, and not just on this woman's side. "How is it you know my face?"

The woman stared at her, drawn-faced and hollow-cheeked, her hand splayed across her child's back.

"You escorted my husband inside the palace," she said. "He didn't come back out."

A javelin of memory struck, driving home a picture she tried not to linger on: a man beheaded, his two pieces left to bleed dry, freshening the stains Tenebrae liked to linger on as he lounged on his stolen throne.

A man with the same golden hair as the child in Briar's arms, her eyes and nose crusted at the corners and nostrils, her mouth open to ease the passage of breath into her lungs.

Raquel walked forward; when Briar shied away, she changed tack, dropping to one knee and bracing her arms on the other.

"I am sorry for your loss," she said. "I did what I could to get him out, but our enemy was faster."

A tear wobbled at the edge of Briar's eye, but did not fall. "What did he do with my husband?" Her voice broke. "Where did they take Nicholas?"

"They didn't. *I* did." She bore down on the howling pain at the center of her, the voice begging to ask the same question, to hear its own answer. "He is buried in a hidden grove on the palace's property. He was treated with all the dignity I could offer."

It wasn't a lie. She had buried him—as she had buried so many others—after carefully binding his body in burial shrouds, doing the gruesome work of ensuring his head didn't part from the rest of him in the grave.

Finn, surprising her, had offered to do it himself. But despite the remarkable detachment he'd clung to thus far, watching Tenebrae's wanton acts of violence as if vaguely amused and nothing more, she knew him well enough by now to have caught the sallowing of his skin.

Trickster and tormentor he might have been, but Finnick Atlas had only recently become a killer. He'd never set foot on a true battlefield, the kind where severed limbs and jutting bone became the norm. He'd not become so desensitized to gore and guts that his nightmares focused not on the sights, but on the smells. The sounds.

The scent of cooksmoke could still send her into fits of trembling, her mind mistaking it for the tar-touched tang of pyresmoke. Kallias had noticed every now and again on their trip from Artem to Skyhaven; she had brushed it off as a chill, and he'd been gracious enough not to point out that she had endured far colder temperatures without as much as a goosebump.

The girl in Briar's arms erupted into a coughing fit just then, a croupy thing that left her gasping; Briar's grief-flushed face dropped, overtaken with exhaustion, and she turned away from Raquel without another word, heading toward the back of the room once more.

She had not answered Vaughn's request—and Raquel couldn't blame her.

"I've got it," chirped another voice—a young boy popped up from beneath a nearby table, gap-toothed and gangly, his eyebrows so pale they were practically translucent. Long-wilted dandelions filled his shirt pocket; their brown-tinted golden heads bobbled together as he hurried her way. "Ma's been teaching me."

"That's very kind," Raquel began, "but I don't—"

"That would be wonderful, Kieran," Vaughn interrupted, offering the boy an easy smile; the corners of his eyes, always squinted in what she assumed to be pain, gentled a bit. "Don't overdo it, though. You remember what happened last time."

Kieran rolled his eyes. He couldn't have been older than eleven, but that look suggested a teenaged attitude might be creeping in early. "Yeah, I took a nap for a day. Big whoop. What's hurt?"

After directing Raquel to sit, Vaughn knelt at the boy's side. "Before we start, you ask her if it's all right for you to touch. Most people are all right with it, but not all."

Kieran looked up at her, hands hovering over her swollen and bruised feet. "Can I touch your toes, or are they too ticklish?"

She couldn't help it; she chuckled. "If you're gentle. Some are broken."

"Oh. I thought maybe you were born with them all crooked like that."

"Kieran," scolded Briar from the back—though her eyes were still glazed and glassy, a mother's instincts never quite ducked out. Kieran had to be hers, too.

"What? She could've been!" Kieran put his hands over her feet, and Raquel steeled herself against the nauseating pain that radiated from bone to bare skin.

"Feel for the break—find the seam," Vaughn coached him quietly. "Not with your fingers—with your magic."

Kieran nodded distractedly, his eyes fixed on her *crooked toes*. "Got it."

And he did—green tendrils of magic sprouted from the creases that marked the first knuckles on his fingers, burrowing beneath her skin. Instinct drew her shoulder blades together, bracing for pain, but none came—she could feel the magic rooting around under her skin, coiling in the cores of her bones, but it didn't hurt.

Honestly, it did tickle a bit.

"Once you find the seams, guide your magic around both bits of the bone—if they're just fractures, not full breaks, you can fill them in instead. You feel them?"

Kieran nodded again. "Yeah. Then I just—"

"Warn her first."

Kieran looked up again, smiling far too wide for the words that followed: "This might hurt a little."

Then, with a curling jerk of his fingers, he pulled those threads of magic taut.

A chorus of sharp clicks sounded, and multiple bursts of pain exploded in her toes—then almost immediately faded, replaced with soft, soothing warmth.

"Got it!" Kieran cried, delighted. "Look, they're straight again!"

Vaughn pressed his lips together, clearly fighting laughter. "Well, would you look at that. All right, let's work on her nose next."

For the next hour, Raquel bore the ministrations of the traitorous Atlas prince-consort and his spirited assistant. Medimancy sought out all the parts of her stripped ragged by Vash and Vidia; the soreness in her veins calmed, her inflamed throat cooled, and the tiny needle-bites closed up like they'd never even been there.

They couldn't clean the remnants of poison from her blood, unfortunately—that skill fell in the realm of sanguimancy, a magic nearly as rare as necromancy. Had Elias been here, he could have helped, like he'd helped Kallias when…

Her throat dried out. She cleared it sharply.

Before they could get to her bruised jaw or blackened eye, Kieran's hands began to shake; his pale brows furrowed in concentration as he hovered over a long cut down her wrist.

Vaughn slid a hand gently over his arm. "That's enough, Kieran."

"But we're not done," the boy protested.

Raquel took the boy's hand. "It's all right—you've done plenty. Thank you."

Kieran looked put out, but his head bobbed in a reluctant nod. He dropped his threads of magic, shoulders slumping, head dipping toward his chest; Vaughn caught him, patting his cheek until he roused. "You're still learning your limits. Nothing wrong with it; we all have them. Go back to your mother."

"Fine," grumbled the boy, rubbing his eyes. He offered Raquel one last smile, then scampered off to his mother, who looked on the verge of involuntary sleep herself.

Raquel flexed her toes; nearly numb from the unusual chill seeping through the floor, but much more bearable than before. "Thank you," she repeated…though it ground uncomfortably against her teeth, leaving a film of grudging grit on her tongue.

"Of course." Vaughn pulled out the chair beside hers, dropping into it with a long sigh; as he massaged his thighs, she could see muscles twitching beneath his linen trousers.

When he caught her staring, he cleared his throat, looking askance. "Kneeling like that can be difficult—and standing for too long."

"Is that an effect of your…affliction?"

"You can speak freely of it—everyone here knows." Vaughn rubbed his brow next. "Yes—my magic often turns against me if I don't use it enough."

"How often is enough?"

"These days? Too often. Two days, at most, before the pains and weakness begin. Three before I begin to grow…unsteady." He shrugged. "With the assistance of herbs, I can sometimes make it a week…but by then, I'm barely in possession of my own mind."

She didn't want to feel sorry for him—not after all he'd done. But… "That sounds like a difficult burden to bear alone, Prince Vaughn."

He cast his gaze to his feet. "It is. But for a very long time, I wasn't alone."

The letter in her pocket practically burned against her thigh. "In my experience, fighting for the sake of others is not enough of a motivator."

"It isn't. But sometimes, they don't give you a choice." Now his lip curled. "Sometimes, even the option to give up is taken from you."

Pain ruptured in her throat, clogging it with a lump that threatened to tear her voice to shreds. So instead, she kept quiet.

She had never been good at loving kindly—when she loved, she loved like a drake defending its hoard, like the things she dared to care for might be taken from her at any moment.

Because, historically speaking, they always had been.

Her family in Skyhaven. Her magic. Her sister. Her battlemate.

Kallias.

Had she been granted the opportunity, she would have robbed him of that choice without a thought. Because she'd promised Finn—because she'd promised herself—because she'd promised Kallias himself.

If you stay, so will I.

Until the end?

Until the end.

But wasn't that love? To fight for someone when they could not fight for themselves? To dig your heels in, to look that darkness in the eye and stake your claim? To say *This one is mine, and you will not have them?*

She didn't know the answer—not anymore. Not after seeing that bitter, broken look in Vaughn's gray gaze.

So she held her silence. And kept holding it, even when chatter began to swell around her again, the people losing interest in their Nyxian *guest* now that she no longer looked beaten halfway to Infera.

CHAPTER 11

FINN

The whole palace smelled of fear.

Its rancid, tongue-curling tang soaked into the layer of humidity ever-present in the Atlas air, base terror replacing brine. Even a hefty dose of perfume—the closest dupe he'd been able to track down for Occassio's signature lilac-and-sugar scent—couldn't fully drown out the stink.

Tenebrae reveled in it. Finn could tell, because since he'd found his way into Jericho's office and sprawled out on the fainting couch, Tenebrae had taken more than one deep breath, followed by contented exhales.

His tongue swelled with the need to mock the Chaos God for it. But his teeth kept their careful clench, trapping the words clamoring for release.

One trip to the past was not enough. Until he could set himself loose with complete confidence, he could not risk it.

So instead, he kicked his ankles up on the rounded arm of the couch, admiring the jeweled cuffs secured around his ankles with a diamond-studded button. These custom trousers had been a commission from his favorite tailoress, Francesca Serna; playing the part of Occassio required a closetful of costumes, and while he could create illusory garments to his heart's content, he was still limited by his own imagination. Francesca brought her vision and talent to the table; those were two cards he couldn't hope to trump himself.

Eyes fixed on the glimmering purple, silver, and turquoise gems, he let himself get lost in his own thoughts for a time…until Tenebrae spoke up, Jericho's borrowed voice grating on his ears. "Your pet is missing."

Finn glanced over at Tenebrae; the god had steepled his fingers together, his bloodred hair tugged back in a messy knot at the back of his head, his piercing gold eyes spearing Finn without blinking.

Finn gave a slow, idle blink. "Which one?"

"The wolfish Nyxian woman. Tempest's special favorite." Tenebrae wiggled his fingers vaguely toward the window. "No one's seen her. She missed her shift guarding our guests downstairs."

Finn returned his gaze to the twinkling jewels at his ankles, their cold gleam reflecting the icy dread flickering through his chest.

Raquel would never miss a shift guarding his parents—not when they both knew how important it was to give them a reprieve from Tenebrae's guards.

Had she not made it home from taking Luisa out of the city? Had Luisa turned on her? Raquel had taken the seer down easily in the shop, but gods knew if Luisa had come up with a better trick on the way out.

This could be a trick. A lie. A test of Occassio's control over Finn himself—after all, after seeing Soren survive Anima's possession, Tenebrae would be a fool not to keep an eye out for dissension from within.

So Finn just said, "Huh."

He lazily spun the rings on his fingers, yawning, refusing to meet Tenebrae's scalding glare.

"You need to track her down."

"I *need* you to remember who you're talking to. I don't take orders from you."

A longsuffering sigh. "It's not an order. It's a necessity. If she's breaking free from your influence—"

"I'm going to try to not be insulted by your lack of faith here."

"It wouldn't be the first time. Ani's little princess managed it more than once over the years."

"Yes, when I was barely more than a scrap of light on the wall," Finn snorted. "You think I can't manage to keep a simple enchantment on someone who's nearly always at my side?"

"I *think* that if you can't keep a leash on your lapdog, I'll have to return her to the kennel."

Finn forced an eye roll, flopping back on the couch and crossing his arms behind his head. "Are you practicing your threats for the next time we see Ani? I'm going to give that one, mmm…"

"Occassio—"

"Five out of ten," Finn decided out loud. "No, actually, four—you get a point off for being *foolish enough to threaten me.*"

Now he made eye contact—met Tenebrae's golden glower with the full force of his own, mimicking Cassi's mocking smile to its exact breadth and might, feeling out how it might look when stretched across a different face.

"I'll track her down when I'm good and ready," he added. "She's still got a mind of her own under all my magic, remember? She may be passed out in a tavern somewhere, sleeping off last night's poor choices."

Tenebrae's mouth bent, but he finally returned his eyes to the object on Jericho's desk—a music box covered in both elegant etchings and childish doodles. The god had absently been winding the lever all morning; the relic's tinkling melody grated at Finn's ears, but Occassio's stolen magic protected him from anything worse than a headache.

"I've set up a new patrolling system," Tenebrae said, shifting the subject entirely. "The guards who've sworn themselves to me will be on rotation throughout the city at all hours. And speaking of lapdogs, I visited the kennels this morning…played the hounds a little music." His grin, lascivious and dark, could have sent a shudder through the most fearless of men. "Those in the city who have yet to bend the knee…they'll do it soon."

"And if they don't?"

"There isn't a choice. Either they bow, or they die." Tenebrae's shrug suggested he genuinely didn't care which they chose. "Regardless, we'll be ready to move on soon. I've sent word out to the other factions throughout the kingdoms—my army is on its way."

"Our army," Finn corrected. Thank the gods he'd so long trained his tongue to run forward on its own when needed—the calculations running through his mind didn't leave room for much else.

Tenebrae rolled his eyes. "Didn't you tell me not to call your followers?"

"That doesn't mean *I* haven't."

"Well, if you haven't, you ought to. But I wouldn't dare step on your toes." Finn didn't like that tone, the teasing that bordered on resentment. "Call on them when you wish, but keep in mind that we'll be moving soon. Very soon."

Very soon. What was *soon* to a god? Tomorrow? A year from now? A decade?

"I'll track down my *lapdog* first," he said. "I'd rather have her do the running around for me."

Tenebrae waved his hand dismissively, returning his attention to the music box. "You never were one to carry your own burdens, were you?"

That wasn't the sort of person Cassandra Medeis had once been—not in his estimation. But he just laughed. "What's the point of being worshipped if you have to do all the work anyway?"

"You make a good point," Tenebrae chuckled, and the sound rang like a victory bell. Round one, survived.

But there would be more rounds to come. And he wouldn't be able to focus on them until he found out what in the depths had happened to Raquel.

CHAPTER 12

R AQUEL

S he woke to the tender caress of a rain-soaked wind.

At first, she wanted nothing more than to curl tighter into the bundle of old, musty quilts Vaughn had scrounged up for her. The cot beneath her had woken new kinds of aches in her hips and neck, but sandwiched between it and the quilts, she felt warmer than she'd been in some time. Even the Atlas palace couldn't chase out the kind of chill that lingered in her lately.

Instead, she unburied her face from her pillow, turned her face toward the ceiling, and welcomed the wind inside.

The storm-birthed breeze unfurled itself over her pillow-flushed face, a cool hand brushing against stifled skin; she breathed in through her mouth, and the taste of petrichor loosened a tension she hadn't realized she was carrying. A string wound near to snapping in her nerves, the piece of her that called to wind and weather and wildness.

The breeze sapped all the heat from her cheeks before ruffling through her tangled hair, coming to rest at her ear as it whispered: *Come out.*

As if echoing the request, thunder rumbled, casting a commanding shadow over the wind's gentle murmur: *COME OUT.*

But she couldn't. Though she'd been treated kindly, healed and fed and given a place to sleep, she knew better than to assume she was free to go. Vaughn might not have been willing to allow the torture to continue, but that didn't mean she was beyond suspicion.

It just meant he still loved his brother-in-law.

Her eyes finally opened, and she gazed at the ceiling until the blur of sleep sharpened into wakefulness. Until the stabbing grief dulled into a bearable ache.

If she didn't make herself move, she might never manage it.

So she tossed the blankets off, letting the damp shock her awake—skin tingling, goosebumps rising, she drew herself into a cross-legged position, bending backward to stretch out her stiff neck.

The eight other cots jammed into this room were empty—no one had been comfortable sharing with her, but Vaughn wouldn't let her go back to sleeping on the floor in her first "room," either. So she'd taken the cot, and tried to ignore her stinging pride until it finally calmed enough to let her sleep.

All this for a woman his brother claimed to love—but not enough to stay for.

Every morning, she promised herself she wouldn't start another day like this—she wouldn't waste her time tracing whorls of ink she could have recreated with her eyes closed, every loop and flourish engraved into her memory with indelible script.

And every morning, she failed herself.

She drew the letter out of her pocket, unfolding it carefully, forcing down the irrational anger that reared its head as she took in its new pieces…the slight crinkle in the bottom left corner, the new teardrop stain beside *You were the one thing I would have been selfish with.*

She hated that Vaughn had seen this. Hated that these words no longer belonged to just her. The poison, the knives, the broken bones…they'd all been lesser violations compared to this.

Her thumb brushed over *My greatest love was you.*

She stroked her fingernail down *Out of everything, you are what I grieve most to lose.*

I miss you. Those words doubled, tripled, echoed far beyond hope of counting. *I miss you, I miss you, I miss you.*

Lastly, when the heat flooding her eyes felt less like anger and more like tears, when her hand began to shake and her breathing grew harsh, she focused solely on his most important request:

Keep my brother safe.

A knock at the door closed her fist around the letter; she shoved it back into her pocket, unfolding her legs and forcing herself up. Her knees held steady, her feet—now shielded by socks, and then by her returned boots when she slid them on—feeling as though they'd never been crushed at all.

When she opened the door, Vidia—the poisoner half of the torture-trained pair—greeted her with an outstretched hand, a shirt dangling from it.

"For you," she said by way of greeting, ignoring how Raquel jolted back a step at the sight of her. "It's my least favorite, so no need to thank me. The color will fit you better, I think."

The shirt was plain black, which would have fit anyone, but Raquel refrained from commenting. "Is it soaked in poison ivy extract?"

Vidia brightened. "No, but that's inspired. I'm going to use that. Look, I would demonstrate that it's safe by wearing it myself, but it's not so convincing once someone knows I'm virtually immune to most things. You don't have to wear it, but you're starting to smell like a dirty sock that died in the drawer."

Raquel took the shirt. She didn't have the energy to do much else.

"There's a washroom down the hall…I think a couple people ran out and got water for it this morning. It's seawater, so don't drink it or get it in your eyes, but it's better than nothing. Once you're cleaned up, come get some food." Vidia held up a hand when Raquel opened her mouth. "No, Officer, it's not poisoned either. I asked; the Prince said no."

"Why are you still listening to him? You know what he is."

Vidia's eyes darkened. She rolled one shoulder in a halfhearted shrug. "No one else to listen to. The King and Queen are captured; we don't know what's happened to Finn." She leveled a pointed look at Raquel; Raquel ignored it. She sighed, then continued: "Look, I'm sorry about…all of that." A gesture down the length of Raquel's body. "Desperate times and all."

She didn't know where the burst of courage—or maybe desperation to know—came from, but before she could stop it, the question threw itself out of her mouth: "Did either of you use Viper venom?"

Vidia shook her head. "No. We probably would have—just being honest," she added when Raquel's fists clenched, "but we don't have it on us. It's illegal to carry it in Port Atlas."

She chose to be grateful for that hypocrisy. "Then I'll consider it forgiven."

"Wonderful." Vidia started walking; after a beat, Raquel trailed after her, hands fisted in the shirt. Looking at Vidia, she could tell it would probably be small—Vidia and her brother were muscular but lean, and since training with the army, Raquel had always been sturdy and tall, her muscle hidden beneath deceivingly soft curves and folds, wide hips and thick thighs.

In Skyhaven, she'd been too thin, too light, trained in magic and poisons and not in weaponry. Food had been served in minimal portions, and never anything indulgent, never anything tempting. Survival, not succor.

Andromeda had been different. Nyx prided itself on its scrumptious treats and hearty meals, everything bursting with flavor and substance; and after one particularly humiliating assessment where she, a brand-new recruit placed in the same company as her year-ahead younger sister, had to confess that she couldn't heft even the lightest sword on the rack, Jakob had started taking her aside every morning for some private training with him and one of the female captains. Together, they taught her how to gain muscle, how to eat to build strength and heft; how a bigger body could be an asset, not a detriment.

Luckily, the shirt's fabric stretched well; it clung to her biceps and shoulders snugly, and she had to tuck it into her waistband to keep it from sliding up and baring her midriff, but it definitely smelled better than the dirty, bloodied, vomit-and-sweat-stained undershirt she'd been wearing.

Well, it smelled like it had been fished out from the bottom of a bag, stale and unworn for so long it had forgotten the scent of its wearer. But an improvement, nonetheless.

"Much better," Vidia praised when she came out; then paused, taking in her dripping hair, only its mourning braids still bound. "Oh. Hang on—here. I know it's not ideal to turn your back on me, but someone's gotta get that for you."

If only because the woman had verbalized her exact concern—then followed it by keeping herself in sight of Raquel's eye, sliding into place behind her with intentional slowness—Raquel allowed her to do so. "Leave the braids."

"I will. If you feel them tug, don't panic—I'm just going to weave them in with the rest."

And that was how, to Raquel's exhausted, vaguely amused consternation, she found herself getting her hair braided by an Atlas Viper.

"Your hair is beautiful," Vidia said, working her fingers through it as they walked toward the common room. Even when she snagged her fingers and cursed, working the knots out with clear impatience, it didn't hurt. Maybe the beatings had rendered smaller pains inconsequential. "How do you get it this color?"

"Nyxian dyes." The blue tinge to her otherwise night-dark hair would be fading soon—though Nyxian dyes were the strongest of any in the kingdoms, much to the frustration and admiration of Lapis, they only held through so many washes. She'd been able to pick up a couple bricks of it on their way to Skyhaven, but Patch had only stopped in one Nyxian town on their way to Sirena, and it had been while she was senseless and struggling in the cabin belowdecks.

The cabin that, over the course of that one voyage, had gone from sickbay to sanctuary.

Silken waves of amber hair fisted in her hand.

The taste of winter and mint, summer and salt, consuming every sense—and her sensible side.

"No crowns," she'd murmured in his ear as she tugged that perfect crown of braids apart, raking both hands through until not a knot or twist remained. She'd bent to claim his mouth again, ferocity guiding her movements, unwilling to waste a second. "No crowns, no thrones, no wars or gods. Tonight, you're only mine."

Green eyes with too much blue, a reminder that no matter what sweet nothings she whispered, she could not hope to claim him from the hands of one of those fickle gods. But for her sake, he pretended; for her sake, he gripped her hips, tugged her close, and broke their kiss to growl in her ear, "As you order, Officer Angelov."

Vidia broke her from her thoughts with a tight squeeze on her shoulder. "You got stiff. Am I hurting you?"

"No." The word came out scratchy, and she cleared her throat. "No. Just thinking."

Thinking. Remembering. Wishing she could stop doing both.

They arrived in the breakfast room just as Vidia released her braid, letting it bounce against her back. "There you are. Feeling more human yet?"

Not especially, but politeness demanded something other than honesty. "Much. Thank you."

"Of course." Despite everyone staring when they entered—particularly Vash, who leaned against the wall with crossed arms, knives palmed in both hands—Vidia seemed perfectly content to keep chatting. She followed Raquel to an empty table near the back, dropping into one seat and kicking her ankles up on the other; Raquel gripped her own seat, turning it around and straddling it, leaning against the back to take pressure off her sore neck.

"So," Vidia said, glancing toward her, "I have to ask—where did you study, to have gained such a varied immunity to poisons? You're the first I've seen with resistance to rival mine."

"I didn't study," Raquel admitted. "I was…part of a community that lives outside the authority of the kingdoms. Our leader got paranoid that we would eventually attract opposition for it, and he insisted we all begin the process of building up immunities to common poisons. But his son…the two of us were close, and his father's paranoia caught on. When I took to the common poisons well, my friend insisted on a more thorough spread…we kept going privately until I nearly didn't survive a session. The physician warned us I couldn't take anymore, and our leader made us stop."

Vidia whistled. "How many total?"

"Enough."

"Fair. We're not friends, I get it." Vidia leaned back, crossing her arms over her chest. "I'll show you mine if you show me yours?"

Apparently she wasn't immune to foolishness, because after a second spent eyeing Vidia for any sign of guile, she said, "Seventy-two."

Vidia slapped the table. "Shut your mouth. You think I've got silt in my skull?"

Raquel blinked at her. "I don't follow."

"You're lying. Is Sanctan confessional oil one of the things you're immune to? Because otherwise—"

"Yes."

Another pound of her fist on the table. "*Damn* it."

"Why?" she demanded. "What's your number?"

The poisoner looked away. "I don't feel like saying."

"I showed you mine. You show me yours. That's the deal."

The stiffness in the poisoner's shoulders didn't let up for a long moment…then they loosened into a resigned sigh and a grumble of, "Sixty-eight."

Absurdly, Raquel's lips tried to curve. "You're a sore loser."

"And you're a *masochist*. We're going to have to compare lists." Vidia hesitated, eyeing her up and down. "Did you kill the bastard who put you through it?"

A blur of howling wind, the snap of a whip, hands clinging to her face. *There she is. Wake up, you.*

"Actually," she said, barely hearing herself, "Kallias did."

At that name, more than a few heads turned back in their direction; she cursed under her breath, rubbing the sleep from the corners of her eyes. Not even a day after the torture had ceased, and she'd already given them more than she had under duress.

A shadow moved—Vash stepping forward, his arms falling out of their cross. He braced his palms against the table without putting his knives away, leaning close, a spy smelling secrets. "What was an Atlas prince doing fighting a Nyxian warrior's battles?"

She met his gaze without flinching. "Not mine. He fought for himself—the same man who forced me to imbibe poison tried to make the First Prince of Atlas kneel. He soon learned why that was a poor decision."

What she didn't say: that Kallias *had* knelt, and had done so willingly, watching her the entire time.

What she didn't say: that he had not fought for himself at all. That he had taken Aeris's whip to spare her and Finn the same fate.

What she didn't say: that she had begged to take his place. That she hadn't been able to bear watching someone hurt him. That she would have scraped every shred of skin from her own back with a dull blade if it meant saving him.

But what really mattered in this moment was what she didn't *see:* that another man had wandered close to their table, wearing a face she didn't recognize and wearing a dagger she should have. A man who'd listened as she spun her tale, passive-faced but keen-eyed, his fingers fiddling with the hilt of that familiar dagger.

A man who stepped into her space, dropped the illusion shielding his true face, and caught her by the chin before she could flinch back.

And only because she recognized Finnick Atlas, golden eyes and all, did she not snap his wrist for it.

Apparently, Vash had some idea of what those eyes meant under most circumstances. Because while everyone else jolted back, parents snatching up children, others brandishing weapons, and Vidia standing with a sharp exhale of Finn's name...Vash threw both of those daggers in his hands.

Finn didn't release her chin. Didn't release her from the piercing power of his gaze. Instead, he cast his other hand out to the side, pinched his fingers together, and twisted his wrist counterclockwise.

The daggers *slowed.*

Like the air around them had suddenly thickened to tar, they struggled through the space between their wielder and their victim.

One, Finn knocked aside harmlessly.

The other, he caught.

She could muster no reaction to that—not while she was too busy trying to formulate the proper string of curses, too busy trying to find the voice to demand to know what he was thinking.

Only because of this inability to find her words did she stay quiet long enough for him to turn her face sideways; she couldn't tell what he was looking at, as he was studying her blind side, but judging by the throbbing pain of his thumb tracing her jaw, he'd decided to probe the tender bruise there.

"Who," he said, pure malice dripping from every word, "did this to you?"

She could only stare mutely, too amazed by his foolishness to answer.

He could not be here. They had agreed—if she got found out, if something went wrong, she was on her own.

Here and there, individuals had lurched up from their chairs, held back by smarter friends, hurling accusations of *kin-killer* and *blood-traitor*. Vidia, eyes flickering between Raquel and Finn, had eased back into her seat, looking stunned; Vash had two more daggers in his hands already, expression guarded, the closed-off coffin to his sister's open wake.

"Raquel." Finn's voice cut through the noise, a razor primed to slit a throat. "Who did it?"

This time, she couldn't control the twitch of her eyes. The traitorous shift that gave him his target.

Releasing her chin, he bent to retrieve Vash's other dagger, his knuckles flexing around the hilt as he stalked toward the assassin.

"Prince?" Vash said cautiously.

"Vash," Finn greeted him.

And then he drove his fist into Vash's jaw.

CHAPTER 13

FINN

God or human, Finn had never really figured out how to throw a punch without hurting himself in the process.

However, he *had* learned how to pretend otherwise. So after decking Vash, he allowed himself a quick shake-out of his throbbing fingers as he said, "Marens, I am grateful beyond words to see you. Really. But you hurt my favorite Nyxian, so, you know—flesh for flesh, bruise for bruise, that whole thing. You look good, Vidia. Vash—you too, for now. Guessing that'll change tomorrow."

Vidia, always faster to see a good thing for what it was, leapt from her seat and embraced him—ignoring her brother's hiss of warning. And pain. "We never believed you were gone—not truly. Not you."

Despite himself, he hugged her back—then hugged her tighter, realizing just how good it felt to be embraced again, welcomed again. "Well, faith *is* newly important to me."

"What?"

"Nothing." He pulled back, shifting his hands to her shoulders, giving her a shake. "I'd apologize for punching your brother, but—"

"Please, you know I couldn't care less."

Before Finn could turn his attention to Vash, a smattering of pink popped and fizzled across his vision, the foamy edge of a wave sweeping across the sand, priming the land before the bulk of it came surging after.

Gray eyes, wide and teary—a trembling mouth, unsteady fingers dashing across it; a voice more broken than Finn's aching knuckles, bleeding shame like someone had cut its artery and left it to spill.

Every notch in his spine filled in with lead, a weighty stiffness that both begged him to run and kept him from doing so.

And just as the whisper of a traitor's voice brushed past the shell of his ear, an echo tumbling in reverse, the real thing reached him.

"Finn?"

He'd thought both his brothers dead.

And though he'd hoped one might prove him wrong, this wasn't the one he'd wanted.

He had forsaken most of his masks by now. They were a tool from another time, regalia for a different role, and they no longer served him the way he needed.

But this…this he would need a costume for. If he wanted to make it out without accruing a debt of compassion, offering sorrow that wasn't his to spend, he needed something solid to hide himself behind.

So, hands slipping in his pockets, mask carefully sealed to every edge of his face, he turned to face Vaughn.

Vaughn clung white-knuckled to the edge of one of the tall tables, one knee buckled, as if it had given out at guilt's nerve-pinching caress. Haggard-looking, but then, he'd always been—Finn had seen him worse than this, though not by much. His clothes were in good enough repair, but certainly nothing like his usual polished button-up shirts or carefully pressed trousers; instead, he wore a beaten pair of pants and a sullied shirt, both stained with drops of blood and spilled tinctures. The sort of stains physicians picked up over the course of the day, not princes.

Maybe once, there would have been emotion—maybe once, Finn would have embraced Vaughn, overjoyed to find yet another soul living when he'd believed them to be long gone.

Instead, all he could feel was cold.

There wasn't even enough heat to muster something that could have expressed itself in a crack of his voice or a curl of his fist—no rage, no loathing, no disgust. He could only stare, numb and unfeeling.

"Surprised you're still alive," he said.

Vaughn's throat bobbed. "Me too." Then: "I heard Occassio had her way with you."

"She did." Finn crossed his arms. "Didn't stick."

"The eyes…?"

"I don't share my secrets with those I trust, let alone traitors who razed the home we opened to them."

Ah, there was the heat—not absent, but slow-building, a trickle swelling into a tsunami.

Vaughn's head bowed—before it could dip all the way, Finn asked one more question, the one question he couldn't seem to find an answer for himself:

"Why should I let you live?"

Vaughn lifted his chin. Held his head high now, gazing at him without pleading, without hesitation. "You shouldn't."

That, he believed. But unfortunately, though sense dictated he ought to listen, there was one whisper he listened to a bit better than logic.

"I will," he said—and noted the slump of Vaughn's posture, the near-disappointment on his face. "Because to do otherwise would be mercy, and unfortunately for you, I'm fresh out."

"Finn—" he began.

"Don't."

That one word, flung like a knife to Vaughn's throat—it stopped him mid-breath, his mouth opening and closing as if it didn't know what to do with the words it had dropped.

A ripple of heat—disgust hate loathing *grief* rage—then back to cold.

"Vash, Vidia, Raquel," he ordered, "with me. We should talk."

Vidia and Vash both dipped their chins—Vash's already looking a bit puffier than usual—and left the room. Raquel hauled herself up as well, but with a hitch to her posture, a curl of her lip that suggested pain.

He couldn't blame Vash for doling out pain to reel in truth—had the situations been reversed, he probably would've done worse. Might still do worse. But the sight of Raquel's pain didn't just drive the cold out of his blood—it made detachment an impossibility.

"Are you all right?" he asked, much quieter—she wouldn't appreciate him asking audibly in front of so many.

"Fine," she answered, curt—he'd expected that. She walked past him, bumping his shoulder with hers—he flashed his hand out, catching her before she could move fully past him.

"Raquel," he said, "now's not the time to be brave."

She ripped her arm away. "I never asked you to throw blows for me."

"Most people say *thank you* after being rescued."

Her teeth ground together, her jaw flexing with the pressure of bone on bone. "I never asked you to throw blows for me," she said again, "and I don't *want it.*"

"I didn't throw that punch for you," he said. "I threw it for Kal—because he's not here to do it, and gods know he would have."

Her breathing halted—then resumed, shallower, like she was trying to breathe around a tender spot in her chest. "I can fight my own gods-damned battles."

"Oh?" He glanced around at the room—at the beams that showed no scars left from lightning strikes gone awry, no sign of having been jolted out of frame by a powerful gale. "Then maybe you oughta start, hm?"

She might not have called a storm here, but one definitely lived in her eyes—fury swirling in a funnel cloud, ready to tear the world out at the roots.

Rather than wait for it to touch down, he turned and left, knowing she would follow. Hearing her trailing footsteps before she ever started walking.

Vash led them all to an empty room, ushering them in—the only furniture inside was a plain metal chair, rusted in places, surrounded by chain and shackle at its legs.

As he got closer, he took a more careful peek at it.

Not rusted. Those patches of reddish pigment were too dark for that.

He glanced out of the corner of his eyes, catching Raquel in his periphery—she'd posted up right beside the door, huddled against the wall, in the best position to run back out of the room if she felt the need.

He'd lied…a little. He hadn't only thrown that punch for Kallias.

He'd thrown it for the woman who'd sworn him a promise on a pirate ship, sealing it with a light punch of her own against his knuckles. He'd thrown it for the woman who had followed the sparest of notes across enemy lines, taking herself into the den of destruction itself to help him save his parents.

He'd thrown it for the woman who had accidentally called him by her sister's name. Who had held his hand and refused to let go when he was too addled to even walk straight. Who had let him get away with pretending to be asleep rather than face Kallias after their fight aboard the *Starsinger*.

And seeing her—Raquel Angelov, she-wolf incarnate, who had never run from any fight—looking as if she wanted to cringe straight into the wall rather than be in this room one more second…

That made it difficult to look Vash in the eye without bruising his knuckles against his face again. Maybe his nose this time. Or his teeth—Finn had never hit someone hard enough to send a tooth flying, and it had always been a dream of his.

But that wasn't what he was here to do. So instead, he grabbed that bloody chair and swung it around, sitting himself down as if it were a throne, ready to hold court.

The mildewed, peeling walls hardly held up to the shining gold and shimmering chandeliers of Atlas's palace, but he'd always been better at commanding these sorts of rooms, anyway.

To Vash and Vidia, both listening intently, he explained the events that had occurred since he'd fled Atlas—their quest to rid Kallias of Tempest's influence, their subsequent failure, their flight from Skyhaven, their reunion with Soren and Elias…and Kallias's sacrifice.

At the news of Soren and Elias, Vidia blew out a relieved sigh, rubbing her brow. "The Heir lives."

He frowned at her. "I don't care for the implication that I made a poor replacement."

"Well, we weren't entirely sure you were *you*."

"Thought you said you never believed I was gone?"

Vidia coughed. "I did say that, didn't I?"

Vash fiddled with one of the handles of his daggers, eyes narrowed. "Speaking of…you wear the golden eyes. Yet you carry no goddess. How is it that you wield Occassio's power, but are not under the influence of Occassio herself?"

"Oh, those were just for show." Finn waved a hand in front of his eyes, forming a brown-eyed illusion over the glowing ichor in his irises. "I've found a way to resist her—it's not without difficulty, but it allows me to wield her blessing without giving in to her."

Vash's eyes narrowed to mere slits now. "You used chronomancy just now—when I threw my daggers, you slowed them."

"Yes. That came from the relic, remember?"

"It shouldn't have been that *easy* for you."

Easy wasn't the word Finn would use. Even that smattering of chronomantic power had sent sweat pouring down the small of his back, not to mention the throbbing pain trying to chisel a chunk out of his skull. Sure, his nose hadn't decided to take another shirt out of his dwindling supply of bloodstain-free clothing, but not giving himself a nosebleed didn't feel like an appropriate metric for *easy*.

He just shrugged. "I'm told I'm something of a prodigy in many areas. Reading. Being a nuisance. Making puff pastry."

Vidia frowned at him. "You can bake?"

He pointed at her. "That's the weird part—no. But for some reason, I can do *that* better than our pastry chef. I swear, she's tried to poison me out of sheer jealousy."

"Puff pastry is notoriously difficult," Vash said, surprisingly serious. "Even professionals can't always get it right."

Raquel stuck one hand out—waved it. "Not to interrupt, but don't we have more pressing matters to discuss? Like being at *war?*"

"I don't know if it counts as a war if there's no army," Vidia mumbled, pinching the bridge of her nose. "We're a resistance, at best—a barrel of fools, at worst. We've tried to contact our companies, but we haven't received word back…or seen any sign of reinforcements. Either the missives aren't making it out, or something's going wrong on the road."

"Are you writing them in code?" Raquel asked.

Vidia and Vash gave her identical glares. "Who do you think we are?" they asked in tandem.

Raquel crossed her arms, scowling. "I think you're two total strangers who introduced yourselves by *torturing me*."

"Enough," Finn said with a wave. "It's probably for the best—Tenebrae told me he's summoned his people here, as well. Between them and him already having spread his influence over the garrison here, we'd be bringing your companies into a hopelessly outbalanced fight. We'd need more—and to summon them, we'd need a signet."

"Does Tenebrae have it?" Vash asked.

"No. My mother was able to hide it—but it's in her office, and I haven't found an opening to sneak in without being seen." Finn rubbed his eyes, flickers of light and color playing behind them, trying to draw him into a vision; he banished them with half a thought. Not the time. "I'm working on it."

Vidia regarded him closely—she sat cross-legged on the floor, hands capping her knees, fingertips tapping against her leathers. "So…the golden eyes. The magic. You're playing the part of Occassio?"

Finn shrugged. "For now, yes."

"And it's working?"

"For now, yes," he repeated. "I'm taking measures to make the ruse more convincing. In the meantime…Vash." The assassin stood straight. "I want you in the dungeon guard rotation by the end of the week. I can give you the schedule, but you're on your own otherwise. I need friendly faces around my parents."

Vash nodded. No questions—only acceptance. He didn't need Finn to hold his hand; it was why Vash had become one of his favorite assets. Finn only had to give him an objective, and he completed it.

"What about me?" Vidia demanded. "Should I be working my way in too?"

"No. I need you with Raquel—she's been bearing the burden of getting people out of here alone, and she's been doing well, but our usual channels may be about to close. The both of you working together may be able to get new ones open."

"We should start here," Raquel said. "These families…"

Finn nodded to her. "Agreed. Vidia, I want all of these people out by morning."

"They'll be difficult to convince," she warned. "They're either too terrified to try to run, or they want to do whatever they can to take back the city."

"Then we'll make sure they know how much worse it will be if they stay. As for the fighters, I admire what they were hoping to do here, but it's a lost cause without an army. Better they find passage elsewhere and join back up when we have a fighting chance. For now, our only priority is my parents' survival."

Small losses to win bigger battles. Small victories to pave the way to triumph in truth.

"Start with Briar," he added to Raquel—he'd spotted the woman amongst the crowd, and it had taken some effort not to let his illusion flicker, bombarded with memories of the auction where he'd seen her last. Memories of sitting with Fidget, laughing together, coaching her on how to read the room—memories of what came after, a dingy alley, his first throat-slitting, his terror that she might have been hurt.

And all along, Occassio been playing him like a fine fiddle.

"Why Briar?" Raquel crossed her arms tighter, glancing at her feet—he couldn't tell why.

"She's got kids. People trust mothers. Get her to help you round everyone up and explain what's happening." He jerked his chin at the door. "Vidia, go with her. These people know your face; they're more likely to cooperate if you're helping."

Both women exchanged glances, then nodded—he suddenly wasn't sure if pairing them together was the best idea, but it wasn't like he had a choice. Raquel slipped out first, Vidia on her heels.

As soon as the door shut, Vash turned to him. "Can the Nyxian be trusted?"

A snort. Finn scratched the side of his head. "Vash, I won't lie to you—I trust her more than I trust *you* right now."

"Is it because I threw a knife at you?"

"Two knives. And no. It's because I've been traveling with her for weeks now, and I could tell you what she's thinking based on how many fingers she's tapping."

Vash stayed quiet for a moment. "Loyalties aside, Prince, if she turns on my sister for any reason, I will place the blame on your shoulders."

"Yeah, yeah. I know." Finn paused, debating—considering how many of Raquel's truths he wanted to give away this early. Considering which of Kallias's sparing secrets he was willing to shake from his sleeves. "She was in love with Kallias, Vash. She might betray me, but she'd never betray him. For now, she's not a concern."

Vash's eyes darkened. "So Kallias *is* dead."

Finn hesitated. "I don't know."

Now Vash looked confused. "But you said—"

"It's complicated. I don't know. I have a plan—Raquel is part of it, but that's not our priority right now." Even if he wished it could be. Even if it was killing him slowly, not knowing where Tempest was, not knowing what he was doing with Kallias's body. Not knowing if his big brother was trapped inside, screaming for help. "Right now, I need your help with something else."

"What would that be?"

Finn crossed his arms and legs, leaning back in his makeshift throne, looking up at Vash through his eyelashes. He let the illusion melt away from his irises, allowing the gold to gleam in the shadows.

"I need you to teach me everything you know about Occassio-blessed magic."

CHAPTER 14

R AQUEL

S he never thought she'd be relieved to be back in Atlas's palace.

Yet, the moment she crossed into her room—a small thing that Finn said had once been kept for one of the captains of the Atlas Guard, painted navy and outfitted with a bed barely large enough for one—she took the first deep, lung-dusting breath she'd managed in days.

But even so…she could not sleep.

After hours spent tossing in this bed, listening to the creaking mattress, pulling the thin sheets over her body and kicking them off again, trying everything to get comfortable, she finally pushed herself out of it, kicking the frame with the back of her heel.

She rubbed her eyes, then glared blearily toward the single window. Moonlight flooded in, carried on a heavily salted breeze; the ocean winked tauntingly at her, waves twinkling silver and ebony, trading its Atlas blues for Nyxian blacks.

It could not have sent a clearer message. A louder call.

She threw it a middle-fingered answer, then marched back to her bed.

Another hour.

Another hour.

Another hour.

The walls closed in. The air, fresh as it was, began to thicken and stifle. The sheets itched. The ocean roared.

Damn it.

Before another hour could pass, while the sky clung to its darkness like a shivering waif clutching their cloak, she blindly threw on clothes and pushed her way out of the palace, ignoring how Tenebrae's guards at the door followed her with wild grins and hooting calls.

She let her feet lead. And as always, the damned traitors led her straight to the shore.

Kallias had whispered to her once of sunsets in Atlas. How, once you saw one, no other sunset could compare. How you'd ache for the sight every night, nothing short of impending death preventing you from taking that journey. How the colors blossomed so brilliantly that the people lined up on the shore burst into applause when it was over, unable to contain their awe.

She had avoided it religiously since she'd arrived. Had hidden herself away in windowless rooms and dank dungeons so she could never be bewitched by it.

And…and because she did not want to see it without him.

She circled her wrist with her opposite hand, staring out at the midnight sea, and breathed.

And breathed.

And breathed.

Sunset was long past—though dawn approached, paling the edges of the sky from onyx to twilight blue, there was no danger of addiction and applause; no risk of mouthwatering oranges or pocket-jingling golds, no blushing pinks or streaks of lavender syrup trailed through the clouds.

No clouds at all, in fact.

And even if there had been, she was so, so tired of playing the coward.

Finn was right. If she could fight her own battles, then she ought to prove it. And this was one piece of proof that couldn't bruise or cut or break.

She left her cloak and boots on the border between city and shore.

The sand cooled her toes—even the dry stuff at the top of the beach held a pleasant chill left behind by the night air. It sifted beneath her heels like powdered sugar dusted on her favorite croissants, coating her toes, and her inexperienced ankles kept trying to roll. Even snow, as forgiving as it often was, had not been quite this pliable, so willing to bend to her will that its lack of fight actually hurt worse than if it had stood its ground.

She almost loved it.

It felt like a battle, or a dance—a series of steps that demanded her engagement, a path that would sweep her ankles out from beneath her if she did not devote herself to it with single-minded focus.

When she crossed over from dry to wet sand, her feet sank to the ankles, consumed in seconds—now the pleasant chill plunged to toe-numbing ice, and the last tendril of tension in her shoulders slipped away.

Like home.

The next wave swept up the shore, lapping at her ankles, and she shivered as she trawled her feet out and wandered deeper into the water.

Ankles. Shins. Knees. She kept going, heedless of her soaked and stiff trouser legs, until she stood waist-deep in the churning sea.

Dangerous, she knew, to be out this deep as one inexperienced with ocean tides. But she felt no fear.

The waves that bore her body up and down, lifting her like she was light as a cork, did not treat her as an enemy—instead, they wrapped themselves around her like an embrace, like a joyful reunion.

Eye of the Storm. Welcome home.

Some part of her, despite its unfamiliarity with the ocean, knew that things weren't quite right. That this deep in summer, the water should have been warm; the wind should have been soft, humid. Her skin should not have been going numb, covered by a coat of goosebumps.

But chaos had cast its net over everything else in her wretched life. Not this.

Not this.

She tugged her hair free from its braid, letting it fall loose around her shoulders; with a surge of recklessness that crested alongside the next wave, she drew in a deep breath, braced herself, and dove headfirst into the water.

The shock wasn't unfamiliar—she'd swum in icier waters, both in Skyhaven and in Andromeda, for fun and for the sake of pride. But this one…this one took her breath away.

She resurfaced with a gasp, saltwater and tears pouring from her stinging eyes. She wiped them away, but her soaked hands only left more salt lining her eyelids.

She kept forgetting that saltwater hurt.

So back to the beach she trudged, grateful no one was there to witness her cursing and crying, even if it came without embarrassing sniffles and sobs. She snatched up the towel she'd brought along, burying her face in its fibers, breathing in the clean cotton scent—

"Saltwater suits you, Raquel Angelov."

She froze, hands fisting in the towel, crushing pain erupting in her chest.

His voice—but wrong. All wrong, with its rumbling undertone, the arrogant lilt, the booming quality that traveled through the air as easily as faraway thunder.

She did not turn. Did not look.

"Why are you here."

"I could ask you the same question." A flicker of golden-red, standing stark against the lightening sky; shoulders draped in wolf's fur, his chest banded in tooled gray-blue leather. "I see you and the ocean have made your peace."

Peace had never been further from her grasp than this. "Leave."

"It's my beach." With a snort, Tempest—God of Nature, God of Storms—circled around her, eyeing her with amusement that infuriated. A fury that only blazed hotter as she took in the cropped hair, the faded freckles, the confident swagger—all the little pieces of Kallias he had taken and shaped to his own liking. "And to answer your question, I've been heading here for some time— took the long way from Sirena, though. I wanted to see what's become of my kingdom while I've been away…felt like we needed to get reacquainted."

Fury roared out of her like drake-fire, noiseless but cataclysmic: "This is not *your kingdom*."

"Nor is it yours, yet you're here." He crossed his arms, cloak shifting in the wind, its edge raking the sand flat. "Raquel Angelov, Eye of the Storm…Atlas's protector. Who would have thought?"

She gripped the bracelet around her wrist. Breathed. Breathed. Breathed. "I told you to leave."

He did not. Instead, he smirked at her, a hint of old fondness—maybe even a hint of sadness—gleaming in his gilded gaze. "You know…I remember a girl, once upon a time, who would have done anything I asked of her. Who would have made any sacrifice, obeyed any order. Now here you are, spitting at me like a pissed-off polecat."

"That girl died," she spat. Worse than died—her chosen family in Skyhaven had ripped out her eye, beaten her to death to kill her magic, then forced her heart to beat again just to toss her out in the cold, hoping she'd be devoured by wolves. "Do you remember *that?*"

His eyes darkened. "Yes."

"Maybe if you'd answered a prayer or two that day, then this would be a different conversation." Or maybe it wouldn't. Maybe the loss of Kallias alone would have been plenty to drive her to *spit* at a god.

Tempest merely gazed at her, calmer and colder than the surface of a frozen lake. "You have that magic back now. Does it feel the same as you remember?"

So she was to be ignored then. Fine.

Through gritted teeth, she said, "I haven't had much chance to use it."

"Well, no better time than now." He jerked his bearded chin toward the water. "Call to it."

She scoffed. Bent to put on her boots. "Go to the pits."

She'd only just tied the laces and started to stand when frigid cold *crashed* over her body, forcing her down to one knee, knocking the breath clean out of her.

She stared at her now-sopping boots through a sheet of dripping wet hair. Her chest began to heave.

When she looked up, she found Tempest smirking down at her, arms crossed again—a challenge if she'd ever seen one.

"Call to it," he repeated.

"No." She forced herself back to her feet. "You cannot—"

Another crash. Another shock. This time, it threw her fully into the sand, skin burning where it scraped against coarse grains and stinging where stray shells left scratches behind.

She glanced over her shoulder, coughing, spitting salt—the waves no longer crashed at an even pace, the tide moving at its scheduled speed. Now they loomed mid-crest, refusing to break—now they stood at attention, soldiers awaiting orders from the god who stood before them, one hand up, fingers bent loosely.

Shivering, shaking with rage, she fumbled beneath her crumpled cloak for her sword. The second she drew it, pain lanced through her palm and up her arm, numbing it—her fingers sprang free of their own accord, dropping the sword back into the sand.

Tempest tsked at her, his other hand crackling with unspent lightning, spears sparking between his knuckles. "This is all he asked for—your magic returned. Do right by what he gave you."

Another order. As if he had any right. As if he had earned that kind of respect.

As if he was not *puppeting* the body of the man she loved.

"You know *nothing*," she snarled, "about what he gave—and what I have done since to honor it. If you won't leave, then allow me that courtesy."

She bundled up her things, a hundred other words coursing through her mind—curses, accusations, threats. But her threats would inspire nothing in a god besides his amusement…or worse, his pity. If the beach belonged to him, fine. She wanted no part of it.

She only made it three feet.

The sand shifted beneath her—not the same shifting she'd enjoyed earlier. This was a *tug*—this carried her forcibly toward the water, the earth returning her to Tempest, who now grinned in truth.

Thunder boomed; lightning flashed. They both looked up to find clouds choking out the dawn…clouds that had not been there five minutes prior.

"I heard complaints about this being the stormiest summer Atlas has ever seen," Tempest chuckled. "Now I see why."

"Let me leave," she seethed.

His face smoothed, impassive as a stone wall. "Make me."

Make me. How could she force a damned *god* to do anything?

"I am fighting enough battles." She didn't mean to say it, but it was there, and it was true. "And you have bigger ones to fight than with me."

The lightning strung between his fingers like a game of cat's cradle brightened; her only warning.

Scalding blue light. Energy combusting in the air.

She moved without thinking, throwing splayed palms outward, heel to heel—muscle memory. Teachings left over from when she and Aeris had trained side by side, private lessons with his father, two twice-blessed wielders honing their strongest magic into an art form.

The lightning struck that space between her wrists, channeling into the bloodbeats in each, and her very veins lit with painful, perfect *power.*

And not just her veins—the lightning split, stray strands of electricity crackling over her soaked skin, forcing the hairs on her arms to stand up straight and salute. The air hummed and popped around her, unable to contain the storm breaking within and without.

"There you are." She barely heard the soft, satisfied sigh from Tempest. "Eye of the Storm."

Raquel stared. And as she stared, pressure bore down on her skin and shoulders, a slow shove toward the ground, knees shaking beneath the weight of the storm swirling into being.

But this storm wasn't his. Not anymore.

This storm belonged to her. And he would regret baiting her into creating it.

Locking her knees, steadying her stance, she pushed her hands out and *shoved.*

The lightning shot out like a javelin, a blinding arc of blue to silver that drove directly into his heart—a strike that would have struck a mortal man dead.

The god stumbled back one entire step.

A victory she'd take.

"Haven't you taken enough from me?" she spat. "Do you get some *joy* from this?"

Now the cut of his grin turned a bit feral. "I promised your prince I would defend his people and family as my own. And letting you mope about on the beach, refusing to touch your magic? I don't believe he'd want that."

"So I'm a tool to assuage your guilt for stealing someone's life."

"I stole nothing. He gave it freely."

Her body trembled with aftershocks from the lightning, her heart fluttering unpleasantly. "Of course he did. You told him he wasn't good enough, and he *believed you.*"

Tempest's knuckles flexed. "Raquel—"

"You don't get to use my name," she rasped, driving herself forward a few steps. "Not with his voice. Not with his breath. *Let. Me. Leave.*"

His eyelids fell to half-mast, assessing; after a beat, he stepped aside, angling his body away. "Hurry home. Seems a storm's rolling in."

She ignored him. Tilted her head away from his body. Bundled up her cloak and stormed back onto the cobblestone streets without pausing to put it on.

And when the rain finally started, so did her tears.

They warmed her cheeks as she stalked through the Port Atlas streets, ignoring glances from rare passersby, ignoring the way they skirted around her, ignoring the hatred in their eyes—their malice toward the hunting hound of the cruel new queen and pretender prince.

But there were some who would not be ignored.

"Angelov!" called a man lurking in the shadow of a tavern; the building's sign had been torn down, the windows barred and dark, yet the man and his two companions seemed content with their perch. The speaker bared a grin, the edges of his gums blackened. "You look like a drowned rat. What're you up to out here?"

Revan, Arcas, and Pyra—Tenebrae's special favorites, a Tallisian and two Artemisians he'd called here mere days ago—were the last people she wanted to speak to, let alone smile for. But she forced one anyway, a grimace dressed up in its best clothes. "Ran an errand and got caught in the storm, that's all. You?"

"Looking for some trouble," giggled Pyra. Her bark-brown hair hung around her shoulders, clumped and tangled like it hadn't met a brush in some time, and her blue eyes sparkled with a now-familiar unsettling gleam. "And if we can't find it, we've orders to make it."

Arcas held up his hand, snapping his fingers—a flame danced between his thumb and index finger. "You're welcome to join, if you've got nothing better to do."

"I serve a different master, if you recall." At their expressions of disbelief and disgruntlement, she forced another smile, doing her best to make it look coy. She'd never been particularly well-suited to that sort of thing, but being around Finn had given her a good example. "Occassio heaps plenty on my plate."

"It is odd," said Revan slowly, twirling one of his dark curls around his finger, "to see a Nyxian woman serving the Goddess of Time."

She gave him a careful once-over. "No odder than a Tallisian—or an Artemisian, for that matter—serving the God of Chaos, hm?"

Arcas alone relaxed, smirking at her in understanding. "Strange times."

"Stranger *all* the time," she agreed.

They turned back to their own conversation, freeing her to continue her cautious flight back to the palace. But the further away from them she went, the louder things became behind her, cackling laughter and horrorstruck screams whispering a tale of chaos being woven in her wake.

It took everything to not turn around. Everything to keep her eyes locked on the palace. Everything to keep walking, one foot after the other, unwilling to even cover her ears for fear of being seen.

Kallias had given his life to avoid this—had granted Tempest everything in exchange for a promise, a currency Raquel refused to trade in.

Even if Tempest chose to make good on it rather than find reasons to taunt her…they were running out of time.

Atlas was running out of time.

CHAPTER 15

FINN

When he tugged the sheet aside from the mirror with a flourish, he did not find Cassi pounding at the glass or whistling inane songs or screaming at the top of her very powerful lungs.

Today, in fact, he did not see her at all.

She was there—he could sense her in the rippling face of the mirror, an invisible stone disrupting the shallow current of a trickling brook, camouflaged in the silt beneath the surface. But that was all—an impression, an effect without a cause, a thing whose existence could only be proved because of the way things moved around it.

He knocked on the frame. "Anyone home?"

No answer.

"I know you're there."

Silence.

"Cassi," he sighed, "this is very unbecoming."

"I'll be *your* unbecoming."

He gave her a vague approximation of applause, his wrists loose as he let his hands clap together. "Ooh, good one. Is it my turn?"

A ripple from the center of the mirror finally revealed her—she sat with her back to the mirror, curls a bit less shiny, dress a bit more wrinkled. She turned her head without turning the rest of her body, glaring balefully at him over her shoulder. "Can't you see I'm busy?"

"Well, not until now, no." He gripped the frame of the mirror, leaning in to peer closer. "I didn't know sitting in a cell counted as being busy these days."

"I'm trying to meditate."

"Difficult, I assume, with someone chattering in your ear."

"Unimaginably, yes."

He tightened his grip on the mirror and rattled it until the glass shuddered noisily in its frame—she clamped her hands over her ears, and he said, "Pretty sure I can imagine."

"I hate you," she seethed.

"Join the club. They meet every other week."

"I'm going to *kill* you."

"Take a number." He made a shooing motion. "Scoot. I have business of my own."

"You know I'm not actually in your way," she groused, turning her head away again. "If I was, I could jump right out when you open the mirror."

"I know, but I find great joy in inconveniencing you."

She crossed her arms. Didn't budge. "Just go."

"You're grumpy this morning."

"Just. Go."

Something about her tone struck him wrong—he'd grown used to her bitterness, grown used to her saccharine pleas and vicious insults, but this time...

This time, something was different.

He turned the mirror this way and that, trying to find a better angle, but no matter how he craned his neck or tilted the glass—even when he took the mirror fully off the wall—he couldn't catch more than a sliver of the side of her face.

The words leapt to his tongue, a demand to know what was wrong…then faded.

He didn't care what was wrong. He *wanted* her bitter, angry, miserable. He wanted her wasting away in that damned mirror. He wanted her to know how it felt to get trapped. To get tricked.

"This is far from my worst," he reminded her. "I didn't bleed you. I didn't break you. This is *kind* compared to what you did to me."

He hauled the mirror up, hanging it back on its hook, ignoring the strange glimmer he caught playing at the edge of her eye.

A trick of the light, that was all.

Without further foolishness, he whispered to the mirror, telling it he was a Sanctaviv sunbeam. And the mirror, being plenty foolish itself, believed him.

This time, stumbling out of the tailor shop's window didn't hurt quite so much.

He caught himself on the wooden beam holding up its awning, cursing as a splinter jammed itself into his thumb.

Not quite so much—but still some.

Sucking on the cut, he hurried into the alley beside the tailor's shop, using his other hand to haphazardly wave down his face and outfit. Though he couldn't see the illusion take hold, he felt the light mist settling over his body, bending the light around his face and frame.

His clothes, he bent in truth; he pictured the style he'd worn last time, but shifted it somewhat, altering color and fabric, cut and embroidery. Once he was satisfied, glancing into a puddle and recognizing little within its confines, he swung himself back up onto the tailor's porch, ready to head toward the Medeis hovel—

A loud *thwap* sounded behind him, and he jumped so hard he drove his forehead into the wooden beam holding up the awning.

"Gods!" he swore, whipping around—then staggering, catching himself against the tailor's window with his fingers splayed, the sun-warmed glass soothing his cut as his ears rang.

Through those spread fingers, Cassandra Medeis's mortal face swirled into focus, gap-toothed grin on full display. "You're back!" she cried, voice muffled through the glass.

He clutched his chest, coughing out a laugh. "You scared the salt out of me."

"Oh, pity. And with you being such bland company already." She rolled her eyes, then gestured over her shoulder. "Come inside! Your head's bleeding."

He blinked. Touched his forehead. Lowered his fingers to find red staining his nails.

Depths. He *was* bleeding.

"Well, that's not ideal," he mumbled.

This was off to a fabulous start. But at least it had been easy to find her.

He did as she asked, opening the glass door; the bell rang cheerily, and she skipped forward to greet him, still grinning.

She looked better today—at least, she looked neater. Maybe others would have found it better, but the longer he took her in—the tightly bound bun, the heavy skirt that fell to the floor in a shapeless sheet of unflatteringly pale green, and the white blouse that, even when tucked firmly into the skirt's waistband, was clearly one or two sizes too big—he found himself frowning.

She frowned back, a mirror all her own. "What?"

"What's a tailoress doing in ill-fitting clothes?"

"I'm just the apprentice." Cassi crossed her arms, craning her neck to meet his gaze, wearing a mighty scowl for such a pert, pretty face. "And if you must know, if we use any supplies on our own things, the cost comes from our wages. I'd rather spend that coin on food—try to fill the gaps with skin instead of stitching, you know?"

There was little he could say to that without sounding like a complete ass, so he just shrugged and said, "Well, could I ask the apprentice for some assistance?"

Now both brows lifted. She handed him some balled-up scrap cloth; he pressed it to his forehead as she said, "Assistance?"

"I," he said, careful to show off the flaws in his illusory outfit—the uncomfortably short cloak, the complexion-souring shade of yellow on his finespun tunic, and the slim pockets, "hate this. I mean, I would rather die than wear it another second. Can you recommend something that will keep me in style, but not make me look like a walking piece of taffy?"

"It is hideous," she agreed—a little too quickly, in his opinion. "I didn't want to say anything, but..."

"I should fire my own tailor?"

"And then throw these clothes in after them, yes."

He snorted. "That bad?"

She giggled, taking his wrist between two fingers and extending it out—she pinched at the garish yellow silk and wrinkled her nose. "Just looking at it makes me a little nauseous. The bloodstains don't help."

"Well, those were your fault."

"Your decidedly low constitution can hardly be blamed on me." She pulled back, still wrinkled. "Sancta save you, this really is brash."

"But you can help, can't you?"

"Well, I can't possibly make it *worse*." She dropped his wrist, pointing to one of the colorfully painted doors at the back of the shop. "Pick one—the store's empty besides me. We're closed for the night."

He glanced over his shoulder at the glass door; the sign had indeed been flipped so the *Closed* side faced outward. "Oh depths, I didn't even see. I can come back tomorrow if you're—"

"No, no—I let you in, remember? Don't worry about it." She shooed his worries away with a shake of her head. "Pick a room. I'll gather some things while you get settled."

Perfect. His relieved smile was only half-false. "Bless you."

"You'd better." She waved him off impatiently. "Go on—I need to concentrate."

So go he did, choosing the door boasting a mural of some slice of forest. Inside was a single lamp mounted on the wall, a block of wood to stand or sit on, and on all sides of the room besides the door…

He tried not to grimace under the scrutiny of triplet reflections, his illusory face looking decidedly less than pleased.

The door itself had several hooks lined up, waiting patiently for garments; he stripped off all upper-body layers, stopping at his cotton undershirt. As he twisted to hang them up, the light caught on his arm…shadows tracing out the ridged pair of scars left behind by undead teeth, a wound that had never truly taken to Jericho's medimantic attempts to heal it.

After knocking to confirm he was decent, Cassi slipped into the room, short arms piled high with different garments, fabrics, and boxes of other supplies. "Sit," she ordered, peeking out above the teetering tower. "It's going to take a minute."

He obeyed, spreading his legs a bit and resting his elbows on his knees; when she turned back from setting her supplies down, her movements stuttered. "I—oh."

He raised a brow. "Problem?"

"No." And yet, she looked troubled. "Do all lords have scars like that?"

He glanced at his arm. "My sister bit me pretty hard as a kid, so—"

"Not that one." As if in a trance, she floated forward, fingers extended…

Her fingertips, soft as the brush of a butterfly wing, traced the scar most people never noticed—the thin seam of raised skin that ran from behind his ear down the side of his neck.

Lucky, to not have many scars to stare at; less so, to have one so tightly tied to a memory he didn't care to share.

Glass hailing down. A thousand cuts too shallow to truly wound. Two or three that sliced deep enough to stick. Kallias screaming his name—anger and fear and the special kind of sickness that came with harming someone you cared about.

"Hard to say," he hedged. "Don't know many other lords."

She gave him one of those know-better looks, the kind where she peeked through her lashes and pouted her lips, as if sulking over the fact that he expected her to believe such a statement. "Lords *only* know other lords."

"Well, maybe I'm bad at lordship."

"Maybe you're being dodgy."

"I know *you*, and you're not a lord." He paused. "Unless there's a secret you want to tell me."

She went to smack her forehead, and Finn caught her wrist without thinking. "Cassi. Please stop trying to put holes in your skull."

She glanced at her hand—she'd layered several pins between her fingers, likely the absentminded habit of an overworked tailoress. "Oh. Oops."

He smirked up at her, giving her wrist two quick squeezes. "We can't have two bleeding heads going at this problem, can we?"

"Right," she said faintly. With a shake of her head that set some curls free from her bun, she turned away from him, shoving the pins back in her pincushion before gathering up some pieces of fabric. "Here, pick between these fabrics, then we'll get into colors…"

While she put herself to task, he watched her—watched the way she treated the dye-stained shop floor like a stage, dancing across it on her tiptoes, never falling back on her heels. Her soft, worn shoes bent easily with the arch of her feet; though they were nowhere near stiff enough to support a pirouette, he could see the itch of habit in the occasional bend of her ankle, a half-attempt at going en pointe before she remembered her footwear.

And as he watched, he worked through what would come next. So by the time she whipped out her measuring tape, several pins clenched between her teeth and several more bunched in her skirt, he was ready.

"So," she began, the single syllable garbled with metal—she let the pins rain from her mouth to her waiting palm, then began pinching and prodding, pinning the loose fabrics until they clung to his body. "What keeps bringing you to Sanctaviv, Lord Ryder? Business? Pleasure?"

"Business." Or something close. "And you?"

She chuckled. "Neither. I was born here. My siblings, too."

"How many you got?"

"Four. Two brothers and two sisters." At his whistle, she laughed again. "I know. You should see how it gets when we're all home—we practically have to sit on top of each other."

"Older, younger…?"

"My brothers and one sister are older. Ani, my other sister, she's the baby."

"How old?"

"Seven." Her brow wrinkled, and she mouthed numbers to herself, flexing one finger at a time as she counted. "Wait, no—eight."

He whistled again. "That has to put plenty of years between you."

"A little over ten." She shrugged. "She was a surprise—our father died about a week before our mother found out she was having Ani. Always called her the family miracle."

"Your mother…?"

"Dead." This time, the answer came quicker, like it hurt to say. "Two years after Ani was born."

"I'm very sorry for your loss."

"Thank you." She worked in silence for a time; he eyed her nimble fingers, watching as they guided the sewing needle. "And you? What sort of family have you got, Your Lordship?"

Gods, what a question.

"Three siblings," he said. "Two sisters and a brother."

"Older or younger?"

Most of them are dead.

"One older sister, one younger," he said instead. "My brother is older, too."

She smiled much easier this time, a slash of sugar-sweetness cutting through the bite of her grief. "So you know what it's like, being in the middle."

"Always looked down on by the older." He flinched a bit at the prick of a pin in the crease of his elbow; with a hurried, murmured apology, she adjusted it. "Yet expected to be responsible for the younger."

She made a soft *hmmm* sound, a gentle note of shared sentiment buzzing against her lips. "Always expected to put your own wants aside for their needs."

"Always forgetting that you were the youngest once, too."

"And you didn't ask to get replaced." She tugged a thread taut, snipping it with her teeth. "And you *definitely* didn't ask for…"

She glanced up at him, lips twisting in embarrassment. "Sorry. *You* didn't ask for a tour of my silly little life."

"It's not silly." In fact, it was exactly what he needed. "I was only youngest for a year or so—my first memory is of my mother helping me hold my baby sister after she was born."

Cassi fiddled with the piece of fabric pinched between her fingers, her brows pinched even tighter. "I don't mean to sound like I resent her. She's a good kid. Just…eighteen and eight, it's quite the gap. And it's hard not to look at her and remember being the one they all loved and protected like that."

"I can imagine." Hopefully he'd be able to mimic it too. "So, which siblings do you like best and least?"

Gasping, she pressed a hand to her chest. "I have no favorites. I love them all equally."

His turn to give her a chiding look. "Come on. What's said in the shop stays in the shop."

A sheepish smile played on her lips—gods, even her *mouth* carried a freckle here and there. "My older brother, Peter—he's my favorite." Her smile flipped, holding itself halfway through a cartwheel. "And my sister Mora…"

"Older sisters," he chuckled. "Think they know best, don't they?"

She groaned, tossing her head back as if locked in throes of agony. "*Always.*"

"I assume she doesn't approve of your more…illicit side work?"

Cassi rolled her eyes. "She approves just fine once I hand her the coin." Another stitch, another sigh. "But she doesn't love the danger it puts me in…or the attention it might attract from the clerics."

"Attention?" That sounded promising. "Why would it matter if the clerics are peeking your way?"

Cassi shrugged, sticking her sewing needle between her teeth as she fiddled with a new spool of thread. She plucked the needle back out, wet the tip of the thread with her tongue, and slipped it through the eye without even squinting. "You may have noticed, but we are…well, we're not exactly lords or ladies. And the clerics have a habit of taking *impoverished* children away in the name of altruism."

"Are you?"

"Am I what?"

"Impoverished?"

She hesitated. "No. I mean, a bit. We get by. But Ani…we give everything to her. The best of it all. She's never wanted for a thing, I swear to you, and we—"

"Cassi—hey. *Cassandra*," he said when she started rambling, watching in amazement as she began to dissolve into *tears* right before his eyes. "It's all right! Hey—it's all right. I believe you."

A slow, tearful breath—her hand rattled at the same time her breathing did, and without thinking, he reached out and took it.

To steady the needle in her hand, too close to his leg for comfort. That was all.

"Hey," he murmured, putting gentle pressure on her palm, thumb against her racing pulse. "I believe you."

She nodded, letting out her breath in a panic-soured whoosh—she wriggled like a snake shedding an ill-fitting skin. "I don't know what it is about you. I can't seem to stop saying too much."

He nearly laughed out loud. "It's my boyish good looks."

She smiled, but fear still drew hashmarks along the corners of her mouth, shading it in terror. "If they take her, we'll never see her again."

"I understand. If anyone took my little sister away, I would do…unspeakable things to get her back." And he had. Would again, too, if the world hadn't learned its lesson by now.

Finnick Atlas stole. He was never stolen *from*—and if someone tried, they would lose far more than they could have ever hoped to gain from the venture.

"Besides…" He leaned in with a wink. "You think I ran across rooftops with you just to turn you in now? I think not. Too much work."

Finally, her laugh shook out the tension in her shoulders. "Lazy lordling," she mock-grumbled, rolling her wrist until he released it. "I suppose I should be grateful for your layabout ways."

"Gods know I am."

She blinked. Tipped her head. "Gods? Plural?"

Damn it. "As long as I'm keeping your secrets, can I also keep mine?"

"Fair play." After a couple more stitches and snips, she moved on to the next piece of this new ensemble. Her fingers practically flew; even pausing to converse, she worked faster than Francesca, and as an apprentice, at that. "What would you like to discuss, then? The weather? Most clients ramble on about that for a while."

"Oh? And what qualities do they find so fascinating as to wax rhapsodical about them?"

"You jest, but you should have *heard* the woman I helped this morning. On and on and on about the rain and how it rusts out her kneecaps."

"Why doesn't she just get better knees?"

"You know, I suggested the very same! In fact—"

"Wait." He held up a hand as she moved toward his pockets. "Do me a favor?"

She rolled her eyes. "I'm not going to rob you again. We both saw how well that went."

"You're not the only pickpocket out there. If I give you some direction, can you do some special stitching for me?"

"What sort?"

"The sort that makes your pockets very difficult to pick."

A curious tilt of her head. "You *invented* this stitch?"

As a matter of fact, he *had* invented it—and had subsequently asked his tailoress to add it to every pocketed garment he owned. But he had enough lies to juggle without throwing too many truths into the mix. "I didn't invent it, but I did help perfect it." With a flourish of his wrist, he held out her measuring tape—the one she'd shoved into the pocket of her skirt moments ago. "Turns out I've quite the talent."

"Sancta's sputtering *flame*," she hissed, snatching it back from him. "How are you *better* than me? Some spoiled lordling—"

"Ouch?"

"—out-stealing a street thief? It's unheard of." She leaned forward, hands on her knees, blinking up at him pleadingly. "How do you know so much?"

"I apprenticed with a magician for a time," he said, reaching behind her ear—when he pulled his hand back, he flashed her one of the pins she'd stuck in her skirt's extra fabric. "Bored lordling stuff. Not much use to me, but nice to have in my repertoire when galas get too dull."

Her eyes gleamed like new coins. "Teach me."

He scoffed. "No."

She crossed her arms, craning her neck back—the only way she could manage to look down her nose at him. "Teach me, or I won't tailor the pockets."

"But if I teach you, what's the point of having the pockets tailored?" he countered.

"If you didn't invent this little stitch, I have to assume your noble friends know of it, too—and that means my marks could become far more difficult to pick off. So teach me, and I'll make sure every pickpocket in this city knows to steer clear of you."

The calligraphic curl of her smirk caught on the corner of his own, forcing a grin in return. "Fine. But no teaching *every pickpocket in this city* the same trick, all right? I'd hate to render this particular invention useless."

"Deal." She held out her hand—no, not her hand. Just her pinky.

Thanks to his time with Fidget, he knew this trick. He crooked his pinky around hers. "Deal."

And that was how, as the sun slowly made its descent toward the horizon line, casting burnished red rays of light through the shop, Finnick Atlas found himself teaching a future goddess how to pick any kind of pocket...even altered ones.

Unsurprisingly, she was a natural. He never had to demonstrate a pick more than twice before she had it down pat, able to repeat it again and again and again, even when he changed the angle or object.

What *did* surprise him was that she had *one* pick she couldn't quite get the hang of: nicking objects from the inner pocket of his new jacket. Her fingers kept catching on the lining, no matter how deftly she dipped her hand in.

"All right," he interrupted after her seventh attempt, which ended in a string of unfamiliar curses and her wringing her disobedient fingers together, "that's enough. No one can pull off every kind of pick, and you're miles ahead of most."

She ground her teeth together, crossing her arms. "I don't understand what's so difficult about it."

"Honestly, it's probably your height," he said—then threw his hands up in immediate surrender when she turned her glower on him. "Don't murder the messenger."

"I'm not *that* short!"

"I've seen twists of hard candy taller," he said.

"You have *not*."

"I have!" He had. His parents had ordered one specially made for him and Soleil one Saltwater Festival, a towering rod of peppermint candy that had stood taller than them both. "I'm not making fun—I swear. Your height determines the angle of your pick, and you're short enough that I won't be much help in adjusting it. It'll take trial and error."

"Trial and error in *crime* usually ends with a barred cell, Lord Ryder."

He smirked. "Just trial, then?"

She groaned, dropping down to her seat and crossing her legs, propping her chin on her fists and pouting up at him. "There has to be a way to make it work."

"You've only been practicing for a couple hours. I'm sure you'll figure it out." He glanced out at the darkening city, watching streetlights flicker to life one by one. "I kept you late—you're losing the light. May I walk you home?"

"You and your manners." She stood and stretched, arching up onto her tiptoes, wiggling her fingers toward the ceiling. "*May I.* No one talks like that."

"Sure they do. Me and all the other fancy lords, we get together every other day for vocabulary lessons. You're welcome to join."

She glanced down at her ill-fitting outfit. "I don't exactly look the part."

"I'm sure you could pull it off."

A smile flickered minnow-swift across her face. "Thank you—for the compliment and the offer. But my brothers will be here any minute to pick me up. I usually have to wait past dark anyhow—the company was a nice enough change." Her gaze drifted past him, and her smile widened. "Speaking of…"

The cheery jingle of the bell behind him chilled him worse than any Nyxian night.

"Sorry we're late!" called the man who entered—a man shorter than Finn by an inch or two, his hair plastered to his head by fresh rain and sodden mud, his grin beaming with energy despite the tired bend of his shoulders. He wore the clothes of a day laborer, his trousers patched in the knees and crusted with dirt and damp, his shirt ragged but well-fit. Behind him, a taller man ducked inside, maybe a couple years younger; they shared Cassi's dark curls and bright eyes, but thanks to their unshaven stubble, he couldn't tell if they shared her dimples or freckles.

Every hair on Finn's body stood on end when the shorter man met his gaze.

"Oh," said the taller man, halting—his hair hung longer than his brother's, longer than Cassi's, tied in a loose ponytail at his nape. "Didn't realize you'd still have a customer this time of night."

"It's fine—we were just about to finish up." Cassi hurried to them, stretching up to give them each a kiss on their bearded cheeks, heedless of the grime. She turned to smile at Finn, patting each of the men on their shoulders as she said, "Lord Ryder, these are my brothers, Peter and Braeden."

Finnick Atlas was the best damned actor in any age. He'd worked his ass off to become so. He'd pulled off many cons more demanding and difficult; he'd created entirely new people with nothing but a brick of dye and a piecemeal costume.

But staring into Braeden Medeis's eyes, he couldn't even manage to fake a gods-damned smile.

At the emphasis Cassi placed on *Lord*, both men quickly dipped into bows—the only moment he had to thaw that frostbitten hatred that had frozen his ever-shifting mask.

Bigger battles. Bigger battles. Focus, gods damn it.

By the time the brothers straightened, Finn just managed to cut his smile loose—it felt wrong, stretched and overdone, but it was that or nothing. "Pleasure to meet you both. Please, the formality's not necessary—you can call me Alex. My friends all do."

And with every gods-damned ounce of will he possessed, he held his hand out to the God of Chaos.

Braeden shook his hand, smile also fixed, wide eyes flickering to Cassi in silent question. Finn's palm burned with the urge to crush the to-be god's fingers in his grip. "The pleasure's ours. A first-time customer?"

"And not the last. Your sister does phenomenal work." He shot a wink at Cassi to disguise the twitch in his eye, releasing Braeden's hand. His fingers smarted as he tucked them into his pocket. "Quick hands."

Cassi shot him a sour look as the taller man—Peter—grinned with pride, dragging her against his side and ruffling her hair. "The most talented of us by far, this girl. She'll be taking over the shop in no time, if you ask me."

Sour dipped into bitter, and Cassi cleared her throat, pulling herself out of her brother's grip. "Let me collect his payment and balance the lockbox, and I'll be all set. Lord Ryder—"

"Alex."

"Sure. Let's get you settled up and on your way."

While her brothers hovered at the door, their gazes drilling into the back of his head, Finn followed Cassi to the counter, watching as she opened the lockbox—not with a key, but with a crack of one knuckle in just the right spot on the drawer. It popped open for her without hesitation.

"You need a new lockbox," he said.

"I've told Mistress Pasha a hundred times, trust me. She's cheaper than a miser at a charity ball." She wriggled her fingers toward him. "Money, please."

"As you wish." He rifled through his pockets. "I know you prefer paper, but will you take gold?"

She rolled her eyes. "Everyone takes gold. I didn't think you were serious when you said other people spent your money for you."

"Yeah, yeah. Lazy lordling, I know." He gave her the amount she quoted for the labor and materials—then plunked two more coins on the pile.

She plucked the extra two from her palm, twirling them between her fingers before offering them back to him. "Don't tell me you can't count, either."

"It's a *tip*. Haven't you ever gotten a tip before?"

She blinked. Looked down at the coins. Blinked again.

"Gold?" she said faintly.

Finn frowned. "Something wrong? I thought you said—"

"This is too much." She held out the coins again. "I don't make this much in tips in a *month*."

Damn. Stingy clientele. He regularly tipped Francesca twice that much, and she never batted an eye.

He reached out, folding her fingers over the coins. "Then I guess you'll be covered for a while if anyone stiffs you, hm?"

The light that lived in her eyes visibly dimmed, replaced by an angrier edge. "I don't need your charity."

"It's not charity. It's what you deserve for good work. Besides..." He unsheathed his best smirk, parrying her hurt pride. "You can use them to practice. Maybe when I see you again, you'll be ready to try that last *stitch* again."

Uncertainty slowed the bend of her knuckles, but bend they did, closing over the coins. "*When* I see you again?"

He winked. "If you're lucky."

Now all he had to do was walk out.

Past Braeden and Peter Medeis…Tenebrae and Tempest. The gods who'd stolen his sister and brother. Who'd manipulated them until they believed the only way to save the things most important to them was to give their entire selves away in exchange.

He held his breath as he left; if he didn't, every secret he kept locked beneath his tongue might come spilling out. Every bloody threat, every promise of revenge he'd dreamed up in the dark, unable to sleep, waiting for morning sun's spotlight to signal his return to the stage.

"Safe journey home," called Peter.

You killed my brother, screamed his mind. *You killed him. You killed him.*

He didn't smile. He didn't call back. He didn't even nod.

And he didn't release the breath he'd been holding until he stepped back into his own chambers, greeted by the gentle popping of embers in his fireplace and the stale smell of cooled coffee.

Damn. So his trips did take up *some* time in reality, then.

He'd brought the cup up just before stepping into the mirror; when he'd left, it had been too hot to sip, curls of steam dancing over its caramel-colored surface.

He stuck a finger into the liquid, testing it—a hint of warmth still kissed his fingertip toward the bottom, but not much. The rest had thoroughly cooled.

So, not too long…but still long enough.

But if he was being honest, that couldn't be helped. He'd needed to know, but not to adjust the plan itself.

Even if the trips into the past had cost him the same amount of hours in the present, it wouldn't have changed anything. He might have adjusted his timeline—might have had to spend less time sitting in tailor shops and giving pickpocketing lessons—but one hour here in exchange for many there? That he could spare to gain the ground they so desperately needed in this game.

He glanced over his shoulder, toward the uncovered mirror—he couldn't see Cassi, but beneath the purr of the fire in his hearth, he thought he could just catch the gentlest hum of snoring.

He peered down at his fingers, flexing them, letting the illusion fall away. Then he set them to task, pulling off his new, custom-made clothes, tucking them behind the hidden panel in the back of his closet.

There was no reason for Tenebrae to snoop in his things—or at least, no real chance he could do so without Finn knowing about it. But better safe than sorry. It wouldn't do for Tenebrae to recognize fashions from his first life.

Sure, he might assume Cassi felt more at home in those garments. But it would invite questions, and Finn didn't have enough answers just yet.

One last look at his strangely-sewn pockets.

Half a glance at the scarf hanging on the wardrobe door…a light lavender coil of cloth that still smelled like lilac. A scarf he'd stolen from a girl he'd now gotten to know thrice in his lifetime.

Not really meaning to, he let his hand wander there, pinching the scarf between his thumb and forefinger.

Then, with a huff and a curse, he slammed the wardrobe door shut.

CHAPTER 16

RAQUEL

She had hoped that once they worked Vash into the guard rotation, she might be able to avoid coming face-to-face with the Queen and King-Consort of Atlas again.

She ought to have figured out by now that hope had no place in this whole mad disaster.

Finn had passed her in the hall, looking distracted—he'd held what appeared to be a sewing kit in one hand, a pincushion clutched in the other. When she'd asked him if he'd decided to join a quilting class, he hadn't even mustered some clever comeback—instead, he'd asked her to take his parents food. And when she'd tried to block him, wanting to know where he was going, he'd waved her off impatiently as he sidestepped, muttering something under his breath about running an errand and minding her business.

They were going to have to have a very long and serious talk about his habit of giving her orders when he got back.

In part, she'd volunteered for that. She'd known this would require a bit of following on her part. But that dismissal, the avoidance of her questions—that couldn't happen.

This wouldn't work if they didn't work together. They both knew that—they'd both *said* it, on more than one occasion.

Still. The temper teasing her fingers into fists suggested a reminder might be in order.

Raquel ground that heated emotion into her jaw, ignoring how it already ached from biting her tongue all evening. She'd spent supper sitting across from Tenebrae's troupe of troublemakers—Revan, Arcas, and Pyra—listening to them cackle too loudly and throw their glasses on the floor just to hear them shatter, demanding replacements from trembling palacefolk.

She could get away with not following their chaos-corrupted example…at least for now. Her status as Occassio's favorite *pet* protected her from being questioned too closely about her calm temperament.

But who could guess how long Tenebrae would be content to let her stay separate?

That troubling thought trailed her down the steps to the dungeon; the task of balancing the tray in her hand while navigating the stairwell only provided a partial distraction. The smell of the pan-fried fish and vegetables and bread on the tray didn't help, either, constantly tugging her thoughts back to supper. Back to that table. Back to watching those people—probably kind once, probably caring, probably frightened before the tune took hold—hurl things and howl at the ceiling and dance on tables when even destruction began to bore them.

It had not been easy to choke that meal down.

And despite the fact that she'd swallowed it all with great determination, forcing it to settle in her stomach whether it wanted to or not, the sight that waited for her at the bottom of the stairs tried to dredge it all back up in one fell swoop.

Ramses sat propped against the far wall of the cell, jaw clenched against the agony that aged his handsome face, drawing out deep creases—mere sketches when he smiled, now shaded and rendered in detail. His torso was bare, his shirt rolled up and clamped between his teeth; Adriata knelt at his side, showing off her own worry lines as she ran something small and silver down her husband's side…a knife.

Raquel glanced to Vash, who shrugged. "His wound needed draining."

She could have guessed that. There was only so much they could do to ease the discomfort of the dungeons…and new clothes weren't one of those things, not without drawing attention from Tenebrae. Which meant King Ramses had been convalescing in his bloodied, muddied clothes for weeks now, making his bed in the layer of salted silt on the dungeon floor.

So while the sight of pus and blood draining from the wound in his side didn't *surprise* her, it did sicken her—and that was saying something, considering all that she'd seen in the aftermath of battle.

"You made her do it?"

Vash shifted his weight to his other leg—the closest he seemed to get to expressing discomfort. "She insisted."

That didn't surprise her, either.

Raquel approached the bars—though Ramses lifted his hooded gaze to take her in, offering a flicker of fingers that might have counted as a wave, Adriata ignored everything but the knife in her hand and the stream of infection draining from her husband's wound.

"Your Majesty," Raquel said—still difficult, offering the respect of a title, but every time she considered testing something else, Kallias's face cringed in her memory.

The bastard didn't even have the decency to give her the consolation of her hate.

Adriata didn't look up. "I am busy."

"I can see that." Her teeth ached, a flood of mockingbird words threatening to tear them out by the roots. "Prince Finnick sent me with food."

"My son would know that he would have to bring food himself in order for me to trust it."

She had made that exact argument to the prince in question. "I'm afraid he's occupied with his own tasks."

Ramses reached up and took the rolled-up shirt out of his mouth, spitting into the dirt beside him. He leveled a cajoling look at his wife…a look so familiar Raquel's throat seized up.

"Adriata," he murmured, tapping an unsteady knuckle affectionately beneath her chin. "Finn trusts her. Kallias trusts her." A pause. A hard swallow. "Trusted her. Let her help us."

Adriata's hand rattled—she only just pulled the knife back in time to keep it from trembling against Ramses' skin. She stared at his bloodstained side, gray eyes unfocused, emotionless.

Ramses settled his hand over her pale cheek. "Addie."

The Queen caught her bottom lip between her teeth; silver flashed in her eyes, there and gone, a blade unsheathed and thrown aside. She closed them, leaning into her husband's touch.

Ramses grunted in pain as he shifted, but despite Adriata's quiet protest, he didn't lie back—he cradled her close, pressing his forehead to hers, hand wrapped around the back of her neck.

"Breathe, my love," he whispered. Words meant only for the Queen's ears, but Raquel had learned to read lips long ago. "Old prejudices have no place in a new war. She's had plenty of chances to harm us; she hasn't. She can't say the same about us."

"That's what I'm afraid of," Adriata breathed back.

"You know Finn—you know how clever he is. He wouldn't trust her if she hadn't proven herself trustworthy."

Adriata's shoulders bowed inward. She caved gently into her husband's arms, weak as they were—and despite the pain, despite the flush to his cheeks and the sheen in his eyes, Ramses did not let her go.

Adriata glanced at Raquel. "Fine. But I'll come to you."

"If you must." It was what Raquel would have done, too.

Adriata nodded, then yanked back the hem of her skirt; soft cotton lining waited beneath, surprisingly free of dirt and grime. She tore it with two quick yanks, then pressed it to Ramses' wound, binding it strip by strip. By the time she was done, Ramses had slipped into sleep, his brows still screwed tightly together.

Only when he was settled did Adriata stand; her tangled, ragged red hair was bound in a simple braid now, swinging well past the small of her back, and the sleeves of her gown were gone—studying the discarded pile of soiled bandages bundled beside Ramses, Raquel could guess at their fate. As she approached Raquel, her foot dragged a bit behind her, like she'd shoved her reluctance and hate down as far as she could…but they still carried weight. Still tried to shy away from Raquel's reach.

Raquel opened the cell door, holding out the tray; her palms tingled with heat. If the tray had been metal instead of wood, it might have leapt right out of her hands.

Once Adriata had a grip on the tray, Raquel tugged her sleeve over her lightning-laced fingers and pulled the door shut. Even with that extra layer of cloth-clad protection, she could have sworn the clicking of the cell's lock sounded far more like a crackle.

"Get that knife back from her," Raquel ordered Vash, deciding to ignore the displeased twist of his face; Finn had named *her* as his second in this hierarchy, not Vash, and Adriata had long since proven patience was not a strong suit of hers. If they allowed her a blade, she might just attempt an escape of her own.

And it would certainly fail.

"Officer Angelov."

Raquel turned to find Adriata still standing by the bars; she held the tray like it might bite her, but her gaze poked and prodded Raquel, steel-gray seeking a seam in the layers of her armor.

"Why are you helping us?" asked the Atlas Queen. "In spite of the war, in spite of everything…my husband is right. You have had every opportunity to take your vengeance. They'd sing songs about you in Nyx's streets; you have nothing to lose by our demise, and everything to gain. Tell me why."

"Why do you want to know?"

Now, that steely composure fell away—now, Raquel caught a glimpse of an almost girlish curiosity, coupled with the sort of frustration she'd often seen in Finn's eyes—the look of a clever mind stumped by the puzzle set before them. "Because it's *weird*."

That word—so unqueenly, so frank, so oddly *Soren*—struck Raquel in just the right place to drive a laugh out of her.

Not a real one—barely a cough, really. But it forced her to pull herself together again before answering. "You are an enemy. But Tenebrae is *my* enemy. He attacked my kingdom; he killed my friends; he killed my *queen*. I will not—"

"What?" Adriata's eyes rounded out in shock; she set the tray aside swiftly and wrapped her hands around the bars, sticking her ear between them as if she thought she hadn't heard Raquel properly. "Enna is *dead*?"

Raquel's voice froze, clinging to the sides of her throat like a layer of hoarfrost. But she forced herself to speak anyway. "Yes."

Adriata stepped back, hands falling to her sides. "How."

"Soren met us before departing for Arborius…she was in Andromeda when Tenebrae attacked. She told us Ravenna stayed behind to face Tenebrae herself; she bought them time to escape the city."

"So she didn't *see* En—Ravenna fall."

"No, but others did." Finnick had told her so when she'd finally gotten up the courage to ask; some of his informants had caught whispers of Ravenna's final fate. He'd warned her it wasn't something she wanted to hear, and she'd listened. It was enough to know her queen was dead…and if the *Trickster God* was too squeamish to discuss it after all he'd witnessed in Tenebrae's court, she didn't really care to know the details.

Adriata's fingers tapped absently against her collarbone, then lifted to her teeth, where she began worrying her nails. "Her daughters?"

"All alive, from what we hear. Two were sent to safety before the attack, and the other escaped to her birth people in Artem."

Adriata nodded, but kept worrying her fingernails—she started to pace, torn skirts swishing, her limp growing more pronounced with every pivot.

This should have been good news to the caged queen—what kind of warmonger fell into such a state at the news of her enemy's demise?

"She got Soleil out…Soren," Adriata muttered into her fingertips. "She sacrificed her life for my daughter's?"

Raquel stayed silent—not because she didn't have an answer, but because she didn't think Adriata was actually asking.

After a couple more seconds of pacing, Adriata stopped, turning to face Raquel again. "What did you mean before, when you said you were protecting Finn for Kallias's sake? What did my son mean to you?" A shaken breath. A hand pressed to her bodice. "Why do you have a letter, too?"

Again, that protective, possessive instinct tried to shove her hand into her pocket. She forced it to stay steady at her side instead.

"You won't be pleased with the truth," she said, "and you won't be placated by a lie. So why bother giving you either?"

"Please."

Now Raquel's blood froze over.

Please—from a queen who'd set out to raze Raquel's kingdom to the ground.

Please—from a woman who had not pleaded for anything, not once in all these weeks of imprisonment.

Please—from a mother who had lost her firstborn son.

"Ever since he hurt his brother," Adriata croaked, "Kallias has chosen his words with incredible care. He says nothing without forethought. And when he decided who would receive his final words, he picked you—all others family, and then you. I want to know *why*."

Elias, too—but Adriata did not know that, did not know the bond that had forged between prince and priest in a torrent of phoenix fire, and it wasn't Raquel's story to share.

Besides, one Nyxian holding a piece of her son's heart was probably enough for now.

So Raquel sat cross-legged before the cell, hands braced on her knees—after a pause, Adriata mirrored her, though she took quite a bit longer to ease herself to the ground.

"Your son," she said, "murdered my younger sister."

And with that, it all came pouring out—how she had spent years plotting and seeking, searching for the First Prince amongst the Atlas ranks, dreaming of the day she would repay him blood for blood, death for death. How the day of that fateful battle in Ursa, she and Soren had promised each other success at last, at all costs—a revenge owed in equal measure to them both. First sight got the kill.

Soren had seen him first. And when Kallias had seen *her*, Raquel knew now, he had immediately recognized his own sister—even ten years older, even wearing Nyxian armor, even trying to drive her blade into his heart.

After that, she knew less—only what Elias had told her of his months in Atlas. So she skimmed over all that, beginning again when whispers had flooded through the barracks in Delphin—whispers that the First Prince of Atlas had entered the city in disguise, accompanied by Elias Loch, who'd been assumed dead after committing treason to chase after his captured battlemate, the poor fool.

She'd snuck into his room that night. Tried to strangle him in his sleep. And if Elias hadn't stopped her, that would have been the end of the story.

Then Artem. Then frozen baths and hostile breakfasts and mutual worry for their grieving friend. Fights and fiery rescues and flirtations that had left her feeling like a schoolgirl still spinning from her first kiss. Stolen shirts and stolen bodies and *He is mine.*

Those things, she didn't share with Adriata—not entirely. Just the barest details, just enough to show where hatred had melted into something even warmer, even wilder, even worse. And when she reached the part about the whipping in Skyhaven, how Kallias had gone to his knees to spare them that pain—

"You love him."

A lightning strike would have been gentler than those words, spoken by Adriata without an ounce of doubt.

Raquel could only look at her. Could only try, with all her might, to come up with some way to say *no*. To come up with some way to say it that didn't feel like spitting on Kallias's grave.

She could not. So instead, she just…looked.

And Adriata looked back. Seeing too much, just like her younger son.

"Love shows itself differently in warriors," she said. "They don't fawn and fuss; they ball their fists and tense for a blow. Every time you say my son's name, you breathe like someone drove their fist into your heart."

The smile that curled across Raquel's mouth…it hurt. And still she could muster no words.

"Atlas royals and their Nyxian warriors…it's going around. First Soleil and her boy, now…" Breathing out slowly, Adriata pinched the bridge of her nose. "My son loved you."

"He was kind to me—kinder than I deserved. That was all." This, she could lie about—for the sake of Kallias's legacy, she could hide this. "He would never have—"

"Officer Angelov." Steel could have been sharpened on Adriata's unyielding tone. "It seems neither of us are women of lies. Do not try to become one."

She did not want to tell her. She did not want to reveal it—especially not to Adriata Atlas, enemy of her people, who had inadvertently whittled Kallias's belief in his own worth enough that he'd believed he was only of value as a sacrifice.

But she was not a woman of lies. And she'd told too damn many lately.

Maybe if she gave up just one truth, just one, it would relieve the ache in her jaw.

"Your son loved me enough that he promised to leave this kingdom if I asked," she admitted in a hush. "But he broke every promise he ever made me in order to protect it. Your son loved you—loved Atlas—more than anything." *More than me.* "Remember him that way."

Adriata didn't speak, but the dungeon did—as the queen and the warrior sat together, neither quite looking at the other, it creaked and groaned in pain, shedding its own tears through leaking ceilings and condensation gathering on the walls.

Even the palace grieved for its prince.

"My son's love was a precious gift," Adriata said finally. "You are lucky to have held it."

"*You* are lucky I held it," she retorted. "It's the reason I haven't killed you myself."

"I guessed as much." Absurdly, Adriata smiled.

A tap on Raquel's shoulder jolted her—she spun to her feet, her sword halfway out by the time she realized Vash had not alerted them, though he still stood nearby, watching the stairwell…which meant it could only be one person.

"I hate to interrupt," said Finn, who definitely did not, "but I have to steal Officer Angelov for a moment."

She frowned, sheathing her sword. "Is something wrong?"

"There's something you need to see." He jerked his chin at Vash. "Stay with my parents. I'll send someone if I need you."

"Finn?" Adriata stood as well. "What's happening?"

"Nothing, Mama," he said—then, when she gave him a severe look that Raquel recognized from her own mother, he hastily added, "Nothing you and Papa can help with just now. I'm handling it. Raquel, with me, please?"

Another *please* from someone who rarely offered such things. A bad sign.

She held her tongue as they ascended the stairs; Finn took them two at a time, his haste giving away the urgency his voice hadn't.

"What's wrong?" she asked once the dungeon door was shut behind them.

Finn stroked his fingers over his mouth, mirroring his mother's nervous tics. "Just follow me. It's easier if you see it."

He led her up two more flights of stairs, stopping when they reached the palacefolk's wing. Bodies crowded the entrance hall; they clustered at every window, stretching to peek over heads and shoulders or ducking to peer past each other. All of them wore similar expressions of horror.

Raquel's stomach collapsed on itself.

When Finn walked toward one of the windows, the group broke apart— some practically leapt aside to avoid crossing his path while others bowed, eyes glued to the floor as they backed away.

Only one had the courage—or the stupidity—to mutter "Kin-killer" as Finn took up position at the window, bracing his palms on the sill.

Finn glanced over his shoulder. "Who said that?"

The entire hallway fell silent.

"I will not ask again," Finn purred, drumming his fingers on the sill, carefully turning the full power of his glare on every huddled mass of palacefolk. "What, can you only speak your mind when nobody's looking?"

Not even a cough broke through the absolute quiet. And in that petrified hush, she finally heard it—a chorus of discordant screams outside.

She joined Finn at the window; everyone took another couple steps away when she approached. She pressed her face close to the glass, shielding her eyes to block any reflection, holding her breath to avoid fogging up the view.

And then she didn't have to hold her breath anymore, because the sight outside stole it all.

Port Atlas was burning.

Sunset hues painted the sky, scarlet and gold streaked beneath every cloud…and the city below blazed with the same sunfire shades.

Rooftops glowed, their shingles molten and crisping, smoke fleeing into the sky. As she watched, one building collapsed, summoning a torrent of sparks and fresh screams.

Beneath the lip of the window, the thinnest draft snuck inside, brushing against her knuckles before darting to her ear.

And in its whisper, she heard triumphant laughter. Dares tossed between torch-bearers to see who could topple homes the fastest. Playful humming roughened at the edges by smoke and frenzy.

"Smile," Finn murmured in her ear. "They're watching us."

She obeyed. "What do we do?"

"You go," he said. "Do what you can—you're less likely to be missed. I'll distract Tenebrae."

"But—"

"*Smile*," he hissed, and she forced a grin; not an easy feat with her blood boiling like this. "Your magic will serve you best out there; mine serves me best in here. Don't let anyone see you leave—don't let anyone out there see your face. But get those fires out."

"What if I run into Tenebrae's people?"

"Then I hope you've gotten better at thinking on your feet." Finn didn't tear his gaze away from the window; unlike her, his smile hung easy on his face, satisfaction glowing from every pore. "Go."

Yes—they were going to have a very, very, *very* long and serious talk about orders after this.

As she walked away, the draft followed her—and when it started whispering about final breaths consumed by smoke-choked air, she began to run.

CHAPTER 17

FINN

Fire.

That bastard had chosen *fire*.

Finn sauntered toward Jericho's office with his hands in his pockets; he worried a bit of lint between his fingers, focusing all his energy on that.

Not the caustic hint of smoke scraping his nostrils sore.

Not the screaming of his people just past the palace walls.

Not the memory of a different night, a different fire, three long days spent watching volunteers recover scorched body after scorched body from the wreckage, waiting for one to be the exact size of his little sister.

He fussed with that morsel of fuzz and forced himself to breathe.

Occassio did not fear fire. Occassio did not care if innocent people were dying outside. Occassio did not care if Atlas turned to nothing but ash overnight.

So the terror trying to beat down the walls of his chest, using his heart as its battering ram…it had to go.

By the time he reached Jericho's office, when he removed his hand from his pocket to knock, his shaking had stopped.

Steady, Finn.

"Come in," called Tenebrae—Finn's stomach flipped at the sound of his sister's voice, shrill with excitement, nearly cracking at the apex of her pitch.

That tone used to be reserved for Saltwater Festival presents and fresh fruit tarts—not the death and suffering of their people.

He slipped inside, shutting the door behind him; the smell of smoke thickened, threatening to choke him as it combined with the tang of dying plants and the smell of…wet dog?

The chair behind the desk sat empty; instead, Tenebrae stood before the large window behind it, watching the chaos with barely contained glee. At his side sat the explanation for the wet-dog note in the air: a hound indeed huddled close to Tenebrae, shoulders hunched, tail twitching. Not wagging—twitching.

The hair on the back of Finn's neck stood straight up.

"Nice view?" he asked nonchalantly.

"The best." Tenebrae flashed him a grin. The hound turned with him, and Finn's spine locked up, chained by chills.

Soren had told him about the wolves in Nyx—how Tenebrae had done something to them, something Anima called *Blight*, a corruption of their very essence that had turned them worse than rabid.

This hound gazed at him with wild eyes, its sclera dyed a sickly green-black; its mouth hung open, baring sharp teeth and gums stained with inky streaks, a purplish taint that seeped from its mouth in strings of tensile saliva. Patches of pink skin checkerboarded its brindled gray fur, revealing teeth marks, like the creature had chewed itself sore. Muscles spasmed beneath its flanks with every shuddering pant.

Finn had never cared much for dogs. This didn't help one bit.

"New pet?" He deserved a damned medal for that detached, steady joke.

"One of many." Tenebrae fondly scratched the hound behind its ears. "Come—come watch with me. It's beautiful out there."

Beautiful. Torment and death, screaming parents and sobbing children—*beautiful.*

He joined Tenebrae, careful to keep the Chaos God between him and the blighted hound. "I thought we were waiting on the rest of your followers."

"We were." Tenebrae smirked out at the destruction; his reflection smirked back, backlit by the spreading fire outside. "They just arrived. I figured I'd put them to task…no use wasting time."

"And what is the task?"

Tenebrae kept smirking, kept staring. "Fear."

"To what end?"

"Does it need one?"

"I like plans to have a purpose."

Tenebrae chuckled. "I know you do. Predictability—that's what you love." His grin turned hungry. "Why limit what could prove limitless? Let's see how far it can go."

Finn's mouth dried out. But he forced a snort. "Do that, and you might not have a city left by morning."

Tenebrae bobbed his shoulders. Barely even a shrug. "I can build a new city."

Not a new people. "Cruel of you, choosing fire. Clever, too."

"Well, I can't take the credit." Tenebrae teased Finn's hair—his scalp crawled, and he clenched his fist against the desperate wish to break the god's wrist. "I learned that trick from you."

Finn chuckled, the sound scraping against his dry throat. "Can't help that I was born prettiest *and* smartest."

"Don't say that in front of Tempest. He's rather attached to that first title." Was that *warmth* he heard in Tenebrae's voice? A touch of true affection? "I'm glad you're here, you know. I feared you might side with him."

Finn snorted quietly. "Believe me, I'd rather be here."

It might've been the first true thing he'd told the Chaos God.

Silence ruled within for a time, chaos ruling without—yet, the louder the commotion outside became, the more at ease Tenebrae looked. After one particularly ear-splitting scream, Tenebrae leaned against the glass window, staring out at the burning city, almost…relaxed.

"Anima should have tried to use her relic by now," he mentioned offhandedly. "And if not now, then soon. Once she's freed the Blight, it won't take long for her to come running back…without her island, she'll have nowhere else to go."

Finn's heart began to pound.

"And Soren?" he asked—then, when Tenebrae cast him a confused look, he rolled his eyes and added, "The princess? You know, Ani's *host*?"

"Right—the other Atlas." Tenebrae rolled his own eyes, blowing a strand of hair aside. "That damned princess has too many names. I can't keep them all straight. I'm not worried about her. The relic is too damaged for Anima to use it the way she wants—they won't be able to separate. And even if she manages a miracle, the Blight will make quick work of her host and that nuisance of a priest."

"That priest isn't just a nuisance," Finn muttered. "He's deathless now, remember?"

Tenebrae's smile slipped, unsteady on its feet. "No one is truly deathless. Not even Mortem; not even Anima. We've seen that."

That shadow passing over his eyes…Finn knew the look of a bad memory when he saw it. Something else he could search for in the past.

"And can't unsee it," he muttered; Tenebrae shook his head absently, but it was agreement, not argument.

It could have been minutes or hours they stood there together, watching fires go out and start again, a battle that no one seemed to be gaining ground in. Minutes or hours of death; minutes or hours Finn had to remember how to breathe through a panic attack without letting it show on his face.

Hours he watched his people burn with a smile.

CHAPTER 18

RAQUEL

She couldn't breathe.

Not because of the smoke, though it didn't help. The heavy blue cloak she'd thrown on before bolting from the palace trapped any extra heat inside, leaving her sweltering, and the cowl wrapped around her face and hair only made things worse.

A necessity, nonetheless—only her eyes were visible now, rendering her unrecognizable, especially in the clamor of fleeing families and the odd shadows cast by the roaring flames.

Too many flames. Too many families. Not enough hands holding buckets; not enough people brave enough to leap into burning houses to save those trapped inside.

But *not enough* was better than *none*. And even one more body would strike the tally closer to *just enough*.

Blown ash and still-pulsing embers crunched beneath her feet as she ran for the nearest building—a tailor's shop, the roof partly caved in, shutters peeling back like teeth bared in an open, blazing dragon's maw. Two girls stood outside it, shivering in their nightgowns—one with golden curls and soot-stained cheeks, the other with skin so pale flecks of ash looked dark against it, her black hair blending against the now-dark sky. The latter had her thin arms wrapped around the former, holding her back; though the golden girl had heft and height on the raven-headed one, the latter dug her bare heels into the cobblestones, refusing to give ground.

"We have to get her!" sobbed the golden girl, raining useless blows on her companion's arms. "We can't—we have to—"

"We can't," the raven-haired girl choked out—an echo and agreement. "She told us to run, Fi, we have to *run*."

"Not without her!"

"Who's still inside?" Raquel barked—both girls leapt back when she rushed up to them, the golden girl's shriek of terror rising above the rest of the calamitous riot.

The raven-haired girl, however, didn't hesitate. "Her name's Francesca. We're her apprentices—we were up finishing our work when the torch came through the window. She told us to run, but she tried to save—" The girl broke into a coughing fit, bending at her narrow waist, a branch set to snap in half beneath the weight of the wind. "*Please.*"

There would be no getting through the door—the flames had devoured it already, and the window to the left was similarly consumed, the glass shattered and scattered across the street. But the window to the right…while she could see flames beyond it, they weren't coming *through* it. The glass remained intact.

She glanced to her side, where a bucket lay tipped on its side—abandoned by a rescuer who'd lost their nerve, maybe. The cobblestones just beyond the bucket shone in the firelight, sparkling with damp.

She might have been too proud to use her magic when Tempest commanded it, but she was not a fool.

So she bent in a crouch, fingers outstretched to the water. "Come to me," she whispered.

And like a loyal hound eager to return to its master's side, it obeyed.

She coaxed it across the cobblestones, pressing her palms flat to the ground—the water gathered beneath her hands, pushing them upward as more and more droplets joined in. Once enough of it had nestled beneath her hands to create a globe, she picked it up and held it to her heart, breathing in slowly.

Then she cast the water across her heavy cloak.

Within seconds, despite the cloak's thick fibers, she was soaked through—the only shield she would receive tonight.

"Go," she ordered the girls. "If she can be found, I will find her—I promise you."

The raven-haired girl nodded, mouthing her thanks as she pulled her companion away—within seconds, the two had vanished into the shadows and smoke.

Raquel could only hope they knew their way around the city. That they had somewhere safe to go.

That they would not encounter anyone with the song of chaos stuck in their heads.

She turned back to the tailor's shop. Took a sharp, shallow breath, all she could manage with the smoke choking the city's lungs.

And with a running leap, she crashed through the window, plunging herself headfirst into an inferno.

One person was not enough to turn the tide.

Though she broke into house after house, shop after shop, she could not save them all—some were already dead when she made it to them, and some of the structures collapsed just before she could make her way inside.

There were many she could save—many she did. Many who sobbed their thanks or coughed it from smoke-stained mouths, squeezing her arm or kissing her cowled cheeks. One young woman even wrapped her in the tightest hug she'd ever received before chasing after her husband, who had their toddler bundled securely in his arms, tears cutting through the grime marring his cheeks.

But no matter how many she saved, the fires kept spreading.

Even when she turned down a street with no fire, smoke shrouded everything, a fog that grated like gravel going down her nose and throat. She coughed into the cowl, squinting through the haze as she staggered to a stop, pressing her back against the side of a house to catch her breath.

The water seeping through her cloak sang to her. The sky above waited patiently.

She could do more. Maybe. If her training in Skyhaven had endured the years she'd spent trying to bury it; if she could call back the muscle memory she'd forced her body to forget in favor of sword maneuvers and battle formations.

She flexed her fingers and closed her eyes, seeking the pulse hidden in the invisible veins of the wind.

After a moment, she found it—that excited, quivering thread of energy that tied itself around her fingers, thudding like a drumbeat beneath her knuckles, begging her to rip it free. Begging her to bring the clouds above to heel with a swift tug of their leash.

She kept her eyes closed for one more moment, soaking in the quiet. Soaking in the solid, reassuring press of stone against her spine.

Eye of the Storm. Power within peace.

She lowered herself to her knees. Raised her hands toward the sky. Paused just long enough to steel herself for what came next.

Then she clenched her hands into fists, seized that thread of power, and *yanked.*

The second her fists struck the cobblestones, the sky split open.

With a booming roar, thunder tore apart the clouds, loosing a torrent of rain so thick, so *cold*, it soaked her to the bone in seconds. But this cold didn't hurt—it thrilled her, exhilarated her, driving the fatigue from her muscles in one fell swoop.

Delight punched a laugh from her chest.

Gods damn it, she had missed her magic.

Not the little displays here and there she'd allowed herself since getting it back; not the storms that gathered without her asking, called by her tumultuous emotions.

Real magic. Real power.

She tipped her head back, ripping down her cowl, opening her mouth to gasp in a clean breath—petrichor drowned out the filthy taste of smoke, rain cooling her tongue and soothing her throat.

The fight wasn't done. The storm would help, but it needed direction. It needed her.

So she pulled her cowl back up, securing it carefully; she took a moment to run a fingertip over her newest braid and the leather band that held it in place.

I've got them, Kallias.

With a sweep of her hand, the swiftly filling puddles swirled upward, tiny twisters answering to her call.

They grew and grew as she sprinted back into the city's heart, clinging to her shadow as they swelled with rain and wind and scattered debris—judging by the gasps of those she passed by, the sight of a hooded individual being chased by a swarm of cyclones just slightly outdid the sight of their city burning to the ground.

Good. Good that they would see this—that they would know someone cared. Someone saw. Someone would fight for them.

Even if it felt like a betrayal to her own kin and kingdom. Even if a small part of her wanted to let this whole damned place burn for what they'd done to *her* home. *Her* people.

But these terrified people pleading for mercy, for a savior…they were not soldiers. They were not strategists. They had no more say in the war their queen waged than Raquel did.

So she set her storms free, dropping to one knee and extending her arms, whispering silent orders to the wind. And each of her swift-moving soldiers obeyed without question.

In the span of five seconds, every flame and spark and ember sizzled out, drowned or smothered to death in the wake of her own cataclysm.

Screams and wails evaporated, rising as gasps and cheers. Raquel stayed on her knee, stone digging into her kneecap, letting her hands fall as spinning spouts of water and wind sucked the breath out of the fires before dousing whatever remained.

And so it went. Street by street, storm by storm, she dredged up the power that had drawn the greedy eye of a tyrant, snaring her within Skyhaven; the power he had honed and crafted so carefully, ensuring she owed every advancement, every accomplishment to him.

This was hers. All hers. And she owed it to absolutely no one.

Still, she gave it—with each new flame that leapt to life, she called a storm to counter it, even as her lungs began to tighten and tremble; even as it got harder and harder to drag herself back to her feet; even as the cold in her bones began to seep into her blood, chilling her, numbing her.

Just as one knee finally gave out, buckling when she tried to make just one more storm sing, strong fingers caught her by the elbow.

A familiar grip.

"Need a hand?" Tempest asked; he, too, wore a cloak and cowl that hid his face, but his was gray. The dullness of it somehow brightened his gilded gaze; his eyes practically glowed.

She yanked her arm away. "What are you doing here?"

"Protecting my people." When she held her glare, he scowled—or at least, she thought so. His brow bent the way Kallias's did when he tried to look angry. "I left, like you asked, but I saw the smoke—"

"I don't need your help."

One brow arched. "You're about to pass out."

"I'm *handling it.*"

He studied her for a moment, then looked to the row of doused houses in her wake—to the people holding each other or sobbing in relief, many clutching children close or clinging to pets. One cat—the most ungrateful animal Raquel had *ever* had the displeasure of knowing—now purred belly-up in the arms of its owner.

It hadn't been so content when it was clawing the flesh from her bones, but holding a grudge against a frightened animal seemed petty. Even for her.

"Why are you helping them?" Tempest's eyes narrowed as they focused back on her. "They're your enemies."

"I made a promise," she snapped—but unfortunately, rage and smoke inhalation didn't combine nicely. Her next sentence fell apart into a crackling cough, and she was forced to bury her face in her elbow, hacking her way back to steady breathing.

Tempest crossed his arms. Turned to look over his shoulder, where much of the city still burned.

"Come on, then," he said. "We've got work to do."

She huffed through her teeth, forcing herself to stand straight. "I said I—"

"Maybe you don't, but *they* do." Tempest caught her by the elbow; when she tried to pull away, he held tighter, but dropped his voice. "One person can't keep up with a thing like fire—particularly intentionally set ones. Your pride will only cost lives, not save them."

Her throat ached with held-back arguments. Held back only because he was right—and only because, when he spoke of lost lives, he didn't look at the people on the street. His gaze stayed fixed on her.

Like her life might be the one lost. Like maybe, somehow, that mattered to him more.

And that made it almost, almost easy to pretend he was Kallias instead.

"Stay out of my way," she seethed. "Cover the streets I can't. And for gods' sakes, don't let anyone see your face."

He rolled his eyes. "For my sake, indeed." The corners of his eyes crinkled, but this time, she recognized the effect of a hidden smirk. "Race you to the other end of the city?"

She didn't answer—she didn't have one. She didn't want to play games with him.

Instead, she walked away.

Somehow, by the time dawn broke against the sky, Raquel was still standing…if only just. She could barely see, a blurred haze of red creeping further and further across her eye; her lungs couldn't seem to get a grip on any breath she handed to them. But she was walking; she was alive, and so were many others.

She hadn't seen any of Tenebrae's people—at least, none she knew. There could have been some hidden among the victims, but if there were, none of them confronted her.

The burns on her legs hurt far less than the burning in her lungs—she barely made it to the edge of the ocean before collapsing in the wet sand, the fresh damp soothing her angry skin.

She tried to drag in a breath. Her chest rejected it, throwing it out with a hacking cough. She tried again; this time, her lungs seized entirely, and a wave of dizziness cast its net over her mind, dragging her toward a darkness she could not afford to indulge in.

Another set of knees appeared beside her, sinking into the sand. "Here."

With a gesture of Tempest's hand, a clean breeze slipped past her parted lips; her lungs opened up at its touch, relief flooding her body as she finally managed to gasp in good air.

For a time, they sat in silence, Tempest gathering more and more fresh air for her to sip from. And much as she wanted to reject his help, it would have worse than ungrateful, considering she needed the air he offered to even try to speak the rejection.

"They're already whispering about you around the city," the god murmured. "The stranger who swept in with storms on their heels and righteous vengeance in their hearts."

She snorted—coughed. Tempest muttered a rough curse, cupping his hand and giving an errant gesture toward her mouth—this time, when she gasped in air, she was able to exhale without a hitch.

"How much smoke did you drink in?" he demanded.

She shrugged. He cursed again, then sighed. "And I thought the prince was overly eager to be a martyr."

If only she had enough energy to snarl at him for that. Instead, she shut her eyes, focusing on breathing. Focusing on cutting every thread of magic loose, letting them drift away like runaway kite strings.

"I mean it, though—they are talking about you. Lucky thing you wore the cloak." Tempest fell silent for a moment, then added, "I wouldn't be surprised if they had a name for you by morning."

She laughed—and when it didn't end in a cough, she gained the courage to test out a retort: "Don't be *ridiculous*."

CHAPTER 19

RAQUEL

"They're calling you the Riptide."

Much to her chagrin—and to Vaughn and Vidia's delight—the people of Port Atlas had indeed bestowed a moniker upon the cloaked, cowled, twice-blessed stranger who had swept in with a storm under their command.

Hopefully Tempest left before he had a chance to hear it.

Vidia spun around, perched on the table, her heels clapping against the seat of the chair in front of her. She grinned broadly at Raquel—broadly enough that the light caught her pointed canines. When Raquel first noticed them, Vidia told her she'd sharpened them herself so she could coat them in poisons and bite down into someone's flesh if she wanted. A Viper in name and in behavior.

Finn later told her Vidia had just lost her baby teeth late, which caused her new ones to grow in oddly.

So when the poisoner said, "People are saying you're Tempest's judgement on those who would corrupt his kingdom," it seemed reasonable to take it with a grain of salt. Or a sea of it.

"Funny, how fickle faith is," Vash grumbled from the corner. "We spent years hating Tempest, calling him a ship-sinker. Now we beg for a vengeful god."

Vidia rolled her eyes, waving him off. "Ignore him, he's sour because *his* goddess turned out to be a traitorous bitch."

"*Vidia.*"

"*Vash,*" she mocked back, sticking her tongue out at her brother—Vash scowled, sticking his tongue out back. A rare show of actual human behavior from the stoic assassin.

Raquel pressed her palms to her forehead. The sweat on her brow stung her blistered palms—she'd suffered a few burns while digging through debris to get to people buried beneath, but nothing severe. "It's silly."

"It's badass," Vidia argued. "Any good rebellion needs a figurehead."

"We're barely a rebellion." More like half a dozen delusional people hoping that they could somehow bring down a deity. "And I'm no figurehead."

"The people of Atlas disagree," Vaughn said from behind her—he was busy slathering the worst of her burns in a slimy salve. The extract of a plant called *aloe*, he said—she'd never seen such a thing in Nyx. Apparently that kind of plant didn't thrive in the cold. "Riptide—it's a good name."

"It's silly," she groaned again. "I wasn't the only one out there saving people—and some of them didn't have the advantage of magic. Why aren't they getting heralded in the streets?"

"Unfortunately," Finn said, turning from his own perch beside Vidia on the table, "people are enthralled by showmanship, not heroism."

She scowled at him, fighting not to flinch as Vaughn spread another layer of aloe across her burned shoulder—it shocked her skin at first, goosebumps prickling painfully over her stinging flesh before it calmed into cool relief. "I wasn't putting on a show."

Finn smirked at her, clasping his fingers loosely between his bent knees. "You know what a kingdom of sailors and sea-lovers fears more than anything, Raquel?"

She could guess. She didn't want to.

"Storms," Vaughn murmured; his breath brushed against her shoulder, colder than the salve coating her skin.

"Storms," Finn repeated, as if Vaughn hadn't spoken at all. "So when a mysterious stranger shows up and saves their lives with a storm at their beck and call…you can imagine it sends a message."

"It wasn't—"

"Gods, Raquel, we *know*," Finn groaned—he sat back sharply on his seat, throwing his hands to the sky in helpless plea. "Rest easy—we all know you didn't go out there with the intention of becoming some kind of hero. We all know you weren't being flashy. We admire you, O Humble Warrior, for your lack of desire for the spotlight. Alas, you stepped into it anyway, and there are consequences for that. I suggest learning to embrace it."

"What are you saying?" She had no patience for his riddles today.

"Tenebrae is barely managing to stick to his ruse right now." Finn stood up on the chair, then stepped onto the table—as their gazes all swiveled to him, he spread his arms, crafting the rickety perch into a grand stage fit for an orator of royal caliber. "He blamed the fires on Nyxian agents, but word is already spreading through the lower city streets about Nyx's fall. The curfew he instilled will slow the spread, but soon enough, everyone will at least suspect that something may not be right in the palace."

"And?"

"*And*, wavering loyalties are uncomfortable. If we give them someone else to put their faith in, they'll latch on quickly." Finn paused, his gaze lingering on her bandages—his eyes darkened a shade. "But that's not a discussion for now. You did well last night—thank you. Take today and rest."

"Tenebrae will notice I'm missing."

"Leave him to me." Finn hopped down from the table, straightening with a quick tug at his shirt cuffs. "Vash, if her condition worsens, you get word to me, understand?"

"Yes, Highness," Vash said—fully drowning out Raquel's noise of protest.

"Good." And with one last nod, Finn vanished.

He didn't walk out. He didn't run. He just vanished.

"I hate that," Raquel muttered, slouching back in her chair—then flinching when her new bandages caught against it.

"He's right," Vaughn told her—he fixed her bandage before circling around to face her, wiping his hands on a rag. Gratitude warmed his tired gray eyes. "You saved many lives last night—lives that weren't yours to save. You deserve a rest…and a pinch of admiration, even if it's uncomfortable."

It was worse than uncomfortable—looking around at these faces she had only just come to know, wonder and grateful smiles replacing the suspicion she'd grown used to…

It wasn't right. None of it.

Even Vash smiled at her when she met his gaze—the barest curve of his mouth, but a smile all the same. From the man who'd tried to carve answers out of her flesh mere days earlier.

Worse than uncomfortable. Unbearable.

She stood up and left without a word.

As she stumbled into the empty hall, the urge to gag gripped her by the throat—she swallowed it down, but it seized her again, sealing her windpipe with memories of poisoned draughts and pyre smoke.

Poison forced down her throat by an Atlas woman. Pyres built for bodies slain by Atlas hands.

The same Atlas woman who'd grinned at her without guile in that room. The same Atlas hands she'd taken last night, pulling them to safety without a thought.

These were not her people. This was not her purpose. She was merely a surrogate; a poor replacement for the person they *should* have been praising in the streets.

Blind with rage, choked by shame, she turned and drove her steel-toed boot into the trim at the base of the wall. It buckled inward, but it wasn't enough; she reared back for another blow.

"You know," said a voice behind her, "many people enjoy being thanked when they do something worthwhile."

Huffing like a wrathful dragon, she wiped a hand across her brow, turning to face Vaughn. He stood with his hands open at his sides, the dark green tint to his fingertips hidden in shadow; when he smiled at her, it was with a look of someone expecting to take a blow for what they said next.

"What's wrong?" he prompted.

"Nothing."

"I think the wall would disagree."

She kicked it again for good measure. "I shouldn't be here." Not in this building, not in this city, not within ten miles of this gods-damned kingdom. "This shouldn't be me."

"What do you mean?"

"This—all of this—it should be Kallias. They're his people. They're his burden. I'm only carrying it because he asked me to." She raked a hand through her hair, scowling at the floor, at her boots, at the trembling fist her other hand had formed. "He should be their savior. Not me."

"Raquel…if I can call you Raquel now?" At her frustrated gesture—which he seemed to take as a *yes*—Vaughn stepped closer, but at her warning look, he halted. He let out a long, rough sigh. "I understand the pain of picking up someone else's burden after they're gone—I understand better than you know. But last night, what you did…Kallias couldn't have done that. Not the way you did."

"You're right. He might have saved more."

He frowned at her, disapproving. "Wallowing doesn't suit you. Neither does intentional ignorance."

She hadn't received one harsh word from this prince before. It halted her in her tracks.

"Kallias is afraid of fire," Vaughn reminded her. "Yes, he would have gone out there—but there were places you went where he couldn't have gone. Powers you wielded that he wouldn't have had. Last night, what you did—that belongs to you, not to him. Not even to his memory."

"But I—"

"If he is gone," Vaughn interrupted, the word *gone* wobbling a bit before it steadied, "from what I understand, it was done of his own volition. You didn't do that to him. My burden…I carry it for the sake of penance. But you don't have to."

She looked down at her wrist. At the bracelet draped over it, many of the gems coated with ashen film.

"You're not carrying on his legacy," Vaughn said softly. "If you ask me, you're building your own. So carry it proudly, Riptide. You've earned it."

He patted her shoulder—the unburned one—then turned and walked away, leaving her to stare at the damaged wall, her fingers anchored around a bracelet that felt heavier and heavier every day.

CHAPTER 20

FINN

His walk home from Vash and Vidia's hideout was not a quiet one.

Though he kept busy as he walked, vigilant fingers folding every ray of light around him to keep himself from being seen, it could only render him invisible—not insubstantial. He could not walk through the world without touching it, seeing it—and what he saw promised to live on in his nightmares for as long as he managed to live after this.

Because while Raquel risked life and limb to save them, a faceless promise that someone out there still cared for the cries of the Atlas people… their prince had watched his city burn with a smile on his face.

Forced. False. But good enough to fool.

Good enough to see half-assed effigies tied to stakes and burned with whatever debris still smoldered this morning. Effigies bearing glasses or ragged coats decorated in bits of false sparkle or thatches of grass dipped in brownish-red wax affixed to the head portion. Effigies hauled up by people who shouted and jeered and cursed his name to the furthest fathoms of the ocean.

Finnick Atlas strolled down a street lined with people playing out a fantasy of his execution.

Part of the game. Not a great loss. He'd never been entirely loved by his people, anyhow…he'd known it would take very little to mangle indifference into infuriation.

But he hadn't expected this.

He hadn't expected them to call for another fire-slain Heir.

He rubbed the lump out of his throat, watching as a pair of boys hauled up another model…this one wearing a crown and a scorched sundress, scarlet cloth sewn to its scalp with thick, vicious, messy stitches.

He couldn't blame them. Their royals had watched them suffer last night, and neither had done a thing to stop it.

But he couldn't help cursing their stupidity, either…not when he knew exactly how Tenebrae would respond to this outpouring of indignance.

The fires, those had been a game. A poorly played one, nowhere near the artful sort that other gods enjoyed, but a game nonetheless.

He didn't want to see how Tenebrae treated poor losers.

Didn't want to see how *he'd* be forced to respond to them, either.

His eyes wandered down different streets as he entered the city square, nearing the palace proper. Even from that cursory look, it became obvious that many of his havens had been lost last night…Francesca's shop, though the woman herself had been saved by Raquel's quick action, a thing he needed to thank her properly for. The Drunken Sun, the Broken Conch, and many other favorite taverns of his had gone up in smoke—he'd taken note of them earlier, passing them on his way through the lower city.

His favorite bakery, Stir The Pot, was also gone—that one hurt worse than others, because he had to assume the recipe for their flawless peanut butter cookies had perished, too. If he had any luck at all, maybe at least one of the bakers had it memorized; that recipe was one heist he'd never quite gotten to, and now it was too late.

Funny, the way small comforts became some of the most intolerable losses.

Shaking his head, he released the shield of light as he stepped inside the palace courtyard. There were no guards posted at the gates…at least, not formally. Instead, a host of Tenebrae's followers lounged about the courtyard, laughing and chatting with each other as they kept idle eyes on the entrance. Most kept themselves busy by tearing the garden apart with their bare hands; others danced with each other or alone; and still others picked at their own skin and yanked out their own hair.

In the center of the courtyard, a brawling circle had formed: an Artemisian woman with a brawny build and flaming fists prowled inside, facing down a slight girl wielding throwing knives—judging by the constellation tattoos scrawled across her shoulder blades, he had to guess she was Nyxian. The two circled each other without care or caution, smiles wide and careless, fingers twitching with anticipation.

He didn't stay to see who would lunge first. Instead, he walked into the palace, ignored by every pair of eyes despite having dropped his invisibility.

What a joke. Last year, he would have given both his big toes—maybe even a finger or two—to be able to go completely unseen at will.

Now he *could*, but why bother? Nobody spared him a second look anyway.

He ground his teeth, wishing the craving for peanut butter cookies would fade from his tongue. It made it difficult to stay on task…difficult to pass by the kitchens, knowing none of the palacefolk would dare question his presence there.

Nor would they question it—at least out loud—if he tracked down a cookbook and set his hands to more calming work, despite the fact that he was a notoriously poor baker.

Besides pastry. He hadn't lied about that. But pastry just didn't fill the same gap that cookies did; pastry was all layers and air, never satisfying even when filled with ganache or creams or jams. Pastry was only meant for showing off.

Probably why he happened to be so good at it.

Finn frowned to himself and paused in the middle of the hall, shoes squeaking against the floor.

He'd just seen his people burning effigies of him in the streets, calling for his demise; he'd just seen warriors from other kingdoms gathered within *his* courtyard, corrupted by chaos magic and maiming each other for kicks.

And instead of pondering any of that, his mind had wandered to cookies and pastries and how unfair it was that this magic only came to him when he hardly needed it anymore.

That either said something extremely concerning about him as a person…or said something about how deeply disturbing the rest of his year had been.

Maybe both. But it worried him regardless.

Still. Time to think on that later. He had a goddess to visit…in the present and in the past.

Last night had gone well—surprisingly well, for how little he'd gleaned so far from his visits to the past. But he had hit a snag or two…particularly when he'd mentioned something about tailoring, and Tenebrae had given him a look of cool concern.

"You hated that job," he'd said. *"Gods, I almost forgot you even had it."*

A slip-up—the one thing Finn absolutely couldn't afford. He'd been able to blame it on mixed memories, getting used to her new host, but that excuse wouldn't hold up for long—not when she'd supposedly been in control of this body for weeks.

So. Another round with Cassandra Medeis was in order.

But today, he needed to tip his hand a bit.

This time, he had the misfortune of arriving at the tailor's during regular business hours.

The line wound out the door; colorful frocks, fine silk suits, and all manner of other fashions glittered and gleamed in the afternoon sun, the patrons who wore them accessorizing with various expressions of distaste and impatience as they waited. Some of them had already sweat through their clothes, blotches of damp decorating armpits and backs and handkerchiefs stuffed into pockets.

Judging by the size of some of those blotches—and the fact that every few seconds, another person abandoned their spot in line—they'd been waiting for quite some time.

Fantastic. He loved waiting.

He shoved his glasses further up the bridge of his nose, sweat already beginning to spread a slick over his skin as he trudged toward the end of the line…then paused when he heard someone call, "Your Lordship!"

When he turned back, he found Cassi sitting on the porch of the tailor's shop, waving eagerly—she sat at the leftmost edge, far enough away from the crowd that she didn't risk getting her skirts trampled on. Skirts that, while still a bit long for her short stature, fit much better today…and shone in an array of pastels, layers of pale rainbow tulle dancing around her bare feet.

When she jumped down from the elevated porch, the skirt flounced past her toes, stirring up a cloud of dust as she landed. She wore a cream linen shirt cinched in around the waist with a corset belt, its golden material embroidered with tiny white flowers; her loose hair covered her self-pierced ears, and her lips were coated in gloss that sparkled in the sun as she beamed his way.

He pointed to the line, one brow raised; she scrunched up her face, shaking her head, and gestured for him to come to her.

Fantastic—*actually* fantastic, this time.

"What're you doing sitting out here?" he called as he strode up to the porch—at the sound of disgruntled muttering rising behind him, he turned and stuck his tongue out in the general direction of the line. A couple of the patrons chuckled; most dug deeper into their scowls.

"Lunch." Cassi gestured back to the porch, where a sandwich sat in a small nest of paper…if it could be called a sandwich. It was either that or a couple croutons with a scrap of meat pinned between them. "What are *you* doing here?"

He flashed her a winning smile, forcing down the discomfort that wormed into his stomach at the sight of her paltry meal…and how that corset gaped around her waist despite being tied to the extremes of its laces. "Do I need a reason to visit a pretty girl on a beautiful day?"

She faked a swoon, fanning her face with her hand. "Oh, to be flattered by a handsome lord! However will I cope?"

"That bad?"

"I mean, it's not the *worst* line I've heard…"

"All right, all right. Truth is, I've got another project for you. But here— finish your lunch while I show you." He gestured to the porch, and she hopped back up to it, settling herself beside the paper parcel and picking up the last portion of her sandwich. He lowered himself to his seat next to her, keeping a polite distance between their hips. "Would you believe that I woke up yesterday morning to find my favorite scarf torn in the center?"

"I hate to be the bearer of bad news," she garbled through her next mouthful of bread, "but most scarves have holes in the center. That's where your head goes."

He slapped his hand to his chest with a gasp. "Why, the nerve of you, being so dismissive of a paying customer!"

Cassi choked down her bite, giggling once it made it down her throat. She put both hands up and bowed at the waist thrice in a row. "Please, mercy! My tongue got away from me."

"You ought to keep it on a leash!"

"Well, sometimes it slips the collar." Still giggling, she drew her legs into a criss-cross, tucking her shirt beneath her ankles and hips. "All right, show me this scarf."

He turned to rifle through his satchel, tugging out the bundle of lavender cloth. He held it out, and she hastily wiped her hands on her napkin before taking it. She spread it to its full width and ran it through her fingers, frowning when she encountered the tear. Her fingers wriggled into it, teasing the edges. "Huh."

"Not exactly big enough to fit a head through," he noted.

"Well, not one as big as yours, certainly." She hovered her nose over the scarf, breathing deep. "That's pretty—what is that?"

Clinging to his casual air for dear life, he gave a careless shrug. "Lilac, I think."

She *hmm*ed, setting the scarf in her lap as she studied the tear. "Fancy taste."

"It's required—us lords, we all have to pick a signature scent on our sixteenth birthdays. It was either lilac or something called *vetiver*, and I didn't have a clue what that was."

"It's another type of plant—the scent's much different. Earthier. A pinch of citrus—"

"Why do *you* know that?"

She planted her fists on her narrow hips. "I know lots of things, thank you very much."

He leaned back, propping one leg up so he could rest his arm on his knee. "I'm learning that. So…can you fix it?"

"*Can I fix it*," she scoffed. "I could stitch this in thirty seconds with my eyes closed."

"Do you feel like proving it?"

"No."

"Because you're bluffing."

"Because I could *definitely* do it, but I'd also *definitely* prick my fingers, and then you'd have blood on your pretty scarf, and I'm not quite talented enough to sew stains out." Cassi reached up and settled the scarf on her head, freeing her hands; then she scooped up the last bite of her sandwich and popped it into her mouth, her head tipped at an imperious angle to keep the scarf from slipping.

"Good balance," he noted.

"Thank you." She wiped her hands one more time before pulling the scarf back down. "But really, I'd better do this with my eyes open. I couldn't launder a stain out if my life depended on it."

"That we have in common." He watched as she pulled a needle and spool of silvery thread from a hidden pocket in her skirt. "You can darn a hole in seconds, totally blind, but you're still just an apprentice here?"

She shrugged, sticking the needle between her teeth as she unspooled the thread, holding the strand along her finger, measuring it against the length of her arm. "Sure am."

"But you do hope to be a tailoress one day?" he pressed. *Come on, give me something.*

She mumbled a garbled response, pinching the thread at her desired length.

He sighed. "Cass."

She plucked the needle from between her teeth with her other hand. "Sorry. No, not particularly."

"Then why take an apprenticeship?"

"It's work, and it pays." A simple answer, but the bitter layer spread beneath suggested something more.

"But you don't enjoy it."

"I don't mind it."

"What would you do if you had your pick?

Unlike her previous answers, this one took its time—it wobbled between her teeth like the needle she was suddenly quite focused on threading. For several seconds, all he got were uncertain hums, the hesitant beginnings of words trailing into nothing.

He chuckled. "Is it that embarrassing?"

"Not embarrassing. Just…private." Yet, when she finally glanced up to meet his gaze, she definitely wore shyness in her smile. "Have you ever walked past the fairgrounds by the shore?"

Shore? They had *shore* here?

"Can't say I have," he said honestly.

"Well, they're pretty popular. Different traveling shows roll in every couple weeks…circuses, carnivals, acrobat troupes, even stage plays."

"Stage plays at a fairground?"

"Well, those usually perform at the theater. But it's closed for repairs right now, so they've been making do with slapdash stages and circus tents." Bashfulness blazed into passion without warning, and she sat forward, toes wriggling excitedly…her hands doing their stitching work all the while. "My father used to take me as a little girl. Everyone else found them boring, but sputtering sparks, I loved them. After he died, we didn't really have the coin for it, but sometimes Peter took up odd jobs at the fairgrounds…he let me come along most times. Once he got me in, I could do the rest of the sneaking myself."

A hint of memory teased him, the ghost of boyhood excursions into unfriendly shadows. He tucked it firmly back in its file, shoving it closed. "Where did you sneak?"

"Where *didn't* I sneak?" Nostalgia slowed her blinks and her fingers, stares and stitches taking longer to break. "I'd hide under the stands to watch the performances…and when the carnies came into town, that was the best. They're close-knit, protect their own first—but they're kind, too. They know the look of an intruder when they see one, but they always took me under their wing. I learned a lot that way."

She tied off the last stitch, handing his scarf back—he took it, then reached behind her ear, pulling a coin out of her curls. "Like sleight of hand, perhaps?"

That smile sharpened playfully, and she plucked the coin from his fingertips, rolling it in her palm. She shut her fingers over it—when she opened them again, the coin was gone. "Yes. And more tricks." Her voice hushed. "Fortune-telling, for one."

His heart skittered sideways in his chest—an attempt to dodge whatever came next. "Fortune-telling?"

"Not so loud!" she hissed, flicking him on the shoulder. "Yes—but the clerics don't approve of such practices. They're considered heresy. They leave the carnies to their business, but if a Sanctaviv citizen got caught…"

"If it's so dangerous, why learn at all?"

"Extra coin." He should've known—that seemed to be the reason for many of the things she did. "Besides, it's not *real*. It's all about reading people…you just have to tell them what they ache most to hear." She smirked, a hint of wicked humor that set his heart's rhythm back into motion. "Or what they *fear* most to hear. Sometimes that's more effective."

A tactic he'd used himself, more than once. He whistled faintly. "You do this for your family, then?"

The passionate gleam in her smile dimmed, and she shifted uncomfortably, fussing with one of the layers of tulle in her skirt. "Not those things. I told you how my sister is…all pious and prudish. Her hair would catch fire if she found out her sister was a heretic."

Gods, if only she realized just how funny that was. "Right. Then what's the coin for?"

"Well, *some* of it is for my family. But I only share the coin if I can share the scheme that earned it." She fussed with her skirt again, blowing out a frustrated breath. "My sister always seems to know when I'm lying. No one else can tell—just her."

He tried not to think of Soren. Of the first time he realized just how *easily* she could peer past his own masks. "Some people know us too well, don't they?"

"Seems so. Anyway, the rest of it, that goes to paying for…" She hesitated.

"What's got your tongue tied up so badly?" What could a pickpocketing tailoress really be spending her money on that could render her *this* shy? "Tell me the truth. Illicit substances? Smuggled liquor?" He wriggled his eyebrows. "Saucy novels?"

She smacked his shoulder, and above his laughter, she groaned, "*No.* Just…things that *I* want. Acting lessons. Training sessions with the troupe of acrobats that have a permanent slot at the theater." A hesitant pause. "Singing lessons. Dancing, too."

"Singing *and* dancing?"

"I know it's silly—"

"Hey." He caught and held her hand against his shoulder to halt her sheepish gestures, her rambling explanation. "Nothing's silly if it matters that much to you."

The echo bounced in his skull, throbbing, angry…threatening to bury him in memories of fireworks and strawberries and lips glossed in champagne.

"My sister wouldn't say so…or my oldest brother." She took her hand back, waving it in front of her face as if dismissing her daydreams from her head. The gesture snapped him out of his own reverie, and he blinked hard, clearing away the sunspots of memory left behind.

When he held his silence, she glanced down at her skirt and frowned, pulling her thread and needle back out. As he watched, she peeled back layers of tulle to reach the silk lining beneath, revealing a ragged hole—with a sigh, she started darning it shut, adding, "Anyway, that's what I would be. If I could be anything, I'd join one of those troupes…any of them. And thanks to all the lessons, I might just make it next time one of them holds auditions."

"That's quite the ambition." Performing wasn't an easy profession to wriggle into in his time, either. "When I was a kid…"

"Let me guess. You wanted to be a magician?"

A chuckle caught in his throat. He scratched the back of his neck before looping the scarf over it. "No. I, ah…I wanted to be a writer, I think. Or a fiddler."

"Those are two very different things."

"I'm a man of varied talents."

"Hmm." This time, she smiled, not smirked—but that sprinkle of wickedness stuck around. "I'm beginning to learn that."

Ears burning—gods, why were his ears burning?—he dug a hand into his pocket and pulled out the coin she'd slipped back in when she'd thought him distracted. He held it out to her. "For your work—and for making you do it on your lunch break."

"You didn't make me, I invited you," she laughed, tying off the last stitch in her skirt before cutting the thread. "Keep it—no, don't pout, I'm serious. The fix didn't even take long enough to charge you our hourly…besides, you're going to need that coin when you have to hire a new member of your household."

His brows furrowed. "Huh?"

"Well, I don't know who, but you're going to have to dismiss someone." She poked the scarf, her sun-warmed fingertip spreading its heat to the skin beneath. "Seeing as that hole had clean edges, nothing frayed…someone cut it deliberately."

Her knowing smile spread, contagious as a yawn; he smiled back, careful to keep its angle sheepish, not smug. He'd hoped she'd be good enough to catch that—and she hadn't let him down. "Damn. Caught me."

"Do you regularly cut your own clothes?"

"Only when there's a tailoress I need an excuse to see again. Look, please let me pay for it—I'll feel awful if I don't, considering I took up your break *and* did so selfishly."

She studied the coin in his hand carefully, eyes narrowed—after a moment, she looked up at him. Behind her brown eyes, he could clearly see cogs turning, clicking into place on some new idea.

"I have a counteroffer," she said. "Will you be in the city much longer?"

"Would you like me to be?"

"I get off early this afternoon, and my brothers will be working for a few hours past…I wouldn't mind if a handsome lordling offered to walk me somewhere afterward."

"Somewhere?" Even knowing her mortal limits, that seemed alarmingly vague.

"To see some friends." Her grin stretched ear to ear. "Friends with similar…interests. A walk to meet them, a pickpocketing lesson or two, and I'll consider your debt paid."

Far more effort than paying her a gold coin. But this wasn't really about the payment—this was about the intentional tear, the repeated visits, her drawing all the conclusions he'd hoped she would.

"Deal," he said. "I'll find a way to entertain myself for a bit. Meet back here…when?"

"Listen for the clock tower—when it chimes five, I'll be ready." She gathered her skirts and stood, offering a curtsy and a wink. "I'll see you then, Lordship."

"Are you ever going to call me by my real name?"

"Sure I will—when you finally tell me what it is." And with a spin that should have swirled her brain into spirals, she flounced back into the shop, leaving him staring after her.

Smiling after her.

With a curse dirty enough to stain a white glove black, he turned away from the shop, pulling at the corners of his mouth until they got back in line.

This was his game, not hers. He couldn't start again with rebellious smiles and flushing skin and misbehaving heartbeats—not *again*.

This girl wasn't *real*. She didn't *exist*. The monster in his mirror had killed her, and he had no hope of saving what had already been buried.

He was the best damned actor in any age—good enough to even fool himself, sometimes.

But he'd lost himself to this role before. Not again. Not this time.

He stormed off, setting himself to a new task—finding a cup of black coffee to clear his head, a cold bucket of water to douse himself in if that didn't work, and maybe—if he was very, very lucky—a bakery stocked with a dozen or more peanut butter cookies.

CHAPTER 21

RAQUEL

Spitting out blood had become a regular part of her evening routine.

The dim kerosene lamp in the bathing room might as well have been a knife shoved beneath her brow bone; it stoked the pulsing ache there until she could hardly bear to keep her eye open. But dimming the lamp further wouldn't help—she already could barely see thanks to the swelling around her sighted eye, left behind by Revan, who had purposely targeted that spot during their sparring session.

She'd known better than to agree to it the first time; and the second, and the third, and so on. There was nobody to blame but herself for the bruised eye, the bleeding nose, and the catch in her breath that suggested a fractured rib.

She'd known better. But to keep refusing their invites and taunts would have drawn a worse kind of attention, the kind of attention corruption paid to things that did not bow to its corrosive touch.

So when they called to her now, she always entered the brawling circle, setting her own rules: no magic. No blades. And no broken bones.

Tonight, Revan had toed the edge of those lines more closely than a tightrope walker balancing on a thread. But a fracture was not technically a break…and the metal loops the mountain-born man wore on every knuckle were not technically blades.

Oddly enough, that rigid commitment to the lines she'd drawn convinced her that he'd once been a good man. Good enough that even chaos magic altering his perception couldn't push him into crossing the boundaries she'd set.

And that made her even angrier.

As she stared into the basin, the flame in the lamp sending a halo of blurred light across her bruised eye, another mouthful of blood swamped every sense in iron. She spat again, twisting the faucet on and bending to drink, swishing clean water before spitting it back into the basin.

When she straightened, looking back in the mirror, her blurred gaze found Tenebrae's.

Before she could shout—like it would have done any good anyway—Tenebrae gripped her by the shoulder and whirled her around, barring his arm across her chest and shoving her against the sink; the ceramic dug into the small of her back, knocking a pained grunt out of her. His other hand shot out and caged her jaw, unkempt nails digging into soft flesh, seeking the bone beneath.

"Hello, Officer Angelov." Tenebrae's smile had a sickening tendency to curl too far across his face, heedless glee stretching his lips near to tearing. "I hope I didn't frighten you."

She did her best to put on a bored stare. "Can I help you, Your Majesty?"

"For your sake, you should hope not." Those nails pierced inward, drawing hot beads of blood. "There are traitors running in my streets."

"If you're referring to the fires—"

"Shhh." The nails in her chin receded, replaced with a slow stroke of his thumb; when he lifted his hand to examine it, blood rolled from the pad of his thumb to the heel of his palm. He looked back to her, lazily licking her blood from his hand.

If he expected her to flinch, to sicken, he would have to do better than that. She'd been tasting her own blood all evening.

"I *refer* to the ingrates erecting idols of me and my sister…and burning them," he said. "I *refer* to whatever mouths spilled rumors of our true nature onto the streets. I have heard my name cursed by those who should not know it."

She held his gaze calmly. "Are you accusing me?"

"I am *asking* you."

"If the people know what you are, it is not by my word." More or less true. "You may want to go and bend your own people backwards for answers. Subtlety is hardly their art form."

His bloodshot eyes flashed. "You've learned much from my sister."

"A compliment."

"An observation." He paused. "You wouldn't happen to know where she is?"

"I answer to her, not the other way around. I wouldn't dare try to keep tabs on her whereabouts." Less true. When Finn got back from wherever he'd gone, she was going to threaten him with a leash if he kept leaving without telling her—and then ask for a better lock on her door.

Tenebrae drew close to her face, scarlet hair blocking her periphery. His breath slithered over her cheek, oddly cold, smelling strongly of fear.

Not her fear. And if she had to guess, not his, either.

This close, the texture of his skin caught her eye…and turned her stomach.

What looked like freckles from afar—mottled specks along the forehead, jaw, and mouth—were actually pockmarked holes. Blackened, necrotic pores that had widened from pinhead pricks to gaping sores; instead of pus or blood or any natural fluid, ridges of purplish scarring branched out from their edges.

Corruption breaking free from its mortal confines.

"Well," Tenebrae murmured, "I suppose you *can't* help me, then, Officer Angelov."

Even after he released her, she did not move—did not breathe.

Had he been human, he would have already been on the ground—had he been human, he would have been dead the moment he touched her. The lightning ever at her beck and call would have forked into his heart without mercy, halting it in a single breathless second.

But he was not human. She was. And she did not feel ready to die…not by his hand.

She didn't know who the satisfaction of her last breath would belong to, but she'd be damned if she'd let it be him.

"At your service, Your Majesty," she said, grateful beyond words that her voice emerged strong and steady. "Please feel free to visit again…but do consider knocking. My time at war did not teach me much mercy for people entering my space unannounced."

His chuckle raised the hairs from the back of her neck to the bruised skin still pressed against the sink. "I have no need of your mercy, Officer Angelov."

For several minutes after he left the bathing room, her body would not release her from the irons of adrenaline—in fact, she didn't breathe again until she heard the third closing door out in the hall, indicating he had entered the stairwell leading to other floors of the castle.

With a quiet but fierce exhale, she slid to the floor, cupping one hand over her mouth and slipping the other around her bracelet.

Breathe.

Breathe.

Breathe.

CHAPTER 22

FINN

In all honesty, entertaining himself in Sanctaviv wasn't that hard.

He spent the first hour doing some of his own pickpocketing, which taught him exactly why Cassi hadn't gotten caught thus far. These people had their noses stuck so far up in the air, it was a wonder they could see where they were going, let alone notice a hand dipping into their pockets or satchels.

However, stealing wads of useless paper did eventually get boring. He might as well have been robbing a library, and this flimsy replacement for *actual* money wasn't half as exciting as any novel he could have filched from those shelves.

So the second hour, he spent his time getting to know the birthplace of his enemies.

In his time, the city known as Sanctaviv didn't hold itself quite as haughtily as this one did. Modern Sanctaviv still showed off its precious metals—it was an Artemisian city, after all—and some fairly impressive figurines depicting their favored deity, but not the way this ancient version of Sanctaviv did.

Here, the "Sancta" in "Sanctaviv" ruled with a gilded fist.

Gold and silver in abundance. Strings of lanterns swung from every building, bobbing in the breeze above every street. Some glowed cheerily, filled with gold or white light—others burned a foreboding scarlet or emerald green or a purple so vibrant it hurt his eyes.

Even in broad daylight, they stuck out. And as he made his rounds doing his best to walk like a man who belonged here, something came to his attention:

The colors weren't random.

He had noted before that the streets leading out from the city square reminded him of spokes on a wheel. Now, taking in the array of colored light, it became obvious that every spoke bore a different color than the one before or after it—some kind of code.

The third hour, he spent cracking that code.

Green, for life—for apothecaries and healers, arborists and grocers.

Red, for flame—for blacksmiths and craftsmen, taverns and bakeries.

Blue, for the trader's market—a street lined with tents and open-air booths, not buildings. A street with sailors and salespeople milling up and down its cobblestones, hawking their catches of fish and caches of treasures. Their collections of oddities and crates of clothing.

Gold, for holiness—for churches, not temples, and shops or stands filled to the brim with worship paraphernalia: prayer beads and lantern charms and strange flowing robes. The city square was circled completely in Sancta's spaces.

White, which belonged to no particular trade: those lanterns lined residential streets. They lit the way home.

And lastly, purple—purple for fabric and gems and finery. Purple for dress shops and jewelry stores…theatres and tailors.

The fourth hour, he spent beneath the glow of scarlet lanterns; moreover, he spent all that silly paper he'd been gathering all afternoon, marveling as the shopkeeps lit up like he'd handed them a heavy sack of gold.

Paper money. Maybe that could be his next long con, if fun ever became a thing he could indulge in again.

The fifth hour, the chiming of the clock tower—five droning gongs ringing out over the city—called him back to one of the purple-lit streets.

Parcels all packed carefully in a new satchel he'd filched—well, bought, but handing over nothing but paper for it still felt like stealing—he strolled back to the tailor's shop, noting its name for the first time: *The Slipped Stitch.*

Cassi waited on the steps, chin rested on her hands, eyes closed—she had her face turned up into a beam of sun, looking for all the world like a dozing cat curled up on a porch step.

Finn slowed, his toe clipping a cobblestone.

The sun coaxed out a spray of glitter across her cheek, likely a work mishap—but it also drew out the trenches exhaustion had dug beneath her eyes. The strain of her cheekbones against her skin. The scabbed-over divot in her bottom lip, the mark that anxious chewing left behind.

Hatred, a now-familiar friend, slid its hands over his shoulders, anchoring him in place…forcing him to take in the girl half-asleep, half-starved, not even halfway changed into the monster that she would one day become.

Look at you, Hatred whispered. *Look at her. Which one looks most like a monster?*

He shrugged off those suffocating hands. They weren't welcome right now—not if Hatred had decided to aim its blows inward.

If he was a monster, then she had made him so—and a monster was the least of what he could become if it meant getting ahead in this game.

Two things could be true at once.

Firstly, Cassandra Medeis did not deserve to be taken advantage of. She did not deserve to be tricked and teased and tempted into sabotaging her own future.

Secondly, Occassio, Goddess of Time, had tricked and teased and tempted him into dooming his kingdom—into dooming himself. And while he had deserved it more than the girl before him did, his kingdom had not—his family had not.

And beyond all of that, worse than any sin she had committed against him and his…she had kept Soren from remembering them. Had forced his sister to live another life when they could have had her home mere *months* after the fire.

Sins committed against him…those he could have forgiven. Maybe. Had he been a slightly better man—or a weaker one.

But sins against his sister…those he remembered. Those he punished.

So when Cassi finally opened her eyes, squinting at him through the glaze of sun, not a hint of shame shone in his smile.

"Five chimes, as ordered." He strode up to her, holding a hand out. "May I?"

"*May I*," she mocked as she took his hand, but her grin was good-natured. "You may, of course. That bag's new."

He patted it with his free hand, then pulled her to her feet, giving her a quick twirl that spun her into giggles. "I did some shopping."

"All by yourself, no servants or anything?"

"I even counted the money all by myself."

She sniffed, miming wiping a tear. "I'm so proud."

Gods, he had to stop smiling. He tapped lightly on the back of her heel with the toe of his boot. "Lead on, then. I'm curious to meet these mysterious friends, provided they don't prove to be imaginary."

"Imaginary friends are the best sort," she argued as she looped her arm through his. The warmth of her sunbathed skin seeped through the sleeve of his shirt; he had to take his next breath slowly. "They only ever say what you want to hear, they follow you everywhere, they never wear the same dress as you to the ball…"

"Attending many balls, are we?"

"Well, if I'm imagining my friends, surely it's fair for me to imagine myself as the sort of person who gets invited to balls."

Fair enough. "Can I imagine I'm the sort of person who always declines the invitation?"

She tipped her head at an angle he'd grown familiar with—she always tilted her head just so when she rolled her eyes. "I suppose a lord would find such events boring. Lavish events are copper a dozen for you, I bet."

Finn considered, absently guiding her around a pile of shattered glass cast across the street—a broken bottle thrown from a moving carriage, maybe. The shards crunched beneath his boots instead. "They do have some redeemable qualities. Good music. Good company, if you're lucky to find the right circle. And the food…"

"Stop," she whimpered. "I don't even want to know."

"I once tasted a cherry tart I'd sell my soul for." At her dismissive snort, he added, "And I once ate my weight in chocolate mousse. That's impressive, too, because they always serve them in these tiny cups."

"I'd take a tiny cup," she mumbled glumly. "Sancta's sake, I'd take a lick."

"Maybe you can sneak in someday and snag one." He glanced at her out of the corner of his eye. "This a long walk?"

"Not particularly. Bored of my company already?"

"Not at all. I just have a game we can play, if you like."

"What sort of game?"

"The sort where we see who can pickpocket the most people by the end of the walk."

She chuckled. "Oh, you are *on*, Your Lordship."

Though he'd said it to buy himself some time to assess the mounting pain in his head, the slow-cranking pressure in his sinuses threatening to sluice blood from his nose, he couldn't help enjoying it. Enjoying how it was actually easier to do this work with her on his arm, enjoying how he only needed to nudge or tug her arm for her to know what he wanted, enjoying how she did the same in return to manage her own picks.

Using each other as obstacles or excuses or distractions, they took turns picking victims until they turned down another street strung with brilliant purple lanterns. However, unlike the other streets they'd walked down, this one looked nearly abandoned.

Most of the street was dominated by a single building: a grand, multi-columned structure that mixed metal and marble and gemstones to create a shimmering vision pearled in silver. There were multiple stacks of steps set on top of each other, staggered all the way up to the building itself; each stair reflected the purple lantern light in its smooth marble face.

Finn could only stare, squinting through his glasses, trying desperately to discern whether the grand theatre before him was real or some kind of mirage. Only when Cassi released his arm to dance up the first stack of steps did he relax.

Not a hallucination—just a bit ethereal.

"I thought you said the theatre was closed," he said.

"It is." She dangled a key in front of his face. "But my brother Peter, he's been working under the foreman for a couple months now. He happened to forget his lunch one day, and I figured, as long as I was dropping by…"

"Poor foreman," Finn chuckled.

"He's awful to Peter. Works him half to death and doesn't pay him enough to afford the coffin." With a shrug, she tossed the key in the air and caught it again, shoving it back into whatever hidden pocket she had in her skirt. "Come on. The key's to the back door."

When Cassi unlocked the door and opened it, Finn had to take a step back. The smells that rushed out told a very confusing story: sawdust and steel, expected of a building under construction; must and mothballs, probably the result of costumes left to sit; and, strangely, something buttery.

"Come on," Cassi urged; she plunged straight into the shadowy space beyond the door, the dim confines swallowing her whole in one bite.

The dark had always been a friend to him; that wasn't what kept him stuck to the threshold, hands pressed to the doorframe, eyes locked on the nothingness beyond.

It was the overwhelming sense of dread that nearly barreled him over, cold certainty brittling his bones.

If he walked into this theater, he would be sealing *something*—some piece of fate that had not yet decided itself, a spinning top only just beginning to tip one way or the other.

He closed his eyes, peering inward…seeking the spill of effervescent foresight that often came with these rushes of somatic knowledge.

Nothing. Even when he prodded at the edges of his mind, reaching into the darkness and blindly scrabbling for a twinkle of understanding…nothing.

Just a *knowing* so terrifying, so true, that he could not make a move to step back or step in.

A pop of color—Cassi reappeared at the door, poking her head out, frowning at whatever look had frozen on his face. "What's wrong?"

"Nothing." Nothing yet. "I…"

I want to go home.

He swallowed that truth, smiling past the barbed pain as it stuck in his throat, unwilling to be buried entirely. "I'm sort of spooked by the dark," he lied.

To his surprise, she didn't laugh or roll her eyes or tug him inside. Instead, she dipped closer, her tiptoed posture bringing her nearly eye-to-eye with him.

"I used to be afraid of the dark," she admitted in a hush.

Gazing into her earnest brown eyes, his mouth dried out, thoughts of impending destiny shuffling into thoughts of a goddess trapped between panes of glass, a sheet cast over her, blocking out all the light.

Monster, monster, monster.

Monsters like the dark, he reminded himself.

"Used to be?" he croaked.

"Until Braeden taught me a trick." She held out her hand, gentle mischief twinkling in the flash of her teeth. "May I?"

He looked past her, over her, into the shrouded future beyond.

There was no telling which path would doom or save him—or if it was even *his* life this choice would change.

He set his hand in hers, and the weight lifted from his chest. The frost thawed from his bones.

As if from a great distance, he could have sworn he heard Occassio—her true self, not the girl holding his hand—crying out across time itself.

No, she shrieked, all pitch and no power—then again, a defeated sob, the echo of bone against unbreakable glass. *NO.*

"You may," he murmured, fixing his gaze on this Cassi. On this moment.

And together, they stepped into the shadows, shutting the door behind them.

CHAPTER 23

FINN

"The secret is, pretty much everyone hates the dark," Cassi told him as she led him inside. Objects bumped against his shoulders, brushed against his ribs, and tried to trip him at the toes; he gritted his teeth, holding tighter to Cassi's hand. "They consider it an enemy. A danger. But the truth is, the dark isn't a danger—it's a defender. If you befriend it, you'll never have anything to fear."

A knob twisted, hinges squeaking—jilted punctuation at the end of a beautiful sentence. Light flooded in, blinding him briefly.

"There she is!" crowed someone past the too-bright light. "Get out here, Cassi, we're just setting up!"

He reached up a hand to shield his eyes, blinking hard—with that shred of protection, he could just barely put together what waited ahead.

They'd stepped onto a stage.

An admittedly fine one, actually—the wood shone like it had been polished in expensive oils, and the plum-purple curtains were sewn from velvet. Real velvet, not the shoddy stuff most theaters used. Silver tassels tied them back, revealing the auditorium beyond.

Rows of seats fanned out in every direction—they lined the ground level until about halfway back, then they began to climb, layered like a cake. To the left and right, he could pick out the boxes reserved for higher-paying clientele, opera glasses waiting on perches for their next patrons.

And scattered across the stage, limbs akimbo, were four of the most colorful characters Finn had ever seen in his gods-damned life.

A scrawny boy sat up when they came in, wide grin beating a hasty retreat when he saw Finn. His hair was shorn on both sides; a shock of vibrant red—too vibrant to be natural—ruffled down the center, falling into an artful twist in middle of his forehead. He wore ragged pants patched in several places with mismatched fabrics, though the stitching itself seemed solid, and he wore no shoes. He paled when he took Finn in fully, scrambling to his feet, making as if to run.

"It's okay!" Cassi called out cheerfully, as if this boy always acted like a jackrabbit with one leg in a hound's belly. "This is my new friend, everyone. He's here to teach us a trick or two."

"Teach *us* a trick?" snorted a girl lying flat on her back, her legs draped over the lap of another boy, who was idly juggling three shoe-sacks with one hand. The small, bead-filled bundles nearly blurred in the air as he tossed them; even Finn's eye, well-trained on stacked decks and shell games, couldn't keep up. "We've got plenty, thanks."

"Molly, manners," warned another girl—this one utterly contorted, her limbs folded in so many wrong places Finn felt the urge to check and make sure all of his own extremities remained in place. Her legs bent fully over her shoulders, her palms flat to the floor—it looked like a handstand gone horribly wrong, her body knotted up worse than a licorice twist. Somehow, impossibly, she was reading a book splayed out on the floor, a pebble wedged in the center to keep the pages from turning; she hadn't even looked up from it when the two of them had entered.

Molly smacked a charcoal-stained hand to her forehead, the charcoal itself still tucked between her fingertips. "Right. Where did I put those pesky things? Do you have any I can borrow, Kit?"

"*How do you do* might suffice," suggested the juggling boy.

"Mm, feels boring."

"Who exactly are you," suggested the jumpy one; though he looked uneasy still, he sauntered back to the group, hands shoved in his pockets. "And why are you dressed like a prince?"

"Critiquing someone's clothes isn't good manners," said the twisted-up girl.

"I didn't ask, Minxie."

"I'm L—" If he introduced himself as a lord here, he'd probably get jumped. "Alex."

"Alex." Minxie wiggled her fingers—he nearly begged her to stop, her limbs already bowed so badly he struggled to keep his stomach where it ought to be. "Good to meet you. I'm Minxie. The one missing her manners is Molly, the one she's using as a footstool is Kit, and the twitchy one's Abbott."

The other three all protested in harmony, varying from curses to reminders that they could introduce themselves just fine and she wasn't their mother.

Minxie rolled her eyes—the first time she'd taken them off her book— and artfully unfolded onto her belly before pushing herself up to her feet. Every movement flowed smooth and slow, languid as pouring syrup; it was a type of grace he'd never seen, the deliberate motions of someone utterly in control of her body.

He couldn't help himself; he applauded. "I've never seen anything like that—I know that doesn't mean much without knowing me, but trust me, I've seen a *lot*."

Minxie beamed, pushing back a strand of white-blonde hair. The razor-clean edges of her blunt bob barely brushed her chin. "You oughta see the professionals, then."

There was nothing he wanted to see less. "Cassi didn't mention her friends were quite so talented."

"Well, unlike Minxie, she knows how to keep her mouth shut when she ought to," laughed Molly. She scooped up her sketchbook and held out a hand— Kit used his free hand to help her up, not breaking his juggling rhythm at all. Molly rubbed a few tight curls from her forehead, leaving behind thicker streaks of charcoal; her ebony mane bounced like a host of springs as she leapt to her feet, the cloudbursts of pale coloration speckled across her dark brown skin catching the spotlight. "What tricks are you meant to teach us?"

Finn smirked, holding up a sparkling bracelet he'd pinched off someone's wrist earlier. "Just a little pickpocketing."

"Really?" Kit snorted. "And what's a fancy kid like you going to teach us about that?"

"Is this a trap?" Abbott glanced nervously to the door. "Feels like a trap."

Cassi scowled. "Why would *I* be setting a trap, Abbott?"

"It's not from the goodness of my heart, if it makes you feel better," Finn offered. "Miss Medeis repaired something very precious to me and wouldn't accept payment. A favor better suited her needs."

"He's better than me," Cassi admitted—the sudden, wide-eyed hush from her friends suggested that confession carried weight. "And it seems that we may soon see an influx of nobles on the street with specially sewn pockets. He knows how to pick around them—and if we don't want to get caught, we need his help. So if everyone could be *nice* to him—"

"I'm not nice to anyone," Kit said.

"—or at least tolerate his presence, then I would greatly appreciate it."

There were murmurs of assent, even from Abbott—they all stared at him differently now, curiosity pushing suspicion aside.

"How's a pretty lordling like you get good enough to out-pick Cassandra Medeis?" Kit asked. His hair, textured and tightly curled and cropped close to his skull, shone a shade lighter than his onyx skin; every so often, he reached up and ran a hand over it, an absentminded habit. His other hand had not yet stopped juggling—Finn wasn't sure if he even realized he *was* juggling.

"My governess always kept candy in her pockets when I was growing up," he said—that drew a laugh out of Molly, but not the others. "The real answer is none of your business. I'm here to help; let me do that, and I'll be on my way."

"Fine," said Abbott with a huff, "but we practice first, Cass. Sancta knows how much time we have in here tonight."

Finn turned to Cassi, brow raised; she smiled sheepishly back. "Remember what I told you about wanting to be a performer? We all come here to practice our, um…acts."

"Acts?"

Minxie raised a hand. "Contortionist—but you probably figured that out. I'm not half-bad with aerial silks or a tightrope, either."

"Performance art." Molly held up her sketchbook, revealing a charcoal rendering of a face. No—*his* face. How in the depths had she even had time—"Usually there's some dance involved."

"Juggling," Kit said with a shrug. "And a trick rider, but that bit's better left to outdoor practice."

"Musician," Abbott mumbled.

Finn hummed under his breath. "What instrument?"

Abbott smirked, his first flicker of confidence. "Anything with strings or keys, my friend."

He was *just* petty enough to be jealous of that kind of talent, even in a boy who was centuries dead in his own time, so he turned to Cassi quickly. "And you…"

"Cassi's a jack-of-all-trades," Molly piped up before Cassi could answer. "She dances, does acrobatics, magic tricks…"

"But Sancta save you if you hand her an instrument," Abbott chuckled—then winced when Cassi landed a punch on his arm. "What? It's true! I've tried everything, I swear, but the girl doesn't have the right ear. She makes up for it with her voice, though—her singing puts the morning birds to shame."

"And her acting…" Minxie whistled through rounded lips, shaking her head as she smiled fondly at her friend. "Even Sancta can't save you from that. She's magic up there. Like she actually becomes someone else."

A chill settled in the core of his spine. "Huh."

"They're exaggerating," Cassi laughed nervously. She sat criss-cross on the stage, yanking pins from her hair, freeing her curls with a quick ruffle and a relieved sigh. "I'm decent, but they're the real marvels."

"Well, he can judge for himself in a moment. Abbott's right, we should take advantage of the stage while we've got it." Molly started stretching, reaching down to her toes without bending her knees. "There's only a couple weeks until the Chrysalis Company rolls into town, and my mam's kitchen is hardly going to suit if I want to impress them."

"*If* they're still coming," Minxie added, casually bending herself backward, catching herself on her palms. She twisted her arms around so they were facing forward; bile began to tickle the bottom of Finn's throat, but he forced it down. "What with the plague and all."

"*Plague?*" That word tickled worse than the threat of his own sickness—a memory that wielded a long feather, teasing the edges of his brain.

A mountain cave. A bonfire. An empress seated across from him, solemn features bathed in flame.

A story about a girl who fell in love with a priest; a priest who fell terribly ill when plague struck the city of Sanctaviv. A girl who burned at the stake when that priest betrayed her for saving his life.

A girl turned Death Goddess.

His throat threatened to close up entirely.

"Plague," Kit scoffed. "Those are just rumors."

"Not rumors," Molly argued. "My cousin wrote us to tell us about it—it wiped out half her village."

"Your cousin who lives out on Spicer Bay?" Cassi stretched out her legs, bending at the waist to reach her toes. "That place is barely even Empire. Look, my sister, she works closely with priests and priestesses—and clerics. One of them claims the threat of illness is far from Sanctaviv still."

"Working more *closely* with those golden-eyed go-hards every day, if you ask me," Minxie said with a wiggle of her nearly-transparent eyebrows—she crawled over to Cassi and nudged her with a contorted elbow. "Considering how many times you've skipped out on practice to watch Ani, since Mora's so busy working the *night shift*."

Cassi playfully nudged her back. "Oh, stop. Sancta's waxy wicks, I *wish* that was why she was stuck there so long. Maybe then she'd loosen her corset strings a bit. She's been such a pain in my petticoat lately."

"Well, that's nothing new," Molly giggled. "Poor uptight thing. Look, either way, we should practice like auditions are still on. Better to be overprepared than under."

"Always better to be over than under," Kit snickered—Molly slapped his wrist, finally forcing his shoe-sacks to drop to the floor.

"As long as I'm here…" Finn ventured, and they all glanced back to him, "I play a mean fiddle myself. If anyone needs music, or if you need a harmony, Abbott, I'm happy to serve."

"Sure." Abbott actually lit up; his shoulders loosened, the last hint of hostility finally sloughing off. "If you can cover the fiddle, I'd love to practice my pianoforte—I'm a little rusty on keys."

"Great!" Cassi hopped back to her feet, bouncing on her tiptoes. "I'll dig up some of the costumes from the back—pretty boy, come with me. I'll show you where to get your instrument."

It took a moment for him to realize *pretty boy* referred to him.

Within minutes, Finn found himself amazed by this oddball group's efficiency; it took no time at all for them to put together pretty decent costumes from the moth-eaten pieces Cassi threw at them. He turned away to give them privacy, finding a perch on a wooden block shoved into the wings; he was in the middle of fussing with his borrowed fiddle, rosining the bow, when he felt a tap on his shoulder.

"Well?" Cassi chirped from behind him. "What do we think?"

Swiveling on his seat, he opened his mouth, tongue primed with something sarcastic—only for it to ram to a halt as he set eyes on her.

She'd exchanged her layers of tulle for a silver leotard, the satin clinging to her willowy form…no, not willowy. Wiry.

Now that he could see the lithe body beneath the billowing hand-me-downs, the muscle tone in her bare legs made itself known, strong and supple; likely a result of many nights spent jumping from roof to roof, fleeing the scene of her schemes. She grinned at him as she busied her fingers behind her back, tying a skirt of transparent chiffon around her waist; it fell down to her bare ankles, nothing but a wisp of shimmering lavender mist cast over her. "Well?"

"Um," he said.

Her face fell. "What? What's wrong?" She glanced down at herself, her ringlets dancing across her shoulders; she'd fluffed them out fully now, no longer trapping them beneath cheap pins or tying them down with cloth bands. "Is there a stain somewhere? I mean, it doesn't matter, no one's going to see it, but—"

He caught her wrist, halting her hand's frantic wandering. "It's perfect."

Those big, breathtaking brown eyes rose to meet his. Molten chocolate, tempting and tricksy—too sweet to resist, sure to scald if he dared try for a taste.

A familiar seizing sensation halted his heartbeat.

"Oh," she said softly. Her breath was warm. It smelled like strawberries; the gloss coating her lips had to have something to do with that. "Thank you."

He dug his teeth into his tongue, hiding the pain behind his close-lipped smile. The sting cleared his head enough for him to force his hand open; cleared his head enough that he could finally hear the voice screaming in the back of it, knocking bony knuckles against his skull.

Too far, it shrieked. *You're going too far.*

Method acting had its dangers…namely, losing oneself so deeply to the role that one forgot the truth of themselves.

That was the trouble, though. This *was* the truth of him: in every time, in any guise, this girl had a way of catching his breath, cupping it between her hands and peering inside to giggle at it. A child snatching a butterfly from the air, refusing to open their hands to admire it for fear of it flying away.

Danger and delight. Wickedness and whimsy. A clever combination that never failed to capture his attention.

The one godsforsaken trick he *always* fell for.

"I have something for you," he blurted—not the smoothest transition, but gods damn him, he needed a distraction.

It seemed to snap her out of it, too; she cleared her throat, stepping back from him, balling her fists in her sheet of chiffon. "For me?"

"Well, I got it for me, but I'll share." And while he did, maybe it would buy him enough time to stoke his hatred back to full blaze.

When he pulled out the bag of peanut butter cookies—along with a box of chocolate eclairs, a sack of cinnamon twists, and a thermos of coffee—the mood of the room shifted immediately, all five of the daydreaming artists scrambling over to start claiming a treat or three.

"Remember that thing I said about not being nice to anyone?" Kit asked through a mouthful of cinnamon-sugar pastry. "I take it back."

After a chorus of laughter, a similar song of gratitude from the others, and several desserts reduced to crumbs that dusted the stage, they all set the treats aside in favor of the implements of their craft. Abbott took a seat at the pianoforte hidden in the orchestra pit, and Finn hopped down to join him, opting for the conductor's platform over one of the chairs meant for the musicians.

Molly went first—she gingerly set a stretched canvas flat on the floor, then stood behind it. She wore a leotard as well, though hers was sparkling white, covering her from the base of her neck to her ankles.

She didn't wield a paintbrush. Instead, she coated *herself* in various shades of paint; first her hands, then her feet, mottling colors together with no clear intent that Finn could surmise.

Abbott came over holding out a couple pieces of sheet music. "This is what we'll be playing for her. If you can't keep up, signal me, yeah?"

"I'll keep up," he promised.

And he did. The music they played was not cheerful; though it moved at a fevered pace—Abbott hadn't lied, he was good—it carried a tone of aggression, anger doused in passion, and Molly's movements echoed it. She *attacked* the canvas, twirling and bending and spinning on her knees, peppering the canvas with strikes from her palms and soles. Before long, splashes of paint soaked the leotard, hardly a hint of snowy satin left.

Panting, Molly halted before her canvas, lifting it to give it a cursory look; when she showed it off to them, Finn had the horrorstruck thought that he was going to have to be the one to tell her she had no talent whatsoever after all. All he could see were oddly blended patches of paint.

Then she flipped the canvas upside down, and his jaw dropped.

She had painted a perfect imitation of this theater; columns and steps and shadows all, capturing the mirage-like quality with nothing but oil paints and her own rhythm.

Molly wasn't the only one to impress; after she exited the stage, bowing and blowing paint-stained kisses to her adoring (if imaginary) fans, it was Minxie's turn. And after she bent herself in so many terrible shapes he had to hug his own shoulders for comfort, Kit took the stage, juggling so many knives Vash would have been jealous, ending his act without a single nick. And then…

Then it was Cassi's turn.

"What're you thinking for this, Cass?" Abbott called out, stretching over the pianoforte to peer up at the stage.

"Aerials," she called back from somewhere in the wings.

Abbott frowned thoughtfully. "Silks?"

As if on cue, two swathes of black silk fell from somewhere above the stage. "And a hoop!" Moments later, a large metal ring lowered in jerky drops between the silks. "Chrysalis Company mostly does acrobatics, from what I hear. Not looking for singers or actors."

"Smart girl. Got music for me?"

"If you can track down *Songbird in Sorrow*…"

Abbott snorted, tapping his temple. "*Track it down.* I've got that one up here." He cast a doubtful look to Finn. "Do you think you can pick it up by—"

"I know that one, too." Surprising—not that he remembered the song from his childhood lessons, but that it had been born this far in the past…and somehow survived all that time. "It's fiddle-forward—you good if I lead?"

"You fed me sugar," Abbott deadpanned. "You can dance on the damn pianoforte while you play if you like."

"Don't tempt me."

Instead of answering, Abbott simply sat down, gesturing to the top of the pianoforte. "Your stage, my friend."

Oh, that really was tempting. But the last thing he needed was to sprain an ankle in front of all these people.

That wouldn't just be a blow to his pride; he'd have to limp all the way to the closest pane of glass, hope nobody decided the poor hobbling lord was an easy target, and somehow get it healed without Tenebrae knowing.

He could probably play it off as some unfortunate consequence of stealing a form with longer legs. But something told him that even in a borrowed body, Occassio would never do anything as human as spraining an ankle.

Especially when she had so much practice waltzing about on her tiptoes— which was exactly what she did as she strolled out from the wings, hair pulled into a single pouf at the top of her head, tied with one of her circular silk hairbands. She was no longer barefoot; instead, she made her way to center stage in worn ballet slippers a bit too big for her feet. She fluffed out one of the silks with a quick shake before fisting the fabric in a remarkably steady hand, flashing him a cocky wink as she called, "Ready when you are, maestros!"

Abbott cracked his knuckles one by one, rolling his neck and shoulders in turn before setting his long, knobby fingers to the keys. "Music or movement first?"

Finn didn't know what that meant, but Cassi called out, "Music," and Abbott did not wait—he immediately began playing the familiar notes of *Songbird in Sorrow*.

The song had never been one of Finn's favorites as a boy; he'd preferred jaunty sea shanties and jig-worthy melodies, every strike of the bow stoking his energy rather than spending it.

Songbird in Sorrow, despite its name, did not mourn with its music—but it still droned in longer, more deliberate notes, a coaxing of emotion that he'd never really enjoyed in his boyhood. But now, as he set bow to string and began leading the song, he understood it just a little better.

Not thanks to maturity; not thanks to the growth of his skill; not because some worldly perspective had been granted to him.

But because when Cassi ascended those silks, he suddenly knew what it was to watch a creature born for the sky dream of escaping the familiar trappings of its cage.

She might as well have had wings, the way she flew up that billowing cut of cloth; she seemed without weight or tangibility as she climbed to its apex, wrapping a length of it around her leg, her back arching in slow, fluid movement, a reflection of the fiddle's wistful call.

She reached for the sky with both hands—grasping empty air, futile and frustrated, aching for freedom and finding nothing.

And then she dropped.

If Finn hadn't seen aerial silks shows before, he might have shouted— and even though he *had* seen them before, his fiddle still struck the next note sideways as he watched her plunge, tumbling down the silk until the length around her leg caught her, leaving her perfectly level with the hoop.

As the fiddle picked up its tempo, Finn's fingers stinging as the strings stamped painful divots into out-of-practice callouses, Cassi leapt from the silk and caught the one dangling from the hoop; with a graceful heft of her arms, she pulled herself up and flipped over, tangling her legs around the silk in an artful twist of her entire body.

His heart pounded. His blood heated. Everything suddenly felt too bright, too real, too *present*—it hurt his head, a lurid pulse that had nothing to do with the fact that he'd never used his chronomantic power for this long before.

Cassi was a marvel up there—nobody could deny it. His fiddle and her form seemed tied by an invisible string; she and the song melded in perfect harmony, her body the definition of grace and command, not a quiver or hitch to be seen as she suspended from that spinning silk.

She didn't cling to it at all; she dangled freely with legs bent, arms spread in a gliding pose, expression filled with such vehement longing that it couldn't possibly be false.

Not entirely.

Not unless he truly couldn't pick up on her tells anymore.

The hoop began to descend as Cassi caught its edge with her hands, flipping herself over and smoothly sliding herself in to sit within it, still spinning. When it got low enough, she lowered herself down to cling to the bottom of the hoop, holding on until her toes hit the stage.

She folded to her knees. Longing twisted into anguish. She released the hoop, palms splayed flat on the stage, shoulders caving in.

The grief of a songbird stolen from its sky.

Why did his throat feel so tight?

Cassi looked up then—out at the crowd. Out at him.

Brown eyes shimmered with tears. Mouth quivered in despair.

The only time I have felt like myself in hundreds of years is the night I spent with you up on that rotting lighthouse!

Now he couldn't swallow. Now he couldn't breathe.

But his hands played on.

Whatever was happening on that stage…he couldn't look away. Couldn't even pretend he wanted to.

Brown eyes cleared. Lips curved into a determined smirk.

She winked at him, and with a sinuous twist of her legs, she rested all her weight on one hip, legs still crossed beneath her—but now, instead of mourning, she looked to be in waiting. Confident and commanding, she lifted a hand without looking, grasping the hoop and bringing it gently around, looping her arms around it. With a roll of her head, the hoop rose back into the sky.

And as he watched, frozen but for his hands, she bent her neck back, slipped her arms from the hoop, and she soared.

Held entirely by her neck bent against the hoop, arms and legs free, she spun in languid circles as the hoop climbed, and climbed, and climbed—until it vanished above the stage, the final crooning notes soaring after her in a scream of triumph.

A songbird set free at last.

Even the burst of applause from her friends, along with a chorus of whooping cheers, couldn't shake him out of his rigid stance. He couldn't lower the bow; he couldn't stop staring at the stage.

Cassandra Medeis hadn't wanted life eternal, magic beyond imagination, a life spent tormenting others.

She'd wanted *this*.

And gods damn it, she should have *had it*.

And he should have had this, too—the comfort of a fiddle tucked beneath his chin, the satisfaction of a spotlight, the power to hush a room with wonder instead of depths-damned *fear*.

The freedom to crawl into a quiet corner in the library and curl up with a book, knowing he had plenty of time to savor the hot chocolate cradled in his hand. The peace of mind to sleep soundly, enjoying vivid and pleasant dreams, nightmares rarely disrupting his rest. The naivete to sit down with pen and paper after finishing a book, believing he could write a better ending than the one penned on those pages.

It didn't matter how good of an imagination he had. It didn't matter that he didn't like this ending, *Cassi's* ending; it didn't matter how little he liked his own, either.

His mind could plead for the story to go differently all it liked. A few hopeful scribbles couldn't fix a future carved indelibly in stone.

Even so...

How different, how beautiful could they have been, if time had been kinder? If they'd been allowed to stay clever rather than cunning, creative rather than cruel?

All this he thought while watching the hoop descend once more, Cassi hopping down and running out to the wings to thank whoever had controlled the hoop for her. Her giggles echoed through the empty theater, shrill with the giddy buzz of stage adrenaline.

Even in this long-gone past, she wasn't entirely a stranger; that skilled performance, her cunning grin, her cutting insight, it all reflected the Occassio he knew now. And as strange as it was to look at her and see truth in her smile…as strange as it was to see her joyful, not jaded…he still *knew* her.

Fidget, Occassio, Cassi—some acts, some truths, but across them all, he could see the common threads. He could put together the pieces of her and see the whole underneath…or at least the sketch of it, the outline of who this adversary of his had been, still was, and would always be.

And every single one made a fool out of him. An amateur con who folded to a schoolboy crush.

He hated that he'd come here at all, necessity be damned. He hated that his game required him to be both her merciless enemy and her traitorous friend.

He hated that it killed him, knowing this time with her was borrowed— that the goddess trapped in his mirror would never give him the nose-crinkling, gap-toothed grin her past self offered as she dismounted the stage and hurried over to him.

And worst of all…

He hated that when he saw that smile, he craved champagne.

Once the little troupe exchanged notes and suggestions—as well as heaps of praise—he took the time to teach them a couple pickpocketing tricks. His mind wasn't in it, but that didn't matter—his body could perform on its own, demonstrating picks without a thought, smiling to those who smiled at him, and even whistling in amazement when Minxie managed to twist her arm around and pickpocket Abbott backwards.

But all the while, his mind danced with memories of champagne flutes and cookie crumbs. Tavern tables and shimmering slippers. Sequined eyebrows and a shining smile that put the stars to shame.

A crystalline dagger pressed to his throat. Splitting pain cracking down the center of his skull. A grin that taunted him for every foolish choice she'd baited him into with a flutter of lashes and a sweet little voice.

A birdcage. A goddess bent before a mortal man. A girl manacled and beaten and humiliated; a girl forced to perform in a prison, her pretty costume a poor defense against her captor's cruelty.

This stage. This girl. This tailoress turned thief turned troupe performer, able to brave the skies and pick a pocket as easily as she sewed a skirt.

Or stole a heart.

All impressive, but the latter most of all, because Finn himself hadn't known he had a heart to steal.

Worse, he'd done everything in his power to get rid of it since, and he'd been so damned sure he'd succeeded…until she wielded those blackmail eyes and lockpick grins, robbing him of something he didn't even want until it was no longer his.

The others left late into the night, still chattering excitedly; by the time they left, even Kit had warmed to Finn, giving him a slap on the shoulder and another word of thanks for the food. Without them, Finn and Cassi were left to finish packing up the borrowed costumes and equipment; and really, he didn't have to stay. Cassi seemed anxious about leaving any trace, not wanting to get her brother in trouble, but she insisted more than once he didn't have to help.

There was no reason for him to linger.

But he couldn't tear himself away.

"So," she asked as she bowed to scoop up her borrowed leotard and skirt, once again wearing her pastel ensemble, "what did you think?"

He crossed his arms, leaning against the patched-up wall of the costume closet while he watched her—she put on a casual air, but she wouldn't look at him. She kept her body bent away, fussing with her ballet shoes like she'd forgotten how to take them off, tying and untying the ankle ribbons over and over.

"You have to know you're magnificent," he said.

A startled laugh. "Go sit on a stake."

"You're kidding, right? I've seen my share of acrobats and aerialists—you're just as good as any of them. Better than some, even. You're easily good enough to get yourself onto a troupe's roster."

She giggled again—when he didn't join her, she looked up, embarrassed smirk melting into a look of surprise when she realized he wasn't laughing. "You're serious?"

"Cross my heart." He jerked his chin back toward the auditorium's door. "You're all good—especially *Minxie*, gods save her. Doesn't that *hurt?*"

"She insists it doesn't." Cassi finally kicked off her ballet slippers, wobbling a bit as she found her balance again. "Listen, you don't have to be kind. I'd rather hear you say I haven't got a prayer than perform in front of a whole troupe and get laughed out of their tent."

"Look at me." When she did, he held her gaze, filled with some foolish, earnest desire to make her believe him. "I don't have the time or the kindness to waste on lies. If I thought you were going to make a fool of yourself, I'd tell you so."

The only fool putting on a show here was him.

Her smile warmed from uncertain to relieved. "Thank you, Lord Ryder."

As she moved toward the door, he pushed off the wall, catching her arm. "Cassi."

She turned to peer over her shoulder at him, frowning. "Yes?"

"Why won't you call me by my name?" He had asked her to call him Alex; she hadn't, not even once, except to introduce him to her friends. Otherwise, she used *Lord Ryder*, and that only sparingly.

Cassi smiled, eyes twinkling, double dimples digging into her freckled cheek. "I'm still not convinced it *is* your real name."

With a pat on his hand and a wink, she slipped away into the shadows, leaving him alone in a closet full of costumes.

None of them half as well-crafted as the one he wore; yet still not enough to fool her.

This wasn't good.

This wasn't good *at all*.

And even worse…

That was not the last time he helped her practice.

When he should have been in Atlas, in his own time, working to save his people…

He kept coming back to play the fiddle for the girl who'd tricked and tortured him to the point of madness.

Against all sense, against all oaths he'd sworn to himself, he came back.

Again.

And again.

And again.

CHAPTER 24

RAQUEL

The Atlas people whispered about a false queen seated on the throne.

Despite her warnings to Vaughn and the Maren twins to help quash the gossip where they caught it, worried what Tenebrae would do in retribution, rumors couldn't truly be capped once they were spilled into the stream of public consciousness.

Even now that some hint of truth had spilled into the current of conversation, the stories varied. Some said Princess Jericho had gone mad in the wake of all her losses; others claimed she and Prince Finnick had conspired together to kill the rest of the Atlas family; and still others uttered the truth: that the gods walked the world again, and the cruelest among them had chosen to gift Atlas a reckoning it would never forget.

They cried to Anima for help. They prayed to Tempest for vengeance.

Atlas's patrons did not answer their prayers. Anima, because she was too far away…Tempest, because he seemed content to bide his time when it came to keeping promises made to their former First Prince.

Their gods did not come to their rescue.

But Raquel did.

Reverent tales of the Riptide had not ceased in the wake of the fires, despite there being no further sightings of that faceless figure. So with Vaughn's words ringing in her ears—*You're not carrying on his legacy…you're building your own*—she had begun taking to the streets at night, putting herself to work wherever she could.

Better than lying in her bed and reciting a dead man's last words. Better than kicking walls or sparring with people who didn't know when to stop or chafing the bracelet around her wrist until her fingertips began to blister.

Tonight, Vaughn had told her about a handful of families who had lost their homes or shops to the fires. Her task was easy enough: drop off packages of food and other necessities on the back doorstep of each inn offering those families shelter, let her cloaked visage be spotted by one or two people if she could, then retreat back into the shadows.

And, with any luck, get more than three consecutive hours of sleep for the first time in days.

After so many sleepless nights, even the solid street beneath her did not feel quite real. As if her next footfall might plunge straight through the cobblestones, sending her plummeting into one of her more common nightmares…a vision of herself falling through the sky, trying to slow her descent through the incorporeal clouds.

Instead, every strike of heel against solid stone brought her back to her body, reminding her of her purpose. Of her mission and its dire importance.

And how imperative it was that no one saw her before she wanted them to.

So she gathered her wits, ignoring how frayed they were at the edges, and kept going.

Even after completing her rounds and walking back toward the palace, she couldn't fully focus. It wasn't just the exhaustion that made it difficult; every second she spent on these streets made it harder to ignore thoughts of Kallias.

She hadn't anticipated how much Atlas itself would remind her of him. But the smell of the ocean brought back the hint of salt once buried in his clothes. The roar of the waves made it easy to understand why he'd struggled so badly to sleep in Artem's quiet caves, but snored through the night on Patch's tossing ship. And though it was a pale imitation of what it used to be, the tatters of the city's former glory remained, just enough to assure her it had once been a sight to behold, worthy of the heartsickness carried in Kallias's voice when he spoke of it.

In this sleepless state, she could almost feel the ghost of his cold hand trailing across the small of her back, shielding the bar of bruised flesh there. She could almost pretend—

A hand gripped her by the cloak, tugging her around by the back of her neck.

She had her sword drawn in half a second, her other hand batting her attacker's arm aside, gripping them by the collar. She tugged them close, ready to drive the sword in—

"Wait!" yelped the man she was nearly strangling—she barely managed to halt her blow, too full of superheated adrenaline, her chest heaving as she met the man's wide-eyed gaze. "Riptide."

Gods damn it.

She dropped him, but he didn't seem to notice—he just kept gaping. "I know you! Raquel Angelov. You work under the Prince…under the Heir, now, I suppose." A nervous laugh. "You're the Riptide?"

Damn it, damn it, damn it. He'd seen her face—he *knew her name.*

"You have to go." Keeping her tone clipped, quick, leaving no room for argument, she threw her hood back over her head. "I'll escort you to the outer limits, but you have to—"

"What? No, I can't—I have nowhere to go. Look, I won't say anything." He stepped closer, ignoring the warning arm she extended, eyes gleaming with glee. "The Riptide is in the palace. You're *close* to them. You can actually—"

"Listen," she snarled, and the man finally stopped rambling, gazing at her as if confused by her hostility. "You have to go. It is not a choice. If the Queen—"

"I won't say anything, I swear on my life!"

"Everyone thinks they won't give in to interrogation," Raquel retorted; streaks of phantom pain ran down the whip scars on her back, a reminder of exactly where she'd learned this lesson. "You have to—"

Another hand circled around the man's throat now, pulling him back— over his head, Finn stared impassively at her.

"Did he see your face?" he asked.

The man's eyes widened in horror, clearly recognizing the voice. "I—"

"I asked *her,*" Finn said.

Every instinct stood on its tiptoes and screamed, telling her to say no. Instead, she nodded.

Without blinking, Finn set his hands over the man's eyes.

Light blazed under his fingers, so pure and painful it might have blinded her had it not lasted a second at most.

When he pulled them away, the man fell boneless, dull-eyed, face still contorted in fear as he slumped sideways. The fount of blood sliding from his eyes, his nose, even his ears pooled in the cracks between cobblestones, filling them in with crimson caulk.

Ringing filled her ears, drowning out everything else. "What did you just—"

"Took his memories," he said. "Just the last hour."

"You don't know how to do that."

"Vash is a very knowledgable teacher."

Perhaps. But all that blood… "You're sure you only took an hour?"

"Yes," Finn seethed.

Oh, the stubborn set of his jaw told her better than that.

"You have no gods-damned idea what you just did to him, do you?" she snapped. "That was *unnecessary*—"

"I disagree." Finn gestured as if batting her protest away, and the blood vanished from his hands, not a speck of red marring his skin. He straightened his coat, gazing balefully at the unconscious man. Hopefully unconscious. "Loose ends will get us caught—and killed, if you've forgotten."

The lack of feeling in his voice infuriated her. "So, what—we're breaking innocent minds now? Bleeding people in the streets? Are you sure you're the one in control here, or did Occassio—"

"*Watch* it."

"I am watching. And I don't like what I'm seeing. Why am I the only one who seems to care about protecting *your* gods-damned people?"

All at once, that unfeeling look shuddered, cracking at the edges—with a sneering glower and bared teeth, it shattered entirely. Finn stepped forward, over the bleeding man, gesturing to him as he did. "*That* was not for nothing. *That* was because you let someone get a look at your gods-damned face. Do not blame me for doing what you made necessary!"

"I didn't—"

"Do you think I'm *enjoying* this? Do you think I like shedding my own people's blood? Do you think I just cut apart a man's mind for *laughs*?"

She could only stare mutely. He chuckled humorlessly, shaking his head…and before her eyes, his grinning anger banked into bitter anguish.

"I am carrying a magic that no mortal is meant to wield," he said. "I spend every day staring into the face of my sister's *corpse*. And I can't grieve her—not her, not my brother, not my *city*, because grief will turn me useless, and Atlas cannot afford for me to be useless right now, Raquel. Nor can it afford either of us to give mercy when we can't spare it!"

"I wasn't—"

"My brother and sister are dead," he snarled. "My parents will be too, if I let myself go soft. I will slit a million gods-damned throats to keep them safe—I will silence any voice that threatens to share the secrets that are keeping us, *all of us*, alive. I am not going to let anything hurt them, or me, or *you*, because you're the only thing keeping me a little bit sane anymore. And if that means killing or stealing or lying, if that means holding a goddess hostage and tricking a tailoress into giving me her secrets, then I will do it. I will do it *my way*, because Atlas needs a defender, and thanks to Kal, I'm the only one it's got!"

Speechless, gutted, wishing desperately she could argue, she just watched…and in the end, she could only find one thing to say.

"A tailoress?" she asked quietly.

A hoarse, hollow laugh shook his shoulders, and he pushed his glasses further up his nose. "She wanted to be an *acrobat*, for gods' sakes. Wanted to run away and join the circus." A beat of silence. "Gods, Raquel, I miss him *so bad*."

The crack in his voice cleaved into her own chest, driving deep into the wound already dealt to her heart.

"We need to hide him," she said—when he blinked at her blankly, she pointed to the bloodied man between them.

"We don't."

"He could die out here, and—"

"And he won't be the first body that's been found out here lately—not the last, either. Depths, the way Tenebrae's been stirring up chaos, he might not be the only one tonight." Still looking shaken, Finn shook his head and walked away; with a reluctant glance downward, she followed. There was no use trying to hide him herself—she'd only succeed in soaking herself to the skin in red, and hope would quickly twist into horror if the people saw their *Riptide* dripping innocent blood.

Or Finnick Atlas walking ahead of her, no disguise to be seen, blinking too hard and breathing off-kilter.

These visits to the past…they might have been helping his act, but they were hurting him in other ways. And she had no idea how to help.

But she had to try.

She quickened her pace to walk beside him, reaching out and touching his shoulder. At first, his muscles bunched, tensing to pull away—then he blew out a long breath, and the tension eased.

"Kallias might not be dead," she said quietly. "We don't know."

"He has to be." Finn's eyes fell to his feet. "Because if he isn't, I won't be able to stay here and do what needs to be done—I'll go and get him. And I can't waste time on that until Mama and Papa are safe."

She had to swallow past the lump in her throat. "When do we move?"

He cleared his throat. Took a breath so deep that his shoulder rose nearly level with his ear. "Soon. Vash is making friends in the barracks, he says, and Vidia's just completed her little project."

That "little project" was a blend of poisons Vidia claimed could be doled out to the soldiers slowly through food or drink, a toxin that would gradually build in their systems until it came to its head all at once. The *boiling frog method*, she'd called it.

Once they dropped, Vaughn would use his particular *skills* to keep the rotations moving, puppeting the dead around the dungeon to keep things from appearing amiss. Provided Tenebrae didn't look too closely or try to visit himself, it should be enough of an opening to get Adriata and Ramses out.

"What are we waiting on, then?" she asked.

"I don't know," he admitted. She hated when he claimed omniscience; she hated when he confessed otherwise even more, because if Finnick Atlas didn't know…in all likelihood, nobody did. "I just…know it isn't time yet. Something isn't ready."

Privately, she worried that *something* was him.

"Finn," she murmured. "Don't forget what she did to you. Don't forget what she tried…what she'll try again, if you let her."

He smiled darkly, but it didn't feel quite true. Like he'd snatched up one piece of that broken mask and tried to glue it back on with water instead of paste. "Trust me…I'll never forget."

CHAPTER 25

FINN

Even in autumn, the Sanctaviv sun was nothing less than *brutal*.

Not two minutes into this visit—ill-advised, ill-timed, possibly about to make him actually ill—and every pit on his person had pooled with sweat. When he finally dove into the sweet, sweet shelter of the theater's back room, he only possessed enough patience to undo two of the twenty-something buttons before ripping through the rest and casting the wadded-up cloth away.

If paper served for money in this odd little empire, whoever had built this theater, they must've had enough paper on hand to put the Atlas royal library to shame. Even the back room's walls were solid marble; he leaned his elbows up against one and bent his weight into it, weaving his fingers into his sweaty hair and staring at the veins of charcoal webbed through sea-salt white.

He hated being hot. Hated sweating even worse. He'd have to lean back out to catch some light in a moment, something to sew up a new shirt, but first—

"Oh, Sancta's moldy *toes*, you weren't kidding when you said you didn't get much sun!"

He refused to startle this time; when Cassi popped out of one of the costume racks, shielding her eyes with a put-upon squint as she stared at him, he shooed her off with a bat of his hand. "Avert your eyes! I'm not decent!"

"The dressing rooms are down the hall. If it's your decency you're worried about, I'd start with shucking off your shirt behind closed doors." She spluttered as he turned in her direction, throwing her other hand up over her eyes, dropping the pile of cloth tucked under her arm. "Don't come closer, you're going to blind me!"

"Ha, ha." He must've gotten sunburned on the walk in—no other explanation for the boiling blood gathering in his cheeks. "I can't help it, all right? It's a redhead problem."

Cassi dropped her hands a couple inches, squinting over her fingers at him now. "You're not a redhead."

Damn it. This girl kept twirling his head around on his shoulders like a gods-damned top. "I was born one—went away when I got older. But the whole *deathly pale* thing doesn't really age out, so get off my back."

"All right, all right, keep your shirt on." She winked, throwing her thumb toward the costume racks. "I'm sure there's something in here that'll suit Your Lordship. I'll meet you out there."

"I'll be the one in…" he looked around at the mess of clothing racks, "…something."

"You'd better be." She recovered her chosen costume, stuffed it in her belt, did an unnecessary cartwheel to the door, and slapped a crooked sign hanging beside it. *NO SHIRT, NO SHOES, NO SERVICE*, it read. "I'd hate to have to call security."

These people would've been scandalized by Atlas shops. Plenty of people came into town straight from the water, wearing nothing but their swimclothes. "Why's that hanging back here and not the front entrance?"

"I don't know *everything*, Lordship." Then she danced out the door.

"Can I get that in writing?" he muttered under his breath.

He didn't have to bother rifling through the racks; he could have conjured something himself. But for the sake of the game, it seemed advisable not to test his imagination on inventing a garment that suited both the time and the place he currently occupied.

By the time he got into the theater proper, Cassi had already taken to the silks, idly practicing the same foot hangs that had nearly scared him out of his skin the first time he'd seen her perform. Even expecting them then—and having witnessed them plenty by now—his stomach still did a passable imitation of her drop every time she tumbled through the silks.

And when she alighted on the stage once more, it took another fall.

She wore her favorite leotard today, a longer one; the sleek fabric hugged halfway down her thighs. The matching chiffon skirt lay in a saffron-yellow pile on the stage, cast aside while she soared up the silks; too much extra fabric was risky for a full aerial routine, she'd explained to him, so she only wore one when the majority of her routine involved the aerial hoop. Two clips held her hair back, shaped and painted like sunflowers.

But that wasn't what had made him so seasick at the sight of her.

"That's dramatic," he teased, forcing himself to hold her gaze. Then forcing himself to look between them, at least, when that failed.

"Huh? Oh!" She laughed, tapping the corners of her eyes…her off-putting golden eyes. "Sorry. Painted contacts. I had them on for a…different activity."

"Not the tailoring, I assume."

"Unless you count all the fortunes I stitched together on the fly." She wiggled her fingers with a spooky coo, then sighed, reaching up to pluck the contacts out of her eyes. Finn turned aside, shuddering, and she scoffed. "Oh, come on. You're that squeamish?"

"Eye stuff creeps me out."

"It doesn't even hurt." A pause; another burdensome sigh. "It's safe to look now, Lordship."

He turned around without thinking—then spun right back around at the sight of her eyes rolled up into her head, her fingertips stretching her eyelids out.

"*Gods* damn you," he cursed as she cackled, rubbing his own eyes until they felt less itchy.

"You're too easy."

"No, no, that's objectively horrifying. I'm not taking any flack for that."

"Sure. All right, it's actually safe to look now."

He didn't turn around.

"I swear! Here, look." Her sweaty hand closed around his, tugging him back around.

He covered his eyes with his free hand, fighting a smile as she tried to pull it down, cursing. She had to hop to get high enough. "Swear on your pointe shoes?"

"Swear on my pointe shoes."

She'd never sully the name of her precious pointe shoes. He finally let his hands fall, laughing when he came face-to-face with a scowling songbird. "Hey, you started it!"

"Picking on the shortie? That's just plain mean."

"I'm going to have nightmares about that face you made for days. I'd call us even." He studied the stage for the first time, frowning. "Where's everybody else?"

"Kit and Molly had work. Minxie's down with a bug—you can imagine why stomach flus and contortionists don't mix—"

"Gross."

"—And Abbott's supposed to be here, so I couldn't say why he's late."

"Want me to play you through in the meantime? I'm passable at pianoforte."

"No. Well, yes, but I actually want strings for this."

He cracked his knuckles, warming up his fingers. "Silks? Hoops?"

"Actually…" Oh, he hated that twinkle in her eye. "I haven't taken the tightrope for a spin in a while."

As previously established on multiple occasions, Finnick Atlas loved heights.

However, he preferred his heights solid, supported by several stories of brick or stone or wood. When he tempted fate, he liked to have the assurance of shingles or thatch or steel slopes under his feet.

But the parallel lengths of sturdy rope tethered to stages left and right, thirty feet above the stage proper? Those draped an uncomfortable set of nerves around his throat, jangling around like fine necklaces.

Not the longest fall he'd seen her take. But there were no silks to tangle her feet in this time; no finespun net like the ones he'd seen when Lapisian traveling circuses came to town.

Not that she'd fallen yet. Actually, she hadn't even climbed up to the rope. But the part of his mind skilled at inventing worst-case scenarios had already slapped the imprint of that future across the backs of his eyes.

Her balance failing. Her fingers slipping from the rope. Her body breaking against the—

"Staring is rude," the present said primly, interrupting the future—he blinked, the Cassi outside his imagination pursing her lips at him as she wrapped the ties of her leather-soled slippers up her calves. "Didn't they teach you that in lord school?"

"Must've missed that day," he said, eyeing her shoes. Well, not *hers*, judging by the poor fit. The sides gaped around her narrow feet. The laces were so worn they kept slumping out of their bowknot no matter how many times she tied them.

Not ideal for walking on solid ground, let alone an inch-wide rope a house's height above the ground.

"Might be better to go it barefoot," he suggested.

"Oh, do you think so?" Cassi pinched the loops and tugged to finish the bowknot once more, glowering at it and mouthing a stern command to *stay*. "I didn't know you were a tightrope expert."

"Doesn't take an expert to see your slippers don't fit. And any fool could figure out ill-fitting shoes and balance don't mix well."

"Well, can any fool figure out why I might choose to wear them anyway?"

Reckless overconfidence, perhaps? A bad case of incurable show-off disease? "Enlighten me."

"You're right; it's dangerous to take on a tightrope with bad shoes." She stood, brushing sawdust from her skirt. The repair crew hadn't done the best job cleaning up after themselves today. "But if I practice in bad shoes, and figure out how to balance in them…what happens when I wear the right ones?"

The missing puzzle piece fell into place. "You won't struggle to balance. It'll feel effortless."

"And look it, too."

Finn crossed his arms, looking up at the ropes. "If you survive practice."

Cassi stood and stomped over to him, grabbing his wrists and uncrossing his arms. "No more pessimism, please. It's irritating."

"So's taking unnecessary risk—oh, *gods*, I sound like my brother." He turned aside, pressing his fist to his mouth, swallowing an involuntary gag. "Never mind. Do what you want."

Her laughter sounded like singing, which always made him wonder what her actual song might sound like. "You all right?"

"No. Blegh. If I ever do that again, stick a sewing needle in my eye."

"Which one?"

"Which needle?"

A menacing wink. "Which *eye*."

After he recovered from his brief fit of horror over hearing his brother's lectures come from his mouth—better than grief, better than rage, better than the little boy that still cried for his big brother when things felt too frightening—he helped her get everything in order, forcing the whole of his mind to the task. Anything less, and his stomach started to ache.

From hunger, probably. Not grief, not rage. Not because her laces had slumped around her ankles again, as good as a tripwire strung sideways across the tightrope.

Regardless, the nausea wasn't helpful when dealing with heights, so it had to go. He forced himself to breathe through it as they both climbed up to the platform affixed to one of the stage columns. She strode straight out onto the tightrope without even bracing or balancing herself, like one might step from one cobblestone to another on a city street.

She had this. It'd be fine.

He made himself sit down. Made himself set his fiddle under his chin. Made himself stop looking at her rebellious laces.

Obviously she wouldn't fall; his time would look a whole lot different if she had. Besides, what did it matter to him if she did? It could only help his cause in his own time.

One of her feet slipped out of its shoe, throwing her off; it tumbled, and in his imagination, so did she. He was half a second from flinging himself out on the rope when she snagged the falling shoe with her toe, cackling, balanced precariously on her other foot. "That was close!"

Finn collapsed back onto his seat, slapping a hand over his chest. "Could you *not*? I just *felt* some hairs go gray."

"But you'll look so handsome as a silver fox."

Sanctaviv sun. He had it to thank for the furious spots of warmth in his cheeks—heat rising and all that.

"Why two ropes?" he asked after she took a few trips back and forth without incident—only across one rope. She never touched the other.

"Oh, that was a little experiment we were testing," called Abbott—Finn looked down to find the tardy musician had claimed his place at the pianoforte, face red with the blood-rush of running, hair red with fresh dye. "We wanted to see if we could get two walkers up there at once, but the routine got too risky. Cass fell twice."

"Once and a half," she corrected, glaring at Abbott when Finn's head snapped her way. "Don't look at me like that, Lordship, it was just a fluke."

"Two flukes?"

"One and a half!"

"One's enough to get you killed!"

"Why are you yelling at me?"

Why *was* he yelling at her? "Didn't mean to." He mimed cleaning out his ear with a fingertip. "My ears get all plugged up this high."

Her cross-armed, squint-eyed scowl suggested she wasn't buying that story in any currency, paper or gold or otherwise.

"All right, Lordship." She walked backwards—*backwards*—to her platform, a predator stalking in the wrong direction. It didn't matter; the challenge in her gaze had already caged him in its claws. "If you're such an expert, why don't you show us how it's done?"

Finn snorted. "No."

"Yes. Put your money where your mouth is."

"I'll pay you a solid gold not to make me walk on that thing."

"Deal," Abbott said, at the same time Cassi said, "*I'd* pay a solid gold to see you try."

"You don't have that kind of coin."

"Don't need it. Your pride will pay it for me."

Oh, he hated how right she was. How right she *always* was.

He set his wretched instrument aside with a dirty curse. "You know what kind of mess you'll have on your hands if I fall to my death?"

"Oh, would you look at the time?" Abbott tried weakly. "I actually have a prior engagement—"

"Sit down, Abbott," he and Cassi said together. The boy sat, scowl strung out with nerves as he tossed his patchy leather duster behind him like a satin tailcoat, fingers dancing across the keys without pressing down.

"Don't tell me you're scared of heights," the girl needled him, like he was some garment she couldn't finagle a stitch through.

He eyed those stretched-out shoes of hers, chewing on words that wouldn't change her mind about wearing them. "I'd call it a *healthy respect.*"

"Didn't you chase me across a bunch of rooftops? I could've sworn you're the same fool who stole my hiding spot."

"I have one of those faces."

"Step up or shut up, Lordship." She spread her arms slow and wide, never wobbling, raising an eyebrow to the precise height one needed to portray judgement. "Make your choice."

No need. The choice was made—there'd been no choice to make.

Never was, when this woman taunted him to her table and offered to deal him in.

So he shucked off his shoes and socks, setting them beside his borrowed fiddle.

As previously established—and referenced again for good measure—Finnick Atlas loved heights.

But he hated being backed into corners.

A carnation cast fell over his vision, a petal-pink play of a memory: a moonlit alley, bloody fireworks sprayed across a dress wrought from opal and amethyst, Fidget's wide-eyed terror as a man twice her size crushed her against a brick wall—

He blinked that memory away, plucking it out and flicking it aside like a sliver.

Not real. A performance orchestrated by Occassio, a part he'd played to perfection despite never auditioning.

This time, the show was his to put on. And he knew exactly how he wanted to play it.

With an exaggerated seethe of breath dragged through his teeth, he set one foot on the rope; hemp fibers needled his bare sole, prickles and frays trying to trick him into making a misstep.

He jerked his foot back to solid ground. Well, solid something, anyway. "Two gold?"

His plea earned him a giggle; she rolled her eyes, then rolled her shoulders before taking another stroll down the tightrope, hands behind her back now. She stopped short of her own platform, leaning down and to the side—unadvisable—to catch his gaze, smiling up at him. "Do you need me to hold your hand?"

"*Maybe!*"

Another froth of giggles, mirth bubbling over into mercy. She offered him her hand. "Come on, then."

He didn't let himself hesitate before he dropped his hand into hers. "Don't let go."

A curious glint flipped through her eyes like a throwing knife.

And when she softly said, "I won't," that knife thudded into the shadowy space between his lungs and his ribs, nicking his most problematic organ on the way in.

No time to patch it up—no time to triage. He'd have to make peace with bleeding until he had time to sit and see why that powerless promise had actually dealt some damage.

Because before he could plug up the hole, she guided him out onto the tightrope beside hers.

No shoes. No net. No looking back.

"Breathe," she coaxed him. "If you hold your breath this whole walk, I *promise* you'll fall."

He sucked in another noisy breath. "I want my rooftop back."

"Tough breaks, Lordship." She lifted his shaking hand to her mouth, brushing her lips over his knuckles with a scrunch of her nose and a bunch of her brows, grin twinkling with mischief and mockery. "Nowhere to jump out here."

Then why, with the warmth of her lips still branded against his knuckles, did he feel like he'd taken one depths-damned dangerous leap?

"What exactly was this routine?" He didn't let go of her hand; step by step, he tightened his grip, catching his breath with each wobble and sway. Every time he stopped in his tracks, Cassi ran her thumb over his knuckles like a lockpick teasing its way through tumblers until he moved again.

It was distracting. He should ask her to stop.

"Tightrope tango," she sighed.

"Pardon?"

"Ridiculous, right? Kit insisted, *alliteration is catchy* and *it's not corny, it's clever* and all that." She dragged her free hand down her face, then grumbled, "We wanted to get two walkers up on the ropes and see if there was a way for them to dance without falling off."

"Dance?"

"A series of stylized movements set to music, often choreographed—"

"I know what it *means*." And she knew it, too, look at that smug little grin. "You're awful, teasing a man while he's testing death."

"Oh, please." She rolled her eyes. "Anyway, we gave it up after a few goes. Not as easy as it sounds."

No, it wouldn't be—in fact, it would be nigh impossible. They'd have to be utterly in sync, both acting as counterweights, tasked with keeping each other's balance as well as their own.

Nigh impossible. Odds entirely stacked out of favor.

By the time they finished their painfully slow trip across the ropes, inch by breathtakingly awful inch, he still couldn't pry the idea from where it'd gotten stuck in his skull.

"There, see!" Cassi twirled up onto her platform, applauding as he practically dove onto his own. "Not so bad, is it?"

He swiped the back of his hand over his forehead, mopping up the sweat. "You're a hazard to my health."

"I'll take that as a compliment."

"I really wish you wouldn't!"

Layers of chiffon unfurled in a goldenrod flurry as she spun back out onto her rope, swaying side to side, purposely throwing herself off-kilter to force herself to regain her balance. The sight made his hands go clammier than a fresh pearl.

"So." He had to cough up the word, wiping another slick of sweat from his forehead. "A tango?"

"Oh, Kit just called it that. No way we could stick to proper ballroom form on a tightrope, so...closest we could manage would be a waltz, probably, but anyone who gives a spark about the specifics wouldn't say it counts."

Finn eyed the two tightropes—the breadth of the gap between them, the hemp's thickness, how much or how little they bobbed as Cassi took a whistling stroll back down the way.

"You'd need some kind of master for that," he mused as she stepped up on the opposite platform, adjusting one of the clips in her hair when it tried to slip out of her curls.

"I don't know that I'd call myself a master, but I'm pretty damned—"

"In fact," he interrupted, sticking his hands in his pockets, "you might just need an expert."

When he walked out onto the tightrope, hands stuffed in his pockets, arms at his sides rather than spread to keep his balance, her eyes doubled in size. "What are you—"

He took one hand out to stifle a yawn, stopping in the center of his rope, glancing idly down at the ground. "You could stand to go up another ten feet, honestly. Ups the crowd's anticipation without upping the danger. Forty feet or fifty, you're toast either way."

Her jaw had fallen far enough to hit the ground from the platform. She didn't speak, just blinked…and blinked, and blinked, like she might be hallucinating.

He tried not to enjoy himself *too* much as he bobbled back and forth, mimicking her balance exercises—then stepping lightly off the rope.

Her cry split through the theater like a bird call—then sharpened into shrill curses as he caught himself on the rope, swinging himself into a handstand, then swinging his legs back underneath him.

"Good tension," he said offhandedly, brushing off his sleeve. "You strung 'em up well."

Cassi sank to her platform, clutching her heart. "You're a *bastard*."

Now he laughed. "You should see your *face*!"

She gestured wildly down to the pit. "You might've killed Abbott!"

He looked down to see the pianist flat on his back on the bench, arm thrown over his eyes, pale as a sunbleached shell. "He's fine."

"Oh, and you're so sure because…?"

"I'm fine," the boy called weakly. "Just resting."

Finn flashed a thumbs-up toward the ground, smirking back at Cassi. "See? He's just resting."

Gods, that sour look on her face was nearly as adorable as her sweeter smiles. "Are you ever going to stop making a fool of me?"

His smile dried out. He cleared his throat, hiding his hands back in his pockets as he made his way to her. "Didn't mean to scare you."

Her scathing glare scrubbed him clean of all guises, and he quickly amended, "Well, not *really*."

"Happy with yourself?" she asked tautly, sticking her chin in the air as if to avoid looking at him. Might've worked better if her head came higher than his shoulder.

"It *was* very funny," he said.

"I'm going to trip you off. See how funny that is."

"But then you wouldn't have a dance partner, would you?"

She paused halfway mounted, only one shoe resting on the rope. "What?"

He jerked his chin back the way he'd come. A silent invitation.

Her eyes narrowed, but the same way his sweet tooth couldn't resist tasting sugar wherever he found it, this girl had a craving for sated curiosity.

So, like he'd known she would, she stepped out on that rope…but she did surprise him by turning around, stepping onto it backward.

A game of one-upmanship. He liked it.

He stepped forward. She stepped back. He folded his hands behind his back. She clasped hers against her front. Pace by measured pace, he chased her all the way to the end of her rope.

There was a joke in there somewhere. Maybe a metaphor. He'd find it later.

For now, he turned to face her at the far side of their tightropes, tipping his hand to her.

"May I have this dance, thief?" he murmured.

She held his stare. Set her hand in his. Smiled bright enough to light up the whole stage without a spotlight. "You may, fool."

Without looking down, he called, "Abbott, play something."

"Play what?"

"Anything," he and Cassi chorused, holding each other's stares like a challenge.

Like they both knew it didn't matter what song Abbott chose for them. The tempo, the pace, none of it. They'd find their way regardless.

Or they wouldn't.

He ordinarily didn't fuss around with fifty-fifty odds. Even splits left room for luck to play a decisive role in the outcome, and he didn't like to rely on good fortune.

But somehow, holding her hand, he felt just lucky enough to roll the dice.

Cassi's throat bobbed, and she licked her lips. It distracted him for some reason. "Is now a bad time to confess I don't actually know how to—"

"Here."

Being in the sky, it always gave him a heady rush, that dizzying glee that woke him up from marrow to muscle—made him feel all kinds of alive. All kinds of reckless. All kinds of invincible.

The only flimsy reasoning he could come up with for why he took his time…why, when he guided her arm around his neck, he didn't simply set it down and let her go. Instead, he slid his palm across her arm, tracing the taut muscles under her sleek skin. He kept a gentle pressure on it, straightening her out from wrist to elbow to shoulder, brushing a fleck of sawdust off her collarbone before setting his hand in the proper position against the back of her shoulder.

"There," he said, certain he'd swallowed some sawdust himself. His voice had gone all raspy and strange, his throat dry as a brand-new tavern table. "Perfect."

It wasn't. Her arm should have been braced against the back of his, her other hand clasped firmly in his. He'd brought her too close.

For better balance, obviously. They couldn't have their elbows out all willy-nilly on a tightrope.

She blinked owlishly, like a daydream had conked her over the head and stolen her lunch money. "Oh."

Oh. Not her usual articulate retort. But before he could tease her for it, their cue came at last.

When the first sinuous swirl of notes swam out of the pianoforte—much less tinny now that he'd helped tune them properly—they both waited for the span of a single held breath. Just long enough to take note of each other's leading foot, where they held their weight, how their balance might shift when they took that first spin—

Then they stopped thinking, because up here, with this kind of impossibility on the line…

Thinking too much would trip them up. Planning ahead was impossible.

They could only trust the other would not miss a step. Would not break formation.

Would not let go, no matter how terrifying the fall might look.

Together they waltzed—or some bastardized version of the ballroom variety—down the ropes, a spinning top of unfailing grace—hers—and fortuitous foresight—his.

Not the magical sort. That felt like cheating, and this…he wanted to win this fair and square.

He didn't peek to see where her foot would land next, if her head would toss or her sole would slip. He didn't prod the future for clues as to where he needed to shift his weight to steady her for the next twirl.

He just knew. He just…did.

Like well-oiled clockwork gears, they spun without a hitch down those mirrored ropes, hand-in-hand, heads bent close, her fingers tightening around the nape of his neck every time they swung into another rotation.

When he dared steal a look at her face, the sight stole his breath in retribution.

He'd never seen her smile like this.

Nose and eye-corners crinkled, teeth bared, double dimples on full display…he'd seen all that before. Seen it plenty. The girl loved to laugh, at his jokes and at his expense.

It was the look in her eyes that made it all new. The thing that beamed brighter than any spotlight that'd ever blinded him. The thing that promised the sparkle in the stars would never impress him again.

Joy.

Unabashed, carefree, reckless joy.

And when she started laughing with the sheer thrill of it all, laughing as they dared gravity to pull them from their perch, his chest went hollow and weightless at the sound of it.

It didn't stay empty. It only made room for that contagious laughter, that infectious joy. It filled his lungs like fluid, pumped into his heart like poison.

Joy. Deadly in high doses, he'd heard. But oh, the way it sang you to sleep…

People paid good coin to feel this however they could: drink, illicit herbs, gambling. Some found it in thievery or grifting. Some found it in hobbies, in reading or writing, in painting, in song. Some found it, so they claimed, in other people.

Finn had only ever felt it while falling. And he refused to wonder if that was exactly why he felt it here.

All this, he'd think of later, cranking the memories around and around through his sleepless mind like a zoetrope, trying to pinpoint the moment it all went wrong.

But as he'd said…when a thief and a fool decided to test their luck on an impossible dance, there wasn't time to think.

Instead, his laughter harmonized with hers, the sound floating up to the rafters in its own whimsical waltz. And when he at last twirled her onto her platform with a flourish, bowing deeply at the waist before stepping up on his own, joy stuck in him like a dagger through the ribs.

"Let's go again," panted the thief.

And like a fool, he did not hesitate before sweeping her off her feet once more.

In the end, they took three turns across the ropes before Abbott begged off, claiming aching fingers and a rumbling stomach. And a fourth with no music, just to really prove they could do it, even without the satisfaction of watching eyes.

Or, at least, none they were aware of until after they'd taken their last bow, both dropping to their seats on their platforms and passing a canteen back and forth, trading between guzzling water and bathing the sweat from their faces with it.

That was when joy took its leave with great haste.

"That's your best trick yet!" laughed someone below; when Finn looked down, drops of water raining from his hair, he found a smudge vaguely shaped like a Medeis brother grinning up from the ground.

He couldn't tell which this far away, not without his glasses, but Cassi laughed, "Braeden! You're not supposed to be here!"

"Neither are you, remember?"

Finn's mood crashed to the ground like a poorly folded paper bird, crumpled beyond repair.

No way around it. He'd have to walk around the bastard to get to the exit, and that meant his best manners needed to make themselves available. Immediately.

"Lord Ryder," Braeden said, sounding surprised when Finn hopped down from the third-to-last ladder rung, holding his hand out to help Cassi. The eldest Medeis's clothes were in passably good repair, but the patches here and there— and the dust dyeing it all a sunbaked shade of brown—suggested Cassi wasn't the only one going without smaller necessities or going out of her way to earn extra coin. "I didn't expect to—"

"He's fine, Brae," Cassi assured him. "No need to tiptoe. He's not going to call the clerics."

Finn was definitely not fine. He smiled anyway, rubbing the back of his neck. "I have no stake here. Just lending my skills to the show."

"Ah." Tension bled from Braeden like a cut artery. "Well, in that case, I should say thank you. Not many nobles would turn a blind eye to my sister's, er…"

"Trespassing," Cassi supplied cheerily.

"Activities," Braeden corrected with a forced chuckle.

When Braeden approached, the most absurd urge to get between the two of them seized Finn's legs like a cramp. He rose on his tiptoes, trying to stretch it out. "Don't know what you're talking about. I've never seen her before in my life."

"Right." Braeden's smile was stiff; Cassi seemed to be biting her lip on a grin. The oldest Medeis frowned down at her, reaching for her head. "Your hair's a disaster, let me—"

"Leave it," Cassi whined, shooing his hand off. "A little chaos is good for you, you know." She rolled her eyes Finn's way, gesturing her brother's way with a thumb jabbed over her shoulder. "Complete control freak, this one."

Braeden coughed out some forced laughter, then squeezed Cassi's shoulder. "We have to get home. Family meeting."

All that flagrant joy extinguished in one fell swoop. Cassi nodded, then smiled at him—the resigned droop of it made all the worse by the wonder he'd witnessed only seconds earlier. "I'll see you soon?"

"Soon," he agreed, watching as she picked up her hand-me-down boots and ill-fitting outfit and trudged to the back of the theater, Braeden herding her with a firm hand on her shoulder.

He wasn't sure if he'd just told her a lie. Worse…

He didn't *want* it to be a lie.

CHAPTER 26

FINN

The missive that arrived the next morning, tucked into his doorjamb by Vash's hand, bore only a single sentence:

I woke to birdsong this morning. The sun shines beautifully through the leaves of their tree.

He nearly sighed in relief—he had to press his lips together until he firmly shut the door, conscious of the palacefolk making their rounds. He pressed his back to the door, reading the note twice more before crumpling it, letting his spine sink into the wooden support behind him.

Vash's contacts had finally confirmed it: Soren had made it to Arborius alive.

Now it was only a matter of whether she and Anima were able to separate—and whether she made it back to Atlas before he could handle their plight himself.

Gods knew his aunt and uncle were stubborn about their neutrality, and if this was a war of mortal men, he knew they would never bend. But this conflict wouldn't be kingdom against kingdom—this would be a battle of humanity against deity. This would be a game of survival, not a disguise thrown over the greed and ambition of queens or kings.

If he'd been betting on it, he would've bet on them agreeing to help. But it might take time—time his parents didn't have.

So if he could get his parents out and steal his mother's signet back on his own, he'd do it. But if Soren decided to wage a war of her own before he pulled off his plan, well…he'd be all right with losing a race to her just this once.

No harm in having more than one plan. Twice the plans, twice the chance of success.

He hoped, anyway.

Despite the letter only bearing two lines—a line of code, at that—there was very little he dared to risk while Tenebrae sat on the throne. So he strode to the fireplace across the room, giving the letter one last good squeeze before throwing it in, watching as the first bit of hope he'd been given crumbled into ash and smoke.

"Burning a missive. I thought you'd be more creative."

He'd almost forgotten Occassio could speak.

Turning on his toes, not rising from his crouch, he raised an eyebrow at her. "Better effective than creative when it comes to covering your tracks."

A girl cut into facets glowered sullenly back at him, one shoulder pressed up to the glass, her arms forming loose chains around her bent knees. Her illusions had grown more fantastical in recent days; today, she could have been a crystal figurine trapped in a music box, her skin glittering diamond, her eyes depthless onyx, strings of amethyst forming a sheath dress over her bejeweled body.

Sometimes he wondered if he'd come across the wrong Cassandra Medeis in the past, after all. He couldn't entirely reconcile her giggly glee as they waltzed across tightropes and ran across rooftops with the sneering creature he saw before him now.

"Wondered where you went off to," he added. Since his first visit to the theater, she had mostly stayed out of sight, even when he ripped down the curtain covering the mirror. And even when she did appear, she wore illusions that boggled the brain more than usual, covering herself in the guise of storybook monsters or wallpaper patterns or twisting her form in grotesque shapes that forced him to look away.

Like she feared what he'd see if she didn't make herself monstrous.

"Didn't have much to say." Her low voice bounced off the glass, giving it a hollow quality.

He strolled to the mirror and spread his arms out, an open invitation. "No threats? Taunts? Jokes about my heinous fashion sense?"

She didn't answer. And somehow, the bravado mattered less when his audience didn't take the bait.

He dropped his hands, wishing he didn't feel so much like frowning. "Gull got your tongue?"

Still nothing. She bent her head away, the firelight dancing playfully between the planes of her diamond flesh.

"This game's not nearly as fun when you won't play it with me," he prodded.

A quiet scoff. "This isn't a gods-damned *game*, Finn."

That tone gave him pause.

No anger or irritation. No mocking or mischief or sneering scorn, all of which he'd come to expect when he and Occassio had their brief sparring sessions these days.

Today, she'd picked up a new weapon: a plea.

A despairing, desperate *plea* that sounded nothing like Occassio at all.

Like she wanted him to believe her. Like there was some reason he *needed* to believe her.

Something swept in on the tail end of that plea and possessed him; that had to be it. Some strange, stupid spirit came and filled his own body with its foolish whim and will, because instead of ignoring this odd mood of hers and heading off to his business…

He knelt before the mirror. Face-to-face with the goddess who had tried to tear his mind to ribbons so she could braid her own soul into the empty space left behind.

And yet, despite her failure, something else *had* definitely taken hold of him. Because when he braced a hand against the mirror's frame, reading the edge of her turned-away face, he didn't call to the goddess at all.

"Cassi," he murmured.

A shudder ran through her form; a fierce shiver that sent shards of illusory gems flying, a disruption of her shield that briefly revealed the girl beneath.

Behind the diamond mask, tears coursed down her freckled cheeks.

He'd long prided himself on his knack for holding a grudge. He kept a well-bred fleet of them at all times, some of them earned, some of them petty, all of them lovingly maintained and precisely polished. Not one of them set aside to gather dust.

He was good at hatred. Talented at it, even.

But hatred forgot itself when it came face-to-face with a goddess's twinkling tears.

"Don't," she rasped. "Don't use that name."

And because he was, of course, possessed, not in control of himself at all, emotions reeling where good sense had once ruled…he reached into the mirror, searching until his thumb touched her damp, warm cheek.

When he brushed at those hidden tears, she froze. So unnaturally still, he nearly fell for her crystalline façade.

"If this isn't a game," he murmured, "then tell me what we're doing here."

His finger sank into a divot—one of her dimples deepened beneath his touch, but not from a smile. A sneer. "You're the so-called Trickster God; why don't you tell me?"

All at once, Finn snapped back to himself—he jerked his hand back out from the mirror, wiping her tears on his shirt, turning away before he could do something really stupid.

Something *else* really stupid.

Whispering her name, wiping her tears—those were bad enough. But if he kept catching glimpses of *her* behind the endless lies, he was going to take *stupid* and invent a whole new variety. The kind that would require a new name to fully encompass the four kinds of foolish he got when he let her into his head.

But as he walked toward the door, his feet stuck to the wooden floorboards. Treacle-tacky reluctance glued his soles in place, the tip of his tongue tingling with words he hadn't planned to say.

"If you ever decide to tell me the truth," he said, "whatever you're hiding, whatever those tears are for…I will listen, Cassi. But only if *you* say it."

Five kinds of foolish.

"No masks," he added, gaze fixed on the door. Not at her—*never look back at her.* "No costumes. No cheats. You, and me, and the truth—those are the rules if you want to quit the game. Until then, you can pass all you like, but I'm going to keep taking my turns."

And because he liked even numbers just a bit better—because six kinds of foolish made a nice, even tally—he waited. For a whole ten seconds he didn't have to spare, he waited.

And when nothing answered him but the fire purring in his hearth, he walked out, shutting the door tightly behind him.

He had other things to do tonight—things that had waited long enough. Things he needed to do if they were going to put his plan in motion at last.

But he had to check on his parents first.

The stairs down to the dungeon were one of the few things in the palace that hadn't changed since Tenebrae had taken charge; they creaked in all the same places, curled his nose hairs with the same brine-and-decay scent driven deep into their planks, and even housed the seventh or eighth generation of the same mouse family that had been living there for over a year. So despite the fact that he now descended to see his mother and father trapped behind iron bars…it was almost comforting, to have that hint of normalcy.

At least, it was, until he crossed from stair to floor, wood to stone, and the smell of rancid flesh barreled into him.

Terror hurled a blow across his knees, a cheap shot that nearly brought him down.

Papa.

The little boy in him wanted to run—to shout—to know *right this second* if his father still breathed, if his mother had contracted an infection as well, if the hourglass he'd been telling time by had broken open without his knowledge.

The prince in him wanted to find Vash and Raquel, grip them by the throats, and demand to know why he hadn't been *told* his parents' condition had taken a turn down treacherous streets, Death circling them like hungry dogs.

But the trickster knew he could do none of those things. The trickster had to walk with silent steps, bracing the boy's shaking knees and the prince's angry fists, composing himself again by the time he reached their cell.

Raquel stood guard tonight; the bruises that mottled her cheekbone, striking through several shades of purple, only wound his hands into tighter fists.

Priorities. They would talk after this.

When he got to the cell, wrapping one hand around the bars, another fist formed around his heart and *crushed.*

He still remembered the days they spent in the country house right after the fire…days filtered through the green light of Jericho's magic repairing the burns on his skin, the film of shock that kept his voice locked up for two weeks after the fire itself, and the empty top bunk he didn't want at all when he didn't have to race anyone for it.

Most severely of all, he remembered his mother; how she'd curled up in the armchair by the window in the den, still in her smoke-stained dress, and stared unseeingly at the shore beyond; how she'd refused to eat or sleep until his father got on his knees and begged her to come back to him, begged her not to leave him too; how her wails had echoed through the whole house at night, and hadn't stopped until Finn had left his bed and crawled into her lap, burying his face in her shoulder, the two of them grieving in silence together.

The look on Adriata's face now…he had seen it before. On a younger woman grieving her lost daughter, holding a son too big to fit easily on her lap, whispering that it was okay if he didn't feel like talking. That he could listen as long as he needed to, if it helped him understand what had happened.

Tonight, it was his father she cradled close; she held one hand pressed to his flushed, bearded cheek, eyes fixed on every struggling breath his father dragged in. Whenever the gap between those breaths spanned a moment too long, she tightened her hold on him, shaking gently until he stirred enough to mutter "Addie…'m all right, Addie."

"Mama?" The word barely made it out, but his mother looked up immediately; he could see the pieces moving, an attempt to puzzle together a brave face, but the reddish rims around her eyes were a tell anyone could catch.

"Please tell me you have a plan," she croaked. "A *fast* one."

"Why hasn't he been treated?" Finn twisted on heel to face Raquel, anger at her and for her clenched within each respective fist. "I thought—"

"He *has,*" she interrupted. "But the infection's too severe. He needs a medimancer."

A medimancer. All of whom had been under Tenebrae's thrall for weeks; at least, all the ones employed by the palace. And convincing any of the others to set foot in here, let alone trying to sneak them in and out of the dungeons unseen…

A stone sailed into his stomach, dread striking each rib as it skipped to the next.

He cursed under his breath, turning away; dragging his hands through his hair, he paced a tight loop before their cell, mind racing down all possible paths ahead of him.

Maybe he didn't ask—maybe he simply grabbed a medimancer and forced them to come with him. But a person dragged in against their will was far less likely to be quiet—far more difficult to sneak *anywhere*. And afterward, there'd be no choice but to kill them, not when they knew his parents still lived…and that he still cared.

When he'd told Raquel he'd spill all the blood he had to in order to keep them safe, it hadn't been a lie. But being forced to kill was far different when it included forethought. Self-defense didn't count for anything if he backed himself into that corner.

He veered down a different path.

They could move up their timeline—but rushing would mean mistakes. He was teasing too many puppet strings already; upping the tempo would cause missteps in the puppet's dance. Strings might even start to snap.

Another turn, another road.

"All right." He steepled his fingers in front of his face, pressing them to the bridge of his nose—it blocked out what little light there was in the dungeon, allowing him to better see the new path ahead, and the pressure of his own hands grounded him. "All right, all right. We can…we'll move faster. Increase the doses. If we can get it into the palace's water supply, that would help. Someone can warn the palacefolk to bring water from home."

Raquel glanced to his parents. "Finn—"

"We can manage it," he said firmly. "Whatever it takes—if we're going to take a risk we shouldn't take, then we're going to take it for him. Your father—he was a battlefield physician?" At her nod, he continued, "How much did you pick up?"

"Enough to help." Her gaze flickered to Adriata this time, and her eyes narrowed, the good one's bruised lid creasing. "If I'm allowed."

"You will be." His mother might have been stubborn and suspicious, but she wasn't stupid…though the look she shot him through hanks of unwashed hair suggested she didn't like the idea. "For now, you're going to keep that wound as clean as you can. Keep it covered, keep it medicated—"

"There's another problem," Raquel interrupted. "Revan told me yesterday that Tenebrae's taking me out of guard rotation."

His teeth scraped together. "Why?"

"I don't know."

"Why didn't you tell me sooner?"

"When was I supposed to tell you anything?" she demanded. "You've been busy with your own tasks. Busy enough to miss our meetings for the past *four days.*"

A puppet string half-frayed.

"We will discuss that later," he said through his teeth. *Once I figure out how to admit you're right.* "I'll handle the guard rotation."

"How are you going to—"

"I will *handle it.* It will just…"

It would just prevent him from going through the mirror again tonight.

Which, judging by how much it bothered him, was a good thing.

"It will throw a few things off," he finished. "But I'll handle it. Mama, for the love of the gods, let Raquel help you. I trust her…more than anyone, I trust her with you."

At that, Raquel's expression softened…if only a touch.

"And I swear on my life," he added, "if she harms a hair on either of your heads, she will regret it."

Thankfully, Raquel didn't scowl at him for that—probably because she knew, just as he did, that it was what Adriata needed to hear.

Adriata swallowed. Hard. But she said, "Fine. Tell me the plan."

Sure, once I finish changing the whole damned thing on the fly.

"We get out," he said finally. No time to wait for Soren to get his message. No time to try and bring troops to the city. "We go to Uncle Roran. Once I have your signet, I'll send word to our generals to abandon anything to do with the campaign against Nyx and head there as well. From there, we all sail to meet Soleil…and we'll figure out the rest once we see what Aunt Gen and Uncle Cy have to offer."

Adriata's gaze darkened. Her fingers flexed against his father's shirt, pausing in their absent circles over his heart. "Genevieve won't help."

"She will. Soleil is stubborn—" understatement of his life, really, "—and I know she won't stop until they give her an army. And if she can't manage it, then *we* will. Together."

Adriata's jaw worked, the frown lines around her mouth deepening; she turned her head toward the back wall of the dungeon, eyes glassy, polished with distress. "We can't abandon our people to this monster."

"We can," he said, "and we will. Small losses win bigger battles, Mama."

Now she sat straight, a hint of fire flickering behind her eyes. "Our people are not a small loss."

"Maybe not," he allowed. "But we've evacuated many of them already, and…compared to what it'll cost us otherwise, you'd be surprised just how small a loss it really is."

It was the wrong thing to say—but he knew that before he said it. So when his mother ground her teeth in return, a mirror to his own tension, he knelt down and reached for her hand.

Throat bobbing like a ship on unsteady seas, she gave it to him. He squeezed it, hard, trying not to think about how cold it felt—how frail it was compared to the hand that had held him steady all his life.

"We're not abandoning them," he promised. "Raquel and the others, they've helped plenty past the walls—and whoever we can't save, we will come back for. But you know the odds—you know what happens if we try to go against an army with nothing but ideals on our side. We need our army. We need our family. We need our Heir."

Her lips pressed thin, but he still caught the way they trembled. "You shouldn't have to carry this alone. We should be with you…we should have been there with *all* of you."

Gods, if only she knew just how much he'd been carrying…and how very long he'd been carrying it.

"I'm not carrying it alone," he croaked, pressing his forehead to the bars, seeking that soothing pressure again. "I have help…and our people do, too." He jerked his head toward Raquel. "She's saved more Atlas lives since we arrived here than I have."

Adriata glanced to her…and her shoulders slumped.

On some, a posture of defeat—on his mother, a posture of ease.

He took that as a good sign. A good enough sign that he could tear himself away from her, holding onto the bars instead of her hand.

"I am so sorry I wasn't enough to save Kal," he murmured. "But I *will* be enough to save you."

His mother's eyes misted over with tears. "I don't want you to take these risks…nor does your father. You should run—both of you, all of you, whoever matters to you. All of you should run, and stay alive."

He had nothing he could say to that—nothing that would take away those familiar tears, the despair of a mother unable to reach her children.

So instead he whispered, "I love you. Both of you. And with any luck at all, the next time we see each other, we'll *all* be running."

CHAPTER 27

RAQUEL

Raquel had always been fond of dogs.

Wolves had been her favorite animal since girlhood; a friend of her father's had kept one as a companion, a gray-furred beast he'd raised after it had been abandoned as a pup. As a child, she'd often been recruited to take it for runs along the man's sprawling property. The creature had been kind, but protective—whenever another beast had crossed their path, he'd planted himself in front of Raquel with a throaty growl, his slavering jaws a reminder of the wild blood in his veins.

The hounds that wandered the streets of Port Atlas were nothing like him.

Tenebrae had left his music box in the rafters of the nearby kennels overnight; by morning, the well-behaved hunting dogs had become howling, frenzied creatures, foaming at the mouth, struck rabid by raving chaos. And after he'd let the strongest of the pack cull the weakest, he'd split them into three groups.

The largest group, he kept sequestered in the kennels; these he called his *war dogs*.

The next, he set loose on the city, a strike back against the citizens who'd made their poor opinion of their new queen known.

The last had vanished overnight, neither hide nor tail of them to be seen. And that frightened her the most.

She didn't know what he had in mind for the war dogs, but she dared not wander into the kennels alone; even domesticated dogs had the teeth of beasts, and she had enough scars to tally these days without adding more to the pile.

The ones on the street weren't any better, but at least being in the open made them less likely to leave the shadows; they were on her turf, and they seemed to know it. All she really saw of them were hints of movement in the alleys and the occasional half-devoured rat…but she heard far more. Their pitchy howls sang a song of bloodlust, stirring a quivering in her belly that mimicked prey instinct. It begged her to duck into a hollow or dig herself into a hole, pressing herself flat to the ground until the predator passed over her.

But she was neither prey nor predator; she was the maelstrom that drove both back to their dens.

So whenever an ichor-stained pair of jaws poked past the divide between shadow and moonlight, drinking in the scent of her fear, she coaxed the clouds above to purr with thunder.

Corrupted hounds they might have been, but they were still hounds—and she'd never met a dog that didn't fear storms.

Even so, when she finally came upon the alley where Finn waited, hood thrown over his head, she said, "You've got company."

The hood twitched sideways, but only slightly—the barest glance wasted on the depths of the alley, where glossy-coated creatures paced in odd patterns. "I think Tenebrae gave them orders not to harm me."

"Are they intelligent enough to understand that kind of command?" Raquel didn't join him in leaning against the wall; instead, she angled herself to keep her seeing eye on the hounds, staying just outside the alley's mouth. One hound lurched toward her with a drunken, staggering gait; Finn swept out a hand, and the animal reeled back into its huddle of packmates, a whine melding with the clacking of its teeth.

"Seems so," he said. "More powerful biomancers have occasionally been known to speak to animals—Jer might've been one of them. Or maybe Tenebrae's strength enhanced her abilities."

She cast a look toward the hounds again, drawing a thread of lightning to crackle around her fingers. "Should I…?"

"I wouldn't. Lightning leaves a certain look behind on bodies." He gave her a reproachful look, tapping his heel in a slow rhythm against the wall. "He'd figure out who did it, and from what you said about the other night, he's suspicious enough already."

The mention of that night scalded her palms with adrenaline, and the lightning brightened, streaking erratically between her fingers. "You can't keep going off gods-know where without telling me."

It could have been brought up more tactfully. But she'd tried twice already, and Finnick Atlas had a talent for pushing off conversations he didn't want to have; he'd parried both attempts.

So when he cast his gaze to the ground, letting the hood conceal his features, she rolled up her sleeves and readied herself to drag the answers out of him if she had to.

Instead, he surprised her by saying, "I know. I'm sorry."

Suspicion sent her fingers on a search for her sword. "Finnick Atlas doesn't apologize."

"He does when he needs to—hand off the sword, please, you're making me uncomfortable."

She snorted. "Have you been comfortable at all since we started this game?"

"Fair enough. Look, it took a while to nail down how time works here versus how time works when I'm in the past—it's shorter here, but not that short. I didn't realize how long you were getting left alone." He let out a long sigh that trailed into a groan as he stretched, reaching for the sky before crossing his arms over his chest again. "But it's working—Tenebrae hasn't questioned me once in all this time, not in earnest."

"How many more trips do you intend to take?"

"As many as I like, and not one trip less."

She glowered at him.

He threw his hands out in exasperation. "What do you want me to say? I don't *know*, Raquel. I don't know how long this game is going to go on, and the longer it does, the more I need to know about her."

"I'm going to say something you aren't going to like."

He rolled his eyes, muttering something under his breath that sounded like *What else is new?*

"I want to know how much of this is actually about the game." Delicacy had never been her strong suit; even if it had been, she'd learned that wielding a blunt weapon was often the way when one wanted to beat something true out of Finnick Atlas. "I want to know if you can pull this off without knowing her—because if you can, then you need to. I've seen what it looks like when she gets in your head."

Finn did not insult her with a quick, easy lie. Instead, he let out a long, long breath, reaching up to rub his temples.

"Maybe," he admitted. "Probably."

"Then why aren't you?"

"Because I don't know for sure," he said. "I might be good enough to pull it off, but I have no gods-damned idea what Tenebrae might say next. I'm studying for an exam without even an inkling of what I'm being tested on—logic dictates that I cover all my bases."

It was a good answer. It might've even been true.

But it didn't strike her as whole.

"How bad?" she asked quietly.

He narrowed his eyes. "Don't know what you mean."

Not a twitch of his features—not a hint of a tell on him. His tapping heel even kept its rhythm.

Still, she held her ground. And she'd keep holding it until he answered in full. "Yes, you do."

She had nothing but raw instinct to rely on when it came to Finn's lies and truths. And she hadn't always been right. But this time, he took off a piece of that ever-present costume; this time, he looked at her with enough emotion for her to read.

And what she read…it spoke of something more than a conflicted conscience.

It scrawled out a story of shame.

Of anger.

Of…

Of something that made him look more like Kallias than he ever had. Something she recognized from too-blue eyes and reddish hair set on fire by the sun and a prince making promises over a periwinkle bracelet.

"Finn," she croaked.

"I know." He cracked a grin. "Always thought Kal was the bigger fool of us—especially when he fell for *you*, murder pact and all." An erratic wave of his hand; a chuckle that made her just as uneasy as the corrupted hounds' howls. "But he only fell for that once—here I am, cheating at a game I've already played move-for-move, and I'm still losing."

She couldn't pretend to understand the game Finn and Occassio were playing; it'd started long before she'd even met Finn, and though she'd seen the effects of the Time Goddess's magic invading Finn's mind, she actually knew very little about her. But what she *did* know was that Finn did not admit to losses easily…and that his care was a hard-won prize.

"Don't go back," she said softly. "You can win the game without it—you don't have to torture yourself."

He kicked off the wall, twisting abruptly and stalking from the alley. "Don't *pity* me."

Pity? Gods, she wished it was simple as pity.

Unfortunately for both of them, they cared about what happened to each other. Even if it was only in honor of Kallias's memory, even if they only took care of each other because he wasn't here to do it, Finn mattered to her…and she mattered to him.

She couldn't stand by and let him lose himself any more than he could have left her to Vash and Vidia's mercy. She'd made a promise.

"This isn't pity, you ass," Raquel snarled, stalking after him. She gripped him by the shoulder and whirled him around, ignoring when he gripped her by the wrist at just the right angle to snap it if he liked. She shoved her other hand into his chest. "If I had to go back in time and see Kallias, knowing how everything ended, not able to warn him, *save* him…" The laugh that escaped surprised her, a dark chuckle that tweaked her throat enough that she thought it might become a sob. "It'd kill me. I really think it would."

Finn's fingers constricted her wrist. "It's different."

"Why? Because you're supposed to be heartless? Because you're supposed to hate her? Because she did irreparable harm to you and yours, and you should want nothing more than for her to suffer?" She yanked her wrist free and spread her arms in demonstration. "Pot, meet Kettle."

He scoffed. "Right. I'm sure it was so hard, falling for one of the best men I ever knew. You oughta be ashamed, really."

"Do you think I *liked* it when I realized I failed my sister? Do you think it felt good, knowing the vengeance I promised her would never come to pass?"

"It is different," he said coolly, "because I am not you. I am *better*."

She let her hands drop to her sides, shaking her head. "In some ways, maybe. But no matter how well you pretend, you've still got a heart, same as the rest of us. And if she's got a grip on it…you can't act your way out of *that*."

Finnick Atlas lifted his chin. Stuck his hands in his pockets. Put on a haughty smirk.

His most common costume.

"Watch me."

And with that, his body wavered, light bending until he vanished entirely.

When she reached the abandoned hostel Vaughn and the others had taken over, she knew immediately something was wrong.

Partly because no one guarded the door, waiting for her whispered password.

Partly because the wind rushed out to greet her when she arrived, bringing with it the smell of blood and steel…and smoke. Smoke tanged with iron.

But mostly because people were shouting.

Heart leaping into her throat, Raquel shoved her way in, beelining for the main gathering room. The closer she got, the higher voices rose—including one that gripped the back of her brain with a horrid ache of déjà vu. She couldn't place it, but she *knew* it from somewhere…a low, rasping feminine timbre that *roared* with fury at whatever was happening inside that room.

She drove her elbow into the closed door, ignoring how the already-bruised bone ached in protest.

Before it had fully swung open, silver flashed—she dropped into a crouch, barely hitting the floor in time to avoid the poison-filled, feather-fletched dart. It jammed into the wall over her head, jittering between the boards.

A moment later, the wood began to smoke.

"Sorry!" called Vidia—but the poisoner's usually cheerful voice seemed inflamed with exasperation. "Thought you were another one!"

Another one?

A quick tally told her there were three too many bodies in this room—one knelt on the ground, hands behind his head, while another stood on her knees before him, arms spread out. Both were bent at an angle that didn't allow her to see their faces.

But it was the third, seated in a wheelchair, that relieved the ache of straining memory in the back of her skull: a woman with deep brown skin, ebony braids, red-and-gold leather armor, and a void-black knife in her hand, the point of which sat level with Vash's navel.

No—not his navel. Lower.

Considerably lower.

It was that blade that dragged the woman's name at last from Raquel's mouth. "Safi?"

Vash, to his credit, didn't flinch when the woman's head whipped to face Raquel—though he did look a bit sallow, squinting in pain. Upon closer inspection, another Artemisian knife stuck out of his arm, pinning him to the wall by fabric and flesh.

"*Raquel?*" Safi Aquila—Elias's cousin, a talented weaponsmith, and a good friend to them when they'd stayed in Artem—beamed at her with ease, as if they had run into each other in the marketplace instead of on the outskirts of a tormented city…as if she didn't have a knife pressed to an Atlas assassin's nether region. "Oh my gods, I am so glad you're here!"

"Raquel? Angelov?" The woman standing on her knees craned her neck to look their way—then shouted again when Vidia aimed her dart-blower their way. "I told you, we are *enemies of Tenebrae*. Raquel—she'll vouch for us. Officer Angelov! A little help?"

"Princess," she breathed. Princess Emberlyn—Ravenna's second daughter, Soren's older sister. Second in line to Nyx's throne, now that Ravenna was gone. "Princess Emberlyn, what are you doing here?"

"Long story," croaked Ember—she glowered at Vidia with all the fire of her birth kingdom's forges, her cropped black curls messy from what must have been a mighty struggle. "One I'd rather tell once she stops trying to poison me and my *unarmed partner.*"

That had to be the man behind her, dark locs framing his frightened face, his hands clamped over her shoulders as if to pull her out of the way of an oncoming projectile. Raquel knew him, too.

Havi Aquila. Baker, pyromancer, and one of the kindest men she'd ever met.

"Stop," Raquel called out quickly. "Vidia, stop! They're friends—Safi, you too. We're all on the same damned side."

Safi snuck a suspicious look up at Vash. "I don't know—he tried to kick my chair over."

"You threw a knife into my arm," Vash ground out.

"What's your point?"

"Weapons down!" Raquel barked. "*Now!*"

Everyone obeyed this time—even Safi, though much slower, grumbling under her breath as she sheathed one knife and reached up toward the other, wriggling her fingers impatiently. "Can I have that back?"

Vash gaped at her. "*What?*"

"I got it." Vidia crossed the room, hand extended.

"Vidia," Vash choked, eyes widening, "Vidia, don't you dare—"

"Relax, I'll count it down for you. Ready? One—"

"If you even—"

Vidia yanked the knife straight from her brother's arm, and he sagged, looking as if he might vomit. He shoved his forearm into his mouth, burying his scream in his sleeve.

"You forgot two and three," Safi said helpfully over Vash's muffled cry.

"Got bored. Math's not my strong suit." Vidia wiped the knife clean on her brother's shirt—which earned her another unintelligible series of indignant noises—and handed it back to Safi. "Good throw."

"Thanks." Safi grinned.

Raquel crossed the room quickly, not entirely trusting the peace to hold—she went to Ember first, helping her up before dipping into a bow. "Your Highness."

"Officer Angelov." Ember nodded to her, then helped Havi stand; he leaned a bit heavily on her, and a flash of concern brought Raquel to his side.

"I'm fine," he said sheepishly as she probed for a wound. "Honest. I twisted my ankle on a loose cobblestone out there, embarrassing as it is."

"A war wound to be proud of," Safi said solemnly. "You'll never walk again, of course, but it can't be helped. I'll make sure they get us matching chairs."

Raquel laughed breathlessly. "Making jokes so soon?"

"I find battle reminds you to use your breath while you have it." When Raquel made her way to her, Safi tugged her down into a tight hug; despite her flippant attitude, her hands trembled against Raquel's back. "I meant it, though…I am *so glad* to see you."

Raquel hugged her back—and retreated immediately when Safi yelped. "What? What's wrong?"

"Static shock," Safi laughed, rubbing the back of her shoulder. "What'd you do, stick your hand on a lightning rod before you got here?"

Blood warmed Raquel's cheeks; her complexion hid blushes, but it didn't stop their heat. She cracked her knuckles to break the buzzing energy out. "Not exactly. Sorry. You're all right?"

"Vash is fine, if anyone cared," Vash muttered through gritted teeth; Vidia had a bundle of cloth wadded against his wound now, stanching the bleeding as best she could.

Raquel crossed her arms, scowling at him. "So you can give it, but you can't take it, I see."

"He prefers to be the one doing the stabbing," Vidia agreed, patting his cheek—he made as if to bite her hand, and her next pat sounded more like a smack. "Hey! Watch it. I'm more than happy to let you do this yourself."

After several minutes more of trading introductions, checking everyone for injuries, and separating Artemisians from Atlas to prevent potential scuffles breaking back out, things finally quieted. Vash sank into a chair nearby, face hidden in his hand while Vaughn stitched him up; ironic, that the skilled torturer and assassin couldn't stand the sight of his own blood.

Ember sat by the fire with Havi, their hands wound tightly together; Havi kept reaching in absentmindedly and rearranging the logs, shifting them to allow more air to feed the flames. Now that the initial conflict had settled, he seemed to have done the same, easing against Ember's side with a wide yawn.

Ember herself remained braced, eyeing the Atlas in the room with great distrust, Vaughn in particular; every time the Prince-Consort moved, she did too, another inch of her shoulder devoting itself to shielding Havi. Protectiveness bristled across every inch of her; Raquel didn't need her magic to sense the tension rippling over the princess's skin, electric all on its own.

Meanwhile, Safi and Vidia seemed to have forgotten the entire thing already—Vidia was marveling over Safi's knives, cooing praises that Safi happily accepted. Within seconds, the conversation shifted to which poisons coated blades best, and whether the two might be able to arrange a trade.

And Raquel could only stand by the wall, staring at it all, trying to catch up to this new stone driven into the spoke of their carriage wheel.

"Princess," she said finally—when she spoke, all other chatter in the room halted, every eye drilling into her. She ignored it, keeping her gaze on Ember. "Why are you here? Soren told us you were going to meet up with Havi and Safi, but she didn't say you planned on coming here."

"We didn't," Ember said, scooting closer to Havi—he rested his head on her shoulder, as much for her comfort as his, if Raquel had to guess. Ember ran her fingers through his locs as she spoke, never breaking Raquel's stare; her other fingers fussed through the rug beneath her. "I meant to find Yvonne and Auralee afterward…most of Andromeda evacuated with them, seeking safety in other cities. I heard my sisters landed in Rosewater, so we—"

"Rosewater?" That name rang another bell in her head. "Isn't that—?"

"It's one of the towns along the Vela." Ember extricated her fingers from the rug, raking them through her curls instead, chewing on the inside of her cheek before she said, "But neither of them were there. One of the generals said there was an Atlas attack shortly after they arrived—our soldiers ran them off, but when the dust cleared, Yvonne and Auralee were both missing."

Raquel caught the alarm that tried to rise into her chest, shoving it back down between her ribs; the bones acted as a buffer, preventing panic from piercing too deeply. "Missing?"

"We thought they might have been brought here, but if you haven't heard anything…" Ember's throat bobbed; Havi rubbed her back with a soothing murmur. "Maybe they got away themselves. Yvonne could've decided to hide out somewhere else, keep her head low…"

Raquel clasped her hands together to trap the nervous energy between them; pressure built in that space between her palms, a tiny storm begging for release.

The eldest and youngest princesses of Nyx were out there, alone, in an increasingly unsafe kingdom—with gods-knew-who, living gods-knew-where. And that was the best-case scenario.

Realization slapped her across the face.

Not the eldest princess of Nyx—not anymore. Yvonne was the *Queen* of Nyx.

"Does Yvonne know about Ravenna?" she prompted.

Ember swallowed, grief throwing a shroud over the blaze in her eyes. A daughter twice orphaned. "I don't think so. The news hadn't reached Rosewater when I arrived."

Raquel didn't know Yvonne well—Soren was the only royal she'd commonly spent time with—but from what little she did know, hiding away without sending word to *anyone* seemed out of character. "And no one saw them run? Not even townsfolk?"

"Not a trace." Ember's hands rattled; Havi reached up and took the one stroking his hair, sitting straight and cradling it to his chest instead, watching her with a worried frown. "It's better than being found in—in some other state, but not knowing is driving me mad. This was our best shot at finding her if she was captured. I should be relieved she's not, I suppose." A quiet, angry huff. "Besides, I wouldn't have been able to rest easy anywhere else. Not while my mother's murderer still breathes."

"He killed my mother, too," said Safi—the quietest Raquel had ever heard her speak, a hushed murmur in the silence of a wake. The weaponsmith twirled her returned knife in her hand, grim gaze fixed on the fire. "Maybe not by his hand, but it was his influence that drove my people to rebellion—it was one of his worshippers that poisoned her. I'll see him dead for that."

"And I couldn't very well let them go alone," Havi added, with an affectionate glare toward Ember. "Though she did her best to leave me behind."

"We both know you're not a fighter," Ember murmured. "I didn't want to—"

"I'm not a fighter, but you are—and we've been apart too long. I couldn't stay there wondering if this time, there'd be no reunion." Havi drew her face to his, nuzzling his nose against hers before kissing the bow of her lip. "We're in this together, whatever *this* is."

"Touching."

By now, Raquel had grown used to Finn appearing whenever he wished—and, often, the wind tattled on him just before he made his grand entrance. But the others were not fortunate enough to have an ethereal scout at their beck and call.

As the usual wave of startles and curses rolled through the room, Finn raised his hands, rolling his eyes and mimicking their shrill scolding: "*Ah! Where'd you come from, Finn? For gods' sake, Finn, you're going to kill someone doing that!* Yeah, yeah, I know, I've heard it plenty, can we move on now?"

"Well, if you bothered to knock every once in a while…" Vaughn teased…then coughed awkwardly when Finn didn't laugh, turning his attention back to Vash's wound.

The brothers-in-law had yet to have a conversation—Finn rarely visited the hideout with her, and even when he did, he purposely left Vaughn out, ignoring him outright even when Vaughn asked him pointed questions.

A better person might have encouraged Finn to at least *try* to forgive the sickly man for sins not entirely his own. But Finn was entitled to that anger, that scorn; it would have been wrong to try and convince him otherwise.

She'd had people try and steal her hard-won anger from her before, claiming it only hurt her, not those who had harmed her. But her rage hadn't hurt;

it had given her power and purpose, a reminder that the things that had happened to her were not her fault.

Finn deserved this fury. So when he again ignored Vaughn's quip in favor of walking in and sitting at the table with Vidia and Safi, she let him.

"I think we met before, if briefly." Finn held his hand out to Safi, and she took it. "Prince Finnick Atlas."

"Princess Safira Aquila," Safi said, not bowing even an inch. "Pleased to make your acquaintance once again."

"Safi," groaned Havi.

Safi rolled her eyes, offering the slightest dip of her head. "*Fine.* Just Safira Aquila. But everyone calls me Safi."

Finn raised an eyebrow, tilting his head toward Vash. "I'm assuming the hole in my Viper's arm belongs to you?"

Smug satisfaction shone in Safi's grin. "That's my handiwork, yeah. He earned it, though."

"Don't worry about it—that bruise on his jaw came from me." Finn kissed her politely on the knuckles, then hopped back down from the table, crossing his arms and facing down the pair by the fire. "And you two?"

"Havi Aquila," Havi said, waving briefly. "We've met, too."

"I remember—my brother raved about your muffins." He jerked his head toward Raquel. "And this one dreams about your chocolate croissants. I think she could literally sell them in her sleep."

Raquel scowled. "Not necessary information."

Ember stood up, releasing Havi's hand to meet Finn in the middle of the room. She held out her hand, chin up, giving no ground—two royals trapped in the center of succession, finding themselves suddenly thrust to the front without any choice in the matter. "Princess Emberlyn Afra-Nyx, born of Artem, raised in Nyx. I met your brother Kallias when he came to Delphin to warn us about Tenebrae."

Finn shook her hand. "Princess Emberlyn…one of Soren's adoptive sisters."

A muscle in Ember's arm twitched, but her voice stayed level. "Yes."

"Well, as my sister's sister, I guess that makes us family…somehow. In a weird way. I don't want to think about it too hard." To her surprise, Finn's diplomatic mask softened enough to let in a smile. "Strange times we find ourselves in, yeah?"

Ember's stiff posture eased, and she smiled back, exhaustion bending her brows together. "Gods, don't I know it. My sister spoke highly of you when we last met—and she speaks highly of very few."

Finn cleared his throat audibly. "She's kinder to me than she should be."

"Doubtful. Soren's not often kind in excess."

"Well, she spoke well of you, too—and despite the awful circumstances, I am grateful she didn't grow up alone. Thank you for caring for her during her years in Nyx."

"It was a gift, not a burden. I only wish it had not come at the cost of so much pain…on both sides."

"You and me both." Finn stuck his hands back in his pockets, slipping back into his lazier skin. "Oddly enough, Princess, your timing is impeccable. I was just coming to inform my friends here of our plan…and as it happens, we may have need of your talents."

Ember frowned. "I'm not sure what need you have for a weaponsmith with no forge, but—"

"Sorry—I should have spoken more clearly. Not your talents." Finn gestured behind her…to Havi, who looked over his shoulder as if expecting to find someone else sitting in the fire behind him. "His."

Havi's eyes rounded out. "Ah—I'm no fighter, Prince Finnick."

"Good. I don't need a fighter." A sinister grin curled across Finn's face, and even Ember took a step back. "I need a baker."

The final plan, when Finn explained it, sounded beautifully simple:

They would not be taking Port Atlas back.

It was, as Finn had said before, a waste—with the barracks full of Tenebrae's loyal soldiers, the stables and streets crawling with corrupted beasts, and no way to summon the armies of Atlas without his mother's signet ring, they only had the bodies in this room…and that would not be enough.

So they would not take the city. But they would take its rulers.

Upon hearing that Adriata and Ramses lived, Vaughn crumbled to his knees, grasping his chest with a mighty sob; Finn did not pause in his speech, but Vash reached out and steadied the necromancer's shoulder.

From there, Finn launched into his plan, stating each step as fact:

Over the next two weeks, Finn would memorize the movements of Tenebrae's new patrols, whittling down their numbers as best he could.

Raquel's task would be to keep the weather poor—and while she watered Atlas with rain, others would head to the barracks themselves, cutting holes in walls and pulling windows off their tracks and prying shingles from the roof, creating drafts and leaks that would render the barracks utterly miserable.

This would drive the soldiers to seek entertainment and lodging in the taverns, so Vidia would find ways to empty the few that remained open in the city until only a couple were left…and only one close to the palace.

This tavern would be Havi and Safi's mission. The two had agreed—Safi eagerly, Havi less so—to take over the tavern and serve the soldiers that came in. Finn would spread praise of their food and drink, drawing attention to them; and all the while, Vidia would work with Havi in the kitchen, finding ways to slowly and subtly taint the provisions with her slow-building poison. And though the soldiers might be reticent to eat after all the issues with the other taverns, Vidia's immunity would allow her to prove their product safe by sampling it herself. Though it would have been more convenient to simply poison the barracks food, it was considerably less likely Tenebrae wouldn't notice a handful of new palacefolk working in the kitchens. Even if Finn claimed to have hired them himself, it would look—to use an Atlas term—fishy. Better to do it the inconvenient way than the imprudent way.

They would need to time it perfectly, Finn warned, but it could be done— once the poison took effect, dropping the guards dead or sickening them past the point of fighting, that would be their only opportunity. Vaughn would puppet the dead to keep up appearances, but that ruse had a time limit; after a couple hours, rigor mortis would set in, making it impossible for Vaughn to puppet their bodies through natural movements.

The entire discussion had Raquel's stomach swirling; a quick glance at Havi and Ember revealed their similarly sickened expressions. But no one raised a protest…because no one had a better alternative.

Once the soldiers were dealt with, they would free Ramses and Adriata. Finn would busy himself going after his mother's signet ring. And with any luck at all, they would all make it out of this city alive.

At that, Raquel finally stood, a niggling concern tugging her up from her seat. "Wait—what about the rest of the city? How do we signal to the people that it's time to evacuate?"

Finn didn't look up, busy sketching out something in the journal in his hand. "We don't."

Raquel's inner storm stilled…the silence within only broken by a thunderous rumble of disbelief.

He'd said as much to Adriata. But she hadn't thought he *meant* it.

"What do you mean, we don't?" she demanded.

"I already told you, we're risking too much as it is with this many bodies— and we just added three more." Finn gestured absently to Havi, Safi, and Ember, then went back to frowning at his notes, chewing on the end of his pen. "There's no way to evacuate the entire city and still ensure our own escape. It will take longer than the window we have."

Raquel gathered a handful of her cloak, directing all her seething frustration into the cloth, grateful she did not have pyromantic powers like Elias or Havi. Her temper would have set more than one fire today alone.

Instead, a new wind crawled in through one of the drafty walls, nearly blowing out the fire in its rush to get to her. It buffeted her body, but she didn't budge; she let it wrap itself around her, teasing her hair, cooling the angry heat building beneath her skin. "I am not leaving these people underneath Tenebrae's boot. Kallias wouldn't—"

When Finn's head snapped up from the journal, eyes gleaming brittle gold, the wind fled for its life.

All the air sucked out of the room with the sharp ruffle of pages colliding. The fire itself did not flicker or fade, but its *light* did…its vibrance dimmed until it barely cast shadows across the floor. Its color followed suit, reds and golds fading into grays and whites.

Fear caught her by the shoulders, trying to tug her back as Finn walked across the room to face her.

She didn't give him the satisfaction of a retreat. But she didn't have to; the quiet intake of her breath told on her just as well.

"I applaud your little show of heroism," he murmured, "but it's unnecessary. You are not him."

Pain raked jagged claws down her throat. "Don't you—"

"You are not him," Finn repeated, still soft, "and neither am I. He is dead. And if we keep playing this part of the game by grief's rules, then we'll end up joining him."

She wanted to spit that this wasn't about Kallias—not all the way. Not anymore.

Her kingdom's queen was dead; their new queen was out there somewhere, no protection at her back, no guards at her sides. Half of Raquel's company had perished in Tenebrae's trap; her birth city, Ursa, had fallen to his plague-like magic too. Her parents could be dead. Childhood friends, kind neighbors, people she'd seen every day for years…all likely dead or corrupted.

And Port Atlas was next.

She couldn't protect her kingdom; she couldn't save what had already been destroyed.

But this city? These people? It wasn't too late for them. Not yet.

They were innocents, most of them. And they deserved someone who would fight for them…even if their princes couldn't.

Or wouldn't.

With his piece said, Finn nodded to each of them and left, throwing his hood back over his head. She didn't follow him out; though her temper begged to pursue, to argue, she knew it would get her nowhere. Finn's mind had set itself firmly on the path to certain victory, not true victory; he had chosen the fight he knew he could win, not the one they needed to win.

So she didn't follow; but Vaughn did.

Before she could decide if she cared enough to stop him from making that horrendous mistake, well-oiled wheels thudded over uneven wooden floorboards; when Raquel looked up, she found Safi watching her expectantly, her hands busy tying her braids into a bundle atop her head.

"So," said the inventor, "how're we getting everyone out?"

Raquel blinked. "What?"

"You don't have to play dumb. I heard the door close—they're gone." Safi leaned forward, hands rubbing together expectantly, clever cogs churning behind her bright eyes. "He's got a plan—that's fine. We can have more than one, as long as the big parts stay the same. So let's hear what you've got."

She looked around the room, throat tightening—Safi was not the only one watching her. Ember and Havi nodded together, an unfathomable understanding stretched between them, minds wound tighter than their joined hands; Vash and Vidia both stood at attention, soldiers awaiting orders, not a hint of hesitation bowing their heads.

They all looked to her. To her, a Nyxian with no title to her name besides that which the tall tales whispered from Atlas mouths had given her.

Riptide.

Nothing but a silly name and a desperate projection of their hopes, their prayers—yet somehow, it had become a thing that mattered.

"I have an idea," she said.

With those four words, the excitement rose so sharply around her that her ears popped. The air began to buzz again, but she batted it away, forcing herself to focus.

"For now, do what Finn asked of you," she added. "I have to check on something before I get everyone's hopes up."

As she walked toward the door, Vidia called out, "Where are you going?"

Nowhere she wanted to go. But wants had to be put aside if this was going to work.

"To pray," she said.

CHAPTER 28

FINN

"Finn, stop!"

He had one rule for skulking where he wasn't meant to be: never walk faster than he had to. Swagger worked wonders, if one knew how to put on that kind of show without being over-the-top.

Over-the-top caught the eyes. Confidence averted them.

But when Vaughn called again for him to stop, his footsteps much too loud, Finn picked up his pace. If there was one conversation he would absolutely *not* be having tonight, it was this one.

Vaughn was the last person in this kingdom he wanted to see right now. And considering that list included, well, the *tyrant god* currently trying to turn Finn's entire kingdom into his own personal circus ring, one could imagine exactly how little he cared to see his brother-in-law.

"I know you can hear me," Vaughn fumed—fumed rather than groveled, that was new—his fingers closing around Finn's shoulder from behind. "You still think you can get out of hard conversations by pretending you can't hear us, I'm standing right here—"

"I'm not interested in whatever conversation you're trying to have." Finn knocked Vaughn's hand from his shoulder. The Prince-Consort's fingers were so cold they bit right through Finn's cloak. "And don't talk to me like that."

"Like what?"

"*That.*" Like old memories mattered at all anymore, his anger stitched with nearly fond nostalgia as he poked for Finn's attention. "Don't act like you know me. I sure as the depths never knew you."

Vaughn grabbed him again, this time by the cloak. Tugged on it, hard, like a puppeteer frustrated by stubborn strings, his marionette oddly unwilling to be danced about. "I'm not the only one who lied about what he was, am I?"

Cold erupted into ruby-red shards of rage. "Don't even *start*. I pretended so I could protect us—us before all. Your lies got Kallias killed!"

Vaughn ducked that blow like he'd seen it coming; he shifted one foot back, hand still holding Finn's shoulder fast, mouth lined with grief, with determination. "Yours may do worse yet."

"There isn't any worse." Finn slapped Vaughn's corpse-cold hand off of him. "Get back inside before I find a little leftover mercy after all."

"You really think you can play a game against the gods?" A breeze blew between him and Vaughn, nearly carrying that low challenge off with it. "And win?"

"I *think*, thanks to you, I don't have a choice."

"You're right," Vaughn said as Finn turned away, flipping his hood up again.

Finn knew that already. He didn't have time to waste on things he already knew. He kept walking.

"You're right," Vaughn repeated, desperate again. "It's my fault—so let me help."

"I don't need your help."

"Ramses does. You didn't say anything about how you're going to keep him alive long enough for this rescue. He needs a physician."

"Raquel's handling it."

"Oh? And when did Raquel graduate from the finest healing academy in the Six Kingdoms?"

Damn him. "What makes you think I'd trust you with him?"

"Because you're not a fool. You never were." Cotton-soft. Strangely knowing. Finn wanted to scratch that softness out of his ears. "You know I would never harm my family."

"You wouldn't?" He had to whisper, to rasp; the words were too brittle between his teeth. They'd break if he handled them roughly. He hooked a finger under his cuff, dragging the sleeve up and bunching it at the shoulder. "Because I've got a scar that says differently."

The color drained from Vaughn's face. Or would have, judging by the guilt-stricken bob of his throat, if there'd been any color left to drain. "That was an accident. I didn't know—"

"When enough accidents pile up, they stop being accidents and start being a pattern." Finn yanked his sleeve back in place, folding the cuff over his wrist with great care. "You knew enough."

A long beat of silence.

"Ramses won't last the week, let alone two," Vaughn rasped. "Let me help. Please."

His lips burned, primed to spit more venom; but he'd made his point. Pride had a bad habit of demanding more than good sense would let him give. He ran the back of his hand over his mouth, then nodded curtly. "Fine. Sort it out with Raquel and Vash."

Vaughn sighed loudly enough to wake the whole damned city. "Thank you."

Finn didn't dignify that with a response. He turned away, walked a few paces—then stopped. His tongue still itched; it wouldn't stop until he scraped that last drop of venom off. "Vaughn."

The Prince-Consort held his breath; Finn could practically taste the bitter dregs of piteous hope in the air.

"One liar to another?" Finn rolled his shoulders. Flexed his fingers. "Lying to yourself doesn't make you innocent. It makes you pathetic. Take some damned responsibility."

Before Vaughn could say another word, he wrapped himself up in a shawl of bent light, vanishing into thin air.

When he was invisible, he didn't have to slow himself to a swagger. And if he ran fast enough, maybe he could escape the needling discomfort of his own words crawling under his skin.

Take some damned responsibility.

242

CHAPTER 29

RAQUEL

With no real idea where to go, she let the wind have its head.

She let it guide her steps, an invisible compass that pushed her this way and that; her hair acted as a sail, each gust blowing the strands left or right, and she followed without question.

The wind, after all, knew its master better than she ever would.

Still, when the wind guided her to the royal cemetery, she started to doubt its sense of direction.

Her boots sank into the spongy grass as she came to a halt at the edge of the gated-in graveyard; though the wind carried the smell of cut flowers and fresh growth, not death or decay, shivers still wracked her limbs as she took it in.

Not from the cold; from the sense that she had trespassed where she was not wanted.

Nyx had no graveyards; instead, they burned their dead on pyres and swept the ashes into whatever receptacle the family requested. From there, it was up to the grieving loved ones what they did with the ashes; some spread them in meaningful places, while others kept the ashes in the home. Others commissioned artists to combine the ashes with blown glass, creating beautiful globes or sculptures.

Beauty from ashes—that had always been Raquel's favorite method. But when her sister had died, she hadn't had a say; despite her and Soren both protesting, begging Jakob to let them make the choice, he'd gently reminded them that Jira had named her parents as the ones to determine her final resting place, not them. And even if her mind had changed, she had not taken the necessary steps to finalize that; his hands were tied.

She had no idea what her parents had done with Jira's ashes. And now that Ursa had fallen, she might never know.

In any case, even if a Nyxian requested not to be burned, graveyards had been abolished thanks to Nyx's superstitious attitudes toward death…and their experience with the scourge of necromancy centuries ago. The closest thing they had were mausoleums, and those marble structures were more closely guarded than the castle itself.

Here, no guards stood on duty—there were no locked caskets or heavy marble doors, no flammable liquids or torches ready to burn the dead should they manage to escape their confines.

Nothing but grass and wind and gleaming white headstones; nothing but flower patches or palm trees grown over graves.

Some of the trees were mere saplings; others towered taller than houses, their boughs vibrant and full of fan-like leaves, birds chirping somewhere in their branches.

Peaceful…beautiful. But so unlike anything she had experienced before that she could not quite relax.

And when her eye caught on a headstone with no garden or grave, she nearly choked on her own heart as it caught in her throat.

First Prince Kallias Atlas, it read.

Below that: *Beloved prince, brother, son, and friend.*

And lastly, etched so deeply that nothing could erode it: *King of the People.*

Grass rustled behind her, stirred by something heavier than the wind.

"Someone carved that just after word of his death began to spread," said Tempest; by now, the faintly accented lilt to Kallias's voice had become familiar enough that she didn't turn or startle.

She just stared, held in place by the sight of that empty grave.

A heavy weight settled over her shoulders, finally drawing her gaze down; a cloak of wolf's fur hung over her, freckle-nipped hands doing up the clasp before she could react.

"You're shivering," he said.

No concern, no warmth; just factual acknowledgement as he walked past her, wearing only ocean-blue leather trousers and a silver tunic belted at his waist, the short sleeves baring his arms to the elements. Despite the hint of cold in the air, no goosebumps graced his skin.

She gripped a fistful of fur and tore the cloak from her shoulders, the clasp ripping open with a loud *pop*. "I'm not cold."

"Suit yourself." He kept walking, not even offering a cursory glance to make her tantrum worth the time.

She would have thrown the cloak down on the dew-covered grass, but her body cringed every time she tried to move; something about the proximity of the dead unnerved her. Like her own bones dreaded the day they would join those buried beneath the dirt.

Throwing things down on graves—even the empty one bearing Kallias's name—seemed like a good way to arrange an unpleasant welcome for herself after death.

So instead, she bundled the cloak around her hands, trying to remind her body it had no reason to fear this particular fate. When Mortem came to take her to Infera or Arcaea, whatever was left of her would be burned, not buried—body to bone, bone to ash, ash to beauty.

If anyone who cared about her survived to see her wishes carried out.

Her stomach flipped itself over, and the swell of sickness forced her feet to finally move, crossing the graveyard with careful steps.

If she stood a second longer over Kallias's grave, she'd either sob or be sick, and she would rather bury herself alive under one of these headstones than do either of those things in front of a god.

Tempest halted in the heart of the cemetery; the wind stirred his hair, dulled from fiery gold to auburn by the gloomy weather. She didn't bother bending her ear for rumors from that playful breeze; the wind never told its master's secrets, no matter how sweetly she asked for them.

As she drew closer, she got a better glimpse of the grave he stood over—the headstone was massive, nearly as tall and twice as broad as him. When he bent to brush his hand over its base, cleaning away dead flowers and dry leaves, she could make out the faintest etching on its surface…a feminine form with no detail, the finer points lost to time.

This grave, while still grand, showed its age. If there had once been text, it had long since faded into unreadable notches; many filled-in cracks showed in its surface, suggesting efforts had been made to preserve it.

"Who was she?" Even her voice seemed reluctant to tread through this sacred space; what she meant to be a demand came out as a murmur.

Tempest knelt before the grave and bent once more, pressing a kiss to its ancient stone. He held that pose for a time, eyes closed; then, with a sigh heavy enough to topple cities, he sat back on his heels, staring up at the faded etching.

And then he said the last two words she'd expected to hear.

"My wife."

There were a thousand questions she could ask—a thousand wounds she could have dealt, or tried to.

Instead, she knelt beside him. "What was her name?"

The answer leapt out as if it had been waiting on the tip of his tongue for centuries, begging to be spoken, to be remembered. Maybe it had. "Athena."

Static buzzed across her palms; she squeezed her hands into fists, trying to grasp that revelation. She knew next to nothing about Atlas history, but she knew *that* name. "Athena *Atlas*?"

He smiled, scratching the back of his neck—a boyish thing, almost sheepish. "Yes. I named the kingdom for her…its first queen."

At her reproachful look—first at his face, then a once-over of his stolen form—he quickly added, "We never had children together. She remarried after…what Braeden did. After we lost our bodies." His voice deepened, harshened, a griefsick timbre that rumbled with ancient pain. "I sailed to meet Mora alone when she sent word that I was needed, and I didn't want to worry Athena. So when I didn't come back…she didn't know what happened, and I had no way to tell her. She waited for years, but there's only so long one can have faith in impossibility. They all came to believe I'd been lost at sea."

"Were you angry?"

"Not with her." A shrug. An absent stroke of his thumb against his ring finger. "She mourned for nearly a decade…waited to remarry even longer. But the kingdom needed an heir, and she deserved to be happy." A wry, decidedly *un*happy smile. "We learned how to take hosts shortly after. I returned to find her married to my former first mate, with a son already toddling and a daughter on the way."

"You spoke to her?"

"Yes."

That didn't sound like the whole of it. "Did you tell her?"

Quieter this time: "No."

"Why not?"

"She was happy. Telling her would have changed that." He swallowed, his throat bobbing like a fishing lure. "And I could never bear to see her unhappy."

"And your first mate?"

"Alexandros?" The name struck her like an uppercut to the jaw, but he didn't seem to notice. "He was…my dearest friend. If I had to trust Athena's well-being to anyone else's hands, I would have chosen his."

"Still. It must have felt like a betrayal."

"No." A firm answer this time, steady and true, a compass pointed ever north. "If the whispers I sought at the time were true, he fought his feelings just as long as her…if not longer. He searched longer and harder than anyone for me when I disappeared, and when they finally agreed to stop searching, he grieved me like a brother…more of a brother than Braeden ever was." He glanced toward her, still smiling, still miserable. "And besides, what kind of wretch would wish his loved ones forever lonely in his absence?"

She had no answers for a god in mourning. So instead, she offered him silence.

He did not keep it for long; after a quiet clearing of his throat, he said, "You sought me out. What made you decide you wanted to see me?"

There would be no better time; no moment better than now, while truth sat between them at an ancient queen's gravesite.

"Is Kallias still there?" She kept her eyes fixed on the headstone, not on him—if she looked at him, she would not be able to ask it calmly. "I know he doesn't speak to you, but…is any part of him alive?"

"You ask because of Anima—because the Atlas princess survived her possession?"

"Not just her."

Golden eyes speared into her, searching, searching—then widening. "The other prince."

She offered no confirmation. But she offered no denial, either.

A sharp breath escaped him; his body began to turn, then stopped, a jilted movement that suggested he'd forgotten himself for a moment. "He survived *Occassio?*"

She was grateful for the secondhand pride that steadied her heart. "He *defeated* Occassio."

This silence went on much longer. "I can't speak to that, but as for the princess…she was coerced and threatened into consent. I never lied to your prince."

"You don't need to explain it or soften it for me." She squeezed her kneecaps tightly to hide the desperate tremble in her hands. "If any part of him lives—if he whispers or thinks, dreams or feels—I need to know. And if he is gone, then I need to know that, too. You owe me the truth, whatever it is."

"I owe you much I cannot give you." A statement that made no sense— followed by one that, unfortunately, she understood all too well. "I'm sorry, Officer Angelov—I truly am. But Kallias Atlas is gone. I believe I would know by now if any part of him survived."

She believed him.

She hated that she believed him.

But if he felt he owed her penance, then she would happily call in that debt.

"If you are truly remorseful," she rasped, "and if you truly did not lie to him…if you meant the promises you made…then I need your help, Tempest."

He pushed himself to his feet, reaching down to offer her his hand; and though it felt like spitting on Kallias's grave, she took it.

Because as much as she hated it, she did not trust her strength to hold. Not against this fresh tide of grief.

He met her gaze without flinching, jaw set. "I'm listening."

She told him the plan Finn had laid out that morning, and the plan she had begun to form after—and all the while, she forced herself to silence the nagging voice that named her *betrayer* and *fool,* that sneered she had never truly grown up from that Skyhaven acolyte who'd given every inch of herself for the love of her silent god.

"We have to evacuate the city," she croaked. "We've hardly made a dent—there are thousands left. We won't be able to get them all out ourselves, not without Tenebrae noticing and engaging us. And that's a fight we'll lose."

Tempest's frown dug into his beard; he'd grown it longer than Kallias liked, but she couldn't think about that just now. These little distractions would be the death of her; she had to point her rage where it mattered. Where it could make a difference.

She didn't need to waste it on ridiculous, petty things like ordering him to shave.

Or carving it from his face herself.

"Let me guess," he said coolly, "you want me to engage my brother. Provide a distraction."

"No." His brow furrowed, but she kept going before he could speak again. "The people know Kallias's face…they trust him." She gestured back toward his headstone; back to the etching that proclaimed him *King of the People.*

Her chest heaved, sore with grief, sick of holding it in.

The King of the People—who should have been there to lead them, to save them, to receive the love strong enough to spark a revolt.

To see his younger sister was not the only royal Atlas adored enough to consider their murder an act of war.

"You took him," she said, "so you will *be* him. They grieve their prince; they pray for a savior. You will give them both, and you will get them out."

"Then who will be occupying my brother's attention?"

"With any luck, no one. Prince Finnick's plan is sound; if everyone moves quickly enough, this will be over before Tenebrae even knows it's started."

At her mention of Finn, his jaw flexed; he looked away, and a trace of foreboding drifted through her.

Tempest was not one to avoid eye contact. If he couldn't look at her, whatever came next…she wasn't ready for it.

"When you say he defeated my sister," he said, "what does that mean?"

She blinked. "Occassio?" That was what he wanted to know about?

Tempest scowled. "Unless he defeated Death herself, and I somehow doubt it."

She scowled back. "He trapped her—shoved her in a mirror, stole her magic as his own, and left her there. Which, after what I saw her do to him, is merciful compared to what she deserves."

A quiet scoff. He rubbed his heart like it pained him. "You don't know anything about her—you don't know what she would count as mercy."

"I thought she stood against you and Mortem—I thought she was your enemy."

"She did," he muttered, pinching the bridge of his nose. "She is. I didn't…I'm not defending her, Officer Angelov. That's not my intention. I merely…"

She had never heard him struggle so badly to find words. "Were you two…close?"

"Once," he said. "Too long ago for it to matter now."

And yet he'd asked.

"We all went through horrible things after we gained our magic," Tempest explained, absently reaching out to her—after a second, she realized he wanted the cloak back. She handed it to him, and he folded it over his arm. "But Cassi…she went through something worse. We didn't…" He coughed, turning his head further away. "I didn't get to her in time, and it changed her. Terribly. I tried—we all tried—but we couldn't reach her past it."

A phantom sting zipped through the scars over her false eye.

"What happened in Skyhaven did the same to me," she said, and he looked back to her, his frown deepening. "But my younger sister…no matter how cruel I was, no matter how hard I pushed her out, she kept trying. And that mattered more than she knew. Maybe if you tried now…maybe if you spoke to her, you could still reach her."

"Kindness from Raquel Angelov. Will wonders never cease." Tempest offered her an unfamiliar smile…one mulled with defeat and spiced with regret, a look she'd never received from Kallias before. It made it easier to look at him without seething. "I appreciate the offer of hope. But my sister…I don't believe there's any love left in her heart. After what happened with that damned ringmaster, she wouldn't risk being manipulated again. And she hasn't been—she's not on Tenebrae's side because he tricked her or threatened her or made pretty promises. She's there because it's what serves her own ends best."

There was a part of her, very small, that considered telling him of Finn's strange pining—that thought about telling him there might be something more left in Occassio yet. But out of everything she'd shared out of turn tonight, that secret felt like a line she couldn't cross.

Finn so rarely trusted anyone with anything, least of all vulnerability. To give that to someone else, even in the name of hope…it would be like him taking her letter from Kallias and reading it out loud to Adriata.

Instead, she folded her hands tightly behind her back. She didn't bow her head, nor did she kneel—this might have been a prayer, but she wouldn't get on her knees before him and beg.

Not this time.

"Will you help us?" The tip of her tongue burned, acrid and stinging; her sister had once joked she was allergic to saying *please*, and in all honesty, she might have been right.

Had it only been her at risk, she would never have asked at all.

"I will," Tempest said. "I made a promise to your prince that I would protect our people, and I do not offer promises lightly. I just don't see why you would trust your enemy with such a crucial piece of your plans."

She glanced toward the palace, its pale silhouette stark against the gathering clouds. "You are not my enemy."

Now he looked at her with true confusion; he stepped closer, frowning down at her like she was a puzzle missing a middle piece. His voice, soft as a receding wave, washed over her in too-familiar tones: "Then what am I?"

What am I, Raquel?

She backed away so fast her boots nearly caught on the grass; she stumbled out of his reach before catching herself, ignoring the hand he reached out to help.

"You are a means to an end." She turned and stormed toward the cemetery gate, refusing to look back. Refusing to give the tears budding in her eye a place to go. "Nothing more, nothing less."

INTERLUDE

TEMPEST

*G*et them out.

Such a small request from one whose faith had once shifted the skies.

He would do it—exactly what she'd asked. But that did not mean he couldn't intervene in other ways. His own ways.

Ways that would provide an answer to the prayer on every pair of Atlas lips tonight.

Ways that would honor the promises he'd sworn to the man whose face he now wore to walk the world.

The God of Nature had no signet ring. No seal or symbol. He had only the wind and the water and the splendor of a storm unleashed.

But for his fervent faithful, it would be enough.

So he sent his favored courier off with clandestine call in hand, a command sailing to soldier and seafarer alike:

Come home.
Come home.
Come home.

CHAPTER 30

FINN

Finnick Atlas did not make mistakes.

Finnick Atlas made choices.

Some of those choices had proven to be the wrong ones; he would admit to that. Some choices had led him down paths that had put his family at risk; others had endangered his kingdom and his people; others had guided him toward his own destruction.

But all of those choices had been made with his best judgement...even when his judgement wasn't at its best. He had never purposely chosen the worse of two options; he had never weighed the pros and cons and chosen the path off-balance with cons. Even the choices that had ended poorly had been weighed carefully in his palm, testing for the costs they would demand and the rewards they would offer.

What he was about to do…it was different.

This was a mistake. A heap of cons and costs with no real reward waiting at the end.

But when he stepped out into the light of a Sanctaviv sunset, the last flecks of auramantic light settling into place over his body, he promised himself that it was the only mistake he would ever willingly make.

The first, the last…and the worst.

But he had to know.

Sanctaviv was a city he'd barely acquainted himself with, yet even he could tell something had changed. Something in the air that reminded him of the day Kallias had dragged Soren home from Nyx…a rare type of tension that corded through cobblestone streets rather than coiled limbs. A city on guard against a change it might not survive.

Whatever Sanctaviv feared today, it had nothing to do with him. This place had come and gone long before his time…and though they'd met under strained circumstances, the trespass was entirely his. He owed it no reckoning dealt by his hands.

He wasn't here to cause trouble.

He was here to see a show…and to say goodbye.

A few well-aimed winks, charming smiles, and flashes of gold later, someone finally pointed him in the direction of the fairgrounds. Once he wandered out of the maze of buildings, he could spot them on his own—unless some other portion of Sanctaviv housed towering tents capped with colorful flags.

Cassi hadn't lied; the closer he drew to the grassy patch of open land currently occupied by the performing troupe's tents, the air began to smell more and more familiar, sprinkled with salt and seasoned with brine. It nearly overpowered the sweet, nutty aroma of roasted almonds and the sugary scent of kettle corn.

Nearly. Not enough to keep his stomach from begging him to veer off course, reminding him he'd barely eaten today.

Maybe once he tracked down Cassi, he'd snag them a treat to soften the sting of his farewells.

The best thing he could've done was to leave without goodbyes—to let her think he'd gone home after finishing whatever business he'd had here, or that his cowardly lordling self had heeded rumors of the plague and locked himself up in his manor.

But something had kept him from making that choice—the same foreign whisper that had warned him about stepping foot in that theater.

Last time, he'd ignored it. This time, he followed its heeding.

He tried not to think too hard about the common factor in both decisions.

Now…which tent would the performers be hiding out in?

The performances hadn't begun yet—he could tell that much from the occasional flash of costumed splendor between the spectators gathered in clumps around concession stands and souvenir stalls. But every time he tried to follow one of those sparks of color through the dull masses, he lost them in the crush of the crowd.

Damn it. He didn't have time for this.

Glancing about, he caught sight of a tent that didn't have any silhouettes moving around inside—a tent with no light warming its belly.

Good enough.

He ducked beneath the flap, only catching a glimpse of garment racks in the sliver of sunset before he let the flap fall behind him, cloaking him and the circus supplies in comforting shadow.

Thanks to the darkness, he didn't even have to close his eyes to keep anyone from seeing his magic flare—he let it shine freely, lavender and lily-pink blossoming more beautifully than any biomancer's blooms.

But when magic settled into a map, it didn't show him a tent at all. Instead, when he asked it where to find Cassandra Medeis, a pastel imitation of the tailor's shop took form.

"Why are you there?" he muttered under his breath.

Golden-red light cut through his violet vision, soaking the future in a bloody glaze. A disbelieving voice entered the tent before a body did, far more familiar after his many nights spent fiddling in accompaniment to her act: "Lex?"

He turned on his heel, forcing a smile for the white-clad woman at the tent entrance. "Molly! Funny, I was just looking for you."

The artist frowned at him as she leaned through the open space, her hands fisted in either flap. "What're you doing in the dressing tent?"

"Being hopelessly lost," he admitted. "I meant to wish you all luck before the show, but I couldn't track down the performer's tent, it's so damn crowded out there. I promised Cassi I'd come and see it before you all left town…" When

Molly's face fell, he trailed off, a marble of dread rolling down a sluice into his gut. "What's that face for?"

"Have you seen Cassi since the audition?" Molly asked instead of answering, a less-than-subtle evasion.

"No." In all honestly, when he'd decided to come, it had been with the sentimental desire to keep the promise he'd made to her at their last practice. He hadn't even considered checking in sometime between. "Why?"

"She didn't make it."

"They didn't take her?" The surge of outraged indignation caught him off guard; his fist clenched closed with the urge to strangle something. What kind of fools could watch what Cassandra Medeis could do and not *beg* her to join their troupe?

"That's not it." Molly didn't look too pleased either, but she looked less rageful and more resigned. "She didn't make it to the *audition*. We even convinced them to stay open another hour to give her more time, but she never showed."

"Is she all right?" Of course she was; she had to be. If something terrible had happened here, she wouldn't be trapped in his bedroom mirror in the future, hiding behind a cloak of diamond deception.

And even knowing that, he still waited with bated breath for her answer.

"She's fine. It's her damned family that's the problem." Molly's lip curled, accentuating the sparkling stud she wore in it today. "Her selfish sister took one too many *night shifts*, and the day before the audition, she slept so hard that their littlest couldn't wake her. Poor thing had to care for herself alone all day. The brothers said enough's enough, so they traded their day shifts for evening shifts to let Mora rest, but—"

"But that meant Cassi had to stay with her younger sister for the evening," he finished—as always, his guess was good. Molly nodded with a frustrated huff.

Gods, this wasn't the way he'd hoped it would go. He hadn't even considered the idea that Cassi wouldn't make it into the show to perform; between the lingering awe after her first practice with him and watching her improve since, adding more and more daring drops to her aerial routine, the only way she wouldn't have made it was…

Well, this. If she didn't show. If something kept her away.

The unfairness of it dug its fingers into his chest muscles and pulled in opposite directions, tightening them until it became difficult to breathe past his anger.

He'd known she wouldn't get to live that life forever, but he'd thought she would at least get to *taste* it.

"Where is she now?" he asked, even though his divinimancy had already showed him. Better to keep up all appearances, even if he didn't plan on seeing this woman ever again.

"Tailor's shop—or at least she should be. She's working late herself tonight—some special project for her mentor. All hands on deck, I guess." Molly shrugged. "She said she couldn't make it to see us perform because of it, but Sancta knows if that's true. She could just not want to be around it, you know?"

"What about the others?"

"I think her sister has the night off tonight, so—"

"No, not them—*your* others. Minxie and Abbott and Kit."

"Well, I'm here, obviously. Kit, too—I guess their juggler just retired. Minxie and Abbott didn't make it through this round, but the ringmaster did give them letters of recommendation for whatever troupe comes in next, so there's that. He liked their stuff—just didn't have spots." Molly glanced toward the rapidly descending sun. "I have to go, but if you do track Cassi down, just…tell her we're rooting for her."

"I will." *If* he saw her.

This could be a boon from whatever higher power ruled prior to the Medeis siblings…a chance to save himself from what would surely be a fool's errand.

It would've been nice to pretend, just for a moment, that the opportunity held any appeal at all. That he gave the idea of taking the out even a morsel of thought.

But he'd spent his entire life turning his nose up at the designs of deities. Why change that now?

Once the crowd swept over Molly like a paintbrush blending in an errant stroke, Finn walked as fast as he could back to Sanctaviv proper, praying to no one at all that he would make it before the sun dipped its head below the horizon, sleeping soundly beneath the cover of night.

When he reached the porch, the wooden boards creaking curses at his feet as he came to a panting halt before the door, the only welcome he received was from the cruel *Closed* sign dangling against the glass.

But the shop itself wasn't dark—the large display window glowed with cheery gold light, casting his shadow sideways on the porch, fending off the encroaching dusk.

He craned his neck around the mannequins arranged in the shop window, cursing whoever chose to build them at above-average height. But just past the elbow of one of the headless humanoids, he thought he could see familiar curls.

He went back to the door, risking a series of knocks.

"We are closed," called out an older, feminine voice—she spoke with a commanding clip that said there would be no bartering for that to change. "Come back in the morning!"

"Forgive me," he called, cupping his hands around his mouth and pressing them to the door, his plea fogging the glass. "I'm not here for business— I'm here to check on a friend. Is Cassandra Medeis in?"

"No one of that name here."

"Tell her it's Lord Ryder."

A series of whispers, followed by shifting objects and something clattering—then a silhouette plastered itself against the door.

"Back up," came Cassi's muffled voice.

He obeyed immediately, and she cracked open the door—though she greeted him with a smile, no dimples appeared. She wore plain gray trousers and a dull brown tunic; neither color suited her, and as usual,neither garment fit. When she propped her shoulder on the doorframe with her arms wrapped around her middle, the collar of the tunic gaped, revealing a hint of glitter smeared across her collarbone. Similar traces twinkled like shy starbursts in a few of her curls.

"You spoiled lordlings," she said, wiping shooting stars of sweat from her brow. "I suppose you think that business hours are a suggestion."

In the past, she'd been the one *suggesting* that he stop worrying about the posted hours on the door, but he'd come to have a different argument—he didn't have the time to waste on smaller ones. "I'm not here for business. I just came from the fairgrounds—Molly said you missed your audition?"

That demanding tone was the wrong way to go; her paltry smile flattened out, and she stepped back, ducking slightly deeper into the shop. "Something came up."

"What *something* could be worth wasting weeks of practice—and a double-dose of talent?"

"I'm sorry I wasted your time. It wasn't my intention."

"Gods, no, I didn't mean—" No, no time for smaller arguments. "Cassi, why didn't you go?"

Cassi squirmed, glancing over her shoulder. "I just…didn't think that troupe was the best fit, that's all. I—"

"Hogwash," scoffed the other voice that had spoken to him—a woman pushed the door open the rest of the way, robbing Cassi of her shield. The newcomer stood so tall and imperious she brought to mind the pillars framing the outside of the Sanctaviv theater—her soft chin folded as she looked down at him through wire-framed glasses set upon a broad nose, her plump cheeks pale and smooth as carved marble. She wore a sky-blue silk ensemble that wrapped around her generous form, a shade darker than the pale blue eyes that stared through to Finn's soul.

He tugged his illusory costume more tightly around him, the same way one might pull a coat closer to hide from a chill.

"Pasha," Cassi hissed, but her mistress held up one finger—a command to hush.

"She didn't do any such thing," Pasha told him. "She gave up that audition to care for her sister, and let me tell you, I have more than half a mind to throttle those Medeis boys for costing her that chance. Mora, too—Sancta knows the girl works hard, but you and I both know she doesn't have to spend so much time in that sanctuary."

He didn't know that, actually, but he nodded along anyway.

"Wants to be a priestess, but they're supposed to be the selfless sort, aren't they?" Pasha continued, pulling Cassi into a sideways hug, heedless of Cassi's pleas for her to *leave it.* "And here she is, stealing her sister's chance at her ambition for the sake of her own. Unbelievable!"

With a toss of her hands, the lead tailoress turned away and swept gracefully back into her shop; Cassi tightened her hold around her middle, lips pursing, brows drawn close.

Like someone else revealing her truths made her nauseous. Or like she was nursing a heart that hadn't stopped hurting just yet.

"Are you all right?" he prompted, striving for a bit more gentleness.

"Sure I am." But she didn't loosen her self-embrace. "There'll be other chances."

Behind her, heads swiveled and eyes narrowed—besides Pasha, two other tailors were working in the shop, all three huddled around a garment he'd occasionally seen on his prior visits. It had transformed slowly from a slip of silk to something far grander, but without his glasses, he couldn't make out all the details—just an amalgamation of sparkle and splendor that suggested a very wealthy client had put in a custom order.

The looks the tailors swapped between them—and shared with him, when they realized he was looking—suggested there would not, in fact, be other chances. Or, if there were, that something would crop up to keep her from seizing them.

"Cassi," said Pasha, "why don't you take the rest of the night off?"

Genuine shock struck Cassi across the face; she whirled away from Finn to face her mentor, who smiled at her over the shoulder of the mannequin. "But I—"

"Don't you *but* me," chided Pasha. "I'll pay you the full wage for the evening—go show that handsome beau of yours a good time. If you pick up your feet, you can still make the show."

A flutter of tension pinched a wrinkle between Cassi's shoulder blades. "Oh, I don't know, I—"

"Cassandra." Pasha crossed the room again to fold Cassi's hands between hers, squeezing—the look the tailoress gave her silenced her protests. "We've all heard the whispers…if I had to guess, it won't be long before that illness strikes out at Sanctaviv. And if it does, there won't be any shows to see for a time. Take the night."

Cassi's shoulders rose and fell in a deep, defeated breath. "All right, all right—if you insist." She glanced over her shoulder to Finn, forcing a smile…still no dimples. "If Your Lordship is willing to be seen with a lowly tailoress, that is?"

"I suppose I could bend beneath my station for the evening," he decided out loud—she rolled her eyes, and a dimple finally took the stage, peering out from the wings of her smile.

His throat strained, and he coughed into his elbow, clearing away the pressure.

That damned dimple.

"Wait," Pasha ordered before he could escape with Cassi in tow—before he could find something else to look at. "If you think I'm letting you strut out of here in that outfit, my dear, you're mistaken. You'll be taking this."

Let me guess…

The tailoress rested her hand on the stunning piece in the center of the shop.

Lovely.

This time, Cassi shook her head so fiercely that he feared she'd shake it straight off her neck. "Pasha, absolutely not. I can't possibly—I mean—it's for—"

"It's for *you*," Pasha interrupted; the other two tailors nodded, smiling mischievously. "It's always been for you. I hoped it would be your quitting present—oh, don't make that face. I'd keep you forever if I could, but we both know it's not what you want. Anyhow, it's yours, and you'll wear it, and if you want to thank me, you'll come back with a good story to tell about this evening."

Cassi's next breath shuddered with emotion; she quickly dashed at her eyes with the backs of her hands, then looked to Finn, smiling broadly. "I know a great view…it even has enough room for two fools, if we squeeze."

No divinimancy necessary to guess where this night would lead them. He forced a smile in return, stepping backward over the doorjamb. "I'll meet you there?"

And there it was…that wicked grin she never failed to flash at him. The mask that had tricked the Trickster Prince. The blade that stopped the heart of a vengeful god.

"I'll be the one in purple," she said.

CHAPTER 31

FINN

The stars gathered in droves to witness Finnick Atlas's final fall.

But much to the disappointment of their prying eyes, he didn't take that fall right away—instead, he teased them by sitting on the very edge of the roof, dangling his feet above the alley below.

If he closed his eyes, he could pretend he sat on an Atlas rooftop instead, that all of this—the gods, the war, the deaths, the schemes—had been nothing but a bad dream, and he'd abandoned his bed to cure his lingering fear with fresh air.

But even a deep drink of night air didn't unknot the tangle in his stomach.

Finn drew his legs up to his chest, but the pressure didn't help—it only shoved that knot up into his throat, choking out his attempts at even breaths. He tucked his face against his knees, burying a curse in them before he let them fall again, feet plunging into open air.

After this, there would be no rooftop adventures or fiddle music or fine clothes torn with the tip of a dagger to buy a tailoress's attention.

There would be no hot chocolate in wine glasses or cheating at card games or peanut butter cookie cravings.

No laughter. No daydreams. No stage shows or tightropes or champagne smiles.

No siblings.

When he returned to his time, he would be returning to a kingdom relying on him to keep it alive…a kingdom filled with people who wished him dead. To a family only he could protect now…a family already half-destroyed, teetering on the edge of compete annihilation.

That wasn't a game. That was real. And it wasn't the sort of game he could win with a hidden ace or a bump of the chess table.

Or by tricking a tailoress into sabotaging herself with simple, silly questions.

And yet, somehow…this rooftop, this ending, this revealing of his hand…it didn't feel like a win.

For the first time in his life, cheating felt like something to be ashamed of.

But this—the guilt, the reluctance, the urge to shake out every card shoved into the creases of his sleeves so he could claim a clean victory—all of it came too late.

And it shouldn't have bothered him this much.

He had chosen this game for himself—had stood on this very rooftop and decided against the safer scheme. He had gambled on anger, on payback, on conning a girl with the same cruel streak as her future self.

He had not gambled on Cassandra Medeis.

"Told you I had a good view," bragged a singsong voice behind him.

For a moment, he considered not turning around.

But that would have been cowardice. And maybe he would have been all right with that, but his magic didn't give him the choice—when he blinked, a flash of pink struck behind his eyes, leaving the imprint of a vision behind.

And gods, what a vision.

Cassi stood behind him with her hands behind her back, her smile tilted at a nervous angle, so deep that it dug out her second dimple. The stars, wretched meddlers that they were, had granted some of their shine to her eyes—they shimmered with mischief and marvel, the impish combination that made her a rarity in this world…and every other.

It probably should have frightened him, the way he trailed his gaze over her freckles and knew he could have spent far longer tracing out their patterns than he ever had observing the constellations. And that was coming from a man whose mind easily lapsed into boredom.

But it was the little details that sapped the moisture from his mouth and left him scrambling to regain his composure, his heart leaping and falling on subsequent beats, a tumble that spoke more truth than his tongue ever had.

The sparkling rhinestones in her hair…and her eyebrows. The crystalline slippers peeking out from beneath her gown, their facets shattering the moonlight and casting its fragments across the rooftop. And the gown…

Damn that gown.

Its silk brocade bodice clung corset-like to her torso, like lavender foiling painted over her with a precise hand. But where the skirt flared out, bits of color invaded the silvery shade of purple.

Not fabric. Not stitching.

Clusters of gems.

They cascaded from waist to hem, a starry sky of a different sort; they increased in number the further down the skirt one looked until they crusted the silk entirely. Silver swallowed by shimmering color.

A music box ballerina long-buried in a dragon's hoard, its jewels sticking to her skirt when someone finally plucked her out.

All this, his magic revealed in the span of a blink. And a blink was not long enough—a blink could not buy him the time he needed to compose himself.

But it would have to do. He had no reason to stall.

A quick end to a long game.

It would hurt. He couldn't pretend otherwise. But the faster he dealt the wound, the faster it would heal.

He stood and turned, lips already rounded in a whistle—even so, it stuttered a bit when he laid eyes on her in truth, a broken bit of birdsong ringing through the night.

Play your damn part, Finn.

"*You've* got the view?" he laughed, shoving his hands into his pockets. "I think mine wins."

Her face screwed up in embarrassment, and she hid her face behind her fingers. The bag resting on her hip jounced with the movement—its hole-riddled, ragged canvas contrasted sharply with the rest of her outfit. "Oh, stop."

"I mean it." He crossed the roof and pried her fingers from her face, tickling the stubborn ones that tried to stay put; she squeaked in protest, but released her hold. He pressed her knuckles to his lips, smirking at her from beneath his lashes. "The moonlight suits you."

She wrinkled her nose, freckles melding together. "It's the dress."

"It's *not* the dress." If it was the dress, he wouldn't have come tonight in the first place. "So…what're we doing up here? I can't even see the tents."

"I know." She dropped the bag and began rifling through it; as she removed the contents one by one, his heart began to slow and skip again, trepidation spilling down the column of his spine.

A handmade quilt discolored with age. A tin with the lid tightly shut. Two chipped mugs. And last of all…

Moonlight nearly blinded him as it ricocheted off the pinkish glass bottle, and Cassi's beaming grin finished the job. "What show's complete without something sweet to drink?"

A rickety lighthouse balcony. Foam running off the lip of a freshly uncorked bottle. Champagne and strawberries and a hint of chocolate.

"Hey…what's wrong? Your face got strange."

"Nothing," he whispered—then shook his head, stretching his grin out as far as he could. "Just wondering how long we have until clerics come running around the corner looking for you."

Her jaw dropped. "I *purchased* this, thank you very much—I even used the gold you gave me."

"Sure, sure—whatever you say."

"I *did!*" she giggled—*double dimples, champagne bubbles, "Finn, can I kiss you?"*

When she offered him the bottle, he tried to take it—he really did. But his hand wouldn't budge from his side.

"What're you giving it to me for?" he asked, biding time.

"You think I know how to open a champagne bottle?" She shook it at him—he refrained from telling her how poor of an idea that was. With that one rattle, that champagne cork had just gone from a harmless projectile to a deadly weapon. "You're the one with fancy tastes."

"You're the one who *bought* it—didn't you have a plan?"

"Yes." She blinked at him expectantly. "To have you open it."

Too simple by two for her, but hey—she was still early in her career. "I see. And if I refuse?"

Cassi frowned, looking down at the bubbles cheerfully leaping from the bottom of the bottle to the neck. "Well, then, I guess I just wasted two months' worth of tips on a pretty bottle. What a shame. I do hope your conscience can bear the weight…"

"Wow. Really? A guilt trip? That's beneath you."

"Nothing's beneath me." She hovered her own hand over her head. "I'm very short."

"You said it, not me," he chuckled. "All right, fine. Guilt trip taken." *Destination reached.* "Gimme that."

When she offered the bottle again, he forced his unwilling hand to reach out and grip the neck…and as his fingers closed around it, they trembled. Tingled.

A refusal to function he hadn't suffered from since he'd taken her magic and shaped it as his own.

If she'd handed him a viper with its fangs primed to strike, its bite pumping venom into his veins, it wouldn't have been half as effective at paralyzing him. His fingers spasmed shut, but they wouldn't release—they wouldn't go through the memorized motions to pop the cork.

"Go on," she called—she'd turned away and crouched down, spreading out the blanket until the corners were even. She took off her shoes and set them on two corners diagonal to each other to weigh it down. "Just don't point it at my ass."

"I am a *gentleman*. I would *never*," he said—thankfully, offense was a part he could play without any input from his greater consciousness. He could only stare at his reflection in the glass.

A quick blow, a quicker recovery.

Somehow, he managed to get his other hand to work, untwisting the rose-gold wire wrapped around the cork.

This bottle held nothing but sparkling wine—the memories, the misery, that all lived in his head. And if it lived in his head, he could command it—he could control it.

Small losses.

He was in control of this con. And after he popped the cork, foam spilling over the bottle's lip and soaking his knuckles in sweetness, he proved it.

He brought it to his mouth and took a sip.

Despite the part he'd cast himself in for this con, he didn't know enough about wine or its bubbling cousin to name the notes buried in its flavor, though he did consider himself a cocoa connoisseur. To him, champagne often tasted of overripe fruit, a cloying mix of sweet and sour that didn't lean deeply enough into the sour.

But the bottle he'd offered Fidget prior to the fireworks show had been different—though he'd chosen it by shopkeep recommendation, it had been perfectly balanced, a dance of citrus and sugar that made him realize that actually, he didn't dislike champagne…his parents just had bad taste.

Or they only shelled out for the cheap stuff whenever they held events at the palace.

Cassi had not chosen the cheap stuff. Even without tasting it, he would have known by the frightening thinness of the glass itself…and the authentic gold foil on the label.

A guilt trip well guided. Shame bubbled in his stomach, souring the almond-and-amaretto sweetness of the wine.

She could have cared for her family with this—could have cared for *herself* with this. And instead, she'd tried to get something she'd thought worthy of his *fancy tastes*. Something that would make him happy.

And in exchange, he was about to break her heart.

Or maybe that was conceited of him. Maybe when he told her she'd never see him again, she'd say her goodbyes with a smile and a shrug of her shoulders, remembering him only as a lazy lordling who'd been slightly more generous than others of his kind.

"Cassi," he croaked when he lowered the bottle, "you didn't have to get this. I would've been happy to just—"

A finger pressed to his lips.

"Shh," she scolded. "The guilt trip's done. I bought it for me as much as you, so hand it over."

He smiled wryly against her finger, passing the bottle back—she tipped her head back and swallowed two gulps before sitting down on the blanket and patting the spot beside her. "Come on. We've got some time before the real show starts."

"Oh, yeah? What can I expect from this special, secret show?" His shoes scuffed on the roof as he lowered himself to sit beside her. "Should I have brought my fiddle?"

"No, no. It's not *my* show." She settled closer to him, shoulder pressed against his—though she didn't shiver, goosebumps prickled through his thin sleeve. She hadn't worn a cloak over her dress. "You could call it a finale, I guess."

"A finale with no performance beforehand?"

"Will you stop with the questions?" she laughed, swaying back and forth to bump her shoulder into his. "You'll ruin it!"

Finn grinned down at her, bumping her in retaliation. "Suprises make me nervous, all right?"

"Facing your fears is good for you." She patted his knee—this time, her cold fingers left no room for debate. He tugged off his cloak and offered it to her.

She blinked at it. "You want me to hold that for you, Your Lordship?"

"I want you to *wear* it, Your Weirdship. You're freezing."

She held up the bottle and one of the chipped mugs. "That's what the champagne is for."

"The champagne is cold, I—Cass. What are you doing?"

She'd started pouring the champagne into one of the mugs; she looked up with a frown, the starry gems in her hair twinkling with merry abandon. "Well, if we keep drinking right from the bottle, we're not going to be able to climb down from this roof safely. I'll tell you that fortune for free."

"No, I mean…" This had to be some kind of cosmic prank. "Wine in a cocoa mug?"

"It's what we had in the shop," she defended herself. "I know it's not what the nobles do—"

"I'm not making fun of it," he assured her; he picked up the other mug and held it out, a silent request for her to pour. "It's just funny. I do this thing…my sister and I, we drink hot cocoa out of wine glasses. It's a happy memory, that's all."

One he hadn't expected to visit here.

She grinned so wide that her nose wrinkled; crinkles even formed around her eyes as she poured him his own mug of fermented fizz. "Hot cocoa in wine glasses? On purpose? I mean, my thing was out of necessity…"

He groaned, but somewhere in between, it turned into a laugh. A real one; real enough that he realized just how rarely he'd laughed in truth these days. "Are you making fun of *me* now?"

"I mean, for the sake of my reputation, I don't actually think I can be seen with you. Word might get out I associate with eccentrics." She went to stand; still laughing, he snagged her hand and tugged her back down.

Maybe it was the sip of champagne tricking his body into tipsy truth—maybe the taste alone had loosened his tongue. But when she fell to her seat, dimples starting to vanish as she opened her mouth to protest, he reached out and pressed his thumb against them, holding them in place.

"You know," he said, the soft words escaping of their own accord, "I think you might be the only person I can laugh with. *Really* laugh with."

Her dimples deepened under his thumb, her grin softening into a guarded smile. "You flatter me."

"It's not flattery." It was the truth, horrifying as that might be. "I'm serious. You make me feel like…me."

She gazed at him for too long; too long without laughing herself, too long without making some quip. Instead, she gazed into his eyes, her own gentling with emotion he desperately feared to name.

"I'm glad," she murmured. "Everyone deserves to be able to live as their truest self…even lazy, spoiled lordlings."

Even wicked, wish-making girls.

Even hateful, heartless goddesses.

He cleared his throat, snatching his hand back like he'd touched his thumb to a stovetop, not her skin. He rubbed the back of his own neck instead, pushing the bottle closer to her. "Hopefully you'll forget that by morning."

"Oh, I don't think so, Your Lordship." That smug little smile…that was another commonality between her, Fidget, and Occassio. Between fact, figment, and future. "Nothing about you is forgettable."

He'd been afraid of that.

This hadn't been the plan—the plan had been to congratulate her on her role, say goodbye, then go find Braeden while she was busy at the show. Even when making a mistake, he couldn't force himself into foolishness without coming up with some sensible excuse—he'd hoped that if he could track down Braeden, he could find one last thing to use against Tenebrae in the present.

Instead, here he sat, the taste of champagne buzzing between his teeth, getting far too close to a girl who held the key to his potential demise in her clever fingers.

History repeating itself before *history* had even happened.

But as long as he was making mistakes…

He fit his thumb back into that dimple. Teased it until the second came out to play.

"Stop, that tickles," she laughed—then blinked, eyes widening enough to catch the reflection of the stars when he set his other hand to her other cheek, drawing her in. Breathing her in. Lilac and sugar burying shame six feet under.

She wasn't the woman who'd made it her immortal life's mission to ruin him, not yet. And here, he wasn't a prince, wasn't a villain, wasn't a trickster.

Just a thief and a fool sharing space on a rooftop. And for once, he wanted to pretend his life was exactly that simple.

Because the Trickster God wasn't playing any trick at all when he whispered, "You should tell me to leave."

"Why?"

"Because if you don't, I'm going to kiss you." And if he did, he'd be well and truly done for.

But that was the thing about fools. They didn't care about things like consequences. Not when a craving like this kicked in.

She'd kissed him before. But it hadn't been real; hadn't been *her*.

Just once. He wanted to know what the real thing felt like—just once.

"If I ask you to leave," she said slowly, "you'll leave."

"Yes."

She shifted until she sat knee to knee with him, her silhouette blacking out the stars. It didn't matter. He could chart the constellations by the sparkle in her eyes.

"What if I said something else?"

For one horrible heartbeat, he wondered if he was about to be made fun of. Too far to turn back now, regardless. "Like what?"

Her smile was nothing short of diabolical. "Like *stop dawdling and kiss me already before I push you off this roof, you fool.*"

She didn't know the half of it. Had not even seen half the fool he truly was.

But in the scale-tipping second when his lips had just begun to brush hers, his mind muddled by the phantom shine of champagne flutes and the softest strain of fiddle music, time took its chance to make sure he couldn't share her ignorance.

A whistling scream. A momentary pause as he broke away from her, searching for the source, not thinking to search the sky until—

A thunderous explosion. A spray of color.

He stopped breathing.

And he waited.

He waited, because that couldn't have been what he thought it was. That couldn't have been…

Cassi gasped in delight, snatching up his hand and tugging him clumsily to his feet—he swayed in place, watching numbly as she pointed and said, "There's our show."

And as another firework fired off into the sky, he realized that he hadn't just made a mistake.

He'd ruined everything.

"You are now the only other person to know about my secret viewing roof," she told him, leaning in and squeezing his arm. "I hope it impresses."

What she'd said to him on Patch's ship…

"I told you one hundred and sixty-three lies about myself when I was Fidget…Somehow, you awful, clever boy, you still managed to pick out the one gods-damned truth that mattered to me."

The lighthouse—the fireworks. That had been the truth that mattered to her.

As Fidget, she'd told him she'd gone to see them with her siblings…that she'd watched these shows with them.

But she'd lied.

She'd meant *this*—this night. This roof. This show.

The one truth that mattered to her…the night that she spent here with *him*.

He was going to be sick.

With every explosion of color across the sky, color in equal measure drained from his face, all warmth seeping from his cheeks until he could have dunked his head into an ice bath to drive *away* the chill. The sip of champagne climbed further back up his throat, drowning his breath in its bubbling bite.

And with a finality that reworked him, remade him, a wave of disgust drowned every other part of him in sickening rage.

The same damned game. The same damned trick. The same damned weakness.

He owed her nothing. Least of all kindness—least of all—least of all—

Gods, what had he been *thinking?*

He ripped his arm away from her, kicking over the quilt as he paced to the roof's edge. "I'm leaving."

"What?" She laughed at first, like he'd made a joke—like he *was* the joke. It only made him angrier.

"I'm leaving," he snapped. "I shouldn't have come at all."

"What?" she said again, but this time she whirled to face him—this time she looked anxious, appalled, distress wringing her fingers around the champagne bottle. "What's wrong? I didn't—is it the—what did I do wrong?"

Emotion hardened like a stone in his throat, loathing that frantic fear, loathing that he'd caused it—but he gripped it with everything he had and *threw*, refusing to feel it. He let it fall so far that he could no longer even *imagine* what it felt like to want this to be different.

Hate. He needed *hate*.

"Nothing." A painful, wrathful chuckle scraped against his throat. "Everything. Getting to know you, being kind to you—it was a mistake, all of it, and tonight…this was the worst of all of them. I have to go."

He expected many different reactions—flowing tears, betrayed rage, maybe even an actual attempt to shove him off the rooftop.

But Cassandra Medeis never did what he expected. So instead, she stared back at him, and a look of bitter understanding passed over her face.

Understanding, when no part of this ought to make any sense to her for centuries yet.

"I knew it," she said.

"Knew what?"

"That this was coming." She shook her head; laughed with such wretchedness he had to look her over from head to toe to make sure he hadn't been fooled again. When he did, she pointed at him. "That! You look at me like *that* sometimes, and—and sometimes you speak to me like you're so angry, and this whole time I've been thinking you had to be seeing someone else's face in mine, that I brought up bad memories of some other person, because—I mean, I haven't done anything to you!"

Now *that* was a joke. "You have *no idea*—"

"You're right! I don't. I have absolutely no idea why you—" She huffed out a shaky exhale, lowering her hands to the body of the bottle, her knuckles paling.

"You hate me," she whispered. "I just don't know *why*."

She would, one day. But for today…

"I don't hate you," he said. "I don't care enough about you to hate you. I mean, come on—look at you. Some wannabe performer in a charity dress? What's there to care about?"

She blinked. Stared blankly. "You said—"

"Sweetheart, I say all kinds of things to all kinds of people. Keeps me from getting bored." He smirked at her—not teasing or flirtatious this time. It was his best scoundrel smile. The one he used when a con was over to really drive the whole thing home. "It's just a bit of fun, you know?"

Her chin trembled. "Fun."

Gods, she sounded so small. So dazed. Like he'd struck her instead of slighted her.

"You were just a game." Dismissive. Haughty. "And hardly my first…though definitely one of my easiest. Which is exactly why I've grown bored of you."

And there they were…the tears he'd been waiting for.

It should have been gratifying.

It wasn't.

"You can't…" To her credit, she steeled her chin and held back her tears. She even added a little anger to the mix. "You can't treat me like that. I won't be made a fool."

This part, he'd practiced—this part, he had played out a hundred times since he'd caught Fidget picking a lock in the palace hall and called her by her true name.

"Oh, Cassi." He walked to her, gently tipping her chin up with a bent finger, smiling lovingly down at her. "You already are."

Her breathing sped up. Her eyes no longer shimmered—they burned, baleful and broken, a starless sky with no moon to brighten it.

The sound of shattering glass broke his stare from hers, his eyes darting down to her hands.

Her *bleeding* hands.

Both her skirt and his shoes were soaked, covered in champagne…and thin, pinkish shards of the broken bottle she'd been clutching. Her hands dripped scarlet, more of those shards driven deep into her fingers and palms.

For half a second, he forgot himself.

He'd heard people compare hatred to seeing red—that it blinded and befuddled, blurring everything except for what existed right in front of them, and they often didn't realize the consequences of what they'd done under its influence until it was far too late.

He'd never been that way. Hatred had been a companion of his for so long that its company never interfered with his good sense.

But that blood, those wounds—the shuddering sob at the end of her exhale—those painted a crimson vignette around his vision.

His hands reached for her of their own accord, hate freezing into horror, his only instinct to get those crumbs of glass out of her nimble, talented hands. "Oh gods. Cassi—"

"Go away," she choked, stumbling back a step, snatching her hands out of his reach—she didn't even look down at them, though they had to be stinging something fierce, the wine finding another way into her bloodstream. "If this is a game, fine—you win, I fold, whatever you need to hear. *Go away.*"

This was what he wanted—so why couldn't he move? Why couldn't he leave? "You're bleeding—"

And then, for the first time, Cassandra Medeis truly helped him.

Because when he took another step forward, she sneered in his face. A vicious cut of her teeth he recognized in his very core. Proof that, despite all illusions and impish smiles, she would one day become something dangerous. Something devious and deadly.

"I am bleeding," she agreed, voice steeped in boiling rage. "And you will be too if you don't *leave me alone!*"

He didn't know how she'd get down from this rooftop with her hands like that. He didn't know how long she had left before the story he'd been told of the gods' origins would come to pass. And he didn't know if she'd forget him and his borrowed face before they met again—if she'd only just now, in the present, realized that the lord who'd broken her heart on this rooftop was also the prince who'd sealed her away.

But there was one thing he did know: that regardless of the foolish whims that forced his hands into fists, the knuckles aching to catch her wrists and tell her he hadn't meant any of it, that he wanted to help, that he had never meant to see her bleed…it was time to go home.

So without another word, Finn turned his back and left her there.

He didn't look back as he slipped through shadowed Sanctaviv streets, asking the light to flee from him this time, transforming himself into a slip of darkness moving through a monochromatic maze.

He didn't look back when he realized how empty those streets were, despite the fact that the show had ended.

He didn't look back when chants of "Heretic, heretic" echoed through the streets…not even when his eye caught on a procession dragging a girl who looked a bit too similar to the other Medeis siblings into the city square.

He didn't look back after catching a glimpse of the pile of wood in the dry fountain…or the stake stabbed into the stone at Sancta's feet.

He didn't look back. Not even when the chanting grew manic. Not even when screams of "Mora!" rose above the frenzy…two male voices, one childish voice, and one…

One that sounded an awful lot like Cassi.

Finn picked up his pace, terror prickling at the back of his neck, an urging to *run run run* until he reached the tailor's shop, slamming his palms against the window, not caring if those still working within happened to see—

And when a roar bellowed over the crowd like vengeance given voice, a war cry that his very spirit recognized as Death calling down a reckoning, he flung himself through that window like his life depended on it.

Heat blazed against the small of his back as he dove into the embrace of his own magic…

And just before he tumbled into his own room, he heard the sickening hush of Sanctaviv meeting its end.

Then carpet. Then the scent of hot cocoa gone stale. Then wood, solid and shining, speeding toward his face—

He barely caught himself on the footboard of his own bed, heaving in breaths of familiar air, the scent of the past and the stickiness of champagne still clinging to his clothes.

He dispelled the magic-crafted clothing with a shaky curse, his skin itching madly until the illusory threads reverted back to his own soft sweater and lounging pants. Normally he kept the clothes he created, but not…not those. Not this time.

Not with champagne stains and glass-torn stitches left behind.

He kept his gaze fixed firmly on the gleaming wood of his footboard, tightening his grip, anchoring himself back in his own time—reminding himself over and over again that the doom that had come for Sanctaviv had not touched him in truth. That even if it had, gods knew if he would have actually died.

Warmth flooded his nostrils. Moments later, a drip of scarlet landed on the footboard and lazily somersaulted toward the floor.

The instant he registered the sight of his own blood, the consequences of his actions slammed him over the head with pain.

Agony rippled outward from the center of his skull, flowing down his shoulders and torso, all the way down to his toes. And when he bent against it, gritting his teeth against a cry, another wave came—

And another.

And another.

His knees screamed out as he crashed to the ground, bent in half, a silent scream wrenching his jaw open as he bent into the pain. Salt and iron flooded his mouth as he coughed, mingling with the leftover tang of champagne—he couldn't tell if he'd coughed up blood or if the fount from his nose had leaked in.

Chronomancy, punishing him for his theft at last.

It took several minutes for the pain to abate, clearing just enough for him to think again—to remember where he was, who he was, and who he was meant to be.

Limbs shaking, body weak and sore and cringing at every movement, he tried to stand—and failed. Instead, his exhausted muscles dropped him back on his seat, a firm order from his body to *sit still and rest.*

He couldn't argue his way out of what his body wanted. He'd learned that when this magic first started invading, forcing quivers into his hands and migraines into his head.

So he stayed on his seat. Scooted backward until his back found something smooth and cold to lean against. Sank against it with a long groan.

It wasn't until something stirred behind him that he realized he'd propped himself up against the mirror.

"That looked bad," Occassio murmured to him.

He couldn't muster more than a grunt—not a show of petulance. Just simple exhaustion.

"Where did you just come from?"

There was no point in lying—it'd already happened. She couldn't change it now. "Fireworks. The rooftop."

"Mm." Her voice roughened in understanding; anger, too, but it didn't reach out to stir his own this time. It simply existed, a reflection of what he'd wielded against her that night. "That was the night we got our magic."

"I heard." He'd never forget the sound of Death made manifest in a city square—he never wanted to hear it again.

"I wasn't there," Occassio said—so softly that he shut his eyes and indulged in a bit of imagination, letting himself picture her human self with her back pressed to his, not the goddess watching him through layers of glass. "I wasn't home when they came for her, because I was out there with *you.*"

"Is that what this has all been about?" A vague gesture at his temple, an attempt to sum up their entire feud in one loose-limbed wave. "Because instead of being dragged through the streets by clerics, you were drinking champagne and watching fireworks with me?"

A harsh, ragged scoff. "I'm not *that* petty, Finn."

He profoundly disagreed.

"It is strange, though," she continued…another shift, and the glass at his back warmed, like she really was sitting against him. After a moment, her nails began to scrape down the glass; not the malicious clawing she'd used to try and torture him those first several days, but an absent stroking, a thoughtless habit.

He could have said something awful to make her stop, to make her retreat—he could have turned and shoved the mirror over—but in all honesty, he didn't have the strength. His spine kept quivering, a structure about to collapse on itself. The added support of her back was all that kept him from curling into a ball on the floor and passing out right there.

"What's strange?"

"To know someone's out there ruining your life, and you can't do a thing about it, because it's already over—it's already happened for you." A cracked, faintly manic laugh. "You already bear the wounds. The memories. And gods know who you'd be if it changed."

He tried not to think about the broken bottle buried in her hands—or whether he'd ever seen those scars polka-dotting her palms.

Like she said, it didn't matter. He'd already done it. And the girl he'd done it to…she was long gone.

"If this is another guilt trip," he muttered, leaning his head back against the glass, "don't waste your time. I did nothing that you didn't deserve—nothing you didn't already do to me."

Now that manic chuckle pitched into a wild giggle. "You still don't get it, do you?"

"Get what?" Irritation boiled beneath his skin, and he twisted to face her. She actually did have her back to the mirror—but when he turned, she did too, peering over her shoulder with eyes of shimmering ichor and a smile primed to kill.

"To me," she said, so softly he could've knit baby blankets from her voice, "*you* did it first, Finn."

He blinked at her. "I didn't…"

"Think about it." She turned aside again, letting her head fall against the mirror with a dull thud. "You went to my past—that little con you played, you played it on me long before I became a goddess…*centuries* before you were born."

Another giggle, but this one sounded like glass bottles breaking, like blood staining a lavender dress. "The sweetness, the stealing, the cookies, the fancy outfits...the champagne I spilled on you that first day, even. The game you lost so badly? I learned it from *you*."

His heart forgot how to beat.

And he just...stared, for a time. Stared and stared and stared, because what else was there to do?

Nothing could save him from this: the stomach-dropping, nauseating realization that broke him right down to his bones. That marred him in mind and in memory.

Because she was *gods-damned right.*

No wonder he hadn't seen Fidget's deception coming. No wonder he'd been so perfectly fooled.

Nobody was good enough to steal from Finnick Atlas—nobody was good enough to con him, either. In the wake of Occassio's betrayal, he'd been left shaken, terrified, convinced her magic had robbed him of his one true talent...

But he'd been wrong.

One person *was* good enough to con Finnick Atlas—one person knew exactly how to steal from him, even with his pockets sewn to repel pickpocketing hands and his senses always alert for the slightest twitch of his coat or coinpurse.

Himself.

And now there were two—because he had taught it to her. Had guided her through the motions of dipping her fingers past that stitching—had shown her how to con the cleverest of minds, even those trained to see the signs of an impending knife in the back.

Finnick Atlas, creator of his own downfall.

"You went back and taught Cassandra Medeis to con. Then she conned you the same way—which taught *you* how to do it, because you hadn't gone back yet." Maybe she laughed again, or maybe she groaned—it was difficult to tell with the ringing in his ears. But he heard the taut tone of dark amusement when she finally stopped, wheezing out, "Isn't it awful?"

Something snapped—not a bone or a branch. Not a temper or a tortured mind.

Something snapped deep within him, something attached to his mind and heart, flooding him with a sensation not unlike the slaphappy sleepiness one experienced when staying awake all through the night...

And then he was laughing.

Not faked, not forced, not a trick or a tool.

He laughed. *Hard.*

Maybe it was hysteria. Maybe he'd finally cracked.

Or maybe his body recognized that if he didn't start laughing, something worse would come out instead. Something he couldn't let the goddess see.

The goddess who laughed with him, her own giggles roughened with exhaustion.

"So awful," he groaned through his laughter. "Gods, Cassi, what are we *doing?*"

"You want honesty?"

"If you can remember how to use it."

Another thud against the mirror, lighter this time—she muttered an *ow*, and he realized she must have tried to elbow him, forgetting the glass between them.

He only laughed harder.

"Honestly," she repeated, her own giggles shaking the glass in its frame, "I don't even *know* anymore."

Unable to catch his breath, laughter robbing his lungs with repeated assaults, he finally turned to face her—he tapped on the glass, a silent invitation.

One she heeded.

When she turned to fully face him, she was back to the Occassio he was used to—not quite Cassi, not quite Fidget. Now that he'd seen her real face, he knew Fidget's had actually been closer to the truth than Occassio's—though Fidget had still been tiny, she'd filled out all her sharper edges with roundness, a gentling of her features that echoed Cassi's—what Cassi might have looked like had she not been half-starving in order to pay for her passions and care for her family.

Occassio, while she too looked healthier, had kept some of those piercing pieces—in fact, she'd altered them to almost otherworldly angles, a standard of beauty set by faerie tales and show makeup.

And abruptly, instead of laughter, words poured unsummoned from his mouth: "You looked beautiful that night, you know."

She smiled, and he saw just enough of her true self in it to swallow hard— to pull himself back from the surface of the mirror, recognizing it for what it was.

A pretty thing to lure him in; a predator playing at the part of prey.

"I know," she murmured.

"Are you going to return the compliment?"

She snorted softly, turning aside—but her smile spread, double dimples coming out to ruin his day. "I prefer your real face."

As he did hers, but he didn't say so.

"Can I ask…" He hesitated, unsure if he wanted to know—but he'd already dragged her gaze back to him, and if he didn't ask, she'd pester him until he did. "What happened to them?"

"To who?"

"Minxie. And Molly, and Kit, and Abbott. Did they…?"

The answer came in her crumpling face; a pain so plainly spelled out that he could have read it with his eyes shut. But she dismissed it with a harsh huff, her features going cold. "Molly and Kit, they were far enough on the outskirts, and the show packed up to move out right after the fireworks…they were far enough away before the cataclysm. Abbott and Minxie weren't so lucky."

Damn it. "I'm sorry."

The last time he'd practiced with them all, they'd been laughing, teasing— promising each other that if they didn't make it, there was always next time. That the good thing about dreams was that they had no time limit.

He had disagreed, privately, but let them have their hope…now, he wished he'd said it, and said it without room for argument, and kept them hours longer into the night until they had no chance of failing. Or that he'd gone to the ringmaster and paid him handsomely to take them in spite of his lack of need for a contortionist or a musician, even if it meant he traded them off to another troupe later.

Dreams had no time limit. But life did.

Even for the young and ambitious—even for those who thought they had all the time in the world.

Death cared not for dreams.

"Neither did Pasha," she added, though he hadn't asked. "None of the other tailors. None of my other…friends." She cleared her throat, a crooked grin slashing across her face. "For a long time, I thought you died there too. I couldn't even be happy about it, you know that? Even after what you said, what you did…I shed tears for you."

"What can I say? I played a good trick," he muttered lamely.

Everyone—she'd lost *everyone* that night.

And among the rest, she'd cried for him.

Maybe. Unless that was another lie.

"The best trick." She leaned back, crossing her legs, her gaze wandering to something behind him—something further away than his bedroom wall. "Not many cons can fool us both, can they?"

"No." Now that his body felt functional again, he forced himself to stand—to grab the cover for the mirror. "I suppose they can't."

She tracked the movement, and he tried very hard to pretend he didn't see the flicker of fear in her eyes. "This is it, then?"

A pang struck him in the heart. Not pain, but…*something*. Something that begged his hand to cast aside the sheet and his rage and his plan, good sense be damned.

In all this time, he'd never really thought that a permanent victory would be possible. Imprisonment, sure—vengeance, of course. But the kind of victory that meant saying goodbye to the one mind that had proven itself worthy to stand against his? The kind that promised every game he played after would never satisfy, leaving him hunting for puzzle after puzzle, chasing the high of unraveling her lullaby lies from her treacherous truths?

The kind that meant he would never see her double-dimpled smile again?

Even with the power of prophecy pounded so deep into his skull that he couldn't separate cleverness from clairvoyance, he hadn't expected that. And he hadn't expected that it would *hurt*.

But he'd endured worse pain. He'd endure this, too.

One day, maybe he'd even find a way to forgive himself for it.

"Goodbye, Cassi," he murmured.

And with a flourish he didn't feel, he settled the cover over the gleaming prison…knowing that if all went to plan, he'd never open it again.

Where no one could see him, where there was no risk of it being used against him…he leaned his forehead against the sheet-covered glass. Squeezed his eyes shut. Tried to understand the hollow place yawning open in his chest.

He'd told the truth. He had no need of her now—in the present or the past. When he and his family fled this palace, this city, he would leave her behind, never to be released. Never to harm him or his ever again.

The mirror game over at last.

CHAPTER 32

FINN

After a good night's rest—the closest he'd come to real sleep since arriving home, in fact—he expected to greet the dawn filled with the familiar glow of victory.

Instead, he drew the curtains of his doze aside to a headache happily chipping away at his temple, encouraged by the world-shaking thunder roaring itself hoarse outside.

Raquel was doing her job well.

Too well.

When a blinding flash of lighting shot across the sky, Finn snatched up his pillow and shoved it over his face—then, on second thought, he flipped onto his stomach and buried his face in his middle layer of pillows, jamming the one in his hands over his ears, desperate for the comfort of quiet and darkness. His brain buzzed like someone had dumped a hive of bees into his ear.

It wasn't just his head that hurt—his skin felt sore, but not the kind that came from being scraped or scratched. Discomfort had taken root between the layers and spread, an agitation he usually cured by sitting alone in his room, replacing lamplight for candlelight and reading with earplugs in.

Too much—too much activity, too much light, too much pretending to be someone else. His face felt stretched out and strained from forcing the expressions other people expected of him.

Deeper into the pillow he dove, groaning into its muffling fluff.

He couldn't afford a day to soothe his overwhelmed body—and that was part of the problem. It'd been months since he'd been able to properly rest…at least, the kind of rest that made him feel capable of putting on a show again. And without time to stop performing and just sink into himself, the itching beneath his skin just kept building.

He couldn't afford a day. But he could afford five damn minutes.

So he shut his eyes, let his face slacken against the pillowcase, and breathed in the calm.

Gods knew when he'd get the chance again.

He never would've made it as First Prince—or, gods forbid, the Heir. Kallias had grossly miscalculated when he decided to shove the kingdom into Finn's hands and sacrifice himself to the whims of a god who'd once been so useless he couldn't even protect more than one sister at a time. Couldn't even feed or clothe her with anything better than scraps and hand-me-downs. Couldn't even—

He jammed the pillow harder over his head.

Stop. Thinking. About. Her.

Even without the help of sleep, he'd done nothing but dream of different ways the night before could have gone—how time might have twisted if he hadn't gone back. Whether that night on the lighthouse would have happened at all…if Occassio would have even bothered with the ruse of Fidget.

But it didn't matter. It was over—all of it was over, and he'd won, and now he needed to focus on winning again.

And instead, all he could think about was the confused, devastated way she'd whispered, *"You hate me."*

All he could think about was the way she'd screamed for her sister, despite telling him more than once how often they fought.

And the thought that came back most frequently, the one that dug the hole in his chest deeper and deeper and deeper…

"To me, you did it first."

If someone charted the impossibly long thread of her life, they would end at the conclusion that Finnick Atlas had been the villain who turned the tide of her tale; if they took a peek at his first, following the much shorter path, they would call Cassandra Medeis the monster who stalked the pages of his story.

So in the end, had she really deserved the pain he'd caused her?

Had she earned an eternity locked in a crystalline cage, a fate she'd escaped once before—a fate that made him sick with rage, the memory of her fettered wrists and ankles still razor-sharp in his mind?

And did any of it even matter, when he knew freeing her would seal his and his family'sown fates for the worse?

He tossed aside the pillow protecting his head, pushing himself up and scowling down at the imprint of his face in the gold silk pillowcase.

So much for five minutes of rest.

The twenty-minute shower he took afterward might have been cheating, but he excused it by reminding himself he couldn't very well have Tenebrae see him wandering around covered in crusted blood and smelling of wine and smoke and Old Sanctaviv.

Or maybe he just couldn't go without the comfort of his favorite soap, hot water, and clean hair for another second.

Once the shower eased some of the ache from his muscles and he managed to get all the blood cleaned out of his nose (yes, he did it exactly how one would imagine, and he refused to be ashamed of it), he dried off and changed into an outfit composed of compromises: just enough finery to appeal to Cassi's tastes, but all made with comfortable fabrics that kept his skin from crawling.

After he'd finished tugging on the deep green tunic and buttoning the jeweled cuffs at the ends of the sleeves, he adjusted the collar in the mirror…then stopped when a slice of morning sunlight cut through the shade tugged over the bathing room window, spotlighting a strange texture coating the lower half of his face.

Slowly, as if he might frighten it away, he reached up and ran a hand over his cheek.

Over his stubble-covered cheek.

He'd never been able to grow a beard. Never.

And really, this was barely a ginger-tinted shadow over his cheeks, chin, and upper lip—not impressive by any measure—but the sight of it closed his throat up with a swell of grief.

It made him look like Kal.

When they were younger, people had commented often on how alike he and his brother looked—but as Kal got older, more and more remarked on Finn and Soleil's similarity instead. Even after Soleil was gone, once Finn's hair darkened—a shift from bright scarlet red to auburn-tinted brown that seemed to happen between one haircut and the next—almost no one compared him and his brother any longer.

But this fledgling beard had been enough to send a surge of adrenaline through his body when he first caught sight of himself in the mirror, thinking— just for a single senseless moment—that his brother stared back at him instead.

With a fierce swallow, Finn shook himself into action, yanking open a drawer and digging around until he found what he needed: the razor his father had gifted him at thirteen, so rarely used its edge remained keen.

He could have pretended it was out of necessity—that Cassi didn't seem the type to keep a beard, and he didn't want to risk the con for the sake of vanity.

That wasn't the truth.

He just couldn't bear to see even a hint of his brother's face in his own.

Despite being out of practice, the razor kindly chose to bend to the guidance of his fingers, bowing to his needs the same way his daggers did. Not as well-balanced or well-forged as the blades he typically went for, but it did the job regardless.

He did not stop until he'd pared every piece of his brother from his reflection.

A quick rinse later, he gave his hair a tousle before slipping out of the bathing room, refusing to look at the covered mirror. The new game had gone on without him long enough; Raquel had been working like mad to keep everything running, but as grateful as he was for her picking up his slack, it was like asking a cook to repair a clock. She had talents, sure, but they were better used elsewhere.

Like ensuring the barracks and the quarters for the palace guards were damned near impossible to live in.

Between the leaks and the drafts and the constant sounds of the sky splitting itself open, many had begun to flee to the taverns for warmth and shelter; unfortunately for them, most taverns were no longer running, either because they'd burned down or because Vidia had laced their food and drink with nausea-inducing poison that quickly branded them as poor-quality establishments.

Which left only one: a cozy little place that had recently been taken over by new management, its metal sign proclaiming it *The Mayhem Den*. The sign had been forged by Safi Aquila herself…one of Finn's new favorite people, now that he'd heard the story of her dragon automaton nearly killing Elias Loch.

And since Raquel was busy there today, it was up to him to make sure his father got the medicine he needed.

As he slipped into the hall, giving a quick glance in each direction, relief loosened his shoulders—no one lurked in the torch-lit corridor. No one he needed to put on a show for.

He should have known that luck wouldn't hold.

As he rounded the corner, the ghost of another sibling halted him in his tracks…only this time, when he blinked, the specter didn't waver away in the mirror.

"There you are!" Jericho's face grinned at him, lips stretching so far that the chapped skin cracked, a bead of blood breaking out. The grayish tint to her pockmarked skin had spread, a necrotic shade branched with dark veins; it crept over the edge of her jaw and the apex of her forehead, a shadow without a caster.

Tenebrae's magic devouring her vitality, throwing her body into chaos.

Finn grinned back. "You look rotting awful."

Tenebrae rolled his eyes, splaying his fingers toward Jericho's borrowed face. "Look, I'm doing my best here. You know how human bodies take to any *real* power."

"Not well."

"Putting it mildly." Tenebrae jerked his chin in Finn's direction. "How's yours holding up?"

"Beautifully, and if you suggest otherwise, I'll cut you." He rubbed his freshly shaved cheek with a scowl. "Though I've got to say, he picked an inconvenient time to start sprouting a beard."

That grin, already spread too thin across his sister's heart-shaped face, inched to grotesque lengths. "Really? I thought you might enjoy it—a costume you don't have to pin on."

"Would you believe it's itchier than the false ones?"

"Trust me, I remember." Tenebrae mirrored his movement, rubbing at Jericho's beaten skin. "Track down some shaving balm, if you can. I'm sure it comes in lilac."

"Ha, ha. Never thought *we'd* be having this conversation."

"Eh, well. I had it with Tempest; not that hard to repeat myself." Tenebrae chuckled before his grin shrank down to a simple smile—then a displeased frown. "And speaking of the others…things in Arborius don't seem to be going the way I hoped."

"One of your plans went awry? Imagine that." Thankfully, smugness had made itself known as one of Cassi's favored outfits. He wore it with pride, more than happy to unleash a bit of condescension where he could. "Do I need to make a few of my own?"

Tenebrae's eye twitched. "Watch your tone."

"I'm watching enough already; one more thing and my eyes might burn out." Finn shielded his eyes as if in demonstration, but in actuality, he needed the excuse to hide his face—to hide how badly he needed to hear the answer to his next question. "Ani's not ready to climb down from her pretty plagued treehouse yet, huh?"

"Seems not. And there's been another…complication." *Complication*, he said, like the growl of one of his corrupted hounds, like the grinding of an earthquake beneath the crust of the world. "Ani and her host were successfully separated—and the host, it seems, has traveled elsewhere."

Finn's entire body hollowed out.

Bone brittled. Breath thinned. Blood evaporated.

And inside the shell that remained, those words echoed in the empty space, over and over and over and over again.

The host has traveled elsewhere.

Elsewhere.

Elsewhere.

"She *what?*" The pitch of his cry startled even him; luckily, Tenebrae nodded grimly, a twisted snarl taking over his face.

"I know. I didn't believe it either, but the little bitch just doesn't quit."

Everything that had gone weightless in him caught fire, and for half a second, he knew with his entire heart that he was going to break his fist—and his ruse—on his sister's stolen face.

But the better part of his brain came back to him just in time; instead of throwing a punch, he threw his clenched fist into his pocket, trapping his temper within.

Paper rubbed against his knuckles; he balled it in the center of his fist, rubbing his thumb over the imprints dug into the note by Kallias's hand.

Atlas needs a defender.

Atlas did. Soren didn't—and she'd kick his ass straight into a shark's maw if she found out he'd compromised everything, ruined everything, because the Chaos God had called her a name.

But where in the depths had she *gone*?

"I thought she couldn't survive that," he croaked.

Yet she had. And if she'd survived separating from Anima…

He tightened his grip on the paper in his pocket.

Hope.

If even a scrap of his brother's soul remained…if any part of him had survived…

Maybe they had a chance.

"You and me both," Tenebrae said.

"Where'd she get off to?"

For the first time, he saw Tenebrae hesitate. Swallow hard enough to make a sound.

"Brae," he prompted.

"I had very few eyes in Arborius to begin with, and the Blight took them all early," Tenebrae muttered. "But the last messenger bird said the Tallisian prince was on the island when they arrived…and they appeared to leave together. My guess? She's got her eye on that god-killer of theirs."

Too many revelations—he couldn't contend with them all.

She was supposed to stay on the gods-damned island, safe with their aunt and uncle—and she'd *left*?

With *Everin Arden,* no less?

Whether Tallis's god-killing weapon existed or not, with Everin Arden in tow, Elias Loch would never survive the trip. Everin held less reverence for the gods than Finn himself, and that was saying something.

"Seems the plan needs rethinking, then," he said, his mind no longer in the room. "More bodies, maybe? Take her back by force?"

"Actually, I'm thinking of sending you."

Of course he was. "I think you mean *asking me nicely* if I would be willing to go."

Tenebrae gave him a baleful glare. "The attitude, Occassio. We talked about this."

"Did we?" Finn tapped his chin, frowning. "I can't seem to recall—"

"Will you *shut your mouth?*"

The walls themselves quivered at Tenebrae's roar, shaking in their trim—the floor shifted with a violent *crack*, the world disappearing from beneath Finn's feet, and open air rushed up to embrace him as—

As the floor opened its gaping maw and swallowed him whole.

He liked falling; but not when he couldn't see the inevitable end to that plunge.

Not when the fall took him, not the other way around.

Instinct spread his fingers wide, and a shout ripped from him, a wordless command—warmth fizzed in his fingertips, bubbling from a low simmer to a rolling boil, and pink light burst into being below him.

His heels slammed into a solid disc of pinkish-lavender power, jamming his ankles sideways in their sockets, and that commanding shout cut into a bark of pain.

Knees buckling, head spinning, he caught himself with fingers still splayed, staring through the transparent pink surface of the auramantic shield he'd formed to catch himself. Far below, he could just begin to make out the dungeon in the darkness beneath.

He blinked down at it, then blinked up at the hole in the floor ten feet above his head.

He had absolutely no doubt how Cassi would respond to *that*.

With a double-handed gesture upward, he propelled himself back up with the auramantic disc. As soon as it came level with the floor, he stormed off of it, letting his tongue loose: "You have five seconds to start *groveling* for forgiveness, or—"

He didn't even finish his sentence before cold, clammy hands came at him—at first, he reared back, a response hammered into him after several attempts at strangulation leveled against him in bar fights and street brawls.

But when those hands framed his face, they were gentle—and when he blinked, focusing straight ahead, he met Jericho's teary eyes.

Tenebrae's teary eyes.

"Are you all right?" he asked frantically, turning Finn's face side to side, then running his gaze down the rest of him. "I didn't—" A hectic, hysterical laugh broke his sentence in half, in sharp contrast to the fear in his eyes and the lingering flush of temper in his cheeks. "I didn't mean to do that. Are you all right?"

It took a moment for Finn to find his voice—then to dig deeper and find Cassi's. "I'm fine, no thanks to you." He shoved off Tenebrae's hands, clearing his throat and straightening his coat.

"I'm sorry." Breathless. Dazed. Almost…genuine. "I am. Damn it, Occassio, that scared me!"

"What're you snapping at me for?" Finn demanded. "You're the one who—"

"I know!" Tenebrae shouted—as Finn watched, having to swallow back his horror, something *shifted* beneath Tenebrae's chest…something solid swelling outward until, with spurts of blood, the invading objects tore through flesh and bone.

A row of talon-like thorns curled over Tenebrae's collarbone, like claws unsheathed, like a palisade erected to defend his clavicle. With every heave of his chest, more blood bubbled out from around them, torn flesh rising and sinking around the base of every thorn.

Tenebrae looked down at them, chest still heaving. With a thick, slow swallow, he set his hands over the thorns, squeezing until they pricked through his fingertips. Until those beads of blood joined the rest.

"I know." Finn could've sworn that crackle in his voice sounded like *shame*. "I'm so sorry."

Finn closed his eyes. Sucked in a bracing breath.

To Cassi, this god was not a monster—to Cassi, this was her oldest sibling, her first protector, a man who'd beamed with pride at the sight of her dancing through the tailor's shop—and, in spite of that pride, had bowed low before a lord to help keep her in his good graces.

And though he couldn't think of it this way…though he couldn't afford the hesitation it might cause…to him, the person before him was his oldest sibling, his first protector, the woman who'd told him bedtime stories through the crack under the door when he wouldn't let anyone in after Soleil died and called him *Nicky* even when he groaned and whined and complained that it was undignified.

What would he say to her, if those eyes gleamed green instead of gold? What would he say if she was the one raging at him, agitated and anxious, on the edge of a full-blown fit of hysteria?

"It's all right," he said softly. "I'm not your enemy, Brae. I'm with you. Tell me what you need me to do."

Tenebrae took in a long, harsh breath…then let out a smooth, steady exhale. With an erratic wave of his hand over his clavicle, those thorns shuddered and sank back into his skin—another pass of his hand, and the wounds closed, though the skin didn't quite heal over. Instead, knots of flesh formed over each wound, a shoddy bit of corrupted medimancy; whole, maybe, but not healed.

"Ani's all we need," Tenebrae said slowly. "Tempest is already lurking, and where all of us are, Mortem's sure to follow. We just need Ani back."

Tempest.

Finn's mouth dried out.

Tempest was here.

Kallias was close.

"When did Tempest get here?" A demand—he tried to soften it, sweeten it. "He didn't even stop by to say hello. Bastard."

"I don't know when for certain, but there have been sightings of the First Prince…rumors that he's alive after all. That he might even be that Riptide nuisance who's taken it upon themselves to calm my chaos." A sneer lifted Tenebrae's lip. "Storms aren't meant to be peaceful."

"I don't know." Finn had to bury a smile. "I've heard the eye of the storm is the most peaceful place one can be."

Something subtle shifted in Tenebrae's face. "You're different, you know…less antsy than you used to be. I'm surprised you haven't gotten bored."

"I'm keeping busy my own way. But I am running out of things to entertain me…a trip might actually be in order. I have a few things I need to see to still, but if needed, I'll go. We have all the time in the world, remember?" A wiggle of his fingers. His best imitation of a certain wicked grin. "We have me."

Finally, Tenebrae loosed a smile. "You're right…as usual. Don't let it go to your head." His gaze wandered back to the dungeon door. "I interrupted you. What business do you have in the dungeons?"

Finn rolled a shoulder, letting out an airy sigh. "Eh. Like you said, I'm getting bored. Thought I might play with them a bit…give them a vision or two, tell them how that last daughter of theirs dies."

A mistake—Tenebrae's eyes sharpened again, and he stood straight. "You've seen that? And you didn't *tell me?*"

"No," he snorted, rolling his eyes—his heart tried to surge forward, but he tugged it back. Even the slightest inkling of alarm might be enough to tip off Tenebrae—especially in this state. "But they don't know that, do they?"

"Clever girl."

"Always have been."

And then, with a cock of his head and a hungry smirk, Tenebrae said the words Finn had been dreading for weeks.

"I think I'll accompany you."

CHAPTER 33

FINN

With every step down into shadow, Finn's mind raced ahead of his feet, frantically tallying every possible action Tenebrae could take against his parents.

Taunting, if he was lucky. A game he didn't mind playing in tandem with the Chaos God, not when his parents were in on the game. He'd spew every horrible thing he'd ever thought if it amused Tenebrae enough to keep his hands to himself.

Torture came next on the ladder, but his mind tried to cringe from it, unwilling to face the very real possibility; with a massive thrust of will, he forced himself to look it in the eye. Ignorance wouldn't save him from it; planning would.

He could distract him, somehow—he'd find some way to get the god's attention off of them, whatever that took.

And if Tenebrae tried to kill them…

Before his mind could reach that possibility, his feet caught up with it, and there was no more time to think.

"Good morning, Your Majesties!" sang out Tenebrae, clapping his hands gleefully as he swept into the dungeons—the guard at the cage, much to Finn's added frustration, wasn't Vash. Because of course nothing could go right today.

That Viper better have one *fabulous* explanation for why he wasn't where he ought to be.

And honestly, any excuse short of being murdered or held hostage or accidentally imbibing one of his sister's more abrasive poisons probably wouldn't satisfy.

Both of his parents rose to greet them, and he had to swallow down his relief…and his apprehension. To see his father on his feet…he couldn't be anything less than grateful for that. But judging by the predatory slant of Tenebrae's head toward him, the god didn't share the sentiment.

"Well," Tenebrae purred, dark curiosity shading his smile, "don't you look better. Look at all that color in your face."

Ramses simply dipped his head. "Atlas heal better than most."

"I've heard. Favored by the Goddess of Life and all that." Pacing to the left—pacing to the right. Tenebrae stalked before his parents' cage with energy pouring from every limb, an excitable friction that made Finn's skin itch.

Ramses' gaze wandered over Tenebrae's shoulder, catching on Finn's face. For half a second, his father's eyelids fluttered, revealing a hint of questioning concern—but Finn merely blinked back twice, a desperate attempt to signal him to *look away* before Tenebrae could notice.

Ramses' eyelid twitched, an almost-wink that could have been a twitch of pain or a flinch against the floating dust in the air. He stepped up to the bars, and Finn clutched firmly at the edges of his mask…the bored, careless queen of lies, not the scared little prince pleading for his older, stronger self to save his papa.

Ramses had taught him his street smarts, how to pull gently at the delicate threads that connected people's desires to their actions—his father's manipulations might have been the loving sort, the kind that drew vulnerable truths from the most unwilling of mouths and emotion from the most reluctant of hearts, but they were manipulations all the same. He had to trust that his father still knew how to wield those weapons…that the pickpocket-turned-prince still lived somewhere under the skin of the kindhearted king.

Ramses didn't cower; Finn had never seen his father cower. Instead, he stood before the cage bars with all the composure his title demanded, hands folded behind his back—judging by the way Adriata leaned in close behind him, peering over her husband's shoulder with wrathful, warning eyes, the two were holding hands behind his father's back.

"Whatever you seek from us," Ramses said, his calm voice dipping into a soothing, measured murmur, "you won't find it. You've already taken all we have."

"Oh, no, Your Majesty. I'm not here to take." Tenebrae smiled sweetly at him, and a tear budded at the edge of Ramses' eye—a clue to his grief that vanished with his next blink. A forgivable slip from a father watching his daughter be used as a puppets. "I'm here to give."

"We want nothing you have to offer, either," Adriata snapped, sliding her hand around her husband's shoulder, an attempt to pull him back—Ramses held firm, standing steadfast between his queen and the predator eyeing them through the gaps in the iron. A prison that now stood as their only protection.

"Oh, you misunderstand. It's not for you—it's a gift to my sister here." Tenebrae stepped aside, and Finn's heart lurched.

If Tenebrae asked him to hurt them…

Ramses met his gaze again, but there was no concern this time—no sign that he recognized him as his son at all. He slid a hand over Adriata's, gripping it tightly. "Occassio."

"Your Majesty." Finn smirked, blowing a mocking kiss to them. His fingertips stung as they made contact with his lips, venomous words burning them with vitriol. "You're looking well for…hm. Not an orphan, exactly, though I suppose you're that too. It's a shame that they have a word for children with no parents, but nothing for parents with no children. Shall we come up with one ourselves?"

His mother flinched.

Finn's ribs squeezed inward, piercing the muscle of his heart, a pain that nearly took his breath away.

He hadn't expected his mother to flinch.

His father, though—he took his place in the dance like they'd practiced it for weeks, like the choreography had been beaten into his muscle memory. "I am always and forever a parent, no matter where my children are. No matter how lost they may seem."

"Even past death?"

"Even then." Ramses smiled without strain; a smile thick with unimaginable grief. "Wherever they've gone, I will be there too, one day—so why would I call myself anything but a father?"

"So stalwart," Tenebrae said—he leaned against the wall now, watching the exchange with a sick, gleeful grin. "Even now that your youngest has gone to the grave."

Ramses's smile dropped away immediately. "What?"

"Say that again," Adriata seethed—she pushed around Ramses this time without resistance, his father staring blankly between Tenebrae and Finn. The uncertain terror in his eyes pleaded for a denial, but Finn could only hold his smirk, the burning touch of Tenebrae's gaze too close to risk even the slightest shake of his head or twist of his mouth.

Don't believe him, he begged silently. *But pretend you do.*

He didn't think he could project his thoughts into the minds of others, not the way Cassi could—he'd tried it with Raquel, but after half an hour of trying and an increasingly painful migraine, he'd given it up as one of the traits only the true goddess possessed. Still, he tried it again now—tried it with all the strength he'd built up in his mental fortresses, an assault he hoped against hope would reach his father.

But Ramses's expression didn't change. Not until Tenebrae cooed, saccharine and sadistic, "Oh, don't look so sad—your little Heir put up quite the fight, I hear. But you poor little mortals…you're just not built for godhood. Care to show them, Occassio?"

No.

No.

The word branded the tip of his tongue, screaming to be let out, shoving back any other word that tried to take its place.

No, no, no.

He had been on the receiving end of Occassio's brazen attempts at driving him mad—had spent too many days and nights with blood leaking from his ears and eyes, his nose and mouth, a gushing fount that spoke of broken things inside his most sacred space. He'd endured the skull-shattering agony, the screams he couldn't keep in, the hallucinations that drove him to wail for his big brother or sleepwalk off the edge of a tossing ship in the middle of the ocean.

He could not do that to his father. He couldn't. He wouldn't, he—

"*You lie.*"

At first, he didn't recognize the voice—even though he saw his father's mouth move, even though he saw the deep creasing of his forehead and the laugh lines that bent all wrong to make room for a snarl, he couldn't imagine that voice had come from Ramses Atlas, who'd never raised his voice in wrath against anyone—not even his enemies.

But at Tenebrae's giggly, heartless obituary for Soren, cast before them as if it couldn't have mattered less to the god who spoke it, Ramses's voice rose to a cold, murderous *growl*.

"My daughter lives," he said when Tenebrae didn't answer—when the god's smile only widened, his jaw cracking with the breadth of his joy, Ramses slammed the bars and roared: "*My daughter lives!*"

As if by shouting it to the skies, it would make it true. As if by the might of a father's rage alone, he could still save what had already been stolen.

Tenebrae merely tipped his head toward Ramses, gaze fixed on Finn. "Go on," he urged. "Show him."

He couldn't. Wouldn't. The refusal to move took up residence in his feet, in his spine, a freezing of body that his mind couldn't overcome...

And then his father met his gaze.

"Go on, witch." Ramses slung the taunt at him like a thrashing wave, its foam-capped might colliding with the rocky surf—but his fingers loosened slightly from around the bars, the bend to his shoulders a message all its own. "Show me what you will."

Somehow, somehow, Finn stepped forward without shaking, without breaking. The rock, not the wave.

Another step. Another. Another.

Until he stood before his injured, aging father, eye to eye, hand to hand. He held the bars just beneath his father's clenched, white-knuckled fists, barely allowing their fingers to brush.

And with his back to Tenebrae, he let his eyes speak to his father, a promise and a plea: *I won't do it. I don't have to do it.*

His father's glower didn't soften. But his smallest finger twitched just enough to touch the tip of Finn's—the only message he could give. The only hint that what he said next was part of the game...permission and promise.

"Do your worst," King Ramses commanded him.

Permission to do what he had to. A promise that it was all right—an assurance that his father would endure.

And Finn didn't know if he believed him.

"Papa." Not a word; not even a breath. A silent movement of his lips that not even a god could hear.

Ramses's eyes drilled into his, a fierce, unyielding demand. "Do. Your. Worst."

Don't you dare, said that steel in his father's eyes. *Don't you dare do anything less than what he wants.*

If he released the bars, he knew his hands would shake—and that would be all Tenebrae needed to see the truth.

So instead, he slid them up lightning-quick, gripping his father's hands tightly.

I'm so sorry, Papa.

And with the same thrust of power he'd once used to tunnel into Occassio's memories, he shoved into his father's mind and dragged a dream in with him.

A nightmare.

Ramses began to scream.

"Stop!" shrieked his mother—she shoved between Finn and Ramses, pushing Ramses back, but it was too late—Finn's magic had taken root in his father's mind, and the contact wasn't necessary. He could do nothing now but watch, stoic and smiling, his lips stiffer than a stone pillar as he watched his father descend into a vision of his mind's own making.

Finnick Atlas smiled as he tormented his father.

And in the darkest depths of himself—in a place where he shoved all his weak and wasted scraps, the traits that could compromise a con if he didn't keep them in check—he knew he'd never forgive himself for this.

Even knowing that his father had ordered him to do it. Even understanding that he'd had no choice. Even when his mind chased down a hundred other scenarios and they all ended in death.

Finnick Atlas had sins and secrets too numerous to count. Many he secretly held as accomplishments, as something to be proud of—and few, very few, he regretted.

This one trumped them all.

This one made him a monster.

Ramses's brown eyes blew wide, his bearded face stark white beneath the red, his jaw gaping in horror; he screamed again, bellowing in rage and terror, veins popping in his eyes. Blood leaked into the whites, crimson paint pressed between pieces of polished glass; despite Adriata's pleading, her hands anchored around his shoulders, the King crashed to his knees. With an atavistic howl, he clawed his way toward something none of them could see, his primeval wails interrupted half-comprehensible gasps of "Baby, my baby, look at me, look at Papa, please please baby look at Papa!"

He could not be here. He could not watch this.

With a swift and violent separation of mind and body, Finn no longer occupied his own form.

From the outside, not one damned inch of him would look amiss—to Tenebrae, Occassio stood at the cell with her hands in her pockets, amused and apathetic, her head tipped back as she gazed down ruthlessly at the groveling king and his panicked queen.

But Finn simply could not be present in this moment—he could not exist here.

He took his perfect memory and built a wall; a box, steel-solid and impenetrable, the sort one used to store things they never wanted found or seen.

And he hid there until the screaming stopped.

When Finn came back to his body, it took a moment for him to remember what he'd fled from in the first place.

A hollow ringing clanged through his eardrums, like someone had struck a gong directly at the side of his head—the splitting pain in his temple suggested that as well. And the blood—so much blood, everywhere, all over the floor and that man and the woman who held him—

He blinked.

Breathed.

His mother. His father. They both sat on the floor, Ramses barely holding himself up, and the blood—

The blood—

All that *blood*—

It dripped lazily from his father's nose and eyes; it gurgled in his frantic, heaving breaths. It stained his fingertips, outlining cracked and broken nails; it stained his shirt, the clean one they'd just provided him with yesterday.

Finn flexed his hand, testing whether it responded to his command—and when his fingers twitched, both his father and his mother cringed away, a broken, sobbing cough cracking open his father's chest.

Finn froze.

Monster, monster, monster.

He couldn't breathe. Couldn't speak.

Oh gods, he couldn't *speak.*

Say something, screamed the voice in his head that handled this sort of thing—the cruel part that knew sometimes, great evils were core ingredients to greater goods. *Say* anything, *fool!*

"Beautiful work," murmured Tenebrae in his ear—he hadn't even noticed the god creep up on him, but he definitely felt that cold, clawed hand slide over his shoulder, squeezing harder than necessary.

The pinpricks of pain anchored Finn's floating, dazed consciousness back to his body—back to reality—back to this living nightmare of his own.

Somehow, he managed to contain his own ragged sob; instead, he sucked in a breath, smiling idly at Tenebrae. "Shall I do her next?"

"No, no—let me take a turn." Tenebrae turned to the cage, eyes firmly fixed on Adriata.

Murder flooded his hands and heart, instinct screaming to rip this god apart, flesh and soul.

He'd tortured his own father.

And his mother was next.

Bile lurched into his throat; he swallowed it down, but it refused to be sated, rising again and again until he felt at war with his own body, every breath acidic.

Helpless.

He was helpless.

He could not stop this.

He could not turn away.

He could not leave.

He could do nothing, *nothing,* but stand in silence and watch as Tenebrae opened the cell door.

As the God of Chaos bent down and dragged Adriata up by her hair, ignoring Ramses's sudden snap out of his daze—ignoring the King's brutal shout that echoed through Finn's numb, ringing ears, the shaking fingers that struck out for his queen.

"Down, boy," Tenebrae said with a bored sigh—as Ramses tried to stand, tried to dive in and snatch Adriata out of the god's grip, Tenebrae gave a short whistle.

With a burst of dust, vines sprouted through the dungeon floor, cracking stone and silt and wrapping tourniquet-tight around Ramses's legs. The thorns dug in, twitching and writhing, dragging scratches through fabric and skin; Ramses didn't even flinch, his gaze glued to Adriata. "*Addie.*"

Adriata twisted to meet her husband's gaze…and there was no fear there. No pleading for rescue.

Only staunch, uncompromising will.

"Whatever he has for me," she said, voice ringing out as if she sat in her gilded throne, not on the filthy floor of their most despicable dungeon, "I have endured worse." She looked to Tenebrae, baleful, defiant.

"You think you can taunt me with her?" she said softly. "You think you will break me with my children? Do you know what I did the first time someone *murdered my baby?*"

Tenebrae smiled condescendingly down at her. "Yes, you started a little war. How utterly mortal of you."

"I broke." Adriata forced her spine straight, unbent, unbowed, baring her teeth in the God of Chaos's sneering face. "I broke…and I broke, and I broke, and I broke. For ten gods-damned years, I woke up every morning newly broken…and it never stopped." She held up her arms. "These? They never stopped aching for my baby girl." She tapped her ear. "These? They never stopped listening for her voice…or hearing her scream." Her chest. "This? It tore open anew every time I saw the color pink. A plate of cookies. A mermaid doll. The sand, the sea, the gods-damned *sun.* So do what you will, God of Chaos—bleed me dry and twist my bones, wrap me in vines or scar my skin—but you cannot break what is already broken." A savage grin—the heathenistic sort that punched him in the chest, an exact mirror of Soren's taunting smile. "And I can't remember the last time I was anything but."

Tenebrae's eyes narrowed. His smile vanished. And with a roll of his wrist, another vine shot up, wrapping around Adriata's neck—

Finn snapped.

Just for a second—not even a second.

Faster than a secret wink, a fleck of lavender light got between that vine and his mother's neck. Just long enough to ensure that it didn't fully strangle her.

And his breathing stopped.

Tenebrae couldn't have seen that—gods, he'd barely seen it, and he'd *done* it.

But if the god *had…*

"You are lucky," Tenebrae murmured, leaning in and running a finger over Adriata's jaw, "that I may have use for you yet. Otherwise, I'd be happy to teach you what *broken* really looks like."

"I should go," Finn announced quickly, dutifully adding on a yawn and a stretch—his only defense against the raging beat of his blood, a rush of heat that couldn't decide if its name was anger or terror. "I have better places to be."

"If you say so." Tenebrae didn't turn to look at him, and he couldn't pick out any suspicion in his voice—relief loosened his shoulders, but even so, air refused to enter his lungs.

If he didn't leave, this would only get worse. Tenebrae wouldn't kill them, not while they still had some use—and if he stayed, he didn't know that he could keep his magic from escaping again.

And if Tenebrae forced Finn to torment his mother, too…

He didn't think he'd come back from that.

He didn't even know if he'd come back from *this*.

With a graceful, mocking bow to his parents, he turned and walked toward the stairs.

The world dipped and tossed around him, a ship forced to sail on a cursed sea; and Finn had never really found his sea legs, despite the best efforts of his father and brother.

Every step up jostled him in ways he hadn't expected—each click of his boots against the stone unbalancing him, loosening his binds on his self-control. Tossing waves of stomach swill swept up the column of his throat, a sickness born entirely of shame, of the soul-deep knowledge he'd just done something utterly unforgiveable. Unredeemable.

By the time he got to the top of the stairs, opening the knob after four shaking tries, he couldn't breathe at all.

Blinded, barely aware of himself, he fumbled back to his room, slamming the door—by some miracle, the thought occurred to him to bar it shut, lest someone make the mistake of entering without a warning knock.

When that barrier clicked in place, his spine cracked against the door, sliding downward until he curled into a ball against it, his body shaking so fiercely that his teeth began to chatter, threatening to leap out of his skull.

He shut his eyes. Buried his face in his knees. Wrapped himself so tightly into a knot that nothing could escape. Not even noise. Not even breath.

And with a gasp that wedged in his lungs like a flung dagger, he screamed into the hollow space until his voice went hoarse.

CHAPTER 34

RAQUEL

Patrols had always been her favorite part of serving in Nyx's army.

Though the others in her company complained about being forced from their usual routines to traipse around the woods by their borders, taking their turns checking for any signs that Tallis had thought to push their luck—and the boundary between their kingdoms—while Nyx was distracted by the more inflamed presence at the Atlas border, Raquel had always enjoyed the break. Though she'd been cut off from her magic well before she'd ever taken her first trip into the mountains, she'd found some small comfort in the ferocity of the wind tumbling down from the snow-capped peaks. The blizzards out there were something to behold, and she'd always taken to the challenge of keeping her and Lily's tent up with vigor, happy to test her mettle against the weather…hoping to prove that even without her magic, she could hold her own against Nature's might.

Patrols in Port Atlas were not the same.

City patrols, they stifled her—the air between buildings lost so much of its core nature that by the time it reached her, it hung weak and wobbling, a breeze that could barely drag the scents of brick and mortar and day-old refuse along with it.

Once upon a time, she was sure it had been different—that the heart of Atlas's capital had danced with breezes that smelled of food and drink, perfumes and forge-smoke; maybe they'd even sung along to fiddles and folk tunes.

But in Tenebrae's city, these things had been driven out, replaced with hollow-eyed houses with boarded-up windows, ransacked shops that sagged with unhealed wounds dealt to their walls, and taverns that smelled of nothing but rat droppings and rotting food.

Luckily, thanks to the scheme Finn had pieced together on the fly, she and her companions were heading toward the one place that might yet hold a candle to Port Atlas's former glory:

The Mayhem Den.

Havi and Safi worked fast, she'd give them that. Within two days of arriving in the city, they'd had the tavern up and running, hollowing out the shell of the abandoned *Squall and Stew* and pouring all they had into making it feel real.

Despite the company she kept—Revan, Arcas, and Pyra, who'd informed her that she was required to accompany them on their patrol, then refused to take no for an answer when they invited her to join them in the tavern after—the tension slipped from her shoulders as she stepped into *The Mayhem Den*, the homey smells of cinnamon and honeyed mead and fresh bread a welcome reprieve. While her companions stormed straight to the center of the crowded space and claimed a table—and by claimed, she meant they forced its current occupants up by the point of their blades or flame in their hands, Pyra going as far as to literally light a fire under the ass of one of the patrons—Raquel quietly removed her cloak and hung it on one of the hooks attached to the wall beside the tavern door. Iron hooks, each one designed with barbs shaped like miniature flames.

The tavern itself smelled of fresh cedar and spiced smoke, deep currents of scent that ran under whatever Havi was crafting in the kitchen tonight. The Aquila siblings had done a wonderful job mixing Artemisian comfort with Atlas décor; though the walls hung heavy with cuts of knotted dock rope and restored anchors, netting strung across the lights hanging from the ceiling to soften the glow, and many of the tables boasted centerpieces made from shells and imitation siren scales and candles that bobbed in clear vases filled with water, there were still traces of Artem hidden in plain sight.

The roaring hearth at the back of the room. The thick rug spread before it, its pattern filled with reds and golds and oranges, all the shapes and lines geometric in design. The metal accents to the furniture. The blown-glass globes that floated from the ceiling, fires flickering cheerily within their confines.

If not for the patrons that frequented the establishment—and the fact that she knew everything served here had a hint of poison buried in its batter or brew—she would have loved it.

"Keep up, Angelov!" called Revan good-naturedly—of the three chaos-worshippers Tenebrae had chosen to constantly hound her, he was the least objectionable. As a former instructor in some elite Tallisian university, she guessed his idea of chaos was more mild than most.

"Don't make us start drinking without you," added Arcas. His thick black mustache curled upward with his grin, framing straight teeth that sparkled in the light.

"Wouldn't dream of it," she muttered under her breath, picking her way toward the table—even in her thick boots, she didn't care to step full-sole on the piles of broken glass and carelessly tossed dirty dishes, or the slack, unconscious faces of those who had yet to rouse after their latest brawl.

Under the guise of thriving on chaos, Havi couldn't set rules about fighting in the tavern—but he did ask that the patrons at least take care of their own messes before they left. For the most part, because even chaos-worshippers couldn't seem to look the baker in his kind eyes and tell him *no*, it worked—but many of them got around the rule by staying overnight, so their "messes" didn't often get mopped up until the next morning.

Raquel slid onto the wooden seat beside Arcas, careful to set herself adjacent to Revan, not Pyra. The Artemisian woman had grown worse and worse in the past days, often lost in humming, and had gained a penchant for setting anything she happened to touch on fire just for the fun of it.

Raquel preferred not to become one of her victims.

"Look what the shark dragged in!" called a familiar voice, though it didn't come from a familiar face—thanks to the amount of Artemisians among Tenebrae's worshippers, Safi and Havi had been forced to disguise themselves, so Safi and Finn had worked together on a little invention of their own: a pearlescent glass bauble dangling on a suede cord that Finn infused with a portion of auramancy every morning. When worn, it altered the Aquila siblings' features just enough to render them into different people—the same coloring, the same bodies, but faces no one would recognize from their home kingdom.

Raquel didn't like it—the melding of magic and objects was a practice that had only recently begun to show promise, and while Safi and Finn were certainly the minds to take it on, it was impossible to predict when that magic might fail them. But for now, it was all they had.

"There's my favorite new friend," Arcas laughed, smiling at Safi as she sped to them, stopping just beneath the lip of their table and propping her elbows on its surface, offering Arcas a broad grin to put his to shame. "How are you this evening, Sabine?"

"I'll be better after I've finished up with your table—I trust you all to be fair." Safi jerked her chin at a table in the corner, scowling. "Those fools stiffed me my tip, can you believe it?"

"I'll shake it out of them right now," said Arcas, shoving back out of his chair—Revan rose too, silent but scowling, eyes already fixed on the rowdy group of men taking turns playing a knife game with each other's hands. The sound of wobbling blades digging into soft wood—or softer flesh, followed by howls of pain and giggles of delight—threatened to turn her stomach.

This was the hard part—when her enemies showed proof that they had once been people. The kind that wouldn't stand for rude customers mistreating tavernkeeps.

But instead of confronting them with calm words and firm demands that they pay what they owed, chaos commanded that they solve the problem with blood and bruises and burns.

"Sorry in advance," Safi whispered once the three were well-occupied with their spat. "We didn't know you'd be here—we don't have anything clean prepped."

"It's all right. Once won't do any harm," Raquel assured her. Odds were she'd be immune to the poison entirely, anyway—and if she wasn't, it would take far more than what they'd laced the food and drink with to cause her any real pain. "How's it going here?"

"Good—Ember's working on those lockpicks Finn asked for, so she's not around, but Havi's hiding out in the kitchen." Safi blew out a breath, wiping her forehead with the back of her hand—somehow, the illusion didn't hide the beads of sweat there. She picked up Arcas's unused napkin, wiped her hand clean, then set it back down without a care.

Raquel gave her a reproachful look.

Safi grinned sheepishly. "Chaos, right? They don't care about hygiene."

"I do."

"Well, I didn't use your napkin, did I? Besides, he's about to get much worse on it." Safi craned her neck to peek at the increasingly violent brawl, grimacing. "His nose is definitely broken."

"Wonderful." Raquel pinched her own nose, rubbing the bridge of it, wishing it would sap the tension from her temples. "And the twins?"

"Vidia's with another table. Not sure where Vash went off to, but he *was* here." Safi referred to the twins by their first names with cheerful abandon; meanwhile, when Raquel had checked in yesterday, she'd heard Vash stiffly refer to her as *Lady Aquila,* followed by Safi snorting so hard she shot water out of her nose. "I haven't seen anyone else. Why're you out here, anyway?"

"I think Tenebrae's losing patience with me—he keeps finding ways to pull me off whatever *Occassio* has me doing and put me with his people instead." Not unexpected, but inconvenient—especially when they were getting down to the wire. "But I—"

A fist slammed down on the table between her and Safi, smears of blood trickling over the knuckles—as the fingers uncurled, the sound of coins piling on top of each other clanged out over the tavern.

"For you," Revan said with a genial dip of his head.

Safi *beamed.* "You're a lifesaver, dear."

Raquel almost snorted—she had to cough to cover it as Arcas and Pyra came back, dropping into their chairs. Arcas did indeed take his napkin and jam it into his broken nose, swearing so filthily even Raquel's hardened ears burned, and Pyra didn't bother with cleaning herself up at all. She eyed the blood beneath her nails with something like wonder, a strange sheen to her dilated pupils that set the hairs on the back of Raquel's neck standing tall.

The next hour or so went by without making much of an impression on Raquel's mind—her thoughts wandered elsewhere as her companions chattered about nothing. Their thoughts, she found, often wandered in circles—they treaded the same ground just for the sake of hearing themselves talk. Repetition better than silence, it seemed.

So when they were halfway through the meal, Raquel dutifully chewing a mouthful of her sandwich, she noticed immediately when the pain began.

It started as a niggling worm of discomfort crawling through her stomach—nothing but a vague shiver beneath her belly button that set off a warning bell.

Something's not right.

The more she ate and drank, the stronger the sensation became—discomfort built into nausea, those occasional shivers building to full-body chills she had to hide with stretches and false yawns.

Chills—yet her cheeks felt flushed, inflamed, like a fever had swept in to claim her while she wasn't looking.

Shivering, sick, she peered down at her plate—and froze.

She recognized this feeling…from early-morning hours spent in secret with Aeris, both of them huddled in their shared cabin, a seventy-third poison fed to her by spoon.

She hadn't asked Vidia which poisons made up the concoction they tainted the food with. Hadn't thought to make sure that they excluded one poison out of hundreds, because she'd never expected to partake in it.

But her body knew the wicked touch of this toxin—a plant known as *gutrot,* named for exactly what it did to the human body. Over time, if given in small doses, it weakened the body's ability to gain energy from food…it could cause starvation in days, even if the victim continued eating regular meals.

When Raquel had tried to build her immunity against it, her body had rebelled entirely. The herb had wreaked catastrophic consequences, nearly killing her in a single night.

And judging by the way her hand rattled around her fork, hidden beneath the tabletop, she'd just consumed it again.

She swallowed hard, slowly setting her sandwich down.

Help—she needed help.

But she couldn't just run, she couldn't just—

"The rest of the troops should be here any day," Arcas announced, shoveling his own meal into his mouth without a care. "After that, looks like half of us will be heading out to Tallis."

"To get the god-killer," Revan agreed—a chill ran down Raquel's back, but it was impossible to tell whether it was from the poison or the mention of that coveted weapon. The one they'd meant to recover by now, before the relics had taken precedence—before everything had gone so wrong, forcing them down other paths. "Once he has that, nothing in the flogging world will be able to stop us."

The note of awe and excitement in his voice twisted Raquel's stomach—then another knot formed. Then another. Until she could hardly bear to sit still.

"The god-killer?" she rasped.

"That's what we were told." Arcas shrugged. "Supposedly the last Atlas princess got it in her head to go after it."

"I wouldn't worry," Revan chuckled, mistaking her hushed intake of breath as alarm. "No one's ever survived the try. She'll be nothing but a corpse to kick out of our way by the time we get there."

"Wherever *there* is, exactly," Arcas snorted. "Tenebrae's awfully tight-lipped about that. Says our guide has to get here first."

A guide. Tallis. Soren was in Tallis; Soren was going after—

Something dug blistering talons deep into her gut, and her hand slammed down on the table, gripping the edge so tightly she nearly dented the wood.

All three of them looked to her with concern—even Pyra, who paused with her fork in her mouth, held aloft by her bloody hand.

"Are you all right?" asked Revan. Across the room, the halt of swishing silk skirts told her Vidia had paused in her own serving, watching her from the corner of her eye.

"Sorry—before I left, Occassio ordered me to pick up some extra pastries for her. I meant to order them already." Sweating, smiling through the shredding of her stomach, Raquel stood up, silently begging her legs not to fail her. "I should put that order in so they're ready in time. I'll be back."

As she made her way toward the door separating the tavern proper from the kitchen, bits and pieces of their conversation followed her…the slightest breeze whispering to her of *a god-killing weapon* and *who could this guide be* and *I've got a good guess, but don't quote me…*

She needed to be at that table. She needed to be hearing this, but—

The walls flew away, replaced by the floor rushing toward her face.

"Raquel!" A strong set of hands caught her by the shoulders—she blinked hard, realizing she'd swooned her way through the kitchen doors. She now stared at flour-coated wooden floors, her nose inches away from crunching against them, and her stomach…

"Havi," she choked, "charcoal. I need—"

"I'm on it—I had it out just in case." The world muddled and swirled around her as Havi hauled her upright—she couldn't even help him as he sat her on a stool and steadied her, blurring into the meld of colors and shapes as he moved away.

Only when the cool rim of a glass pressed to her lips did she manage to move of her own accord—she gripped the glass tightly and recklessly gulped down the liquid inside, heedless of the awful flavor or the grimy texture, only caring to get it into her stomach as quickly as she could.

"I am so sorry," Havi fretted. "If I'd known you would be here, I would have—"

"I know," she mumbled—her teeth gritted uncomfortably, and she did her best to lick them clean. "It's not your fault—one of the poisons, it's…" Gods, she couldn't even get the explanation out. "It's not your fault."

"Just sit tight—rest a moment. I'll have Safi tell your friends I'm hogging your attention back here."

A kind offer. Hopefully it worked.

Raquel bent in half against the lingering pain—this would not be an instant cure, but with any luck, she'd be able to walk out under her own power—and tried to breathe. She braced her elbows on her knees, staring at a divot in the floor, making it the anchor she clung to with every wave of new agony that ripped through her stomach.

It could have been minutes or hours before Havi came back—all she knew was that when he did, he placed a hand gently between her shoulder blades.

"You are remarkable, you know," he said. "For being here. For protecting a people not your own."

A dry, heaving sound—even she wasn't sure if it was a gag or a laugh—ground out of her throat. "People keep telling me that. It's not *remarkable* to do the right thing…to do right by your promises."

"That isn't true. It is…certainly remarkable, to protect those who wouldn't offer you the same. To put yourself in harm's way for those who have been at war with your people for a decade." A pause. A gentler tone. A comforting circle between her shoulders. "Just like it takes remarkable courage to forgive a man who killed someone you loved."

Now the agony twisted within her chest instead.

"How did you figure it out?" she murmured in the direction of the floor.

"I didn't. Safi did." A hint of laughter in his kind, deep voice. "She did catch you two standing nose to nose, after all."

Raquel laughed in return…but it faded within seconds. "You know what the worst part is?"

He waited, a silent invitation to enlighten him.

"I wish I'd kept right on hating him." The admission fell from her lips like stones thrown at a grave; a defilement of what Kallias had meant to her. "If I had, I wouldn't be here—this wouldn't hurt so much."

At first, the baker stayed quiet—then he crouched before her, blocking the piece of flooring she'd been staring at. He held her gaze with a gentle smile—to her relief, her vision had cleared some, returning his features to their proper places.

"Maybe you'd be in less pain," he agreed, "but there would be more of it—just spread out amongst these people. It would have multiplied through this city, because you wouldn't have saved all the lives that you have."

"I don't know what that makes me," she confessed. "A traitor to my kingdom, at the very least."

"I don't think so." Havi glanced toward the door, then back to her, bracing his hands on his knees. "I've had the privilege of being in the company of many royals, both born and made… in my own kingdom and others. You may not be him; you may not be of royal blood. But as I've watched you speak with the people in our little group…as I've watched you lead them…I see the bearing of an empress." He paused again. "Sorry, wait—a queen, here."

Now she laughed in earnest. "You're joking."

"No, I mean it. Isn't a queen her kingdom's first defender? Her peoples' protector? Does she not stand for them when they cannot stand for themselves?" He rose, forcing her to raise her chin in order to hold eye contact. "Kallias was the same, from what I understand—a king not in succession, but a king regardless. I've heard some call him the King of the People…and if you're here because of him, if you're here to fill his role, then that makes you Queen of the People." His eyes gleamed knowingly. "The riptide that sweeps the wreckage away. The eye of the storm where your people can shelter."

She was going to throttle Finn and Vaughn for telling stories about her behind her back.

"Atlas isn't mine." It was all she could think to say—all she could manage past the lump in her throat and the burning in her stomach.

"Are you certain?" He raised an eyebrow at her. "Because if I recall, their prince is the one who deemed his people as an acceptable loss…you're the one who stood your ground and refused to abandon them."

Her heart fluttered. Failed. Tried to take off again, like a bird with a broken wing, desperate to flee.

"Atlas isn't mine." This time, she didn't let the pain punch all the breath out of her—she slammed it down in time with her heels, forcing herself back to her feet. The kitchen tried to tip sideways again, but she scrunched her eyes closed, counting to three—when she opened them again, everything stood upright…if a little wobbly. "I have to go."

"You should give the charcoal more time to—"

"I know, but they won't wait forever—and if I try to make them, they'll wriggle their way in here and contaminate your kitchen." She patted the baker's hand, forcing a smile…and forcing herself not to fold in half when lightning-sharp agony shot through her center. "Thank you for the help."

As she lurched back toward the swinging door, Havi caught her by the wrist. Something warm and paper-wrapped nestled into her palm—on instinct, she closed her fingers around it. When she brought it around, the decadent smell of warm chocolate and flaking layers of pastry tickled her nose.

"They're clean—just pulled out of the oven. I had a batch tucked in the ice box to make today for you." The subtle lilt in his voice promised a smile waited somewhere behind her…but she couldn't bring herself to look. "Besides, you told them you had to get something from me—it would look odd if you walked out empty-handed."

She should have thought of that. "Thank you."

"Raquel…" A squeeze around her wrist. "I am sorry for your loss—Safi and I, we grieve for him too. You're not alone."

You're not alone.

Tears nipped at her eyes; she blinked them away, blaming them on the pain, the poison. "Thank you," she repeated in a whisper.

Havi wasn't wrong—she wasn't alone. But sitting at that table until the others had finished their meal, smiling through her sickness, listening with dread as the commotion around her rose from commotion to cacophony…

She was certain she'd never been quite this lonely.

CHAPTER 35

RAQUEL

She made it two blocks before she had to make excuses to her patrol, telling them she'd forgotten something at the tavern and had to turn back.

The tacky air stuck to her skin as she stumbled back the way she came, a humid mingling of salt and sweat that trapped heat rather than relieved it. And while she'd come to enjoy the constant presence of moisture in the air, if only because it meant she always had a weapon to call on, it had chosen the wrong night to plant a ring of damp kisses over the crown of her head. The wrong night to grip the nape of her neck with a sweaty hand, soaking into the hair at the base of her skull.

She flung herself into the safety of alley shadows just before a rib-cracking retch broke her body in two.

With one palm braced against the cool stone wall, she fumbled at the clasp of her cloak with the other hand—her sluggish fingers racing against the second retch already building, desperate to free herself from the extra layer of weight before—

Three things happened at once.

The cloak dropped to the ground around her ankles, soaking up the sick already spattered over the ground.

Her stomach tried to throw itself out of her throat, a violent surge that forced her to gag again, despite having nothing left inside her but bile and charcoal.

And something seized her from behind, frigid fingers circling around her now-bare biceps.

"What's wrong with you?" Tempest demanded harshly—the huff of air against her neck chilled the sickly sweat gathered there, several notches colder than the weather itself. She shivered, swaying sideways, and his voice only rose in volume and violence as he held her steady. "Officer—*Raquel.* What's the matter? Are you hurt?"

"No," she groaned—then gagged again. "Gods *damn it.*"

"Damning is actually my sister's specialty, but—" When she sagged, her knees plunging toward the puddle of vomit, he cursed fiercely and caught her up in his arms, one against her back, the other beneath her knees. "Where are you hurt? Tell me!"

"Nowhere. Put me down," she commanded.

"Tell me what happened," he commanded back.

The two of them glared at each other—a contest she would have happily won, had his face not begun to shimmer and blur about three seconds in.

"Poison," she admitted. "I am—I got—poisoned."

His golden eyes practically glowed with molten fury. "*Who*—"

"I had to eat some of the food at the tavern. I did it to myself." And she'd much prefer to do this by herself, too—especially because the sight of Kallias's face, even blurred, wasn't helping the pain any. "I'll be fine; you can leave."

Tempest snorted, derisive—far above their heads, thunder grumbled its own complaints. "I'm not leaving you to die in some rat-infested alley."

"I'm not *dying.*" Lightning flashed. Raindrops kissed her cheeks. She squinted up at him, blinking the water out of her eyes. "Put me down, or I'll—"

"You'll what? Vomit on my shoes? You already did that."

"I vomited on the *ground.*"

"And then I stepped in it." Gods help her, was that a rumble of amusement in his voice? The way Kallias suppressed laughter sounded so different, gentle and genial, withheld not by immortal detachment but by regal grace. "With my shoes."

"I didn't ask you to come storming in."

"Mm." Though her eyes were only open a squint now, she felt the bobbing motion as he started to walk—carrying her out of the alley. "Was that a pun?"

She couldn't begin to think of what he could mean. "What?"

"*Storming in.*"

Bastard. "I don't appreciate being mocked."

"There's that unfailing sense of humor," he deadpanned. "Save your breath, Officer. I've got somewhere we can go."

She was sure he did. But the very last thing she wanted to do was go there—wherever *there* was—and have to writhe her way through these fits of illness while he watched.

"I will scream." A bold bluff; her throat rubbed against every word like a sheet of sandpaper, buffing her voice until it barely crackled out. But maybe, maybe it would be enough to free her. "I swear on my life, I will scream so loud the whole city will hear."

He craned his neck to the left—to the right—over his shoulder. Such a gods-damned show-off. "If you feel that's necessary, by all means. But it doesn't look to me like anyone else is keen to rescue you."

She seethed. Shivered again. Begged the storm above to sweep her away. But it only continued to pepper her face with fat, sea-fed raindrops, too gentle to wash her anywhere. "This is not a rescue."

"What would you call it?"

"Being taken hostage?" When he chuckled, she tried to push off his chest, but the muscles in her core cramped together, forcing her body to buck. The spasms wrenched a groan out of her; she couldn't stop it, but she could at least shape it into words. "I *don't need* your help!"

"And yet, you have it," he said—his voice echoed with finality. "You're sensible enough to know you won't make it anywhere safe alone. You'll end up on the street overnight, and when Brae's hounds go on the hunt, you'll be sitting on a silver platter. You don't have to thank me—"

"I won't."

"And you don't have to be happy about it—"

"I'm not."

"But this *is* a rescue, and you have no choice in the matter, so *stop squirming.*" A huff of breath, an exhale chilled with petrichor and ice. "You're the last person I would have expected to put on such a childish display."

Humiliation held out its hand, an offer to share the burden of this moment—she smacked it away, clinging to righteous indignation instead. "I'm not squirming. It's—"

Her teeth slammed together involuntarily, a grinding attempt by her body to brace against the rebellion of her insides. Some panicked corner of her dizzied mind imagined a stomach filled from top to bottom with fanged snakes, her muscles growing scales and teeth as they tried to throw her out of Tempest's arms.

Luckily—or unluckily—the god had a good grip. He barely flinched as she convulsed, spitting curses. "I'm not sure what else you'd call this embarrassing tantrum of yours—"

"Muscle spasms?" she ground out through her locked-up jaw. "From the *poison?*"

He fell silent for a moment. Then: "Ah."

The next breath she choked out had the audacity to come out as a laugh. "Yes. Ah."

"I apologize." Judging by the smudge of warm pink now blooming across his cheeks, he'd taken humiliation's offer of companionship. "That was…"

"Rude."

"I was going to say *insensitive.*"

She squeezed her eyes shut. "For a deity, you are incredibly petty."

"For a mortal, you are incredibly bossy."

After that, she did fall silent…not because he told her to, but because the smile softened his voice too much, and it wasn't raining quite hard enough to hide the moisture gathering in her eyes of its own accord.

INTERLUDE

TEMPEST

When he and his wife had built their home, he had never imagined he would one day regret building it within view of the sunset.

But then, one would have needed a depths-damned *depraved* imagination to predict the events that had carried him back to this ancient cottage, nestled out of sight of the palace and as close to the shore as he could convince Athena to let him build it.

Events like the violation of laws holy and natural. A punishment handed down to him not for the crime, but for the simple sin of failing to stop it. The simpler sin of shoddy timing adding injury to insult, bringing him back to his chosen family just in time to watch his brother in all but blood kiss the woman who had once been his bride.

He had not hated *them* for it. Neither of them, not for a second. But hate had been there, regardless.

Of all the things he'd loved and lost, hate had been the hardest to let go.

Nature had no heart; hope and hate, love and loss, guilt and grief, he could afford to give none of them ground. Bias was a blessing for mortals and messier gods.

If Nature had a heart, it would grant mercy where none had been earned. It would lay waste to the necessary evils which kept the world in balance. And…

It would rage, as any ordinary man might, over what had been done to the woman sleeping under his second-best quilt. More woman today than most days; she spent so much of her time as a storm wearing skin, he often forgot the flesh and bone still mattered. That blessed to his fullest measure or not, she could still fall prey to mortal misfortunes. Could still suffer.

Could still die.

Something pulled taut and tremulous within his chest, a rope snagged by a splintered scrap of ship-wood; with a thump of his fist and a pipe-smoker's cough, a result of poor boyhood habits, he rattled it loose.

For an empty chest, it could mimic the reactions of a human heart a little too well for his taste.

But even the wildest hearts came to heel eventually—he would master it soon enough.

It bucked again at the kettle on the stove wailing for mercy from the heat, the steam flowing from its spout reminding him of early mornings spent swimming alongside whale pods as they migrated from colder climes to settle in Atlas's warm waters for the winter. An honor and a privilege not afforded to most.

Then again, most couldn't breathe underwater. Nor could they command the ocean to carry them to safety if its unpredictable nature saw them surrounded by something meaner than a handful of massive, meandering mammals.

After he swiftly plucked the kettle from the stove and set it atop the clamshell-shaped potholder on the counter, he crossed the kitchen like he'd once crossed through dangerous currents, breath held and shoulders braced. But when he leaned over the back of the couch to check on his guest, he did not find her locked in that fitful sleep she'd fallen into on their way here, failing to rouse no matter how many times he gave the order.

He found her awake, blinking with worrisome slowness, stern brow smooth for once as her gaze skimmed over her surroundings like a skipping stone. Never lingering long in one place. Never sinking into awareness before leaping elsewhere.

Until her gaze crashed against his, ripples of emotion breaking the surface of her glassy-eyed stare.

A mortal could have drowned in those dark waters.

"You're here." A faint curve to the corner of her mouth.

The mooring line tied to either side of his ribcage pulled again, so sharp and sudden his lungs went rigid.

Yes—a mortal would be utterly doomed, damned to die by that sirenlike smile. The lure hiding a terrifying set of teeth.

"Yes." No blood washing her lips, only a pinch of slur salting her words—good signs, but not enough to be sure. She'd consumed some charcoal, and she'd vomited earlier—a mark in favor of the poison being out of her bloodstream—but he didn't like that look in her eye, nor the shallow rise and dip of her chest. "Are you in pain?"

Her head bobbed to the side like a buoy caught in a passing ship's wake, sinking against the dusty pillow pinned beneath her. "You're *here*?"

Unease hummed through his bones. Beyond the window, smudges of soot shaded in the clouds, replacing a saccharine sunset with a sinister storm.

"I am. And will be, for the foreseeable future, so if you plan to try and snap your teeth and scare me off, save your strength." A press of his thumb between her brows proved his concerns correct—her fever hadn't broken. If anything, it raged to new heights, a tidal wave rising with no recourse. "Your fever is worsening."

As a mortal man, Tempest had been struck by lightning only twice—once when he'd first been given his magic and had not yet learned how to leash lightning properly, and again when…

Well. It had happened again. He couldn't remember when, but he knew it had.

When Raquel Angelov's feverish hand collided with his, a clumsy fumble of fingers that left her knuckles loosely locked around his, it didn't feel like lightning at all.

Lightning couldn't hold a candle to this.

"You're back?" A raindrop fell from her cloudy eye, rolling down to kiss that shifting, shaken corner of her lips. "You're staying?"

Mystified, completely confounded by that touch, that *tear*, he gave the only answer he could. "If you ask me to."

Nature had no heart.

But if it had…if it *could* have, even for one selfish second…

The crumpling creases between Raquel Angelov's brows would have broken it.

"Stay," she commanded. Lightning leaped between clouds outside the window, whooping its glee as it struck the shore like the tines of a trident; rain battered the paned glass, a host only half as harsh as the second tear that fell from the Eye of the Storm. "Don't go. Whatever h-happens, whatever comes…promise me you'll stay."

And Nature, which had no master and obeyed no order, whispered, "As you order, Officer Angelov."

The words were not his, but they belonged on this tongue, regardless; they surfaced without call or cause, as if this body only knew one way to answer her call to action. To oath. To obedience.

She shut her eyes. Smiled again, stern, satisfied, siren.

"If you ever try to leave me again," she mumbled, "I'll track you down and kill you in your sleep, Kallias."

As she slipped back into her own fitful sleep, her fingers followed suit— and when they fell away from his, landing in her lap, he did nothing to stop it.

Yes. It was a very, very good thing he was not mortal.

CHAPTER 36

RAQUEL

The world came back in shades of warmth.

The brightest shade boiled in her stomach, a seething nausea that told her she'd been sick too fast for the charcoal to do its work…yet hadn't been sick soon enough to purge the poison.

Next came the flush of heat in her face—not a blush that built, but a wavering warmth that came and went, like it couldn't decide whether it should draw closer or back away.

Then the softest warmth—the all-over warmth of an old quilt wrapped tightly around her, its musty scent just strong enough to finally drew her back to the waking world.

Raquel opened her eyes to a home.

At least, it looked like one—it had none of the fine trappings of the palace, none of the soaring ceilings or golden décor or fine art. Instead, the walls were crowded with knick-knacks displayed on driftwood shelves, not one of them matching; from where she lay, she could just make out a jar of sea glass, a conch shell bigger than her head, and a pockmarked stone carved with two swirling letters: *P + A.*

There were bigger pieces that couldn't fit on the shelves—a handled net hung on a hook by the chipped-up sea-green door, along with a ring of leather she recognized as a dog's collar. Above the mantle, where a small fire burned—the source of the more hesitant warmth against her face—a bodyboard hung, stretching almost the entire length of the wall.

She only knew what they were called because Kallias had described them to her—she didn't know if this one was unusually long, or if the room was just that small. But regardless, its stripped-silver surface dominated the space.

The open window to the far right allowed fresh air to leak in, bringing the smell of fresh rain with it—the cornflower-blue chiffon curtains swayed gently with every breeze, an ethereal dance that looked like some kind of worship.

She eased herself up, breath held, grimacing as the sofa beneath her squeaked—her palm pressed down against a hole in the upholstery, finding spongy stuffing that padded a stiff spring beneath. The blue-and-white gingham had clearly seen better days.

"Don't get up," called a voice from behind the sofa.

When she flipped over, she found Kallias—*Tempest*—with his back to her, hovering over a stove. The living area flowed directly into the kitchen; just behind the sofa, the floor shifted from wood to tile, leading right to the round dining table. It appeared hand-hammered, hand-carved, all rough edges and rustic charm; there were three seats set up around it, but only two plates. "I'm making you something that will help."

Between the haze of pain, the disorientation of going to sleep one place and waking up in another, and the utterly bizarre idea of a god occupying such a simple space, she could only come up with one thing to say: "Where are we?"

For several seconds, only the crackling of the hearth and the sound of something boiling answered her.

"My home." The confession seemed to cost him; his shoulders drew tightly together, then eased apart, a flinch and a sigh. "Mine and Athena's."

She looked at the table. "Three chairs?"

"I said not to move."

"I didn't move."

"Talking counts as moving."

She could have argued, but somehow, it felt wrong to fight in this quiet, peaceful place…like it had spent so long in silence that it now preferred it, and to raise her voice against its wishes would break its gentle heart.

So she swallowed her temper in favor of crossing her arms over the back of the sofa and settling her chin on them, watching him bustle around the kitchen.

All she could see of him was his back…and the occasional glimpse of his face, allowing her to catch his rounded lips as he whistled lowly to himself, a shanty-song that dipped so low that his whistle occasionally rumbled into a bass hum. He'd discarded his own cloak, though she didn't see it anywhere—instead, he wore a long-sleeved knit shirt that slouched in the front, baring a cut of his muscular chest and clinging to his lean biceps.

It was too easy to lose herself in a soft-edged daydream; too easy to pretend that when he turned around, he'd be wearing sea-green eyes and a smile to shake her world.

She pressed her lips flat against her arms, burying the urge to whisper his name…the senseless wish that maybe, if she said it just right, it would summon him back from wherever Tempest had sent him.

She didn't have the strength to waste on delusions.

When she couldn't bear it another second, she cleared her throat, forcing herself to spit the first question she could think of: "You lived here, not the palace?"

The whistle cut off. "Not exactly. Officially, yes, we lived in the palace, but palaces take time to build. We lived here in the meantime, and when it came time to leave it behind, we just…couldn't." He scrubbed the back of his neck with one hand. "We split our time as needed, but most nights, we snuck back out here. Gave our bodyguards a heart attack or twenty."

She tried to picture it: two giddy young rulers escaping their own palace, racing to spend their happiest moments in a cottage smaller than the room Raquel had stayed in since arriving in Atlas. "And…the third chair?"

"For guests," he said—when she held her silence, glaring at the back of his neck, he turned and smirked at her, still stirring the pot on the stove. "Fine. We had a dog—a completely useless dog, all fur and no brains. Athena loved him more than she ever loved me, and gods, she let me know it."

She coughed out a laugh—then grimaced, curling more tightly over the back of the sofa, bracing her spasming stomach against it. "What was his name?"

He turned away from the stove, stepping toward her—he rocked a bit when his eyes fell on her face, and he swallowed thickly, the dripping spoon held loosely in his hand. "Are you—"

"Just keep distracting me."

Tempest's mouth knotted sideways. "His name was Prince Barkley Ophelius Atlas. And before you start, my *late* wife named him, so keep your thoughts to yourself."

This time, she didn't feel guilty for laughing—because gods above, even Kallias couldn't blame her for this one. "I don't believe in refusing to mock the dead simply because they're dead. And that's a *terrible* name."

He cleared his throat, turning back toward the stove—but not before she caught the fisherman's crook of his smile. "It really is, isn't it?"

"I had a dog once." Not hers, but close enough—she'd loved him like he was. "Well, a wolf."

"What was his name?"

"Atticus."

"A noble name."

"Better than *Barkley*," she mumbled under her breath—and he burst into laughter.

Shoulder-shaking, nose-pinching, back-bending laughter.

He braced his back against the counter, still laughing—he ran a hand over his beard, giving her a helpless grin that flipped her heart upside-down before crossing his arms over his chest. "Sea swallow me, I hate that you can do that."

The way he said it crackled like static in her ears. "What?"

"Make me *talk*. Make me want to tell old stories." He shook his head at his feet, as if asking the floorboards what to do with her; they evidently offered no answer, because when he looked back up, he had a wrinkle to his nose and a pinch to his eyes. "You make me want to prove something, and I don't rotting know what."

Whatever feeling blossomed in her stomach at those words…she liked it even less than the rollicking sea the poison had made of her gut. And maybe it made her a coward, but she had to look away—had to busy her fingers with the well-loved quilt wrapped around her, rubbing its worn threads between her fingertips. Deep in the folds of patchwork blue and ocean green and aged cream, burrowed beneath centuries of stale air and dreamy dust…she could've sworn there were notes of coconut and musk hiding in the threads. Traces of a new god and a new queen, first of their names and lines, who loved their seaside shack so deeply that they would not trade it for a palace filled with splendor and sunlight.

"What was Atlas like?" she muttered into the quilt's storied folds. "Before…when you were king?"

The pause that followed held weight. It pressed down until she couldn't breathe past it; it bent her head to avoid his gaze, though she could feel it lingering.

"Home," said the god.

It was a privilege not offered to many, she supposed—to be regaled with firsthand tales of history so old it had aged into myth. To be handed a steaming mug of tea made by hands that held the power to halt the unceasing tide; to be told stories by a voice that could command the currents to swallow ships whole.

She almost felt guilty for wishing she was sitting with someone else. Someone human.

Someone who spoke of Atlas, *this* Atlas, with the same fiery passion in his gaze. With the same enthusiasm that turned his hands into puppet frames, his fingers putting on a show because his words weren't enough.

Still, wishes weren't words; if she could keep her tongue under control, the malicious discontent robbing the wonder from this moment could not make itself known.

So as she alternated between gulping water laced with charcoal and sipping the warm, honeyed tea that soothed her raw throat, she simply listened…and did not tell him how she wished she'd never been given the privilege of sitting at a god's hearth.

And in exchange for her lie of omission, he told her tales of young gods delirious with newborn power; how, in a fit of unbearable homesickness, he'd towed the ocean of his birth city across the continent, leaving behind a sprawling desert. How Mortem had been so furious with him for it that her magic had blackened that sand for hundreds of miles, creating what Artem now called the *Onyx Desert*. How Anima had spent days on end with her hands buried in the sea, spreading the roots of her power deep beneath the surface, ensuring it teemed with life. How Occassio had begrudgingly spent those same days cross-legged beneath a satin parasol, hiding from the sun while she tried her hand at crafting shells and sand and sea glass, all because he'd told her how badly he missed them.

He told her how he met his wife years later: a freckled, fire-haired sailor with a mouth salty as swill and a singing voice that could lure sirens to land. An explorer who dreamed of chasing the sun to wherever it made its bed at night.

The woman who brought the God of Nature to his knees.

And just as the sea-roughened storyteller's cadence melded with the warmth of the tea, a wave rolling gently into the one that came before…just as the pain finally eased its grip on her guts enough to let her lean back comfortably, the embers in the hearth lulling her toward something close to sleep…he asked a question of her.

"What about you?"

She blinked heavily at him, frowning; she leaned away, sinking deeper into the quilt's protective embrace. "What about me?"

His gaze drifted to the window, where the curtains still swayed; ballroom skirts with no one to waltz in them. "Tell me what life was like for you…whenever you had a place that felt like home."

Though it could have been another order, a demand from god to mortal, he instead shaped it as a plea. And somehow, that made it easier to tell him her own story—much shorter, much harsher, but peppered here and there with scraps of happiness. The games she and Jira played as little girls, laughing together as much as they fought; the first time she'd successfully wielded her aeromancy and aquamancy in tandem, everyone in Skyhaven whooping and cheering her on, Aeris whistling so shrilly that the glass broke out of a nearby windowpane; the moment she snapped a solid wooden board in half with just the heel of her palm, and she'd wept into Jakob's shoulder, finally believing she might have strength worth using…even without her magic.

It became so easy, in fact, that she nearly wandered into whispers of a seaside town and a sunset kiss and promises she'd never quite believed.

Almost, but not quite—because he asked another question first.

"Why didn't you destroy them?"

The drowsy fuzz over her vision cleared with her next blink. "Who?"

"That little cluster of heathens that tried to kill you—the ones that fancy themselves favorites of mine." This time, the curtains did not dance—they *fled* from the harsh wind that forced itself into the cottage with a furious howl. Tempest cleared his throat, standing in a jilted rush—the least graceful movement he'd demonstrated in her presence—and shut the window, latching it without looking. The absentminded movement of a man familiar with his home and the way it needed to be handled.

"Why do you want to know?" She'd always assumed the darkest pit of her life—one so unfathomable she had believed for some time she would never crawl back into the sun—had been beneath his notice. That he had either abandoned her to it, or had not even seen it happening.

"You made this…remark…on the beach. About unanswered prayers." He stayed by the window, leaning his palms against the sill, staring out at something she couldn't see. "It's…bothered me."

"Why?"

"Because I *didn't* answer them. I didn't have to." Gilded eyes lanced into hers, burning away the last of her weariness. "I had already blessed you double—then doubled it again. You needed no answers…you were your own rotting answer. So why didn't you use it? Why didn't you *decimate* them?"

It should have taken longer to answer. It should have taken searching, scouring, ripping apart the whirlwind that had swept up her life in Skyhaven and dropped whatever remained of her in the furthest reaches of the Nyxian woods.

"Because they were my family," she whispered. "Because it was my home."

And even when they hurt her—even as they *killed* her—she loved them still.

Loved them even as they tore the flesh from her back.

Loved them even as they ripped the golden eye from her skull, the pain nothing compared to the sudden silence where her magic used to sing.

Loved them with her whole heart, even when they stopped it from beating.

Tempest watched her. Unwavering. Never looking away.

Maybe he never had.

"Then I think you know," he said quietly, "why Kallias Atlas made the sacrifice that he did."

She curled up into a tight ball. Clutched her knees to her chest. Ached, badly, to cover her ears and wait until all the voices who knew Kallias Atlas's name fell silent forever.

Even if it took a lifetime. Even if it took many. Even if she went to her pyre still covering her ears, just in case the fire remembered the Atlas prince who feared it so much.

"You don't get to talk about him," she whispered.

But he did anyway, walking back toward her, forcing her to see that face. That *look*. The one that had riled her temper more times than she could count—and riled it again now, even though she could barely keep her eyes open to see it. "He hated to leave you. Of all the things he lost, you were the one he most grieved."

She squeezed her eyes shut. "Stop."

"You were right, when you told him he wouldn't give up his kingdom for you—that it was a promise he couldn't keep." A weight settled in the center of the sofa, the cushion sinking two inches deep—a hand settled over her knee, so cold it stung through the quilt. "But he would have tried. And that says more, I think—that he tried."

She tried to open her eyes again, tried to glare—but her body had decided it was done. Her eyelids were iron boxes, locked shut with keys she'd never touched. "Why are you telling me this?"

"Because I want you to know that I will make his sacrifice count for something." The hand on her knee pushed downward; another settled on her shoulder, and she only realized she was being made to lie down when those hands disappeared. "That I don't take it lightly."

The weight vanished from the sofa, leaving her with a sense of weightlessness; the sense that she was floating away, the ceaseless current of sleep tugging her out to where no one could swim or sail.

Except for her lips, sluggish and slow as she said: "I will never forget him. And I will never forget that you took him from me."

A quiet sigh. A brush of warm lips against her clammy forehead—Nature, unkind and unbowing, offering softness for her sorrow.

"I know," Tempest murmured against her brow.

And then he was gone. And she was alone again, left in the care of a cottage filled with dust and dormant dreams, the latter layered twice as thick as the former.

Nature didn't feel pity; Nature didn't apologize. It simply acted, and the consequences—no matter how dire or deadly—were entirely the fault of those who put themselves in its unerring path.

But with those two whispered words…

They made her think that maybe there were times, however rare, that even Nature wished it could halt its course.

CHAPTER 37

FINN

He didn't really mean to go looking for her.

But after what he'd done to his father earlier today, he had to find someone to talk to. Run-of-the-mill madness had been bad enough; if he spent the night with his father's screams looping through his head, he'd become something worse than mad.

And even without that, the problem with a quiet, calm night was that it forced him to think about just *how* quiet it truly was…not just in his room, but in this hall.

His parents' room, torn asunder from the eaves to the floorboards. Jericho and Vaughn's room, even worse thanks to Tenebrae's gleeful take on ownership. Kallias's room had been untouched for weeks before Finn had left the first time, and Soren…

Soren's room, neighbor to his, had ached with silence for years. But tonight, even now that they were only separated by an ocean rather than a grave…

Somehow that gulf seemed even wider than the last.

And that was all without paying the covered mirror in the corner any consideration.

It was that loneliness he got lost in. The exhausted, thrumming desperation for the company of someone he didn't have to pretend for. Someone he *couldn't* pretend for, because she'd catch him in the act before he even started it.

He was sick of lying. Just once, just tonight, he wanted to tell someone the truth.

Which was how he got pulled down a path of thought he had no business walking, a path whose gray-toned bricks began to blush as he crossed them. A road so rarely traveled it got shy around strangers.

Not the branching trail of foresight, but the winding lanes of a dreaming mind. Hazy, clouded by lavender mist; the further he walked, chasing a memory of merciless wit and inexplicable understanding and a bond thicker than the blood they shared, stars began to appear through the clouds.

Just ahead, the brightest star of all blinked out a game of peek-a-boo. There and gone and back again. Blinking, blinking—

No.

Not blinking—fading.

Maybe he should have worn his glasses. But no, this was in his head—wearing his glasses wouldn't help him *imagine* better. Instinctively, he reached to rub his eyes—then stopped, because that was just as ridiculous. And the star—the star was still blinking out, taking longer and longer to regain its light each time.

Something was wrong.

He ran faster, cobblestones tearing at his soles, reaching for that star like a little boy trying to nab a lightning bug in his fingers before it could flit away.

When his fingers closed around it, water burst through his lips, gushing down his throat before he could hold his breath. He hacked, gagged, but the water didn't rush back out—it just kept coming, pouring in through his lips, his nose, strangling him, drowning him—

No.

Not him.

Soren.

Darkness surged over his head like he'd tried to take a wave taller than he'd expected, frigid and fresh…no salt in the water, no sun in the sky. When he struck out for the surface, he caught rippling glimpses of distorted stone, eerie green light, the shadow of a sailboat bobbing out of reach.

He dove out of that place with a gasp that swept from his lungs to his toes, his entire body tingling with the ecstasy of breathing. Not being dead, that was his favorite surprise these days, but he hadn't expected to experience it here.

He dragged one hand down his face. Clammy. Cold. Like he really had been drowning.

Drowning.

Panic jostled him back into his kneeling position, hands upturned, meeting his own horrified gaze in his mirror pendants.

His sister was *drowning*. Not in a dream, not in a memory. *Now.*

He had to help. Had to get her out. But she was an ocean away, and even if he could guess exactly where she was, the likelihood of there being a reflective surface to walk through in a churning body of water…

Think. Think.

She wasn't dead. Dreaming somehow, but not dead.

He couldn't save her. But maybe he could help her save herself.

He shucked off his mirror pendants, muttering to himself as he flipped them glass-up on the floor, then sprinting to the bathing room—he had to slam his palm down on the sink to make himself skid to a stop, yanking every drawer open until he found a hand mirror. Something spasmed in his leg as he flung himself back down by the smaller mirrors, spreading them out until…well, until they felt right, for lack of a better explanation.

This wasn't cleverness at work; this was instinct. And while he was reluctant to rely on it most days, he had to take what help he was offered these days. Beggars, choosers, that whole thing.

He placed his palms over the mirror pendants, then bent his forehead against the hand mirror. With a focused burst of auramancy, he filled the panes with light, blinding them as best he could.

And while they were distracted, he slipped through them to chase a drowning dream.

The water tasted like flowers and rot and the scum that grew at the bottom of the palace pool—don't ask how he knew—and as soon as he took form in it, he wanted out of it.

He could barely see. Everything was shadow and silt and sickly green, grinning skulls watching him from several feel below.

Where in the *depths*…?

This wasn't Arborius's part of the ocean, he'd bet his life on that. Better— he'd bet his entire bookshelf. He'd plodded along behind his siblings to every stretch of shore on that island, had struggled to swim up and down each one until he'd begged Kallias to play on the sand with him instead, and they'd never come across anything this ghastly. That kind of childhood trauma would absolutely have stuck around.

One shadow caught his attention—one that thrashed and spun, treading water in the wrong direction, swimming down instead of up. Bubbles exploded in a column above it, the telltale sign of a swimmer's breath abandoning them moments before the watery inhale doomed to follow.

She was swimming for one of the skeletons. One with its arms out in supplication, its grin picked clean of gum and lip, leering like it mocked the girl it beckoned into its embrace.

Not dreaming, but something close. Hallucinations.

Fine—that was fine. He could work with that. Madness was his specialty now, after all.

Finn was not the strongest swimmer of the Atlas brood. But thanks to Soren's ten-year sabbatical, he at least wasn't dead last any longer.

That made it easy enough to cut through the water, get his hands around her head, and drag her into a daydream of a different kind.

One splashed across the stage of a memory.

Sun-warmed saltwater replaced ice-cold snowmelt; when he kicked out for solid ground, his toes brushed ceramic.

And when he hauled his sister to the surface of the swimming pool, déjà vu slapped him over the head for his trouble.

"I'm feeling like we've done this before," he spluttered, dragging himself out of the pool entirely. He plopped onto the edge, trying not to flinch at the sopping wet *squelch* of his clothes. He let his feet dangle, smirking down at her as he knocked water out of one ear. "Still trying to drown yourself, kid?"

She stared at him like a little girl lost in the market, clinging white-knuckled to the edge of the pool. "Finn."

"Oh good, she still remembers my name." He did his best to tease, though the befuddled look in her eye had actually scared him for a minute. "Do you remember me teaching you how not to die in the water? Because I did. It was, like, the second actual conversation we had after you came home. Not counting the one right before your lover left a dent in my handsome head."

Soren swallowed, studying their surroundings in a dreamer's daze. "I'm…I'm not supposed to be here."

"No, you're not." But gods, he wished she was. He looked up to the ceiling, blinking his burning eyes; he waited until they cleared before he looked back down, patting the tile beside him. "Come on out. The water's *not* fine."

For once, she didn't argue; she pulled herself out of the pool and sat beside him, shivering, staring down at her own sopping clothes.

"So," he said, propping one leg up and resting his elbow on it, "where are you supposed to be, if not enjoying my sparkling company?"

"Tallis, I think. What are *you* doing here?"

Tallis. Tenebrae had been right.

Had his aunt turned her away, after all? That didn't seem like Gen, but he couldn't come up with another reason why Soren wouldn't be in Arborius.

Or why his visions would have shown him his missive landing in her hand if he sent Luisa to the island. Depths.

He'd worry about it later.

"Looking for you." A one-shouldered shrug. "Didn't think I'd find you doing a shoddy impression of a whale, but—"

Against all odds, a laugh cracked out of her chest, and she elbowed him in the arm. "Excuse me?"

"What?" Finn put his hands up, laughing as he ducked out of her range. "Do you want me to tell you that you did a *good* impression of a whale? Because that's a lot ruder, if you ask me."

"I wasn't doing any impression of a whale."

"Could've fooled me, with all that flopping around." He dipped himself to and fro, clapping his arms together. "So graceful! So elegant!"

"That's a *seal.*"

He was pretty sure it wasn't, but he shrugged and waved her off, which was as good as conceding the point for him. "Same thing."

Oh, he knew that face. That was the scrunched-up, indignant face of his whale-obsessed little sister who'd tried to beg off school in favor of whale-watching voyages every single day. "They're *so* not."

Finn pushed her toward the edge, forgetting himself for a second; she caught herself with a yelp. "Like you'd know. You were raised by wolves, remember?"

She shoved herself back on her seat and stuck her tongue out. "At least the wolves taught me manners."

They hadn't taught her one damned manner, let alone multiple. But he caved with a laugh and let it lie; he didn't want to argue with her. Not when they only had these few stolen seconds.

He couldn't even give her the gift of Atlas as it was. He'd had to settle for a slapdash daydream of his own: his ideal summer day, lounging beside the pool while the sun stayed safely outside, enjoying all of the beachside splendor with none of the sunburn or sand-chafe.

But it wasn't real. And as much as they both needed a reprieve… "You can't stay."

Soren looked up at him, a funny kind of flinch to her face that made his stomach hurt. "Why not?"

"Because this is just a dream." Because past this pretty lie, past his desperate wish to have her and her cocky defiance in the face of all awful things at his side for this game, he could still see the truth.

A shadow sinking in faraway waters, sung to sleep by a bounty of bones.

"You're still drowning." At least he broke it to her gently. "And we both know Elias is useless in the water, so I'm sorry to tell you, but you're going to have to save yourself this time around."

Her irises flickered briefly—about to peek and see what he was looking at, he thought. But she stopped at the last second, settling on glaring at him instead. "Then why'd you bring me here? If I can't stay, why bother?"

Because you're my sister. Because you get it. Because I'm at my best with you.

Because I needed to remember just how much Occassio took away from us.

He wanted to tell someone the truth. But that was a little too much truth to dump on a drowning woman's head.

"I just miss you, is all," he admitted. "I wish you could be here…well, no, I don't. It's all going to the depths here. You're better off where you are, trust me."

At first, when her eyes went glassy, he feared he'd lost her to the other dream again; but then that glass shattered with her next blink. And the trust went with it.

Oh.

"There it is," he mumbled. No one to blame but himself for that.

"What?"

"I was wondering when you'd remember I'm supposed to be dead."

Alarm broke the glass this time. "Don't give up."

Oh, gods, she had no idea. He couldn't give up this game if he wanted to.

He didn't mean to laugh. But he did, and he felt all kinds of guilty for it when she balled his shirt up in her fingers and shook him, half anger, half terror. "I'm serious. Don't give in to her. We're getting the god-killer, and we're—"

God-killer? No, no, no time. She had to go. He'd brought her here—he had to make her go. "Soren, I'm the last person you need to worry about right now. This has been fun and all, but I don't need saving—you need to wake up and save yourself."

Her chin trembled. "Why did you let her in? I just got you back, both of you—you told me to *trust* you—"

That rambling pain in her voice broke his heart—almost as much as it did to pull away when she tried to hold on, to make her go when he wanted nothing more than to make this all okay again.

Still, he'd brought her here to tell her the truth. He couldn't give her the whole of it, not without ruining it, but…

She was drowning. In more ways than one. He could see it in her pallid face, her broken eyes. He felt it in her iron grip on his shirt.

She was drowning. But he could give her something to hang on to.

So he curled his fingers under hers. He held on, tight as he could, looking her dead in the eye. "I did. I did tell you that. And I'm telling you again now. So *you* tell *me*—can you keep it up, kid? Just a little while longer?"

She stared up at him. He stared back, willing her to understand. Willing her to believe in him. To *believe him.*

And when she nodded, her jaw clenching, he saw truth shining in her steely glare.

"Good." He pried her fingers off, giving them one last squeeze. "Then trust me—and *wake up.*"

He released her without warning. And with a rush of ice and terror and poisoned perfume on his tongue, he watched as she came back to her senses. Shook off the haze. Swam for safety, for the sailboat that had finally drifted back in reach.

He held on to the dream with both hands. And he didn't let go until he saw her break the surface.

CHAPTER 38

RAQUEL

"You were *what?*"

She couldn't decide if Finn and Vaughn's cries, given in chorus, irritated or warmed her more—so she went with a scowl just to be safe, drawing her knees to her chest and scooting closer to the fire.

"Poisoned," she repeated. "*Barely.*"

"Severely," Vidia corrected; she didn't look much less infuriated than Finn and Vaughn as she checked Raquel's pupils, forcing her to look into the fire so she could measure their dilation. Finn was pacing already, fingers raking through his hair; Vaughn had dropped into a crouch barely a foot from her chair, rubbing the bridge of his nose between two fingers, his eyes squeezed tightly shut. "Why didn't you *tell* me you were deathly allergic to ribcage roses?"

"We called them something different where I came from."

Vidia swore, releasing Raquel's arm to get up and join Finn in pacing. "Seventy-two gods-damned poisons to work with, and I picked the one that could've killed—"

"It's not your fault."

"No, it's not. It's your fault for eating that stuff in the first place when you knew it was laced."

Once again, Raquel tossed up an idle prayer of thanks to Mortem—she was still on their side, wasn't she?—that Havi wasn't here tonight. This wasn't his fault, either, and the last thing she wanted was for him to become the target of Vidia or Finn's wrath.

Even if it was…nice, almost, to see someone incensed on her behalf.

Say the word, and he is dead.

Kallias had been the first to show rage on her behalf since her sister had died. Her late battlemate never had much cause to, and though she suspected Jakob might have felt some kind of way about how Skyhaven had treated her, he'd never shown it to her face. Only in longer and longer reports handed off to Soren after he came back from patrols near that border, Soren doing a terrible job of avoiding Raquel's sight as she hurried those reports directly to the Queen's desk.

She didn't require another's rage as her shield; she didn't need someone to hold her sword for her. She'd learned some time ago that she was allowed to be angry for her own sake. But that anger, it meant someone else cared to see her treated well…and did *not* care for seeing her harmed.

That mattered. Even in the middle of all this, that mattered.

"But you're all right now?" Finn demanded. "Because I swear to the gods, if you try to pull a Loch and martyr yourself on me—"

"Let me examine you," Vaughn pled, pushing up from his crouch with a grimace and a harsh breath pulled in through bared teeth. One knee buckled—Vidia lurched, but she was at the other end of the room, and—

And Finn lunged faster than any of them could, anyway, one arm finding its way around his brother-in-law's waist, the other guiding Vaughn's arm over his shoulders like he'd practiced it. Like he'd caught Vaughn exactly that way a thousand times before.

"You need to use your magic," Finn said under his breath. It was the softest she'd heard him speak to Vaughn—still cold, but a vein of some other emotion bled through. "That's the third time you've gone down this week."

Shock flashed in Vaughn's eyes. Then betrayal. "How—"

"Vash tattled. Which is what I *pay him for*," Finn reminded when Vaughn turned his glower—not an impressive one—on the assassin posted against the wall in the darkest corner of the room, who shrugged, unapologetic. "Save it. I would've found out anyway. I lived in the same hall as you for a decade; you think I can't see when you've got an episode coming on?"

"And where do you suggest I practice my craft?" Vaughn's voice took on an edge of temper. Unfortunately for him, everyone in this room had been on the receiving end of far sharper ones. "In the graveyards already torn asunder by Tenebrae's army? In the alleys where the blighted hounds have been dragging their kills? Out in the field where Raquel has been digging shallow graves for our people?"

Finn's knuckles whitened as his grip flexed on Vaughn's wrist. "Would you prefer I had Raquel *actually* chop them into shark chum? Because that's the only—"

"I would *prefer* there be no bodies to bury!" Vaughn pushed out of Finn's hold, stumbling, catching himself on the opposite wall; he flashed one hand out when Vidia took a step in his direction, his bloodshot gray eyes boring into Finn. Jaundice had begun to seep into the whites…or maybe it was a trick of the firelight. "I would prefer you stop sitting on your ass while that monster slaughters our people. I would prefer you start doing your own damned dirty work instead of letting Raquel carry your burdens for you. She *could have died today!*"

Yesterday, actually. But that would require explaining that she'd spent the night in a god's ancient cottage, so she held her tongue.

Finn watched. Expressionless. Quiet. Not even blinking.

"What was it you said?" Vaughn's voice hardened, chipped with rage, brittle as calcified bone. *"Take some damned responsibility?* How's this: I will when you will. I was half a kingdom away when Kallias died. Where in the depths were *you?"*

Ice thrust through Raquel's heart, trickles of snowmelt chilling her veins.

And Finn just…kept staring.

Then, so quietly Raquel had to lean in to catch it: "You're right."

"What?"

"I said you're *right.*"

Oh, gods. Finn's voice broke.

Raquel exchanged a look with Vidia, who'd gone wide-eyed, the closest to panicked the poisoner had ever looked.

Go, Raquel mouthed silently; Vidia didn't argue. With a nod and a gesture, she and her brother slithered out of the room.

"I have asked too much of her—of you," Finn said, tilting his head her way without taking his eyes off his brother. The lack of feeling on his face wasn't unusual, but paired with his threadbare words, each unraveling even as they left his mouth…that frightened her. "I should be taking those risks. Do you know why I'm not?"

"Because you think you're playing a game."

"Because I *am* playing a game—and if I use my king to make every move, I'll *lose.*"

That was twice now Finn had confessed to coming anywhere close to a loss.

Not a good omen, when they needed him at his absolute best more than ever.

She swallowed her dread, hiding her hand behind her back, fiddling with the draft always crawling through the damaged window behind her, its glass painted over with tar. She looped it around her fingers, tying it in knots to keep her nerves from manifesting as static instead.

Vaughn slammed his fist against the wall behind him. "We are not your gamepieces!"

"Yes, you are—we all are. Including me. I'm the King—if Tenebrae takes me, the game is over." Finn pointed to Raquel. "She's the Queen—the most powerful piece I've got. And yes, I want to keep her protected, but I also need her out there. I need her to take the fights I can't so I have a clear path to checkmate. And sometimes, to make both of those things happen, a pawn or two gets sacrificed. And yes, it's a loss—but without that loss, we don't just lose a couple pieces, you get me? We lose the whole board. Do the damned math!"

"Is that what you did with Kal?" Oh, that hushed murmur, the resigned set of his jaw…Vaughn was pissed. "You did the damned *math?*"

Finn's lips jerked to one side. He snorted…smiled. Shook his head with a chuckle and a drag of his hand down his face.

"Yeah," he said softly. "I did the math. I've done the math a hundred times."

"And what answer did you come up with?"

"All the ways I could have stopped him." Finn shoved his hands in his pockets, one forming a fist. She knew exactly what he held. "All the reasons it's my fault."

An ache spilled down her throat, the bitter chaser to an acidic brew. "Finn…"

His smile widened. His eyes brightened. He gave one firm nod, sniffing, shaking his head as he paced back a step. "Yeah. No, it's all right. He's right. It's my fault."

"Finn."

A low, awful chuckle. "I made my father scream."

Now it was her and Vaughn's turn to trade wide-eyed looks; his vitriol melted, dripping away like candle wax, replaced with the quivering flame of fear. Raquel got up, her stomach finally holding steady. "What?"

Finn blinked at her, his brows slowly bending, like he didn't understand what she was asking. "I made my father scream."

"Tell me what that means." For some reason, she knew she had to be gentle—for some reason, when she approached Finn, she did it with back slightly bent and palms flipped outward. The way she'd been taught to approach wounded beasts. "What did you do?"

Finn looked at her hands, then at her face—and when he met her gaze, his smile shattered.

When he broke down on his seat, she was already there, on her knees, hands out—and when he grabbed them, sobbing like a small boy, she held fast and did not let go.

It was over in an hour. But at the end of that hour, something had shifted.

Finn had regained his composure, not one blotch or tear-track to suggest he'd ever broken down out at all; she hated him a little for it, but she comforted herself with the reminder that it was likely the assistance of auramancy. He hadn't said a word to her after he'd choked out the story of Tenebrae forcing him to torture his parents; instead, he'd looked at Vaughn, something like exhaustion dulling his clever gaze.

"I'll see to them," Vaughn promised, without Finn saying anything. "Vash will get me in."

None of them questioned how. Vash hadn't failed them yet.

Finn nodded. Let his head roll back. Stared at the ceiling.

"I don't forgive you for the part you played in this," he croaked. "Gods, I may hate you for the rest of my life. But what Kallias did, that's not on you. I shouldn't have said that."

It was the closest thing to an apology Vaughn would get, and he seemed to know it; he dipped his head, guilt of his own shadowing his brow as he rasped,

"No. You were right…about all of it. I did not mean to harm you, but harm was done regardless. I lied to you all about what I was. I let Jericho go too far trying to save what couldn't be saved, and now…now we have lost so much more." He shook his head. "Us before all. *Us*—all of us. I should have run when you did. I should have been there when Kal…"

"There was nothing you could have done," Raquel interrupted, sick to her soul of hearing his name. There was nothing any of them could have done. She knew, because she'd tried everything—had promised everything—and had still lost him.

She stamped the forget-me-not charm into the pad of her thumb. It needed cleaning—the blue gems had gone foggy and dull.

Breathe.

Breathe.

Breathe.

"I mean it," Finn said to Vaughn; when Vaughn frowned at him, he groaned, muttering under his breath about *keeping up* before he added, "You need to find a way to use your magic before we kick this off. If you can't walk under your own power to the palace when it's time, we might as well ask if we get a say in scheduling our executions. Personally, I call the sunset slot. I'm not getting up at dawn just to die, you know?"

"I'll do what I can," Vaughn muttered, ignoring the stab at humor.

"You'll do what I said," Finn corrected. "Or I'll tell Papa you're not taking care of yourself, and the next time he sees you, you'll get an earful about empty cups and trying to pour them out for other people."

Fondness pinched Vaughn's lips into a reluctant smile. "Fine."

"I'll be in the palace from here on out, so if anything needs adjusting, Raquel can get word to me at any hour." Finn caught her swift, surprised look, parrying it with a shrug. "I ran out of past to search through. I have enough—I can play the part. That game's over."

It had to be her imagination, that hint of regret in his eyes.

"It's over," he repeated, a little too quiet. "I won that battle—now it's up to us to win the war." A brief flash of amusement. "Us *for* all."

"Why do you keep saying that?" she demanded. It'd been long enough now—it was time for someone to let her in on the joke.

Vaughn glanced sidelong at her, almost smiling. "Us before all…it's a vow we swore to each other, the four of us, after Soleil—after Soren was taken. We protect each other over everything. Over everyone." A determined clench of his fingers, his jaw; then he reached out, setting his hand on the arm of the chair she'd taken when her body reminded her she hadn't eaten in nearly twenty-four hours. "In Kallias's absence, I make that vow to you on his behalf. I will do everything in my power to ensure you make it out of that palace alive."

"I have no need for secondhand loyalties." She set her hand over his. "Do everything in your power to ensure Adriata and Ramses live—that is our only goal."

It wasn't a lie. They, the people in this room, had only one goal. Tempest would be handling the rest.

"Us for all," she muttered under her breath.

She almost liked how it sounded.

CHAPTER 39

FINN

At first, they were only hallucinations.

They began with glazed, colorless eyes, no more alive than chips of pottery. Limbs so horribly distorted that the skin twisted like a wrung cloth, flayed bones in place of frayed threads. Cheekbones dented in, crushed porcelain dimpled with droplets of bruise and blood. A gaping mouth framed in torn ribbons of skin, lips shredded from the inside out.

A queen slumped on a golden throne; a thing so utterly, desperately broken that to see it draw breath inspired more horror than to think it dead.

And it *did* draw breath—at least, the chest rose and fell. But the longer Finn watched, gripped in place by the back of his head, his body refusing all commands to let him look away…the more he realized that the movement wasn't breath at all.

Beneath the queen's skin, something crawled.

It slunk its way from chest to clavicle; it wriggled up the column of her neck in spurts of struggle, dragging itself upward.

And behind the shreds of skin framing her mouth, a shadow built…not the hollow of a throat, but a swarm of corrupted power, a sickly-green gathering of what had once been lauded as a gift. Healing power twisted inside out by chaos; what once put bodies back together now unraveled them at their basest parts.

Not a shadow, but a crook-legged beast, spider-like and skittering…

Clawing its way out of Jericho's ruined body.

Objectively horrifying—no one could blame him for how deeply they disturbed him.

What disturbed him far, far more was how much worse it felt to watch the *other* vision.

A mirror girl on her knees—a mirror girl kneeling at his side, hands pressed to his chest, weeping diamond tears.

She spoke to him—she tried. But though he knew her voice—knew it like he knew his own, knew it like he knew he'd put a swift and violent end to whatever had caused those tears—he could not understand her. Every word came out garbled and strange, a code his mind refused to unravel.

He tried to tell her. He tried to tell her he knew her, that nothing could make him *not* know her, but he did not know what she was trying to *say*, and something hurt, something hurt so badly that he could not think past it, could not speak, could not remember her name or his—

And the longer his silence lasted, the more she wept. Fortunes of fear gathered in her fingers, fistful by fistful.

Her glittering gaze drifted from his chest to his head.

"No," he tried to tell her—but he couldn't remember how. Couldn't remember what that word even meant.

She bent. Pressed a kiss to his brow.

And with a whisper made of language that outdated the fabric of the world he knew, she shoved that priceless hoard into his chest, their facets cutting him straight to the core.

He'd jolted out of the nightmarish visions already in the throes of nausea, his body utterly rejecting what he'd seen, what he'd heard…and that wasn't even the worst of it.

He didn't sleep. Yet somehow, he'd started sleepwalking again.

Little bouts at first, nothing too alarming—blinking to find himself already standing by his bed, or partway to the bathing room, or tripping over the shoe he'd accidentally left in front of his closet door.

Then it got worse.

Blinking to find himself already dressed.

Blinking to find himself walking toward the covered mirror with purpose in his gait.

Blinking to find himself already wearing a face that wasn't his, braced to leap into the quicksilver pool.

He *did* try—no one, not even Raquel with all her skepticism and scowls, could say he didn't try. The first two times it happened, he simply threw the cover back over the mirror; the third, he clamped it down with sturdy steel clips made to hold fishing supplies; the fourth and fifth, he went as far as locking the mirror away in a trunk, hiding the key where he *definitely, absolutely* couldn't retrieve it without being fully conscious: Soleil's locked bedroom.

The sixth time, when he woke up to find the mirror back in its place, the key to his sister's room placed neatly on his bedside table, and his auramancy buzzing expectantly over the surface of his skin…he got tired of trying.

If he had to finish his business in the past before it released him fully to the future, so be it.

When he dipped his fingers into the shimmering quicksilver, he told it no lies—instead, he gave it a command.

"Take me where I need to go."

And with a gentle pull on his hand, the mirror obeyed its master.

When his foot settled on the ground, something cracked.

Brittle in break but soft in sound, it could have been anything—a twig, an icicle, even a particularly crisp leaf.

So when he looked down and found himself ankle-deep in a ribcage, his shoe coated in white powder, the gagging and the curses were more than justified.

He shook himself free of the bony snare, hastily crafting a scarf over his mouth as that white substance puffed gently into the air, the cloud threatening to invade his airway. Swallowing back another gag, he blinked away the last few flecks of sparkling magic, squinting against the sunlight to take in where the mirror had brought him.

Motes of dust bobbed peacefully in the sun, a shimmer not of magic's making cast over the world. The sky above gleamed brilliant blue, brighter than a robin's egg, surface unspoiled by clouds. Even the breeze seemed to sigh in contentment as it rolled over his shoulders, teasing the lifted hairs there, as if lazily inquiring over what all the fuss was about...

As he stared out over a *decimated* Sanctaviv.

He only knew it to be Sanctaviv at all because in the center of this empty space—miles of what had once been a bustling city now an empty plain painted in white—the fountain remained untouched.

He approached the statue of Sancta, his throat swelling tighter and tighter as he waded through the fine powder—at least a foot deep, nearly spilling over the edges of his boots. He reached up, running his palm carefully over the stone.

The carved lantern still hung around the statue's neck; its hands still faced outward, ready to pour blessings or curses in the measure one was due; its empty gaze stared impassively out at something no one could see.

But Finn could have sworn that bend to Sancta's brow—the vaguest sketch of sorrow, or maybe anger—hadn't been present before. And worse, he could guess why.

Because the motes bobbing through the air were not dust. And the white powder coating the ground was not snow.

Sanctaviv had been swallowed by a sea of ash.

The city had tried to burn one of its most faithful. And its most faithful had burned it right back.

The skeleton he'd stepped in was not alone, though there weren't many— as he picked through the destruction, catching glimpses of a reaching arm or a half-charred jaw parted in a scream, it became clear that the explosion had reduced most of the bodies to nothing.

The buildings, the people, the streets...Mortem's fire had consumed them all.

He waded shin-deep through human remains.

He had to stop. Had to take a deep breath—well, not a deep breath. A very shallow one through the protective fibers of his scarf, the best he could get without sucking down corpse dust.

He didn't *have* to be here. He didn't *have* to see whatever his magic was so intent on showing him. He could turn around right now, put himself back to bed, and accept that sleepwalking would just have to be part of his life from here on out.

But then he'd have to start bunking with Raquel, because someone would have to keep him from coming back here. And he knew how early she rose most mornings—and how likely it was that she'd let him rot in bed until his preferred hour of *whenever he felt like it.*

"It's just ash," he mumbled to himself, taking one more step. Then another. Then he started shuffling, an attempt to keep the ash from choking the air so thickly. "It's not blood, it's not guts, it's barely even bone. We have stepped in worse. We have absolutely stepped in worse."

He'd never been great at lying to himself. But it was enough to get him through the city square, slowly making his way in the direction of the singular dark spot that stood stark against the field of white, a charred bone cut against the beautiful sky: a familiar hovel.

The Medeis home.

Still standing, despite its rickety supports and weak walls—still standing, when everything else around it had disintegrated into dust.

When he set foot to the porch, trying not to look too closely at the open space to either side…the door swung open.

A trick of the wind, he thought at first—but then a small hand wrapped around the edge of the door. A small hand with dirt caked under its nails, its fingertips alight with the same sun that had nearly blinded him when he arrived; a hand that trembled as it clutched the wood. Between those fingers, tiny plants took root, sprouts wriggling their way out and reaching for the sky.

When the hand got its bearing, a face peeked out after it.

A little girl, no older than eight or nine; her chin quivered as she gazed up at him, her plump cheeks painted haphazardly with the scrubbed-away remains of tears.

Those eyes blazed with golden brilliance…a glory not content to stay confined to her irises. Her sockets spilled over with sunshine.

Some parts of her, he recognized from meeting those she shared blood with—the tilled-soil hair, the smattering of dark freckles against her rich brown skin—and other traits he knew from watching her live in Soren's body, such as the timid tuck to her chin as she gazed up at him. And though he'd never clearly seen her true face, guesswork could jump to the conclusions past experience couldn't reach.

"Please help," begged Annelisa Medeis—whom he knew better as Anima, Goddess of Life. "My brothers and sisters—I think they're dying, and I can't make it stop."

Dying.

That word thumped into his chest like a javelin thrown into a target, driving itself into its mark so hard that it came clean out the other side.

"I'm a friend of your sisters—of Cassi's," he croaked, though she seemed past caring about the inherent danger of letting a stranger into one's home. She hadn't even asked who he was or where he'd come from. "I'll help. May I come in?"

She nodded, a relieved gasp mingling with a sob as she shoved the door open all the way. "They're all sick, but I can't make them better. Mora's too hot and Peter's too cold and Brae's bleeding all over and—" She hiccup-sobbed, gripping his hand and dragging him in faster, pulling him through to the bedroom in the back. "Cassi's crying. All the time. And she's talking but I don't know what she's saying, a-and my stomach hurts and—"

"Hey, whoa—whoa whoa whoa." He knelt down, bringing her around to face him with a gentle tug on her hand. Gods, she was so *tiny*—tinier even than Soren had been at her age. When he ran his thumb soothingly over her knuckles, he might as well have been counting a row of ladybugs. "Take a deep breath—can you do that for me, Ani? That's your name, yeah?"

She sucked in a breath, her head bobbing rapidly. "Uh-huh."

"My name is Lord Ryder, but you can call me Alex. Your sister's told me a lot about you," he lied, smiling as kindly as he could. Had she been older, he might not have bothered—had she been closer to the goddess who'd stolen his sister's skin and stretched it out so badly she could barely keep it together any longer, he might have even been cruel.

But it didn't matter how corrupt he chose to become. He would never set his anger loose on children.

Ani sniffled, smiling shyly. "She told me about you, too."

"Did she?"

"Mmhm." Ani took her hand back, fussing with her fingers—moments later, tiny petals began to fall. "You ripped your scarf so she could fix it."

A rough chuckle jammed uncomfortably into his throat...beneath an auramantic imitation of that very scarf. "I did. That was silly, huh?"

Ani nodded, her gaze drifting toward the room behind her—revealed by the pause, the sounds beyond that threshold promised nothing good waited for him. A woman groaning in pain; someone coughing, the kind of cough that suggested the entire lung was trying to come up through the column of their throat; and a wailing scream that seized him by the heart and ripped it clean out.

He knew that scream.

Had known it in a Port Atlas alley, when he'd slit his first throat rather than risk her blood coating his hands instead.

Had known it just after abandoning her on a Sanctaviv rooftop, chants of *heretic* nearly drowning it out as he forced himself through to the future.

Had known it in the worst of the waking nightmares, the ones that woke him with a knife in his hand and her name on his lips.

"You lay down and rest," he told Ani—the girl's eyes, bright as they were within, were stamped in dark divots from lack of sleep. Gods knew how long the little girl had been working to keep her siblings alive. "I'll help them for a while, and I'll wake you when I have to leave, okay?"

Her fingers sped up their invisible crocheting, cherry-pink petals lengthening and darkening into black dahlia blooms. The wisps of scarlet-ebony drifted to the floor, so silk-soft they didn't even whisper as they settled on the flimsy floorboards. "But I…I promised them I'd take care of them."

"Can I tell you a secret?" He tapped her twice under her tucked chin, and she lifted it just a smidge, staring into his eyes without blinking…a newborn goddess gazing into his very soul. "The words we use when we make promises matter a lot less than the intention—that means it's more important that they get taken care of than it is for *you* to be the one caring for them. So here…"

Wrapping her fever-warm hand in his, he guided her to the bedroll crumpled just past the door to the back room. He'd seen it before, when Occassio had first shown him a glimpse of her past—in that memory, the nicest bedroll by far out of five had been wrapped tightly around a little girl hugging a doll made of candle wax and spare cuts of cotton.

As he guided Ani into it, he caught a glimpse of a tiny honey-yellow head buried inside…the doll herself, staring out with thumbprint eyes and a smile that looked like someone had carved it out with their fingernail. But half her head now slumped into dripping layers, like she'd been left in front of the hearth by accident.

Or she'd been touched by a superheated hand.

The second Ani's head hit the bedroll, those golden eyes flickered shut, magic extinguished by simple sleep. And once she slept, he was up and moving, pushing his way into that back room.

Finnick Atlas had known a few times that he was in over his head—that he had joined a game with too few cards up his sleeves to win. That he'd chosen the wrong character to wiggle his way into a mark's good graces. That he'd miscalculated, made a misstep that would see his opponent to checkmate before he could get there himself.

This was worse.

This was a wonder not meant to be witnessed by mortal men.

Luckily, he was no longer anything as simple as a mortal man.

So he walked in without pause—walked past the convulsing man nearest to the door, a mess of contorted limbs and frothing lips and wild, sightless eyes. Beneath Braeden's skin, bone and muscle *moved*, joints and tendons roaming where they wished; the foam at his lips was tinted darker than the dahlia petals stuck to Finn's soles, and despite the horrid cracks and squelches coming from inside him, he did not scream.

He tried. Finn could see him trying in the occasional gape of his mouth, the desperate crackle of breath and spray of spittle that emerged. But there was no voice.

Perhaps his vocal cords had also wandered away from their post.

Finn's stomach felt ready to follow their example. But as tempting as it might have been to dump his guts atop the monster at his feet—then to drive his heels into the god's ribs until they broke, to twist every finger so fully they would never find their way back to proper orientation, and maybe draw something unflattering on his wrenched-up face—it didn't feel worth it, not when the god wouldn't remember who'd done it to him.

Not when someone who *actually* mattered waited just a few steps away.

He ignored Mora, the only Medeis he hadn't met in the past or the future; she lay utterly still, no breath filling her chest, outlined in a foot-tall barrier of flame. A body on a pyre; yet her eyes darted wildly beneath her closed lids.

He ignored Peter, who lay so close to his sister's fire his clothes had begun to smoke and steam; despite the teasing nibble of the flames against his sleeve, a frigid ombre crept from his fingertips to his bottommost knuckles, frostbitten black to pallid blue to a truly colorless white.

In comparison, the girl huddled in the back hardly merited attention.

A thin shawl draped over thinner shoulders, patterned in polka-dots and streaked with dried blood, too small to belong to her. A jeweled gown tattered and scorched at the hem, the once-colorful gems blackened with soot. Hands buried in clotted and frayed hair. Her head thudding against the wall like she was trying to beat something out of it. Jagged nails repeatedly scraping layer after layer from the bloody furrows in her scalp.

A warbling, woe-is-me song unwinding from her lips.

O songbird in sorrow,
Don't sing of tomorrow,
You're better off stretching your wings
It's one thing to mutter,
Intention's another,
And humming won't bring you a breeze

Heart lodged firmly in his throat, he knelt beside her. Wrapped his hand gently around her wrist, halting her idle but dogged scratching. "Cassi."

She didn't look up—didn't act like she heard him at all. She sang on without a hitch or a hush, and gods damn him, how could she have a voice worthy of sold-out performance halls even while clawing her scalp away from her skull?

"Cass," he tried again. "Hey…can you hear me? Look at me if you can hear me."

She didn't turn her head. Didn't answer. Didn't even blink.

Just sang and sang and sang. A broken bird with a broken mind, a broken bird with a perfect voice, doing all she knew to do when everything else abandoned her.

When a mind came to its furthest extremes, it defaulted to what it had been made for. And Cassandra Medeis had been made to sing—to shine.

And him, well, he was no songbird—but he knew how to put on a show. He knew how to play pretend.

So he knelt on the musty floorboards, claiming every inch he could until his kneecaps brushed the tips of her bare toes. He reached past her drawn-up knees and cradled her cheeks, forcing her to stop tossing her head against the wall, teasing his fingertips beneath her hands until he could wind his fingers underneath hers.

When he extricated her hands from her hair, they began to tremble—he shushed her gently, rubbing his thumbs over her knuckles, ignoring the half-dried tack of blood. Wishing he could ignore the knotted skin sealed over what felt like beads, glimmers of glass catching the light—glass that had healed *inside* her skin.

And when she finally tipped her head up, eyes screwed tightly shut, he pressed his forehead to hers and tried so very hard to not feel foolish as he sang with her.

Maybe if he plunged into madness with her, he could find a way to pull her back out.

O songbird, my darlin'
You must try to bargain

So gather your treaties and pleas
The housecat is cunning,
No mercy is coming,
And dreaming won't buy you a leash
O songbird in sorrow,
You've no strength to borrow,
You wasted your time on a tune
Your clipped wings are failing,
Your heart's quick to breaking,
And wishing won't grant you a—

A sharp gasp drew her note up short of his, leaving his half-decent voice to finish the verse—adrenaline hummed through his bones, and he tightened his hold on her face, whispering *stay with me, stay with me* until she eased out of her rigor with another gasp and a sob, her voice wandering into a hum before it stumbled into the last verse.

He was no singer—his skills lay in things he could manipulate with his hands, and he couldn't reach into his throat and pluck the strings of his own vocal cords. He couldn't fix whatever kept them out of tune, no matter how many singing lessons his former fiddle teacher had put him through. She'd always said he had a lockbox voice—that he should have been good, great even, but something kept his voice sealed up.

Whatever lock kept that box shut, he couldn't pick it. But in this ramshackle shed a thousand years in the past, for once, it didn't matter if he was good—it didn't matter if he put on the perfect show or made the perfect choice. It didn't matter if he forgot to smile at the right time or laughed when he should have frowned or broke his voice trying to sing over the nightmares babbling in a goddess's bleeding ears.

All that mattered was that he did it, and that she heard him, and that he stayed.

He stayed—because somehow, no matter how many times he tore himself away, no matter how many times he tried to rid himself of her for good, no matter how many locks he put on his door or pins he put in his shoes or lists he made of all the things she'd done to shatter his mind and break his heart…he ended up right back here.

So he stayed. And he sang; even when her voice failed, even when her gaze tried to roam, even when she tried to tug her head away, he kept singing, kept calling, kept hanging on.

And as the last note faded, a shuddering, wet breath had him drawing back, fear bolting his voice to his tongue. Without letting go of her face, afraid she'd start bashing her head again if he did, he leaned back and searched for the source of what had to be pain...

And instead he found her staring back at him, eyes leaking lavender light and viscous scarlet tears, tremulous panting parting her lips.

"You," she said.

Her entire heart beat within that one word. Betrayal and hate; sadness and hurt; relief and confusion.

It throbbed in the air between them, then paused—skipping beat after beat as it waited for his answer.

His heart followed suit. But they couldn't both put them out in the open, raw and vulnerable—one of them had to keep their senses.

And today, wonder of wonders, it was him who had the upper hand on sanity.

"There she is." It took everything—*everything*—to play at sounding chipper as he released her face to trail his thumb over her coarse brows, scraping blood from them; once they were clean, he started scrubbing dried clots from the furrows in the bridge of her nose. "Gods, look at you. You're a mess. What happened? Did those pretty eyes of yours blind a bird? I've seen them crash into things before, but this is...I mean, it's grisly."

Her face crumpled beneath his touch, and she let her head drop forward—he had to catch her chin to keep it from colliding with her sternum. A wholehearted sob bent her into him, and she moaned into his palms: "*Please kill me.*"

"Of course. Whatever you want," he murmured, humoring her—and muffling the panicked lurch of his heart as it broke down to its knees. "But you'll have to be more specific, you know. Lots of ways to kill someone. I can't be expected to narrow them down on my own."

She giggled—whimpered—then hummed, rocking back and forth, lurching out of his grip as she wrapped her arms tightly around herself. "Lazy lordling," she murmured absently—the first sign she really *could* hear him. "Lots of ways to die. Not enough anymore. You have two faces. You burned—didn't you burn? *Dying in body, heart filled with folly*—you filled my hands with light. Do you remember?"

With every looping tangle of thought she babbled into the air, his heart sank deeper and deeper—and he wondered, over and over, why he stayed to watch this. Why his magic had brought him here. Why any of this mattered.

Finnick Atlas didn't like things that were allowed to be true without some kind of logic backing them up. He didn't like laws, not even natural ones, that he couldn't follow backward from establishment to conception in one straight line.

But he couldn't walk his way through this one. Not forward, not backward, not even if he took the long way around.

He didn't know why it mattered. He didn't know why he stayed.

But it did. And he did.

So he held his hands out to her, waiting—for what, he didn't gods-damned know, but it seemed like the thing to do. He waited as a goddess pleaded with him to end her life, to snuff her out, to end the pain, to douse the light…waited as she begged and screamed and laughed and sang and murmured nursery rhymes that would survive to his own childhood.

And all at once, silence fell.

Silence—and stillness. Like the hovel they huddled in had been holding its breath, waiting for something it might never see; like it had held it until it had gone blue in the face, but finally had to empty its lungs of wasted air.

Echoing that exhale, Cassi broke from her rocking crouch. Blood dribbled from her nose and eyes as she bent forward on hands and knees, crawling without looking…

Right into his lap.

Right into his arms.

Right up to his heart, where she buried her face in his chest and clung to his shirt, knuckles wrapped in the cloth like she'd been swimming for days and finally found a life raft. Like if she let go, the ocean would swallow her whole.

"Kill me," she pleaded again, defeated this time. Like she already knew the answer was no…or maybe realized that even he tried, he couldn't possibly succeed. Not with Ani in the next room.

So instead, he braced his hand behind her head—she crumbled completely into that support, like a ragdoll who'd just remembered they hadn't stuffed any bones under her stitches. He pulled her all the way into his lap, hating how easy it was—hating how he could feel where every bone led to the next, her skin doing nothing to mask the structure bearing up her body.

"Please," she begged, trying to lift her head—her neck wobbled, and he eased her head against his chest again. Gods, there was just…nothing left to her. No strength, no sparkle, no smile. "Just *try*."

"Sure, sure—in a minute," he murmured, distracted by her blood seeping through his shirt—when she groaned, a frantic whimpering sound, he shushed her again, tugging on a curl far from her bloodied temples. "Patience is a virtue, you know. And when one asks for a favor, it's impolite to rush the completion of said favor."

"You're being *mean*," she mumbled into his shirt—so absurdly *pouty* that he had to laugh.

"Oh, forgive me," he muttered as he freed one of his hands to card carefully through her curls—once he found the divots in her scalp, he began pulling the loose hair away from them. He gripped his sleeve in his teeth and tugged sharply, tearing off a strip—he pressed it to her bleeding head, and though a shiver ran through her from head to toe, she didn't make a sound. "Didn't mean to bully you before I murder you."

"You should be dead," she said softly; when he looked down, he found her staring off into nothing, that lavender light in her eyes swirling with strands of golden power. "Both of you—both faces. You're dead, and he will be. This is just a pretty dream."

"You dream of me? That's adorable."

She didn't laugh; didn't roll her eyes; didn't show off her double dimples. "Oh," she said instead, like it all made sense—then again, softer, sadder: "Oh."

"Oh?" He focused on stanching the bleeding, but something about that *oh* set every instinct of his on high alert. Her hair coiled around his fingers as he worked, snakes winding themselves around hapless prey, tangles pulling them tight enough to pale the pink in the pads of his fingers. "It's a nice enough letter, I suppose, but I find it does better with company. Care to add a few more? Maybe enough to make a word or two?"

"You're not real." Her voice rounded out with knowing, and she smiled…a smile that split her chapped, chewed-raw lip, cherry-red blood leaking from the tear. "Of course you're not real. You burned."

Clearing his throat, he untangled his fingers from her strangling hair and held up his hand in front of both of their faces, flipping it this way and that. "Do I look burned?"

She swayed back, muscles still pulled so taut they trembled beneath her skin; when she gazed at his hand, foggy-eyed and frowning, confusion pinched her brows together.

Then she laughed. And when he lowered his hand, she only laughed harder; the wider her grin stretched, the more tears spilled from her eyes, both bloody and clean.

"Cassi," he croaked. "You need to try to—"

"You're not *real*." Another laugh—a harder sob. "I want you to be *real*."

He swallowed. Forced a smile. "I'm as real as you are."

She stared at him, her smile shattering faster than the glass buried in her knuckles had; she sobbed so soft and sweet it could have been the first note of a song. "Prove it."

Not a challenge or a tease—a plea. A wish.

"Tell me how," he said, "and I'll do it."

It scared him, just how much he meant it. Just how much he'd do to make those tears stop.

She leaned in, still crying; when she pressed her hands to his chest, they shimmered with light, the glass splinters in her skin reflecting her own gaze back to her. She tapped her fingers erratically against his shirt; a moment later, she scrunched it up in her fists, trying to tug it open.

Finn didn't stop her; mostly because he had no depths-damned clue what she was trying to do, but also because he didn't want to frighten her and end up with a scratched-up chest or clawed-open hands he'd have to explain to Tenebrae later. But as she kept tugging, her breathing taking on a frantic tempo, he finally risked wrapping his fingers around her wrists. Her head came up with an unsteady jerk, her breath rushing out in a frustrated whimper.

He gave her a pointed look. "Most people ask before they try to rip someone's clothes off."

Cassi blinked at him, a total lack of comprehension showing on her parted lips and dazed eyes.

The urge to joke and tease his way around this suddenly held no appeal at all.

"Cassi," he murmured again, relaxing his hold on her wrists; he rubbed his thumbs along the backs of her hands instead, trying to loosen their bowstring-tight grip. "Tell me what you need, and I will find it for you."

She blinked again. Her throat bobbed.

"I need to feel your heart," she whispered. "Real things have hearts."

That might be difficult, seeing as those teardrop-soft words had crushed it into powder.

She could have asked him to dance a jig on top of her twitching brother and he would've done it faster. To bare his heart to this sharp-fingered, glass-tongued girl…one who'd already proven she'd happily drive a dagger through it if given the opportunity…

Every instinct that had kept him alive in Atlas's festering underbelly screamed that if he showed her where he hid his most vulnerable piece, she'd rip it out with tooth and nail.

But the heart itself did not bow to instinct's ranting. Instead, it shushed those suspicions with bruised fingers to bloodied lips, grin doused in crimson as it whispered, *It's all right. I'm ready to try again.*

Again. A word only good for proving that risks like this didn't often end in his favor.

He folded her fingers shut, one by one, until he held her fists between both of his hands. He kissed her knuckles, protruding glass catching on his lips—not keen enough to cut, but enough to remind him it was there.

Enough to remind him who put it there.

"I'll help you," he said. "Rest your hands."

And she did. Though she fretted with her fingertips, she kept them folded in her lap, kneeling in the swaying stance of a dreamer only half-roused.

One by one, he fumbled through his buttons, thumbing them slowly through their holes. Magic couldn't be blamed for his clumsiness this time; these were nerves, pure and simple, the kind an ordinary man might have suffered while removing his shirt in front of an ordinary woman.

Gods, if *only* these nerves were caused by anything that silly. But rather than blushing uncertainties or thoughts of what she might think of him without the help of his costumes, his skin ached furiously with the anticipation of a wound soon to be dealt.

Sometimes, fear of pain could be so strong that even when the wounding didn't happen, the pain still did. And though he had a better grip of his mind than most, it still played its own tricks every so often.

So when her calloused fingers rasped over his bare skin, seeking the beat of his heart beneath, his mind told him they were forged from steel.

Steel so cold it burned.

Finn's heart leapt into his throat, fleeing the oncoming blow—with a harsh swallow, he forced it back down, his steadying breath pushing his chest against her palm.

She didn't claw or tear or pour purplish light into his eyes; instead, she rested her palm atop his heart, eyes glued to it with unbreakable focus, not even blinking as her lips moved in silent count.

Numbering his heartbeats.

"See?" he croaked. "Real as you."

Her brows drew together, and she blew out a shaky breath, nodding once. "Real things have hearts," she said again, like she was convincing herself, reminding herself. Then: "I want to sleep. Can I sleep?"

The imaginary, anticipatory pain leeched out of his skin, replaced by a gentle warmth as her fingers soaked in his body heat. He wrapped his hand around hers and squeezed, guiding her back to the floor. "Of course you can."

When her eyes closed, they didn't open again—despite lying flat on splintered wood, she immediately dropped away from consciousness when he set her head on the boards.

With a brief drag of his finger down his own chest, he put together a new shirt, illusion shifting into reality as it took on weight and texture. The one he'd come in with, he folded and left under her head; unclipping the cloak around his neck, he cast it over her shivering form, absently rubbing over her arm to try and push some extra warmth into the cloth.

Something *tugged* on his mind—such a clear yank that his head whipped around in that direction, sure someone had pulled his hair or called his name. But all he found was an ash-frosted window, one of the few that still had glass in its frame.

He glanced back toward Cassi; she didn't exactly look *peaceful*, but she'd at least gone quiet, sleeping without muttering or screaming. She'd tucked her face against the makeshift blanket he'd made of his cloak, her fingers strangling the fabric like someone might steal it from her.

Maybe this was all he'd needed to do; maybe she'd just needed him to get her through this one moment, and now he could go. Now he could leave her behind.

But that insistent *tug* didn't feel like permission to return home.

Regardless, he couldn't stay here; the second and third eldest Medeis siblings were beginning to stir, their frozen and burning bodies struggling toward wakefulness, and he had an educated guess on what they would do if they spotted a stranger in their current state.

He strode to the window and pressed his hand to it, telling it he wanted to go home. But as he stepped through, he could've sworn the glass giggled; could've sworn it named him *Liar* as he slipped between its panes.

CHAPTER 40

FINN

Shocking no one, least of all him, Finn didn't step out into Port Atlas. However, something *did* shock him—enough that he pulled up short on his next step, hovering halfway in and halfway out of whatever sheet of glass he'd traveled through, taking in the sight before him as fast as he could manage.

Which needed to be *much faster*, actually, because if anyone saw a man bisected by glass, they might start to scream. And he was hardly an expert on chronomancy, but he assumed that someone witnessing this sort of magic before it technically existed might cause some pretty serious problems.

All he knew for sure was that this *definitely* wasn't Sanctaviv—neither the ancient version that had burned, nor the new city built in its place in modern-day Artem.

Instead, he found himself standing on the outskirts of what appeared to be an outdoor market—rather than brick or stone shops, colorful tents and tarps loomed in irregular rows, hawkers standing in front of racks of wares, people milling between them in various states of excitement or overwhelm. Most of them wore thin, gauzy garments in rich colors, wraps or brimmed hats protecting their faces from the sun.

When he peeked around and behind him, he found he'd walked through one of several framed mirrors—the sort that stood on their own. The tarp-covered stand nearby had a sign propped on it that read *Back Shortly*.

Lucky break.

Hot, abrasive air smacked him full in the face as he stepped all the way out of the glass, a dry grit that smelled of sunbaked earth. Heavy summer heat draped over him like a cloak, shoving the lingering cold out of his skin; he squinted against the blinding sun, probing his surroundings for shelter.

There—a tarp-covered board driven into the ground beside the dusty path winding through the market, covered in tacks that pinned down fluttering scraps of paper.

The shade did little to sap the heat away, but at least it would protect him from sunburn. He carefully arranged himself within the thin sliver of shelter, tucking every inch of exposed skin into the shade; he rolled his sleeves up and cropped them there with a subtle bit of illusory tailoring. He kept the overall look of the outfit—simple pants and a simple shirt—but altered the material to something lighter in weight and color. Something that would breathe in the oppressive heat.

Now to find out where he was.

He turned to the board, skimming the papers quickly—most of them were job postings or instructions on what to do if one suspected they'd caught the plague currently traveling through the Empire.

Not too far removed from Sanctaviv, then. But that didn't—

A scrap of handwriting caught his eye. Handwriting he recognized from notes taken on his measurements.

Mouth drying out faster than the sandy breeze tugging mightily on the folds of his shirt, he plucked the tack out of the board and caught the paper before it could fly off, skimming the text with haste:

Miracles Await All Who Ask

Whatever your ailment, whatever your need, bring it to the New Gods of the Empire.

The sweat on the back of his neck turned cold in an instant.

Beneath that text, the flyer spoke of the sorts of miracles waiting for those who dared answer its summons, but none of that mattered—not when he caught sight of the names listed at the very end.

Anima.

Mortem.

Tempest.

Tenebrae.

And lastly, in swooping script that sparkled just a bit when the breeze pushed the tarp aside, allowing a ray of sunshine to strike it: *Occassio.*

He crumpled the flyer in his fist, sharp corners of folded paper stabbing into his palm.

He didn't need his magic to lead him this time—he could guess exactly where the Medeis siblings had chosen to display the might of their magic.

So he followed his instincts—and the crowd—and wove his way toward the gathering host of people just past the market's end.

The crowd hummed like a host of cicadas as he pushed through the net of sweaty limbs and vulnerable coinpurses and desperate eyes.

These were not the idle patrons taking leisurely turns about the market, weighing bits of sparkle and judging their quality by eye and by touch; these were people who ached with need.

They all wore hope on their sleeves—and their chests, pinned over their heart like a standard. They held it plainly in their hands, fussing fingers counting their meager coins or pieces of paper over and over and over.

But it wasn't hope that buzzed in the air.

It hadn't taken long at all for him to memorize the exact frequency of a building frenzy. Even though Occassio's stolen magic protected him from the infectious melody plinking from Tenebrae's cursed music box, the chaos it coaxed into the world was a palpable thing.

To feel it here…and to feel it this strongly, with no tinny notes tweaking his ears the wrong way…

He should have brought his damned daggers.

Shoving a hand into his pocket, he summoned a tidbit of magic into his fingertip before scraping at the pocket lining, deepening it until he could hide his hands past his wrists. Once they were tailored to his liking, he let that fizz bubble outward until the entire underside of his hand shimmered with the magic of making.

Even if he and fire had gotten along, he wouldn't have been able to forge a blade of his own. Luckily, all auramancy required was a forging fueled by imagination.

And he had a damned good imagination.

As he dipped and bobbed through the crowd, a cork set free on the tide, he squeezed his eyes shut. And while his body found its own way forward, his steps guided by the firm hand of foresight, he imagined a weapon.

A dagger, plain but functional—one that would meld to his fingers like they were two halves of a whole, just the right weight to strike fast and strike true.

As the carved-bone grooves of its hilt settled against the creases in his hand, his lungs loosened up, allowing him a deep draw of desert-dry air. But only his lungs relaxed; his muscles bound themselves in iron, snakes tensed to strike, ready to draw his weapon the second the swarming energy broke open over the crowd.

Above the cicada-song of antsy chatter and scattered magic, a voice boomed, turning heads and ears in unison toward something Finn couldn't see. He stretched on his toes to try and seek a path ahead, but the crowd just kept thickening.

He glanced down to the path under his feet. Scowled.

Well, he'd done less dignified things in his life, but this would definitely be up there on the list.

His knees protested as he forced them to bear the brunt of his weight; his palms protested in turn as he started crawling forward, swinging his arm wildly about, knocking aside legs and skirts.

"So sorry!" he yelped to the angry glowers that drilled holes in the top of his head.

"Dropped my last copper," he rambled to the one kind woman who stopped to set her hand on his shoulder, asking after his well-being.

The people who kicked him as he passed, he said nothing to—because they wanted a fight, firstly, but also because the only piece of them close enough to attack was their ankles, and he didn't feel like becoming a *literal* ankle-biter just to get to the front of this mass of miracle-seekers.

And before he knew it, he'd shoved himself out into open space—a twelve-foot stretch of it between him and a platform of gnarled tree trunks, their branches tangled thickly together to form a somewhat stable surface.

"Oi!" barked a voice—oil-black boots appeared beneath Finn's nose just before one kicked at his chest, driving the breath from him as it forced him back into the throng. "Wait your turn."

Finn bit down a grunt of pain as he skidded back on his seat, dust leaping into the air to escape his slide—when he looked up, he found a uniformed man scowling down at him, dark russet skin streaked with what looked like soot across his cheeks. His square features—broad nose, broad mouth, broad brows—all bore creases that didn't exactly translate to *cruelty*, but they certainly didn't leave Finn thinking he might be able to simper and sob-story his way into being allowed to cut the line.

Even though what existed behind and around him could hardly be called a *line*.

"Apologies," he croaked instead, throwing his voice to match that strange Sanctan accent. "Got lost."

"Well, get lost again. They take their audiences as they can, and cutting won't buy you any miracles."

Finn dipped his head, keeping his eyes down as he stood and swept off his palms and pants; better not to pick fights, not when he had no idea who exactly he'd be picking a fight with. A bodyguard, maybe, or a city guard paid extra to keep the crowd in check.

It made sense—when one made such bold claims as to be selling miracles, one would be foolish not to keep some extra muscle around.

Once the man stomped his admittedly fine boots elsewhere, Finn took the chance to wind himself up on his tiptoes again, peering over hands thrown out in supplication.

Braeden—Tenebrae—paced the platform with tangible excitement. His dark curls, twin to Cassi's, seemed to have a life of their own; they leapt this way and that with every whip-quick twist of his ankle, more of a mess than when he'd shown up at her shop after a day-long shift of hard labor.

In contrast, his clothes were of incredibly fine make; the charcoal-gray satin pants were cinched at the ankles and waist with rows of gold buttons, and his matching see-through shirt showed off the whorls of golden ink painted over his torso and chest.

That gold also painted his nails, his eyelids, and his cheekbones—even his lips gleamed like fresh-ground gold dust as he grinned broadly, spreading his hands and shouting, "Your prayers are heard, friends! You have begged and wept for too long to be answered with Sancta's silence—you have waited *too long*. The new gods hear—the new gods answer!"

"Praise the new gods!" shouted a handful of scattered voices amongst the crowd. Others muttered uneasily, fiddling with the lantern tokens looped around their wrists or necks; but no one left. No one accused him of the reckless, almost *gleeful* heresy he threw out like a scream of triumph.

Past Tenebrae's shoulder, four tents loomed, crowding out the horizon—large, expensive tents.

One dyed green, painted with the same golden swirls as Tenebrae's skin and covered in creeping ivy; one dyed the same shade as the ocean on the clearest summer days, also accented with gold; one dyed such a deep, sanguine red it could have been soaked in blood, gilded accents few and far between; and one vivid purple, decorated in silver and pink, its common threads of gold much thinner.

These tents didn't sit on dead, scorched earth. Instead, verdant grass cradled each one in its cushion, proof that their claims were not entirely false. Proof that some new power had been born into the world…a power that had now come to visit this little desert town.

Before the green tent, Anima knelt in the grass, her hands pressed to the still chest of the child lying prone before her. Bile stung Finn's throat at the pallor of the child's face.

He'd never seen any living child, even ill or injured ones, lie so still.

The weeping pair kneeling by the girl's head confirmed his suspicions. The woman had her forehead pressed to the girl's, her tears running down the girl's cheeks; the man was rambling to Anima, his hands anchored around the woman's shoulders, his eyes glazed with the sort of shock that only struck in the wake of sudden loss.

Finn knew that glassy shield. He'd seen it fall over his father's gaze more than once over the years.

Anima was older now, not by much—maybe twelve. But compared to the sleepless little girl he'd settled in her bedroll a mere hour ago—at least, an hour ago for him—she might as well have been a different girl entirely. Her cheeks were round and full of color, and though her frame still leaned willowy, he couldn't see her bones peeking out anymore. Health and happiness glowed from every pore; even as she frowned in concentration, her eyes sparkled.

The flowers twined in her crown of braids boasted new buds. No roots, no water or soil—yet they grew.

At the same time the little girl's cheeks bloomed with blood-blush, her lips parting to gasp in new breath, those buds burst open.

As the parents collapsed over their daughter, sobbing and kissing her face clean, Finn forced his gaze away, an old, jealous fury scraping at the backs of his gritted teeth.

In front of the sea-green tent, Tempest listened patiently to farmers explaining their struggle to keep their crops and themselves properly hydrated; before the red tent, Mortem ran her fingers over the veins of a man who couldn't hold his head up for drunkenness, another man sitting close by, watching with a haunted glaze to his eyes. And the purple tent…

No one sat outside Occassio's tent. Everyone whose needs required an audience with her entered alone; and when they left, they didn't look quite like the same people that went in.

Some more literally than others; more than one person came out with a different face, an illusion Finn could just see wavering at the edges.

He'd have to go to her, then.

He could have conned his way in—he could have found a way to get rid of the next man in line, then illusioned himself to look like him, leaving the guards directing the miracle-seekers none the wiser.

But that would take too long. So he just made himself invisible instead.

Sure, maybe the sight of feet pressing down the grass without any *feet* visible could have given him away; maybe the sight of a tent flap lifting itself could have given the onlookers pause.

But they were all so fixated on Tenebrae's rousing, rabid speech that no one saw a thing.

People were all the same. They never looked for the little tells—as long as you gave them something loud and shiny to stare at, they'd never notice you robbing them blind.

Finn paused at the entrance to the tent. He set an ear to the canvas and closed his eyes, listening. When he heard nothing, he reached for his magic, asking for a peek—

And it flinched back from him, skittering away like a kicked hound pup.

That wasn't promising.

He tried again to grab it, snatching for its scruff, but it fled further from his reach. No matter how he coaxed and cajoled, it wouldn't come to him; it wouldn't obey its new master.

Maybe because it sensed the old one lurking nearby.

Fine. He'd do it blind.

He didn't let himself wait another second; he let himself into the tent, releasing the bent light that shielded him from view.

The inside of the tent was doused entirely in rosy light; auramancied orbs bobbed gently above his head, perfect spheres crafted from trapped magic, a luminescence that stirred dizziness like the dust of the road outside. He rubbed his eyes as he took another step in.

Somehow, it seemed smaller on the inside—the draping curtains and standing shelves surrounding the crystalline desk in the center gave the impression of walls where there were none. Beneath the desk, a glass tank showed off a snake slowly slithering from one end of its habitat to the other—a three-foot creature with shimmering lavender scales, its snout upturned at the end, its eyes taking on the pinkish sheen of the light surrounding it. A long-haired cat dozed beside the tank, its creamy fur pressed flat against the warm glass, its blue-gray muzzle tucked against its paws; when Finn walked in, it stood and stretched, prancing out the back of the tent. And behind the desk, seated on an iridescent stool, her back facing him…

"Welcome, traveler," purred Occassio, Goddess of Time. "What have you come to ask of me?"

At first, his voice fled the same way his magic had, both of them terrified to face someone who'd once commanded them; someone they'd since betrayed.

Someone who'd hurt him immeasurably.

Someone he'd hurt immeasurably in return.

As he scrounged around for any hint of breath, of cleverness, her head tipped to the side. The jewels embedded in her lush, lovely curls had to be worth more than all the gold he'd ever held in his life—the metallic silver gown she wore dripped down her body like molten ichor, accentuating dips and folds that spoke of health returned, full curves flourishing where sharp angles had once cut into her skin.

One hand rose, fingers bending, beckoning. "Go on—I don't bite. Unless I'm asked."

She might change her mind when she saw who waited for her. But he didn't say so—instead, he came to stand before the crystal desk, glancing down at himself in its reflective depths.

Hundreds of illusory eyes gazed back at him…hundreds of reflections of this face he'd crafted on a whim his first day in Sanctaviv. A reassurance that his mask hadn't slipped…and a reminder of the part he played today.

"You've come a long way from pickpocketing lazy lordlings," he said lightly.

She leapt from the stool, twirling so fast she almost tripped—it might have made him laugh, if the expression on her face hadn't fallen open, spilling out emotions he hadn't expected to see.

Shock, he'd guessed at—anger, he'd assumed.

But the tears…those he hadn't counted on.

And even though they were barely more than a frosting of silver piped over her lower lids…even though they blinked out of existence as fast as they'd blinked into it…he still saw them.

"You." The word fell like a flipped coin from her lips, an echo clattering between them—when he didn't stack a word of his own on top of it, she slid slowly back onto the stool, staring like he was a dead thing her sister had puppeted through the door. Her eyes kept darting behind him like she expected someone to own up to pranking her. "You're…you're dead. You died—everyone *died*."

She didn't remember him being there as her magic took over, then. Good. That was…good.

"Apologies. If someone had bothered to tell me, I wouldn't have spent this long walking around. Can you point me to the nearest graveyard?"

She spluttered. "It's not a joke, you—you ludicrous—you awful—"

He scratched his chin, grateful all over again that he'd shaved. "C'mon, you have to be more creative than that."

She bent over the desk, palms flat on the crystal—light flickered inside, leaping from facet to facet before extinguishing. "I *grieved* for you, you haughty bastard."

His smirk froze in place, waiting for her to laugh—when she held his gaze without blinking for several seconds, lips pressed in a furious line, it thawed into a frown.

"Oh," he said lamely.

"*Oh?*" she repeated, voice quivering with barely contained rage. The desk flared with sourceless light once more, nearly blinding him from below.

"I thought you were dead too," he lied in a hurry—if clever comebacks had abandoned him, at least he could always rely on lies. "I left the city right after the…after…"

"After you broke my heart and abandoned me on a rooftop with my hands full of glass?"

Abandoned. "Technically, you told me to leave."

She scoffed, shoving off the desk and turning her back on him. She brushed both hands over either side of her head, smoothing the curls down; they bounced back the moment she released them to sweep her hands down the sides of her skirt instead. "You left. Then what?"

"Then I heard about what happened a couple days later, and I figured you didn't make it out." He buried his hands in his pockets to keep himself from running his hands through his own hair. "I'm glad I was wrong."

"The sentiment isn't shared." She turned to flash him a smirk over her shoulder; no dimples to be seen. "If you're just here to mess around…"

"No, no. I'm a paying customer." He took his time taking in the tent—the floating lights, the piles of loose gems and jewelry, the array of mirrors—and rounded his lips in an impressed whistle. "You've gotten your hands on some great props, I'll give you that. Which hoax do you recommend?"

Her eyes glittered, a frigid gleam that reminded him too much of her future self—but she sauntered back to the stool with something gripped in her curled fingers. "It's not a hoax anymore, Lordship. I'm sure you've heard what I can do, or you wouldn't be here. So tell me…what does a man like you desire from a woman like me?"

"More goddess than woman these days, I hear." He cocked his head. "How'd that happen?"

She used her empty hand to summon another ball of light, spinning it idly on the tip of her finger; belatedly, it occurred to him he probably should've acted surprised by her little show. "Long story. Too long to waste on you. Here's what I can offer instead…"

In a fluid movement, a graceful uncoiling that mirrored the slithering of her snake in its tank, she rounded the desk—then rounded him, a predator hunting for weaknesses in its frozen prey. "I could show you your future…" Fingers trailed behind his neck, not quite touching, just close enough for the warmth of her to raise goosebumps down his spine. "Or change your appearance…" She paused in front of him, gazing up into his eyes with a shrewd, almost teasing twinkle. "Though it seems you already know that trick." A pat on his chest. "I could even wrap you up in a shield of light, make you practically invincible for a bit. You could jump from, say…a rooftop, and land without a bruise to show for it."

He held her gaze, raising an eyebrow. "Impressive."

"I know." She backed away, hopping up on the desk and crossing her ankles, extending one arm in invitation. "So? What miracle will you ask of me, *Lord Ryder?* What does the lazy lordling want?"

Finn chewed on that for a good minute, weighing his options—in the end, he settled on the truth. "I think I want the hoax."

An odd answer, maybe—a risky one, definitely. He was taking this magic of hers in stride far too easily.

But with all that hurt still boiling behind her eyes, he couldn't muster the motivation to push his con that far.

She blinked, a few times too many and far too fast—she hadn't yet learned how to fully mask her surprise. But then she smiled—not a full one, not enough to draw both dimples out of hiding, but one of them made a shy attempt at an appearance.

"Sit down, then," she said brusquely. "I'll need a moment to set the stage."

He sat down on the wooden chair on the other side of the desk, gesturing around the tent. "Please—by all means. Take your time."

A bold remark to toss at the Goddess of Time, who certainly didn't mind stretching out the seconds as far as she could. It felt like hours that he sat there in that uncomfortable chair, forcing himself not to fidget as she set up an incense burner and lit it, coaxing the flame to life with a gentle purse of her lips and a few careful breaths rather than summoning her fire-gifted sister. She called each bauble of light down to her, one by one—when she blew on them, rather than brightening the way the incense fire had, the illusory baubles dimmed. She rubbed their tops counterclockwise, and the color swirling inside shifted from a pastel pink to a smoky purple.

After releasing them back into the air, letting them float to the top of the tent, she sat on her stool and set down the object she'd been hiding in her other hand…a deck of cards, purple with gold foil on the back.

He glanced up at her, an unspoken question perched on his tongue; she bit her scarred lip on a smile, and in that softening, he caught a glimpse of the Cassi he'd come to know.

"I had a feeling you'd pick the hoax," she said.

"May I?" When she nodded, gesturing to the cards in a silent *be my guest,* he picked up the deck and began thumbing through them, frowning at the unfamiliar designs.

"These look like tarot," he said.

"They are."

"But I don't recognize the cards." He knew his way around most tarot decks, even those that originated from centuries before his lifetime—Luisa had taught him the meanings behind most of the cards, explaining how he could twist their messages to his liking when he used them on jobs. They were useless on the majority of religious marks, and most people thought they were a harmless bit of fun, but they'd come in handy more than once when his mark was deeply superstitious—or an Occassio-worshipper.

Now she beamed with pride—a true preening that straightened her spine and lit up her eyes. "That's because it's my personal deck. Here, look."

All at once, that crystal-cold shield cracked—she stretched gracelessly over the desk to snatch a card, laying it on the desk and hovering her hand over it, shedding light from her fingertips to help him get a better look.

"See those paint strokes?" At his nod, her nose scrunched up with smugness. "Every single one of these is hand-painted—one-of-a-kind. I made them myself. You won't see any of these cards duplicated anywhere else."

"They're beautiful." Another truth, but one he didn't mind giving—they were gorgeous cards. The paper had heft to it, the kind only quality parchment offered; the corners were perfect, not one of them creased or bent. And the illustrations themselves invited staring; the eyes of *The Songbird* refused to let him loose, her sorrowful gaze dark as despair, her hopeful smile showing off a familiar gap in her two front teeth. *The Treasure* glowed with cherub cheeks and bright eyes, her childish hands clinging to a skull with a crack straight down its center; the flowers winding through her hair stood in sharp contrast to the macabre find cradled in her palms. And when he flipped to the next card…

It was, perhaps, the greatest feat of acting he'd ever accomplished—that he looked at that card for a full five seconds without dropping his mask. That he took in the shushing finger, the wicked smirk, and the familiar jacket of *The Trickster* without flinching. That he only brushed his thumb briefly over the glass shards painted in fierce strokes in the background.

"I thought Molly was the painter," he said finally, giving the cards a quick tap on the desk to bring the deck into alignment. He handed them back to her, and she took them, absently beginning to shuffle.

"She is. But she taught me a thing or two."

What he really wanted to know was who'd taught her to shuffle—the way she handled her deck, he would've thought they were trick cards strung together with thread, the kind magicians used to do their fancy bits of eye trickery. But he'd held them himself, and no string joined them together—Cassi just possessed that level of mastery over her cards. They seemed to levitate between her palms, their mistress whistling mindlessly as she went through the motions.

When she finally fanned them out before him in a perfect arc, he couldn't help applauding, and she laughed—the bubbly giggle that always tugged out a chuckle of his own.

Especially when that second dimple finally came out to play, invited by her eye-crinkling grin.

"You know," he said without thinking, "I meant it, when I said you were the only person I could really laugh with."

That easy, honest smile disappeared. "Did you mean it when you said getting to know me was a mistake? A *game?*"

Again, the truth, too much and too late: "Yes."

Her throat bobbed. She cleared her throat, lowering her eyes to the cards. She walked her fingers across the desk, drawing one out of the pile with the tip of her middle finger—she flipped it over, pushing it toward him.

The Trickster taunted him with that scheming smile.

"Well," she said, "that doesn't need much interpretation, does it?"

"I'm pretty sure I'm paying you to tell me what it means," he said.

"I'm pretty sure you know what it means."

He grumbled, but didn't argue as she flipped over the next card. This one he hadn't seen before—*The Liar.*

The illustration here had no face; instead, it showed the side profile of a woman. She had one hand outstretched, palm open and inviting; the other hand rested behind her back, her fingers crossed.

"This feels a bit pointed," he said. "And petty."

"Hush. This one's different." Cassi leaned over to study the card from above, frowning to herself. "*The Liar* doesn't pop up when you're lying to someone else—she means you're lying to yourself. Usually about something important…and usually, you know exactly what the truth is." Her gaze flicked up to his. "You're hiding."

His chest tightened. He sat back in the chair, crossing his arms over his chest. "Next pull."

A frown danced across her face. "My prices aren't cheap, you know. You oughta get your full reading."

"You were happy to skip over the first one!"

She rolled her eyes. "Look, do you want the hoax or not?"

Well, not *anymore.*

He scowled, but tried not to slump—acting like a petulant child wasn't going to win him any ground here, and something told him whatever had drawn him here…it hadn't happened yet. "Next pull."

She huffed, but did as he asked.

This time, she flipped the card—but despite the lack of drafts in the tent, *something* caught its edge. It fluttered back from Finn, tumbling to the center of the desk before finally landing on its back…the exact same distance from him as from Cassi.

The Mirror.

This card's illustration split in half in the center, but both halves were exactly identical…just reversed. Two faceless people, both posing with one hand raised and the other lowered, palms facing outward; both had open chests, revealing hearts wrapped in gold-foil thread. That thread stretched between both hearts, but it was difficult to tell whether there truly *were* two hearts, tied together with one string…or if the thread was a trick of the reflection.

Cassi stared at the card, and the look in her eyes frightened him—it reminded him far too much of the empty, uncomprehending look she'd given him while lost to her magic's maddening touch.

"Cassi?" he prompted softly.

She blinked. Shuddered. Sneered.

"It's Occassio now," she said stiffly.

"Right," he said slowly—that look hadn't quite gone away, and he couldn't peer past it. Couldn't figure out what had spooked her about this card in particular.

He'd asked for the hoax. Yet she seemed to be the one fooled.

"*The Mirror's* a bit of a joke card," she said, shaking herself again; she sat back on the stool, gripping its edges tightly, still staring at the card like it might crawl across the table and bite her. "I usually use it for people asking about their romantic lives…people like to believe in the idea of soulmates, and they tip better when I give them hope in that."

"So…what, there's romance in my future?" With a snort, he pushed the card back into the pile—

And it jolted back out. Right back to where it had landed before: perfectly divided between him and Cassi.

They both stared now.

"I don't believe in soulmates," Cassi murmured. "All that stuff about someone else completing you…it's silly. We're all whole on our own."

"So why make the card?"

"Because I don't believe in soulmates, but I believe in *something*." She shrugged, crossing her arms over her heart. "People who don't complete us, but *match* us…souls that reflect our own. Perfect mirrors." A huff, again—but this time, a huff of laughter. "I'm not explaining it well, but…you know those people you meet for the very first time, and you just…you don't know how, but some part of you *knows* them, and they seem to know you better than people you've known your whole life, and it's almost terrifying?"

"Can't say I do," he said. Trying not to look at her. Trying not to look at that damned card…or *The Liar* still laid out by his hand.

"Perfect mirrors," she murmured. So hushed he barely heard her, even in the silence of the tent.

With a sharp clearing of his throat, he stood up, pushing the cards back toward her—this time, they stayed where he put them. "How much do I owe you, then? For the hoax?"

"I…" She stood too, hurriedly sweeping the cards back together. Though she didn't look down at them as she did it, they somehow ended up in a perfect pile. "Fifty gold. Or a hundred notes, but I know you prefer the shiny stuff."

"Well, clearly, so do you." He rapped on the desk with his knuckles, then dug into his left pocket, pulling out a heavy coinpurse.

Creating gold from thin air. He could've pulled off some serious schemes with that skill.

After counting out her fee, he slid it across the desk—she took it and swept it into a bag of her own, not even batting an eye at the chorus of clinks.

From practically fainting at the sight of two gold coins in her palm to charging fifty without flinching.

"Goddesshood suits you," he offered. "You look…"

She planted a fist on her hip. "Think carefully about what you plan to say next."

"I was going to say *radiant*."

"Mmhm." With another roll of her eyes, she turned aside, pulling out a lockbox and tucking the full bag of coins away. "Goodbye, Lord Ryder."

He hesitated—hovered.

Something didn't feel finished here. Something that itched at the bottom of his brain, refusing to let him walk away.

"Maybe I'll come again tomorrow," he threw out recklessly. "For one of the truths this time."

"Don't bother." She shut the lockbox with a sharp *clap*. "I'll be gone at first light."

He blinked. "Gone *where?*"

The harshness of his voice surprised him—surprised her, too, judging by the way she stood straighter, tilting her chin up. "The ringmaster of a traveling troupe approached me yesterday and offered to take me on."

"Oh." *Get it together, Finn.* He forced his lips to spread into a smile. "Congratulations. What will you be doing with them?"

The sound of a canvas flap folding back alerted him to someone entering behind him, and a voice followed—male, smooth and sweet, lilting with a hint of amusement. "Anything she likes, really. The extraordinary can't be asked to fit into an existing act."

With a horrendous, ear-splitting *crack*, Finn's skull cleaved entirely in half.

He had grown used to visions. They now came when he called, and even when they nudged their way into his head uninvited, they rarely came with pain.

This was not a vision.

This was a portent. An inevitability that had called him to witness its ascension from potential to promise.

And the agony it brought with it…it wasn't his.

Flashes of lurid color wavered and winked, images crowding in without waiting their turn.

Tents and wagons and faces bearing smiles beneath terrified eyes. Strange wine that tasted of slumber and citrus and sugar-rot, its cloying flavor numbing to the tongue and the limbs and the mind and the magic.

Magic.

Magic.

Where had her magic gone?

She tried to call it but it hurt, it hurt, that wine was an axe in her skull, digging until it hit dead center and then—

Nothing.

Nothing.

Nothing.

A cage.

A cage, and a crowd, and dirty white grins flashing in the spotlight burning her scalp. Bars and barterers that would not bend to her begging, voices ringing out with offered prices for the songbird who sang of things yet to come.

A violin raised its voice above all the rest, crooning through the chasm carved into her head…

Not a violin. A fiddle. A fierce accompaniment to her favorite routine, his song urging her to fly higher, fly faster, fly until she fled into the sky—

But it wasn't sorrow pinning her wings in place. And with nothing more than a memory to provide the music, she could not find the strength to soar.

Bets. Barters. A beaming grin as the key to her cage dropped into a waiting hand, traded for a coinpurse heavier than her.

Her toll come due at last.

"Let's go home, pet."

Pet.

Pet.

Pet.

Cage. Bars. Darkness.

No one coming. No one looking. No sound, no song, no fiddle.

One song.

All around the songbird cage, the future chased the goddess. Her master thought 'twas all in fun—

Mad goes the goddess.

Mad goes the goddess.

Mad goes the goddess.

Mad goes the—

A hand gripped his and shook it—shook *him* out of that place. Two quick blinks cleared away the fuzz, revealing a charming grin and kind blue eyes, laugh lines crinkling the corners so precisely Finn had to imagine they'd been drawn in.

"Pleasure to meet you," said the man, and it almost sounded true. His handshake was firm and friendly; his ringmaster's uniform was well-tailored, colorful accents mixed with a blue fabric that matched his eyes. He carried a flower in his pocket, a daisy—he turned to Cassi after greeting Finn, plucking it from his pocket and offering it with a bow and a flourish. "For you, milady."

A perfect gentleman. Perfect manners. Perfect laugh lines.

Finn knew what it meant to stumble across perfect people.

There were no such things. And if you found one, then congratulations…you'd found a con man who'd perfected nothing but his act.

He should know. He'd played perfect for nearly a decade now.

And he knew, with perfect clarity, that he was going to murder this man if he got one inch closer to Cassi, who leaned against her desk and sniffed at the flower.

Cassi, who smiled like a lovelorn girl as she tucked the gift behind her ear.

Cassi, who *hated* daisies.

"I didn't catch your name." Though the man had probably offered it; had probably held it in the palm of his hand when he shook Finn's. A clumsy comment—and had he more time, he might've come up with something better—but it'd have to do.

The man turned back to him, flashing another easy smile. "Apologies—I must have spoken too low. I'm Jeremias Claude. You?"

Finn stared him straight in the eye, mirroring that smile as he said, "Alexandros Ryder."

Jeremias blinked twice. Smiled just a bit wider.

Con recognized con. But Jeremias didn't realize who he'd just come up against with this particular trick.

"If you don't mind," Finn added, "I had a bit of business to finish up with the goddess. I paid good coin for a miracle, and I prefer to get what I paid for."

"A trait we share, Mr. Ryder."

"It's Lord, actually." Fine, that was petty. But pettiness was the least he could leverage at this sea-scum.

To his credit, Jeremias didn't crack, didn't stiffen. He just smiled again, offering a quick but polite bow. "Apologies, again. Cassandra, dear, we'll speak after?"

"I'll find you after I close up the tent," she promised.

Finn's palm prickled like he'd grabbed a school of lionfish by the fistful.

If anyone would be finding that marble-eyed, silt-blooded *bastard* after this, it would be him. And he'd fill that empty chest pocket with something considerably deadlier than a daisy.

The second the tent flap fell back into place, shutting out the man who would one day sell a caged-up girl like her worth could possibly be numbered in any kind of currency, Finn whirled back to Cassi.

His feet made their own path. He didn't command them—nor did he resist as they took him straight to her. As his hands anchored around her arms, a madness twirling through his head that he'd only rarely met.

A madness so reckless it could not be reasoned with. A madness born not of torturous magics or the crushing weight of divinity, but by pure, simple *feeling*.

"Do not go with him," he said.

Cassi's arms tensed in his grip, but she didn't pull away—not yet. She stared up at him, her dragon's-hoard-gold gaze hazy with confusion…then molten with rage.

"You're joking," she said flatly.

He snatched that wretched daisy out of her hair, throwing it to the ground and grinding it under his heel without looking. Without ever looking away from those venomous, vehement eyes.

Damn the future. Damn the truth. Damn time and its insistence on printing itself in indelible ink, a story he couldn't rewrite with all the imagination in the world.

When he didn't like an ending, he came up with a better one. And he *hated* this one.

"Go anywhere you like," he added, the words wheedling out of him like a wagon wheel set loose on a city street. He couldn't catch them once they started. Maybe he didn't even try. "Stay here, go back to Sanctaviv, go across the continent—depths, cross the oceans and never set foot here again for all I care, but do not go with *him*."

Her fury caught like a firework's wick. And when it burst into a spray of scalding embers, he stood too close to dodge the shrapnel.

"You cannot be serious," she seethed—she shoved him back, and he let go immediately, though his hands still burned with toxic, terrifying fervor. He would not hold her here, he would not trap her, but if she didn't listen…

Cages and auction paddles and leering grins. Manacles and mirrors and madness.

"Serious as a stroke." He folded his arms over his chest—not his usual defense, but for some reason, it felt more important to hide his heart than to hide his hands.

The sound that came out of her wasn't a laugh, though it got close—it shook her shoulders like one. "Let me get this straight. I finally have what I've always wanted, and you—you, who's supposed to be dead, who won't even tell me your real *name*—think you can just saunter through that door like you rotting own the place and tell me I'm not allowed to go after it?"

"He is a *con man*," Finn snapped. "A damn good one, sure, but I know a con when I see one, and he—"

A dark, hysteria-tinted chuckle. "Oh, I know a con when I see one, too. You wanna know who taught me *that?*"

Burning shame blistered his lips, nearly swelling them shut. He forced them to move anyway. "Cassi—"

"Say that name *one more time*—"

"Fine!" he spat, throwing his hands to the sky. If she insisted on being theatrical, *fine*. He'd play along—he'd play whatever game she liked with whatever rules she set as long as they made her listen. "Occassio, Goddess of Time, How Mighty Is She, Praise Be To Her Name, whatever you rotting want to be called, if you listen to one damned thing I've ever said, listen to this—you *cannot go with him.*"

Dragon's-hoard-gold glittered with topazine ire.

"Do not," she said, in a voice so soft one could have spun it into candy floss, "act like you care what happens to me. You made it very clear you feel nothing but contempt for me when you left me on that rooftop. You are selfish. You are cruel. You are incapable of love, or kindness, or compassion—and you are a *liar*. That is the truth of you, whoever you are, and I will not be fooled by you again."

In that moment, for the second time in his life, Finnick Atlas made a mistake.

Because he laughed.

He couldn't help it. He couldn't stop that cracked, frenzied sound from shaking his chest, a cackling wheeze that would've made music of a dying cat's yowl.

Because it was ridiculous—no, worse than ridiculous. Absurd.

Absurd, because she ought to have been right. Because if anyone had told him such a thing a week ago, he would have wholeheartedly agreed with her assessment of him—bragged about it, even, just for good measure.

But now?

Now she was *depths-damned wrong.*

So with that cackling, crackpot laugh and a fierce rake of his hands through his hair, he stormed right back up to that desk—and when she did not stop him, when he held out his hands and she did not hit them away, he planted them on either side of her hips and stared the Goddess of Time in her mind-breaking eyes.

Truths had always been harder for him than lies. But if this truth would keep her wings unclipped, he'd sing his secrets until they got stuck in her head for days.

"You want truth? All right, fine, Goddess—here's the truth. I don't know *what* I feel for you," he said. "And you're right about one thing—I wouldn't know love if it shook my hand and introduced itself by name. But I know this: every time I hear *your* name, it feels like this." He rapped his knuckles hard against his heart, a driving blow that knocked a bit of breath out of him, thinning his next words: "And every time I try to be done with you, something drags me back and dumps me at your mercy. And every time you smile at me—your *real* damned smile, Cass, not that fake little thing you flashed at him—it's like I downed that bottle of champagne you bought us in one draw."

Madness. He'd fallen to it in truth, now—no, he'd bent to it, bowed to it, allowed it to crush his mind between its greedy fingers.

Because when he took her face in his hands, holding her the way he had as she sang through the shattering of her mind, there was no thought behind it. No grand scheme or choreographed waltz or complicated plan to tease that anger in her eyes until it melted into something sweeter.

The Trickster God had no trick to play. Not for this.

He got closer because he wanted to. He said these things because he wanted to.

He told her the truth—because he wanted to.

And worst of all...

Because he wanted *her.*

"I don't know what I feel for you." The echoed confession held more heft than its predecessor. It weighed so heavy on his tongue he thought his knees might give out, seeking some kind of altar—and when he did manage to throw it over the edge, it dropped like an anchor between them, dragging his brow against hers. Her breath, cherry-tart and sugar-sweet, warmed his lips—and the secrets that spilled from them. "But I know this: you are something I would kill to get back if you were stolen from me. You are someone I would offer any ransom, make any trade, pay any price for. I would tell any secret I have to make you safe again. And that *terrifies me.*"

Her breath halted in its tracks.

"I am a liar," he promised—an echo, a tease, another weapon she would one day use against him. But if he changed it here, fixed it here, none of that would matter. "I am a liar, and a trickster, and a con to end all cons. I can number the truths I have told you without using up all my fingers. But I am not lying about this. You cannot go with him. He will *destroy* you, and you will *never* be right again. You hear me?" He shook her gently, like he could jostle the visions he'd been given from his mind to hers. "Cassi, please, I am begging you…trust me. Just this time—just this once—*trust me.*"

Had he ever begged? To anyone, for anything?

Maybe once—to a different goddess, when his baby sister had been burned to ash and buried under rubble.

This was different. Those pleas, he'd been a boy when he'd made them— just a kid so desperately lonely, broken beyond his years, that he could do nothing but *beg* for someone to give his baby sister back.

And after, he had done everything in his power to ensure he would never be that helpless to shape things the way he wanted ever again.

He had never begged as a man. As a prince.

As a god.

But he begged now.

Trust me, the Trickster God begged the Goddess of Time. *Trust me.*

But that was the problem with liars.

By the time they told the truth, everyone had already decided they weren't worth listening to.

Cassi's lashes caught the light as she pushed in, pushed back—she stood up from the desk and walked him back, still brow to brow with him…a claiming of ground that didn't feel much like a compromise.

More like an ambush.

"That's a nice speech," she murmured…so close her lips brushed his, warm and sticky with glimmering gloss. "You may not know what you feel for me…but I know what I feel for you."

"And what's that?"

The cruel, cunning smile of Occassio, Goddess of Time, speared his heart with a fishhook curve.

When she cradled his jaw in her palms, drawing him down to whisper in his ear, that hook twisted in without mercy.

"Nothing," she said. "Nothing, because that is what you have earned. Now, if you don't mind, you've stayed well past the welcome your coin bought you."

When she tapped his chest, a silent request for him to step aside, it rang hollow—a knock reverberating through an empty chamber.

He had given it all—laid his truths out like a sacrifice in her temple, a prayer at her altar—and she had not believed him.

Fine.

Fine—because he did not believe her, either.

So he took a step back as asked. Folded his hands in front of him. Arched an eyebrow into a question-mark curve. "Still lying, hm? Even now, when I know all your tells?"

Her smirk cooled, smelt chilled into impenetrable steel. A lock that practically dared him to try and pick it. "I don't have tells."

"Everyone has tells…even me. Even you. Would you like to know what yours is?"

Oh, she wanted to. More than anything. The way her brow twitched told him that in no uncertain terms. But she didn't say so.

"See, the thing about liars…it's hard to learn how to read them, because you have to find a way to pull out their truth to be able to see their lies."

He didn't step closer; she did. One crystalline slipper after the other, she inched her way back to him, drawn in by his promise to reveal her façade's failings.

"But I'm a lucky liar," he said, "because I met you when you were human—when you were still honest. And once I saw the truth of you, Cassandra Medeis, the tell was easy."

Her jaw flexed, teeth grinding like she was chewing on a stone. "Is that so."

Instead of answering, he held one hand out, his fingers so close to the corner of her jaw he could feel her pulse leaping out to meet them.

"May I?" he murmured.

She blinked. Nodded.

"You can say no," he added—he didn't know why. But with that cage in his head and the demands of her master ringing in his ears, he couldn't *not* remind her that she had a choice—that he would never force his hand on her, not when they weren't performing their mutual dance of destruction. Not when it wasn't life or death that demanded he steal choice before she could steal it from him.

"I know." This time, she didn't blink; this time, she raised her chin a bit, offering it to him. "Show me."

He took her chin between his fingers like a jeweler plucking a diamond to appraise, thanking Sancta—the only supposed god that hadn't fully screwed him and his family over—that his fingers didn't tremble. "You smile when you lie. But you know what's funny about it?"

"You're putting on quite the show," she breathed.

Wait until she saw the finale.

"Tell me again," he said, stroking his thumb idly along the length of her jaw, "that you feel nothing for me."

"I feel nothing for you," she said, her smirk not budging an inch.

Caught her.

She smiled when she lied. But she smiled when she told the truth, too. And there was one particular detail the two smiles didn't share.

He tipped her head to the side, pressing a gentle kiss to the corner of her mouth. He didn't think he imagined her hushed intake of breath.

"Look at that," he murmured against her skin. "No dimples."

Her skin flushed hot beneath his lips. Five-pointed pressure dug into his chest—her fingers, splayed over his heart. A silent request for him to step back.

He obeyed immediately, hoping he retreated quickly enough to keep those fingertips from sensing the thundering of his heart. A storm worthy of any Tempest-blessed.

He was in such gods-forsaken trouble.

"Leave." The single hushed word bore more strength than it should—it barreled into him, shoving him back another step, an irrational burst of panic splaying his fingers in helpless plea.

"Leave *with* me," he said—and really, he didn't say it. Saying involved some kind of voluntary choice, a scripting of sorts, and that invitation—that plea—wasn't what he'd planned on.

But it had come out regardless.

And for one frozen, beautiful moment, he thought she was about to say *yes*. Thought her lips were curving toward agreement, rounding out into an *okay* or *all right* or even *well, if you insist…*

But then the tip of her tongue hit the roof of her mouth. A hard consonant—the prerequisite to a refusal.

"No," she whispered. "I can't."

His heart sank faster than a ship with a hole in its hull. "I actually don't believe that there's anything you *can't* do."

Even with that bait, she didn't come at him with anger—only a screwed-up, bitter smile, like she'd stuck a candy drop in her mouth to discover that it was actually a salt lick. "I *can't*."

That should have been it. That should have been enough to cool the feverish hysteria urging him past every line he'd ever drawn—including the ones he'd carved in stone after the others were far behind him.

But as she slipped around the desk, heading for one of the mirrors in the back, renewed visions tumbled through his mind.

Cage barter beg pet sing please please please please please—

"Cassi," he ground out as he followed her, "*wait—*"

She stepped into the mirror, ignoring him. And without thinking, he followed her—stepped straight through the glass without even telling it a lie.

On their own, mirrors weren't cruel—they only took what you handed them and reflected it without guile, doubling whatever you had to offer. It wasn't their fault if you gave them something you didn't want to see.

So when Finn forgot to offer a kinder lie, it took what he did have—and took him to the very last place he wanted to go.

CHAPTER 41

FINN

He'd been in this room before.

Not like this—not fully present in his own body, able to move under his own power without the slog of dreaming weighing down his limbs. But he recognized it the second he tripped into its dusty, spotlit confines...and this time, he could see it all.

He stood in the midst of a dragon's hoard.

But there were no piles of gold or jewels—no dried-out bones of would-be thieves or loose scales glimmering like the heart of a flame. None of the things he'd come to expect from a proper hoard, thanks to inhaling innumerable storybooks throughout the happier half of his childhood.

There was gold. There were jewels. But the gold had been molded into a form that made his wrists and ankles ache; the jewels adorned those forms like crowns set atop the corpses of long-dead queens. An attempt to beautify what could only ever horrify.

What *should* only ever horrify. But his last visit had reminded him that some people didn't care for *should*, not when faced with a spectacle to satiate even the most ravenous boredom.

He stood in a forest of glittering cages.

Some were no bigger than his fists set together, containing small shadows that shifted ever so slightly—others were bigger than the dungeon cell his parents now languished in, housing beasts he also recognized from the pages of storybooks…beasts that constricted his throat with fear stronger than any noose.

One particularly expansive cage, a rectangular thing that took up the entire broad side of the chamber, contained something called an *elephant*—the kind-eyed creature swayed idly on its log-like legs, its massive head hanging low enough that its trunk swept over the floor of its cage. Every illustration Finn had ever seen had depicted these animals as proud, heads held high, intelligence gleaming in their gazes—this one looked to be barely conscious, its eyes fishlike, filled with no more life than glass marbles.

The wyvern in the tall cage against the other wall, however, had not yet lost its fire…figuratively, anyway. Though it didn't share that fabled weapon wielded by their four-legged dragon or drake cousins, it vaulted up the vertical bars in a frenzy of bat-like wings and taloned back feet, snapping at the bars at the top of the cage. Its teeth scraped off the metal with a horrendous grinding sound; seconds later, a series of plinks suggested a few of those teeth had shattered and scattered.

For every cage, a creature: the elephant, the wyvern, a panther with fur blacker than Vaughn liked his coffee, a crocodile soaking in a miserably small pool…

A juvenile phoenix, pacing and agitated; wherever its paws dragged, scorch marks followed. Its feathers—burnished scarlet swimming through depths of inky black, a flash of red that only came out when one of the spotlights swept over it—spat sparks every time it ruffled them.

Too many beasts. Too many cages—he couldn't see into all of them, couldn't tell what this monster of a man had added to his collection, but he didn't have to in order to know what this was.

An abomination. A gods-damned crime.

And when something earned the title of crime from Finnick Atlas, that said something about just how awful it was.

Especially considering he reached that conclusion long before he spotted the birdcage in the heart of the collection.

A birdcage with a different kind of creature crumpled inside, cradling her manacled wrists in her lap, staring at nothing at all.

He had to stop and cover his eyes with his hands for a moment.

Too much color. Too much light. Too much *feeling*; too much to unravel each individual emotion, unspooling the threads until he could follow them back to their source.

Not here. Not this. He didn't want to see it.

But if he tried to leave, would he find his way home? Or would it take him somewhere worse?

It could be days; it could be weeks; it could be *years* later that she would slip her shackles and choose to stalk through nightmares instead of dancing through dreams. But if he went through the nearest reflective surface and came face-to-face with the more violent version of her, gods knew what he'd find himself embroiled in.

He'd already risked too much. If he risked an uncertain destination, knowing this moment had already come and gone…

He forced his lungs to open up, pulling a breath in…even though it came kicking and screaming, tweaking a muscle in his chest on the way. As the air rushed out of him, dizziness rushed in, proof he'd spent too long holding his breath.

This was nothing he hadn't seen before. He'd face it, force himself through it, and then he'd go home.

Atlas needs a defender.

He *had* to go home. *Had* to go back to the family he'd sworn better promises to protect.

So he'd see her freed, and then he'd go.

But that was the odd thing, he realized as he approached—footsteps quiet on the polished marble floor, the stone under his feet doing nothing to soften or warm this museum of a room.

The cage wasn't locked. The door hung wide open, gaping at the magic trick the goddess had just performed; no one but him wandered between the cages, and any beast that might have hunted her or halted her flight had cages of their own to be concerned about.

The songbird could set herself free. Yet she stayed huddled in her prison, making no move toward the open door.

He crept closer, instinct whispering something was very wrong. Goosebumps prickled up his arms as he made his way toward the hanging cage, unsure if she heard him approach…unsure if she cared, because even when he let his sole scuff the floor, she didn't blink.

She was facing the back of the cage, not the door. So as he moved around to it, he lost sight of her face—but he caught sight of her back.

And then cold became nothing but a memory. Instead, acid rage poured through his blood, stinging his veins with its flaring burn.

No more creeping. He hurried now, hastening to the opening of the cage and gripping the bars in tight fists.

Up close, the picture painting itself in front of him took on a horrific cast.

Just like his vision, she wore a costume sewn from sheer fabric that shimmered gently in the harsh spotlight.

Fabric that let every cold draft leak in…

And made every scar stand out.

Her back was a *mess*. Not whip marks like Raquel bore, but something darker. Something sinuous and pitch-black slithering beneath her costume.

When she sat up, her shoulders rolling back into place, the picture came together with a suddenness that spun his head.

Tattoos.

Feathered wings had been etched with needle and ink across her shoulder blades and the backs of her arms. The fabric cast them in mist-like shimmer, but did nothing to hide their shape…or the lettering beneath them. A pair of initials: *HM*.

The same ostentatious script that fluttered on the banner above the door.

Her captor had *branded her*.

"Who's there?"

His ribs pulled taut around his heart at that plaintive warble, and he leaned in a bit further. "Can you guess?"

She didn't turn around. Instead, she reached to either side and gripped the bars, holding herself up as she sagged forward…spreading her wings, but not to fly. To steady. To brace.

"The door is open," he murmured. Low. Soothing. A creature in a cage was easily frightened—and the murderous sediment clogging his veins and voice would definitely be a fright. "You can come out."

The muscles in her shoulders flexed. She didn't turn her head.

"Cassi." Softly, softly—he had to come at this softly. So in a whisper walking on its tiptoes, he said, "Why won't you come out?"

A shallow breath, an up-and-down bob of her shoulders. "Do you know why they put mirrors in birdcages?"

An answer shaped like a question—a weapon they both loved to use. No harm in letting her wield it, at least for this round. "I don't."

"It's a trick; birds like to flock. Birds of a feather and that whole thing." A ragged giggle—a deeper bend to her spine. "The poor little things, they'll die if they're left to themselves. Just waste away without a friend in the world."

Her shaking fingers reached out above her, plucking absently at the mirror propped against the back of her cage. Her nails scraped at the jewels and engraving, teasing at the riches anchored into it.

"They put the mirrors in to trick the birds into believing they aren't alone," she whispered, eyes fixed on her own faceted reflections. "You're a mirror, too— a mirror my mind put up. You're not real."

"I'm not—"

"You're not. You're not real." Cassi curled in on herself like a wilting flower, rocking and chanting to herself, the rhythm of realities those who fell to madness had to memorize: "You're not real, you're not real you're not real you're not—"

"*Hey.*" The bars went slick against his palms, sweat gathering the harder he held on. He ignored it. "Maybe I'm not real…but this door? It's open; that's real. You don't have to stay here anymore."

Silence.

"I don't know where to *go*," she whispered, anguish muffled in her matted curls, in her hiding-place hands. "Where can I go?"

"I don't know," he admitted. "But why don't you start by coming to me?"

"But you're not—"

"So?" He held his hand out, even though she wasn't looking. "Maybe I'm not real—maybe I'll disappear. But you'll still be free, and that's what matters, isn't it?"

She uncurled herself slowly, crawling around to face him—she dropped onto her seat, her back pressed to the rippling mirror, and raised her hollow eyes to him.

Tears spilled in broad, blood-sullied rivers down her bruised cheeks.

"I don't want you to disappear," she pleaded.

I want you to be real.

Finn kept reaching. Refused to let his hand waver—refused to let her down.

"I won't disappear," he said. "Not until you tell me to go."

"You promise?"

"Would you trust a promise from me?"

She sniffled. Smiled. "No."

"Then why don't we call it a deal?"

"That's the same thing."

"Mm-mm." He smiled back at her, winking. "Promises are one-sided—those I break. But deals, those I keep, because if I don't, then I don't get what I need out of them. So let's make a deal: if you come out of this cage, I'll stay until you tell me to leave."

She stared at his waiting hand, hesitating.

He wiggled his fingers. "If I'm real, I won't disappear—and if I'm not real, then you're the one making me up. So it's really up to you if I hold up my end of the bargain, yeah?"

When she sighed again, a spark of life flitted through her eyes. She clenched her fists at her sides, frowning in thought as she watched his hand. "I hate when you say things that make sense."

Maybe it shouldn't have relieved him so much to see that hint of spite, but it did—enough to dump a vial of neutralizing base into his blood, muzzling the acid's rabid bite. He forced a chuckle, holding out both arms. "Well, if it helps, it's a rare occurrence."

Finally, she began to crawl forward, eyes averted from his—shame brought into plain sight by the spotlight ever-trained on her face. She squinted against it, new tears escaping as the manacles around her wrists bumped against bone.

The second she got within reach, he slid a finger beneath her chin and coaxed it upward.

"Don't do that," he rasped.

"Do what?"

He tugged his sleeve down with a quick roll of his shoulder, covering his fingers up to the middle knuckle—he wiped her tears away with it, gentling his touch when he had to dry the trails that ran over her bruises.

"Don't be ashamed that you have to crawl thanks to someone else's chains," he said. "Be proud that he did his best to crush you…and you're the one crawling away from the carnage."

A sparkle of understanding pierced through the dusky shade pulled over her eyes. And though it wobbled, she raised her head, straining to meet his gaze.

Pride warmed his voice; he didn't try to hide it. "Hey, there you are. Remember me? The con man who chased you across rooftops and tightropes?"

Cassi exhaled heavily, the sound just barely tinged with laughter. "You'll have to be more specific," she muttered, a rambling pitch to it that scared him a little. "I attract so many con men, it seems."

One more shuffle brought her to the lip of the cage; she tried to jump down, but the fabric caught on some sharp piece of the cage, and she spilled right over the edge. He caught her instead, and her body jerked in pain, a hoarse cry jamming against her gritted teeth.

"Sorry, sorry," he muttered, kneeling on the floor, ignoring how unkindly the stone cradled his kneecaps. As he sank down, she shifted—to leap out of his grip, he thought, and he got ready to steady her…

Instead, ragdoll arms flopped around his neck, too weak to get a proper grip. But when her fingers fisted in the back of his shirt, they could have been cut from diamond. Sealed in stone. He couldn't have pried them free if he wanted to.

He didn't want to.

"You were right," she whispered into his shoulder. "I shouldn't have gone with him."

The petty side of him felt like a massive *I told you so* would be the appropriate response to that. But he'd have to be worse than petty to gloat at a girl half-faded already, her colorful countenance bleached to a ghost of its former self. "You had no reason to believe me."

"I had every reason." A dull blink; a shallow shrug. "I just didn't care."

Every reason had to be an exaggeration of impressive proportions, considering he couldn't come up with even one for her to have followed his lying, cheating ass out of that tent. But he worried that an argument, in this state, might shove her back over the edge he'd just coaxed her away from.

"Well…in any case, you pulled a pretty good con of your own there." When she made a confused sound, he tapped her shoulder and pointed at the mirror—its quicksilver surface had stilled now, but knowing what lurked beneath was enough. "Not bad, Goddess."

A warm puff of laughter against his shoulder. "I learned a lot in that rotting cage." A pause. A tentative pat over his heart. "You're still here."

He folded his hand over hers. "We have a deal. Not till you tell me to go."

She swallowed so hard he could hear it. "If you're not real, I can *make* you go."

"Hmm. Can you now? I'd like to see that trick."

For half a second, her fingers tightened, strangling wrinkles into his shirt.

Then, with a nod so slow he wasn't sure she'd be able to raise her head again after, she pulled back and looked up to his face, touching her fingertips to his cheek.

And he didn't realize he'd just made a horrible mistake until her eyes flared pink; until she jolted back from him like he'd burned her, another hoarse scream shattering out of her at such a pitch that the glass in one of the aquariums fractured, water spitting out from the cracks. She practically somersaulted backwards out of his lap.

"Cassi!" Alarm bells rang in jarring chorus in his head as he leapt up, reaching out when she staggered back, clawing madly at her own eyes…

And froze at the sight of his hands.

His hands.

Freckled. Fiddle-worn. Still sporting bruised knuckles from punching pain into himself to make up for the agony he'd wreaked on his father.

He looked up to find his true face staring back at him in her mirror pendant, mouth agape with horror.

Then he found her, and he saw something worse.

Terror. Terror that seized her utterly, shaking her by the shoulders until her teeth chattered. Terror that kept her face hidden behind her fingers, a cage of her own making—a cage to protect, not to trap.

But that wasn't the *worse*.

Because past the terror, past the finger-cage…

Recognition paced behind flesh-and-bone bars.

Like she knew his real face just as well as his false one.

"No," she said—then again, a plea to a scream—"*No!*"

Confusion swarming in his mind, buzzing so loudly he could barely think, he took a step forward, hands up in surrender. "I can explain—"

"Not you. Not you, not this, I knew it, I knew you were a trick, I *knew.*" Her feet tripped over themselves—she caught herself on the cage bars, crawling backwards back into it.

"Don't! Cass, wait, you don't have to—"

"*I will not watch you die!*"

He had *never* heard her like this. Had never heard her *scream* that way, not even while being tortured by her own mind. Not even when her sister had been dragged to her execution.

She wasn't in her right mind. He'd known that, but depths, fleeing back into the cage—that proved it.

So he followed her. It would scare her, and she might even lash out with worse than her voice; but had she been fully cognizant, she wouldn't go anywhere close to this thing. Especially not for safety.

"You need to breathe," he tried—when she kept babbling, kept wailing, kept yanking her hair by the roots, resignation gave him a boost, helping him haul himself into the cage after her.

"Don't," she sobbed, one hand out, the other still over her eyes. "*Don't make me watch you die.*"

"Who said anything about dying? Look at me—look. I know it's not the right face, but it's still me, all right? I swear—I *promise*—"

"You *break promises*," she snarled.

And before he could stop her, she hauled the mirror around and thrust it at him.

He ducked his head on instinct, the same way he curled up to cannonball into the pool back home, boyhood terror remembering the cutting hail of glass pelting his back.

I can't save you!

I won't watch you die!

The mercurial wave trapped in the mirror crashed over his head, swallowing him into its fathomless depths. And when he tried to scream for his brother, metal coated the inside of his throat and lungs, silvering his shout into silence.

CHAPTER 42

FINN

Warmth.

The first thing that roused him…a light-fingered caress of heat over his cheeks, his forehead, the bridge of his nose. Not sun—something softer.

When he tried to open his eyes, something stopped him: a stickiness that clung to his lashes, gelling them together. No matter how hard he tried, he couldn't drag them apart.

Finn stretched out his hand blindly—his fingers jammed against something hard enough to jolt the bones back into the joints, and a groan scraped out of his throat.

A groan that rattled like something died in his throat.

Great.

He rolled onto his stomach and coughed—then coughed again when the first one stopped short, that death rattle repeating itself.

Something was stuck in his throat.

It took him a couple seconds longer than it should have to realize he couldn't breathe.

So he coughed. Then retched. Then retched again, clinging to sense when adrenaline tried to drug him into the kind of hysteria that got people killed.

Panic could yank the breath from his lungs on a good day. It would hardly help him when something tangible had decided to block his airway.

Finally, with a final ugly hack, the clot in his throat expelled itself, air rushing in to replace it.

It probably would've been helpful to be able to *see* whatever monstrosity he'd just hacked up, but he'd take blindness over not being able to breathe.

He reached up to explore the glue sealing his eyelids shut next. Two attempts to peel it off with his fingernails failed; the sticky *something* definitely came off, but not enough of it to get his eyes open.

Nothing for it. This was a job that called for soap and water and the old, rough rag he used when he needed to exfoliate.

But before he could track those things down, he needed to know exactly where he was.

First, he shoved himself up to his seat, taking in another deep breath through his nose—it whistled like he'd caught a cold, but he could just catch familiar smells past it. Hearthsmoke. Ink and parchment. Clean sheets.

Good. He'd made it back to his room.

Though, judging by the taste of fresh blood in his mouth and the pulsing pain in his nose and head and, let's see—*everywhere else*, he'd be lucky if he made it back *out* of his room.

I won't watch you die!

Suddenly grateful he'd done his once-weekly purge of clutter from his floor before going to bed the night before, he stumbled somewhat successfully to the bathing room, finding his way with spread fingers and only two stubbed toes.

I can't save you.

It took two minutes to find the knobs on his sink. Another minute to tug the rag down from the towel bar. He wasted two minutes tracking down the soap only for it to fly out of his hand, skating off to some unknown corner of the bathing room.

Atlas needs a defender.

The fibers of the washcloth stung his eyes as he scrubbed, but bit by bit, the crusted substance flaked off his lashes.

Do your worst.

His lungs hurt. When had he started holding his breath again?

You break promises.

A cry of frustration clawed at the backs of his teeth; he bit down on his sleeve to muffle it, scrubbing harder and harder until he could finally pry his eyelashes apart.

He opened his eyes to the faintest bit of light—the bathing room nothing but a charcoal outline, shadows on shadows, his own reflection barely visible in the mirror over the sink. He fumbled with the lamp's knob, twisting until the wick caught.

He looked up to find a beaten man staring back.

Nostrils crusted in crimson. Cheekbones sprinkled in flecks of the dried blood he'd scrubbed from his eyelashes. Purple and gray bursts of bruising decorating his skin. When he winced, he caught a flash of bloodstained teeth.

But no glass. No cuts, not even when he twisted around and yanked up the back of his shirt, searching for any evidence of stray shards.

Relief shuddered through him, and he bent over the basin, bowing his head. Focusing all his attention on breathing.

Spitting out another clot of blood.

The message couldn't be clearer: if he tried to drag himself back into the past again, his body would make him pay for it.

Luckily, he'd just run out of reasons to try.

He had no idea how long he stood there staring at nothing, his mind reeling through the events he'd just witnessed over and over and over again. The birth of new gods; Cassi walking away from him, straight into the cage of a con man; Cassi screaming at the sight of his true face, thrusting him into the same mirror she'd used to trap her greatest tormentor.

Cassi.

Her name struck his skull like a clap of thunder, and he rushed to finish cleaning off the blood before bolting back in, the firelight stoking his headache to greater heights as he hurried to the mirror.

Though it still sat uncovered, he couldn't see any hint of the goddess lurking at the back of its frame—no rhinestone curls, no sundrop freckles, no mirthful grin.

Because the mirror had covered *itself*.

A frost of silver had spread its cloak across the glass, shielding its former mistress. Like an ex-lover who still harbored some protective nature, it cast that pearlescent curtain between pretender god and false goddess.

"Let me see her," he commanded the mirror.

The mirror defied him.

That frost whitened, thickened, until he could have been staring out at a Nyxian blizzard—the kind that swallowed men and buried buildings. The kind that made sledding hills out of villages.

Damned stubborn thing. Gullible glass might be, but one thing it didn't do was bend to another's will...not even his own. It would shatter before it sold out.

And somehow, he didn't think he had enough coins in his purse to bribe something that had no need of money.

Fine. Glass might not bend without breaking, but he was made of sterner stuff—he could play along. He'd allow this spat of resurging loyalty if it bought him a clue as to what exactly it was protecting.

He pressed his ear to the glass, fingertips dancing across its surface. A distraction—a lure.

His father had taken him fishing with worms once or twice, before they'd come to the conclusion that Finn's stomach couldn't handle the whole ordeal. He hadn't even been able to watch his father bait the hook without his stomach churning.

But that hadn't ended the fishing trips—Ramses had simply changed tack, literally. He'd taught Finn the art of using false lures...a bit of shimmer and shine that caught a fish's eye.

Movement is the key, he'd told Finn after casting. *Not so much that you frighten the fish away, but just enough that they believe the ruse. Just enough that it looks alive.*

So he baited the mirror with a friendly wave...and a flicker of firelight that caught on the mirror bracelet around his wrist.

"I am a moonbeam," he murmured, "and I wish to greet my mistress. Will you let me see her?"

Much to his dismay—and rapidly mounting dread—no matter how carefully he set his hook, no matter which lie he recited from his overfull stash, the mirror wouldn't wipe its glass clean. Even when he gave up on lies and tried the few truths he was willing to spend, he couldn't earn back its trust.

Maybe he couldn't see...but fog and frost couldn't muffle sound.

So he closed his eyes and listened.

At first, he thought it was the wind. That he'd left his window open and the air had decided to play a prank of its own, mimicking the frantic tugs of air into tear-flooded lungs.

But he'd never heard the wind *whimper* before.

He gripped the frame, the silver so cold it dug serrated teeth into his palms, a warning bite that promised worse would come if he didn't let go.

Let it try. Let it freeze every print from his fingers. It would find that Finnick Atlas didn't quit a game over something as pathetic as pain.

"Occassio?" he called into the fog.

The mirror echoed him, bouncing her name off its paper-thin walls. *Occassio, Occassio, Occassio.*

She didn't answer any of the echoes. Not even the ones that picked up the brittle, breakable emotion he couldn't keep a cork on.

He didn't have time for this.

Another lie, whispered his mind, a taunting lilt it rarely used on itself. *You think you can fool yourself better than you can fool a mirror?*

No, he didn't think that at all.

The truth was, he had all the time in the world. What he *didn't* have was the composure. The patience. The restraint.

Not when he couldn't *see her.*

He propped the mirror up against his footboard, kneeling as if to pray. And in a way, maybe he was—praying for a goddess to reveal herself, even if it hardly counted as a miracle.

"Cassi," he growled, "I can hear you in there. You're not fooling anyone."

The mirror shivered again. And this time, that gentle disturbance let a hint of true sound out.

A hushed sob.

He knew that sob—knew it intimately. It was the way someone wept when they didn't want to be heard. The way someone fell apart when all they wanted was to keep their pieces stitched together.

That did it.

"*Cassandra.*" He leaned his forehead against the mirror—not quite touching, but hovering close, nearly blinding himself hunting for any glimmer of her in the quicksilver sea beyond the glass. He unraveled the steel thread wrapped around his voice, swapping it out for silken softness. "I know you can hear me. I won't come in, but please just let me see you, I can't—'"

Without warning, a palm smacked against the mirror's surface, fingers splayed.

Crooked, freckled fingers.

All at once, the mirror's façade fell away, its lying surface dropping like a curtain crumpling to the floor. A cloak thrown to the ground like a gauntlet…or a flag lowered in surrender.

And in its place, Occassio knelt knee to knee with him.

She'd locked her mouth behind a cage of unsteady fingers, lips streaked with blood just beyond the bars. Her other hand put more and more pressure against the glass, her palm paling the harder she pushed.

All that, he could have borne.

But what awaited him when he finally found her eyes…that killed the last of the liar stone-cold dead.

What lived in her gaze, it wasn't hate—or anger, or scheming, or even that curious look she sometimes gave him that made him want to spill every secret he'd ever kept.

It was panic. Wasted, delirious panic that blazed bright, the kind of supernova that could kill any star or sun.

The kind of cataclysm that could turn a goddess into a madwoman. A trickster into a truth-teller.

Or…

Or turn a vengeful god into a weak, wretched fool.

He'd caged her. Of all the things he could have done—of all the ways to torment her—he'd *caged her.*

Less than she deserved, he'd told her. The least of the punishments he could have picked.

He'd called it *kind.*

How many days and nights had she spent with fear's sweaty, too-tight hands wrapped around her wrists, refusing to make a sound in case it drew him to investigate? How many hours had she trembled like this, suffered like this, all while putting up a sneering, careless mask in front of him?

And worse—better—no, gods, *worse*—

Had he obliterated even the sliver-thin shards of Cassandra Medeis buried in Occassio's skin, flickers of color and life that only sometimes caught the light?

"There you are," he whispered. "Can you breathe for me?"

She shook her head. Shoved harder against the glass.

"Leave," she gasped out.

"Hey, now—this is my room, remember? My mirror, too. And let's be honest, we both know I don't take orders so well." He pressed his hand over the glass, palm to palm with her. "Breathe, Cass. Try to breathe."

A suffocated snarl of frustration rattled her—her body, her voice, her cage. The glass vibrated between their palms. "Don't you *pity me*."

"I don't pity you." He'd never pitied anyone in his whole damned life, least of all her. "I just want you to—"

"*Leave!*"

Both of his palms lay flush against the glass now. And despite the flood of adrenaline stoking his blood into a whirlpool, they didn't shake. "I'm not going anywhere, Cassandra Medeis. Not tonight."

Her voice rose in a pale imitation of divine wrath. "Occassi—"

"*Cassandra Medeis.*"

Not Fidget, the figment of imagination she'd allowed him to name. Not Cassi, the nickname he'd used to mock and charm her alike. Not Occcassio, the divine title her brother had thrust onto her, forcing her into a role she'd never auditioned for.

Occassio, he'd learned, was an Old Sanctan word. The translation wasn't easy; most texts seemed to agree it had often been used to describe a moment in time, but they disagreed over the implication. Some said it referred to an opportune moment, a kind of kismet rarely gifted; others leaned into more ominous meanings, saying an *occassic event* was a moment in time that could not be altered. That no matter how one tried to avoid it, no matter how one fought against it, that moment would always arrive against all odds, against all will.

In one text, it had simply meant *fate*.

But Cassandra…

In Old Sanctan, Cassandra meant *shining light*.

They'd played a good game. But he was done playing, done pretending. Done acting like he would be just fine if that light never shone on him again.

He knew the girl behind the goddess. Knew her truths, her tells, her tears.

And he wanted her back.

His hand slipped through the mirror, ripples ringing out across its surface as he reached around and grasped the hand she kept pressed to the glass.

"Hello," he murmured. "My name is Finnick Atlas. I wanted to be a fiddler when I grew up. I lost my baby sister when I was ten, and it almost killed me. I drink hot chocolate out of wine glasses, and chess bores me to death, and I think you're beautiful."

Her brows came together. "What are you—"?

"I can't sing to save my life. Can't draw, either. My art instructor, she actually quit the profession entirely after trying to teach me, that's how bad I was. I love peanut butter cookies, and I can't bake them, but our palace baker makes them for me whenever I ask because I'm the one in charge of ordering stock for the kitchens. And I know this is going to hurt your feelings, but I really, really, *really* hate champagne."

She blinked at him like a dreamer. Like a bird that had collided headfirst with a too-clean window, dazed beyond the ability to fly.

Then she laughed.

Just once. Just a jerky, half-formed thing she had to cough up.

But a breath followed it. A deep enough breath that he could hear it.

So he kept going—now that he'd popped the cork on his secrets, there was no capping the flood that poured out, a foam bubbling with everything true he'd ever told her and a few too many things he hadn't. Every threadbare scrap of himself that still existed beneath years and years of masks; things he could just barely remember if he peeled away the layers still stuck to his true skin.

"I can read a hundred pages in an hour. I bought flowers to bring to your performance, and I threw them away—they're still there, in that wastebasket by my desk." He jerked his head in that direction, but didn't dare rip his gaze away from hers. "I trained half the Vipers in our army on daggerwork, and my parents don't know—they still think I might cut myself when I use a butterknife at breakfast. When that circus bastard handed you that daisy, I wanted to throttle him—and you. I mean, come on, you don't even like daisies. You like sunflowers."

She laughed again, a perfect droplet of water escaping her eye, plunging toward her chin…until her dimple caught it. She raised her hand to shield her whole face, hiding the rest of her tears. "I never—how did you even know that I like—"

"It killed me," he said. "It *killed* me, watching you smile at him like that. Knowing what he was going to do. Knowing I couldn't stop it."

Her breath halted again. "You tried."

"I failed." Honesty upon honesty. "I failed before I ever went into that tent."

"You—"

"Tell me why you didn't come with me."

"I wanted to," she admitted. "That was the worst part. I wanted to."

"But?" he prompted.

"But I kept thinking of the rooftop." Another grind of her teeth—her dimples vanished as she smiled wretchedly. "And how you hurt—"

"Ah, ah." He squeezed her hand once, a warning. "No lies, not for this."

"You rotting bastard," she cursed—almost sounding like herself again, despite the panic still pulling her breaths short. Finn chuckled, and this time, she smiled in earnest. "Fine. I could see how upset you were, how much you wanted it—how you wanted it just as badly as I wanted to make you feel the way I felt that night. I wanted you to know how it felt to get left."

His last truth, he almost swallowed rather than speak—even though it would have burned, the confession higher proof than the Nyxian whiskey Kallias had once snuck home after finding a flask abandoned in the aftermath of a battlefield and subsequently dared him to taste.

But the end of a game wasn't the time to bluff or to fold—it was the time to go all in. To risk it all…and hope the cards fell in his favor.

"Leaving you on that rooftop almost killed me, too."

Time sat between its master and mistress, refusing to budge. The seconds of quiet stretched into what could have been hours of silence, their breathing the only thing that dared breach that no man's land.

Inhales and exhales that now released in tandem. Like somewhere in the midst of this dizzying rush of truth after so, so many lies, something between them had synchronized. Fallen into a rhythm.

Finn wouldn't be the one to force time back into motion. The blood caked between his teeth and the woodpecker-worthy throbbing in his head were enough reminders of what happened when he pushed time too far.

So it was Cassi who spoke next; Cassi who covered her face once more as she whispered, hand rattling beneath his like a bag of bone-dice: "Hello. I am…"

Her voice hitched, breaking over a heap of nerves.

Like she hadn't introduced herself by name in so long, she'd forgotten how to recite the lines.

He smirked at her past the glass. In its topmost pane, he could just see the ghost of his own reflection, the smirk reversed back at him.

You're a fool, it seemed to say.

Shut up, he said back. Then, out loud: "If you pick this moment to let me beat you at something—especially something as silly as who can introduce themselves the best—I swear to that stuffy god that came before you, I'm going to throw a hissy fit the likes of which you've never seen."

Ah, there it was: that glimmer of wicked mischief that had first stirred him from boredom to fascination. The hint of cunning that had called to his own like a siren set on a sailor, singing until he hardly knew the difference between dancing and drowning.

He could barely see it thanks to the way she peeked between her fingers. But barely was enough.

"Hello," she repeated firmly. "I am Cassandra Medeis."

She lowered her hand from over her eyes…and Finn's heart gave up on beating.

Because the costume she wore as Occassio—the razor-sharp cheekbones, the taller frame, the wrathful cut to her every smirk—had disappeared.

Occassio was gone. And in her place, Cassandra Medeis wept without end, her cheeks sticky with fresh tears layered atop dried ones, her soft features showing her pain plainly, and her eyes—still gold, even without her costume—rimmed in red.

Something in his chest loosened, a thread of tension cut by the sight of his favorite face.

He had almost wondered if she had forgotten it. If, like him, she'd worn too many false faces over the centuries to find her way back to her own.

"I *do* love sunflowers," she said, "and I hate daisies. They smell terrible to me. My mother used to weave wildflowers in my hair before I went to school in the morning because I loved them so much. I'm so rotting sick of purple—my favorite color is yellow. I still see my friends' faces every time I close my eyes, and I watched my sister burn too, and I miss my cat, and I tried *so* hard to hate you."

A smile, unexpected and entirely unbidden, stretched his lips out. And even when he tried to force them back in line, they just kept going, a goofy grin he couldn't shove down.

"Hello there, Cassandra Medeis." Gods, he sounded ridiculous. Happiness had this awful way of making him sound rambly. "It's a pleasure to meet you."

Her throat bobbed, the ghost of a smile leaving her face, fleeing to haunt some other corner of the palace. She took another deep breath. "You know most of my truths, but you don't know this one, so…do me a favor and brace yourself, will you?

He really couldn't think of anything that could shake his foundations more than what she'd already done and said…but she knew that. She knew, and she gave that warning anyway.

Best not to ignore that.

So with a deep breath of his own, he adjusted himself to sit on his knees, anchoring himself to her with a firm grip, his thumb bent uncomfortably around the fragments of glass that shifted around her knuckles.

"Do it gently," he said. "My nerves are shot."

Her eye roll stood in sharp contrast to her quivering frown. "I wish you'd stop making jokes."

"But I'm so good at them."

"Passable."

"Prodigious."

"Finn," she groaned. "I can't laugh about this."

That stupid grin only grew. "I like it when you say my name."

"I will punch you in those perfect teeth."

Finn ran his tongue over his teeth, testing them. "You think they're perfect?"

"*Finnick—*"

"Hey, look at that—it worked." He released her hand to wipe away the last traces of tears from her cheeks. "You're not crying anymore."

Cassi tilted her head, giving him a look; a look so unfamiliar it stirred a fluttering flock of nerves in his belly.

Wait…no. That wasn't right. He did know that look…just not on her.

He'd seen it on his sister, when she poked and prodded at her battlemate until she cracked through his darker moods; he'd seen it on Elias, too, when he calmly gathered the threads of Soren's more temperamental outbursts and helped her bind them into solutions.

It was a piercing, perfect knowing. A recognition no mask or act could fool.

"It baffles me," she whispered, "how nobody else realizes just how much you do for others. Even when you're being a rotting *dumbass*—"

"Why does every compliment have to end in an insult with you?"

"—which is *most of the time*, you're doing it to patch the holes in everybody around you. I mean, Sancta's rancid breath, Finn, how can any of them think you're just…*ordinary?*"

He cocked a grin at her. "Well, you may not know this about me, but I'm a damned good actor."

The look she gave him next was far more familiar, because it was a fed-up glare, and he'd received those from just about everyone he'd ever met. "No kidding."

"All right, I get the message—enough stalling." He pulled his hand out of the mirror, shaking starbursts of silver from his fingertips. They fell toward the floor, vanishing into mist before they could collide with the floorboards. "Tell me this truth of yours."

Cassi nodded, shifting her own bearing into a storyteller's sit—criss-crossed legs, hands braced on her knees, head held high as she met his gaze.

Two tricksters, face to face for the first time…no lies left between them.

"A thousand years ago, my very first vision showed me your death."

CHAPTER 43

FINN

In all honesty, Finn had never really thought much about death.

Not his own, at any rate. Soleil's demise had always overshadowed all other contexts for the concept; whenever thoughts of death came to visit, they were thoughts of hers, a lack of closure chasing his thoughts in circles around her empty room.

Death happened to her, not him—he was the one who'd been left to Life's careless hands instead. So whenever he thought about the bad things, he thought about life.

Instead of halted hearts, he worried about his rushing ahead of him, a hammering beat that would drown out the whispers of his marks on the other side of the table. Instead of ever-closed eyes, he worried about not blinking too much, keeping his gaze locked on his opponents when he lied. Instead of robbed breath, he worried about taking deep ones, keeping them even to hide one of his actual tells.

He had a bad habit of holding his breath when he thought too hard for too long. And right now, he was thinking harder than he ever had, lungs begging for new air as he stared at Cassi, searching for any hint of untruth.

The first time he'd ever *prayed* for her to be telling a lie.

"How…" *How does it happen? How bad is it? How do I stop it?* "How long?"

She didn't break his gaze. "I don't know."

"You're the *Goddess of Time*—"

"Yes," she interrupted. "Of *Time*, not Death."

"A thousand years, and you never asked your sister for a hint?"

Her forehead dropped against the glass with a dull *thunk*, her eyelids crinkling up in annoyance. "You weren't *born yet*," she said, punctuating each emphasized word with another *thunk, thunk, thunk*. "There was nothing for her to *look at*."

The next question—the obvious, inevitable question—waited its turn patiently, allowing other questions to cut in front of it in line.

Rather, it waited while Finn kept shoving those less important questions forward…like if he just crowded out the one that needed to be asked, he could avoid it forever.

He didn't like delays, most times—even when that delay stalled something unpleasant. Better to get it over and done with. But this wasn't something he wanted *over and done with*; this was something he wanted *unfinished and happily prevented*.

So he sat with that cowardice for a moment…an allowance for the boy he'd been, the prince he'd been, before war and tyrants and yellow-bellied brothers forced him to become someone worse…someone braver and nobler. Someone who had to be willing to die when told it was time.

If time would soon turn on him, then he needed to squeeze every last damned second for all it was worth. And he needed to know—didn't want to, but needed to.

So he let that question make its way to the front of the line…a question that had waited so long that when it finally emerged, it had aged into a withered whisper.

"What did you see?"

Foggy memories tainted her gaze, muddying their golden gleam until they nearly resembled the chocolate shade that had left him captivated, craving. Those clouded waters teemed with flicker-fish…winks of silver that wet her lower lashes.

Candy-floss pink flurried out from her pupil, a pinwheel spin of possibility that left him dizzy.

"I don't know—no, really, I don't know," she insisted when Finn gave her a warning look. "I don't even remember what it was the first time anymore…I've seen it so many times since. Arrows to the neck, poison in a cup, a cracked skull, a living body with nothing there behind the eyes…death of the body or death of the mind, it's always shifting. But it's always death; no matter which way we turn, you don't survive what's coming." A breath she drew close and held like a bastion; a roll of her manacle-scarred wrist. "And it's always, always my fault."

You don't survive what's coming.

It was one thing to fear the possibility of death—to know you were taking the first step on a journey that must be seen through to the end, regardless of what that end entailed.

It was another entirely for death to become a promise, not a possibility, after you'd already set foot on the path. To have the hope for a happy ending snatched away when it was too late to turn back.

"What is it now?" He'd seen that pink flurry of magic—she'd seen *something*. She knew *something*.

Occassio pressed her fingertips to the glass, breathing out—her breath fogged the surface, and she idly traced patterns in the mist, avoiding his gaze.

"If I tell you, that makes it real," she whispered. Another swirl of her finger. A tighter scrunch of her nose. "Don't make me do that."

His temper cut itself on his fear, a stinging slice that bled anger. "If you knew I was going to die all along, why even bother with all this?"

"At first, I thought I wanted it." No shame—just truth. "I thought you deserved it. But things changed after…after the lighthouse. Then I thought I could at least make it quick. Make it merciful. At least save you suffering. But you fought me every step—like I knew you would. Once I knew *Alexandros Ryder* and Finnick Atlas were one and the same…" She smiled thinly. "I knew that was a game I'd never win."

He coughed out a laugh; disbelief clotted that free-flowing anger. "Really? Because according to my tally—" and he *did* keep a tally, wins and losses slashed in purple ink across his favorite journal's final page, "—you won most of our rounds."

"Not the ones that mattered." Before he could dig into that further, she buried her face in her hands. "I tried to change it…after the lighthouse, I tried so hard to change everything, I swear." Her hands dragged over her forehead, digging through her knotted curls. "I thought I *did* change it, when I took your body. For those couple weeks you were quiet, I kept waiting for my memories of you from back then to just…go away."

"Go away?"

"Well, you hadn't gone back in time yet when I took over, so I thought everything that happened would just…" She snapped her fingers and fanned her hands out, mimicking a *poof*. "But I never forgot. Didn't know why until you put me in here."

Her voice wavered a bit on the *here*.

Suddenly, he couldn't quite swallow around the lump in his throat.

Suddenly, he heard a series of thuds outside his door.

Suddenly, he wanted to curse chronomancy for not giving him the gift of better timing.

Those sounds weren't knocks or footsteps. Those were the heavy, foreboding kind of thuds that came from bodies colliding with the floor.

Now? Really—*now*?

He thrust himself to his feet and darted to the door, ignoring Cassi's questions and triplicate series of knocks against the glass—when he flung it open, throwing his gaze left and right, his suspicions were confirmed in short order.

Four guards lay scattered down the hall, limbs splayed, eyes fixed unseeingly ahead. Their expressions betrayed no hint that they'd anticipated their deaths—one was even smiling, halfway through telling a joke whose punchline would have to wait for the afterlife.

He'd been in the mirror longer than he'd thought.

The hourglass on their escape had just flipped.

His muscles strained—his legs toward the dungeon, his heart toward the mirror.

He didn't have time for this. His family didn't have time.

But he ran back anyway. Stood before her anyway, wringing the nerves out of his hands until he could uncurl his fingers without any trembling.

"One more question," he whispered.

She stood to face him, folding her hands behind her back, watching him with the cautious mistrust of a creature caged. "I highly doubt it'll ever be jus*t one more question* with you."

"Our game is over." Though he could no longer say with certainty which of them won…if either of them. This didn't *feel* like a victory. "So what do we do now?"

"I don't kn—"

"Then *guess*, girl, gods."

She pressed her lips together, pinning a smile between them. "We stop acting like fools," she said, "and we accept what time's been trying to tell us."

"And that is…?"

"That in any time, with any name, with any face…I am always your downfall, Finnick Atlas." Abject misery seeped out with her smile. Chilled adrenaline bubbled in the chamber of his chest. "And you are always mine."

Truth. It rang through the room like a gong struck, a trumpet blown. A clarion call that couldn't be mistaken or ignored.

Truth struck harder when it came from the mouth of a liar. And he'd taken a punch or two in his time—he knew how to handle the ringing ears and full-headed dizziness that followed. He knew how to carry himself through a concussion just fine.

But this blow didn't daze him; it brought everything into crystalline focus, so sharp and detailed he had to blink in order to bear it.

And right then, he knew what he had to do.

Or maybe not *right then*. Maybe he'd known since he saw her crumpled in that birdcage, heart and bones so fractured she would not even crawl the few feet to freedom…

Or maybe he'd known earlier than that.

Maybe he'd known when she'd spent her meager coin on a bottle of fancy champagne to suit his blue-blooded tastes. Maybe he'd known when she'd turned a half-repaired stage into a royal theater, soaring on winds wrought from music and wings sewn from silk. Maybe he'd known when she'd thrown down her hood on a Sanctaviv rooftop, challenging him to a duel of fools to stake her claim on the spot.

Or, if he was being very, very honest…maybe he'd known when he'd seen her standing at the end of a line of Lapisian Mirrors, fidgeting in place, her gap-toothed grin a better lure than any bit of flash he'd ever dangled in front of a fish.

Always and forever his downfall…right from the very start.

But he was Finnick Atlas, after all—would he have had it any other way?

Kallias had Raquel, fierce and steady as the sea. Jericho had Vaughn, calm and gentle as the gardens. Soren had Elias, ever-present and unkillable as the stars.

He had the giddy terror that only came with falling. Off of rooftops, off of tightropes, off the edge of the chasm that separated feeling from sense.

He had Cassi. Dazzling and distracting as the view from great heights. Treacherous and thrilling as the plunge toward the ground. Addictive and addling as the adrenaline high that came after.

He had her.

And he couldn't have her anymore. Not like this.

He smoothed his hand over the glass, using the cuff of his sleeve to wipe away the condensation left by his breath—the fog parted to reveal her eyes, now squinting at him, confusion drawing tiny wrinkles between her eyebrows.

"What are you—"

"She is no longer your prisoner," he told the mirror, interrupting her question. "Let her out."

It was impossible to discern whether the sound that came next was the cracking of glass or a gasp from the goddess behind it. But either way, the mirror obeyed him.

Bare feet came first—as they settled on the floor, tiptoed and cautious, he took two steps back. Then one more, for good measure.

Her hand came next, wrapping hesitantly around the mirror's frame. As she pulled herself through, her joints cracking from too long spent in disuse, her fingers trembled.

Finn braced himself, quickly gathering every puppet string threaded between his knuckles and his magic, ready to tug it into its half-practiced dance. And if those strings snapped, if that power broke free of his binds and ran back to its mistress, he'd go for his daggers next…or the door. Whichever would be fastest.

Freedom for her meant a fight for him—a fight he'd have to win, if he intended to see his parents safely out of here.

Or, at the very least, a fight he'd have to successfully flee from.

Cassi's eyes stuck to the floor, fixed on her toes—she tapped them timidly on the floorboards, like a child's first shy attempts at plunking on piano keys.

"You let me out," she said, like he might not have noticed.

"I *did?*" he gasped, like he might not have noticed.

Playing along with her had become worse than habit—it had become natural as breathing, as scheming, as lying.

And despite that tenuous bond, he knew she would do whatever it took to reach freedom in full, no matter what strange half-truce they'd just come to. So when she lunged for him, he was ready.

Ready for pain. Ready to fight off whatever hallucinations she shoved into his mind. Ready for—

Her arms locked around his neck.

Not hurting him—but *holding* him. And yet, his breath halted like she'd wrapped strangling hands around his throat instead.

Fine, he'd admit it: he hadn't seen *that* coming.

"Go," she whispered in his ear, squeezing a hug into his neck—in the next breath, she released him, striding back to the mirror, meeting her reflection there. The mirror's surface had returned to its usual state with no prisoner to guard; with a sharp huff and a mutter of, "Rotting ribs, what a *wreck*," she ruffled her curls and blew on the glass.

With a sparking *pop*, twinkling trails of pink appeared, zipping through her hair; wherever they weaved, limp curls fluffed and brightened, styled like she'd just waltzed out of a salon with a fresh cut. Those tendrils of light whirled from her head to her toes; skirts flurried outward before folding in, closing like the petals of a flower, forming pants of black satin and a top of sheer violet chiffon with a black overbust corset underneath. With a swift tug on the sheer overlay and a nod of grim satisfaction, she turned back to him, face set with pinched determination. "What're you gaping like a gargoyle for? *Go.*"

"Go where?"

"The *signet*, Finn—go hide by the office." She went to walk past him, chin high—even stretching her neck that way, she only reached his shoulder. "I'll distract my brother. You can figure out the best moment to sneak in."

"Whoa, hold on." Finn flashed his arm out, barring her from her exit— when she kept her gaze straight ahead, he leaned into her eyeline, forcing her to look at him. "What are you talking about?"

"You need a distraction—no, don't shake your head at me. We both know you do, and we both know you're pretending you don't because you know whoever goes in there isn't coming back out." She wrapped both hands around his wrist and pulled it to her lips, pressing a kiss just above his pulse point. "But I *will* come back out. So I'll be your distraction."

His mouth dried out. "No."

"I'm not asking."

"Neither am I."

"You need—"

"Maybe I do," he interrupted, catching her by the chin to hold her darting gaze on his, "but why would I trust *you* to do it?"

And why wasn't that the real reason he was saying *no*?

She tipped her head sideways, squinting one eye at him in a glare that almost felt playful. "Finn, we're *never* going to know for sure if the other is telling the truth…but we have to hope, don't we?"

"I'm not big on hope."

"Then call it a deal." A flash of memory cut across her eyes, a dagger drawn and thrown. "I get something, you get something. You get your kingdom the help it needs…and I get to see my brother's stuck-up face when he realizes he's been duped."

Oh, he didn't like this.

He didn't like it even a little.

But he didn't have to like it for it to be a good plan. And he didn't have to like it to know she'd do it whether he agreed or not.

He shut his eyes so he could think, rummaging through the pieces of his plan, holding them up in the light of this new idea to search for flaws. "How long can you keep him distracted?"

"Half an hour, tops. And that's if he's sated himself on enough chaos to hold still that long."

Half an hour. That was half as long as he'd expected stealing the signet to take—but with a distraction in play, it might be worth the loss.

"Cass," he said, "if he realizes you've tricked him too early…"

"You think my big brother has half the brain he needs to catch *me* in a lie?" Cassi snorted, rolling her eyes—and her shoulders, as if readying for a fight. "Please. He's not *you*."

He couldn't resist smirking. Rarely could, with this gods-damned girl. "Was that a compliment?"

"You don't have time to crack jokes." She ducked under his arm, twirling to face him as she walked backward to the door, gripping the doorknob with a half-cocked grin. "Good luck, Your Lordship."

"Wait," he called when she twisted the door open—she paused, looking back over her shoulder.

Finn wouldn't know love if it shook his hand and introduced itself by name.

But he knew this: watching her walk away to face down her brother, weakened as she was, made him feel like a fish being gutted alive. Like he'd been slit from neck to navel by some rough-handed fisherman who now dragged his insides out piece by piece, leaving the heart for last, forcing him to feel every tug and tear.

He knew this: she wore fear differently than anyone else he'd ever met, as a sparkling accessory that tricked the eye; a smile that bared her gleaming teeth, or a wink that ignited a twinkle in her pupil. Her gaze could have passed for a fireworks show all on its own as she looked back at him now.

And he knew this most of all: that he had never wanted, did not want, and would never want anything more than he wanted to pull her back to him and convince her to stay however he had to. That every selfish bone in his body ached to keep her at least ten leagues away from her bastard of a brother.

But he didn't know how to say any of that. So instead, he made his latest in a quickly lengthening list of mistakes.

He prowled across the space between them, seized her face in his hands, and kissed her.

Kissed her like he should have in the tent. On that rooftop. Center stage in that empty theater. Walking down a tethered tightrope. Against a desk littered with hand-painted cards.

No champagne stinging his lips. No false faces. No fireworks.

Just him.

Just her.

Cassi's back hit the door, slamming it shut—slamming him back to sense.

Breathing hard, head spinning like a top dropped into a whirlpool, he broke the kiss to reach past her shoulder and lock the latch. Just in case Vaughn— or gods forbid, *Raquel*—veered off course and tried to track him down.

Cassi only stared, her lips still slightly parted.

Ever the shameless thief, he couldn't help himself; he bent one more time, stealing one last kiss from that wicked mouth, letting it linger; letting it dangle like a pilfered necklace, a treasure he had to admire a heartbeat longer.

Even if it risked getting him caught red-handed.

Even if it risked his own ruin.

The pulling away happened slow and steady; when his lips finally lost contact with hers, he opened his eyes to find her still staring, owl-eyed and lightning-struck.

"Sorry," he rasped. "Maybe I—"

"Oh, shut *up*, Finn." And with a lunge that proved she hadn't lost her acrobat's reflexes, Cassi seized him by the collar, dragged his head down, and stole that kiss right back.

He let it go without a fight.

For a moment, his entire world narrowed to this: to her lockpick fingers fisted in his hair, her lying lips coaxing his into a languid dance, his thumb tracing her telltale dimples.

If this was a theft, he might just let her rob him blind.

But even gods and goddesses had to breathe; with uncanny synchronicity, the two of them pulled apart with hushed gasps, pressed so close together he could feel her heart colliding with his.

"Well," Cassi whispered, eyes glowing faintly in the shadow he cast over her, "we've really done it now, haven't we?"

Gods, he hated how greedy that golden gaze made him. What terrible things he'd do, how much precious time he would waste, just to keep it where he could see it.

"You're free," he whispered back instead of answering, releasing the doorframe to trace the line of her jaw. The muscle fluttered beneath his finger, tensing; but judging by the way she leaned in, nudging his cursory touch into a caress, that tension didn't come from fear or discomfort.

So he let his finger continue its path, his knuckle drifting down to the hollow of her throat; there, he tapped her mirror pendant, making the glass tremble in its frame.

Or maybe that was her measured, careful inhale. Like a gasp she only just managed to leash.

"You can run," he added softly. "Depths, I might even want you to. So why are you staying?"

Her smile spread, tight-lipped and tricky, about as revealing as a triple-locked safe.

"You're so clever," she reminded him, giving the bow of her upper lip a coy tap. She then curled that finger under his, prying it away from her pendant; when he stepped back, she unlocked the door and turned its knob in two quick twists of her wrist. "Why don't you try to guess?"

"Wait," he said—when she did as she was told, wonder of wonders, he ran to his closet, tearing through costume after costume until he found the one piece of *real* underneath.

If she was off to con on his behalf, he couldn't let her go unarmed.

He returned to her with his hands behind his back. "Eyes closed."

"Don't love that."

"Just do it, will you?"

It took two quick tugs to get his purple sweater over her hair—when her head finally popped out from the collar, her eyes were open again, wide with wonder. "What are you doing, fool?"

He waited until she got both arms through the sleeves, then wrapped his fingers around her left wrist, holding it up. Rubbing his thumb over the card tucked into the cuff.

A trickster should never go anywhere without an extra ace up their sleeve.

"For luck," he said.

A small, sly smile. "You never cease to surprise, Finnick Atlas."

With a wink that flashed and faded faster than a firework fuse—and with a graceful, extravagant bow any showmaster would be proud of—she shut the door behind her.

And no matter how hard he tugged at its strings, the future refused to tell him if he'd just sent her to her doom…or to his own.

CHAPTER 44

RAQUEL

Raquel marched through corridors patrolled by the dead.

Slow and steady—every pause between her next footfall lasted exactly one second, no longer, no less. She counted out every one with silent precision, forcing herself to ignore her sprinting heart, to not let it govern her sweating feet.

She couldn't run. If she ran, one of the living few might realize something was deeply amiss.

So she marched. And she breathed. And she prayed her brow wouldn't betray her with the beads of sweat that gathered when she suffered from rare fits of restrained nerves.

Get to the dungeons, get the keys, get them out.

One second. Step. One second. Step.

Get to the dungeons, get the keys, get them out.

Three simple objectives—so simple a child could have memorized them.

One second. Step. One second. Step.

I'm getting them out, Kallias.

One second. Two seconds. Three seconds.

She'd stopped walking. Shaking herself, she returned to her march.

One, step. Two, step. Three, step.

She could see the dungeon door. Could see the guard posted by it, leaning against the wall like a bored man inching toward the end of his shift.

Could see the pallor in his face and the dead-eyed stare that betrayed his true fate.

Vaughn had thought of everything—the man's chest rose and fell. His eyelids blinked in seemingly random patterns. He even chewed idly on the inside of his lip, a fidgeting habit that the dead rarely engaged in.

But the wind knew better. The wind whispered warnings about the man's chest rising and falling without pulling in any breath; it begged her to notice the stench of death that corrupted its breezes.

Not the odor of rot that came with decomposition. It was too early for that. But the wind knew, just like she did, that death itself carried a smell. That a body without a soul was just *Other* enough that the air could tell—and it tattled on the body that had the audacity to play as if it still held life in its confines.

Raquel was the one it tattled to.

But Raquel already knew. And when she begged the wind to keep the body's secret just a short time longer, the wind reluctantly agreed.

As she approached, feeling as though her boot-soles had been cast in iron, the dead man gripped the dungeon door and pulled it open for her.

"Officer Angelov," he greeted her. Toneless; too even. A harsh sound at the end, death trying its hand at sorcerous work of its own, transforming the greeting into a snake with a rattle at the end of its tail.

A warning to the living that even Vaughn couldn't hide.

Raquel was not so skilled a performer. Unlike Finn, she couldn't forget herself in the muddled lines between mask and truth; her skin repelled facades the way her most expensive winter cloak repelled moisture, lies rolling off of her back like droplets of snowmelt.

So when her returning nod jounced on her neck like a gearspun carriage jumping its track, it hardly surprised her; the absurd urge to grip herself by the sides of her neck, however, took her off guard.

Irrational fear tried to tow her hands from her sides, insisting they needed to hold their head steady…but she kept her fingers loose, letting them sway with her gait as she stepped through the open door.

Lax fingers, less suspicion. Pale knuckles and readied fists didn't look like they belonged anywhere but a training circle.

The chill of the dungeon air bit deeper than usual—its fangs struck straight to the bone, bleeding goosebumps over the surface of Raquel's arms despite her borrowed Atlas uniform.

Not a palace guard's uniform, but a military one—darker blue, thicker fabric, better suited to fit around additional armor. Armor forged with input from Safi and Ember—Artemisian and Nyxian craft weaving their fingers together to forge something wholly unique.

When she'd asked how in the pits they'd gotten access to a forge, let alone the materials, Safi had merely winked and said something about never revealing her secrets. Raquel hadn't pushed.

The chainmail pressed between her undershirt and uniform helped ease the pressure on her chest, despite the extra weight—even though the uniform itself held no malice toward her, every chafe of its cuffs against her wrists felt like phantom manacles. Like her imagination had turned a blind eye to necessity, to truth, and named her *traitor*. Named her *betrayer* and *turncoat* and…

Eye of the Storm. Power within peace.

She drew in a long, salt-crusted breath through her nose.

They cannot touch any piece of me I do not offer.

The next time the cuffs gripped her wrists too tightly, she slid her fingertips underneath to loosen their hold, clinging instead to the much thinner tendril of chain looped around her wrist.

Not forged by two kingdoms. Not meant to spare her a blade through the ribs, the sternum, the heart.

This chain would stop no weapon smithed by traditional means. But it might parry the ones her mind tried to hurl at her.

Raquel Corentine Angelov.

The caress of warm lips in the hollow of her throat. Reddish-gold hair teasing her nose with the coarse scents of salt and petrichor.

Only yours.

Sailor's-knot callouses skimming down her bare back. Teeth testing the waters, nipping at her neck.

You were the one thing I would have been selfish with.

His hand snatching up her hair, wrapping it around his wrist the same way she'd seen him brace his arm against a mooring line. The full might of his grin, fearless for the first time since she'd known him, knocking her breathless.

You're beautiful, she'd told him then. Not slurred by pain and the herbs that killed it; not a confession eased by the blur of delirious dreams. A murmur she pressed into the permanent worrier's well dug out between his brows, cradling his too-pretty princely face in her steady hands. *What are you looking at me like that for? It can't be the first time you've heard it.*

It's the first time I've believed it.

She would have laughed at him for such an obvious lie, had a single tear not followed it; she'd thumbed it away while he cursed himself, laughing it off. But she'd caught his chin and forced his gaze up, diving into the saltwater there…knowing with sudden, striking clarity that she would ford any depths, swim any current, sail through any storm if he waited on the other side.

You're beautiful, she'd told him again. And again, and again. Until hearing the words stopped being enough, and he towed her in by her hair to taste them on her tongue instead.

These were not the depths she'd expected to ford; this was not the current she'd expected to sweep her off her feet.

But it didn't change anything.

She paused on the bottom step, rocking back and forth on her heels, a hesitation they couldn't afford—not a hesitation, really.

The creaking wood beneath her feet, the must of dried saltwater, the cramped walls of the stairwell…they could mimic the cabin of a ship, if she stoked her imagination to its greatest heights.

So she shut her eyes. Yanked down her sleeve. Pressed her thumb against the forget-me-not charm until its imprint lingered, the pain of its metal brackets nothing compared to the comfort of carrying it that close.

I will save them, she vowed to Kallias. *All that I can, I will save. For you.*

And somehow, she knew he heard. And just like in that cabin, he believed.

She was no god, nor would she pretend to be one. But maybe faith bolstered anyone it was offered to; maybe belief could make her something more than human.

Gods, she hoped so. Somehow, she doubted the task before her would not succeed without a little *something more.*

So she tugged down her sleeve. Tugged up her cowl.

Eye of the Storm.

Raquel Corentine Angelov.

Riptide.

Unmatched power. Deathbed promises. Answered prayers.

She stepped into the dungeon with her head held high. And when the guard at the front of the cell looked up at her, blood and saliva bubbling from his gaping mouth, he gurgled, "Help—"

She curled her fingers around a tine of lighting. And when the guard's eyes sparked with realization that she had not come to help, but to harm, he opened his mouth to try and shout through the slurry of blood and stomach bile—

And she threw the lightning straight into his chestplate.

His metal chestplate.

It did not take long for the gurgling to stop.

A second bolt melted the lock on Adriata and Ramses' cell into molten dross; Raquel ignored the scalding silver droplets that flew as she wrenched the door open. There wasn't time to worry about pinprick burns.

"We have to move!" she barked, dismissing the lightning from the bars before Adriata grabbed them, heaving her husband up with her. Thanks to Vaughn, the King didn't huff for breath or look around with a wandering, feverish look— instead, he pinned Raquel with a sharp glare.

A glare that was only a glare because of its intensity. No malice or suspicion met her there; only a passionate gratitude she didn't deserve.

"Thank you," the King of Atlas told her, catching her head and giving her a fatherly kiss on her brow.

Or at least, what she imagined a fatherly kiss to be. Her own father had never bothered with little affections like that.

Why did she let him do that? Why didn't she pull away?

Why did it make her eyes sting?

"Hurry," she rasped. "We don't have much time."

With the same sad smile he'd passed on to Kallias, Ramses let Adriata drag him up the stairs; every stumbling step cranked open the floodgates on Raquel's adrenaline, ice floes cracking together in her veins as she bit down insistences that they move faster.

No use giving those orders. Ramses couldn't follow them, and Adriata wouldn't; even under the threat of death, she'd probably slow her steps on purpose just to vex Raquel.

She'd love to begrudge the queen that pettiness. But had their positions been reversed, she would've almost certainly done the same.

So she kept her mouth shut, and not just to repress her own impatience; the wind kept bringing her the last breaths of the fallen guards like cats bringing dead prey to their owners, proudly showing off its catch, not understanding why she fought a retch every time the scent of death passed by her nose.

It took less than a minute to free the King and Queen from the dungeons, but that was the easy part. Half a palace stood between them and freedom—and while the corrupted guards were all dispatched or desperately ill, they weren't the only people in the palace who worshipped the god sitting on the Atlas throne.

But somewhere in this palace, there were palacefolk who served only because they feared. And if they were anything like her people, she had to hope that they would rally when they saw their king and queen still lived.

But that was several plans down what Finn called the *something has gone horribly wrong* ladder. With any luck—any luck at all—they would make it out with *nobody* seeing them.

"Officer Angelov." Adriata's hand, joints worn down to the knobs, closed around her shoulder. "My son?"

Which one?

She resisted the ache in her neck, a crick that would only be relieved by bending toward the window. To see if Tempest had kept his reluctant promise.

"Finn has his own part to play." She forced her hand to close over the Queen's. "And we have ours. The best way to help him is by not getting in his way."

Raquel knew how to sight a storm…in the sky, on the horizon, in someone's eyes. And the roiling gray in Adriata's gaze promised a reckoning would rain down any moment now.

A queen unused to being placed on the sidelines by anyone but herself.

Raquel couldn't begrudge her that seething unrest—had she been forced to stand aside and allow someone else to defend what was hers, she would have chafed at the bit, too. But it didn't change anything.

Adriata didn't have to like it. She just had to move.

And move they did—a painstaking crawl down corridor after corridor, willing herself not to look too closely at the dead palacefolk—those under Tenebrae's thrall who hadn't been warned to avoid the food and drink—still playing out the motions of their chores. Willing herself not to grow too impatient with the wounded King's lurching gait, somehow less steady than the puppeted palace guards keeping to their patrols.

She'd say this for Vaughn: to keep so many puppets dancing at once had to take considerable power. If someone had asked her to stir up storms in dozens of separate cities, she would have been well spent by the third.

The grand foyer doors greeted her with a gaping grin; they'd hung open ever since Tenebrae's claiming of the throne, an open-faced dare for anyone unfond of the new regime to come and make their displeasure known. Finn had made his opinion on Tenebrae's reckless taunts clear early in his tenancy—under the guise of Occassio, of course—but the god had only laughed.

Today, Raquel tossed a nondescript prayer of thanks to the sky for Tenebrae's pride. The gift of an unguarded door was exactly what they needed to pull this off.

Home free. All they had to do was walk out the door.

There was only one problem.

Finn wasn't there waiting for them.

She chewed on her indecision, wasting a much-needed moment looking over her shoulder for a flit of purple clashing against navy. A cherrywood flash of auburn hair. Anything to suggest the prince might be here…just biding his time. Making an entrance.

Spending that second bought her nothing. Finn wasn't there.

"Go," she muttered to Adriata, white-knuckling her heart to keep it from racing past those doors. "Vaughn is waiting in the courtyard; he'll take you to the harbor. The ship is waiting. If we're not on it by sundown, don't wait."

How long exactly that ship had been waiting already, she wasn't sure. But Finn had arranged for it to arrive with a window behind and before it—something about foresight never outweighing good common sense.

As Raquel slid her arm away from Ramses, Adriata slid inward to brace him. "Is this part of your plan?"

"No." No use lying. "But I want to give your son more time."

Understanding flickered in her eyes, lightning-bright. With a nod, she guided her husband's head to her shoulder; he shut his eyes, every breath dragging in like it weighed a thousand pounds. She did not look up as she whispered, "Thank you."

That softspoken gratitude cost the Queen in pride. And it cost Raquel something to bow her chin and accept it; to let them stumble out that door to freedom. But it would have cost her more to leave with them, knowing Finn remained; it would have cost her any hope of sleeping in peace for the rest of her days, haunted by Kallias's plea that she watch over his brother in his absence.

When Raquel Angelov gambled, she gambled carefully. So she ought to have known better than to make this bet…to halt mere steps from salvation, from the success of Finn's precisely timed plan, and let hope try to bluff itself into a better position. To trick the other players into folding with nothing in its hand but false confidence. Nothing in its purse but pocket change and a stray prayer.

A bad bet on bad odds.

She ought to have known better.

"Angelov!"

A jolt of adrenaline scrambled the even gait of her steps; she stopped and spun in a clipped about-face, scowling at the pair of men marching across the tiled foyer. "Can I help you?"

"I sure flogging hope so," spat Revan. His axe swung from his belt, no sheath or guard in sight. Reckless. "Pyra is dead."

"*What?*" She dropped her arms out of their cross, her best attempt at affecting shock. "How?"

"Not just dead." Arcas's brow was so deeply furrowed, it looked like he'd thumbed soot between the creases. He paced sideways as she came to a halt, circling toward her back; she swiveled with him, more concerned about letting him escape her periphery than Revan. She'd hear the Tallisian's heavy axe coming; the Artemisian's fire, not as likely. "Keeled over, hacked herself into oblivion…then got back up and went right on walking. They're all like that—dead eyes, no words, but still walking."

"Except you," she said.

A mistake, inviting suspicion into the conversation. It made itself at home in Arcas's narrowed eyes.

"And you," he countered softly, words claiming their ground like a boot settling in pyre-ash. "Funny how that works…a palace full of corpses, and you heading for the door."

"I wasn't heading anywhere. You two were the ones in a hurry." Retreat wasn't an option—Adriata and Ramses likely hadn't even left the courtyard yet. She advanced instead, stoking up her best scowl. "It's *all* of them, but not you?"

"One of the benefits of sanguimancy." Bloodred robes ruffled around his ankles; a murderous sneer of his own took shape, frenzy bleeding through his skin in spasms and shudders. "Poison doesn't take too well."

Revan didn't make a sound behind her, but she sensed his shadow looming over her shoulder. Her hackles rose, skin prickling, adrenaline pouring awareness down every inch of her back.

Still no sign of Finn.

Had he escaped by some other route, finding his own way to the harbor, trusting her better sense to keep sentiment's hands off the reins? Was he here now, late but loose from Tenebrae's clutches, watching these wolves surround her from the shadows?

Had he been caught in his ruse and killed, a fate she would soon share?

"Kill me without proof or permission," she snapped, "and Occassio will not be pleased."

"Relax, Angelov. I don't plan to kill you." Arcas cracked his neck, then his knuckles—then his scowl, rearranging it into a hungry grin. "Where's the fun in that?"

Lightning purred in the very tips of her fingers, boiling her blood until her skin threatened to blister from beneath. She dug her nails into her leather sword belt, refusing to give her wayward power a channel. "I don't have time for this. We're being attacked. If you want to toss blame, you and Revan feel free to play catch—I'm going to warn Tenebrae, as *you two* should have already done."

The key to pulling off a costume, Finn had told her—the best way to be ignored was to act like you belonged.

She did not give them the satisfaction of shielding against their suspicion; she walked away without looking back, making for the stairs. Away from the exit. Deeper into danger.

Any rational person would have thought twice about their accusations; anyone with a lick of logic to their name would have followed her, at most, to make their own case before their god.

But that was the problem with chaos.

Chaos didn't care about her mask or how well she wore it. Chaos cared about *mayhem.*

And that was exactly what broke loose when the *snick* of an unhooked weapon screamed a warning at her back.

Mayhem.

Maelstrom.

Lightning leapt from her fingers when she ripped them away from her belt; her muscles stiffened, shook, then went slack as her magic sapped the pent-up electricity from her limbs. One bolt flew awry, forking out to crack against a nearby column; like a whip with too many tongues, it wrapped around the column's girth twice before sparking out.

The other bolt caught Revan's axe.

It should have lanced right down the handle to Revan's hand; it should have left him a smoking, silent husk, freed at last from Chaos's thrall.

Instead, he tightened his grip around the axe's leather wrapping…while the axe itself danced with deadly power, crowned in a frisson of stormfire.

A weapon made to capture blows fueled by magic.

Damned Tallisians and their never-ending suspicion of those blessed by the gods.

Step by step, she kept backing toward the stairs—but Tenebrae's two favorite toys matched her step for step. Stride for stride.

Panic tried to flood her body, to burst the dam of her composure—but she patched it with a harsh breath.

I am the Eye of the Storm.

They could touch no piece of her she did not offer…and she would not offer them her gods-damned dignity. They would not break her at the end of it all.

Death knew her face. Nature knew her name.

Now Chaos would know her wrath.

"Here, little stormcloud," coaxed Arcas, scuffing his fingertips together, clicking his tongue. "Let's see what you're hiding under all that bluster."

The scars carved into her temple and torso stung like someone had ripped them back open, knuckling salt into the stripped flesh.

Salt.

Through those open doors, a wet breeze stumbled in on tattered feet; torn by weather not of her making, it only just made it over the threshold.

Just far enough for her to smell the sea on its breath.

Riptide. Tempest's judgement on those who would corrupt his kingdom.

They'd stolen her storm…but the storm was not her only weapon.

When she closed her eyes, it was not because she feared what was coming.

Spring-green eyes, winter-bright blue dyeing them dangerously dark. Her first taste of the sea in his eyes, on his lips, by his side.

A reckless plunge into open water. Yet she'd felt no fear.

Show me how to swim, Kallias.

In the shipwrecked ruins of partly-sworn promises and borrowed time, the memory of an ocean-blooded prince answered her call. *As you order, Officer Angelov.*

She reached out her hands as if in supplication, in prayer, opening her eyes to see Arcas and Revan advancing, practically salivating for her suffering. A wall of steel and bloodthirst and turmoil trapped in two bodies.

Perhaps it *was* a prayer, of a sort. But not to any god, self-appointed or otherwise.

To freckled skin and gold-spun, fire-laced hair. To cold hands and seafaring songs and a whip-beaten back.

To a prince with no crown. To a king on his knees.

And with a scream fierce as a summer squall, she tore the tide free of its bindings.

Seawater gushed through the doors, the cracked-open windows, the locked-up windows—anywhere water could possibly leak through, the ocean found a way. And at her behest, it grabbed her assailants by the ankles and pulled, a beast that attacked with tides instead of teeth.

Arcas went down, spluttering, screaming—Revan hit his knees, but while Arcas was swept back, thrown against the wall with a painful *crack*, Revan struggled back to his feet. Planted them against the raging current, raising his axe once more.

Raquel threw another wave at his knees; he wavered, but kept his feet.

Those damned steel soles—they anchored him to the floor. Built-in balance.

She stumbled up one step; he swept his axe in an arc, and two tines of lighting tore loose, spearing toward her chest. She jerked up one fist as if tugging a rope; a wave reared up from the invading ocean, catching one tine and sending it streaking across the flooded tile.

The other drove into her shoulder, deadening it instantly.

Pain would have been better—pain she could have pushed through. Instead, her arm went limp, her dominant hand spasming into a stiff, useless claw.

The bolt that drove into the water should have shocked Revan senseless, if not killed him outright. Instead, he pulled his arm back, readying another strike.

She wasn't going to make it.

All this power, all this work, all this hope—and she wasn't going to make it.

But that didn't mean it was over.

She shut her eyes again. Clung to her numb, trembling arm.

Laid down her pride at the only altar she could offer—her own sea-sopped boots—and hoped against hope Nature would deem it adequate.

If you can hear me, she prayed, *please get them out. Keep your promise to him…to me. Get them out.*

Silver light burst across her vision. Pain sang through her teeth, through her skull, a shock that burned like frost.

Thunder boomed like a battle cry. Like a call to arms. Like someone roaring her name.

Swift, brutal blackness swept her away—the kind most everyone feared. The kind people clawed and kicked at, treading its viscous current.

The kind that carried them off anyway, borne on swift waters to a shallow grave.

But not her.

They were kindred spirits, her and this blackness. Force to force. Savior to savior.

Riptide to riptide.

She let it take her without a fight.

INTERLUDE

TEMPEST

R aquel Angelov, Eye of the Storm, had a…*charming* habit of issuing a command and calling it a prayer.

You took him. So you will be him.

A summons he would have answered no matter what name it went by, damn this body and the slow decay of his own sanity and a chronic stumble in his heart's steady gait that his middle sister would have smugly referred to as the *staying power of memory.*

Memory. Nothing more than that. Nothing that belonged to him, not truly; and though the survival of his kingdom had demanded this affront to nature and life and plain, simple morality, he could not bring himself to take anything more from the prince who had already given everything. From the woman who had not had any say in what that choice took from her in turn.

The rest of this body had bowed to his will. But the heart? That hadn't been Kallias Atlas's to give.

Raquel Angelov held fast to it, that last perilous piece of her prince. Her hand still guided its rudder; her orders still set its course.

This heart wasn't his. And he would not rip it from her grasp.

But his mind was his own. And though she made quite the cunning general, for being the face of this revolution, she knew little of its ways. War was war, but revolt played by different rules.

He ought to know. He'd led one, after all.

Same battle, different blade.

For all her bluster, the Eye of the Storm's failing faith held truer than she believed. True enough that she'd asked him to do the impossible alone—and had not considered for a moment he might need more than two hands to see it done.

He suffered no such illusions.

So it was good he had issued commands of his own…and his whispers had fallen upon willing ears.

From fathoms afar and battles unfinished. From landlocked kingdoms and ever-sailing ships. From the hidden hovels of deserters and the gilded offices of retired heroes taking a rest well-earned.

Sailors and soldiers. Defectors and deserters. Nobles and nobodies.

From every corner of the wide-open world, the faithful answered Nature's call.

And because they answered, only a fraction of Port Atlas's people would sleep in freshly dug graves tonight.

Still too steep a loss. One he would repay tenfold once he got his own hands on his rotting brother.

But not until she got out.

The wind waited with bated breath, crouched at the palace door, slavering with the anticipation of carrying good news back to its caller. It had nearly bowled him over merely half an hour earlier, trying to knock the small boy he carried out of his arms; after he'd seen the boy and his father safely onto one of the waiting ships, young sailors urging them on while grizzled men in uniforms well past their glory days defended the docks from corrupted forces in varying states of ailment, he'd given the breeze a good scolding before sending it back to its post. The breeze had sheepishly delivered the news of the Queen's escape before scampering back into the maze of Port Atlas alleys, taking the scent of sick and spoil and tepid death with it.

Impatience aside, he spared a breath of relief for the survival of Athena's bloodline. Her loss had nearly set him on a similar path as his brother; only her memory and a scant handful of years spent with an old friend afterward had kept him sane. Her legacy—their legacy, Alexandros and Athena—could not come to an end under his watch.

It should have been him guiding them out, not the necromancer. But he knew his late wife—he knew where she would have wanted him to be.

So he stayed in the city, ushering innocent after innocent onto boats flying flags both familiar and foreign.

Even after that half-hour sailed in and sailed off, and he had yet to see cap or crest of this city's valiant Riptide.

A mortal man would have buckled under the weight of the massive, black-bellied cloud Tempest held aloft and arrested, its woolen hem sagging under its own sopping weight; so it was good he need only curl his fingers open and shut to squeeze out that burdensome cloud. Good he could treat a hurricane like a handkerchief, wringing it out when he had need of it, tucking it back into his pocket when it no longer served him.

Those first years, the mortal years, he'd pushed himself beyond the borders of his power more times than he could count. Summoning a storm like this would have left him with contusions the size of conch shells, battered by wave after wave of hail; every lightning strike would have sapped the heat from his bones, dumping him in a shivering heap; every gust and gale would have left him bedridden and breathless, lips bruised tart-taffy blue, looking like he'd snuck the last confection from a carnival trip.

Today, he rubbed the itch of dust out of one eye while snapping a nine-tongued lash of lightning, dropping a handful of Tenebrae's foolish faithful.

Easy, all of it.

Until the wind careened into him a second time, frost mingled with fear on its icy breath, and his head spun like he'd stuffed the hurricane between his ears instead.

Keep your promise to him…to me. Get them out.

The heart in his chest fell further than the sea floor.

Raquel.

CHAPTER 45

CASSI

Cassandra Medeis had never been sorry, and she wasn't too keen on starting now.

Sorry wasn't the word for the razor-edged shears sliding beneath the seams of her skin, snipping the threads of the costume she'd sewn herself into. *Sorry* couldn't hold a candle to the starlight beating through her spectral veins, shielded by sweater sleeves so long she had to cuff them twice just to find her fingers again.

Liquid supernova. Wishing-well water. The unknowable sky-stuff that had obviously shriveled her good sense.

But it was to be expected; Finnick Atlas had an uncanny knack for getting under her skin and staying there, no matter how many times she tried to excise him. Like a splinter that only dug deeper when you tried to pry it out with a pair of tweezers.

And now it had come to this: to wearing dusk instead of daydreams, to shaping each step into a kind of claiming, to winding up the cogs of old memories and older talents to play a brand-new part.

She had never played Tenebrae's enemy before. Even at the height of her power, the things her brother could do…she'd never cared enough to test the mettle of glass and light against undiluted chaos.

Fire and death—those she would happily pit against imagination and time. And erosion was the only weapon that water and weather could wield against crystal and glass.

But the grime of corruption, the contortion of natural law—she didn't know what that could do to her.

Yet here she was: marching off at half-presence and half-power and half-sure that she'd just met a new kind of madness.

All for *Finnick rotting Atlas*.

Not for Alexandros Ryder, the charming lord who played the fiddle like it was his first language, who could pick a pocket better than the best thieves ever trained by Sanctaviv streets. Not for the blond-haired, bearded man who'd looked at her scrappish lunch with a worried crinkle to his nose and brought a bag full of decadent desserts to a theaterful of dreamers. Not for the sneering con who'd made her feel her most beautiful and her most pathetic in the span of an hour, only to sneak back into her life years later and beg her to run away with him.

For Finnick Atlas.

For the brown-eyed boy who'd sprinted to save her the night of the Drunken Sun auction, who'd clung to her elbows and asked over and over if she was hurt, if she was all right, long after conscious thought had left him. Even when his eyes had gone glassy, lost in the haze of shock and mind-magics, he hadn't let go of her. Hadn't stopped asking. Hadn't stopped checking her hands and face and heart for wounds he couldn't see, dewdrops of blood dripping from his rigid fingers as he wiped the scarlet spray from her cheeks.

For the trickster whose roguish grin had a most curious talent for stopping her heart in its tracks, who could slip into different skins without a flicker of auramantic power, who had knelt before her mirror and poured out his dearest and most damning truths…just to stop her from gods-damned *crying*.

For the prince who'd picked the lock on her cage. Who'd made a fool of himself by holding a gone-mad girl's face and singing her back to a semblance of sense.

Who'd kissed her like a starving thief teasing the tumblers on a chest full of jewels. Like nothing else mattered if he didn't pull off this particular pick.

I wouldn't know love if it shook my hand and introduced itself by name.

Unfortunately for them both, she didn't share the same ignorance.

She had no talent for music, but she could play love like it was *her* first language; her own special instrument, strung with lies and varnished in loose-lipped smiles, tuned to enchant each listener like their own personal siren's croon.

And when the real thing dared show its face, there was no mask on earth that could disguise it from her.

Which was why, when she finished strolling the gilded halls of Atlas and scaring the pants off of the living palacefolk with winks and blown kisses and auramancied fangs flashing in her grins, she did not hesitate when she marched up to Tenebrae's office door and knocked her knuckles in a *one-two-three one-two-three* beat.

And when the door swept open, halting with a stuttering back-and-forth swing that betrayed her brother's surprise at seeing her—*her*, Cassandra, not Occassio—she flooded her face with all that sky-stuff, lighting her gaze and her grin with the love she couldn't spend anywhere else.

"Surprise!" she sang, spreading her arms out in her best showwoman's pose. Of all her memories, muscle memory never failed her—the ghost of the sky-hungry songbird spread its wings with her, lending a swooping grace to the bow she presented to her brother. She could practically feel the tickle of feathers at the tips of her fingers. Or maybe it was those stretched-out sweater sleeves. "May I come in?"

Tenebrae's eyes narrowed as he took her in. Suspicion slated like a spotlight across his golden eyes.

But her heart did not stumble out of its steady, self-assured beat.

Compared to the full might of a certain Trickster God's knife-sharp knowing, her brother's doubt could not crumple her confidence.

A songbird in sorrow no longer, but a goddess in love.

"Of course," he said, standing aside. Behind him, his office swam in false twilight, blues on grays on blacks.

But hidden in that layered darkness were flickers of purple, too. The color of performers and tailors and a gemstone dress. The color of the lanterns that once lit her way to her friends, her ambitions, her sanctuary; the color that reminded her of a girl who danced on her tiptoes and soared over rooftops and sang for the pure joy of it.

The color her trickster had armored her in before sending her off to this most risky of ruses.

To be herself—that would challenge her more than any figment she'd ever invented.

But she'd never been one to duck a challenge.

So she stepped inside, stretching to plant a fond kiss on her brother's cheek, smiling through the swell of nausea at the texture of it—the pockmarked holes, the rancid freckles.

And she prayed it would be enough to delay her Trickster's inevitable future just a little while longer.

CHAPTER 46

CASSI

"You've been busy."

The empty desk paid tribute to her wandering hand with a palmful of dust; a suggestion to the contrary. But paperwork and planning had never been tenets of her brother's schemes.

And the wallpaper was patterned in blood.

Old blood, new blood, in-between blood. A tailoress's swatchbook stuffed exclusively with shades of red.

Like he'd handed his keys and his coin and a handful of cowering prisoners to a decorator whose favorite medium was *carnage on crepe paper*.

This room remembered them. Their screams. Their silence.

The unsatisfied sighs of a craving chaos god.

"As have you." Her brother propped himself on the desk, knocking the woven wicker jar of writing utensils to the floor. He didn't flinch when they scattered with a noisy crash; neither did she. "*What* you've been doing, I haven't the slightest, since you've been too busy prowling around to come see me."

Oh, fun. They were playing the guilt game. She was rotting fantastic at that one.

"Do you know how much *work* it takes to stop riots from breaking out in a city this large?" Because she didn't. But she'd known this would be a test of her improvisation. She slid hip-to-hip with him on the desk, knocking her elbow against his. "If I wasn't out there *prowling,* you'd actually have to get off your ass and do something clever."

"Us forbid." An old joke of his; it bounced off her heart without even cracking the crystal. That version of her brother had been dead for eons, and impressionists were her least favorite sort of performer. "So why are you here now?" A dangerous drag of his eyes down her form. Not even one layer of costuming to keep her safe. "And why are you...*you?*"

Her heartbeat kept to its choreography, cued by the hands of her invisible clock. *Tick. Tick. Tick.*

Not a slow or skip in her pulse. Exactly one beat to every second. Never faster, never slower.

"Borrowed skins itch after a while." She pinched a loose eyelash off her cheekbone, blowing it like a birthday candle. Flimsier than fire, but better to wish on. Besides, luck did plenty of fragile things some powerful favors. "It's good to let the real one breathe."

She'd been in the game far, far too long not to notice when one of her tricks didn't stick the landing. And this one tottered on impact, failing to find its balance in Tenebrae's flat gaze, his inflectionless *hmm.*

"You haven't worn your real face since Sanctaviv," he said. "Why now?"

Why now, indeed.

A blithe shrug. "You trust me more like this."

Truth could be wielded like sand to the eyes, if one knew where to aim. It caught people off guard; distracted them, blinded them. The lies had time to slip by unnoticed.

Tenebrae laughed, startled—and pleased. "Plans like that work better when you don't *tell* people about them."

"Maybe." She flashed a smirk like a flask hidden in a hollow textbook, like a dagger sheathed under a slit in her skirt. "What about you? How long till this skin wears out?"

"Not long." A fleeting glance at his hands, at the rot embedded between the knuckles. "But I won't need it for much longer."

Once upon a time—a time not so far from this one at all—that would have set her heart purring with anticipation.

Instead, it alchemized from crystal to lead, weighing down her songbird bones.

All thanks to Finnick *rotting* Atlas.

"It's going to be strange, wearing our bodies again." Stranger and stranger still. Even this shape was more costume than corporeal; already her skin had begun to slough layers of reality, tangibility cut from her body like flaws from a gem, eradicating her soft parts in favor of severe angles. Cutting away the human to free the divine.

Only felt, not seen. But it wouldn't be long before this con came to a close. *Find the character, Cassi.*

A softer slump to her shoulder; a cross of her knees, not her ankles. Allowing her eyes to wander, forcing herself not to watch her brother's minute movements in her periphery.

Trust. Forced and false or not…she had to show him trust.

If he read the tension wrapping her up like the ribbon on a pair of pointe shoes, he'd take some of it for himself. Like he always had, a thief in his own right, snipping away piece after piece of them all to serve his own ends.

For all the things they said about her, Cassi had one over on Tenebrae: she had never, ever stolen from one of her siblings. Ever.

She had tricked them, yes. Conned them into giving things away, every once in a while. But she had never outright stolen from them. Not even from Mora.

Even wicked things drew lines here and there. But evil never watched where it stepped.

"You have something on your mind," her brother said.

She gasped, gripping the sides of her head. "What? Where? Get it off!"

"Ha, ha." He rolled his eyes. "Spit it out, Occassio."

Occassio.

Rarely Cassi; never Cassandra.

Always the lie, never the truth. With him, with her worshippers, with everyone.

Everyone but the brown-eyed boy who counted her dimples and called out her tells.

"I don't like not knowing where Tempest is lurking," she admitted. Another truth, or something close. "I thought I was done looking over my shoulder centuries ago."

"You're always looking over your shoulder."

"Well, I prefer it as an old habit, not a necessity."

"It's good he's here. We're going to need him when all this comes to a head."

A piercing disquiet itched in her ankles, nerves getting dancy in the anticipatory silence of a missed cue. "You remember he's trying to *stop* us, don't you?"

Tenebrae's smile would have sickened a seasoned torturer.

"Not for long," he promised. "He's here to reclaim what's his…and everything he wants, I have. When he shows his face, it will be as friend, not foe. You'll see."

"And what do you know about what he wants?"

"What we all want—the things we lost the first go-round." Tenebrae drummed his fingers on the desk; he hopped off, leaving her alone on her perch as he paced the worn-down rug. "His home. His crown. And his queen."

"His queen is long dead."

An erratic wave. "I found him a new one."

"I'm on the edge of my seat."

"Angelov and the Atlas boy were already dancing around each other before Tempest took him. I'm sure it won't take much of a push on his side, and any resistance she has, well…you'll take care of that."

Rage and disgust got their hands on her script, ready to tear it to shreds, but she was a goddess—and before that, she'd been a woman. She knew how to save herself with a smile. How to laugh at sickening jokes to make sure they wouldn't test the punchline out on her. "Not a bad plan."

And if she'd had any hope of succeeding, she would have killed him for it.

For thinking it. For saying it. For saying it to *her*, knowing what had been done to her, knowing what she'd survived.

But she didn't have long to consider killings or conspiracies or all their implications. Because between rolling over and showing her proverbial belly to her brother and him bursting into seesaw laughter, pitch rising and dipping, something else rose and fell in the silence.

A scuff, brief and benign as a clock-tick, a lock-click, a pocket-pick.

A cowardly floorboard snitching on a sneak.

Her heartbeat, unmoved since the beginning of her long tenure as Time's mistress, lurched a half-step ahead of the clock's long hand.

But what moved her brought her manic brother to a halt. Stock-still, head tilted, squint straining through the mottled midnight colors splashed across the far wall.

"Did you hear that?" he asked.

"No."

One of the lies she had practiced the very most. One she could tell in her rotting sleep. One of the only two lies with a perfectly even chance at being believed or not—fifty-fifty. Half and half. Probability's own perfect mirror.

When luck served at her beck and call, it took nearly nothing at all to tip those odds the extra one percent.

But luck had left her; a different master held its leash. And out of pettiness, out of anger and fear and wretched *spite,* she hadn't taught him the commands he needed to bring it properly to heel.

Maybe she'd blame it on the metronome misstep of her pulse. Maybe she'd blame it on too much truth-telling tuning her vocal cords to the wrong key. Maybe she'd blame it on having to perform on this shoddy stage, framed in by a slapdash set.

Blame would have to go somewhere. Because her pretty, practiced *no* lost its footing as it dropped into its final plié…

And her voice cracked.

The best liar in this whole rotting world—and in the moment it mattered most, her voice cracked.

She had known Sancta would come for them all, someday. That when his light caught her up again, it would press in like a sunbeam through a magnifying glass, narrower and narrower until it speared her like a tack through a butterfly's wing.

She'd just hoped that somehow, if she was clever and quick enough, if she hugged her own shadow as tightly to herself as she possibly could, she might spare Finn from the reckoning she'd more than earned.

But he'd found a way to step back into that shadow, over and over again…just like he stepped *out* of the shadow cast by the sunny yellow waterboard propped up in the corner, batting aside the cobwebs strung up like spider hammocks between the board and the wall with an affected gag. "All right, so not my best skulking job. I made it a good five minutes, though, so what would you score that—an eight? It's gotta be at least an eight."

Tenebrae, eyes wide, looked between the two of them. "Occassio, what is this?"

"Oh, please—like she would have pulled this one on you without some *encouragement.*" A cut of perfect teeth, a predator smiling in the dark; his golden eyes nearly glowed as he stared Tenebrae down. "Can't blame her for the slip, though. This is the first time I've let her out for some exercise—she got restless all cooped up in her cage. Thought I'd let her go on a fly-about."

The lightest powdered-sugar dusting of emphasis on *fly.* A tap of his thumb against his pocket, the rest of his fingers hidden inside.

Oh, fool.

Her fool.

"Brae," she said, letting her voice shake in its boots as she scrambled behind her brother's back, "he made me, he's had me for—for weeks. I don't know how but he put me in a mirror, he locked me, caged me, I couldn't get *out.*"

Impressionists were her least favorite performer. A truth that doubled down when the unscrupulous god's face—borrowed as it was—took on a darkness thicker than backstage shadows, a havoc of fury kicked up by Finn's tactical truth. "Did he hurt you? Did he *touch*—"

Finn took a fearless step forward, ticking his finger in time with his *tsks.* "Not my sort of game, Captain Chaos. No point breaking a caged bird's wing, is there?"

Fly away. His slanted words, his refusal to look at her, his body between Brae and the door—*fly away.*

He knew what he was doing, her Trickster Prince—and she knew, too.

But there was one thing he didn't know.

I wouldn't know love if it shook my hand and introduced itself by name.

That by letting her out of her cage…he'd clipped her wings all the same.

CHAPTER 47

FINN

If he survived this, he was going to burn this pair of shoes—and encourage his mother to refloor this office with *great* prejudice.

Sloppy. He'd gotten distracted by stupid sentiment, seeing red after Tenebrae voiced his intention to offer Raquel up for Tempest's *use,* and he'd scraped his sole on one of the imperfect boards in his mother's office. The ones he had mapped out backward and forward in his head.

It hadn't been the worst offender among them. And if Cassi hadn't *also* stumbled, he might've had a shot to sneak all the way behind his mother's desk to recover her signet.

But even the foremost among liars and thieves had their off days. Unfortunately, it seemed they'd decided to share this one.

Even less fortunately, for the first time, it felt like he and Cassi weren't reading the same page from the same playbook; he kept hinting, shifting, poking at the predator crouched in front of her. Stirring up the memories she'd need to lead her down his path of reasoning; distracting the cat so the bird could take flight.

But she wouldn't take the leap. She shrank into her brother's borrowed shadow, golden eyes wet as wishing coins fished from a fountain, lip quivering just enough to affect fear without crossing the line into dramatics.

Come on. His hand curled into a fist in his pocket. *Come on, make your move.*

"You have *got* to be kidding," Tenebrae seethed, scratching viciously at the back of his head; a clump of Jericho's scarlet hair tore out of his scalp when he dropped his hand. "First the rotting *Heir,* now *you*—what's next, is your brother going to march his worthless *skin* through the door and tell me he locked Tempest in the hold of a ship?"

Like he was fool enough to take *that* bait. "If your bad luck holds out, maybe."

The traitorous floorboards started to shake. The first harbinger of chaos. Finn rolled his eyes. "No new tricks, old dog?"

"For you?" Tenebrae split Jericho's lip open with his snarl, inky discharge dribbling out instead of blood. Veins swollen with pure spoil. "I'll get *creative.*"

Whatever cue Cassi was waiting for, he didn't know how to give it— unless she wasn't waiting for a cue at all. Unless those crocodile tears were part of her final change of heart, shedding the last of the water thinning out the blood-loyalty to her brother.

It wouldn't be a surprise. But it would be nice not to die because he'd been the exact kind of starry-eyed idiot Kal always became around a certain lightning-licking Nyxian woman.

All this, he was able to ponder in the span of a second—and when that second ended, the wall clock marking its passing with a crisp *tock,* chaos came for him.

From the floorboards—depths-damned snitches, one and all—slithered the god-queen's signature vines watered in ichor. An adversary he'd faced before.

The vines tied around his ankles, trying to tug him off balance; with a strum of one of chronomancy's strings, his counter-blow swept down so fast even he didn't see it happen. One moment the vines held him fast; the next, they writhed like headless snakes around his shoes.

"Old tricks," Tenebrae mocked.

"Well, if it's not broken…"

"It's not broken?" A menacing twinkle. His fingers rose to his mouth, his lips pursing oddly. "I'll fix that."

Passably funny. Finn might've even laughed if he'd been in a better mood.

And if a pitchy growl hadn't come from behind him, roughly at ass-level.

Even with chronomancy strung like cat's cradle between his fingers, he only had enough time to spin and raise his dagger, not dodge—the overgrown claws of the corrupted hound sank into his chest, so severely curved they hooked in and back out of his skin.

All right, he'd give that one to Tenebrae—that was new.

"Watch it!" he sputtered, swiping his dagger outward; it slashed across the hound's muzzle, its panting jaws parting in a garbled whine. "My mother's going to have some choice words if I show up with piercings in my—"

The hound reared up, raking its claws from Finn's mouth down his torso; streaks of brand-hot pain tore through his shirt and skin, blood leaking into his mouth.

A clearer *Quit being clever and focus up, fool* had never before been spoken by the universe.

"Good boy!" cooed Tenebrae. He flashed his fingers at Finn, revealing a slim cylinder perched in Jericho's delicate fingers. A dog whistle, copper coated in corrosion the color of mildew. "Music's been known to tame even the wildest of beasts. I figured, why not see if it could do the opposite?"

He could come up with at least a dozen reasons why not. But he'd get to that later.

Finn tipped his wrist toward the candle on his mother's desk, catching the bobbing light; a disc of auramancy unfurled parallel to the mirror tied around his wrist, fire catching the pink, tinting it coral. He swung his arm as hard as he could without adequate room to wind up, striking the hound off; it reeled, more out of shock than pain, its head wagging as it coughed through another growl. A gob of purplish gunk slid off its lolling tongue.

Finn rolled onto his stomach, letting the pain of his punctures propel him up. "All right," he panted. "New tricks."

Both wrists out. Both mirrors angled to the pendant around his neck. His reflection split between the three of them.

One bolt of auramancied light. A triangulation of magic that thrilled him like few things could these days. A theory he'd only chanced testing now.

As did the look of absolute *loathing* that claimed Tenebrae's features as he took in Finn's favorite new trick.

As three Finnick Atlases broke rank from the first, taking on life of their own. Three forgeries indiscernible from the original.

He hadn't dared steal a peek at Cassi again yet. But pickpockets couldn't resist the itch for long; and when he finally let himself look, he could've sworn her eyes glittered with delight.

It should have been difficult, one mind stretched across four bodies, even when three were nothing but candlelight and imagination. It wasn't.

The hound growled deep in its chest as it circled back to its prey, hackles bristling. Its glass-marble gaze clicked between him and his copies.

"Not such good odds for you anymore, huh?" he chuckled through one of his copies.

Finn—the original—crossed his arms. "Arithmetic was never my longsuit—"

"*Our* longsuit," corrected another copy.

"Sure, whatever—but one against four, that's looking a little bleak."

Cassi broke character just long enough to mumble, "Are you seriously bantering with *yourself*, you absolute—"

He flashed a grin her way. One of the copies winked. "No one else can keep up, Fidg."

Were her cheeks going pink, or was it just the auramancied light in the room?

Tenebrae circled to the left; one of Finn's copies followed, the other tipped to the right with a taunting whistle at the hound, and Finn flung himself through the gap that left Cassi exposed.

If she wouldn't run, he could at least help her keep up the ruse of remaining on her brother's side.

If it *was* a ruse.

He swung one hand up, catching the candlelight; with two swift cuts of the imagination, he forged a dagger from nothing but a daydream.

And when he swung downward, never expecting it to land, Cassi proved him right by swinging her own arm across her front, her wrist parrying his, their blades not even glancing off each other.

"What are you doing?" he hissed over their locked wrists, both of them shaking as they tried to shove themselves through the stalemate. Without the knives, they could have been preparing for a twirl across a ballroom, not a collision of powers past the mortal imagination.

"What are *you* doing?"

"Buying you time to run!"

"Run where?"

"*Anywhere!*"

She ripped her wrist away, ducking as he finished his swing; when she stayed low, lurching into his breathing space with her blade angled for his heart, he strummed a chord of chronomancy to step exactly one inch out of her reach. He plucked another just to measure—then plucked her dagger neatly from her hand. When he tossed it carelessly at the ceiling, it stuck—then shimmered, dissolving in a fizz of shooting stars.

He pressed the last of his advantage to steal her hand instead; with a brush of his lips so light it barely counted as a kiss, he spun her in a starstruck circle and pinned her to his chest, arms banded over hers to keep her from picking or poking her way out.

Worth it. Even when his vision flooded scarlet, a film that thinned with his next blink, bloody tears his sacrifice at chronomancy's own altar …worth it.

"Cheating." Even breathless with bruised ego, he knew her smirk when he heard it. When she twisted her head to the side, freeing up her ear for whispered secrets, the divot in her warm cheek pressed into his shirt.

This was awful. If Kallias and Raquel had been this distracted their entire journey from Artem to Skyhaven to Sirena, it was no wonder they'd failed at half the pursuits they'd planned.

"Make yourself scarce, Songbird," he muttered in her ear. "I need to concentrate."

She gave an infinitesimal shake of her head and reached back under the guise of trying to claw at his face, wiping some of his bloody tears instead. "Not the boss of me, Lordship."

"Cassi—"

"Take your *stake-burnt hands* off *my sister!*"

Talons flayed into his throat, something squeezing, cutting off his air; panic strangled whatever air was left as he clawed at the vine noosed around his neck. Tearing it was out of the question; the damned thing was as thick around as his wrist. And even he didn't trust his own skill enough to risk trying to slice something so close to several *very important* veins.

He'd cut a throat or two in his time. He'd prefer not to add his own to the list.

Tenebrae, however, had no such qualms.

Finn hated the glottal gagging sound the vine squeezed out of him as it dragged him into a backward stumble. He had to banish the daggers he'd built to get his hands around the vine, groaning through his teeth as he shoved his thumbs under the vine, relieving just enough pressure to sip in a thin breath.

Tenebrae wasted no time punishing him for it.

The ground disappeared from under his feet, reappearing just as quickly under his head as Tenebrae slammed him onto the floor.

He heard the sound first, a crack like someone had thrown a spark-nub—a small, round firecracker of sorts—onto the nearest available brick.

Then the pain caught up.

The arch his spine curved itself into would've been impressive if he hadn't been occupied with the dizzying explosions going off in his back, his shoulders, his neck—and the finale filling his head with nauseating whirls of color.

A chorus of snaps, and his right hand went entirely numb.

A sound like someone munching gravel, and his left hand followed the right's example.

He might have screamed. Gods, he hoped he hadn't screamed. He'd rather die than give Tenebrae the satisfaction, but pain had filled his head with temple bells; he couldn't hear a damned thing past all the ringing.

His vision cleared just in time for him to watch as Tenebrae's heel ground the mirror pendant into his chest. Something crunched; gods knew if it was the glass or his sternum.

His copies—one now fending off two hounds, the other with his own illusory dagger buried in Tenebrae's side—vanished, extinguished like blown-out candles. Tarry blood stained the torn silk over Tenebrae's ribcage, but he didn't even seem to notice; his famished stare was locked on Finn.

All right, he'd admit it—this wasn't going exactly the way he'd hoped.

One of the hounds lay where it had fallen after his figment vanished, too still to be playing dead; the other limped over with one shoulder hitched, neck bent low, head cocked so far it nearly dragged its face sideways across the ground. Its shrill whine went off-key more times than Finn could count as it waited for Finn to try and push himself up—then pounced.

Those claws shredded through his skin like he was made of wet paper.

"Occassio." Almost a purr. "Hold him down, will you?"

Finn twisted his head and coughed, copper-soaked spittle spraying from his lips; even swallowing, breathing, and weeping his own blood, nothing held more of his attention than the wispy brush of dancer's feet over old wood. The fool's gold no longer playing pretend in her eyes. The undimpled smile.

The hound did most of the work—its weight kept him flat on his back. But those were her hands holding his head in place, forcing him to look her full in the face as she betrayed him one last time.

"You missed the point of the song," she breathed to him. Her thumbnail flicked a drop of blood from the corner of his eye, like wiping a tear. "The songbird spends so much time dreaming that it doesn't think ahead. It wasn't made for the sky. It never could have flown away."

And this was better? Staying just to watch him die?

Or did her vengeance still matter to her, after all—enough that she needed to know she'd played some role in his final fall?

"I didn't miss it," he rasped. *I just hoped you'd trust me to catch you.*

Tenebrae didn't bother with the vines this time. When he came to stand over Finn, dismissing the hound with a clipped whistle, metal winked in the dying candle on the desk—his mother's letter opener. A stiletto blade she'd repurposed for a more menial task.

"Three down," Tenebrae murmured. "One to go."

In all honesty, Finn had never really thought much about death.

Even with Cassi's whispered truth gummed into his brain—*My first vision showed me your death*—it didn't feel quite real when Tenebrae dangled that blade over his throat, playfully swinging it like a pendulum, a metronome, a ticking clock.

Counting away Finn's final seconds. *Tick, tock, tick, tock.*

Death happened to other people. His sister—his brother. Not him.

Whenever he thought about the bad things, he thought about life. But this time, with death dangling from his traitorous sister's puppetted fingertips—and a strange glimmer of light in her right eye—he wanted one of life's good things instead.

Finn closed his eyes and whispered the name of his Sanctan songbird.

When the pendulum snapped, Time itself thrummed with pity. The blade strafed Time's cords as it cut through the air, aimed to sever his own thread in the weave—and Time spared a second of its own to mourn. To whisper his name in return.

To *shout.*

"Stop!"

Something tore away from his neck, and for a moment, he was reasonably sure that *something* was a thin strip of flesh, the sort that meant a slit throat. That any moment, he'd leave his body behind for whatever unknowable thing came next.

That any moment, he'd hear his brother lecturing him about taking on a god face-to-face without anyone trustworthy backing him up. Feel Kal's fist against his shoulder—then his embrace, fed up as he might be with Finn's bad habits, bad bets, bad hands.

He'd gone all in with nothing up his sleeves—no cheats, no spares, no aces. His only face card a queen, and her liable to shift suits if she so desired.

And in spite of it all, when he did hear the voice of a disappointed older brother…it wasn't Kallias's at all.

"*Oh.*" The bones of the world shook beneath the weight of the contempt in Tenebrae's voice. "I see. Damn. And here I thought you above such base distraction."

He should probably open his eyes and see why he wasn't dead—and what in the depths *that* meant.

The shining point of the stiletto blade nearly blinded him; he jolted in his own skin, goosebumps erupting in the hollow of his throat as he beheld the blade aimed straight for his jugular.

Aimed—but not falling.

Frozen.

The stiletto blade hung suspended in midair, flickers of iridescence wavering in and out of sight around it. Ripples of light splashed across thin air.

Cassi no longer held him down. Because her hands were occupied with two stolen things, a pick she'd pulled without pockets:

In one hand, she held his broken mirror pendant.

In the other, she held his life. Because the other was tangled messily in Time's matted threads, halting their flow around the stiletto.

"Bravo, Prince Finnick." Tenebrae gave a mocking round of applause; with a low whistle, he ordered the hound on top of Finn away. It retreated to sit beside its master; Tenebrae stroked its ears as he tilted his head Finn's way. "Tell me, how did you pull this off?"

He'd love to brag about it, if only he could figure out for himself exactly what he'd *pulled off*.

"Leave it," Cassi snarled, but Tenebrae kept talking, frenzy stoked in his eyes, practically foaming at the corners of his rabid grin.

"No, no—I *have* to hear this. Tell me, Trickster Prince…how did you manage to trick my one heartless sister into falling in *love* with you?"

Finn scoffed. Might've laughed, too, if not for the blade nearly kissing his throat.

Cassandra Medeis didn't fall—not from tightropes, not for tricksters. That would be a depths-damned marvel. He'd applaud *himself* if…

If…

Why wasn't she laughing?

No knife held to her throat; no bruised ribs warning her against deeper breaths. Yet Cassi didn't laugh.

Not a flicker of humor broke the shadows in her eyes as she tore her hand off the mirror pendant, releasing the threads of time just to thrust her hand outward, neatly plucking the stiletto from the air before time lost its grip on its hilt.

Graceful, as always. But the trickles of blood pouring from both nostrils and one of her ears thrust a bolt of base fear through his chest.

He had her magic, her strength, her *divinity*—and even with all that, he'd still taken a beating for using that power. Chronomancy could hardly touch her as Occassio, but Cassandra Medeis didn't have the same privilege.

She didn't laugh. She didn't even smile. But her crooked snarl brought out her telltale dimples as she stood up and stepped around him, one arm spread to the side while she palmed the stiletto in her opposite hand. Wiped her bleeding nose on the back of her wrist.

"I warned you when we started," she hissed. "You can take whatever you want from the rest of the rotting world, I won't try to stop you—but don't you dare touch what's *mine*."

Finnick Atlas wouldn't know love if it shook his hand and introduced itself by name.

But even a fool—even the prince of them—could figure out what it meant when the queen of thieves called him *hers*.

When the Goddess of Time turned on the God of Chaos against her own best interests, winnowing into his space like a flighted shadow, knife winking Finn's way as she drove it toward her brother's chest.

As her blow landed true.

The stiletto blade slid in so easily, as if Jericho's chaos-battered body offered no resistance at all. Slid in right to the hilt, where it finally caught on a rib, abandoned there as Cassi scrambled back, wrath painting her face with familiar shadows.

The God of Chaos looked down at the dagger in his heart.

And laughed.

Laughed and laughed and laughed and *laughed*, like he'd just heard the best joke anyone had ever told. Like he'd never heard a joke before in the first place. Like that dagger was a set of fingers intent on tickling him to death instead.

"I love you," he wheezed as he ripped the blade out, grinning like a fool as he set it back on Adriata's desk. "You act so superior, but look at you! Look at this!" He threw back his head in another giggle fit, forming a fist and driving it into his own wound. It came away dripping in brackish blood; he shook it idly before dragging it down the side of his face, grinning up at the ceiling. "Gods, you and Ani, you really are twins ten years apart. Getting soft over your mortal skins. Trying to put me down to protect them. You know it won't work."

"You won't hurt me," Cassi sneered, backing toward Finn, one hand still splayed; with panic and pain putting on one horrendous harmony in his veins, he forced his feet to get back in the game, finding them with only minimal attempts by his body to gag up more blood. He had to save up all his strength; had to spend it wisely. This escape would not be easy, and he could not afford to slow her down.

But he only spent one step before Tenebrae decided it was his turn to try a heist.

With one blow, he stole all that strength Finn had piled into his pockets. One blow—a vine snaring Cassi around the waist and trapping her hands, thorns tearing through fabric and skin, squeezing until she screamed—a primal thing that woke a terror in him he hadn't known he could feel.

Worse than watching her wobble across a tightrope in worn-down shoes. Worse than watching her figment tremble in Tomas's shadow. Worse than watching a bottle break in her hands, glass slicing tendons so deeply they'd never really heal right.

In the heart of this castle turned crypt, Finnick Atlas learned the difference between ichor and blood.

Ichor was to blood as ink was to dye; as wine was to grapes; as hail was to rain.

As blood was to water.

He and Cassi bled the same searing red, bright as a bolt of crimson costume silk as it dripped from his lying lips, her pretty hands…but his blood did not sing like hers.

Even spattered on his mother's favorite rug, that blood thrummed with power. Every drop cut from Cassi's skin hit a high note in his brain, a peal of panic that resonated from his throbbing head to his broken fingers.

He didn't know if she could die.

Not by a mortal hand, sure—they'd tested that much. But another deity, might against might? And her without full command of her magic, at that?

He doubted it. *Highly* doubted it. Would've bet his life on it.

Wouldn't bet hers, though.

"Stop!" he shouted; his lungs shuddered out a cough, and he hacked up another mouthful of blood, wiping it on the back of his hand. Hopefully the damage wasn't as bad as it looked. And sounded. And felt. "Just…stop. Don't hurt her. Tell me what you want, I'll give it to you—name your price."

The most dangerous deal he had ever offered.

Tenebrae's eyebrows rose; a tell of genuine shock from the God of Chaos.

Even if there was, the horror in Cassi's voice would've disqualified him, anyway. "Finn, it's fine, it's *fine*, don't—"

"Anything," he interrupted firmly. Never looking at her. Never looking away from Tenebrae. "Name your price."

If he didn't follow through, he got nothing—if he went back on this deal, she'd bleed.

He wouldn't watch it happen. Not because of him. Not again.

Even if the cruel, giddy gleam catching the light in Tenebrae's wild gaze made him want to laugh it all off. To call the god gullible for thinking he'd ever give up anything, *everything*, for the goddess who had conned him into giving the enemy a foothold in his kingdom.

Or maybe he was the gullible one, for thinking he'd ever be able to quit this game of theirs once it started. That he wouldn't crave it, covet it, cash in every flicker of good sense just to chance another round with Cassandra Medeis.

"You know…once, a very long time ago, I was privileged to witness a performance most would deem impossible." Tenebrae's smile bent at a sickening angle. "I think an encore might just be in order."

CHAPTER 48

FINN

Thanks to their poisonous little plot, Tenebrae could put on all the shows he liked—there wouldn't be much of an audience around to applaud for it. But he escorted them in with all the pomp and circumstance of any respectable showman anyway, dragging Finn by his nape like a naughty kitten scruffed by its mother, whistling his way to the dais.

"I'm losing my patience," Cassi sneered, following as Tenebrae ascended the dais, the latter driving a steel-toed kick into Finn's ankle when he tried to hook his shoe against one of the steps. Nothing broke, but *gods* did it smart. "Tell me exactly what show you're spouting off about."

Nothing like her usual sort. No graceful aerial ascents or high-wire waltzes. He'd bet the entire treasury on that.

Pressure released the back of Finn's neck, and he dropped flat on his soles—before he could even think about thinking about running, five fingernails pierced his jaw, hefting him back into a tiptoed stretch just to lessen the pain.

Tenebrae made an errant gesture, an impatient sort of summons. With his head craned back, Finn had a front-row seat to exactly what kind of show Tenebrae expected from them.

A spoiled vine uncoiled across the space, anchoring itself from one wall to the next. Without his glasses, he couldn't be sure, but it looked…studded with something. Typically, Tenebrae's vines came into being fully thorned.

The throne room's soaring ceilings set that vine—that *rope*—well above the one they'd danced across in the theater. Finn's stomach swooped like it had fallen from an even greater height.

Tenebrae tipped his head upward. His jagged nails dug into Finn's jaw. "Climb up."

Cassi's face fell, a coin dropped in an empty wishing well. "What?"

"You heard me." Pain, pressure—they both came together to pop Finn's jaw, the precursor to a devastating break. "Get up there."

Cassi's wild eyes flickered to the horrific mimicry of a rope. To him. To Tenebrae. Back to the rope. Thoughts skittered and somersaulted through those clever eyes, sparks fleeing a firework's wick as they twirled toward an unavoidable end.

Tenebrae's hand lowered as his voice did, crushing Finn's throat instead. *"Now."*

Not a chance in the depths.

He'd worn plenty of costumes, played plenty of characters in this time-tested game of theirs. Fool. First-chair fiddle. False god.

But he wouldn't be the weapon held to her throat.

He held his breath of his own accord; if she heard him strangling, fighting for breath, fear would rush her to the wrong choice. The faster he faded, the better for both of them.

But he'd forgotten.

Until Cassi's gaze swept up to catch his, two blades connecting at the crossguards, he'd forgotten what had happened in the moments after they'd come clean to each other…the way time had stopped in their chests, a pause that abated with a breath they took as one. The way their heartbeats had joined hands and swept into their own precarious, perfectly balanced waltz.

A set of metronomes set face to face, pendulums swinging in flawless alternation. Two clocks set by copycat keepers, sneaking peeks at the other's instrument to tune their own. A tightrope trip taken in twos.

Time and her Trickster.

His heart counted off the *tocks* to her *ticks*—and when his stumbled, slowed, hers kicked into double-time to make up for the missing seconds. He could *hear* it.

She took one step toward the wall where the rope had anchored itself.

"Cassi." Like a beggar who knew he wouldn't survive the night, he spent all he had on that little indulgence: all his air for one taste of hope that he might still be able to save her from this.

She took another step.

He tried to say her name again. Tried it over and over and over.

But he'd run out of breath. None left to save, none left to spend; none left for her to steal.

The third step brought her to the wall. She didn't look at him; she looked at Tenebrae.

"I'm going to kill you for this," she promised.

Tenebrae's smile dripped indulgence. "Sure you will."

She tapped the wall impatiently. "Unless you expect me to fly…"

Tenebrae lifted a hand in an elevating gesture. Golden tiles rotted to bronze-and-charcoal powder, and through that metallic mimicry of soil, bulbous roots dragged themselves up the wall tooth and claw, filament and thorn. Marble shrieked in protest as the corrupted roots dragged turgid, tuberous bellies over its slick surface before branching off into spidering tendrils of smoke and barbs.

Finn had to choke back bile as they tussled and wove around each other, forming a lattice that came to an abrupt end just above the treacherous tightrope.

Without hesitating, Cassi began to climb the trellis.

The laces on her left boot were untied. He could see them dangling from here. Could see them catching on the barbed plants as she climbed without a sound, leaving traces of ichor winking against the wall.

He was going to kill someone. Anyone. *Everyone.*

"Don't worry." Tenebrae's breath was hot and wet against the shell of his ear, almost sticky—or maybe that was the blood leaking from Finn's head. "This won't be a solo performance."

A forceful thrust, and Finn tumbled down the dais, wrist and fingers and head screaming with pain as they broke his fall. He pushed himself onto his fractured hands and unsteady knees at the bottom, spitting blood and bile on the floor he'd taken his first steps across.

His blood, now joined with that of so many examples he'd deemed worthy losses in his single-minded drive to save his family.

Maybe he deserved this. Maybe they both did. But—

"Go on," Tenebrae said, draping himself over the Queen's throne with an errant gesture upward. When Finn dragged his head up, he caught the tail end of another trellis clawing up the opposite wall. "Up you go, *Trickster Prince.*"

"That wasn't the deal," he said, spitting more blood. He couldn't be clever through a mouthful of iron swill.

"There was no deal. Get up there—or I let the vine wither."

Which meant Cassi had already mounted the damned thing.

His swollen knuckles grated painfully against each other as he pushed himself up and limped to the other trellis. Something stung when he grabbed hold of it, though the thorns didn't start until much higher up—when he checked, he found tiny filaments bristling over the surface of the root-like base of the trellis, not entirely unlike jellyfish tentacles.

New tricks. All right, he'd take the blame for that one.

"Don't look down," Cassi called when he reached the rope, eyes smarting, palms tingling like he'd shoved them into a hive and tried to make off with some nasty-tempered bee's honeycomb.

"Wasn't planning on it." The desire to look down from great heights was one he'd never understood. It made no sense from a survival standpoint. Sure, you'd see the danger—but you'd also get too dizzy to see straight afterward. He'd take his chances on ignorance this one go.

"The trick is simple!" Tenebrae called up from below, tone so sweet Finn felt a toothache coming on. "If both of you make it to one end or the other, you both live—I'll keep you prisoner, of course, but you'll live. However, if one of you falls…I'll let the other go free. No strings attached." A sparkle of glee joined the party when Tenebrae added, "Foul play is *not* forbidden."

His and Cassi's gazes snapped upward at the same time, catching each other's stares.

If one of you falls, the other goes free.

Simple rules. Simple subtext. Cassi could redeem herself. She could go free…if she made sure Finn fell to his death. If she proved her loyalties ran in the right direction.

But if she let him live, she'd be punished with her worst fear: another cage.

"Trap," he called across the rope.

She rolled her eyes like he'd just made a terrible pun, not a very perceptive observation. "Traps imply an element of surprise. This is a test."

He smiled. Couldn't help it. "Still the cleverest girl this side of Sanctaviv."

"Goddess."

"Gods, you can't even let me *compliment* you without correcting me?"

A shallow, nauseous laugh. "Well, if you weren't always a little bit wrong…"

Harder to smile when she looked like she might vomit over the side of the vine. Nothing at all like her fearless foray across the rope in the past, netless and nettling him about his own thoroughly reasonable fear.

"Hey," he said when Cassi glanced downward, breaking his stare—her head bobbed back up, and he shook his as hard as he dared this high up. "We know it's a trap—wipe that look off your face, Cass, semantics aren't the hill to die on. It's a trap. So let's figure out how to pick the lock."

Her jaw worked. But she nodded anyway. "Really, though—don't look down."

If he angled his eyes just right, he didn't have to look down to see the trial that awaited him. Snaggletooth thorns corkscrewed out of the vine like bared fangs, thick enough to pierce their soles and sink deep into their flesh. The ends were barbed like fishhooks; they'd have to rip themselves free with every step.

If either of them was to save the other, they would have to destroy themselves doing it.

"Finn."

He hated the way her voice drew him in. He could never ignore her call—not really. No matter how many lies he told himself.

When he looked up, she wore a smile that disarmed his heart with one swift shoulder-check.

"What did I just say?" she teased.

He kicked his sandals off, wishing she'd do the same with that loose-laced boot. No use leaving them on—they were more slippery than his bare soles, and the thorns would go right through them anyway. "My name."

"Don't be smart."

"Can't help it."

"Stop looking at my rotting shoes." He could've paid any ransom in the world with the hoard of diamonds clinging to her lashes. "Don't. Look. Down."

She was right. Any distraction would prove fatal up here...and she couldn't bend to tie them now anyway.

Get ahold of yourself, Finn.

He took his first few steps out on the line. Refused to scream when the thorns sank deep into his skin. Forgot why it mattered when he had to tear his foot free from the hook.

Pain heightened every sensation, every sight—everything went warm and bright, so luridly colorful it hurt his eyes. He felt every minute stretch of muscle and skin as his lungs expanded, drawing in the breath he needed to push himself into ripping his other foot free.

The entire world flushed with pigment, like blood rushing into reality's head. He sank his teeth into his tongue until he tasted fresh blood.

Kallias had taken a whip to the back and had not screamed—not even once.

A lashing he'd taken on Finn's behalf—a burden Raquel had shared. Neither had raised their voices. Neither had screamed for mercy, for help...not even for the simple relief of letting some of the agony out.

These thorns flayed his feet better than any whip. But his brother wasn't here to take this beating for him.

It was his turn to be brave for someone else now.

"Not all that difficult, if you ask me." He flashed a smile Cassi's way, disguising his grimace in that cut of teeth as he took another step. "Maybe we should waltz to the other side?"

Her humorless laugh was not the one he wanted. Better than nothing, though. "Don't taunt him."

"I'm taunting *you*. You call that a tightrope walk? Your form's terrible. You've let yourself go in the last millennium."

"You're the one who's slouched over like a dying flower."

"That's my reader's hunch. It's a sign of—"

When he stepped down next, the thorns *bit*.

They grew in a seizing lurch, writhing sideways and wrapping around his foot.

They pulled.

Rushing air. An icy splash of adrenaline. Cassi shrieking his name.

His own cry when he threw out one hand by instinct, catching himself on the vine...and a thorn stabbed straight through his palm.

"Well," he choked, either through a sob or a laugh, "that's ac-actually helpful, a little!"

"Get back on!" He hadn't heard her so thoroughly lose her composure since the cage. "Get back on *right rotting now!*"

"I'm trying," he panted. Too hard to lie like this.

Thank the gods for all the time he'd spent leaping from—and falling from—rooftops. He managed to wrap the fractured fingers of his other hand around the vine in such a way to avoid the thorns, then pulled himself back up, screaming through his teeth as he swung his feet under him. Plunging them both onto more thorns.

Gods, everything *spun.*

"Oh, you thought it'd be that easy?" Tenebrae's laughter rang sickeningly through his swimming head as he wrenched his hand off of the thorn stabbed through it, a nauseous chill prickling down his arms. "The more you water it, the thirstier it gets."

Oh, gods. The more they bled…

"Keep going." Cassi's voice had gone flat, not a single note of laughter to lift it. "Almost halfway."

He couldn't think of anything clever to say. Anything to make her smile again, or laugh, or stop watching him like she'd seen this show before…and she didn't like the ending.

Two more steps. Ragged shreds of his skin snagged on the thorns when he tried to lift his foot, a gag jolting his entire body off balance.

Do not throw up. One more step. *Mama will kill you if you throw up on this floor.*

Silly. So much worse had already stained these floors during Tenebrae's short but impactful tenure as false queen. But it was just silly enough to keep his stomach where it ought to be as he shoved his foot down on the next thorn, sinking his teeth into the scream trying with all its might to break free.

If he couldn't go free, neither could it.

Gods, his ears rang. From somewhere below, tinny music trotted out to join the show—an ear-tweaking *plink, plink, plink* that barely counted as music at all. Louder than it should have been from this far away.

Don't look down. Whatever was happening down there, it wasn't his problem—and it wouldn't become so until he survived this. *Don't look down.*

Instead, he looked up.

But the view still stopped his heart.

Cassi's progress had slowed—she'd only made it one step in the time it had taken Finn to cover three. Her arms hung at her sides instead of reaching out for balance, and something about that look in her eyes…

He'd seen her suffering under magic and madness, both her own. This didn't look like that.

This looked like…

The ringing in his ears rose in pitch, in pressure—like it was trying to push past his eardrums and chisel into his skull.

It made him itch.

It made him want…

Oh gods.

He looked down.

He couldn't really tell, not without his rotting glasses—he *had* to start keeping them on at all times again—but it looked like Tenebrae had something in his hands. Something small.

"Cassi!" he shouted. "Cover your ears!"

Despite his current ownership over her divinity, some resistance to her brother's magic must have been ingrained in her still; she covered her ears immediately, eyes widening a fraction.

"No show's complete without a little music!" laughed Tenebrae. "Isn't that right, Cassi?"

They'd almost reached the center points of their respective ropes; he could almost reach out, almost touch her, almost test for himself just how much chaos roiled under her skin. If the hunger for discord had already settled in her stomach, he was done for. She'd push him off just for the joy of hearing him scream.

Which wasn't all that different from how she usually acted, to be fair, but things had changed rather dramatically in the last couple hours. He liked to think they were past that now.

She didn't call back to her brother; she fixed her gaze straight ahead, lips parted, fingertips digging into her curls. She shook her head once—then again, over and over, like trying to shoo a persistent fly.

"Hey." His throat ached. His feet burned. If he reached for her, would she let him? Or would he learn why the rest of the world refused to leap for fear of the fall? "Look at me—hey, not there, not at him. Look at *me.*"

They were perfectly even now, perfectly mirrored—mere inches separated his hand from hers.

It would take nothing—a gentle push, a gentle betrayal. Gentler than the one he'd already dealt her. He could go free. He could survive. He could see his family again.

He reached out and, as gentle as he'd ever been, cupped her cheek against his palm. Turned her head slowly. She had more freckles now than in the past—fifty-eight speckled over her right cheekbone. It used to be forty-four.

He teased her lashes with his thumb until they fluttered open. And when she finally looked at him, fear singing a duet with frenzy in those pretty eyes, he held her stare without blinking.

"Sing," he mouthed; her brow furrowed, and he repeated, "You need to sing. Drown it out. *Now.*"

"I can't."

"You're never going to fool me with that one."

"I *can't.*" The last word groaned through her teeth as she ground her palms harder against her ears. She stepped back, stumbled—

He sacrificed his own steadiness to hook her wrist in his hand, holding on until they both found a steady spot. "Stop! Stop it, stop moving."

Frenzy drowned out fear's melody as she glanced at him, then at the ground. Her fingers twitched; she reached up, screwing them more tightly into her curls. "I want to…"

"I know." The safe thing, the smart thing, would've been to get away from her as fast as possible. "And you know how to make it stop."

Her head tipped sideways, almost lazily; she looked at him, then at the ground, then at him again.

He held his breath. Prepared to learn what the songbird felt like as it plummeted from the sky it loved so much.

"I know how to make it stop," she repeated, an uncanny mimicry, her voice rising and falling in all the same places his had. "Keep walking."

He didn't move. "Are you—"

She pulled her arm away from him. "I'm calm. Promise. Keep walking."

Both fear and frenzy had abandoned the stage, that much was true—but peering into her eyes, he couldn't tell what had stepped into the spotlight next.

She smiled, flashing one dimple—then lifted the arm he'd caught, tapping the hidden ace up her sleeve. "Trust me. I know what I'm doing."

He didn't trust her…but he did trust her tell. He started walking again.

He made it two more steps before a wave of dread poured down his back, such a powerful shudder it nearly threw him straight off the rope. A chill that took him back to a Sanctaviv theater, to a doorway and darkness and a murmured discussion of childhood fears.

He looked over his shoulder to find Cassi's gaze on the ground again.

"Cass!" he barked; she startled, which only scared him more. What had dragged her that deep into her head? Why did that hazy, teary look she wore make him want to scream more than the thrust of thorn through flesh? *"Don't* look down!"

Her shoulders rose; fell. She turned back to face him, balanced on one foot, her gaze darting between him and the ground.

"He's not playing fair," she said softly.

"So?" He tore up his feet to turn back to her too, huffing through the pain to keep himself from screaming.

"He's not going to let us win." Oh, he liked that determined look even less than the stricken, wide-eyed one. "He won't let us reach the end—one of us is going to fall."

"Neither of us is going to fall." Another truth. He'd make it a gods-damned truth. "That's chaos talking. Don't listen to it, all right? Keep walking."

Cassi lowered her arms to her sides. Then lowered her foot to the vine, tiptoed, her bootlace swishing just shy of a thorny spindle.

"Cassi!" Terror pounded through his veins, beating all awareness of pain out of him. He staggered another step—two, three, *gods* he could barely see— *"Keep walking!"*

"Will you *listen* for once in your rotting life, Finnick Atlas?" Her voice broke on his name. It almost broke him in turn. "One of us is going to fall. He's going to make sure of it, and he's going to make sure it's *you."*

"No," he snapped. "No, no, we're not doing this. Focus. We can beat this, just…tell me a lie. Tell me your very best lie."

They'd told too many truths—enough to throw any trickster off balance. A lie would center her. A lie would—a lie had to—

Occassio took a deep breath through her nose, her eyelids drifting shut. Good. She was thinking. Even the world's best liar would need a moment to come up with her *best.*

When she opened those eyes, setting two beautiful tears free…something in him knew he'd lost. The corroded little piece of his gut that told him when a bet was about to go bad, when a table had gone cold, when someone else had stacked the deck before he found his seat at the table.

But he'd never been able to turn down a bad bet when it came to Cassandra Medeis.

So when she prepared for the fold, he didn't understand what it meant—not at first. When she crossed her arms over her chest, hands over her own shoulders…so close to the deathbed pose they set corpses in, but more deliberate. More dramatic.

"Cassi." Couldn't think fast enough, couldn't talk fast enough, could barely talk at *all*. The breath kept jamming against his swollen throat, cutting off his air. She needed to tie her shoes. "C'mon, where's that lie?"

"How about a secret instead?" A tear fell, caught by one of her dimples. "You were the only game I ever wanted to lose."

And with a wink worthy of a ringmistress, she tipped backwards off the rope like a trustfall.

CHAPTER 49

FINN

He didn't see her fall. He didn't see her break.

But he felt it.

His chest crunched in, a punched-out hole of crushed glass, of razor wire that wrapped around his heart and *tore*. Heat rushed to his face like someone had flipped him upside down and poured his head full of blood; his nerves snapped like fiddle strings pushed past their limit, discordant pains bursting like fireworks under his skin.

Pressure built and built and built inside his skull. His ears rang, one long, shrill note, a chime stretching on like it might never stop.

He didn't know how he got down from that rope—if he crossed it while Tenebrae was distracted by Cassi's stunt, if he'd been fetched somehow, if he'd sprouted wings and flown to the gods-damned floor. One blink, and he was on the ground—another blink, and he'd fallen on all fours beside a mess he couldn't make sense of.

She'd folded her arms before she'd fallen, but they were splayed now, spread like wings waiting to catch the wind. She'd fixed her gaze on the sky, longing even now, glazed with tears she'd never shed. Her hair was a mess. Something had spilled in it. It stuck to her cheeks, her forehead—it stuck to his hand when he pushed it all out of his way, irrationally angry, sick of not being able to see her face.

Gods, she looked so small—absolutely swimming in his sweater. Her boot was untied. He couldn't let her go anywhere with the laces like that. He'd told her. He'd *told* her to keep her shoes tied.

Fingers shaking, he took up the limp laces. *Over, under, pull it tight. Make a bow—*

The laces slipped through his fingers. He cursed, starting again. Lapisian silk, too damned slippery…*over, under, pull it—*

The bow fell apart in his hands. The laces were white when he started—they were red now. Diamond to garnet.

"I *told* you." His voice—something was wrong with it. Something spiny and swollen had lodged in his throat. He twirled one of her curls around his finger, tucking it away with the rest. Teased the tiny rhinestone winking amongst a cluster of rubies by her brow. Wiped her last tear with the cuff of his sleeve. "You knew…you knew…"

He couldn't breathe. Rubies, garnets—she wore so many of them. Cassi hated red. It was everywhere. He couldn't get it off of her. He couldn't tie her damned *shoes*.

"That wasn't supposed to happen."

Ruby, garnet—fireworks, blood.

Blood.

Shock frayed like a sawed-through rope. And between one tick of the clock and the next, the frosted glass protecting him from the full picture shattered into the cruelest clarity.

Not rubies or garnets or fireworks.

Blood.

Her laces, slick with blood. Her face, bejeweled in blood. His hands…

He lifted his gaze from those gore-gloved hands to find Tenebrae staring at his sister, brows mildly furrowed. The god pointed steadily at his sister, not a lick of fervor on his face. Untouched by the frenzy that battered Finn's thoughts until his mind felt bruised.

"You were supposed to die," Tenebrae muttered...so damned *calm*. "Not her. Why did she die?"

That word. He couldn't make it fit with the woman bleeding new stains into the floor.

A goddess couldn't die.

A goddess couldn't die.

A goddess couldn't *die*.

But songbirds could.

Songbirds whose clipped wings had failed them, songbirds who fell—no, who *dove* out of the sky, songbirds whose graceless descent had drawn such uproarious applause he hadn't even heard her body break.

Songbirds whose magic and might had been stolen by a merciless fool.

He hadn't even seen her hit the ground. He could barely see her now, not when his vision blurred between every blink.

"She wasn't supposed to die." Another death throe wracked the palace, the chandeliers screaming in jangling chorus. Chips of crystal rained from the ceiling as Tenebrae came closer. "She wasn't supposed to...for *you?*"

Fire caught in Finn's periphery. A kerosene lamp, shaken from its post, had rolled across the dais, leaning into the curtained partition for comfort; while the curtain soothed it, the flame inside had taken advantage of the distraction, creeping up its wick to thread itself into the curtain's simple stitches.

Numb wasn't quite the right word for this. Not numb, not dazed, not empty...

Vacant.

When the Atlas throne room caught fire, when he watched his home go up in flames again, when he searched in vain for Cassi's heartbeat and found only bloody fabric and cooling skin, Finn's own heart *vacated* his chest.

Good. He didn't need it for this. Better it stayed out of the way.

Tenebrae forced a rattled laugh, still fixated on Cassi's body, tears budding at the corners of his eyes, a grin budding at the corners of his mouth. "All right, Cassi, that's enough. Good one. Get up." A beat of silence; that grin twisted into a tangle of bared teeth and trembling lips. "Get up!"

Those tears couldn't touch him. He couldn't care less who they belonged to.

He couldn't see Jericho's face at all anymore. Just the bastard that had broken his perfect mirror.

"She can't," he said—and when Tenebrae asked again, he shouted. "She *can't!* Do you know why? Huh?" The laugh that came out of him crumbled in his lungs; he had to hack it out piece by piece, staggering to stand up, burning hot breath seething through his teeth. "She's dead. She's dead. You killed her, do you get it? You killed her!"

"We can't die." Finally, fear bled back into Tenebrae's voice as he stumbled for his sister. If the god tried to take her, to touch her, Finn would double the tide of ichor washing over this gold-plated shore. "I made us that way. I made *sure*…I made sure!"

Perhaps he had. Perhaps he had spun their immortality with failproof fabric, a net waiting to catch them when death dropped them, ready to courier their divine souls to better bodies.

But they hadn't counted on a Trickster God meddling in matters not meant for mortal hands. Hadn't counted on a fool turned saboteur stealing the safety net from under her feet.

"You killed her," Finn snarled, the taste of blood and frenzy foaming in his mouth, "You killed her, and you can't *save her!*"

That scream drove him to the floor, falling to his knees and fists.

And in return, the world sang a dirge of destruction.

A shower of crystal-clear slivers fell from the sky, silver rain with the rainbows trapped inside. Every facet caught the light as they pelted Finn's back, his head, his arms—everywhere he was exposed.

He couldn't even feel the sting.

A breeze tentatively tapped him on the back, as if trying to apologize; shaking, not sure if he remembered how to blink or breathe, he forced one cursory look over his bleeding shoulder.

The wall of windows at the back of the throne room had exploded inward. Had utterly unmade themselves.

Not one solid pane of glass remained in those iron frames. Only fragments here and there, hanging like chipped teeth punched out of socket, clinging to their roots for dear life.

"I made sure," Tenebrae repeated, calm again; he had no need to create more chaos. Finn had provided enough to sate them all—to curb even Tenebrae's voracious appetite for madness.

He wanted to scream again, to make the god understand what he'd done, what he'd broken, what they'd just *lost*. But his tongue wouldn't work. His mind, his heart, his hands—none of them worked.

He just tightened his hold on Cassi's hand, swallowing a gag when the broken bones shifted in his grip. His or hers, he didn't know—he just knew he couldn't let go.

He should've held on when Tenebrae tore them apart. Finnick Atlas never let anyone take what was his—why hadn't he fought harder? Why hadn't he *tried?*

He knew the answer: because he'd thought they could win. That Tenebrae was the fool for putting them on the same side. That no force in existence stood a chance against Time and her Trickster.

When he'd offered that deal, he'd done it expecting that they would do what they did best: find a loophole. Stack the deck. Lie or steal or cheat their way out of it—together.

All the divinimancy in the world couldn't have convinced him Cassi would ever lose *willingly*. Least of all…not for…

This was why he rarely took chances with anyone but himself. When he got it wrong, people suffered. People *died*.

He shook his head again, breath seething through his teeth as he circled around to kneel by Cassi's hips instead. He rolled the cuffs of his sweater up to her elbows, feeling for tricks up her sleeves. When his fingertips skidded through a slick of lukewarm blood that suggested something had abrupted the skin under the yarn, they fled the scene before he could encounter the damage hidden by the thick sweater. Her pockets were the same—infuriatingly empty.

Nothing but a bent, bloody card stuck to the inside of her wrist.

Come on. Come *on*. This was Cassi—she had to have something. There had to be *something*.

Some trick. Some illusion. Some way to unveil her perfect ploy and *get her back*.

She wouldn't have taken that fall without a backup plan. Not for him. She couldn't have…she wouldn't…not for *him*.

She was so still. So small. No eager fidgets. No champagne giggles. No keyhole grins.

No dimples.

No. *No.*

He needed more time. Time to take a breath. To reckon with reality. To *think*, gods damn it.

Think, you useless bastard. We can fix this. How do we fix this?

He needed more time. He needed—he needed to go back. No, he needed…

An unlocked cabin. A chess table with only one chair. Cassi holding his wrist, her thumb over his watch. "Again, from the top!"

He needed to start over.

Time could be hurried, if he tried. Time let him pretend his way into the past, if he told a good enough lie. But to persuade it to unmake itself…

He did not know what it would cost him. But…

Any ransom. Any trade. Any price. He hadn't lied.

He would pay that cost in full. He would dye all his ledgers in damning red, in ink or in blood if they asked, if it bought her back.

But he needed time to think. And he only knew one way to get it.

He thrust his palms into piles of glass, relishing the bite as he screamed, one more time, "*Stop!*"

Silence dropped like a guillotine blade.

Pain landed with a back-splitting thunk a moment later. Like the guillotine had bisected him rather than beheaded him.

When that blow landed squarely on his shoulders, his elbows gave, dropping him into the sea of glass; gritting his teeth, he shoved himself back up on his forearms, skull and spine straining under the pressure.

When he blinked, the air shimmered like a summer daydream.

Time hung suspended in the air around him, no longer flowing threads but frozen raindrops; flecks of eternity glittering like a spray of confetti. Like some fool had thrown a fistful of glitter they'd never finish sweeping off the floor.

Like Finn had fallen into a bottle of wine stirred with edible sparkle, swirled just so before its artful pour.

A tip of the wrist. A flex of the fingers. A sleight of hand like any other.

And it hurt like the putrid, dismal, desolate *depths* from which all evil and ghastly things had crawled.

But Tenebrae had frozen mid-stride, mid-shout; his hand reached in Cassi's direction, brow still furrowed like he didn't understand what he'd done.

With a hard swallow and a curse far too plain for Finn's liking, he raked in handful after handful of the crystalline chaos around him until the fragments coalesced into a shimmering, deceptively pretty pile nearly an inch deep.

Splintered glass winked up at him when he finally turned his swollen, purpling hands palms-up, letting moonlight seep over his skin.

Her blood looked darker in the silver light. More like ink. He had to pretend it was ink, because the more he thought about it—that it was blood, that there was so much of it, that it was hers—his throat pulled tighter and tighter. Panic scrubbed every damned bit of cleverness he'd ever cobbled together right out of his useless skull.

If he squinted upward, he could connect the dots in Cassi's constellation; the threads were still there, just scattered amongst brighter, beaming stars. But they were sagging, drifting, dull and dead and slack as cut puppet strings, and he could only catch them one by one the way he couldn't catch her, and he—

And he—

And he—

And he shut his eyes. Breathed in deep.

Called for a vision. Called for the light.

Color and brilliance shone a spotlight in his mind, and there she was.

On the rooftop in Sanctaviv, the sun dancing in her hair and a challenge dancing on her lips, inviting him to play their very first game.

Darning the hole in his scarf, needle pinched perfectly between the gap in her teeth, giggling until her stomach hurt at the jokes he'd written when she was Fidget; he'd stayed up through the night coming up with them, coffee in hand, driven by a madness he did not understand. A madness that made him crave her smile at any cost. She was not the figment he'd written them for. She laughed herself hoarse at them anyway.

There she went again, cartwheeling across a tightrope, mocking his false fear of heights; looking at him like she never wanted to blink again when he waltzed out onto the rope himself, asking her for an impossible dance.

Her smile fragmented, bathed in firework flame, blue and red clashing on purple cloth, on spectral glass. A shattered bottle; a shattered heart. He pulled it off like a magic trick. He left feeling like a fraud.

Her smile just before she stepped off that thorn-studded mockery of a tightrope and stumbled into the sky, grinning through a broken heart, dimples filled to the brim with tears. *"You were the only game I ever wanted to lose."*

"I am always your downfall, Finnick Atlas…and you are always mine."

Mine.

He lifted his gaze to the dimming threads. One by one, they flickered out, drifting out of reach. He couldn't hold them much longer.

In the end, when he broke it down to its sparsest parts, the scheme was very simple.

Once, he had invented a special stitch to stop anyone from stealing what was his.

He had done it once.

He could do it again.

He had her magic. That made him more than mortal. It had to be enough.

It had to be.

So he gathered those broken, bleached threads of Time, one by two by three. He wound them around his fingers like spindles on spinning wheels, knowing he could never sew the impossibly long weave of her beautiful, burdened life back together.

But he'd been wrong before. He prayed he'd be wrong today.

He clutched the tattered ribbons of Cassandra Medeis's life as if his own depended on it. Like he'd tried to pick Time's pocket and come away with only the purse-strings tangled through his fingers.

Even the best of thieves sometimes crumbled before the whims of fell, fickle luck.

But if luck tossed a lot or two in an unlikely direction, even the worst of fools could find a way to fly.

In that moment, luck found itself masterless, missing its leash. And before a figment and a fractured future had dealt the cards so far out of his favor, a certain Trickster Prince once had a way with that wily, willful beast.

So he held Time in one fist. Scooped up powdered glass in the other.

"This isn't right," he whispered against the glass, letting it bleed the lies from his lips, soaking into his fistful of fairy dust. "You got it wrong—but I know how to fix it. If you take me back, I can fix it."

Lying to glass was easy.

Lying to Time was not.

But Finnick Atlas was a damned good liar. And maybe, just maybe…luck picked favorites among fools, after all.

Because when he told this lie, his *best* lie, the world remade itself to make it truth.

Agony. Fire. Ice. Blood. Thorns. Glass. Singing. Sobbing. *Agony.*

Color and light exploded around him—sizzling crimson, dazzling cerulean, gentle jade, sunny dandelion, steely gray, molten chocolate...a maddening, mesmerizing ribbon of violet.

Someone was calling his name. His name, over and over and over, until he wasn't so sure it *was* his name anymore. Like reading the same word until it stopped looking like a word.

With the foreboding chime of a clock calling out the hour, his best lie opened wide and swallowed him whole.

CHAPTER 50

FINN

His mother's office was pitifully easy to get into.

Pitiful—and painful, because it *shouldn't* have been easy. His mother nearly always kept her office locked, even when she was inside, and there was usually a guard idling around in the hall to announce any visitors.

Tenebrae never locked a damned thing.

It helped, of course, that Cassi had gone in ahead of him, leaving the door cracked open just a slit. It also helped that his mother hated nothing more than she hated squeaky hinges, which meant every door in the royal wing was oiled with a devotion that bordered on religious.

And that he sent out a curtain-call coaxing to every shadow in the room, though he took no bow as they draped over his body, shielding him from prying eyes.

Tenebrae and Cassi sat against and atop his mother's desk, respectively. Tenebrae watched her with a birdlike tilt to his head, curiosity and suspicion chasing their tails in his gaze; Cassi held her perch like she'd claimed a throne, not a tell to be seen, watching the wall with glossy boredom pasted over her—

Eyes glazed with tears she'd never shed. Hair clumped with a spill of wine. A bejeweled brow dotted with rubies, not rhinestones.

Like a shove to the side, that swirl of memory robbed his balance; he wobbled, foot still in the air, throat closing up when the toe of his boot scraped the surface of one of the noisier floorboards.

No weight fell on it, thankfully; the board didn't sound the alarm. But even when he settled his sandal back on safer ground, he couldn't find his breath again.

The tightrope. The throne room. The trick. The blood.

Time unraveling itself in shame when he claimed it had made a mistake.

His heart was going to dislodge itself straight from his chest cavity if it kept pounding like this. He rubbed the heel of his hand over his heart, silently begging the muscle there to loosen. To let him breathe.

If he could just look away from Cassi, who blinked and breathed and spoke and *breathed*, maybe he could have been more convincing. Distraction never did him any favors.

She was going to die. If he didn't get ahead of this right now, she was going to—

Stop. He cut each panicked thought out of his brain like a maggot wriggling in still-living flesh. *Keep moving.*

"You haven't worn your real face since Sanctaviv," Tenebrae was saying as he crept in, mapping out every floorboard in his mind. Two squeakers framed in a board that could carry him quietly—he sidestepped, tiptoeing along that narrow piece of the herringbone-patterned puzzle with his breath held. "Why now?"

"You trust me more like this."

The first time he'd heard that, he'd almost given himself away with a laugh. This time, the urge didn't even come close.

Tenebrae scoffed. "Plans like that work better when you don't *tell* people about them."

"Maybe." She took a smirk for a spin, leaning back on her palms, kicking her feet gently in the air. "What about you? How long till this skin wears out?"

"Not long. But I won't need it for much longer."

All he had to do was get to the signet. All he had to do was be absolutely silent, and she would live.

He hadn't even gotten to open the drawer last time.

"It's going to be strange, wearing our bodies again." Cassi's voice teased his attention as he sketched a course through this maze of potential traitors. Only one section of boards would test the limits of his legs, but it only would take one to set the future back where it belonged.

Senseless. Utterly senseless that all he wanted to do was look at her, waste all his time watching her breathe, when it would require all his attention to make sure she didn't stop.

While Cassi tittered on, effortlessly hooking her brother's attention with jokes and eye-rolls and strategically placed truths, he kept his own focus fixed on the trial ahead of him. That cluster of shrieky boards behind the desk, under the mounted hooks his mother used to hang her waterboard on…problematic. The saltwater damage left behind by his mother setting the board back in its place had warped nearly the entire span of wood leading up to the inner portion of the curved desk. The board itself might have been propped against the opposite wall, but the damage had already been done.

A ghostly pain prodded his feet as he arched up onto his tiptoes, seeking the safest place to try for it. The wounds were gone—had never been dealt at all, technically—but immortal power or not, his body was mortal, and chronomancy couldn't erase its memory of the damage dealt.

He set a toe to one of the boards with its varnish mostly intact. It let out the softest of groans, almost like a hitched breath.

"Did you hear that?"

Another hitch. Not from the board. "No."

Cursing silently, Finn lifted his foot again, looking up—and freezing when he came eye-to-eye with Tenebrae.

Light and shadow, some said, were total opposites…one could not exist without the other, but they could not be trusted to let the other be, either. Light only existed because there were places it did not; shadows only existed if light was held at bay by something solid. Wherever the two touched, they both destroyed and created the other.

Mutually assured destruction. Symbiotic existence.

He caught Cassi's eye over her brother's shoulder.

Light and shadow had one thing in common: they did what they were told. And as long as he commanded them, they would not allow him to be seen.

But she always saw.

This wasn't over. He could still save it. He'd just have to be faster. Better.

He breathed in, willing his invisibility to hold. Willing her to have one of her brilliant ideas that went hand-in-hand with his.

"What'd you hear?" she wheedled, hopping off the desk and tapping Tenebrae's shoulder. "Brae?"

Maybe it wasn't fair to expect *brilliant* every time. But hey, if it worked…

The exact second that Tenebrae's attention flickered to her, Finn strummed a flossy thread of Time, swearing at the top of his internal monologue's volume as bone strained under the weight, as his knees tried to find the floor, as his spine screamed a warning that it could not bear a single second more—

He picked the lock swift and simple as a wink, snatching the signet in his fist before he actually thought about grabbing it. Then he vaulted the desk and hooked an arm around Cassi's slim waist, panting through the dizzying pain, refusing to let the thread of chronomancy go until they hit the hallway.

When he released it, it snapped back like a cut fishing line, whizzing off into nothing.

No time for acts. No time for showing off. They had to go—they had to *fly*.

"We have to go, we have to go, go *go go go go*—"

"You're bleeding!"

"You're beautiful!"

"What?"

"Sorry, I thought we were stating the obvious!"

An incredulous shriek: "Are you *flirting* with me right now?"

Tenebrae's roar shook the hall—shook the *palace*. The floor lurched under his feet—his stomach lurched the opposite direction.

Yeah, no, she was right. Not the time.

"Go," he gritted out, shoving her ahead of him, but she wouldn't run— she stuck to him like a string tied their ankles together, staring at his face like she was trying to solve a puzzle in the three seconds they had before they lost this game for the second time. "Cassi, for *gods'* sakes, *run!*"

And they did. They ran like they had through Atlas alleys and Sanctaviv streets, like they were sprinting for the lip of a roof, like they'd need all the speed they could get to lift them across the gap to the next building. They ran, this thief and this fool, the same way they had been running their whole lives.

Running across rooftops and tightropes and timelines. Running from and toward and beside each other.

And it still wasn't enough.

When thorny tendrils of bramble vines chewed into his calves, yanking him to his knees, he knew it was over.

He still tried. When Time pieced the script he'd shredded back together, playing out the same choreography, allowing Tenebrae to set the stage with all the same props...he still tried with all his damned might to keep her off that rope.

He tried to taunt Tenebrae into killing him instead of using him to bait the hook. He tried to tell Cassi not to climb that damned trellis. He tried to get her to tie her shoes. He tried with all his wretched might to get her to sing over chaos's croon; tried everything, *everything* to get her to trust him, to get her to keep walking.

It happened so fast. The fall. The flight. The ruination in his chest that chronomancy couldn't hold a candle to.

Rubies and garnets, fireworks and blood.

Shattering glass. His hands filled with a generous offering of his own rubies. His body wailing in terror as he clenched his teeth and whispered his best lie one more time.

One more time.

Just one more.

His mother's office was pitifully easy to get into...or at least, he assumed it was. Because when he arrived in the past this time, he was already inside.

And he very nearly lost again in that first moment. Because for a moment, he almost forgot he couldn't scream.

Fool Time once, shame on him. Fool Time twice, and you could *forget* shame, because he couldn't feel a damned thing besides pain.

No, pain was too gentle a word for this. Even agony didn't come close.

Torture. Every cell in his body had wrenched themselves into impossible knots. Every bloodbeat lit his veins with fresh fire. Every movement felt like his bones were separating from his joints.

But he was back in his mother's office. And there was Cassi, laughing with her brother, not a splash of red to be seen.

Relief ached almost as badly as chronomancy. He sniffed, wiping his nose, not looking as he wiped his hand off on his trousers—not wanting to know if it was blood or snot stirred by the prickling burn in his eyes as he watched Cassi breathe. Watched her for seconds he didn't have.

He hadn't made it as far back this time. He was already halfway to the desk; a boon, partially, but a hint of dread crept in alongside him as he snuck closer.

It had taken more strength, more pain, to turn the clock back this second time—but he hadn't turned it as far back as he had the first time.

Even with Time itself strung through his fingers, he was still running out of it.

He couldn't afford to fail again.

Signet ring first.

Across the tattletale boards. Around the dusty, long-neglected waterboard. Right up to the drawer sealed with a complex lock; one he'd picked enough times that he could do it in his sleep.

Especially good news, since he could barely see past the blood welling in his eyes.

He blinked hard, forcing himself to shed those sanguine tears, breathing slowly through his nose as he dropped into a crouch by the drawer.

No chronomancy for this bit, not this time. It wasn't worth the consequence that might follow, and it hadn't worked last time, anyway. He could do this quiet—it would take longer, but he could do it.

So he waited—waited until Tenebrae lifted himself off the desk and began to pace, putting a little more distance between him and the tumblers Finn was about to tease open. He could do it quietly enough to hide it under their voices, but they'd still feel something click inside the desk if they were touching it.

This time, he let Tenebrae's threat against Raquel steady his fingers as he set himself to task. The anger stabilized him, ice clashing with heat, rage putting out panic as he went all the way back in his own past…back to the twelve-year-old boy who needed official papers out of his mother's desk to learn how to forge her signature. The fourteen-year-old boy who needed to know where his brothers and sister were going to be stationed, back when they were all still allowed to partake in active service. The sixteen-year-old boy who checked his mother's private missives every day the year Kallias turned twenty-one—and burned every inquiry about alliances sealed by arranged marriage to make absolutely certain no one took his brother away.

He could pick this lock in his sleep.

So he shut his eyes and let muscle memory guide the lockpicks.

With his eyes closed, he let the pounding in his head pulse deeper, harder—he leaned into it, not away, the pink shimmer of divinimancy stirring dizziness into the migraine mix.

Foresight caught him just as he was about to turn the last tumbler. *Wait.* He held his breath.

"I'm sure Tempest will be thrilled with the…gift." The way she said *gift* poured acid in Finn's ears. Tenebrae didn't seem to notice. "And Mora? Ani?"

"Mora will have her throne and her mountain. And when it's *convenient*," gods, how that last word *seethed* with contempt, "you'll be going to fetch Ani yourself. So I suppose it's up to you how we bring her back in."

Now.

At the same time Cassi threw back her head and laughed, boisterous and bright as a mockingbird, he turned that last tumbler—and was rewarded with a series of clicks as he pressed his palm against the drawer.

The drawer slid open right when Cassi's laughter faded into a light, amused hum. "You really think *I'm* the best one for that job?"

"I think you might be the only one who can talk any sense into her now."

Tenebrae kept talking, but Finn was done listening. He plucked the signet out and slid it onto his finger—better than letting it rattle around in his pocket.

As he rounded the desk, heading for the door, elation sent another wave of heat flushing through his face. Almost out. Almost out, and then she could sneak out after, and they would be—

That rush of heat gushed through his nose. Gushed *out* his nose.

No!

He rushed to stanch it, but there was no halting the flood. Even pinching his nose shut, even shoving his sleeve against it—

A drop fell to the floor, escaping his shield of light and shadow.

Tenebrae stopped pacing. Stared at the blood speckling the floor.

The god crouched down and swiped a finger to it. Touched it to his tongue.

His gaze came up to find Finn's.

"Clever trick," Tenebrae murmured.

No. *No.* Come on, they were so close, so gods-damned *close*—

Tenebrae's taloned hand flashed out, missing his throat but getting quite the grip on his shirt.

"Show yourself," the God of Chaos ordered.

The rest of the story has already been told.

The fight. The failure. The rope. The fall. The blood. The fool who thought he could fix it all.

If one was clever, one might think the fool missed the obvious solution, the sure solution: to take the fall off the rope before the thief could steal her moment.

But that wasn't a victory. That was a draw. And the fool didn't want a draw—he wanted to *win*.

So…one more time.

Just one more.

This time, he arrived at the tail end of his fight with her and Tenebrae.

Bleeding and bruised, stuck on his back, Cassi holding the blade that practically dripped light, drooling for a taste of his throat. Blackness outlined the edges of his vision like someone had taken a kohl pencil to the wrong part of the eye.

Oh, and he couldn't breathe.

Well, depths.

When Cassi stood, some awful noise thumped out of him like someone had struck him between the shoulder blades—half-groan, half-cough. He rolled onto his stomach, trying to stand with her; he couldn't even straighten his knees before he started gagging, and another one of those horrifying clots flew from his throat.

"Finn!" His name echoed shrilly through his skull, pain and terror taking turns bouncing off bone; Cassi crumpled back to the floor with him, holding him by his face. Her gaze darted over him, questioning, confused—then carefully blank.

"Chronomancy," she said.

"Don't worry about it."

Something hot trickled from his nose. Cassi wiped it without breaking eye contact. "How many times already?"

"Don't worry about it. Just follow my lead."

"If you keep trying it's going to—"

"Will you just *trust me*, please?" He palmed her cheek, thumb aching as he brushed away blood that didn't exist yet. "I can do this."

"Oh, bra*vo*, Prince Finnick." Again, that mocking applause; the hound had already fled this time, circling its master with a creased muzzle and bloody teeth bared. "Tell me, how did you pull this off?"

With all his strength, he pulled off a classic Kallias move: he cast his arm around Cassi, pushing her behind him. She cinched her arms around his chest, hands clasped over his heart. "Leave it."

"No, no—I *have* to hear this. Tell me, Trickster Prince…how did you manage to trick my one heartless sister into falling in *love* with you?"

Love. It seemed no more possible than when he'd asked the first time.

Was that the name for it, this feeling—this *madness* that kept thrusting his hands into pools of glass, that made it impossible to imagine letting Time have its way with her, that sent him back again and again and again…a madness that did not care this magic was going to kill him?

He put his hand over Cassi's, shutting his eyes, so lightheaded he feared his skull was about to detach from his spine. Her hands held steady; his shook worse than they ever had.

Hadn't he lived this moment before? Hadn't he…hadn't it been…

She was going to die. He knew it. But he didn't know how he knew it. Everything hurt, everything was…why was he in his mother's office? Where was his mother?

"One more," he muttered, the words slipping off his tongue unbidden. "I can…just one more…"

"Finn." A hand slipped out from under his and covered it, squeezing the shakes out of it. That hand, he knew the girl it belonged to, her name was…the girl holding him, she was… "One more and you *break.*"

One more.

Terror struck like a lash, and he followed suit. He lunged through that choking fog, clawing his memories back like some rabid creature, nearly shredding them in his haste to save them.

Cassi, the signet, the tightrope. One more and he'd break.

If he stayed, she died. If he somehow found a way to run…unforgivable. But maybe kinder.

Kind. *He'd called it kind.*

A spotlight flickered on in his brain, shining straight through that damned fog. And right there, center stage, presenting itself with pride—

The worst idea he'd ever had in his entire depths-damned life.

Not because it was foolish. It was clever, and cunning, and it might very well work.

But it wasn't kind. And it certainly wasn't forgivable.

If the girl with her thieving, greedy hands splayed over his heart truly loved him, it would not last long. This idea would see to that.

"Turns out," he wheezed, "she'll do anything you like, if you stick her in a cage for a day or ten."

Cassi's body stiffened against his back, her hands falling away. Tenebrae cocked his head. The hound sat at his side, mimicking its master's pose. "Oh?"

"What, you've never tried it?" Gods, it hurt to laugh. He forced through the chuckle anyway, but his stomach churned in protest. "A few days in that mirror, and she snapped like a fishbone."

"Finn—"

"People devote themselves to their captors all the time. It's down to a science. You just have to know what you're doing." Finn raised his chin, glad for the blood that stained his teeth now. It'd make a great costume for this particular role. "And I *know* what I'm gods-damned doing."

This would be the delicate piece. Not just the bravado…but letting the tactical truth leak out behind it.

Tenebrae studied him closely. Good. Finn held his gaze, slipping halfway into the skin of Alexandros Ryder…letting Tenebrae see *everything*.

The lies. The truth. The careless lord who'd strung Cassandra Medeis along. The prince who'd pulled off the impossible to have his revenge. The way his gaze almost flicked to the mirror on his mother's wall before bouncing away.

He'd tricked Cassi once. All he needed was to convince Tenebrae he'd been clever enough, cruel enough, to do it again.

"Fascinating," Tenebrae said slowly. "What a clever idea."

This time, Finn was ready when Tenebrae grabbed him by the throat— but he stayed still, letting the god haul him to his feet. Letting himself get dangled in front of Cassi like a piece of bait.

"In," Tenebrae purred, gesturing toward the mirror. "Now."

Cassi's eyes widened. "What?"

"Get in." Tenebrae tightened his grip. Blackness rushed in, then ebbed, then rushed again—a riptide trying to drag Finn down.

Not yet. He couldn't let go yet.

Gods, the way she looked at him…

Champagne and stars and a roof sprinkled in glass.

This time, instead of holding his breath, he held her gaze.

Trust me. Trust me.

She didn't blink as she took one step toward the mirror. Another. Another.

With each footfall, he willed her to take another, refusing to blink even as darkness began to bleed back over the world. *Trust me. Trust me.*

She swallowed hard, then put on a show of her own as she looked at Tenebrae: chin high, grinning so fiercely it brought both sets of double dimples to the stage.

"I'm going to kill you for this," she promised.

The promise echoed backward through his brain, dizzying, trying to terrify him. He shook it off.

This time was different. This time would be *different.*

Tenebrae flashed the same indulgent smile from myriad futures. "Sure you will."

Occassio stood before the mirror and crossed her arms over her chest, hands over her own shoulders. Deathbed pose.

His heart stopped. And for one slow tick of the clock, there was silence.

Trust me, trust me, trust me.

"Don't worry," she said with a wink. "Songbirds know how to take a fall."

She tipped backward before he could look away. Her best trustfall yet.

One more time.

The lights went out before Finn could see if she made it safely to the ground.

CHAPTER 51

RAQUEL

She lost track of how many of her bones broke under the brutal ministrations of her captors.

Spindle-thin fingerbones, no match for Revan's metal-capped boots. Cheekbones cushioned by storm-toughened skin, easily cracked by staggered blows thrown one after the other by both men. Ribs wrenched by muscles pulled apart by Arcas's sanguimancy, his discordant daze faltering only once: only when she rolled onto her back after he pried the internal structures of her body apart, gagging on her own bile and blood, and still did not cry for clemency.

For the full span of a snowflake's life, he stared, swallowed, struggled—tongue floundering around an attempt at remorse—but the song of chaos rooted ever deeper, breaking the banks of his resolve like a river fit to burst with floodwater.

But shattered bones meant nothing to a woman like her. A woman who had borne worse, been broken worse, at the hands of people far more precious to her than these.

If this was to be her end, she would bear it—and would not bow.

She stood up in spite of the pain. Shut her eyes and imagined an Atlas sunset. Blue and green and coppery gold.

Until the end.

When blessed blackness finally tore her out of her beaten body, it found her unbowed, unbested…unwilling to greet death on hand and knee.

Raquel had never understood what people meant when they compared a ship's sway to a mother rocking her child to sleep.

Ramira Angelov had never rocked her to sleep. At least, not to her memory.

From the time her magic had made itself known at the tender age of three, a rarity that labeled her a prodigy even before the whirlpools in her baths were joined by roaring rainstorms, she was marked for Skyhaven. And her mother, the matron over one of Ursa's orphanages, knew better than to cuddle and coddle a daughter she would soon send into the arms of strangers.

Bedtime stories became brisk kisses on the forehead and stern refusals to allow Raquel into her parents' room, even when nightmares left her sobbing at their closed door; night after night she'd fallen asleep with her cheek pressed against it, soothed only by the patter of rain on the roof.

The one comfort her magic always brought; when she wept, the sky wept with her.

Jira, they rocked; Jira, they soothed and sang and told stories to. When Jira grew out of her crib, their parents' door never fully shut, let alone locked; when Jira woke, blinded by nightmares and crying for their mother, she didn't have to go looking. Their parents took turns retrieving her from her bed, calming her whimpers with back rubs and promises that she was safe.

When Raquel woke to the sensation of being rocked, she did not think of a mother. She thought of the water.

So when the first aching shards of consciousness slashed across her awareness, cutting through the blackness with bubbling surges of icy silver, she misunderstood what it meant. When the cold cradling her body began to sway her back and forth, she kept her eyes shut.

It was not the first time she'd dozed off floating on her back in the Vela's current, a thin coil of rope looped around her ankle to stop it from sweeping her away. The river rocked her better than any mother's arms; she could never resist floating in its embrace for a time, even though it frightened Aeris. He worried she'd drown in her sleep.

In case he was watching, just to prove she could, she sucked in a deep inhale.

Water knifed into her lungs, panic knifed into her heart, and her eyes flew open to the blur of a world submerged.

She scrabbled for something to hang on to; her fingers collided with metal, and she pulled herself upward, rearing her neck back until she broke the surface.

When air collided with the water pooled in her lungs, they convulsed, a bronchial spasm forcing out the water she'd swallowed. Salt and brine dribbled past her lips as she squinted her stinging eyes; moonbeams and twilight battled for ground in her vision, every clash sharpening her headache.

Her eyes cleared before her lungs did; still coughing, she twisted against the bindings tethering her wrists to the ceiling. Not rope, but chains. Manacles just loose enough to scrape her wrists raw.

They'd thrown her in the drowning dungeon.

But something was wrong; the water never rose *this* high. Even when she hauled herself up by the chain, she had to press the top of her head to the ceiling just to keep her chin above water.

Something solid bumped her ankle; animal terror seized her by the innards, and she plunged her face back beneath the water, wildly seeking out whatever lurked beneath.

Kallias had woven too many yarns about the creatures that swam beneath the ocean's surface…and the serrated teeth that filled their jaws.

But the gaping mouth she found through snatches of moonlight didn't belong to the awe-inspiring silver-skinned beasts who sailed the undercurrents of the sea. It belonged to Arcas, who sailed nothing but the absentminded whims of the water flooding this barred chamber.

Arcas, who was dead.

In the muddle of chaos and shadow, she couldn't begin to guess at *what* had killed him. Him and Revan, who drifted facedown near the silted floor. But she could guess that if she didn't figure something out *fast*, she was going to join them in their mysterious repose.

Two painful pulls, the effort tearing at her shoulders, and she broke the surface again, barely—she couldn't get her chin fully out of the water unless she tipped her head all the way back. She forced herself to take slow breaths, deep ones, as she fit her fingertips to the metal ring drilled into the dungeon's ceiling, testing it for any give.

None. But that made sense for a ring meant to dangle prisoners from the ceiling. She'd expected that.

She'd had to try anyway.

The sea cradled her chin, caressing her lower lip. Then swiping its icy touch across her entire mouth, as if wiping away any lingering hope.

Shh, it whispered. *Let me rock you to sleep.*

Was this what Kallias heard before he broke all his promises to her? The gentleness they ought to have been granted by their mothers? The ocean cooing lullaby lies in his ear?

Would he be waiting for her if she let herself believe them, too?

His name gasped from her lips as she sank—a pointless waste of her final thought. Her final breath.

Because the ocean did not wait for her belief before it swallowed her whole.

For a time, she drifted.

And in the drifting, memory dragged her into a dream.

Instead of floating weightlessly in the invading ocean, she lay on damp, cold rock. Instead of contusions and fractures and bruised pride, she bled from whip wounds, her skin laid bare, her back flayed open near to the bone.

And above her head, the wind whispered.

No—it howled.

Raquel, open your eyes, look at me.

Not this time. Kallias couldn't reach her here.

There would be no sailing away on a stolen boat. No twilight dances or hateful kisses or sunset promises sealed with flowers real and rosined.

Come on, you beautiful terror...

A stroke of lightning. A calamitous roar.

Raquel Angelov, I know you can hear me. Open your rotting eyes.

Even drifting, even dreaming, even drowning, she couldn't help creasing her brow.

That wasn't the right voice. Not the one she wanted. Close, *so damned close...*

But not right.

Breathe. That is an order…damn you, Raquel, breathe!

This time, the lightning struck her chest. Heat and light seared through her veins, drawing her up from the floor in a rigid arch, forcing her lungs to obey that furious command…

But there was no air.

Heat again—heat rained blows down on her chest, striking again and again and again before landing a softer, stranger blow to her mouth.

Strange, but familiar. She recognized the taste on her tongue…ice and mint and salt, but twined with something else…something ancient and mighty and unused to being disobeyed.

So when that order came again, a storm snarling in her ear—*"Breathe, Raquel!"*—she surged upward again, grasping desperately for any errant breeze, any bit of air that might heed her call.

She found a cold, broad hand. And when it clasped hers, she felt it—a pocket of air dancing between their palms, eager and full of life, ready to go wherever she asked.

When she summoned it into her lungs, all the water she'd swallowed fled from its touch.

Tempest ripped her sideways as she hacked up water, spilling the sea back over the floor; he wrapped her long hair, torn out of its braid by the beating Arcas and Revan had given her, around his forearm with a familiar motion. A sailor twining a mooring line around his wrist.

"Breathe," he commanded again when she stopped, holding her breath against another gag; it forced its way free anyway, another storm surge that soaked into the cracked, quake-shattered floor. "Breathe."

He wanted her to breathe? Fine.

"What," she *breathed*, flipping onto her seat to face him, "are you *doing* here?"

"You," he muttered in return, "are *welcome*."

"You weren't supposed to be here—you promised me—"

"I made other promises." The way he stared at her, searched her gaze, soaked strands of muddied auburn hanging in his eyes—the oddly frantic edge to his movements as he teased her own hair out of her eyes with one fingertip—

Her senses rushed back all at once, and she scooted out of his reach; all around them, the drowning dungeon wept unceasingly, remnants of the ocean's nightly visit dribbling from the ceiling. Soaking the silt and stone under her bruised fingers. Puddling around the two dead men lying facedown by the gap in the wall where the water must have rushed in—and rushed back out.

Or *fled* back out with its tail between its legs, if the thunderous look on Tempest's face was any indication.

"Can you walk?" Emotionless. Clipped.

She did a quick tally of her injuries—broken ribs on both sides, a stiff hip and ankle with little range of motion, so many small agonies she couldn't identify them all—and nodded.

"Good. Get out of the palace—the streets should be safe enough." Tempest stood; when he cracked his neck, thunder rumbled through the sky, through her chest.

"Where are you going?"

A glance at her swollen bottom lip. A flex of his jaw.

"To kill my brother," he said, "if I can. Distract him, if I can't."

She hauled herself up, legs barely holding; but hold they did. "I'm coming with you."

"You are getting as far away from here as humanly possible."

"I'm *coming with you.*"

Tempest scrubbed his hands down his face with a muttered, ancient curse. "You're half-drowned, half-*beaten*—and even if you weren't, you have no place in a battle between gods, Officer Angelov. He—"

"I think he has Prince Finnick." Fear and rage surged like another lungful of seawater; she ground her teeth together, swallowing them instead of spitting them out. "Kallias's brother. I made promises, too—maybe I have no place in the fight, but neither does he. I'm not leaving without him."

A slight softening to his harshly drawn brow. A tap of his knuckle under her bruised chin, so swift she nearly missed it. "Riptide, indeed."

None of her wounds pained her the way that touch did. Or the way that he snatched his own hand back from her as if remembering who he was—or *forgetting* who he used to be.

"Lead on, Tempest," she rasped.

He did not touch her again. But he did say, so softly she almost thought she was still dreaming: "I am...sorry. That I didn't reach you faster."

There was nothing she could say to that. Nothing she could do but nod as he swept out of the dungeon, climbing the stairs without a backward look.

CHAPTER 52

FINN

When he woke up, the first thing he smelled was blood.

Dried. Cloyed with the abrasive odor of cleaning substances. But still blood.

Some fresh, too—the bright copper tang of the new clashed with the rusted-iron reek of the old. That surprised him less; his nose had put on a decent act as a faucet plenty of times lately, though he couldn't quite recall why. Not because he'd forgotten; it was there, prancing just past the boundaries of his consciousness, giggling as he swatted for it past the slowly stirring confines of his mind.

He'd find it soon. But *soon* wasn't fast enough.

"About time," groaned his older sister's voice—distant, ringing like a tin bell struck by an idle knuckle. "I thought your lazy little habits were supposed to be an act."

"Jericho," he mumbled, half a whine. Why was she in his room, anyway? He'd told her last time that if she set a toe past his door before noon for any reason other than *actual life or death,* he'd sneak past *her* door while she slept with a pair of shears, reckless confidence, and absolutely no hair-cutting experience whatsoever. "Leave me alone."

"Oh, no," she chuckled. "I hope you didn't go too long without breathing. This isn't going to be as fun if I already broke you."

Broke him?

Light spidered through the well-spun shadows darkening the recesses of his mind, bringing memory into sharp, horrible relief.

The office. The squeaky, snitching board. His fingerbones, his mirror crunching under Tenebrae's heel. Cassi—

Cassi.

The cotton-spun kindness of strangled sleep fled his mind, and he thrust himself up from the floor by his palms, swallowing a surge of bile when his wrecked fingers screamed anyway.

In a blink, it all came rushing in: grimy golden floors and intact windows filled to the frames with a dying sunset, bleeding color until the sky grayed to dusk.

A set of empty thrones. A dais in disrepair.

The God of Chaos, smiling down at him from his mother's throne.

But no tightrope.

At the same moment the thought crossed his mind, he realized how odd a thought it was—why would there be a tightrope in the throne room?

He must have hit his head when he'd fallen. He was getting his past and his present muddled.

No sooner had he bobbed to his feet than something hooked around him from behind; two of Tenebrae's thorn-dappled vines shoved him back down to his knees, a third snagging in his hair and forcing his head down.

"You played a good game as my sister's double." A slow, mocking round of applause from up the steps. "Really, I'll give it to you—you had me fooled. Not easy, that."

Finn spat blood on the floor. It freckled his knees in brighter red, crimson speckling the cardinal crusting of hour-old wounds. "I heartily disagree, but please, continue. This little soliloquy habit of yours never gets old."

"Oh good, he's still clever." Tenebrae descended the dais, spreading his arms out to his captive one-man audience.

The dais buckled under his steps; not broken, not enough for him to fall or fumble, but a wrenching of metal that showed where his footsteps had fallen. A working of chaos in what could not be corrupted by music and magic.

"You lost," Tenebrae sang, a sweet little tune thrown in Jericho's voice. "Whatever scheme you and my little sister dreamed up, it's over. If you...."

The Chaos God kept talking—something swollen-headed and belittling, no doubt—but Finn didn't have time to waste on being mocked. Or caring about being mocked. Because once this speech was over, Finn's life would be, too.

And as ridiculous and exhausting and *complicated* as that life had gotten lately, he was still pretty attached to it.

So he didn't look for the slips in Tenebrae's speech, the little places where a more talented tale-spinner could sneak in and unravel the whole thing from start to stop; there was nobody in this room to witness his defeat, nobody he needed to show off for, nobody who needed him to play his princely part.

Instead, like a fool, he looked for a mirror.

Tenebrae wouldn't have stuck Cassi somewhere he couldn't see her; he was an arrogant silt-sipper, but not that much of one. Even that bastard of a curiosities collector had kept her underneath his menagerie's brightest spotlight, eliminating any sleight-worthy shadow.

And while he searched for the mirror, he coughed up a cackle that was *almost* stage-worthy.

This was why it had to be him. He wasn't his brother; he wasn't Raquel; he wasn't Tempest. He wasn't any kind of noble prince or folk hero or avenging god. He could not save his people.

But the Trickster Prince could do this much; he could sit on his knees, let his enemy's taunts float through one ear and out the other, and put on a gods-damned *show*.

"Oh, gods," he groaned, throwing his head back; the thorny talons twisted up in his hair wrenched tighter, threatening to yank clumps out by the roots. He just grinned through the pain, pulling his cheeks so taut he could barely feel them. "Do you ever stop *talking?*"

A dreadful moan rumbled the palace down to the roots with Tenebrae's next step.

"And that's coming from me, too," he rambled, darting glances around the room. "I'm a chatterbox, me, especially when I'm scared out of my special-sewn seal-leather shoes. It's a disease, honestly." *Where are you, where are you, where are you?* "But you, you're giving me a run for my money. And I really don't like to run anywhere, so—"

There. Tilted against the arm of his usual throne, pane faced away, half-hidden under the curtain partitioning the back of the dais from the private hall they sometimes used to enter and exit unseen. If she was watching, he couldn't tell from here.

When he looked back, still running his mouth without watching where it was going, Tenebrae wasn't smiling anymore.

With a curl of Tenebrae's fingers, the vines tugged him across the floor—still kneeling—with a careless force that tore straight through cloth and flesh, skinning layers of fabric from his pants, layers of skin off his knees. He let them; it got him closer to that dais, to that mirror.

And to Tenebrae, looking down at him with his sister's scar-pocked face, her mouth straining between a cruel smile and a bored sneer.

"Right again," Tenebrae sighed. "I talk too much. Show off too much. That's Occassio's play. Why don't I take a page from another sister's book?"

Tenebrae shoved his palms outward as if pushing someone over—a push aimed for the glass wall at the back of the room.

A horrendous *crunch* made his muscles cringe away from his skin.

The transparent glass utterly *sundered,* frosted through with breakage.

Chimes of falling glass rang through the room like the world's worst-conducted orchestra, Tenebrae's hand the baton that commanded a host of woodwinds to scream a battle cry; and with a spasm of Tenebrae's fingers, the sparkling rain fell in reverse, broken glass floating into the air in droves.

Wine and wrath and wild eyes. "I can't save you!"

Rubies and bowknots and a dimple drowned in blood. "You killed her—and you can't save her!"

No. He swept that memory aside like a stage curtain. *Not now, not now.*

The curtain swept back over his eyes, this time tinted pink.

"I'm coming, Finn. Just hang on."

"You couldn't save me…but I can save you. Let me save you."

He gritted his teeth, banishing his vague-as-all-depths sprinklings of foresight. *I said, not now!*

His magic listened, if reluctantly. But panic didn't care for propriety or pride. And as Tenebrae guided the mass casualty of crystal over his head, panic squeezed his lungs shut until he could barely get a sip of air.

Not now.

Not with that mirror out of his reach, not with his parents waiting at the harbor, not with so much still left to do.

Where are you?

He tipped his head back, taking in the cloud of razor thin shrapnel taking aim for his half-broken body. He'd heard certain sorts of suffering be described as *death by a thousand cuts*, but he'd never taken it quite this literally.

Déjà vu dizzied him, spinning a vision of the stiletto blade Cassi had caught over the longest of those glass shards. *Old tricks.* For a force of chaos, Tenebrae's lack of creativity was in danger of making him predictable.

But that only mattered if Finn lived long enough to keep predicting.

The glass twinkled like starry champagne and stolen wine, like a Sanctan rooftop, like his older brother's tear-filled glare. They reflected his face back at him: impassive, unimpressed.

Calm on the outside, at least…that was good. He didn't want to die like he'd seen so many die in this room, mouths gaping in grotesque masks of terror, eyes nearly popping out of their sockets, spittle seeping from their open mouths. Death having its way with their dignity.

Tenebrae ascended the dais with an absent wave of his hand. Not even looking when a wall's worth of glass plunged downward, aiming to make a pincushion of Finn's body.

Finn didn't know which came first: the wind, or the water.

The wind, which swept most of the glass aside in a screaming gale, banishing it to the other end of the room; the water, which arced over him like a cresting wave before stiffening. Solidifying.

Freezing.

He gaped up at the arch of ice now bent over him like a shielding body; in its crystal-clear confines, several leftover shards of glass gave menacing glares his way.

"Tenebrae!" A storm-tossed shout that echoed through the chamber with a bone-shaking *boom*. Another torrent of wind crashed through the empty windowpanes, rattling their metal cartilage like prison bars. Like the world wanted in, and it wasn't taking no for an answer.

Nor was the man who thrust through the throne room doors like a calamity all his own, head held high like it carried a crown, wearing all the confidence it ever carried every time he stepped into this room.

Kallias.

CHAPTER 53

FINN

In most other parts of this palace, of this life, Kallias approached with his head already hung. Wearing an apology nobody had even demanded yet.

Not here. His brother came alive in this place of politics and power in a way the rest of them never had. And when the throne room's ivory doors swept aside for him at the insistence of a hurricanic wind, Finn forgot himself.

Just for a moment, he forgot.

"Kal!" Hope broke its leash, running for its master; he had not meant to call his brother's name.

But Kallias didn't look at him.

Another cry of his brother's name shattered against the backs of his teeth, swallowed like a mouthful of the broken glass frozen above his head. He caught hope in one hand; crushed it, firmly, by tallying everything wrong with the picture.

The short, tousled hair; Kal hated wearing his hair short. The indifferent slide of his gaze over Finn and straight to Tenebrae; a suggestion that Finn was nothing but a very fortunate stranger who happened to be in need right when the god had a miracle to make. And if none of those tells had been enough, the golden eyes would have sealed the deal.

Not Kallias at all.

"You," seethed Tempest, God of Nature, "are in my rotting *seat*."

Tenebrae stood, grinning from ear to ear; he swept a hand over the seat before jogging down the dais, arms spread out like wings. "Finally! It's about time you showed up! Forgive the mess, I didn't know you were—"

"Are you alone?"

Tenebrae blinked, brow creasing; his steps slowed on the final stair. He gestured at Finn, still ducked under a shield of unnatural ice. "It's rude to ignore a guest."

"You know what I *mean*." Tempest did not ease from his rigor, his ready stance, teasing a thread of lightning between his fingers. "Where's Occassio?"

"What am I, her keeper?"

"Mirror," Finn rasped; this time, Tempest looked, and he pointed with a jerk of his chin.

Tempest's throat bobbed. He turned slowly back to Tenebrae; that lightning between his fingers popped. Struck the floor. "Why haven't you let her out?"

He still couldn't see her. But he thought he heard her say something; he definitely *saw* Tempest's hand curl into a loose fist.

"Don't worry about her." Tenebrae breezed across the room, arms still extended, all interest in Finn gone; Tempest rocked back a step when the Chaos God pulled him into a hearty embrace, clapping him on the back. "It's good to see you."

Tempest tore out of his hold, teeth gritted, Kallias's face wrenched into a poor-fitting mask of fury. "Good to—why is she still in there? What are you doing?"

"I'm trying to have a nice reunion with my little brother. What are *you* doing?"

"This is not a *reunion*." Finn had never been big on respecting the gods, but the fury quaking Tempest's limbs—a seething, stony rage that could not be contained by skin alone—yeah, even he didn't quite feel like testing that. "You hurt my kingdom. You hurt *my people*. You hurt…" A flex of his jaw. A stuttering blink. He shoved his finger at Tenebrae like poking a sword at his face—Tenebrae's abruptly smug, knowing face. "I am here for my throne. Move aside."

"Gladly." Tenebrae put his hands in the air, still gods-damned *grinning*—like this was all part of his own game, one none of them had volunteered to play, one with no rulebook or gameboard or arbiter. Only powerless pieces set and scattered according to the god's whim. "Oh, please—you can't have thought *I* actually wanted this kindling-heap of a kingdom. I just needed my host—the rest is for you."

As Tempest strode toward the dais, gaze flicking furiously between his brother and the mirror propped on the dais, a cold hand seized him by the back of the collar and tugged.

On instinct, he flailed for his assailant; she bent his arms behind his back, pressing in closer than most dared to rasp in his ear: "Out the door. *Now.*"

Raquel.

"You're supposed to be *gone*," he hissed, letting her pull him out from beneath the shield of ice, eyes riveted on the collision of gods before Atlas's throne. He dashed sprinkles of glass from his knuckles; not even the pretty *plink-plink-plink* drew Tenebrae's attention.

"You were supposed to get the signet and *run*."

"I got delayed."

Static stung his wrists; his ears popped. "You call this a *delay*?"

"It's a delay until proven otherwise." And he wasn't about to make up any time. "I'm not done here."

"And I'm not doing this." Raquel yanked him back another pace; he dug his heels into the floor, an old practice from boyhood. Except back then, he'd been dragging his heels to keep his mother from pulling him *into* the throne room, not *out* of it.

"I have to get that mirror," he hissed.

He could not see Raquel's face. But he *felt* the pause as she turned his words around in her head like a costume jewel fished from a pile of stolen gems, second-guessing its appraisal as something worth her time; he practically heard the gears in her head grind to a halt as she realized what he meant. "No."

"Not asking you."

"Not letting you." Gods, this woman must've stuffed bands of iron under her sleeves; even throwing his most subtle tantrum, she managed to drag him out the door and into the hallway.

The decimated hallway.

Broken ceramic and tipped-over stone pedestals had been flung every which way; seawater soaked the tile, puddling in the caulk, making it impossible to keep up the digging-his-heels-in method. When he tried, his sandals sank into piles of silt, sand grains and dirt clods sliding under his heels; it took all his self-control not to kick off his shoes. Instead, he indulged that urge by yanking away from Raquel. "Pull me again, and I'll—"

"Oh, you wouldn't *dare*," she hissed.

How could she know? She hadn't even let him finish the threat.

Not that he could have. The sight of her battered face and bloodied clothes shoulder-checked it straight back down his throat. He had to swallow before he could speak again. "*Who*—"

"Someone else beat you to the punch," she interrupted. "And you can't kill them twice, so leave it and *move*. Your parents—"

"It would be like leaving you with Aeris," he said—when her breath seized, he drove into that pause, thrusting his next words in like his mother's letter opener, a dagger disguised in plain sight. "I'm not doing that to her."

"She's *your* Aeris."

"Not before I was hers."

A short silence—barely enough time for him to steal a look back inside.

From here, he could just pilfer a peek at the mirror's prisoner. A flirt of tied-back curls and frightened eyes.

Her fear never failed to stoke his fury. And Finnick Atlas's fury might not be enough to shake the earth or summon a storm or set the sea loose within a palace's walls…but it was enough to make courage out of cowardice. To replace self-preservation with reckless risks, a counterweight measured out with a cavalier hand.

He had willed her to trust him. Had tricked Tenebrae into putting her back in that mirror for…for…

Why had he done that?

Reddish grime rusted his brain…every memory sticky and strange, every thought tarnished to the point of near-incoherence.

But the *why* didn't matter. He could not leave her. Simple as that.

A cursory look over Raquel gave him the numbers he needed: three open wounds at least, possibly four, one definitely deep enough to require stitching. And soon.

He'd never seen her wear quite this much red before. The color didn't suit her.

"You go," he said. "Thank you for staying—but you need to go. You kept your promises. What happens now, that's on my head, not yours. And if Kallias wants to have words about it, he can crawl out of whatever hole that god kicked him into and have them with *me*."

Periwinkle-blue lightning wove around her head like a wire crown, striking thrice before dissipating. "This isn't about him. You're not leaving without her. I'm not leaving without you."

There was an air of defeat, not determination, in her ragged voice; maybe she knew, like he did, that this moment of distraction gifted by a god of shipwrecks and storms was their only shot at escaping a room with two gods going at it. He didn't have to be clever—though it certainly didn't hurt—to know that when divine powers dueled, the mortal and mundane could not survive.

Or maybe she was reckoning with the same straining realization that closed his throat on a *thank you*. That the idea of dooming her hurt almost as much as the idea of abandoning his shining light to sputter out under the heel of another malevolent master.

"So?" she demanded under her breath, impatience shoving through sentiment. "Tell me the plan."

"Don't have one." He turned to flash her a grin that hopefully didn't look as wild as it felt. "Can't plan for chaos. We're going all in on luck."

Raquel didn't blink. "I don't know about you, but I'm fresh out of luck."

But Luck had learned to come when called. And with its mistress sealed away behind gullible glass, it came running right to him.

A pink-tinted tide crashed over his gaze, swallowing Raquel's face; the scowl, the bruises, the bloodied lip that made him itch to draw a dagger.

"I'm coming, Finn. Just hang on."

Silent bootsteps on tile floors. Sea salt and hibiscus swept away on a rush of darkwood needles and mountain wind.

A shuffle of shades and saviors, dealt in droves across a hidden hall.

A pair of venom-green eyes colliding with his, peering out from behind a drawn curtain.

Finn grinned so depths-damned hard it split all his masks straight down the center.

Because sweeping the dais curtain aside, dripping wet curls splashed across her brow, scowling and surly and looking *far* healthier than she had last he'd seen her, was the last chesspiece he'd been waiting on.

And she had not come alone.

Elias was right on her heels, grim as always—this was the first time he'd ever been *glad* to see that grovel-happy bastard and his big sad eyes—and behind them…

Actually, he didn't know *who* that was. But when she strode past Soren and Elias and stopped at the lip of the dais, fists curled against her hips, brown eyes the exact color of strawberries coated entirely in milk chocolate…he could just begin to muster up an educated guess.

He'd only seen her as a girl in Cassi's past. But even older and clad in Arborian leather armor, the woman looked enough like her siblings that he could give her a name.

Anima, Goddess of Life, trembled in every limb as she glared down at her brothers; her brothers, who had both stopped circling each other in the center of the room to gape up at her.

"Anima?" Revulsion writhed in Tenebrae's gilded gaze; he took a full step back from the dais, lip curled. "What happened to you? What did you *do?*"

"Braeden," she greeted him instead of indulging his dramatics, perfectly calm—she'd trapped all the shakes inside her skin, not one tremor sneaking into her breath. Not at all like the timid, terrible actress who'd tried to play his little sister's part. "Peter."

"Ani," Tempest looked spooked—like a ghost had drifted out, haunting center stage. "You're—"

"Ani?" Finn's heart, damned useless thing, surged at the sound of Cassi's echoing cry.

Anima's eyes widened, and she spun, taking one stride toward the mirror. "Cassi?"

"Soren!" Soren announced; when the divine siblings all swiveled to look at her, she shrugged. "Felt left out. This is nice and all, but hey, here's an idea— how about you all get out of my siblings, then *get the pits out of my palace?*" A pause. "Ani excluded."

"Did I not make myself clear last time, Anima?" Syrupy-sweet mocking drizzled over Tenebrae's voice as he glared at Soren. "No pets allowed."

"Damn," drawled another voice from the back of the room; Finn actually almost lost his grip on his jaw when a golden-haired, fully armored man strutted out, two other men—one familiar, one not—right on his heels. "That's Wolf out, definitely. Think we can pass Kess off as a helper-hound?"

What in the depths was *Prince Everin Arden* doing here? And Wolf—that *was* his eldest Arborian cousin emerging just behind another woman with Arborian armor who stood slightly apart from the Tallisian trio, golden-brown gaze bright with fear and fury behind her glasses, sighting her shot down a drawn arrow.

"One chance," Soren said. A violent promise glittered in her stare as she looked between them all…Tenebrae, Tempest, Occassio. "Set my family free. Whatever cage you have them in, minds or cells—you let them out."

"Or what?" Tempest, not Tenebrae; he could not seem to rip his eyes off of Ani, who stared back at him with a stern scowl and mystifyingly mortal eyes.

It was Elias who stepped forward now. Elias, who stood shoulder-to-shoulder with Everin Arden—a famously faithless man—and did not lower his head as he addressed the divine host before him. "Or we will *break* them out. Starting with you."

Something zapped Finn's shoulder; he kicked the back of Raquel's boot. "Calm down."

"I'm calm," she said, releasing his shoulder to cling to the wall instead, fingernails digging in. Fabulous—now they'd have to repaint on top of everything else.

"Forty more seconds."

"What happens in forty seconds?"

No clue. Chronomancy gave him the clock, not the agenda, and divinimancy didn't seem to be in a giving mood.

"Do you trust me?" he hedged.

"No."

"Well, I trust *you*." He owed her that concession—and couldn't begrudge her withholding her own. "And when all depths break loose in there, I trust you'll have my back."

"What do you expect me to do?"

He raised an eyebrow. "Your worst, Riptide."

That made her smile. If one could call the near-canine twist of teeth Raquel put on when she was feeling bloodthirsty a *smile*.

"Last call," Soren sang, doing an impatient little dance across the top of the dais—a half-stalking, half-skipping gait as she paced before the thrones.

"What'll it be, boys? You're welcome to test your luck, but as you know…us Atlases don't die easy."

"Good show," Tenebrae said, sounding profoundly bored. "But you don't have anything that can hurt us—and I *really* don't think you're ready to see just how easy dying can be for you mortals."

"Ten seconds," Finn whispered, gaze fixed on the mirror.

"Finn, *what* is going to—"

"Can't blame a girl for trying. I did warn you." Soren shrugged. "Elias?"

"Three," Finn breathed. "Two…"

Elias flew down those steps like a raven borne on swift sea breezes.

A scion of flame. A specter of death.

Finn didn't have time to let the chill make it all the way down his spine.

Five moves happened at once.

The Phoenix Priest took the God of Nature clean off his feet, sending Tempest sprawling in the inch-thick sea of broken glass.

Bishop takes Rook.

The Prince of Heathens cleared the dais in one leap, landing so hard his steel-soled boots cracked through the tile, flashing the God of Chaos a lethal grin…a taunt a thousand years in the making. His two companions followed without hesitation, flanking him like a swallow-tailed shadow.

Pawns attack King.

The Heir of Atlas, the lost-and-found princess, stepped back from that fight…a step so out of character it almost distracted him from his own strategy.

Knight bides her time?

The Trickster God, prince over fools and fibs and fiddles, flew for that mirror-cage like a songbird set loose.

Free the Queen from her trap.

Last but not least, the Riptide, Atlas's mysterious savior, stormed into the fray with a roar that rattled the chandeliers above his head, raining dust and debris over them all.

Two queens on the board. Cheating.

But this game had no rules. No board. No arbiter.

And these powerless pieces had just flipped the whole damned table.

CHAPTER 54

RAQUEL

Raquel had no gods-damned idea what just happened.

After he'd finished ferrying every innocent palacefolk out with directions to head for the harbor with the help of an army that seemed to have materialized from thin air—*his* army—Tempest had promised her two things: the distraction she needed to get Finn out of the room, and the time for both of them to throw themselves on the ship waiting to carry them to safer shores.

In return, he'd only asked for one promise of her own: that when she ran, she would not look back.

She'd sworn it with every intention to keep it. To run into the ocean's open arms without a backward look…and, once safely carried in its embrace, to at last lay Kallias to rest in her heart.

But Elias Loch had sailed that same sea, there and back again…had carried that same burden of grief, there and back again.

He had not laid anything to rest. And he'd done one better than steal a look over his shoulder.

He'd challenged the God of Nature at the foot of his own damned throne.

A challenge that now saw him tussling with Tempest on the tile floor; no battlemate guarding his back, no weapon in his hand, no fire in his eyes. What smoldered in his stare now frightened her like fire never could…a razing force she could not douse with rain.

She didn't know what to call it. But she knew it would not be enough.

Not when this throne room remembered who it had been built for.

Tempest threw Elias off of him, his arm swinging like a battering ram; his fist collided with Elias's chest, and the dull *crunch* of knuckle to rib nearly drowned in the jingling clatter of glass. The tile floor itself quaked as the God of Nature reclaimed his feet, advancing on Elias, fists curled. Fingers dancing with static slivers of blue and white.

"You're fighting the wrong battle, Phoenix Priest," Tempest rumbled, cracking his neck. "Don't you know the enemy of your enemy is your friend?"

Elias looked up through frayed strands of ebony hair, already breathing hard; he coughed out a cloud of smoke before pulling himself back up, only barely favoring the ribs Tempest had absolutely broken. He tipped his head back, looking down his nose at the deity despite Kallias's body standing an inch or two taller than his.

"Kallias Atlas is my friend," he spat. "And anyone who harms him? They are my enemy. His battles are mine. I will fight for him every time."

"You'll lose."

Elias smiled, faith melding beautifully with malice. He drew his scythes; instead of the fire she was used to, scarlet and gold bleeding from blade to hilt, his fire lit in lurid cerulean heat…a blazing double-pour of Atlas blue.

"I won't," he said.

Both men—one a god by name, the other a god by proxy—lunged to land the first blow at the same time.

Why was she just standing here—why, instead of running to one pocket of conflict or the other, did her feet feel like someone had shoved one of those glass shards through her boot and into the floor?

Why couldn't she *move?*

All she could do was watch, not breathing, as Death and Nature met in the middle of the Atlas throne room; Elias a dervish of ebony steel and cobalt flame, Tempest a hurricane of black ice and stormfire. Blue and black and white so bright it hurt her eyes.

Tempest dropped under Elias's first swing, hair stirred by a boiling breeze; he slapped his hands down into the seawater that had shoved open the door for him, heralding his entrance better than any palace crier could have. The water rolled in reverse, a tide turned inside-out; it coated his hand just in time for him to throw himself flat on his back to avoid Elias's second swing, rolling through glass just before Elias stabbed downward, jamming his blade between sheets of gilded tile.

Tempest stood, water roiling as it poured back down from his hand, a deluge that flowed fast at first, then sluggish…then stopped.

Raquel's knees ached as Tempest hefted a blade of his own making. One forged entirely from ice.

Ice that, if she had to guess, would not crack or melt when it met steel and flame.

"I'll give you one last chance," he said, "because I admire your loyalty—and I know what it is to lose a friend. This will not bring him back. Sheathe your blades, and I will gladly lend mine to stopping the *real* threat in this room."

Elias didn't try to yank his other blade back out of the floor; he abandoned it there, lifting his other scythe instead. Splaying his other hand for Tempest to see.

Fingers dipped in frostbitten black. A sight that drizzled a new kind of mortal fear into Raquel's stomach, though she didn't know exactly why.

"Maybe I can't bring him back," he said softly. "But I can put him to rest."

Tempest snorted. "I would love to see you try."

Finn might have been the cleverest man in most rooms—much to Raquel's chagrin—but Elias was often the wisest. And he proved it by not taking Tempest's taunting bait; instead, he drove in faster than she'd ever seen him move, face arranged in determined calm, scythe stoked so fiercely that a slice of heat struck *her* when Elias swung, aiming for Tempest's arm.

Tempest batted the blade aside with his, then swept splayed fingers through the air, attempting to hurtle Elias off his feet with a violent gale of ice-cold air.

Elias's boots skidded across the floor, shrieking—but he didn't fall. His stance didn't even buckle.

She glanced at the boots. Steel soles. *Tallisian.*

But even those weighted boots couldn't keep Elias upright when Tempest drove into him bodily, another gale giving him all the momentum he needed to send Elias crashing to the ground.

Raquel staggered forward a couple steps, suddenly remembering herself; adrenaline woke her feet back up as Elias slammed into the base of the dais, barking out a cry of pain.

Out of the corner of Raquel's eye, she saw Soren rock forward, as if about to sprint down the steps…then she steadied. Stayed put.

A cry went up from two sides of the throne room—one from the blond man in the trio taunting Tenebrae, the other from the two Arborian women who'd rushed down the dais, taking up posts behind the columns on either side. Both women nocked arrows to their bowstrings, sighting down the shafts, but Elias held a hand up.

"Don't," he panted, staggering back to his feet. "Eyes on your own fight, Everin—Medwenna, Ani, that goes for you too!"

"Quit getting thrown on your ass, then!" the blond man yelled back. Tenebrae's hands struck out, fingers bent in jagged claws; some of the knuckles had popped out of place, but it didn't seem to hinder his aim with his bloodthirsty vines. The blond swung his hatchets in arcs so fast the blades melted into silver blurs in the air, slicing each vine before it could find purchase in the gaps between his armor plates.

Elias spun back to face Tempest, his single scythe flaring as he rolled his shoulders. "*Now*, ladies!"

Both women hesitated, heads turning toward each other…then the shorter one lowered her bow. The taller one shifted to aim at Tenebrae instead, letting two arrows loose in quick succession; one sailed over his head, but the other dove deep into his shoulder joint.

When Tenebrae's head snapped in her direction, a vine followed, striking out with hooked claws.

All three Tallisian men moved at once—the dark-haired one to cut the vine, the mouthy blond to swing his hatchet toward Tenebrae's neck with a furious shout, and the lanky redhead to get between the vine and its intended target.

All three succeeded.

Tenebrae reeled back, the hatchet slicing his cheek instead of his neck. The vine slackened, cut off from its master—but not before the other end struck true.

Not before it wrapped around the redhead's arm like a tourniquet and *pulled*.

All she could comprehend before her view was blocked by the taller archeress and the dark-haired Tallisian was a spray of blood. A wet, grinding *pop*. A howl strung out with such visceral agony she nearly covered her ears.

An arm lopped off at the elbow.

"*Kessen!*" Soren. The princess only made it down two steps before the dark-haired Tallisian pointed at her, barking some order Raquel couldn't make out past his heavy drawl. Soren shook her head, taking one more step—this time the blond spun her way, baring his teeth like some feral beast, and Soren cursed at the top of her voice before bolting back up the stairs.

No, Raquel had no idea what was happening at all. And she didn't like it one bit.

But she did know that she was of more use on one side of this fight than the other—and whatever alliance she and Tempest had struck by necessity over these weeks, it did not outweigh her loyalty to her brother-in-arms. Nor would it allow her to set her anger, her grief, aside like she had before.

Kallias had deserved her mercy.

Tempest did not.

As Elias paced back into Tempest's space, adjusting his grip on his scythe, the flame flickered red. Then…

Raquel's throat dried out when the flame sputtered black. Then red. Then black again, ebony fire dancing up the blade before it livened up, bursting back into a flurry of oranges and golds.

"Chaos lingers with you still." Tempest narrowed his eyes, the slits of gold glowing nearly as bright as Elias's blade. "That explains why you're set on picking a fight you can't win."

"This is not chaos. This is the gift a true god gave me." Another rippling shift of color, the blade coated in shining shadow. "He gave me a new name, too. Would you like to learn it?"

That certainly sounded like chaos-rambles to Raquel. But Elias did not twitch or scream or dance on his feet; though wrath coiled from him like smoke, his gaze pierced like a blade all its own, clearer and colder than any body of water she'd ever set eyes on as he sliced the scythe through the air. Black fire arced outward, rushing toward Tempest like a dragon's furious bellow.

A wave crested up to meet it; steam erupted as the two collided, a haze settling over the room as Elias and Tempest circled again.

As the two of them began another dance, a torrent of black and blue that bruised the wall in mottled light, Raquel reached for power of her own.

Elias didn't want interference. But she wasn't going to let him get himself killed for nothing.

A sickening, rib-snapping *thud* doused the light; the second scythe skittered across the floor, steel clanging against gold. Elias hit the dais step a moment later with another nauseating crack, his scream seething through his teeth, his hand flying to his shoulder—but Tempest was already on him.

Tempest fisted his hand in Elias's shirt, towing him up off the floor; then *thrust* him back down into the dais stairs.

Thunder boomed. Cracks spidered up the walls. Raquel's ears popped.

Tempest lifted his blade of ice, aiming the tip at Elias's heart. Cerulean light darkened his features like a shadow; his golden eyes cut through the color.

They held no remorse. No reluctance. No horror.

Nature did not apologize. It did what it must.

And so would she.

Every hair on Raquel's body stood straight up as she swept a hand down her woolen sleeve, skimming every fizzle and pop of energy out of its fibers—and aimed a blade of her own at Tempest's.

A bolt of lightning arrowed into Tempest's blade, shattering it into nearly as many pieces as the wall of windows.

When he looked over his shoulder at her, his gaze leapt first to her smoking fingers, then to her narrowed eyes, his own round as a full Nyxian moon. Filled with genuine surprise.

That surprise only locked her resolve in place.

If he'd thought saving her life would be enough to pay for taking Kallias's, it was his own foolish fault. It was not an equal trade.

"Leave him!" she shouted.

And for some foolish reason, when Tempest's gaze shuttered, she expected *his* knee to bend. *His* head to bow.

Instead, it was the only warning she received before the ice blade's decimated remains melted and surged across the floor.

Faster than she could run; faster than she could wrest control of that water for herself, if she even could have overpowered a god's iron grip on his own element.

Unbearable cold clamped over her body like a set of piercing jaws, swallowing her from ankle to neck. When she gasped, her breath plumed with silver mist.

He'd encased her in ice.

He ignored her screams, her threats. He ignored her cries for Soren to *do something*, her blood running hotter and hotter as Soren just kept…staring. Staring, jaw tight, one hand tucked behind her back.

Elias was about to die. And Soren seemed content to stand by and *watch*.

"Enough."

Something moved behind Elias…a smoke-stain imprinted in the air. A ripple like heat emanating from a stovetop.

The ethereal shadow of a woman on fire.

"Took you long enough," Tempest muttered—he'd curled his fingers under the lip of Elias's armor to hold him still, but at the sight of this specter, he released his prey.

Raquel's heart skipped a beat. And as long as she stared at the visage of Death herself, it refused to start again.

She could have sworn Elias's bruised mouth curled upward.

"Not him," commanded Death, the very mouthpiece of divine wrath. But there was an odd jitter to her form, almost quivering. A ghost frightened of its own shadow.

Tempest hauled Elias back to his feet and shoved him forward. Elias stumbled, dropping to one knee before Death herself, tipping his head back.

It took Raquel too long to realize why that pose seemed strange: Elias had raised his chin instead of bowing his head.

Defiance, not deference.

"If you'd stop speaking in riddles and give your clerics clear orders for once," Tempest said crossly, "perhaps I wouldn't have to put them in their—"

"I was not speaking to you, Peter."

The notches of Raquel's spine chattered like teeth when Mortem's shadow billowed out and up, looming over Elias. Sparks of amber and scarlet played shooting star deep within that core darkness, flaring in paired pulses of heat. Like a handful of heartbeats held captive.

Elias lifted his chin another inch. His throat bobbed. Smoke drifted lazily from his open wounds; overheated iron and smelt-smoke coated the back of her throat. The blood in those wounds…it bubbled. Simmered, like soup spilled across a stovetop. "He killed my friend."

"If you kill him, our chances of victory die as well," snarled the phantom of flame and soot. "Your vengeance is nothing. Your fight is elsewhere. Not. Him."

Oh.

Raquel's fury cleared—then struck with a vengeance.

Mortem had not come to rescue her chosen cleric. She had not come to see the thieves in this room punished for their trespasses.

She had come to save her gods-damned brother.

Elias gazed at his goddess, jaw set. Raquel couldn't read the intentions roiling behind his eyes, blacker than the bitterest coffee.

With painstaking slowness, the Phoenix Priest straightened his bent knee. He did not break his goddess's gaze, no more than embers and wrath embedded in endless shadow. He did not bow his head.

"He took a host." Soft as a confession echoing off temple walls, yet it rose above the din of faithless warriors fighting a losing battle against a rogue god. "He murdered an innocent man and stole his body as his own. Is that not the sin for which you've condemned Anima to die?"

"If we were tallying sins, hers would number far higher than—"

"He *killed my friend.*" She had only heard that hushed, deadly rage in Elias's voice once: when he'd told her Anima had taken Soren away from him. "I owe him justice—I fight in his name. You would deny me that right?"

"I would have you obey the command of your *goddess.*"

Elias ground his teeth, his jaw flexing. His hands lowered. His tattoos extinguished.

Raquel's heart hammered, torn between fury and relief. Hating he'd given up. Hating that she couldn't hate him, not for this. Not when he'd merely taken her place in a line she'd never wanted to stake her claim in.

The last in the long line of people who had let Kallias Atlas down.

"Good." Death's darkness shrank into itself, shifting like a cyclone that had sighted a new town to tear through. Shifting toward the smaller Arborian woman, whose shoulder dropped with a prey-animal flinch. Her bowstring slackened, the arrow dipping out of place. "You know my command, Phoenix Priest."

"Elias?" Soren's voice, tremoring like the air after a lightning strike.

Elias bowed his head, ragged breath seething through his teeth. He rubbed at his shoulder—possibly dislocated—over the strap of his sheath, then took a few steps away. Abandoning the fight. Slinking away like a kicked dog, bending to retrieve his closest scythe.

His gaze, resigned, utterly cowed, drifted to the young Arborian woman. Raquel didn't know her face, but she didn't need to—not when she knew where she'd been aiming her arrows.

By his goddess's order, Elias's weapon now aimed askew. At one of their *allies.*

"Don't," Raquel snarled. "Elias, *do not!*"

Do not obey. Do not give in.

Do not fail him like this. Not like me.

She had no real faith left to her but this: that whether Kallias Atlas was alive or dead, whether some unreachable spark of his noble heart still kindled in the core of the storm wearing his skin or not, he deserved better. He deserved everything.

Their lives for his cause. Their blades for his kingdom.

Her heart for his soul.

What power could a mortal woman wield against the order of a goddess? What might could she delude herself into believing she bore, that her unmitigable will could reach a man so devoted to Death that years of hazing and barracks-banter could not break his zeal, that he answered to *Pious* more reliably than his given name?

What insanity had seized her, that she had given her god an order—and expected him to heed her?

Elias wouldn't—or couldn't—look her in the eye. He only walked toward the smaller bow-wielding woman and her off-putting guardian, the Arborian man armed to the teeth with an array of beautiful blades.

The woman said something—Raquel couldn't hear her over the din, but her lips seemed to shape Elias's name.

Elias kept walking. Raised his scythe in a ready position.

The world around her turned inside-out, pressure thrumming over her skin. Pushing and pushing and *pushing* until her bones shuddered and strained. Until her teeth hummed with heat and energy and *need.*

Her next shout erupted in a roar of sky-sundering thunder.

"*Traitor!*"

That earned her Elias's gods-damned attention. But when he lifted his eyes to hers, she did not see a gutless man's cowardice disguised as faith staring back.

Only a calculated calm she had seen a hundred times. In Finnick Atlas's company—never Elias's.

He made as if to sheathe his single scythe with one hand, a movement designed to distract. The other he set over his chest, palm to sternum, fingers splayed. The gaps precisely spaced to reveal a braid of Atlas blue looped around the chain he'd worn since she'd left Delphin with him and Kallias.

He might as well have grabbed her by the throat.

They might not have been battlemates, her and Elias—but they'd still served in the same company. Had trained and sparred and played barracks games together for nearly five years. Had witnessed each other's brightest and darkest phases. Had been dealt near-identical wounds by weapons forged of paper and string and a prince's perfect handwriting.

She was not his battlemate. She could not read him the same way Soren could.

But their twinned hurts spoke a different language. And with that one gesture, over and done almost before she could see it, she understood.

He had a plan. But he needed a distraction. He needed…

She knew what to do.

Her magic knew nothing about time and its dealings. She could not ask the unseen to slip secrets up her sleeves or count her opponent's cards before they were dealt. She could not travel between mirrors and millenniums by making a fool out of gullible glass. Not the way Finnick could.

But she was the Eye of the Storm. The Riptide. Chosen by the tempest.

Her skin was tuned to the ebb and flow of energy in the world. And just before the storm broke, the world always held its breath.

All she had to do was wait for the inhale.

So she shut her eyes, and she waited.

And when Mortem's ethereal form coalesced into something almost human—a death-touched shade bearing striking resemblance to the woman she'd marked for death—the air froze in its tracks.

The heat swarming under Raquel's skin ignited.

Power erupted, ice cracked, and a shriek—Raquel didn't know if it belonged to her or the storm, did not know if there was a difference anymore— popped the pressure in her ears. In her chest. In her bones.

Eye of the Storm. Riptide. Raquel Corentine Angelov.

With a battle cry worthy of battlefields far bloodier than this, Raquel Angelov broke the sky open.

Lightning punched through the empty window panes, frigid wind colliding with white-hot power. Not one bolt. Not two. A host, a battalion, thrice as many bolts as there were bodies in this room. A storm unstoppable.

Tempest wanted to see the truth of her. What she was capable of when she stopped holding back.

The girl she'd been in Skyhaven hadn't been brave enough. Hadn't understood her own worth and worthiness. Hadn't been ready, not for this.

But they were warring against powers beyond fathom in this throne room. And if she did not turn this tide, it would sweep all that remained of Kallias's beloved Atlas away with it. His home.

And not just his, but Vaughn's, and Finn's, and all those who'd lent their skills to this mad scheme of theirs—the defiant, devoted souls who had chosen their kingdom over themselves. Whose loyalty to Kallias had kept them fighting.

Who had trusted Raquel, enemy and all, to do the same. Because she'd loved him, too.

Her lungs burned. She couldn't see. Every hair on her body stood on end. *Too much, too much.*

Not enough. Never enough.

No. Enough did not exist—not here, not today.

She would not settle for enough. She wanted it all. And if the powers she had worshipped so long would not give it to her, she would take it.

She threw her head back and let the storm speak for her. Scream for her.

All her fury. All her grief. All her strength poured into this one barrage.

For Kallias. For Nyx. For *Atlas.*

With one blow, she stopped Death in her gods-damned tracks—and drove her back an entire step.

Had she been facing an enemy of mortal caliber, that would have felt like a failure.

Not today. Today, Raquel Angelov faced down Death—and Death dared not step within her reach.

But she wasn't done. For Elias to do what he needed to do, what she believed he was about to do, he needed more.

He needed time.

She held that wall of lightning fast. Refused to let the energy drift and die.

Not a strike, but a shield.

All of it. All of it. All of it.

Gods, everything hurt. Magic skittered down her arms, climbing her armor like briars scaling a brick building. Golden ivory brilliance danced through her bracers, her steel-studded knuckles slavering sparks, salivating for another chance to strike.

Stop. Strike. Rest. Rage.

A body at war with itself.

She could dismiss the power devouring her from soul to skin. Spare herself the agony, the exhaustion, the gods-knew-what that would come after as a consequence for this.

Rest. Rage.

Something warm coursed down her cheek. A tear. A raindrop. Blood. She couldn't tell which.

I don't know how much longer I can do this, Kallias.

A spark played hopscotch through the chain around her wrist.

A pinch of sea salt sprinkled the tip of her tongue.

Not forever. Just long enough. Just until it's over.

War-wrath dissolved into gentler, jarring emotion, a humming frisson of grief that brought her breath up short. That knifed into her chest and carved, searching, seeking her heart.

Rage against anything that would see you to ruin.

Rage. Rage. *Rage.*

Just long enough. Just until it was over.

And when she saw Tempest tried to skirt her storm, moving to intercept Elias himself, she knew how to end it.

Swaying, half-blinded by her soldiers of skyfire holding the line, she stabbed a finger in Tempest's direction.

And with a breathless prayer uttered in a dead prince's name, she called down lightning on the God of Nature's head.

White fire. Searing energy. Ecstatic pain singing in the roots of her teeth, the marrow in her bones, every seam where a break or fracture had fused back together.

This time, her spear of lightning did not land true. It crumpled inward, writhing and jittering as it bent unnaturally.

Tempest beheld her with something like wonder as he reshaped her weapon, molding it into a ball like a crumpled piece of paper. "You can't have thought that would work."

No. But it had served its purpose.

Failures could be tactical, too. Another lesson learned in the wake of Finnick Atlas's special sort of madness.

She hadn't needed to hurt Tempest; she'd only needed to perform a little time-stretching of her own.

Just long enough.

And when she finally lost her balance, legs numb and tingling, her knees not even registering the impact as she collapsed, she refused to let her eyes close. Refused to divide her attention, even when the God of Nature called her name with the voice of someone she loved.

Not yet. Not until she knew if it had been enough.

Cheek pressed to the tile, reveling in the relief of icy rainwater against her smarting skin, she bore witness as the Phoenix Priest stepped into the space she'd made for him. As he stood in his goddess's warpath, onyx steel dancing with midnight flame. As his eyes…

Raquel's heart thundered—then stopped.

Last he'd looked her way, his eyes had been exactly as she remembered: one coal-dark, one a gold-ringed goddess eye.

But as he interposed himself between Mortem and the woman she'd commanded him to kill, that goddess eye was no longer ringed in gold.

Nor had it faded to black.

"I gave you an order, Phoenix Priest!" Death spoke with the wrath of every mourner standing vigil at an unearned pyre, her shadow reaching new heights, long and lethal. "Your goddess—"

Elias Loch looked up at the Goddess of Death, his eyes haunted by grief unfathomable.

His *golden* eyes.

"You are no longer my goddess," he said. "And that is not my name."

The Goddess of Death *recoiled.*

Like bonfire smoke given breath, Mortem's whisper hung in the air, hoarse, horrified: *"Godkiller."*

CHAPTER 55

ANIMA

Annelisa Medeis had not been built for battles, and she would like it very much if her friends would stop finding reasons to drag her into them.

Having the eldest Arborian prince at her back with his crossed bandolier and belt full of bloodletting blades should have made it better. Instead, every scrape of steel being yanked from its sheath marked another hash in her mental tally, her worry mounting with each weapon lost to a perfectly aimed throw.

"You need to use your magic," she panted when the tally dropped from eighteen to eight.

"Mixed company," he reminded her, as if she could have forgotten the faithless friends in their midst.

She risked a look over her shoulder, her next arrow not quite primed to shoot. His dark hair had struggled free of its tie, only half still held in its tail; the rogue strands stuck to his face, damp with sweat. Perspiration not summoned by exertion, but by restraint.

As Ani had witnessed, battle could break even the strongest of wills. And her prince was fighting not one battle, but two.

"You're exhausting yourself twice as fast by fighting it!" Those fairy circles of fatigue had already formed around his eyes; for every weapon he freed from the bandolier strapped across his chest, its weight was replaced with a labored cough and a fist thudded over whichever lung pained him.

Every rotting piece of her cried out to help. To heal. To lay hands over his own rebellious body and pour all she had into him.

But for the first time in her very long life, her cup was empty.

No, worse—she had no cup to pour from at all.

"And if I give in before I must, I risk worse when my well runs dry!" he snapped.

Wolf had never raised a hand to her in fury, not even when Blight had its way with him; only his voice, and nearly never with true anger. And still, cowardly to her core, too close to every loved one who had ever turned against her, Ani flinched.

"I know my limits." His voice first, soft; then a swift brush of knuckles over the small of her back, softer. "Eyes on your target, love."

He was right. She had so little practice with limits—he had lived his whole life managing his own.

Nock, draw, aim, shoot.

She had only made it halfway through *draw* when a chill spidered up her arm. A creeping vine of hoarfrost she had only felt in one place.

Twice she had escaped the grave. And today, the grave had come back to claim what it had lost.

Aim.

The leather bracer strapped around her wrist scraped her darkwood bow as she pivoted, sighting down the shaft of her arrow.

Ani was no hunter. But she knew a predator when she saw one.

There was no mistaking what prowled in her direction now.

A huntsman clad in fire and shadow; a dark-eyed priest with a cloak of ire and soot swept over his shoulders.

Elias Loch walked in the shadow of Death. And with every step he took, that shadow stretched. Sought. Stalked her like a hound on a scent.

"Elias?" she whispered.

He didn't look at her. But his shadow did.

When mortality had claimed Annelisa Medeis, it must have alchemized somewhere only base instinct could reach. Because when the goddess who had once been Mora Medeis set her sights on her, her hand did not shake—but the very depths of her spirit quailed.

This was not part of their plan.

Wolf's arm swept across Ani's front, pushing her back two paces before he yanked two more knives from the sheaths at his belt. His bandolier now hung empty.

"Whatever's gripped your head, lad," Wolf warned, "you'd best pry it off."

Her heart broke all over again for this man—this man who had emptied pocketfuls of pebbles into her palms just to see her smile. This man who'd carried her heart in his pocket ever since. This man who stared down Death like he'd found an expected but unwelcome guest at his door and had no intentions of letting her in.

Over Elias's shoulder, Raquel Angelov shouted at his back, teeth bared in a bestial roar: "*Traitor!*"

Elias turned back, lingering on the soldier for only a moment; but when he aimed his attention toward Ani again, Raquel's eyes had shut.

Defeat.

Anima lowered her bow.

"Let me speak to her," she begged Wolf. *Let me try.*

Wolf squared his shoulders.

"Wolf." She dug her nails into his shoulder, trying to haul him aside—he didn't budge an inch. Rotting nonsense. Even weakened by necromancy, she stood no chance of moving him. "*Please.*"

If her sister wanted her, so be it—she *would not* have Wolf Olivander. Not today. Not so soon.

The shadow over Elias's head shrank, rippling in reverse until it shaped itself into a mimic nearly as sickening as the one Ani had laid to rest mere weeks ago in her own kingdom. The ghost of the girl who used to tuck their single fleece blanket around Ani's ankles and keep vigil by the hearth on the coldest Sanctaviv nights, stoking their sparse pile of firewood, throwing her own clothing atop the embers on the most dire of days.

Ani opened her mouth to beg her sister's mercy—and in that pregnant pause, the air banked sharply cold.

When the world went white, she knew it was too late.

Silence roared in her ears. A gale blasted her backwards, the chill cutting right through her wool-lined Arborian clothes. Someone's hand struck out for hers, but the wind tore her away, spinning her around and around and around until—

Until color bled back into the world. Until sound seeped in, too, Wolf's voice muttering a frantic chant in her ringing ear, his hand cupped under her head. She couldn't tell what he was saying. It might have been her name.

When she opened her eyes, fingers spasming around her fallen bow, understanding petered in like sap drawn from a near-empty tree.

Whatever force had swept through the throne room had flung her to the floor; not just her, but nearly everyone. The Tallisians still knelt beside their fallen friend, all three conscious members bent over him with arms twined and heads bent, shielding him from the squall. Tenebrae seemed to be recovering too, shaking his head as he struggled to his feet. Even Tempest had fallen to one knee, one arm bent to shield his face, staring in bald-faced amazement at the only person left standing in the aftermath of her storm.

Raquel Angelov, swaying on her feet, tears evaporating into tendrils of steam the second they touched her skin. Whose armor and weapons and prosthetic eye all sparked with trapped lightning. Who steadied herself just long enough to point all that power at Tempest's chest—and release it.

The little sister inside her almost forgot herself when lightning hurtled for her brother's exposed chest. Almost screamed for Peter to run.

But she remembered the real threat in the room when the throbbing blindness faded—revealing Elias barreling toward her, blade still drawn.

As a gust of sunbaked wind and stray embers replaced Raquel's rain-soaked gale, she allowed herself the single weakness of holding Wolf's hand. Of shutting her eyes, so she would not have to see Death come for her.

But her sister's cry was not one of victory.

"I gave you an order, Phoenix Priest! Your goddess—"

Darkness.

The soft kind. Not oblivion, not nothingness, but shade. A shield against sunburn and heatstroke and a hundred other ways too much light could kill.

And a whisper, even softer, even colder: "You are no longer my goddess. And that is not my name."

Oh, rotting *roots*.

Ani squinted one eye open.

At first, all she could make out was her own reflection, distorted across a plate of pitch-black armor. Then Wolf pulled her back a step, and the picture became terrifyingly clear.

Elias. Holding one hand to the side, a protective pose, placing himself in front of her…and holding his scythe out in the other.

Pointing it straight at the Goddess of Death's ember-bright heart.

Mortem's shadow stilled. Solidified. Became something so near to human Ani could make out the horror in her eyes. The withered scars climbing her arms. The same nose and chin and funny-shaped upper lip Ani had seen in the mirror every morning since she and Soren had conquered the Arboretum Absolute.

Elias did not introduce himself. He did not have to.

Because Mortem took one look and whispered, *"Godkiller."*

Elias didn't flinch like he had when he'd confessed what he was to Ani. He only inhaled, slow and steady—and when he let it out, the onyx tint of his blade seeped into his fingers.

A wave of cold washed over her. It had only been weeks since she had willingly set her life in those hands. To be this close again now, even with that hand extended to someone else…

"I won't hurt her," Elias rasped. "But I do not want to hurt you, either."

Mortem's shadow lost itself in light. An inferno of scarlet and sunfire and sunflower. "You *betrayed* me."

Ani waited for that blow to land. For Elias to hit his knees and pray. For holy men's habits to prevail.

"Forgive me, Goddess." Black ice. Old grief. Fresh yet fetid rage. "I am not above such things like you. I am still a mortal."

Mortem stopped blinking. Stopped blazing. Went dull and dark as a stomped-out firefly. "You spoke to Evan."

Was that *remorse* poking holes in her sister's spiteful shadow?

Elias's next breath hissed as he drew it in. Like it had to scrape through his teeth. "Don't you dare speak of betrayal with one breath and speak his name with the next."

"Had he followed my order—"

"He would not be your weapon," Elias interrupted, "and neither will I. I know what I am—I know *why* I am."

Ani's fluttering heart bleated in panic when Elias lowered his scythe, stepping to the side—leaving her vulnerable.

"I will not hurt her," he said softly. "If you want her dead, you will strike that blow yourself."

Heat clung like burrs to the backs of her eyes.

We trust him, she reminded herself. *We trust him, we trust him, we trust him.*

Elias would not have stepped aside if he did not know, somehow, her sister would not—or could not—strike that blow. If he did not possess some certainty that Ani certainly did *not*.

"Mora," she pled. "I'm not here to help Braeden. I couldn't even if I wanted to."

Her sister's disbelieving huff stirred a thousand embers to life in her shadow.

"Look at me!" Her voice broke. "Look me in the eyes, Mora!"

And with a shock that would have bleached bloodred roses white, she watched her sister do as she asked.

The look they shared stretched across centuries. So much time, too much time—yet the blood they shared, the bond of birth, it still mattered. Ani could no more have raised a hand against her sister as she could have driven a knife into her own heart.

"I want to fix this," she whispered. "You're still my sister. Let me fix this. *Please.*"

It still mattered. It still meant something. It had to. It—

"You are right, Elias," Mora whispered. "This task is mine."

Her sister vanished. And in her place—

Smoke and fire and the shadow of death.

Ani spun and thrust Wolf away from her with all her might.

"Annelisa, *no*—"

The best goodbye she got before agony ruptured her heart.

Wait. Death never hurt before. *Let it hurt, let it hurt.* It wasn't supposed to hurt, why...why did it—

"Annelisa!"

Weight, warmth—*Wolf.*

No, no, no, this wasn't right. Why was this—why did he have time to— why did it *hurt?*

His broad hand clutched the back of her head, holding her face against his chest. His voice rumbled under her cheek, ragged—with relief?

"Don't look. Don't look, love."

Had Mortem revoked even her devotion to mercy? Had she chosen a weapon over magic just to make certain Ani suffered?

"Let me see," she rambled. She needed to know. She needed to see it. She didn't know why, but *need* was the word for the panic building like pressure between her ribs, *need* was all she knew besides the pain, the pain that didn't belong, the pain that made no sense from her mercy-minded sister— "Let me see!"

She wrenched out of Wolf's hold so hard she fell, landing on one knee as she felt for blood or bone, as she searched for the weapon, as she lifted her gaze to—

Oh.

Annelisa Medeis had two graves to her name. An undug hole with an abandoned headstone somewhere on the outskirts of New Sanctaviv. An undying shrine with a crownless queen as its warden.

Yet this was the first time she truly knew what it was to feel the life drain from her body.

Elias Loch had always been quick. As long as she'd known him, as long as *Soren* had known him, the man moved like a specter when he wanted to. Soren had complained once that if he got any faster, she'd have to secure a set of wheels to her boots.

But the princess had never thought him fast enough to outrun Death.

So it took too long for Ani to understand why Elias stood before her once again, a shield of adamant and Artemisian steel. Why she could see the scythe's hilt wrapped up in his white-knuckled hand, but she could not find the blade.

Because beyond the hilt, molten smoke had swallowed the scythe right up to the crossguard.

Because that blade had been thrust straight into Mortem's heart.

CHAPTER 56

RAQUEL

Raquel had not expected to see a deity die today.

Mortem, Goddess of Death, stood at the foot of Atlas's dais. In a palace once razed by her element, raised back to its former glory, refusing to fall prey to fire again.

A curved blade bit through her center. A blade bathed in blazing black.

It was impossible. A goddess could not fall to something as simple as steel, and yet…

As Raquel watched, clinging to the consciousness trying so desperately to abandon her, Death itself slipped into oblivion.

Smoke evaporated. Flame extinguished. Shadow frayed at every edge, unraveling, unmade…

Until only Elias remained, still as stone, his arm still bent as if ready to shove further into an unstoppable heart.

And there he stayed. Not breathing. Not speaking. Frozen.

"Mora!"

Shock weighed her skull down like it had been poured full of wet, stodgy sand; she couldn't lift it off the ground. She could only watch Tempest's shadow as he leapt over her, tearing toward his sister—where his sister had stood only moments ago—bellowing a war cry.

Had Kallias made that same sound when his little sister had vanished into thin air, nothing but ash left to her name?

Kallias.

His name burned through the fog like a lighthouse beam, and she shoved herself up on her elbow, screaming for Elias to snap out of it. To move.

Soren screamed too—but not for her battlemate.

"Kal, *no!*"

Tempest, already well on his way down the warpath, jerked like a hound whose leash had been tugged—stumbled backward, swearing, beating his fist against his own chest before bolting ahead once more.

Elias's eyes cleared at the sound of his battlemate's voice—or maybe Kallias's name shone a light through his clouded mind. But even then...

Even then, it was too late to take shelter. The tempest had already blown in—and the tempest was *pissed.*

The man who had just slain a god went down in two rib-crunching blows. And this time, when the God of Nature loomed above him, the shadows held their peace.

Elias squinted upward, head tipped into the dais step, fresh blood painting his head as Tempest came to stand over him. As his lips moved, fingers shaking as he ran them over the braids of cloth hanging beside them on a separate chain. His fathomless gaze searched the god's, like he might yet have hope.

Raquel *could* hate him for that, that senseless hope. Could hate him for holding on to it when she had not.

Hating, more than anything, that she had not.

Heat consumed her eyes, flooded her face—tears or blood or simple rage, simpler terror, she couldn't tell. All she knew was that she lost her breath at the same time Elias lost the fight; at the same time Tempest dropped to one knee and leaned over Elias, fist winding in the cloth collar sticking out above his armor.

Elias lifted his hand, and for one moment, the entire world slowed...stopped, leaving her breathless, riveted on those charcoal-dipped fingers. The hand that had just dealt Death a taste of its own medicine.

But as she watched, Elias's fingers began to fade to russet. By the time he set that hand to Tempest's cheek, that abysmally frightening power had vanished. Not one lick of it left to try and save himself.

"Kal," Elias whispered. Deathbed soft. Clotted with blood and pleading and that pointless, powerless hope. "Get up."

A flicker passed over Tempest's gaze. It almost looked like pity—even for the man who'd murdered his sister.

The fist he held ready, lightning splitting through the skin stretched over his knuckles, death of a different sort racing itself in circles…that did not look like pity at all.

"Kal," Elias growled again through gritted teeth, a waste of his last breath; he wove his fingers into Kallias's hair, holding on so tightly his knuckles paled. *"Get up!"*

Raquel thought one of the Tallisians roared Elias's name as Tempest drove that fist down toward Elias's face—thought Soren might have screamed, too, her incomprehensible composure taking flight just as it was too late to change anything.

But she couldn't be sure. Because instead of screams, all she heard was thunder, a cataclysmic *boom* that shook the earth and shattered windows in their frames and burst eardrums beyond repair…

Thunder that roared its defiance to the skies. A wordless, primal *no.*

Then a horrendous crack. Bone crushed beneath a fist. Another death blow decisively dealt.

Except…

Except it wasn't.

Instead of a triumphant god and a dead friend, a miracle met her when she got the courage to blink again.

Tempest, gaping at his fist…the curled, lightning-ringed fingers that had slammed into the throne room floor, cracking the tile instead of Elias's skull. Molten gold pooled around the shards of true tile hidden underneath.

He had missed.

Tempest, God of Nature, Ship-Breaker, The Eyeless Storm, Lightningsmith, Tide-Tamer…he had *missed.*

Her heart took off at a full-tilt sprint.

No. Not missed.

He'd been *stopped.*

Elias bared his teeth in a grin like she'd never seen before—vicious, bloodthirsty. *Excited.*

Almost frightening.

"Got him," he breathed through scarlet and exposed bone. Then again, a shout this time: *"I've got him!"*

Then, like a breeze had blown in and infused him with fresh vigor, he surged up and rammed his forehead against Tempest's.

"Sorry, Kal," Elias coughed as he wrenched the god's arms behind his back. Tempest snarled, bucking against his hold, but Elias shoved him down at the shoulders, straddling his back and screaming, "Soren! Now!"

A sunbeam severed the darkness chaos had thrown over the room.

Raquel squinted against it, instinct trying to pull her hand up to shield her eyes, but exhaustion kept it pinned to the floor. Though it could not have been, not at this hour, that brilliance struck her eyes like daylight. Like she glared directly into the sun, daring it to strike her blind.

This light did not blind. It…amplified, almost. She could have sworn she could see more clearly with that light scalding her eyes than she could on any given day; could have counted the dust motes dancing on her exhale, the beads of sweat and blood streaking Elias's wonderstruck face, the skitters of lighting still arcing through Tempest's splayed fingers.

She could have named every emotion in the god's golden gaze as his head snapped over his shoulder, finding her, hissing her name. Could have mapped every stolen freckle, worry wrinkle, laugh line. Could have tallied every pits-scorched piece he'd have to answer for when justice came to call.

And justice, it seemed, had chosen its moment well.

Soren stood on the dais, abandoned by every ally, entirely alone. Stars twinkling silver-bright in her eyes and on her shoulder. The sun held aloft in her steady hand.

A sun thrumming in the heart of a lantern.

In a battle against forces greater than human, seconds cost something; when placed at odds with powers past reckoning, mortals could not waste a moment on dramatics.

But if anyone had earned a second to show off, she supposed it was Soren. And even if she had not earned it, she would have taken it regardless.

The lost princess met Tenebrae's flagrant, frenzied gaze across the throne room. Stepped up on the throne that was hers by blood, hers by water; hers by fire. Held the sun aloft by her star-stitched shoulder.

Golden light spilled over her green-eyed glare, shrouding her in the divine. Painting her in equal measure to her enemies.

"Hey, *Braeden*!"

The throne room held its breath once more, waiting for its lost Heir to say her piece. For her to call down the fury of a queen upon her enemy's head. For her to reclaim what was hers—by blood, by water, by fire.

Instead, she thrust her middle finger in the air as if jamming a dagger into Tenebrae's windpipe. With the particular zeal only learned in the trenches of Nyxian barracks. With the crescent moon tattooed on that finger cutting through the light as light cut through darkness.

Then she spun her arm in a full, fierce circle, flinging the lantern to the floor with all her might.

CHAPTER 57

SOREN

Every night since they'd departed the island-kingdom of Arborius, making a mad dash for the Atlas coast by invitation of a coded note, Soren Loch had slept with the glowing gift of a god clutched against her heart.

Its light held darkness of a different sort at bay. Neither bad dreams nor anxious thoughts dared trespass on her resting mind while she held it. Its heatless flame flickered in perfect time with her heart, protecting the precious hope buried inside like a box of priceless treasure.

Finn's alive. Finn's alive. Finn's alive.

Her husband's gentle cautions against letting that hope fly too high fell on deaf ears. She pretended not to hear the hissed warnings to *shhh* from her trio of Tallisian friends, given to their historian handler whenever she tried to sensibly remind Soren that the note must have been sent some time ago, and anything could have happened since. And when her own melancholy came to call, needling her with reminders that one brother might yet be lost to her, she'd hugged Sancta's gift to her ever tighter.

Not just to her. To them. To their cause. But the way Sancta had looked at her as they'd set it in her hands…

It might have been a shared boon. But whatever was to be done with it…that would fall to her. She knew it down to her bones.

So the night before they'd made landfall, she'd held a conclave of sorts on the topdeck. A circle of odds-and-ends allies from all stretches of the continent gathered under a whole host of wishing stars.

Almost enough to carry all the wishes they each held precious in their hearts.

The Queen of Nyx and the King of Tallis had sat side by side, both uncrowned yet unbowed; a heathen historian and a pious priest had exchanged notes beneath strings of lanterns, solemn of look and resolute of spirit; a pair of proud Tallisian warriors had sat shoulder to shoulder, axe and shield to their king, ready when the call to arms came; a mortal, magicless woman and a hunter-prince had leaned into each other for support, fingers folded together and heads tipped temple to temple; and a pirate captain had held their course true as a lost princess paced his deck, both of them eyeing the sky like the map to their destination had been scrawled in starlight.

And together, they had come up with a plan.

Free her brothers. Gather the gods. Shatter the lantern.

Anything sounded simple when you broke it down in three steps.

But after slipping in through the poolhouse's glass doors, dashing through the door that led to a hidden set of corridors within the walls (a door that had been conveniently left unlocked), and storming out from the hidden alcove behind the dais, Finn had *already* been freed, if he'd ever been a prisoner in the first place; and as they'd thought, as they'd feared, no glimpse of Kallias could be seen past Tempest's influence.

So they would have to draw him out.

They had debated for a short time whether Soren or Elias had the best chance of reaching him; but Soren could not tussle with Tempest and ready the lantern at the same time, and she could not bear to set it in anyone else's hands.

Even if it meant her husband challenging a god alone.

In the end, it had made the most sense, strategically speaking…the Godkiller had a better shot at walking away from this than she did. Especially considering what it might take to wake Kallias up.

Elias had volunteered knowing it would mean taking a beating of some kind. Her reluctantly-told tale of clawing back control of *her* body to stop Ani from killing Finn—a tale generously sprinkled with apologies and guilty looks from Ani herself—didn't leave that to guesswork. There could have been other ways, but they didn't have time to try them.

So even without the lantern, Elias's deathless nature and death-dealing power would have made him the better bet. And for her own sake, she wouldn't have allowed it…but for Kallias, she had to let him try.

So the plan came together.

Elias would take Tempest. The Triad would get Tenebrae's attention and keep it however they could…and ensure he didn't get close to Soren and her sacred gift. Medwenna would ensure none of the gods strayed out of the lantern's reach. And if all else failed, Anima would step in herself to play the distraction and the bait, Wolf standing ever at her side.

"You three are her battlemates today," Elias had told the Triad before they'd departed the ship in a hidden cove, out of sight of the main harbor…Patch's generous contribution to the plan. *"Do you understand? I don't trust just anyone with her. I need you to be me. I need—"*

"Hey. Relax," Everin had told Elias…not grinning or goading, but serious as she'd ever seen him, his hand finding Elias's shoulder and his brow briefly bumping his. A gesture of affection she'd seen the Triad trade a time or two amongst themselves. *"We've got her. No one's getting through us."*

Killing Death had not been part of the plan.

Betraying her, yes…the one part of the plan she'd been hesitant to draw out in front of Elias, knowing what it meant to him. What *Mortem* meant to him.

But she hadn't expected it to go like *that*.

No skin off her knees—she'd never liked the Goddess of Death. Not as the *maybe-real-but-probably-not* silent spectator to Elias's gradual demise who'd refused to hand even half a miracle to her most faithful follower, and definitely not as the self-righteous sister set on sending Ani to her own sulfuric pits.

But Elias…

He'd leapt to Ani's defense without a damned thought—had almost definitely done it for Soren's sake, for the friendship she and Ani had forged in the unlikeliest of circumstances.

Elias the Pious had murdered his goddess. And then he'd frozen.

Not part of the plan at all. And with his goddess dead, without any idea if his power over death could still protect him from its touch without Mortem's blessing behind it...

Seeing the God of Nature strike out for him again had drop-kicked the mission straight out of her head. And she'd done the only thing she could think to do: she'd screamed for her brother.

An optimistic onlooker could have pointed out the stumble in Tempest's stride. A more sour spectator could have argued Kallias's name had reminded Elias of the mission at hand, slapping him out of his shock.

Whichever way one looked at it, it had worked...even if watching Tempest throw that lighting-spiked punch at his face nearly killed *her* stone-cold dead.

But it worked, nonetheless.

And Elias's throaty shout, his wild grin when he thrust Tempest to the floor with all his might and screamed her name like a battle cry...

It was the only cue she got.

Naturally, she milked it for all it was worth.

And the look on Tenebrae's wretched face just before glory swept through the room like a summer tide, soothing but swift, rearranging everything in its wake...

That made everything, *everything* they had gone through in the Sanctum Infidelium worth it.

When the sun finally set, it set on a world irrevocably changed.

There were three extra bodies in the room.

A man rose to his knees close to Elias...a man crowned in sable curls, blinking and squinting like he'd just been bashed over the head. A woman had dropped out of thin air a short distance from the dais, too still to be called anything but a corpse; a woman she recognized from the day Nyx fell, her soot-streaked face far less menacing without the help of ethereal shadows wavering at her back or eternal flames skating through the stitching of her skirts. Another man absolutely *writhed* on the floor, screaming like Sancta's light was still searing through his veins, unmaking all that made him more than human...screaming, and scratching, and sobbing like a hysterical child in the midst of a tantrum.

"What did you do?" Braeden Medeis wailed, looking first to his fallen sister, then whipping around to stare dead into Soren's soul, lips peeled back from his teeth. Devastated. Deranged. "What did you *do to us?*"

"I didn't do anything." Her veins sang, shone, still flowing with light and purpose and power. She was not afraid of him. "Did you think Sancta forgot about you?"

The Chaos God drove his fists into the floor like a toddler throwing the world's most destructive tantrum, screaming like someone had set him on fire before he rolled onto his stomach, throwing himself into a stumbling stand and hurtling for her.

"Oh, I don't think so!" Everin's steel-bottomed boots shrieked across the tile as he leapt in Tenebrae's way, spinning both hatchets, teeth bared. "You and I aren't done."

Everything jolted, then swayed. She staggered one foot forward, catching herself, reaching for her head to find the injury, the blood, but found nothing.

It wasn't a head wound. She wasn't dizzy. It was—

Another lurch. Another sway.

The palace itself swooned under her feet.

Oh, gods.

"We need to get out," she gasped as Elias cleared the last few steps up the dais himself, searching her face with a frantic look she didn't like. Especially not when he used *golden* eyes to do it. "Now!"

"Tell me where to go." As if he couldn't find the path without someone pointing the way.

Later.

"Triad." She couldn't see Kessen anymore—not past Medwenna and Matthias, both of whom had stayed behind to guard their fallen friend, his screams raking jagged knives of panic over her ribs. Everin alone stood against the God of Chaos. "Kess is hurt—his arm. It's bad. Get it cauterized and get them moving, then help Ev."

He nodded and drove back down the steps. Instinct screamed to chase him, to guard his back, to not let him out of her reach…

But right now, her family needed her.

Finn first.

He'd crashed to his knees on the other side of the dais while they'd brought their own kind of chaos down over the palace and hadn't looked up since, not even to witness a goddess's demise.

Instead, he knelt over a mirror laid out on the floor, the glass facing up. He kept jamming crooked, swollen fingertips against its surface, cursing at the top of his voice when they thudded into the glass. Bruised, pale as snow, bloodier than she'd ever seen him, he looked like he'd taken twice as many beatings as she had during her first year in barracks training—except he'd taken them all at once.

"We have to go," she panted—when he waved her off impatiently, she seized his shoulder and twisted him toward her, trying to shake his senses back to the surface. His golden eyes froze her fingers on his shoulders for a moment, but—no. No, this was her brother. She knew it in her bones. It had to be different—like Elias. "Finn! Enough with the mirror, we have to go!"

"I can't get her out," he said.

"What?"

He struck the glass with an open palm; this time she looked, and her mouth went dry, utterly sapped by the sight of that rippling silver pool…and the goddess that stared back at her from its depths.

"Good." If not for her suddenly dry mouth, she might've spit on Occassio's smug freckled face. "Isn't that what we want?"

Finn shoved her to the side. "If you're not going to help, get out of the way!"

"Finn!" Oh gods, this wasn't good. She leaned over the mirror again. "What did you do to him?"

"I told him to leave," Occassio snapped. "He's not listening to me, either!"

She knew better than that. "Tell me what you did to him, or—"

"Soren, *I* did this to *her*." Finn pushed her again, gently this time, but he kept his fingers splayed out—kept her at a distance as he bent back over the mirror, hissing at the glass like he was telling it a secret. "I am a chandelier's shadow. I am the light in the heart of a lantern. I am a depths-damned moonbeam, so let me in. Let me in!"

Occassio's brow crumpled as she bent her head to her side of the glass. "Finn, just *go*."

"None of that. You'll spoil my cover." His forehead dropped against the reflection of hers. "Come on, come *on*…I'm a moonbeam. I'm a lantern. I'll be whatever you want me to be, just—"

A shudder beneath their knees—another sideways *jolt,* followed by the sickening sensation of tilting, swaying, the first rock of a boat hitting a storm swell.

"What is that?" she demanded.

"Tenebrae shifted the damned palace. The foundation's shot, at least beneath this wing, I can't—" Another curse, and Finn ripped back from the mirror, tore his hands through his hair—then stopped. Huffed in a deep, angry breath.

"Fine," he rasped. "I fold."

"What?"

Her brother dropped and gripped the mirror in both hands, rattling its frame like prison bars, lips pulled back in a terrified snarl she'd never seen on his face before.

"Fine!" he shouted. "Fine, gods—*I love her!* I love her, you wretched awful thing, now let me *in!*"

Soren's stomach turned over, then flipped back the other way with the next death throe that rattled the bones of her childhood home.

When Finn thrust his hands against the glass, they met no resistance. He dove so far into the mirror that he nearly submerged his own head; then, with a wordless shout through gritted teeth, he tore himself back out—and dragged its prisoner out with him.

Glass crunched of its own accord, shattering inside the frame as Finn sprawled on his back, Occassio landing on top of him with a muffled hiss of pain. Of disbelief.

The two of them stared at each other, panting, caught red-handed with a senseless secret spilled between them.

Soren was going to *throw up.*

"Tell me that was a lie," Occassio pleaded.

"'Course it was a lie." Finn palmed a few curls out of her eyes. "You're all right?"

"'Course I'm all right." Occassio wiped a drop of blood on his cheek with her thumb. "You're a mess."

"I don't suppose you figured out how to launder bloodstains out in the last few centuries?"

"We don't have time for this!" Soren yelled; both of their heads snapped toward her as if guided by one neck. "You can flirt outside!"

Or don't! Don't do that, ever!

"Were we flirting?" Finn asked as Occassio towed him to his feet, looking a little dizzy. "I can never tell."

Occassio looped his arm around her narrow shoulders; despite her small stature, even shorter than Ani, she steadied Finn with only the slightest stoop to her back. "What am I going to do with you, Trickster?"

"Hard to say. I'm guessing either murder me or marry me, but—"

"Oh, shut *up.*"

Soren's thoughts exactly. But it'd have to wait.

"Ani!" Soren shouted; her friend spun up and away from the limp body she'd been kneeling beside, and Soren's heart jammed up into her windpipe.

Jericho.

In all the chaos, the single-minded sight on her brothers…she had not allowed herself to consider her *sister* at all.

But there she was. Her body spent by Chaos. Her healer's hands mottled in purple. Her scarlet hair matted and frayed.

Soren pointed; she could not muster any words. But Ani understood.

"She's alive," Ani called. "Breathing, but she won't rouse."

"Kal, too," Wolf called across the room; he'd already dragged her eldest brother up by the arm, bearing his entire weight across his shoulders. Raquel held Kallias's face in both hands, fingers curled under his jaw, measuring his pulse. "Alive, not awake."

"Hear that, Ev?" She couldn't see Kessen, but hearing him had never been a problem—her knees wobbled, relief almost knocking her on her seat at the sound of his weak, shock-slurred laugh. At least he wasn't screaming anymore. "I th-think you owe her some gold!"

"Damn it!" Everin yelled; but he shot her a grin across the battlefield, if forced for Kessen's sake, as he hacked a corrupted vine trying to tie a noose around Matthias's neck. The latter hauled Kessen to his feet with Elias's help; Kessen's feet dragged on the floor, his eyes fighting to close, but he was moving—he was alive. They'd worry about the rest outside. "Looks like miracles run in the family after all, Princess!"

She wished she could laugh, but the crushing sensation in her chest wouldn't allow it; an iron bar of relief that belonged only to her brothers and Kessen. She did not look at Jericho as she said, "Ani, get them out—take them and follow Finn."

Ani's disbelieving stare flickered to the retreating pair. "Are…is Cassi coming with us? Uh, Occassio?"

"Seems so!" A mistake she'd figure out how to correct later.

Raquel shrugged under Kallias's other arm despite the thick fog gathered in her remaining eye, on the edge of unconsciousness herself; Wolf glanced at her, then to Ani, indecision warring in his eyes.

"Here."

Raquel's gaze snapped to the man who strode up to Wolf, one arm out, his dark curls constantly stirred as if by a phantom breeze. She dragged her blade back out of its sheath, barely managing to heft it between them and the approaching stranger. "Take your vengeance somewhere else. Your sister earned what she got."

Tempest met her glare with a longsuffering look, hands up in a gesture of surrender.

The pause between her challenge and his answer measured exactly how long it took for those gathered to realize what this meant…what Tempest's raised hands and uneasy assessment of Raquel's blade suggested about what had been done here today.

A blade through the heart was a mortal fear.

"You can't carry him by yourself," Tempest said at last, "and between the eldest Atlas and the Tallisian boy, the others have their hands full. Let me help him."

The two of them fought a battle between their eyes alone; then Raquel surrendered, shoving her sword back into its sheath and tossing her glare to the floor instead.

Tempest spun into Wolf's place, bearing Kallias's weight with ease; once Wolf made it to Ani and helped shoulder the burden of Jericho, Tempest said, "Follow me, all of you. This was my home once—I know the fastest ways out."

Ani nodded to her elder brother, though wariness bristled in her bunched shoulders, her abruptly stemmed tears, her flat frown. "Let's go."

"Hey!" When Tempest looked at her, Soren pointed square at his chest, hoping it looked intimidating enough despite the way she shook. "If *any* of them don't make it out, it's your head, you hear me?"

He stared at her, unblinking. Almost owlish.

Weird. That wasn't how most people took her threats.

"Do you *hear me*, Tempest?" she barked.

He blinked; shook his head. "They will be safe." A stolen look at Raquel. "You have my oath."

So nearly all the gods had gotten sappy on them, then. Fantastic.

A chorus of shouts—Everin, Matthias, and Medwenna, Elias's voice notably missing—spun her away from half her precious few to face the rest.

Fire had leapt to life around Tenebrae, a barricade between him and the Tallisians. Her throat dried out; she nearly screamed her husband's name before his shadow circled around the outside of the wall, his stare severe, fixed on the center of the inferno.

She knew that gods-damned look.

"Elias!" When he looked up, eyes glassy with firelight and fury, she shook her head. "We don't have time!"

The Godkiller could end it all here. But this palace had already taken a mortal wound—and it wouldn't last long enough to finish that fight.

Ani looked back over her shoulder, but Wolf herded her toward the doors, a silent but firm agreement; and with a shaken nod, Ani ran, Wolf following with Jericho. Occassio and Finn were already through; Tempest went next, him and Raquel bearing Kallias between them. None of the Medeis siblings looked back.

The Triad and Medwenna started to follow—then, as one, they paused. Everin tore back around, searching until he found her and Elias.

"Not leaving without you, so you'd better move your asses," he yelled over the din, feet planted like he didn't intend to take another step until he got an answer he liked.

Gods, she was going to give him the most embarrassing hug when they got out of here.

"We're with you!" Elias yelled back; to her relief, he abandoned the wall of fire, waving them forward with one hand and taking hers with the other.

She would have stayed if he wouldn't have left. But she'd desperately like to avoid the irony of burning to death.

She didn't miss how he kept casting looks back at Mortem's body, abandoned amidst a dozen growing fires closing in on the dais. But his grip didn't loosen as he ran with her to the throne room doors.

And for the second time in her life, Soren fled from the palace she'd been born in, the smell of smoke suffocating any thought beyond *run.*

Run. Run. Run.

CHAPTER 58

SOREN

Her temper, it turned out, had limits.

She would not have thought so; nor would anyone else on this boat, if she had to guess. But after hugging Everin tight enough that he groaned about her trying to break his rib—then sitting with Kessen until Wolf promised her it was safe to walk away, that he would call her if the boy took a turn for the better or the worse—she didn't say a single word to anyone before dragging herself to the nearest shadow and crashing into a dreamless hour of sleep beside Elias, who'd passed out before they'd even weighed anchor.

After the vastly inadequate nap, when she could finally feel her feet again, she left her still-sleeping husband behind to drag them step by arduous step across the deck until she reached her brother: also barely awake, also barely upright. Finn squinted up at her, leaning heavily against a stack of crates, still panting despite them having been on the water for nearly two hours.

Occassio slept on the floor beside him. But that was a problem for Tomorrow Soren, who would be well-rested and ready to pick yet another damned fight with a goddess for trying to take what wasn't hers.

"If you're going to hit me," Finn groaned, "can you wait until we get to the island full of medimancers? I don't know how well I'll take it just now."

Instead, she threw herself down next to him, wrapped her arms around his middle, and sobbed herself dry against his shoulder. And he held her, jokes and jabs nowhere to be heard, utterly solemn as he murmured apologies to her and settled a single kiss on the crown of her head.

"I thought you were dead," she managed through hacking, hysterical sobs.

"Yeah…been there." He hugged her tighter. "I'm right here, kid."

"Don't do—don't do that *ever again*."

"I won't if you won't."

"Shut up." She sniffled. "Mama and Papa, they're—?"

"Alive—safe. Got em' out before everything went, well…" He mimed an explosion with his hands. "Y'know. The way it usually does for us."

"You're sure?"

He tapped his temple; his eyes flickered pink. "Positive."

As if he'd shared that flicker of foresight with her, they both looked to the door that led belowdecks at the same time; Tempest had helped Raquel carry Kallias somewhere within, then had emerged moments afterward alone. Raquel had yet to show herself.

"Loch said he saw Kal fight." Finn's voice was nonchalant; his fists curled tightly against his knees. "Think he's right?"

"Elias isn't really prone to wishful thinking." Even when Ani *and* Finn had both told him the truth, he'd never really believed Soren had survived her own possession until she'd broken out to tell him herself. And if hope hadn't been enough to fool him then, she doubted it doubly now.

"Faithful men believe plenty of things without proof."

"Well, his faith is sort of…in flux, at the moment."

"Because he just murdered his goddess?"

"That might be part of it, yeah."

Now they both looked to a different portion of the deck…a portion guarded by two Tallisians trying very hard—and failing even harder—to look as though they hadn't arranged themselves deliberately in a wall between her and the unconscious woman prone on the deck, a thin blanket the only kindness bestowed on her.

Finn must have been the one to give it to her, since Soren certainly hadn't; even if it made her awful, she hadn't lifted a finger to care for Jericho, who had not stirred since Tenebrae had been torn out of her by Old Sanctan miracle-magic.

It was sweet, she supposed, seeing Everin and Matthias worry for her safety. In their own way. Even if they were only standing there because Medwenna had ordered them to go be useful somewhere else and let her and Wolf take care of Kessen. Yet they held their vigil without any sign of impending sleep tempting them away.

"Vaughn's alive." No inflection bent Finn's voice one direction or the other.

Soren didn't know which way she bent on that one herself. So instead, she matched his monotone. "Elias and I got married."

Finn blinked. "Weren't you two already married?"

She laughed. He didn't.

"You're kidding," she said.

"Wait, you really weren't married? He's just *like that* about you, nothing legally binding or any—""

She elbowed him, hard. "You *are* kidding."

Finally, he cracked a grin. "Had you going for a second, though."

"You had me going to throw myself off the edge of this boat."

"Good thing you learned how to swim, then."

She could have wrestled him facedown on the deck for pulling attitude like captains pulled rank. But right now...

Right now she was too damned tired to do anything but put her head on his shoulder again.

"I saw you," she said softly. "In the Sanctum. I thought it was a dream, but…"

She didn't know what she was trying to ask. But the two of them had never really needed words.

He squeezed her shoulder, leaning his temple against hers. "Told you to trust me, didn't I?"

Thanks to Patch's expert navigation—and fine, maybe a little bit thanks to carrying the actual God of Nature on board—they shaved off nearly a third of the typical journey back to Arborius.

And even then, every minute chafed at her patience, sharpening her temper like steel against stone. Elias had to herd her away from picking fights with the former deities—Ani excluded—more than once. And when he wasn't lecturing her on all the reasons why picking a fight with them was far worse than foolhardy, which felt *monumentally* hypocritical after what he'd just done in Port Atlas, he was busy giving Everin the same lecture…and keeping an eye on Medwenna, who hovered in the Medeis family's periphery whenever she wasn't on Kessen duty, her taught terror locked in a grisly battle with her insatiable need for knowledge.

Curiosity killed the cat. But Medwenna was no feline stalking from the shadows; she was a shark on a scent. And thanks to Sancta's relic, these former gods were as good as blood in the water. This would be a fight between their millennium of practice keeping their secrets against Medwenna's dogged determination to discover ancient truths yet unknown to her.

Soren's money was on Medwenna.

In any case, it was a relief in too many ways to count when Yvonne hollered a confident "Land, ho!"…and when they all looked to Patch to confirm, as Yvonne had already given them two false alarms, the captain nodded his confirmation and offered an exhausted thumbs-up.

Soren and Finn both collided at the bow, shoving for space and bickering without any real bite until they jostled into a position that allowed them both to see. And when they laid eyes on the harbor…

Soren's throat closed.

Arborius's harbor was one of the more colorful ones she'd seen in recent memory; the ships sailing in flew all kinds of flags, some unmarked, some bearing kingdom crests, all welcomed with open arms to the island of exceptional healers.

But she hadn't seen a ship flying an Atlas flag at these docks since her childhood.

Not until now.

Blue and gold fluttered proudly in the wind, the sun-and-sea crest stamped against the graying sky. The sight of it nearly kicked her to her knees.

Bodies still milled on its deck, too far for her to tell if any of them wore familiar faces. They must have just recently docked themselves.

How they'd gotten here just as fast, she couldn't be sure. But when she turned to search for Elias, she found Tempest watching her first…then dipping his head as if to say *You're welcome.*

She didn't feel like thanking him for…whatever he'd done. However he'd done it. Not with her other brother still unconscious in the sickbay belowdecks. So instead, she turned back, gripping Finn's sleeve. "Please tell me that's…"

"Mama and Papa's ship," Finn breathed, relief dropping him back to his seat; he shielded his face with his hands. "They made it. They made it."

Mama. Papa.

As soon as their hull scraped the dock spoke, Soren made a break for the gangplank.

CHAPTER 59

SOREN

The moment her feet hit the Arborian docks, she was nine years old again, lost in a sea of bodies and confusion and hysteria.

Shoulders thudded on shoulders, elbows drove into ribs, hands grabbed for her sleeves. Bruises on bruises. Fear on fear.

The past tried to drag her under, ashen panic drying her voice to dust. She'd never done well treading these kinds of waters, her body remembering exactly how it felt to get swallowed up and spat back out by a crowd, locked in a burning ballroom.

But she was not nine years old anymore. She was a soldier; she was a general.

"Out of my way!" she roared over the crush of refugees and rangers. "Move—*now!*"

And just like that, a path opened up before her.

"King Ramses! Queen Adriata!" she barked, spinning side to side as she stormed through—dazed, exhausted gazes skimmed over her, some bouncing back when recognition struck. "Someone tell me where I can find them!"

A handful of voices rose in awe, in tearful relief, hailing her by her Atlas name; she ignored them all. Any other time, she might have offered at least a cursory smile for her birth people—any other time, and she would have fought her way *to* them instead of *through* them, offering help where she could.

But she couldn't be anyone's princess right now. Not until she knew she was still someone's daughter.

"Princess Soren!"

That cry caught her attention—the only one who called her new name, not her old one. She spun to find a man she didn't recognize…or maybe she did? His face made her brain itch just enough to tell her she'd seen him *somewhere* before. He towered over the crowd, just unusually tall enough to stand out; his black locks swung as he pointed toward the tree line.

"That way!" he called—definitely an Artemisian accent. Interesting. "They were escorted to the gates!"

She'd figure out how she knew him later. For now, she threw him a wildly off-kilter salute of thanks, then sprinted for the gates.

The path to the gates wasn't any less congested, but at the very least, she could veer off the beaten path—literally—and aim straight for the towering entrance into Elderwood Forest. The uneven terrain barely gave her mountain-beaten body pause.

What a difference from the last time she'd flat-out sprinted for these gates, blood clotting every breath, her dying body losing the fight to hold her spirit and Ani's in the same skin.

Her lungs failed her this time, too. Because the sight of scarlet hair in the knot's center mercilessly ripped her breath away.

So she couldn't scream or shout to summon their attention. She tried— she tried so hard, but she could only sob, choking on her own voice.

But parents had a sense about these things.

That scarlet-crowned head started to swivel first. Then the copper-crowned one beside it. Like they'd heard the cry she couldn't give.

More white streaked through both than she remembered. Stardust through fire; bone through blood. She had to get to them. She couldn't move.

Ramses found her first, his hand covering his bearded, bruised mouth; half a second later, Adriata spun around, blackened eye searching, searching—

She and Soren locked gazes, and Soren forgot to be afraid. To be careful. To remember that this woman had not been her mother in over a decade, and the last time she'd confronted her without her siblings at her side, she'd threatened to burn the palace down a second time if they didn't free her battlemate from the drowning dungeon. Had called her *Majesty*, not *Mama*.

One look, and she was Soleil again, one last time. Soleil, soaked from head to toe in seawater and sand, too tired from a full day of swimming to put one foot in front of the other…but not too tired to lift her arms up, pleading without words for her parents to pick her up and carry her home.

"Mama!" she shouted, shoving bodies out of her way; cursing when another wave closed around her, holding her back from her parents. "*Mama!*"

If Adriata shouted back, Soren couldn't hear it; but something told her the queen hadn't wasted time on it. Because Soren only had to throw elbows twice more before her birth mother broke through the crush of refugees, of cure-seekers, of medimancers and rangers trying to put everything back in order after the unexpected influx of arrivals.

"Mama," she sobbed before Adriata crashed into her, crushed all her breath out of her with a hug that nearly knocked her to the ground; instead, her mother caught her up in her arms, clutching her close by her hair, hiding her face there as she wept.

"You're safe," the Queen of Atlas cried into her curls. "You're *safe*."

Not a question, but an oath sworn fiercely enough to rattle the ground under their feet.

"I didn't know," she rambled through her own tears as Adriata pulled back, wiping at her cheeks with unsteady thumbs, shushing her before she'd even finished her apology. "Mama, I didn't know, I didn't remember—"

"I know, love, I know—let me see you, are you hurt? Oh gods, your face—"

"*Soren!*" Her father's broken laughter cut into her chest, her heart seizing up when she saw how badly he limped. Rather than swimming against the current, he had to let the crowd carry him to her; his crimson-splattered shirt barely clung to his shoulders, and the bare stripe of skin over his ribs had the telltale sheen of a medimancer's recent work. But his eyes shone like the gods-damned sun as he stumbled into her and Adriata's joint embrace, grabbing her face in both hands and kissing her fiercely on the forehead. His tears fell in droves, speckling her skin like sea spray. "Oh, thank the *gods*. We were so afraid…"

"What happened?" she demanded, shaking them both off to grab for that pathetic storm-torn sail parading as a shirt; her rigid heart overcorrected, stumbling into a sprint, when she took in the full measure of that just-healed wound. "Did anyone here get a look at you? Where's Sage—let me find—"

"I've been tended well enough. Let me see that." He turned her face gently to the side, gaze darkening as he took in the nasty weal across her cheek. "Did no one help you with this?"

"My face is *fine,* Papa. You're both hurt. You need…I need you to—"

Her voice broke down—then her knees. The adrenaline that had pumped false wakefulness through her veins for most of the voyage must have taken its leave.

Warm hands smoothly caught her under her elbows, steadying her before her parents could see her fall; she leaned gratefully into Elias, who muttered, "I could've sworn we talked about you not running off without me anymore."

"I knew you'd catch up."

"We'll discuss it later." Code for *you're still in trouble, but I've got bigger deer to skin.* He shifted to hold her by her waist as he cautiously regarded first Adriata, then Ramses. "Your Majesties."

Matching veils of suspicion fell over her parents' faces; instead of stepping back, they stepped in toward each other, Ramses looping his arm around Adriata's shoulders. A united front.

"Officer Loch," Ramses greeted him. "That was your name, wasn't it?"

"The real one, that is," Adriata said stiffly. She eyed Elias's hands like she'd prefer to see them detached from his wrists, not touching her daughter. "The one we learned after my son found you out as a Nyxian spy."

Oh, pits, she'd forgotten that part. This was going to be a fun conversation.

"It's actually Captain now, Your Majesty." Elias did not let her go—possibly because he knew she'd fall if he did—but he gave the best bow he could without loosening his grip. "Captain Elias Loch. I regret the circumstances which led to that…*unfortunate* first impression, unavoidable as they might have been."

She could've kissed him for those pretty manners—and she would. Later. When her parents weren't standing right there.

"He really wasn't spying." The words rushed out of her, undammable. "He only came to save me, which…well, you can figure out why that got complicated."

Adriata didn't look away—nor did her glare soften. "And why is he *still* here?"

Soren snorted; bad idea. Her head spun with the force of that off-kilter breath. "He's still here because the next thing that tries to take him from me is getting its fingers ripped off with my bare *teeth*."

Elias subtly pinched her side. She ground her heel into his toes.

Ramses coughed into his fist. Adriata's fingers flexed at her sides.

"Mama." Gods, where were these nerves coming from? She drew one of Elias's hands over her heart and twined her fingers with his, squeezing until her knuckles started going numb. "He's…"

All at once, this didn't feel funny at all.

She'd never been talented at explaining Elias to others. To say she loved him felt too common—plenty of people fell in love without feeling *this*. But to say the rest…how could she bare the soft underbelly of her heart to anyone like that?

He is the best thing in my life—he's the better half of everything I am.

He is the keeper of who I am when I cannot be trusted to hold it. When I misplace myself for the hundredth time, he is always patient…he always helps me look. He never lets me give up. He never stops until he finds me.

He is the maker of half the miracles it took to bring me back to you.

If the choice is between him and you, I will walk away from you. And you won't catch me looking back.

"*I* am grateful you both made it safely here," Elias stepped in when she failed to finish her sentence. "And I know there are conversations to be had and stories to be shared between us all. But while I understand your concerns for your daughter, my concern for my wife comes first."

Her mother's eyes doubled in size.

Oh, gods, they were so dead.

"Nice," she hissed at him. "Very tactful. We're just going to say it like that?"

Calm as ever, he held her mother's gaze like he'd faced down more intimidating creatures on any day of the week. "I don't know any other way to say it."

Damn. No arguing with that.

"Give us a couple hours," Elias added. "We'll find you once we've seen a medimancer and seen to our companions. I swear it."

"We can spare that much for you, Captain," Ramses interrupted, earning a baffled look from Adriata as he held his hand out to Elias. "You risked your life, infiltrating our palace to reach her…and from what I've been told, you've risked far more to return to and remain by her side. I cannot question your devotion to my daughter, nor can I be anything less than grateful for it."

Elias took her father's hand and shook it. "I did nothing for her she would not also do for me."

It could have been humility. Or a warning. Either way, her father met Elias's solemn stare with one of his own. "As for the timing…there is much to see to tonight, not least of all our own hurts. Is this conversation the sort that can be slept on, Captain?"

Elias glanced at her sidelong; she nodded, and he did the same, his lips twitching faintly. "Seems our patience will keep another night."

"Let's hope mine will do the same." Ramses finally cracked a knowing smile—then he looked to her, smile fading as he traced her wound again. Not just that one—older ones, too, dispensed by Atlas weapons and goddess-glory; Chaos-corrupted creatures, friends, foes; trials and tribulations conquered within the Sanctum of the Faithless, dealt last, not least. Silently tallying her new hurts and fresh scars with an anguished pinch to his brow that pinched her heart in equal measure.

"I'm all right, Papa, I swear." She stole his hand from Elias and squeezed it. "Finn, too."

As one, her parents slumped in relief; Adriata croaked, "Where is he?"

Shame flashed through her, scalding hot; she'd run too fast to notice where her brother had gone. "Um…"

"He went with Kallias," Elias said. "I saw Wolf take Jericho, so—"

"Jericho?" Adriata's glare snapped wide like a caught sail. Before, she'd regarded Elias with her sneer unbent by his manners, his *Majesties*; now, she hung on his every word. "Kallias? I…" A wet, shaking breath. A hand pressed to her bodice. A more composed question: "You were able to recover their…their bodies?"

"We were," Elias said—misunderstanding what her mother meant. But before she could correct him, he charged ahead, unaware of the hope he carried like a weapon…unaware he was about to plunge it into Adriata's heart without proper warning. "They're unconscious; we haven't been able to wake them yet. Soren's recovery came under different circumstances, so we're unsure—"

Adriata seized Ramses's arm so swiftly Soren flinched. "They're *alive*?"

Her mother's cry shattered across the harbor—the clamor died almost immediately, gazes drawn to the raised voice of a queen. Even the crowd still gathered near the ships went still.

Elias's eyes widened. "I apologize. That was thoughtless, I should have—"

Adriata surged forward, seizing Elias's arms now—but no anger, no violence fogged her glassy eyes. Only tears. "*My children are alive?*"

Soren's muscles hummed with fierce, learned warning—a terror that screamed to shove between her mother and Elias, to pry her hands from him finger by finger if she had to.

Instead, she sucked in a breath and set her hand on her mother's wrist. "They're alive, Mama. We don't know what state they're in, not yet, but…" Her throat swelled shut; she had to whisper this time. "We're alive, Mama. We're all here."

"They're alive," Elias agreed; her heart did a somersault when she watched how gently he held her mother up, how steadily he held Adriata's gaze, how he gave hatred no space in his own as he murmured, "Your family is safe— and they will stay that way. I will see to it personally."

A swift, harrowed inhale. "I want to see them."

"Aunt Gen can take you." Soren took her mother's hands once more and guided them away from Elias, wedging herself between them. When the relief wore off, there ought to be an obstacle between Adriata's vicious streak and the nearest known Nyxian in the harbor. "Have you spoken with her yet?"

Something guarded reclaimed its post in Adriata's tear-glazed eyes. "No."

"I'll help you find her." She looked at Elias. "I know we need rest, but—"

He set a hand to her back, grazing a kiss against her curls. "You don't have to ask, smartass."

Adriata's jaw dropped, ire searing her cheeks pink.

"It's a joke," Soren promised in a hurry, turning her mother away again— biting her lip on a laugh when she saw her father raise a fist to his mouth, coughing into it. "Trust me, I've called him much worse. Right, jackass?"

"Your mother called me a cod-kissing son of a sturgeon once," Ramses said. "Remember that, dear?"

The Queen of Atlas blushed to the roots of her hair. "I did no such thing."

"She was in labor with Finn at the time," Ramses confided in Elias, winking Soren's way as he pulled Adriata back to his side, leaving room for Elias to slide in and claim his own place beside Soren. "It's supposed to get easier with each, but the boy got himself stuck, and—"

"*Ramses Atlas*," Adriata hissed. "Is now really the *time?*"

"Would you rather I waited until Finn's around to hear how many times you said we should have stopped at two?"

"Stop that. You're making up nonsense."

Ramses shielded his lips, mouthing *Seven* at Soren over Adriata's head.

Soren couldn't hold it anymore; a guffaw brayed out of her, startling a brace of birds from one of the trees—and startling a handful of refugees into leaping away from the gate.

Maybe it wasn't the most appropriate moment. But her siblings were alive. Her parents were safe. Her Elias, her *husband* had his arm around her waist, his thumb stuck through one of the leather loops in her sword belt. They hadn't won the war, not yet—but they'd certainly won the battle.

The weeping would come later. But for now, she'd earned a good rotting laugh.

CHAPTER 60

FINN

However Astrid Thorne might have changed in the years since he'd bade her a quiet farewell on Port Atlas's dawn-soaked docks, neither of them daring more than a hidden squeeze of their hands before she dismissed her tears with a commanding sniff and strode onto her ship home, she had one unbreakable bad habit: she never found her way into bed before midnight. And thanks to the helpful chime of some faraway clock, counting off eleven bells before falling sweetly silent, he knew they had plenty of time to track down the one living soul he could confidently call a friend. The only one he didn't share blood with, anyway.

Raquel didn't count. He didn't really have a name for that particular bond, but he wouldn't call it a friendship. Didn't think she would, either.

The one living soul he didn't share blood with that he might consider calling a sister.

Plenty of time. Still, as he led Cassi through hallways thrumming with torchlight—really, torches? They lived in a tree, for crying out loud—he couldn't contain the urgency that kept tugging his gaze over his shoulder, seeking any sign of pursuit.

Their enemies were made of something more than mortal now. And though the two of them made quite the team, he simply didn't have it in him to deal with yet another near-death experience. He'd more than had his fill.

Convincing Cassi had been harder. But with a Godkiller walking around, his family in various states requiring sickbeds, one goddess left dead in their wake, and Cassi herself at half-strength, his unwillingness to leave her without a friend or fool at her back clashed irreconcilably with his need to handle a hundred other things before he could withdraw himself.

And Astrid Thorne was the only person he trusted implicitly to favor his word over his family's opinions.

Still, when she opened the door with a tired smile that collapsed when she realized who exactly had come to her door, the sensation that socked him in the stomach caught him entirely off guard.

He'd expected the relief, the flood of ease that came with knowing he'd reached the asylum of an ally. Cassi couldn't hope for a safer spot to hide out for a few hours while he got his own affairs sorted.

He *hadn't* expected the sight of Astrid to leave him winded like a fall gone bad, caught up by five years of only letters to get him by without his friend's clever counsel.

He'd missed her—just hadn't noticed until the missing was over.

"Hey, you," he croaked.

Those diamond-blue eyes misted over. "Hey, too."

Finn welcomed hugs from very few, but he welcomed this one with open arms—metaphorical and literal. Especially when it hit him that somehow, without his notice, he'd grown taller in the last five years. Not especially, but tall enough to just barely wedge his chin against the top of her head without stretching.

He looked forward to being smug about that later.

"Don't you ever scare me like that again," she scolded him. The crackly, holding-back-tears thing sort of ruined the effect she was going for, but he offered a contrite nod anyway. He owed her that much. "Do I need to bother with the lecture on just how foolish it was to go fiddling with godstuff all by yourself?"

"Not necessary, Lady Thorne."

"Good. I'm worn thinner than a shorn sheep as it is."

"Who's at the door, love?" came another familiar voice, groggier, his brogue so thick with sleep Finn could barely understand a word he said.

"Come see for yourself, lazybones! Forgive Sage for taking his time, he sleeps hard enough I might as well carve him a coffin to nap in." Astrid smiled, but her gaze darted over Finn's shoulder. "And who's this, then?"

"A long story," he hedged, pulling Cassi around to his side; he tossed a casual arm around her shoulder, glancing over his own for any winking steel or shifting shadows behind them. "Can we come in?"

Concern shaded slight lines between Astrid's brows. But she stepped aside, holding the door open. "I'll start the cocoa. I'm guessing you still prefer a glass?"

"How did I survive this long without you around?"

Astrid winked. "You're far from the first to ask. Come in, get settled— I'm dying to hear what sort of trouble Finnick Atlas has stirred up now."

As he could have predicted, the cocoa was exquisite, and the company even better.

Neither Sage nor Astrid got bug-eyed or brazenly accused him of falling fully to madness when he introduced Occassio; for her part, she shook Sage's hand and smiled at Astrid with the warmth of a kindred spirit. And to her credit, by the time the grandfather clock chimed in and reminded them of the late hour, he'd only had to steal back two of Sage's belongings; a pen and an unopened twist of caramel candy, both plucked from his older cousin's pockets as he meandered sleepily past them, mumbling his way through brewing a mug of midnight coffee.

The pen went back where it belonged. The candy went in his own pocket, much to Cassi's scowling chagrin. The coffee went down Sage's throat, and the chagrin migrated to Astrid's subtle glare as she eyed his older cousin with a squint that would've sent smarter men—or less groggy men—running for their lives.

And once Cassi had been settled in the guest room, rolling her eyes when he asked for the third time if she was sure she didn't mind if he left, Astrid walked him to the door.

"She's not what I expected," she said, with the kind of withheld curiosity that implied a question.

"Me neither." Never had been, probably never would be.

"She's perfect for you."

A left-leaning smile tugged at his mouth. "I'd love to return the sentiment, but everyone knows you're too good for my cousin."

An ocean of sterling-blue stars shimmered in her eyes. "A pretty face makes up for a heap of hooliganism."

"Don't I gods-damned know it." Where cleverness failed, charm never did. "Send for me if she needs anything…or if you do."

"This is my kingdom—you're our guest. You have no need to fuss on my account."

"You know I will anyway."

"I know." She clasped his hand and squeezed thrice. "You're still my second-favorite person in the world."

"The first being yourself, right?"

Astrid's eye rolls were nothing less than expertly given. "Now you're third."

"That's fine. You fell to fifth when Soren came home, so—" He dodged when she tried to smack his arm, laughing as he ducked out the door, hands up. "Fine, fine, I'm going. But really, you'll get me if—"

"I'll do what I deem best and not a mite more or minus, mister. Get before I call my husband to shoo you off with our dustiest broom."

"Letting a *man* fight your battles for you? Who are you and what have you done with Astrid Thorne?"

The door shut in his face while he was still laughing. And when he turned away, he found himself grateful there was still one person he trusted enough to turn his back on.

Maybe even two.

CHAPTER 61

ELIAS

The hot, humid rain pattering against his bunched shoulders felt like blood. It snaked down his bare back in running-river branches, the heat only heightening the sheet of ice that coalesced over his skin, refusing to break— refusing to thaw beneath blood-water's mulled caress. Errant streams collided with the wall, misdirected by the crooked creature huddled on the floor; the backlash misted his cheek like arterial spray.

In his waking mind, he knew the truth: there was no blood, no wound, no cut veins or sanguine rivers or iron-flavored rain. Knew he'd gone to bathe off the battle-grime still caked on his skin after days of sailing from the scene of his crime. Knew he'd intended to hop in and hop out after a hasty scrub-down, ready to rejoin his wife in their bed. She'd already done her own washing up and sent for some food to be brought to the room, and he'd thought…he'd *hoped* that the promise of cool sheets and candlelit curls and her fingers wandering aimlessly through his hair would be enough to keep his mind where it ought to be: here and now. Her and him.

But somewhere between shucking off his sullied gambeson, stepping into the porcelain bath, and turning on the showerhead, his mind abandoned *here and now* to seek out *elsewhere and elsewhen*. Coaxed by the stench of sweat and the adrenaline draining from his muscles and the heady exhaustion quivering through his limbs, his mind crawled through trenches and sprinted down snow-covered hills; it fell to its knees beside a boulder just large enough to shield a bleeding body in its shadow, drawn there by heat and terror, damp and dread, unable to separate blood from bathwater.

She was dying, and he had no one he could beg to save her this time. No miracle to plead for.

No one to pray to.

"Elias?" Thudding knuckles on solid wood. "Did you hear me? Food's here."

"Elias. Don't go."

Just like then, just like Ursa, her voice sputtered and died in her throat, a death rattle that shook him to his soul.

He couldn't leave. He couldn't stay. He'd watch her die if he didn't move now. She'd die all alone if he left.

No matter which way he turned, Death kept vigil over her. Ever present, ever patient, knowing its vengeance was close at hand.

The moment he let his guard down, it would have her.

He could not let it have her.

Warmth and snow and salt.

Iron and death and sundered steel.

Her beautiful armor he'd made by hand, shredded by an Atlas blade; her beautiful face streaked with scarlet, traced in starlight.

"I'm sorry…my armor. You worked so hard on it."

The curtain pulled away, but he hardly noticed. Hardly cared.

His battlemate bathed in her own lifeblood. What worse could this intruder do?

"Don't go."

Cinnamon pastries and rose-and-peach shampoo and new yarn.

Death.

Home.

Soren.

Her hand announced her presence first, a slow, soothing rub between his shoulder blades. Then her forehead, cool against his shoulder. Then her lips, chapped but gentle on a cauterized scab, some trite little scratch his magic had burned into something worse.

Not all miracles were kind.

"Where are we?" she murmured.

All wrong. This was all wrong. She lay before him, flayed from sternum to stomach, not enough skin left to hide her insides from view; she leaned against him, hand on his back, cheek against his shoulder. He could feel her holding him, real as his own racing heart; he could see her dying breaths plain as day.

Terror noosed his neck; his fingers noosed her wrist. "Don't go."

"Not going anywhere, jackass." Her chin dug into the knob of bone where his clavicle met his shoulder. Her breath warmed his neck. Her blood warmed his hands. "I'm staying right here. Now tell me where *here* is."

"Ursa." It made sense she couldn't remember—a wound like this, a death like this, it would kill slowly enough for shock to shroud everything in merciful mist. "I'm so sorry. I'm so sorry, I only looked away for a second."

To pray. But…why? Why had he bothered, when he knew no one would answer?

When that absence of answer was *his* doing?

Sour bile spun up his throat.

Soren's fingers seized his hair, tipping his head downward. "Aim for the drain."

He only had a moment to worry about how softly she was speaking to him before his stomach purged itself.

Nothing but swill—he hadn't eaten anything today, and barely anything at all since leaving Atlas shores. Only when Soren asked, and only *because* she asked.

Everything tasted like ash. Like dust. Like the chalky remains of a pyre.

Like death.

"It's all right." The circles between his shoulders resumed, her calloused palms as familiar to him as his own. He could have mapped each and every crease blindfolded. "It's the shock catching up. You're all right—we're both all right."

Blood coating his fingers, his prayer beads. Terror coating her eyes, her trembling smile, her bloodsoaked breath.

"You're not." So much blood. His hands couldn't hold it all. Couldn't hold her together. "F-find…you need to find—"

"My anchor?" Her hand slid up to cup the back of his neck—a cool, firm pressure that drained some of the dizziness out of his head. "Got him right here. Now find yours."

Find your anchor.

It had started as a joke, handed down by higher-ups with similar senses of humor to Soren's—using an Atlas implement against them. But the grounding technique had proven more effective than anticipated—in moments that brooked the gap between living and dying, between fighting and fading, thinking of everything you had to fight for…it took too much. Too much a dying soldier didn't have.

One person. One place. One memory.

"The Sanctum." Even with all that had gone so very wrong there, it'd take far worse than shock to steal that place away. "You're asking me to marry you. I can't say yes fast enough." His throat tightened. "You're so beautiful."

The rosy glow of a Lapisian lamp matched his heart inch for lovesick inch. That glimmer of pink erased the pallor and exhaustion on her face, igniting a spark in her driftwood-and-double-dare gaze. He'd waited so long, had lost hope and found it a hundred times, and now…now he couldn't bear to go one more gods-damned second without being wholly, entirely *hers*.

"Stay there." Another kiss, this time on his cheek. Her fingers twined in his hair at the same time her forehead met his temple; she didn't seem to mind the showerhead raining on both of them. "Stay here—stay with me."

"Elias. Don't go."

But the blood—she needed help—

"Hey—what'd I just say?" Two hands on his cheeks now, turning his head away from her feeble, failing breaths, her closing eyes—turning him toward her worried smile, her creased brow, her green—

Not green. Gold.

A foreign smile on his best friend's face. A foreign look of fright when he lunged for her throat.

That same look of fear in a new friend's eyes as the Goddess of Death lunged to take her life.

That same look of fear in the Goddess of Death's eyes when his blade sank into her heart.

A cry caught in his throat as he scrabbled back, slamming hard into the porcelain tile, slick with steam. *"No—"*

Soren cursed. The thing pretending to be Soren cursed. No, it was her, it had to be her—

She wove her fingers behind his head, getting between him and the tile. "Shh, shh! Elias, it's me. Our eyes, they changed in the palace, remember?"

Our eyes.

He scrubbed water and tears and steam out of his own, squinting until he found hers again.

Gold—but not fully. When she tipped her head from side to side, slices of shadow fell over her gaze; where the darkness lingered, the gold dimmed, sun swallowed by clouds. And under the blinding sheet of sun, the shade of green he'd long since memorized still waited beneath.

He still didn't know what that change meant for them. He didn't *want* to know.

"Still me," she whispered, pulling in the hand he'd thrown up between them and pressing it to her cheek. "Still me, see?"

His thumb tingled as he traced the constellation of familiar freckles over her cheekbone, and a shaky exhale wound out of his throat. *Soren.* His Soren.

This was not an unfamiliar dance; the part of his mind not fully adrift in memory knew that, too. Fugues like this, they happened to many soldiers; they'd all been trained in helping their battlemates through them, though there was no tried-and-true standard. Each soldier needed to be grounded in different ways; each one had a different path back to themselves, and their battlemates had to memorize the steps to walk them home.

Thanks in part to walking those paths together so many times, the two of them were fluent in the language of each other's bodies; that trembling stroke over her cheek told her what to do. Humming lowly—a Nyxian lullaby she'd often hummed to him on nights when he struggled to rest, one she'd learned by listening to his mother sing his youngest sister to sleep—she tenderly anchored his fingers into her wet curls, placing his hand at just the right angle that he could keep running his thumb in soothing, repetitive strokes over her cheekbone.

His Soren. His battlemate. His wife.

Not dead. Not dying. *Not going anywhere.*

He nuzzled his nose against her curls, cradling her chin, letting the drumbeat of her pulse set the pace for his own. "You're not hurt?"

"I'm not hurt," she promised. "Swear on your socks."

He scoffed. Laughed. "Swear on your own socks."

"There you are. Works every time." She kissed his forehead before pulling back; when she made eye contact with him again, his stomach settled at the glimmer of understanding waiting for him. No reproach; no fear. "You with me, jackass?"

"With you, smartass."

Slowly, the iron flood drained from his tongue and nose, replaced by the overwhelming aroma of rosemary-lemon soap spilling into the drain. Somewhere in the hazy moments between entering the shower and exiting reality, he must've dropped the bottle.

He shut his eyes, breathing in the citrus steam, resting his head against his battlemate's.

Once upon a time, he might have apologized for this; might have cringed over her seeing him so vulnerable, so lost. But between Soren's night terrors and her occasional loss of footing in reality, he had plenty of practice coaxing her back from distant, dark places. And she'd walked him back with terrible jokes and shoulder massages and murmured recitations from his holy book just as many times as he'd walked her back with soft reassurances and logic untangling her fears and fingers untangling her hair.

They were well beyond apologies or debts or shame. For this and every weakness they carried between them.

"I killed her." Only in the safety of his battlemate's shadow could he at last make the confession. Only with her holding him fast could he finally face what he'd done.

"Yes." A careful response—uncharacteristic of her. "How does that…feel?"

How *did* it feel?

"Wrong." Like every bone had been turned inside out, marrow scrubbing against flesh. Like the fire he carried inside had dwindled three sizes smaller. Like he needed Kallias to wake up and remind him just how slippery a slope shame could be. "But not…I don't know. I don't know."

Soren's lips left a fleeting impression on his cheekbone as she untangled herself from him. She twisted the knobs attached to the faucet, shutting off the water; when she reached to him again, he reached back without pause.

Wherever she led, he would follow.

She didn't go far—only to the ostentatious darkwood sink against the wall. Ostenatious not in design, but in decoration—the simple basin boasted a solid sheet of gold inlay, unetched, unadorned. The real thing.

Real gold. In a sink. In one of over a dozen guest suites.

He'd never understand royals and the joy they took in owning ridiculous objects of little use.

He stared at his reflection inside the gold as Soren set the plug, then filled the basin with water. Not steaming like the shower—when he tested a fingertip against the surface, he found it cool as a freshwater stream.

"Here." A cloak of black terrycloth tossed over his shoulders—a robe. He slipped his arms inside, tying it shut as Soren bustled out the door—when she came back, she tsked, shaking her head and holding up what she'd gone to retrieve: a small physician's kit. "Waist down only. I want to check those burns."

"They're fine."

"Strip down and shut up, jackass."

He did as his wife ordered.

For a while, the silence helped; the only sounds were the occasional muttered curse from Soren when she fumbled the bottle of burn ointment or her caught breath when she stumbled across a particularly grievous welt branded on his side, skin taut and red and hot as a stovetop just extinguished.

"What did—"

"Tempest broke some ribs," he said. "Think one broke the skin."

"Elias?"

"Yeah?" Then, before she could say it: "No, you can't kill a god to make us even."

"You don't know that's what I was going to—"

"The answer's no."

"*Jack*ass."

That set him just right enough to smile. "Smartass."

Another silence, this one stretched like a bandage readied to wrap around a limb. "So you…can you still—"

He picked up the discarded razor on the lip of the sink and sliced it over the back of his wrist.

They both watched, not breathing, as blood welled along the shallow slice…and kept coming. Seeping over his wrist. Dripping into the basin. Staining the water red as it swirled down the drain.

"Ah." His wife blew out her held breath. "Well…damn."

It was the least he deserved for what he'd done. Besides, if the gifts he bore now had been granted by Sancta…well, the god didn't strike him as one to make the same mistake a second time.

Deathless no longer. The fire remained, but it came with mortality returned.

He could accept that. Even if he no longer knew where he would go when he took his last breath. No longer knew who would greet him when he got there.

Soren's hands abruptly fell away from his back, replaced by her head snugging into the space between his shoulders. Her arms wrapped around his middle and squeezed.

"I'm so sorry," she whispered. "I know she was…everything, for a while. For pretty much always."

His throat closed up. He set his arms over hers, shutting his eyes.

As long as he stared into the sink, he could pretend the gold was a trick of the basin's lining. But if he looked anywhere else…

"I don't know who I am now." The part that scared him most, shook him most. The grief, the loss, he understood them enough to nearly get his hands around them, to carry them. But the *other* thing he couldn't excise from his chest, the *other* thing sticking out like a broken rib…

He didn't know what it made him.

He hadn't wanted his goddess dead.

From the time he'd been introduced to her faith as a boy, he had been taught of Mortem's mercy. Her gentleness. To save life, not take it, was to honor her. To kill was a choice that should only be undertaken in the direst of circumstances.

He'd believed with his entire heart—the heart devoted to her for well over a decade—that she would show mercy. That she would spare the life of her sister.

He'd been wrong.

He had put his faith in her, like he had since he was eight years old— and he had been *wrong*.

And if he hadn't acted as quickly as he had, Ani would have paid the price for his mistake.

He *hated* what he'd been forced to do. Hated how it had left him, his soul half-untethered, afloat in the empty place where faith once found a home in him.

But the unseemly thing stuck in his chest…it wasn't shame. Not when he sat down and looked at it closely. Not when he was honest.

Because he hadn't done anything wrong.

Conviction. It pierced him, pieced him back together, promised he had not sullied himself beyond saving.

He had done the right thing.

But gods, he still *hated* it.

Soren wrapped her hands around his wrists, stepping back to make room so she could turn him to face her. Her hands slid down to grip his, her thumbs rubbing over his knuckles.

"I know exactly who you are," she murmured. "Would it help if I reminded you?"

His throat ached; he had to swallow hard before he could whisper, "Please."

She opened her arms to him. "Come here."

He crumbled into her without a second thought.

"You are the only person I trust to fight and stand and sleep beside me." A light kiss against his hair. "You are loyal, and passionate, and *good*—annoyingly good. You make the rest of us look bad, you're so good. And you *believe* in things—in people, in miracles, in doing the right thing even when it's the last damned thing you want to do. I know you think that's thanks to her, but it's not—it's you. It's your faith that makes you who you are, not who you put it in. And that's still here. You're still you."

Elias shut his eyes, letting the tears fall. They burned gentle trails down his cheeks; Soren kissed them away, then tapped under his eye until he looked at her again.

"I know you, Elias Loch." Her stare held him captive, offering no alternative, allowing no argument. "And I know you *never* would have done what you did if you had any other choice."

"I'm…" He couldn't ask. Couldn't bear to hear the answer.

Soren frowned. "You're what?"

"Nothing. Never mind." It was the smallest part of all this—too small to make him feel so much.

"You know you can't lie to save your life. Why are you even trying?" She wiped another tear from his cheek. "Tell me."

"Do you…" His composure failed him; he had to breathe through a sob. "Do you think my mother will forgive me?"

Soren's eyes softened. "Oh, no. We're not going down that road."

"She loves Mortem more than I…more than I did. More than my father did."

"She loves you more."

He wasn't so sure. But no matter how closely he searched for it, he found no doubt in his wife's steady stare.

So he sank back into her arms, letting her confidence steady him in turn—and just for tonight, just for now, he set everything aside but her.

What came next…that decision would keep until morning.

CHAPTER 62

SOREN

"**K**ing Denali is *dead?*"

In the stunned silence, she and Everin locked gazes, his teeth bared in a very tactful wince.

They probably should have come up with a more strategic way to bring that up.

To be fair, when she'd been dragged away from the first quiet dinner she and Elias had been able to have in gods-knew how long by the summons to a meeting in her aunt's office, she'd expected the line of questioning to follow the fact that she'd just turned the gods back into mortals—and her husband had, you know, *killed a goddess*.

The events of their Tallisian trip felt like they'd happened *decades* ago. To be perfectly honest, she'd forgotten she hadn't had time to unpack the whole thing before they took off for Atlas.

So when Genevieve had requested they start at the beginning and work their way forward, she and Everin had immediately—and overconfidently—begun taking turns sharing and squabbling over the details of their Sanctum Infidelium ordeal, all the way up to the point when Soren breezily sailed over the bit where she murdered the King of Tallis in his own throne room.

Until Everin kicked her ankle under the table, she didn't realize the other royal-blooded bodies in the room had gone still. The kind of still that told her she'd just gotten herself in trouble.

"In my defense," she said, slowly raising her hands, "he *was* a complete ass."

A laughing snort—from Occassio, of all people. She glared at the goddess, who replied with a subtle shrug. A silent *My bad.*

"Please," said Astrid, her head in her hands and a faint note of nausea in her voice—the first time Soren had actually managed to break her diplomatic poker face, a feat Finn was about to owe her a handful of gold for. "Please tell me you did not assassinate a monarch for being—forgive me if I quote this verbatim, Queen Genevieve, for the integrity of the record—*a complete ass.*"

"Of course not," she muttered.

"Good."

"He also refused to acknowledge my rank and title."

Astrid set her head fully on the table. Sage reached over and massaged her neck, peering over his spectacles at Soren. "For the sake of my wife's health, would you mind terribly skipping to the part where you had a perfectly valid and defensible reason for putting a foreign king to the sword after announcing your political tethers to Nyx, Atlas, *and* Arborius? In front of his entire court, no less?"

"She acted in self-defense, nothing more," Everin stepped in again, finally—the smug bastard had just wanted to see her sweat, she could absolutely tell—warning off arguments with a stare of rime-coated stone. "My father has grown increasingly volatile and unreliable in matters of diplomacy as of late, and regrettably, he suffered a break in sanity when faced with the prospect of an oncoming war with the God of Chaos. In his delirium, he threatened Princess Soren; she acted accordingly. And as Tallis's Heir-Apparent, I can assure you we will leverage no retribution against any of her allies or allegiances for her actions. The trespass was ours, and I cannot apologize enough."

Gods, he was good. More proof she would never make it as Atlas's Heir. She couldn't have made her story sound that rational if they'd given her three days to write it down.

Though now that she thought about it…they *had* been given a couple days of downtime. And Everin happened to have a walking lecture on inter-kingdom law nearby just about always, so…odds were he'd cheated. Copied off of a certain hyper historian's paper.

She slumped in her seat, scowling. *Bastard.*

Elias stuck his fingers between the gaps in the back of the chair, tapping on her curved spine. She bent even further. He tapped more insistently, and she reached back to smack him off, pinching his hand until he hissed under his breath.

Everin shot them both a look that screamed *behave,* which felt doubly hypocritical.

"Heir-Apparent?" Astrid raised her head again. "What of Raini?"

"My sister is away from the capital at the moment," Everin said, more tactful than she'd ever heard him, "on her yearly sabbatical to visit our mother's relatives. She is not expected to return for another month or two. In the meantime, my best advisors are searching through my father's effects for his statement of succession. I will be returning to Tallis once matters are settled here to ensure all is properly documented myself."

Translation: *I'll be returning to Tallis to make sure that statement says exactly what I need it to say, and any document suggesting otherwise will be unceremoniously fed to the nearest goat.*

In theory, she had very strong opinions about assassination and manipulated inheritance and thrones being taken from those they rightfully belonged to. But in this highly specific case, the ends did justify the means.

Everin and his men had shed blood and tears on her behalf. Raini's representatives had harmed her in ways she still couldn't bring herself to talk about. Ways that could have been unfathomably worse, she knew, but still set a weight on her heart she hadn't learned how to carry comfortably. Wasn't sure she ever would.

While traveling back from Tallis, she had asked Everin why he'd never killed his father himself. But as usual, Medwenna had been the one to eagerly offer up the answer: Everin's father had refused to officially file his statement of succession into record, allowing him to redraft the document whenever he saw fit…which proved to be whenever one of the twins defied or demeaned him. Without that document, the right of inheritance could not be confirmed.

In that scenario, a quorum of Tallisian lords would have been gathered to vote on the issue of successorship…and if the King's death came by Everin's hand, that vote likely wouldn't have fallen in his favor.

"Which is exactly what Raini's hoping for," Everin had drawled, rolling his eyes like his sister's very existence gave him a raging headache. *"So in deference to cooler heads and wiser counsel,"* there, his eyes had flickered to Medwenna, *"I have stayed my hand."*

Translation: he would have done it a hundred times over, throne be damned, had Medwenna asked or allowed it.

Soren could respect that.

So when the assembly around them exchanged glances with those they trusted at this table, ranging from understanding to uncomfortable to outright unconvinced, Soren glued her spine to the back of her chair, forcing herself into a posture so perfect it made her neck ache. "What's done is done. We don't have the time or the breath to waste on a dead king—unless you'd like to dig him up and ask him to sit in with us. But if that's the case, I'll have to insist we all arm ourselves with clothespins for our noses." And, because she was just petty and reckless and downright stupid enough, she let her gaze slide to Tempest. "It already smells like rotting fish in here. I'd rather not add more corpses to the mix."

Everin coughed. She could have sworn another snort came from Occassio's general direction.

Elias just cleared his throat. Loudly.

Fine—she'd already made her point, anyway. She looked away before Tempest's glare could freeze her into a block of self-satisfied ice. "Let's return to the discussion at hand. Arborius and Tallis have made their numbers known—I'd like to hear what Atlas and Nyx are able to offer. And more importantly, I'd like to know what help we can expect from the former deities in the room."

"With what authority do you demand such answers from us?" Tempest tipped his chin back, studying her down the bridge of his too-perfect nose. "You are neither goddess, nor queen—you claim to be Heir of Atlas and Princess of Nyx, yet you ask after their forces as if you are a stranger to both. You spin lies on the wind of justified killings and successions shaped by your hand, then demand solemn promises from those who outrank you in every way. By what right do you claim a place at this table equal to ours? Blood or rank? Title or glory?"

She could have painted over her bored stare with something more diplomatic, but quite frankly, between stealing her brother's body and giving Raquel those weird little looks, Tempest didn't deserve that kind of effort. "With what authority do you call mine into question? From where I'm sitting, you're neither god nor king—and you're certainly not in line to be Heir of anything."

"Good use of *nor*," Elias muttered beside her. Everin whispered something she couldn't make out, followed by the *thwack* of a tome against his arm.

"Thanks, lover." But she didn't tear her gaze off of Tempest.

His nostrils flared. But where she'd expected anger, she found only…assessment. "I would know who I will be fighting this battle beside, if I do choose to fight it. You and yours murdered my sister—the only one who fought for *your* best interest her entire tenure as a goddess. Answers are the least I can ask for. Humor me."

It wasn't his scrutiny that drizzled sweat down the column of her sticky spine, nor the handful of power brokers awaiting the proof that she was owed a place at this table—*another good use of nor*, she congratulated herself—but the knowledge that her parents sat only two chairs down from her.

Whatever answers she gave here, whatever claims she made…they could not be taken back.

But she had made her choice.

"I am Heir of Atlas by blood," she said. "And Princess of Nyx by…circumstance. But I am a *general* of Nyx by my own choice." She thumped her fist twice on the quintet of stars stitched on the shoulder of her uniform. "Any of the three would give me the right to be here. I have my preferences, but please…do feel free to choose the one that suits you best." She leaned back in her seat, tipping the front two legs off the floor—her stomach swooped as the chair wobbled, but Elias's hand snapped over and caught it by the seat before it could topple over.

Not the first time he'd saved her from looking the fool, and definitely not the last.

"Heir, princess, general." Tempest tipped his head to one side. "Yet no say in what your kingdoms bring to the—"

"I've been a little busy trying not to die while pursuing alliances elsewhere," she snapped, patience finally abandoning her. "And speaking of your sister, if you want to keep arguing this point, I'll remind you that my battlemate has already demonstrated *exactly* which matter demanded our full attention for the past several weeks."

Tempest's nostrils flared.

"Condolences for your loss," she added. For poor Astrid's sake.

"You have no right to question her place here." At first, Soren thought Occassio had spoken up in her defense—which somehow felt less impossible than realizing it was *Ani* who had snapped at her brother in such icy tones, her rich brown hair swaying down her back as she stood, palms splayed flat on the table as she leaned in her brother's direction. "She has done more to set Tenebrae back in his plans this year than any of us have in *centuries*. Where have you been? What have you done?" Her brown eyes leapt from Tempest to Occassio. "What have *any* of us done to fix what we broke in the first place?"

"I just called down a damned hurricane to drive him out of Atlas," Tempest muttered. "Not to mention summoning a slapdash army of my own."

"And in the millennium before that, Peter?" Occassio asked, saccharine sweet.

"Watch it." Tempest glared at his sassier sister, then turned back to Ani. "I didn't ask to be made a god. I had no part in it. When you all tried to reach for what we couldn't have, I lost *everything*. What have you done to fix what you broke in *me*? What have you lost that was not given in service to your own cause?"

Habit said to step in, but instinct stayed Soren's hand. There were some battles people had to fight themselves.

A similar tension rippled through Wolf's shoulders. But he, too, held himself in check. Ani's throat bobbed. "Look into my eyes and tell me again how little I have lost."

A tide of cold rolled over the room, static popping under her sleeves. Elias's expression slid into a lethal focus that made the hairs on her nape bristle, his hand sliding just far enough to the left to brace in front of her. Everin's smile vanished; he took in Elias's posture with a single blink before sliding one elbow onto the table, leaning his chin casually on his palm as he angled himself ever-so-slightly in front of Medwenna.

Medwenna, of course, remained blissfully engrossed in her work, eyes glued to her journal as she scribbled notes at a frightening pace. Soren had barely seen her blink since the gods had joined their little company.

"I didn't do a damned thing," Occassio said, her frankness catching Soren's suspicion off guard. "And neither did you, Peter, so for Sancta's sake, leave her alone and let her do her job."

This time, Soren and Ani were the ones trading looks. But Ani only shrugged, looking as surprised as Soren felt.

"I appreciate circumstances are tense," Astrid interrupted finally—Soren could've kissed her, both their husbands aside, for that fearless reclamation of the room. And for saving her from having to *thank* Occassio for anything. "But personal matters are best left at the door when it comes to war rooms. I would appreciate if you all kept your tempers and kept your focus on the matter at hand: tallying our numbers and plotting our next steps. You can sort out who owes a sorry or two later."

Soren had to give it to the diplomat: the woman had guts. For someone with no experience mediating a gathering of gods, she showed no fear; she stared them down until they averted their gazes, Ani blushing, Occassio sheathing a smirk, Tempest scowling so hard she had the delightful thought that it might just get stuck like that. Would serve him right.

"Nyx's army is scattered throughout many of our larger cities." Yvonne was the first to speak up, frowning at the map of the continent spread out before them, nearly spanning the entire table. Genevieve's desk had been shoved against the back wall to make room for the twelve-foot table Wolf and Sage and a handful of rangers had hauled inside, and even then they couldn't all fit around it; Sage himself stood behind Astrid's chair, cross-armed and calm, his cool demeanor belying the shrewd warning in his hawkish eyes as he prodded each face in the room for their intentions. His hands rested on his wife's shoulders, not his weapons, but there was no mistaking the message: *Come for her, you go through me.*

Then again, maybe he *did* have his hands on his best weapon.

"It will take time to summon them all," Yvonne continued, glancing over her shoulder at Patch; Soren wasn't sure why *she* was the one getting interrogated about her rank when the pirate had waltzed right in behind Yvonne unchallenged, but she'd pout about it later. Preferably over a steaming cup of hard cider or three. "But if Captain Douglas is amenable—"

"*Douglas?*" Soren burst out before she could think better of it.

Patch speared her with a look venomous enough to flip a lionfish belly-up. "Mind your business, Princess."

"Mind your *tone*, pirate." Everin's lazy drawl stood in contrast to the nasty edge wielded in his glare.

"Oi, you're not king yet, mountain man." Patch thumbed his nose Everin's way. "And even if you were, you're fifty fathoms far from being mine. So, with all due respect, shove—"

Yvonne whipped around so fast Soren almost expected to hear her spine crack. "*James.*"

Patch's mouth shut with an audible *clack*.

Yes, hard cider was absolutely in order—and she'd pour as much of it down Yvonne's throat as she had to in order to get the whole of her story post-rotting-haste.

"As I was saying," Yvonne said, cold as the Nyxian lakes when the deep freeze fell over the kingdom, "if Captain Douglas is amenable, he and his crew can cover a greater distance in less time than any ground patrol could—if we send a handful of battle-ready couriers along, the *Starsinger* can carry them to every town along the Vela River. It is too small a vessel to carry any significant number of soldiers, but it's one of the quickest. We'll save…" A pause. A softer, less certain glance over her shoulder.

"At least a month," Patch finished for her, rearranging himself into something close to proper posture. She almost startled a second time when she finally took in the jacket buttoned snugly over his chest: starchy Atlas-blue cloth. Golden buttons tarnished by salt and sea air. A wave with two crests stitched into the shoulder.

Oh. *Captain* Douglas.

"That's an Atlas navy coat," she muttered in Elias's ear, turning her head to shield her lips from anyone perceptive enough to read them.

"What poor fool do you think he stole it from?"

"I don't think he did. Look at the tailoring." The fit was too perfect, the measurements too exact. "A crew of deserters, remember?"

Elias blinked. "Pits."

"You're telling me." Atlas navy were not chosen for their posts lightly. Deserters were nearly unheard of.

"What are we whispering about?" Everin leaned around Elias, stretching his arm across Elias's chair as he bent his head in her direction. "I hate when you two gossip without me."

"We were just talking about how terrible your uniform smells." Soren pinched her nose, wincing at the gray dress uniform that still wore its wrinkles from being stashed in one of Everin's bags. "Did you wash it in stinkbush sap?"

"That's not a real thing."

"It is," Elias said. "Sage warned us about it when we got here."

"You're both hilarious. Remind me why we're even here?"

"We had the misfortune of being born royal."

Everin tapped the back of Elias's neck. "And why's he here?"

"He has the misfortune of being married to me."

"Care to share with the class, you two?" Sage called across the table; she and Everin both retreated to their seats after trading eye rolls behind the shield of Elias's shoulders.

"Tallis has five battalions on route," Everin said without missing a beat, "and Arborius has committed three, with the expectation my people will take part in training them. Assuming the worst, Your Majesty, how many can we expect from Nyx?"

Yvonne folded her hands on the table, thumbing Ravenna's signet ring. "Two at worst. Five or six at best. Tenebrae's progress in Nyx has been halted thanks to the efforts of Captain Douglas's crew and myself, but we suffered heavy casualties in Andromeda proper, and I cannot be certain how many we've lost elsewhere."

Everin's gaze swung to her parents. "And Atlas?"

"Two companies are already here," Tempest answered out of turn. "As for the rest…Queen Adriata?"

"I have yet to properly assess those numbers," Adriata said, voice flatter than Artem's desert plains. She fussed with the pen beside her pile of papers, tapping an erratic rhythm, gaze straying to the door more than once. She'd pointedly avoided looking Yvonne's way thus far, but that was a problem for a more private room. "Other matters demanded my immediate attention. I could make an educated guess, but our efforts may be better served by certainty." Distraction turned dangerous, gaze sharpening to spear Tempest through. "Two of my children remain in poor health. They are my priority until further notice."

"I can speak with Finn—Prince Finnick and Officer Angelov." The lump in her throat made it difficult to get the offer out. "They'll have a better idea of what we're dealing with."

Astrid nodded approvingly her way, but added, "You are also recovering from your recent trials, Princess. I'm happy to speak with them as I can. Focus on seeing to yourself and your family. I'll reach out when I'm in need of you."

"Thank you." Gratitude weighed her down in ways she wasn't used to. Exhaustion going by some other name.

When she dared a glance at each of the Medeis siblings again, she found Tempest and Occassio watching each other from the corners of their eyes, their frowns uncannily similar. Ani's attention darted in uncertain spurts between each of them like she couldn't decide whose side she was on…if either of them. Soren couldn't see her and Wolf's hands from this angle, but judging by the brush of their shoulders, they were holding hands beneath the table.

"We are all weary in our own ways," Genevieve said at last, standing to her feet; the rest of the attendees followed suit, even the pantheon. Perhaps the former deities were just as eager as she was for a good night's sleep and food that hadn't been trawled out of a ship's galley. "Queen Yvonne and Captain Douglas, I trust you'll send word when you've made your arrangements—Arborius would be happy to lend our messenger birds to your efforts if needed. Addie—"

Adriata's glower shifted to her sister. The table creaked; Ramses and Cypress, both silent spectators seated between their wives, exchanged discomfited looks.

"Queen Adriata," Genevieve corrected softly, "you are right—you should be with your children. Astrid will report to you once she's met with Prince Finnick and Officer…Angelov, you said?" she checked, and Soren nodded once. "As for the rest of you…send your missives. See to your people. And let us all hope this defeat sets our enemy back far enough to buy us the time we need. We'll convene again in a few days."

A few days' respite from politics seemed nearly too good to be true. But she prayed with all her might to a better god that it would hold.

"We're heading to Kess once we track down some food," Everin muttered to her once they reached the safety of the hall, he and Medwenna hot on their heels as she and Elias bolted out the door. "You two should head that way once you're done with your family."

"How is he?" Elias's hand tightened against her hip.

"Bad," Everin said bluntly. "But I'd like to see you do any better after losing half your arm."

"They were able to wake him up this morning," Medwenna offered more helpfully. "They were working to get his pain under control when we left."

A necessity Everin hadn't liked. She could read the sullen guilt in his downcast gaze better than any book.

"We'll come by in an hour or so." As much as she wanted to go now and see Kessen for herself, if she didn't check on her brothers first, she'd worry herself sick the whole time she was away. And the last thing Kessen needed was a nauseous princess losing her lunch at his bedside. "Tell him he'd better arm himself before I get there so I can fight him for scaring me."

"Soren," groaned Elias, "that's *awful.*"

"What is?"

"*Arm* himself," Everin chortled, pinching the bridge of his nose. "That's a good one."

She cursed herself. "Oh, depths, that's not what I—"

"Relax, Princess. It's Kess, he'd laugh too." Everin clapped his hand over her shoulder and shook her. "Go see if your brother's back from wherever that asshole was keeping him. We'll be around."

Her heart slowed just enough to allow her a deeper breath. "Thanks."

"Yeah, yeah." Everin ruffled her hair, then jogged away from them, casting his arm around Medwenna's shoulders and steering the still-scribbling scholar in the opposite direction she'd been walking. "Wrong way, Winnie."

"Mmhm," Medwenna mumbled, following his lead without looking up.

Elias toyed with one of her curls, frowning uneasily over his shoulder at the open office door. "That went about as well as I thought it would."

"At least Tempest didn't snow us in." Soren reached up to play with the hair at his nape. "C'mon, lover. We've got a prince to peek in on."

CHAPTER 63

FINN

He had never been so afraid in his entire gods-damned life.

He'd been dithering outside his aunt's office while the royals and the gods—former gods—debated with each other for over an hour now, wearing the shadows like a security blanket pulled over his head. Darkwood was the bane of his existence—it made any room nearly eavesdropper-proof, which made life very difficult for a prince whose primary source of entertainment was to drop from a few eaves here and there.

Honestly, it was a terrible term. *Eavesdrop.* Any spy worth their sea salt wouldn't be dropping from any eaves; they'd be clinging to them for dear life and jotting mental notes on any spare bit of brain matter. Unless it was meant to suggest that they dropped from the eaves *after* the spying was done, but by then the referred-to act was already *over*, so why not call it—

He caught his own thoughts by the collar before they could tumble further down the crab hole. His terror was making him loopy.

The terror *itself* was loopy. He'd spent his past few weeks waging shadow wars against divine forces. He'd traveled through time. He'd turned time backwards. He'd made himself a god with a fib and a fiddle, and *this* was going to give him a panic attack?

The door opened, and all thoughts of eaves and terrible spies and terrible words fled for their useless, cowering lives as the gathered gods and royals left the room one by one.

Soren and Elias fled first—nobody surprised about that—followed swiftly by Everin Arden and the spectacled woman who couldn't seem to decide if she belonged to the Arborian or Tallisian contingents here. Anima bolted next, Wolf on her heels, his hand pressed to her back with that *I'm-rushing-you-but-trying-to-make-it-feel-romantic* thing some people did when they were trying to balance their partner's feelings with the need for a swift getaway. Tempest left alone, silent but stewing with so many unsaid thoughts he could *feel* the bubble of tension swelling around him, then—

He shot one hand out and swept Cassi into the shadows, clasping them around her neck like a cloak, tugging a hood of darkness over her lackluster hair. "Hey."

"*Hey?*" She slapped him on the shoulder. "You're lucky I see the future, or you'd be wearing a new necklace right about now."

"Let me guess—a dagger?"

She tapped the loop of shimmering wire twined around her throat like a coiled serpent. "Garrote."

"Nice." He paused. "Wait. You're wearing a garrote around your neck?"

"That's what I was implying, yes."

"But wouldn't that make it easy for someone to just—"

"Don't try to distract me." She dusted his hands off of her, rolling her eyes; with both of them shrouded in dusk, he couldn't tell if she was teasing him or actually didn't think it was all that dense to wear a *strangulation weapon* around her *throat*. "Why are we lurking?"

Fear wrapped its hands around his throat. Maybe it was searching for a garrote.

"Not here," he said.

"Everyone's gone, and no one can—"

"Just—not here, all right?" He tugged her along by her wrist. "Come with me."

Cassi groaned, but let him pull her along. No one spared them a second look as they passed. "I thought we were done with secrets."

"Not a secret. Just asking you to wait."

She gave a grumpy hum. "I don't like waiting."

Big shocker, the Goddess of Time not caring to follow its rules.

Luckily, she didn't have to stoop to a mortal's level for long; his room wasn't far from his aunt's office, as the royal wing of the tree-palace was arranged much like home. Perks of his aunt being Atlas-born.

While they walked, he said, "How did that all go?"

"As expected." She waved dismissively. "Lots of staring. Lots of awkward silence. Astrid is just as sharp as you said."

"I told you you'd like her." He put his hands in his pockets. "Sorry I didn't sit in with you."

"You needed to be with your brother." She glanced at him. "Is he...?"

"No." So far, Kallias hadn't even had the decency to blink. "Did you and Peter get into it?"

"Does a fiddle have four strings?"

He paused. "Well, sometimes. Some have five. Others can—"

"*Yes*, we got into it," she groaned. "Because he's being a self-righteous ass, and he deserves to hear it from someone."

"Thought he was your favorite."

"He didn't have very stiff competition." She looked away. "Even less now."

He didn't know what to say to that. "Sorry."

"You're not. And neither am I." She shrugged with a flippant smile. "You ask me, my sister burned at the stake a thousand years ago."

No hesitation. No hidden tears. But no matter how closely he searched, he couldn't find a dimple.

Still. If she wanted it dropped, it could stay on the floor until she felt like picking it up. Not his place to nag.

When they finally stopped at his door, the nerves came surging back. But he turned to face her anyway. "I...I need to ask you something."

"The worst way to begin a conversation," she sighed. "It wastes both of our time, it's unnecessarily vague, it creates suspense where there's no need—"

He framed her cheeks with his hands, resisting the urge to rumple her curls until she begged for mercy. "Will you stop critiquing my conversational skills for *ten seconds?*"

She scrunched up her face, lips moving slowly; after a moment, he realized she was counting.

"You're *so* annoying," he groaned.

"Oh? Then I suppose, if you're so annoyed, I ought to take my leave." She broke his hold and spun like they'd choreographed it, sticking her hand straight over her head and waving back at him as she began to sashay off. "So much for that thing you needed to—"

"Cassi."

She twirled back, too graceful for words. *Mean.* "Yes?"

"I…" Oh, gods, he couldn't breathe. He'd dropped the breath he'd been holding, and now he couldn't seem to stuff it back in his lungs no matter how hard he shoved, and—and—

"I want you to stay," he blurted. "Uh, here. Tonight. All night."

Her eyebrows catapulted straight into her hairline.

Finn clung to the lining of his pockets to keep himself from outright palming his face. *Stupid, stupid, stupid.*

"I mean, not *all* night," he laughed nervously. "Half of it's gone already, anyway. And only if you want—uh, want to. Or don't mind, at least. It's, it's not for—it's not because—you can still stay with Astrid if you—"

"Hey, Finn?" She patted his cheek. That didn't help. "You're not breathing."

Ridiculous. He'd shared a room with her for weeks in Atlas, and she'd been his *enemy* for most of that. How could this be worse?

"I know," he moaned. "Gods, this is embarrassing."

She giggled, the shadows sinking into one of her dimples. "Deep breaths. Try again. You want me to stay…here? In your room?" Her gaze flickered to the bed. "You want me to *sleep* here?"

"Yes."

"With you?"

"Well—not exactly. Well, maybe. Well, not like—"

"*Finn.* Breathe?"

He sucked in another mouthful of air, equal parts grateful and irritated for the reminder. "I want you to sleep in here, yes. But it doesn't have to be with me."

Her dimple stuck, but her smile phased into a frown. "I don't follow."

Yeah, he couldn't blame her, considering he wasn't making any godsdamned sense.

He didn't know how to explain that he had never slept *with* anyone before. Not in any interpretation of the phrase.

He'd never been the kind of kid who crawled into his parents' bed after nightmares; the closest he'd ever come were the nights and Soren had spent on Kallias's floor, but they'd always dragged in their own blankets or sleepsacks. He'd always been too particular about his sleeping space to share; he needed the right arrangement of pillows, sheets sewn from the right kind of fabric, the weighted quilt his aunt had made for him, all the little and larger comforts of his routine. Anything less or more would send sleep running for its life.

But for some reason, the idea of her sleeping somewhere alone made his heart race. Not in a good way, if heart palpitations could ever be considered *good*. His family meant well, and he couldn't begrudge them their skepticism on his behalf, but…he didn't know what they'd do if they realized she was alone.

He didn't trust them with her. And gods, how ironic was *that*?

"You snore," he said instead of explaining any of that. "Got used to it, I guess. Too quiet without it."

Her mouth popped open in a perfect O. "I do not *snore*."

"You do."

"I do not!"

"I suppose you could have been sawing down trees in your sleep…"

"Why do you really want me to stay?" When he didn't answer immediately, she pushed, "*Do* you really want me to—"

"Yes." He laced his fingers behind his neck, studying the sky for gaps— it had to be falling, after all, for him to be inviting a girl back to his room. "I want you to stay."

She didn't ask him to look at her, which was good—judging by the itchy flush spreading through his face, he was either allergic to or thoroughly humiliated by this conversation, and either way, he didn't want to look her in the eye while he made a fool of himself in front of her.

Not the first time, not the last. But perhaps the most honest.

"I can sleep on the floor," she offered.

Tempting. But just like the first time he'd let her sleep in his space—when he'd made his first kill on behalf of her figment, when she'd stayed to clean the blood off his hands—the manners his mother had drilled into his head since boyhood wouldn't allow it.

And even if his manners might have, he knew exactly *why* she could offer such a thing with no pinch of martyrdom in her voice. Knew this hearth-warmed, rug-cushioned floor wouldn't bruise or bite like the bottom of a birdcage.

Not tempting at all. Actually, the idea made him queasy.

"There's a windowseat—I'll take that. You can have the bed." He'd spent plenty of lazy afternoons dozing in his favorite reading spot back home; he'd manage one night here.

Her thumb settled in the divot driven into his chin. "Tell me why you want me to stay."

He still couldn't look at her. Every time he tried, his gaze bounced off her like a ball tossed against the wall.

"Just want to keep you where I can see you," he said, with just enough playful suspicion poured over it to make it sound like a jab. Or a joke, depending which way her ear bent.

Not a lie. Just…a white lie, of a sort. More like a gray truth.

"Only fools sleep soundly beside people they don't trust."

Damn it. "Why do you need to know?"

"I don't." Indifferent, almost. But the curiosity swirled into her voice sweetened it somehow. Like caramel syrup stirred into coffee.

He'd always had an awful sweet tooth. Couldn't resist the stuff. This was no different.

Now he had to force himself *not* to look at her. To let that craving lure him off the edge yet again.

He shut his eyes like it might save him when he let his head fall, burying his face in her curls, breathing in lilac and sugar. A trace of ichor and madness underneath.

Sugar and poison. The two always came in tandem with her.

"I know we have…a lot to sort out between us, you and me. But my family and friends," he said—what a marvel, that word, *friends*—"are *very* convinced you've melted my brain into lovesick mush, and I'm a little worried they're out there plotting how to rescue me from you. *Your* family is still acting like you're in Tenebrae's pocket. And while I think it would be quite the entertaining exercise to watch you foil them all…the odds might be bent out of your favor this time around."

"Ah." Understanding rounded out the word. "Mortality."

He nicked a curl from beside her ear, teasing it between his fingers like a lucky coin before tucking it away. "That's the one."

Something flitted through his head, tickling his memory like a butterfly wing brushing his nose.

Untied shoes. Unshed tears. Unsaid secrets.

You were the only game I ever wanted to lose.

He swung for the memory like he might catch it in a net; but the moment he tried, it fluttered fully out of reach, leaving behind nothing but the lingering dread he sometimes got stuck with in the middle of the night. The sort where he woke up gasping, knowing he'd had a nightmare but unable to remember what had scared him about it.

For all his family feared, it was *her* whose voice lilted with lovesick laughter, not quite singing when she cooed, "You're *worried* about me."

He groaned into her hair. "Don't do that."

"You *are!*" She drove tickling fingers into his abdomen; he swore, flailing back like she'd tried to drive a knife into his heart. "You're worried about me!"

"I'm not proud of it!" he moaned, batting her hands away as she tried to poke at his ribs. "I just—it's only—*will you stop it?*"

He caught her by both hands—she beamed up at him, still laughing, smiling so hard it showed off both sets of dimples. The gap between her teeth. The crinkles carved in the bridge of her freckled nose.

She blinked, crinkles migrating between her brows as she stared up at him. "Why are you looking at me like that?"

Depths. He needed new masks…all his old ones had cracked and warped. They weren't half good enough to fool her.

To hide how that smile had softened every sharp edge carved into him by his own hand…edges he'd cut himself and others on countless times over the years. Edges that kept him safe, kept him sane.

"I thought I'd never see you smile like that again," he confessed.

He didn't know which damned him worse: that he'd told her, or that he'd thought it at all. That it had mattered. That it *still* mattered.

Her gaze softened, too. "Oh."

"Yeah, I know." He dragged his palms down his face, then stuffed them in his pockets. "I'm not letting anyone hurt you anymore, all right? I did enough damage."

And I couldn't think straight the whole time you were out of my sight.

"So did I." Guilt occluded gold as she fixed her gaze on his pocketed hands.

He took one out to tip her chin up. "I'll make you an offer."

"I'm listening."

"New game." He smirked when her eyes narrowed a smidge. "Clear the score. Reset the board. We'll come up with the rules together so we don't cheat."

She pursed her lips, skeptical. "We'll still cheat."

"Well, *yeah*, I know that, but we have to at least pretend, all right?"

"Does this game include those cute little squinties around your eyes?"

Oh, gods. "*Squinties?*"

She set her thumbs over the outer corners of his eyes. "These. The little wrinkles you get when you worry."

"They're not called *squinties*."

"Well, what are they called, then?"

He opened his mouth—then paused. "They're…well, they're…my father calls them *sunsquint*. But that's not—"

"Huh, weird! That sounds awfully close what I said."

"Are you going to keep me awake all night arguing about this? Because I might change my mind about—"

"You started it." She mimed something out above her head…like squishing two knots of curls. "With that *poufies* nonsense."

He blinked at her. She blinked back at him.

"Have you actually been waiting a millennium to get me back for that one?" he asked.

"A little over, actually." She started counting on her fingers with a frown, lips fighting a tattletale twitch. "Eleven hundred years, give or take fifty or so…"

He stole those crooked fingers and kissed each one, counting off the five kinds of foolish he got when he let her into his head…into his heart.

Into his room.

"As fun as this is," he murmured, "I'm going to crumble like a stale cookie if I'm not in bed in the next twenty minutes, so…"

"You'd better get going, then." She steered him toward the bathing room. "You need at least fifteen to do all your fancy face stuff."

He caught himself on the frame when she tried to shove him over the threshold, sticking his head back out. "Skin care is important."

"Go," she giggled through a groan, kicking one foot up and pushing him all the way in.

And with the door closed, he finally couldn't ignore the buzzing hive of nerves rattling around in his stomach.

Whatever poets and romantics felt when they swooned about butterflies in the stomach or flutters of the heart, it couldn't have been this. He wanted to unzip his skin and crawl into something more comfortable—something that didn't buzz until his bones hurt or itch in ways he couldn't scratch or bombard him with misinformation about what it needed to feel normal again.

But this was the skin he was stuck in. So instead, he settled for a shower, blueberry-scented soap, and pajamas that didn't stick to him like flypaper.

None of it quite right; none of it entirely helpful. But better than nothing.

It had been such an abominably long day.

An abominably long week. Month. Year. *Life.*

When he came back out, glasses hanging in the pocket of his sleepshirt while he dried his face with a towel, he found her with her curls wrapped in a silk scarf, lips pressed tightly together as she rubbed something into her skin…a serum of some kind, maybe. Her skin shone like a rain-soaked stone; when he tossed the towel in the wicker basket at the foot of the bed and sat beside her, he caught a subtle whiff of jasmine.

"This feels hypocritical," he said.

"It is." She cracked a yawn. "Feel better?"

"A little." He rubbed his eyes. "Sleep's what I really need."

"How long has it been?"

How long *had* it been?

"Sirena, I think," he mumbled. "Before you…before we…"

"I didn't sleep for a year when we first got our magic."

"Do you have to beat me at everything?"

"Isn't that why you like me?"

That word, *like*. It paraded between them, ostentatious as could be, a much more frightening word hiding under a threadbare set of stageclothes.

He didn't have it in him to unmask it—not when he so badly needed to unmask *himself.*

"I don't mind sharing," she added, a little too quickly to be casual. "The bed, I mean. I shared a floor for the better part of my mortal life, so…" A laugh, higher-pitched by an octave or three than usual. "Can't be too bad, right?"

Nervous. Perfectly mirrored, even in this.

And that made him brave enough to say, "Scoot over, Songbird. I need room to stretch."

Her laugh steadied, finding its pitch, and she did as he asked—after putting on quite the pout. "I should've shoved you off that roof."

"I should've tripped you on that tightrope."

She yawned, reaching over her head in a leisurely stretch. Not a lick of fear. "Which one?"

A puff of neroli and citrus shot up his nose when he plopped facefirst into his pillow. The scent loosened up his lungs, letting him draw a full breath. "I don't know. You pick."

He'd had a spare pillowcase packed for ages—along with any of his little and larger comforts that could fit in the bag of essentials he'd stowed on their getaway ship. Pillowcases. Shampoos and soaps. A few articles of clothing. His comb. A handful of favorite books.

Some would call it spoiled. Let them. He knew what he needed.

But then another head dropped onto the pillow beside his. Jasmine and starlight and a skosh of lilac.

He forgot how to breathe when he turned over and found Cassi's nose an inch from his…then remembered again when she scooched down with another yawn, making her own pillow out of his heart.

He couldn't see her face. But he could feel her silent, tremulous breath…could feel the loose fist she formed around a handful of his sleepshirt.

He covered her hand with his and squeezed. "I'm real, Cass."

She went stock-still. "How did you—"

"Doesn't matter." He shut his eyes before she could search them out. "I'm not going to disappear, all right? Get some sleep."

That worked about as well as he'd expected—cold swept through the gap she left behind when she sat up, poking his forehead until he opened his eyes again. "No. Tell me how you knew."

"Tomorrow." When she groaned, he added, "Tomorrow, I promise."

"You *break*—"

"Not anymore. Not to you." He drew her in to kiss her forehead. "I'll tell you everything tomorrow. Trust me."

Her brow scrunched up under his lips.

"All right," he chuckled. "You let me go to sleep now, and I'll tell you everything in the morning. Deal?"

Her breath was warm as it skated over his skin, but his neck didn't seem to know that—it broke out in goosebumps as she grumbled, "Deal."

Despite his confused skin throwing up strange signals—possibly white flags of surrender, utterly boggled by the sensation of another body being held against it—when he settled his head back on his own pile of pillows, adjusting until it finally sank into a comfortable position, a blanket of ease fell over him. Cotton-soft. Cool and calm as a tide pool.

Her presence didn't set off the itchy *awful* that wriggled under his skin when things weren't exactly the way he liked them, the inexplicable agony that made him long for escape from his own body.

In fact, he had a sneaking suspicion she might have just become one of those crucial comforts. The ones he couldn't sleep without.

"Lie to me," she murmured sleepily.

He should've known she wouldn't be content until she filched the last word from his pocket. Finn kissed the rhinestone sparkling at the arch of her brow. "I hate you."

She smiled. "I hate you back."

Look at that.

A smile of his own crept in uninvited.

No dimples.

CHAPTER 64

RAQUEL

It didn't matter.

It didn't matter that nature had brought her a peace offering: a fat-bellied host of thunderclouds darkening the horizon as fast as it had begun to brighten, storm swallowing the sun whole.

It didn't matter that the wind showered her in petrichoric kisses, pleading for her forgiveness in whispers that smelled like fresh water and sediment stirred up from the beds of nearby rivers and streams.

It didn't matter that Nature himself had not left his post outside the rosined wooden door she'd shut with the finality of a drawbridge yanked back by its chains; as if an uncrossable moat stretched between her and Tempest, not two inches of Arborian darkwood with no locking mechanism sealed inside its knob.

It didn't matter, any of it. Because Kallias had not woken up.

If she'd been in a more generous mood, she might have said exactly the opposite—that he *had* woken, and relatively quickly, after a couple days and nights of slumber in the Starsinger's familiar sickroom. But *waking* was not the same as *being awake,* and while his accomplishment of the former had given them all a surge of cruel hope…he had failed to do the latter.

Well, don't just sit there gawking, Prince Sage Olivander, Kallias's cousin, had urged her before he'd left the room, spectacles donned and clipboard in hand. Like a generous prophecy of what Finn *could* grow into, should he change roughly two-thirds of his personality and decide to try his hand at something as benevolent as healing. *Tell him off for letting a god into his head. Tell him Sage has one hearty I-told-you-so waiting when the walking martyr complex with a nasty case of people-pleaser-pox decides to rejoin the living. Read him your market list for all I care, but if you keep treating him like a corpse, he'll keep acting like one.*

It had been hours now, and she hadn't been able to spit one word out.

Maybe the spiteful side of her had not fully let him off the hook, after all. Because there was some satisfaction, small and sour and shameful as it might be, in holding her silence the way he held his; a promise that so long as he refused to let her hear his voice, he would not have the pleasure of hearing hers, either.

Or maybe it was just easier to pretend that he had only held his silence so long because she had not yet coaxed him to break it. That one word from her would call him back from the brink of death dealt by a divine hand.

He'd woken up before her this morning…had fallen asleep tonight before her, too. She'd dozed off in the chair beside his sickbed last night, gaze riveted on his face until her eyelids grew too heavy to hold; she'd woken to his vacant stare resting idly on her.

When she'd moved, he had not; even when she strafed a thumb over his beard, teasing the corner of his maddening mouth, he did not smile. Or turn his head. Or blink those pale green eyes, no blue, no gold, no godly influence to blame for this extended leave of absence.

She hadn't dared test a *good morning* on that dull, stony stare. Not when to do so would relieve her of the final weapon in her sparse supply.

This was all right, though…sitting beside him on the bed instead of the chair, a comfortable inch between them, a book in her lap and a mug of cold coffee on the nightstand despite the late hour.

When she'd asked for coffee poured over ice, Sage had looked at her like *she* was the strangest thing he'd seen over the past handful of weeks rather than…well, whatever Soren had said, something about a sickness and giant spiders and the island coming to life. But he'd fetched it for her regardless—and, after gaining her permission to take a sip, had declared it a revelation.

The coffee was passable. The book, well…she was halfway through and had very little idea what it was about. A romance of some kind; the forbidden sort centering on a prince and a palace baker. One of the Tallisian prince's people had ducked in just long enough to hand it off to her that morning, saying Soren had tasked him with delivering it. Something about knowing a thing or two about bedside vigils.

A kind gesture—doubly so considering that Soren was not a reader, and Raquel had done her best to keep her own habit hidden from the rest of the company. But there was only one prince she had on her mind just now.

"Book's not helping, huh?"

Raquel looked up from that very thing to find Soren hanging from the doorpost; out of the Atlas siblings, she certainly looked the best at the moment, all hale cheeks and bright eyes and the closest thing to a real smile Raquel had seen in months. But when she found Kallias, the sun set in her eyes. "Still nothing?"

Raquel shook her head. "Nothing."

She kept her head turned away from Kallias. Just so he wouldn't think she'd spoken to him.

"What a *jerk*." Soren rounded the bed, scooting in on Kallias's other side; she wasfar less delicate than Raquel, dragging her brother's limp arm aside and snugging up to him. She poked his cheek, scowl deepening. "I know you can hear me, Kal. You're really sticking snowballs in my sheets with this whole silent treatment bit. Elias is a gods-damned mess about you, and I'll give you one guess who's got to clean that one up."

Kallias didn't stir.

"Yeah, *me*. And I'm not so practiced at that, as you might have guessed, because anyone who's ever been within five miles of us can tell I'm the hot mess half of the pair. I couldn't even get him to come in and see you just now—he's probably out there crying his eyes out. And don't even get me started on the whole deal with Finn and *Cassi*." Soren dropped her head against Kallias's chest, rolling her eyes to glare toward his chin. "You *so* owe me when you snap out of it."

When. How could a word Raquel couldn't even *think* strut out of Soren's mouth so confidently?

"How's your Tallisian friend?" A change of subject would be necessary if Soren planned to stay for some time.

"Kessen? Not sure yet." A worried crease deepened along the bridge of Soren's nose; Raquel didn't remember those lines being there before. The princess rubbed her temples—a habit she must've picked up from her battlemate. "They kept him sedated for a while, but Medwenna said they woke him up earlier today. We're heading to him next."

"And…his arm?"

Soren's teeth sank into her bottom lip before she shook her head. "Nothing they could do to save it. Everin's already been meeting with Safi and Sage to discuss options for prosthetics, but it's…not a quick process."

"I'm sorry."

"It's Kessen," she said, like that meant anything to Raquel. "He'll be all right."

"And have you visited…her?" She still couldn't quite bring herself to say Jericho's name, even knowing Tenebrae no longer resided in the First Princess.

A harsh swallow; one shade of color stripped from Soren's skin. She cracked her neck, avoiding Raquel's gaze to play with Kallias's fingers instead. "No. But I asked Sage—no change there."

No hope to be found outside this room, either, then.

She felt rather than saw Soren glance at her out of the corner of her eye. "What's-His-Face won't leave, by the way. Every time I walk by, he's pouting by the door."

Raquel grunted, noncommittal. What Tempest wasted his time on wasn't her business.

But apparently, Soren thought it was hers. "You wanna tell me what that's about?"

Raquel slapped the book shut and tossed it onto the nightstand, trading it out for her coffee. "Would if I could."

Silence. Raquel sipped, letting the cold, bitter brew distract her from the cold tingling in her fingertips. The static popping in her ears. The frisson of tension in the air, a storm begging to break.

"He keeps looking at me like I'm a gods-damned ghost," Soren announced loudly. Clearly she wasn't concerned about being overheard. "And that's the new normal for me, sure, but it's weird that *he's* doing it."

A flicker of graveyard dirt and ghostly stone flashed behind her eyes. "You probably remind him of his dead wife."

"Oh. Yeah, that makes sense." A pause. Soren flipped onto one hip, leaning over Kallias to catch Raquel's gaze. "Wait, hang on, I just heard you. I probably *what?*"

"Long story." Raquel downed another gulp of her coffee, wishing the buzz in her bones came from caffeine, not the anticipation of lightning. "The first Queen of Atlas was his wife—Athena. Your great-great-great…you get it."

Soren's nose crinkled. "Ew. Does that mean we're—?"

"No, you're not related. She remarried after he and the rest of the gods lost their bodies."

"Oh." Oddly, she didn't look relieved; almost disappointed. "Damn it."

"What?"

"That just would've been a really easy solve for the Finn and Occassio problem."

A snorting laugh startled her, almost spewing her next sip of coffee across the bedspread; she swallowed in a rush, rolling her eyes. "Unfortunately, no blood shared between you all. We'll just have to come up with some other reason."

"Since the fact that she's *actually the worst* isn't good enough, apparently."

"Apparently."

They both sat silently for a bit; stewing over alternative solutions, she thought, until Soren suddenly spoke up. "Thank you—for being there when I couldn't be."

Raquel turned to look at her. "In Atlas?"

"Not just there. For being with Kal and Finn in Nyx, too—and with Elias, in Artem, when I was…gone." Gratitude had never looked so grim as it did painting Soren's scarred, shaken smile. She reached over and squeezed Raquel's wrist. "I owe you the lives of my battlemate and my brothers. I won't forget that—not ever."

Gods, she didn't know what to do when people said things like that. So she employed a Finn tactic: misdirection. "Are you sure? I hear your memory's a bit more fallible than most."

That smile toughened back into a scowl. "Damn it, Raquel, I'm trying to have a nice moment here—can you let me have that? Just once, can you let it be nice?"

Raquel almost, almost smiled. "I'll try."

She waited until Soren left to see to the rest of her business before she stopped allowing herself to indulge in cowardice.

Tempest was obviously waiting for something. And she'd have no peace until she either denied or satisfied him.

Which she chose would depend on what he wanted. But there was very little he could ask for that she'd be willing to give…even if he'd kept his promises. Even if he'd saved her life.

She wouldn't pay debts she hadn't accrued of her own volition. The protection of Atlas, he'd promised to Kallias; she hadn't asked him to offer that protection to her. She owed him nothing.

He still stood to the left of the door when she cracked it open, exiting as quietly as she could. Even when she shut the door and stepped to the side, taking up a parallel post on the right, he didn't look in her direction.

"Eye of the Storm," he said. "Riptide. Skybreaker."

A delicate shiver tiptoed over her shoulders. "That's a new one."

"The survivors of Port Atlas brought many names for you." A slight lift to the left corner of his mouth. "Those are only my favorites."

Odd, how it didn't feel like standing watch beside a stranger. She didn't know him in this body, with its black-ice hair and sleek sienna skin and a jawline so sharp he kept it sheathed in a beard grown just past the point of needing a trim. It shouldn't have been familiar.

But when he finally shifted, one shoulder hiked against the doorframe, she knew exactly what he would say before it left his mouth. So she didn't waste either of their time by letting him say it.

"There's been no change," she said. "He's still…not here."

Not here felt better than *gone*. Less final, somehow.

"I am sorry," Tempest said after a beat. "I wish I could help."

"So do I."

Another beat.

"I *am* sorry," he said again, in a rush this time, a storm surge gushing downriver. "I did not lie to you. I never heard him. He never spoke. I never felt…" He trailed off, reaching up to rub the back of his neck, cracking it with a resigned growl. "*If* I felt him, I did not realize it. I thought I was…that is, I believed…"

She barked a single halfhearted laugh. "Did your body come back with a hook in the tongue?"

He growled again, but this time, the note of warning was almost warm. Irritable, yes, but…

She looked away. He did too.

"Looking back on it," he admitted, "there may have been signs. But I did not recognize them for what they were."

"Signs?"

"There were…dreams." Every other word dragged slowly from his lips, like they were too heavy; like he had to haul them out one by one. "Errant thoughts. Some…unexpected sensations."

She narrowed her eyes at him. She hadn't removed her dagger from her belt, even while sleeping—she thumbed its pommel now. "Sensations?"

His jaw worked, drawing the words through his teeth like shards of glass embedded in his tongue. "*Emotions.*"

"Ah." She said it like she understood. She did not. A trick she'd learned from the Atlas siblings.

Tempest knocked his head back against the wall. "I misunderstood their meaning. I…took them as something they were not. For that, I am sorry. I did not intend to mislead you."

Raquel had never been a person overly susceptible to curiosity—it was rumored to be a killer, after all. But the temptation of questions gathered like dewdrops on the tip of her tongue, ready to fall into open air.

She wanted to ask…but found she did not want to know the answer.

She hated secrets. But maybe some things *were* better left unsaid.

"I believe you," she said instead. "I know you would not lie to me."

A test he passed with a nod and a long, resigned sigh. No guilt. Just acknowledgement. "No. No, it seems I wouldn't." He slipped his gaze to her like a gold coin slid across a bartop. "Would you offer me that favor in kind?"

Raquel did not feel inclined to offer promises of any sort. She simply canted her chin, waiting.

"What will you do if he does not return to you?"

"You already know the answer."

"Not the whole of it."

"You know enough." Enough to spare her from searching for the whole of it herself. How could she give him what he wanted—the truth—if she couldn't even give herself that kindness? "I should get back."

Thankfully, for once, he abandoned the fight. "And I should go." He slung a sideways scowl down the hall. "Someone has to breach the silence between me and my sisters, and we all know it won't be those bull-headed girls, Sancta save me."

Really, he should have gone after he'd helped her haul Kallias to the healers here. Instead…

"Before you go…a favor in kind?" she murmured.

Curiosity gleamed in his narrowed eyes. He flicked the ragged edge of his sleeve. "If you ask it of me."

A meaningful push on the word *you*. Another for *ask*.

"Why did you come looking for me?" A chill dripped down her back, snowmelt poured from a bent bough. She rolled her shoulders until the shivers left her. "Why did you stay and face him after?"

A low cough. Another crack of his neck, like he'd slept on it wrong.

"In that regard," he muttered, "I believe the best favor I can offer is my silence."

She bristled. "Why?"

"You will not like my answer."

"I've hardly liked any of your—"

When his hand came up in a gesture to *stop*, another petrichoric gust swept over her face, through her hair—it cooled the insistent, oily heat that came with sickbed vigils and an overabundance of sleep.

A different kind of cold sapped the adamance out of her when he said, watching her with the tired pain of a man pleading for mercy, "*I* do not like my answer. As long as we're dealing in favors…do not ask for it. Because if you ask, Raquel Angelov, I will give it to you."

Another secret. Another unwanted promise.

Another truth better left unsaid.

"You should go," she murmured.

He cleared his throat and nodded, turning aside; thunder called out for her to take caution, and when she peeked, soot-dark clouds reigned unchallenged in the island sky. No stars.

"Goodnight, Raquel Angelov," he said over his shoulder.

She didn't know what possessed her—she couldn't blame the gods anymore, nor could she name any other entity that might have made off with her tongue to use as its own. But something came over her in a rush she couldn't resist, an impulse better suited to the reckless Atlas brood than their unflappable, unwilling guardian.

Because in return, she said, "Goodnight, Peter Medeis."

He stopped. His shoulders rose, stiffened, his fists curling—then they fell, his fingers loosening again.

He walked away without looking back.

CHAPTER 65

FINN

Four nights after their arrival in Arborius—four nights he'd spent with Cassi tucked under his arm, her soft snores a passable replacement for the roar of the ocean outside his window back home—he woke to the rattling crash of a doorknob slamming into the wall.

Steel kissed his throat at the same time his dagger whispered against someone else's skin; when he finally blinked the sleep out of his eyes, Cassi blinked back at him, her sleepy squint off-puttingly adorable for someone holding a dagger to his throat.

Someone who *also* had a dagger held to her throat. His dagger.

"Sorry," they said as one, both spinning their weapons away—then spinning up from the bed. Cassi dropped into a crouch, her auramancied dagger shimmering in the sliver of light from the cracked door; Finn threw himself off the bed entirely, drawing a second dagger from under his pillow, flipping both around to face—

"*Gods*, Raquel!" he swore, whipping the daggers back just before their tips drove through Raquel's sternum. "If you're trying to put your death on my conscience just to spite me, I applaud the effort, but for gods' sakes—"

"It's Kallias." Grim terror widened Raquel's eyes to the whites. "Sage says he's dying."

"Tell me *exactly* what's happening," Finn demanded, heart pounding as he bolted after Sage and Raquel like he had one of Tenebrae's war dogs on his heels. "And don't try to make it sound nicer than it is, all right? Makes me itchy."

Sage fell back to walk beside him, letting Raquel take the lead. "It's called having a bedside manner, and you could stand to sprout one, kid."

"I'll pass. Tell me."

"Breathing's poor," Sage finally obliged, no compassion coloring the words in. Every edge kept sharp, not sanded down by sentiment; just cold, calloused fact. Exactly how Finn liked to hear it. Exactly how he needed to hear it. "Slow, shallow. Bad sign. He won't rouse when we roughhouse him—pokes, prods, nothing. No response to pain. That's worse."

"Damn it." He curled his fingers into his hair and pulled, trying to tug an answer out. All he got was another "*Damn* it."

"They won't help him," Raquel said tersely, not turning her head. He had to jog just to stay on her heels.

"We're keeping up with the regimen, but not much good it'll do now," Sage corrected. He scrubbed a hand over his beard, shrugging apologetically when Finn shot him a look of reproach. "Not a lot we can do for a body that's decided to die."

"Is it…I mean, is there a wound? A sickness? What can we—?"

"None of that. He's healthy enough, strong enough. It's the will that's missing. Nothing there to tell the body to fight." Sage shook his head. "Sometimes the body can be right as rain, but none of it matters if the mind's gone bad. I've seen it. Bloody unfair, it is, but I've seen it. An arrow through the heart, a blade through the belly, people understand that, yeah? They know how to grieve that. But if they can't see the blood, they can't see the wound."

Humor dried up like a jellyfish left to die on the sand. "The mind's dead. So the body's playing copycat."

Sage nodded. "Aunt Addie's with him. Your da's off fetching Soren and her lad."

To say goodbye. That explained Raquel's refusal to turn around, the stiffness in her shoulders, the uneven tugs of breath. The way she kept her hand braced over her heart like she was stanching a stab wound.

Small losses, bigger battles. He'd had to focus on getting his parents out. He couldn't have gone traipsing after Tempest to demand the god release his brother without sacrificing their lives, and even if he had, he would've only been fed a mouthful of lightning for his trouble.

Small losses. Bigger battles.

But this wasn't a small loss. Not by a long shot.

His steps slowed. "Not sure there's any point in me—"

"Rip that root right out of your skull," Sage scolded—not unkindly. "You're not squirming out of this. I'll drag you in by your hair if I have to."

To say goodbye. To say goodbye to *Kal*.

Panic grabbed him by the throat. He stumbled, gripping his own neck like he could strangle the panic right back. "No."

Raquel spun. "Finn—"

"I can't." The bob of his throat under his palm, the trembling vibration of his own voice, it all made his stomach swim.

He'd never been the strongest swimmer. And if he started to drown in that room, his brother wouldn't be there to pull him back out.

Sage didn't touch him; he'd been around Finn enough to know he hated that kind of comfort from most people. The sensation of another's hands on his already-crawling skin made him want to scream—and as a child, before he'd discovered how to expel that pent-up awful in less disruptive ways, he often had. Instead, his cousin faced him with his back straight, gaze even…meeting him there like a man, not the little cousin who'd nuisanced his way into a mentorship on mischief.

"I have stood where you're standing," Sage told him, a stormcloud of emotion drifting through his gaze, "more times than I have fingers to count 'em on. And I'll tell you what it taught me: there's nothing you can say to him that will make it feel like enough. Nobody's invented the right words to say goodbye to a brother. But it's important that you try."

Sage was the only person he'd ever met who could be gentle with him without making it feel like coddling. But that didn't make this any easier.

He didn't want to walk into that sickroom. He didn't want anything to do with it. He wanted to demonstrate the flawless about-face his Uncle River had taught him years back and march straight back to his bed, where he could bury his face in his pillow and beg Cassi to make him forget he'd ever even had a brother.

But out of all his little luxuries he'd smuggled out of the palace, cowardice was the one he couldn't keep, confiscated by Kallias's decision to die for them all.

Finnick Atlas made it a point never to indebt himself to anyone. But Kal had given him a goodbye, poor as it had been—they wouldn't be even until he paid him one in kind.

"Thanks," he said. He'd never meant it less.

"Ach, don't mention it, kid." Sage held his hand out, pausing; Finn dipped his chin, and Sage clasped his shoulder, giving it a light shake. "I'm so rotting sorry I can't do more."

"Not your weed to whack."

The creases around Sage's eyes shifted...frown lines easing, laugh lines deepening. "You got that from Astrid."

"Got a lot of things from Astrid." He cleared his throat. "She's smarter than both of us stacked together."

"You can play mockingbird with that one."

Finn blinked. "Lost me."

"You can say that again," Sage translated with a chuckle. "Get on then, kid. Before your sister stampedes straight over you and doesn't stop to scrape her shoes."

Finn waited until his cousin disappeared around the corner, Raquel on his heels; then waited even longer to hear a door slam shut. And only once he was certain he was out of their sight did he peel panic's sweaty fingers from around his throat, retreating into his mind and rummaging around for the tools he needed.

Indifference. Detachment. Anger, no—anger held too much, kept him too close. Anger would keep him too warm. He needed cold—he needed *numb*.

Sage was right. He had to go. Had to say goodbye.

But that didn't mean he had to feel it.

Dim light greeted him with a muted, halfhearted flicker as he forced himself into his brother's sickroom, step by aching step. He'd thought moving under the burden of chronomancy hurt, but this…

This felt like walking to his own grave.

But he'd toed that grave's edge plenty since he'd flown a false flag of surrender in Sirena. Had crossed far more precarious lines in the time since…and in a time before.

Raquel now sat on the floor under one of the mounted kerosene lamps, head tipped back against the wall; if not for her ticking jaw, he would've thought she was asleep. He'd expected to find her in the bed with his brother, like he had during each of his prior visits—but it wasn't hard to see why she'd chosen a different spot.

The blankets had been tugged down to his brother's ankles, bunched precariously at the foot of the bed; the rumpled pile could go at any second. Someone had washed Kallias's hair and changed his clothes; the damp scent of cedar tickled his nose as he shuffled to the side of the bed, sniffing hard to stop the itching. He had to be allergic—his eyes stung, and warm patches splotched his face. The closer he came, the less he blinked. The harder he breathed.

A pair of medimancers circled the bed as they prodded his brother, pressing their fingertips gently into his sides, his chest, his jaw; one wielded a small hammer-like tool, tapping his brother's kneecaps to test his reflexes.

A test Kallias failed.

His throat swelled, closing up around a lump so tough he couldn't cough it up.

The medimancers had to work around his mother, who refused to move no matter how pointedly they stared or how many times they "apologized" for bumping into her. She held Kallias's hand with both of hers, bloodshot eyes dry but puffy. Her hair was a mess, twisted in a knot that had frayed halfway out of its tie already. Her lips were moving, but he couldn't make out a whisper over the medimancers' chatter. He could have read her lips, but…

He tore his gaze away from her. Unfortunately, that left him with very few other places to look—and he found Kallias's face first.

The lump in his throat calcified to stone.

He looked *fine*. Tired, sure—maybe a little pale. Maybe a little thinner. But he wore no bandages. No fever radiated off his body. No stitches marred his skin. He was *fine*.

But he was dying anyway.

"Mama," Finn rasped.

And the way her gaze flitted first to Kallias, hope widening her eyes before disappointment closed them…more than anything else, *that* was the thing that killed him.

"Tell me they're not serious," seethed another voice behind him—Soren shouldered into the room so hard the door slammed into the wall and rebounded. It would have hit her right back if Elias's hand hadn't shot up to catch it. "I don't care what Sage said, we can't stop, so someone needs to tell them—"

"We're not stopping," Raquel said flatly, eyes still shut. "He is."

"So make him *start*."

Denial. Yeah. He'd tried that already.

Elias, however, seemed to have skipped straight to anger; he bent over Kallias, brow to brow, lips drawing back in a furious, tearful huff. "Damn it, Kal."

A latch clicked softly behind Finn. His father's hand brushed over his back briefly as he walked to join his mother, who just…watched Kallias breathe. Like she was counting every inhale, measuring every exhale.

Body's alive, brain's dead.

But how long until the body caught up?

How long until his mother had nothing to count?

Soren stalked past them all, dropping into a crouch to argue with Raquel; Elias sank down to one knee beside the bed, head bowed, fingers digging into Kallias's shoulder. Ramses kissed Adriata's temple, then closed his eyes, hiding his face in her hair as he put his hand over hers and Kallias's.

And Finn just…stood there.

I can't save you.

He shoved his hands into his pockets. Took a deep, sharp sniff.

I can't save you.

Raquel shoved up from the floor, pushing Soren out of her way; she crawled up on the bed without a word, settling in on the same side where Elias knelt. She set her ear over Kal's heart, empty gaze fixed on the wall; a tear trailed down her impassive face, staining the oversized infirmary shirt they'd dressed him in. Her thumb teased the forget-me-not bracelet chained to Kallias's wrist, clasped at the very furthest loop and still straining not to snap.

Abandoned in her anger, left with no place else to spend it, his sister turned on him. But just before he took the brunt of that blow, it softened, saddened—by the time she faced him fully, devastation had taken its place.

"Finn," she begged.

He held out his arms. "Come here, kid."

She collapsed in his arms like a badly balanced card tower. He almost wished she'd started shouting at him instead.

Another violent opening and hasty closing of the door, and suddenly Vaughn was there, breaths divided between wheezes and sobs as he stumbled to the bed. "Is he—"

"Not yet," Adriata, Ramses, Raquel, and Finn all chorused. Soren was crying too hard to catch her breath; if Elias's hitching shoulders were any indication, so was he.

Vaughn wiped his face, dropping to both knees beside Elias. He took Kallias's wrist, hand extended to Raquel; wordlessly, she undid one of the braids pinned against her temple and handed off the leather tie.

"Hey, brother," Vaughn rasped, looping that tie below the bracelet, securing it with a slipknot. He then clasped Kallias's wrist, shaking it with a sharp inhale. "We're all here. All of us."

Vaughn looked up—not at Ramses, not at Adriata, but at Finn, gray eyes uncertain—and Finn nodded his permission.

Us before all. The one promise Finn would never break.

He knew Kal—and he knew no matter what Vaughn had done, if these were Kallias's last hours alive, he'd want their brother here.

Jericho, too, probably. But from what Finn had heard, though she'd finally woken—and shown more improvement than Kal—she had yet to respond to anyone who'd bothered to visit her. Not even a nod or a frown to tell them she was cognizant. Not even for Vaughn, who had spent every moment at her bedside since hearing they'd brought her back with them.

Later. She wasn't the one dying in front of him.

He kissed Soren's head. "You should talk to him."

Soren shook her head. "I can't...I can't say—"

"I know." Gods, he knew. "Me either. But we have to try."

Damn Sage.

Soren clung to him a moment longer; then, with a quiet but vicious curse, she tore away and crawled onto the bed opposite Raquel, hiding in Kal's shoulder as she wept and muttered what he could only guess were threats against the integrity of his hairstyle if he failed to wake *right damned now.*

And then it was Finn's turn.

Us before all. Everyone—everyone but Jericho—now sat with Kallias. Holding him. Crying over him. Trying their damnedest to tell him everything they ought to have said while he could still hear them.

And Finn couldn't do it.

It wasn't cowardice. He'd left that at the door. This was worse—this was the one thing he could not abide, the one thing he could never allow.

Helplessness.

Nothing he did—*nothing* he did, no deathbed whispers, no mourning tears, no empty threats—could bring his brother back.

No aces up his sleeves. No weighted dice. No stacked decks. Even gods-damned chronomancy couldn't undo this.

Even the Trickster God couldn't trick death.

He had nothing to arm his brother with. No daggers, no cheats, no aces. Nothing he could use to fight it.

Fight it.

A slow tingle started at the base of his skull; it fizzed upward, cresting over the top of his head, and when it hit the center—

Wait.

Wait.

"Soren." Her shoulders shook as he grabbed them, peeling her away from Kal; he cupped her cheek, urgency burning any guilt away as he met her disbelieving stare, gleaming with grief. "What made you fight?"

"What?"

He shook her, just a little. Not enough to make her guard wolf pounce. "You said you almost let go, when Anima had you. What made you fight?"

"Um…" Her fingers drummed on her thigh, then reached up to fuss with her hair. "I heard you talking to me. I saw her hurting you, I saw you needed me, and I just…I had to stay. I had to get back to you."

That was all he needed.

He couldn't cheat at this game—but maybe he didn't have to.

He attacked her forehead with a fierce kiss, then turned and bolted out of the room, running for his gods-damned life.

Running for *Kallias's* gods-damned life.

CHAPTER 66

FINN

"I do not like the look on your face," Soren sniffled when he came back to his brother's sickroom and dragged her off the bed, pulling her into the furthest corner.

She'd like the idea that came with the look even less. Finn crossed his arms, bouncing on his heels to dispel the nervous thrum in his legs. "I'm going to do something, and you'll want to say no, but you've just got to trust me on it, all right? Don't yell at me."

Her tearful squint did not exactly scream *trust*. But she nodded, and that was good enough for him. "All right."

First, Finn checked her hip, her shoulder, her thigh—anywhere he'd seen her hang a sheath. "Are you armed?"

"Do I need to be?"

That sounded like a *no* to him. So he strode back to the door and opened it, wedging himself between it and Elias—just in case. "Come on in."

Cassi's curls had barely bobbed into the room before Soren snapped, "Oh, absolutely *rotting not!*"

"What did I *literally just say?*" Finn demanded.

Cassi crossed her arms, scowling over his shoulder—well, under his arm, actually, since he'd extended it to block Soren's path to her—at his sister. "I told you they wouldn't let me help him."

"That's fine, because you're not helping him. You're helping me." Finn strode to Kallias's bed. "Everyone move."

"If you think I'm going to let her—" Elias began, but Raquel stopped him with a fist around his collar; she dragged him up and back, clearing the path to the bed, her gaze fixed on Finn.

"Thank you." He took a step forward, but Raquel followed suit, halting him with a hand on his wrist. Static buzzed up his sleeve, prickling something awful.

"What are you doing?" she asked under her breath.

"Same as always—something mad." He swallowed the lump in his throat. He'd never suffered stage fright before. "What am I supposed to do, watch him die? What do you *want* me to do, Raquel?"

Raquel did not release him from her hold—neither her gaze nor her hand loosened their grip on him. But the longer she looked, the more that piercing look began to soften.

"Your best, Trickster," she said.

His *best*.

But which best? Which trick, which con, which *lie* could he spin convincingly enough to make his brother believe he wanted to live?

And if none of those did the trick…

Could plain, simple truth possibly be enough?

He looked to his sister.

Soren watched him from across the bed. No fear now. No doubt, either. Just that intrinsic understanding she'd always had about him—the one that had frightened and infuriated him when she'd first come home, convinced he'd been cursed to suffer his sister's corpse under the same roof.

But he'd been wrong then. And now, he needed that understanding—needed her to let him do this.

He didn't have to ask the question for her to answer it.

"If it's you," she said softly, "I trust it."

The trust he'd asked for, back in a sunny Sirena inn. The trust he'd asked for, already planning how he would break it. The trust she'd given him when he had done nothing to deserve it…when he'd done much, in fact, to ensure he would *never* deserve it.

Discomfort simmered like stew in his stomach.

To be trusted by a mark, that was gratifying. To be trusted by someone he loved, someone depending on him?

Finnick Atlas was many things. *Trustworthy* was not one of them.

But when he'd asked in Sirena, his sister had left him to his plans, making it possible for him to pull this mad scheme off at all. Had taken on dangerous trials and despotic kings and the bottomless depths of grief, all without him there to help her swim those treacherous waters.

When he'd asked, Raquel Angelov had abandoned her brother and sister-in-arms to help him steal lives and loyalties from under Tenebrae's nose, putting her faith in nothing but a note. Had shown up armored his brother's shirt and a new mourning braid and a world-shaking, sky-breaking fury.

Both had trusted him, against bad odds and better judgment alike—and here they were again, watching him, waiting for him to once again pull off the impossible.

He owed them, too. He owed them his best try.

And if not them, then certainly Kal.

He gestured for Cassi to join him; with a slow tip of her head, she obeyed.

"What *are* you doing?" she murmured to him as he climbed onto the bed, kneeling beside his brother's inert body.

"Give me your hand." When she did, he lifted it to his lips and kissed it. "You remember how you told me if I did the impossible one more time, I'd break?"

Her fingers curled around his with a warning squeeze. "Yes."

"Here's hoping you're wrong."

With another quick kiss, a different kind of pickpocket trick, he siphoned some of their shared power back—then let go, grabbing Kal's head in both hands.

One swift cut of his magic, and the world around him turned to dust and dark and the sound of falling rain.

"Come on, Kal." He ground his forehead against his brother's, refusing to scream against the searing purple pain throbbing through his temples. "Remember me."

CHAPTER 67

KALLIAS

When he dove into a catastrophe of ice and storm and earth, the first thing to go was a name.

A name. A pearl. A precious thing swallowed by a creature more adamant than oyster or clam. A pearl passed down from king to prince, from father to fishermen, from history to present.

The name abandoned him first. And without it, he was left adrift, his soul dissolving in a salt solution.

There were no bones, no breaths, no memories.

He closed his eyes and let himself sink.

"When does falling feel like floating?"

"When you're sinking."

"It's supposed to be a metaphor for love, Kal. Don't be depressing."

"Love doesn't feel like floating."

"Then what does it feel like?"

Coffee-dark eyes. A murderous mouth. *"Is he still there?"*

No life, no lungs. Yet she still took his breath away.

"Love feels like drowning."

"You don't get on your knees. Never again, not for anyone. Promise me."

A promise. A lie.

Coffee-dark eyes scorched black with fury. Night-sky lashes twinkling with diamond tears, twice as rare and half as desirable as their gemstone twins.

A dream. Nothing but a dream.

"You promised me, Kallias Atlas."

A name that pealed through him like lightning, like the path of a shooting star. The light carried another name with it, one just *barely* out of reach, teasing, testing, taunting him with its nearness…

But to catch it, he would have to swim. And he'd been drowning for so very long now…

"Promise me you'll stay."

He couldn't remember if he'd ever known how to tread water at all.

"Set my family free. Whatever cage you have them in, minds or cells—you let them out."

No name. No voice. No heart.

No mind. No soul. No sense.

Yet he heard those words.

"Or what?"

"Or we will break them out. Starting with you."

A call to surrender. A call to arms.

A call to memory.

Lightning forked through darkness. Darkness stained darker with blood. He could taste it. Blood. Blood and smoke. Ash and anger.

Death.

Knuckle against bone. Knuckle against flesh. Knuckles laden with lightning.

A hand against his cheek.

A name.

"Kal." A whisper. Deathbed soft. Clotted with blood. *"Get up."*

Get up.

Get up.

Kal.

A name.

And it wasn't alone.

Eli.

A name.

A friend.

A brother.

"Get up."

The name would not stay.

The dark kept coming back, kept devouring, kept sinking its teeth into the name until only tatters floated on the surface.

Kal.

Here and there and gone again.

No name to call. No water to tread. If the tide could not carry him home, what hope did he have left?

He had fought enough, tried enough, waited enough. Had saved enough.

The name was gone. What more did he have to give?

But then…

Light.

Light and bruises and freckles. Purple and wine and tears of glass.

"Come on, Kal. Remember me."

That voice.

That *voice.*

He knew that voice.

He *remembered.*

CHAPTER 68

KALLIAS

Finnick Aurelius Atlas was born on a rainy autumn day.

For his sister, the day wasn't worth the dramatics; she already had one little brother, after all, and all the medimancers had advised the queen to expect the arrival of another boy. The princess would remain the Heir; the kingdom was to have a Second Prince.

Every group of palacefolk, however, buzzed with the same current of excitement; anticipation spun like a whirlpool through the walls, drawing everyone who came near into its inescapable swirl.

But there was not a single soul in the entire palace more excited than the little boy racing up and down the cordoned-off hallway, pausing every now and again to peek through the rain-wracked windows at the tossing sea. The little boy who was also a little brother; a little brother who was about to become something even better.

"Kallias?"

The little boy stopped in his tracks when his father leaned out of the room, smiling from ear to ear.

"Would you like to meet your new brother?"

"Why's he crying?"

The little boy scrambled up on the couch, anxiously craning his neck to peer over his mother's arm as she adjusted the bundle settled in the crook of her elbow, cooing sweet nonsense over his heartbroken wails.

"He's all right, love. Just a little grumpy."

"I can—um—what if I tell him jokes?"

"How about you take a try holding him instead?"

The little boy lit up, scrambling to sit on his seat, arms extended ramrod straight in front of him. His mother gently handed the bundle over, keeping one hand safely tucked behind his neck. "Careful with his head."

The little boy gasped. "He's *heavy*, Mama!"

"That's because he decided to get stubborn and overstay his welcome. Sit back a bit…there you go. Great job."

His mother settled on the couch beside him, slow and sore, but she hid it with a smile as she leaned over her two sons, teasing a fold of the baby's blanket away from his face as his cries quieted.

The little boy marveled at the warm, heavy bundle laid across his lap, giggling when his brother's mouth gaped wide in a yawn.

"Oh, big yawn," cooed their mother, reaching in to tickle his chin.

"Big yawn," the little boy agreed, sticking his finger directly in the baby's open mouth.

"Oh, no, Kal—" His mother hooked a finger around his, fishing it neatly out of his little brother's mouth. "Gentle hands with the baby, remember?"

The little boy took his hand back, sticking it in his own mouth instead as he stared at the baby. The longer he looked, the brighter his eyes became…until his mother realized that brightness had overflowed, streaming down the little boy's cheeks.

"Kallias! What's the matter?"

"I didn't mean to," the little boy sobbed.

"Didn't mean…what do you mean, love?"

"My hands!" he wailed, garbled around his fingers.

The boy's parents exchanged the sort of looks parents wore when their child was being absurdly funny, but they couldn't risk letting on.

"It's all right," the boy's mother said, her promise tight with restrained laughter. "You didn't hurt him!"

"I didn't mean to!"

"You didn't. Here, look." Adriata towed her boys into the shelter of her arm, carefully bracing the little boy's arm curved under the baby. "You see how soundly he's sleeping? That means he feels safe with you."

The little boy sniffled, scrubbing his nose with the back of his hand. "He's—I m-make him safe!"

"That's right!" The little boy's mother teased his hair back, kissing his freckled forehead, smiling against it as she glanced up at her husband. "You're his big brother. And a big brother's job is to make sure his little brother is safe—just like Jericho makes sure you're safe when you go play in the water."

The little boy blinked up at her, uncertain—but when he looked back at his baby brother's face, his own scrunched up in the indomitable determination of a four-year-old given his first taste of responsibility.

"It's *okay*, Finn," he mumbled, kissing his brother's head the same way his mother had kissed his. "You're safe. I keep you safe. Promise. Here!"

The little boy set his pinky in his brother's hand. One small finger wrapped up in five smaller ones, a fist that clung on like it might never let go.

"Promise," the little boy whispered once more.

"Kal! Kal, it's me, are you awake?"

The boy, not so little anymore, stared at the floorboards through the telescopic glass of a near-empty wine bottle. The rounded periwinkle glass warped the lines between boards into curls that stirred his head in a lazy whirl…or maybe the contents of the bottle were to blame. Either way, the touch of seasickness brought him his first deep breath since they'd arrived in the newly rebuilt palace earlier this afternoon, dust and new paint burying the salt-and-sand smell of home.

The builders had done a commendable job. The rebuilt portions looked…almost identical to their predecessors. Eerily identical.

Just eerily enough that he'd almost forgotten what they'd lost. A hole no one could fill with new walls and fresh paint and a dash of play-pretend.

His baby sister was dead. Her cheeky grins and wild cackles and little hands that never failed to find his when they crossed the streets in the city proper, all gone.

Had they cleared away all the ash before they'd begun to build? Did any of the dust in the air belong to her?

A stronger wave of sickness doubled him over, bending him across his knees. "Go 'way."

"Can I sleep in there with you? I-I brought my own blanket. I won't kick or anything."

The knob squeaked. The swish of a heavy quilt and the soft patter of bare feet announced Finn's arrival, and the boy lifted his head, squinting through the generous haze wine had poured over the world.

His brother needed him. He could…he could try. For him. He could try to be—

"We're not supposed to drink that," Finn said, his feet shuffling anxiously; he was staring at the bottle. "Mama said not until we're eighteen—"

The wine might have tempered the grief, but it also tempered his self-control—when the anger came, he couldn't bail it out of his head. "I don't give a shit what Mama said."

Finn slid back a step. Like the boy had frightened him. "We're not supposed to say that word—"

"What're you going to do about it? Run to Mama and tell on me? Do your worst."

As the boy shifted his weight, the sway to the world brought back that soothing seasickness…the closest he'd get to using his sea legs until his mother let them out of her sight again. And gods knew when that would happen.

He set the lip of the bottle to his mouth, letting the must of old fruit and sugar cloy the bitterness he couldn't seem to wash off his tongue.

Even blurred by drunkenness and the dark, the fear in Finn's rounded eyes pinched the softer side of his heart. "No. I just—I—"

"Why are you here, Finn?"

Finn ducked his head like he was embarrassed. "I had a nightmare."

The tide of anger rushed back out to sea.

His brother needed him. Like so many nights since the fire—since before the fire, even—Finn had fled the clutches of nightmares to seek shelter with the brother who always protected him. Who'd promised he always would.

But he'd promised his sister, too. And look where that had left her.

Anger washed back in with a vengeance, high tide claiming the entire shore. He launched himself into a stumble, strangling the neck of the bottle in one hand, the other striking out uselessly for the window on the opposite wall. He needed fresh air, the smell of the ocean—anything to wash this rage away. "What do you want me to do about it?"

In the brief silence that came next, the boy dragged his hands over his eyes, then his ears—his head swam so badly, the anger mounting into a tidal wave towering stories above his head, and he couldn't stop seeing his sister's face in the wall of water, and she was gone and it was his fault, it was all his fault, he'd promised he'd save her and now—

"I just…you said, after the fire, you said if I needed you, that I could—"

The tidal wave crashed down, consuming everything in its path.

"What is it? Huh? You want me to fix it? To kiss it better? Do you want me to *save* you?"

The boy couldn't save anyone. He'd been ready to die trying—and he'd still failed.

He wished he'd died trying.

Maybe then his baby sister's ghost would leave him alone. Maybe he'd stop seeing her terrified little face everywhere he turned, every shining surface reflecting his guilt.

"I can't save you," he sneered at the ghost in the window, the words burning his throat like liquor, like poison. "No one can save you! Stop looking at me like that! Stop *looking at me*, Soleil!"

He spun, the wine tugging him off-balance as he threw the bottle as hard as he could.

He didn't see his brother had moved until the lip of the bottle kissed his fingertips goodbye.

As long or as little as he lived, he'd never forget the way his baby brother screamed.

A torrent of glass and the last dregs of wine. Anger fled for its life, bone-chilling terror taking its place when he called his brother's name and got no answer; when Finn just *laid* there, covered in glass and wine and—

Oh gods. Oh gods. Blood. His brother was bleeding, and he'd—

He'd—

No.

"Oh gods, no, no—*Finn?*" The boy dove to the floor, lungs spasming with near-sobbing breaths as he rolled Finn onto his back, reaching for his pulse.

Brown eyes met his, the whites gleaming in the dark.

"Oh, thank Anima. Thank Anima." The boy broke—his voice, his anger, his heart. He'd hurt his brother. He'd hurt him. "Oh gods. Finn, I'm so—I'm so sorry, I didn't know you were—I didn't see you move, I didn't—"

When Finn found his voice, he didn't say a word to the boy at all—instead, he wriggled out from under the boy's hands, screaming for their mother.

Screaming. Like the boy was a danger to him.

No longer his protector, but something he needed protection from.

And he was *right*.

Sickness well and truly claimed the boy, and he fell back on his heels, too dazed with drink and dread to defend himself when his mother stormed into his room, demanding to know what he'd done. Shielding his brother from him with her hand on his head.

He'd hurt his brother.

He wished he'd died trying.

That day, the boy became a man. And when the man had another chance to save the ones he loved…

He made sure he would not fail again.

So the man became a martyr, and the martyr became a god. But then the god became a man too, and that…

That made the man nothing at all.

No name. No voice. No heart.

No mind. No soul. No sense.

And for a little while, nothing was…nice.

Until *something* came to find him.

"Kal."

A name. A voice. A hand on his face.

"Come on, Kal. Remember me."

But remembering meant remembering all of it—the broken promises, the broken glass.

"We need you to come back."

We. Come back.

"I can't," he said—then blinked.

A voice. He'd found his voice.

"Sure you can. It's nothing, right? Just follow me home."

Home. A replacement palace, an empty room, a missing princess in ten years' worth of portraits. His throat hurt. "Why?"

"We need you."

They needed him. For *what?*

Was there another god waiting for him to give up his body? Did they need an alliance, and no one else was willing to sell themselves for it? Or was someone holding a whip, and they needed a back for them to break?

A long beat. Then Finn ventured, "Soren's waiting for us."

Soren. His sister's new name—he remembered that now.

His heart quickened. So it was still beating, after all. "Soren...she's here?"

"Not just her." Finn hadn't cried in front of him since the incident—but there was no mistaking the tears running down his face now. He could see it, his brother's image wavering against a silver-touched mist, his brown eyes bloodshot and ringed with bruises.

Someone had hurt his brother.

"What happened? Are you all right?" That mattered—that mattered enough to try to stay, just for another minute. Just to know he was safe now.

"Don't worry about me. Worry about us. We're all here—me, Soren, Elias, Raquel. Mama, Papa, J-Jer's here somewhere, and Vaughn...everyone's here. We all came back—we came to get you."

All...all of them?

Slowly, the warmth against his skin started to make sense.

Hands on his face. Hands holding his. A hand on his shoulder. A hand around his wrist.

A head over his heart.

But he couldn't go to them. Not the way they wanted.

"I can't save you." Not the boy, not the man, not even the god anymore. *Nothing.* "I can't save any of you."

"Oh, for *gods'* sakes, Kal—" Finn's mouth jerked downward; he sniffed, steeling his jaw, and for the first time, he wondered when his brother had grown up. "Fine, you can't save us—you can't save *me.* But I can save you."

They were all here. Not asking to be saved—asking to save *him.*

The boy's mistakes had made him a man. The man's guilt had made him a martyr.

But this...this made him *loved.*

This made him remember.

His voice. His family.

His name.

Kal, get up.

I know you can hear me, Kal.

Hey, brother. We're all here.

I'm so sorry, son. I'm so sorry.

I know my son. He is not done fighting yet.

Kal, get up!

Tonight, you're only mine.

"I can save you," Finn promised, desperation shattering like glass through his gaze. Tears spilled like wine, dripped from his cheeks like blood. "Let me *save you.*"

He is not done fighting.

And for the first time…he didn't want to be.

Kallias reached out and held his brother's face. He wiped those tears like he should have done that muddled, wine-soaked night; and when the darkness tugged at him, trying to pull him back out to sea, he held on so tightly his fingers ached.

"What do I do?" he asked.

Finn broke into a boyish smile. One Kallias hadn't seen in nearly a decade. "Just follow my voice. Follow me home."

Home.

It had never felt so far away. Not even with deserts and tundras and forests driven between him and his beloved sea.

But his brother was here. His brother had come to get him. To save him.

And for the first time since he could remember, he wasn't afraid when he stepped into the dark. Not with his brother by his side.

CHAPTER 69

FINN

Madness shattered the world into flakes of splintered glass.

Darkness throbbed in shades of bloody black behind his eyes, a second pulse showing off its skill at keeping a beat. But in that pool of clotted tar, shards of iridescence swam for their lives, crying out in voices he'd once or did or might one day love.

A glass bottle in his hand. A glass bottle broken against his back. A glass bottle embedded in a tailoress's best tools.

"Let me have him, let me have him…give me my brother, that's my *brother!*"

Wine spilling down his throat. Wine spilling down his back. Wine spilling down her skirt.

Clammy hands over his heart. Under his jaw.

"Is he dead? *Tell me he's not dead!*"

Oh gods, was he dead?

Let me help you.

I can't save you.

Let me save you.

A body on the floor. His body on the floor. *Her* body on the floor.

Broken glass. Bloody cloth. Battered heart.

Time only knew one way this story could go.

"Finn, can you hear me? Make a fist if you can hear me." A cold, sweaty bunch of fingers captured his, waiting—squeezing, then waiting. "Can you move your fingers?"

So many gods-damned questions. Did they usually ask dead men this many questions?

"Come on, Finn." Another desperate squeeze, so firm his fingers ached. "You can't drag me back just for you to go next. Move your damned fingers. Make a bad joke. Just show me you're—"

"Gods," he moaned—that one breath grabbed a broom, nearly shooing him back into the shadowy nothing he would have liked to nap in for a few years or so. "I forgot how *bossy* you are. Five more minutes, all right?"

A set of sighs gusted over him like a brewing storm in need of a breath mint.

"I hate him," fumed a voice as sweet and severe as a silver bell. *Cassi.* "I rotting hate him."

Relief scrubbed away the traces of nightmare splashed against his subconscious in warped whorls of spilled paint…messy streaks of bloody curls and lusterless eyes and her pretty dimples locked behind death's unbreachable door.

This once, he let that memory flee into the murky depths of his half-maddened mind without a fight.

Not real. Not anymore. No reason to remember what had never been done.

"You have five seconds to open your depths-damned eyes," choked his older brother, not sounding particularly patient, "or I'll have Elias scorch the silt out of your toes."

"I keep my toes clean as a whistle, thank you," he mumbled, put out. What was the point of all those pedicures if people weren't going to pay attention?

"Finn!" Soren snapped, half frightened, half furious. "It's not funny!"

Under ordinary circumstances, he'd dig his own grave before surrendering his commitment to a bit. But not when his little sister needed him. Never when she needed him.

"Hey…I'm fine. I'm fine, kid." Lamplight sliced across his eyes when he finally pried them open. He turned his head with a hiss, squeezing his eyes shut and rubbing the glare out of them as he groaned into the…quilt? No, a rug. They'd moved him to the floor—right underneath the brightest lamp in the room. "All right, who did that? One of you did that on purpose."

Two shaking hands gripped him by the biceps and hauled him up, dragging him into an embrace that reminded him where he actually was.

His brother's sickroom. His brother's deathbed.

His brother's arms.

"You shouldn't have done that," Kallias said, voice slogged with tears, thumping him on the back like he couldn't decide whether he was hugging Finn or hitting him. "You should *not* have done that, I can't believe they all let you pull that stunt, but…I'm so gods-damned glad you did."

I Should Not Have Done That could be the title of his autobiography.

"Oh, you wanna talk about things we shouldn't have done?" He shoved Kallias off of him, expecting his brother to shift an inch, maybe two—when Kal fell onto his back instead, coughing like Finn had knocked the breath out of him, the world wavered around him again. His eyes burned. "How bout we start with *handing yourself over to a god after we all specifically told you not to?*"

"This may be the wrong fight for you in particular to pick," Cassi hummed from somewhere off to the side.

"*I* had a plan." When Kallias pushed himself up, the fatigue he wore like a shroud knotted up Finn's throat; anger pulled the knot tight, then stabbed Finn's finger into Kal's chest like blade of flesh and bone. "*He* had a death wish!"

The sad, soft look in his brother's eyes only made him madder. "I'm so sorry."

Sorry didn't mean a damned thing to him. Not right now.

"You would've been dead. You get that?" Something was stuck in his throat again. He coughed, growled, tried to swallow it down—all for nothing. His voice sounded wrong. His cheeks were warm, wet—had his nose started bleeding again? "You should be dead. Without me pulling that *stunt*, you are depths-damned—"

"I heard you the first time." Kallias reached for his face, and he slapped him away, sniffing hard. Swallowing harder.

"Don't do that again," he rasped. "Don't make me be you, all right? I don't know how."

"Can we—" Kallias's throat strained, then his lungs, his breath coming in shallow, labored huffs. "Can we argue about it later?"

Finn didn't want to argue about it. He wanted to yell about it with considerable gusto and receive absolutely no retort whatsoever. But it seemed Vaughn agreed with Kallias; he pushed through the knot of onlookers, avoiding Kallias's gaze.

"Everybody back up—let me through. Finn? You know the drill. Eyes open, look at the light…"

Only Elias ignored Vaughn's request. When Vaughn knelt to guide Finn back, supporting him with one hand braced against his chest before peering into his eyes to check for gods-knew-what, Elias dropped to both knees and seized Kal by the side of his head, forcing him to look his way instead of Finn's. "Kal?"

"Eli." Relief washed over Kallias first—then horror splashed in, drowning the light in his eyes as he reached out for Elias's face…but stopped short. His fingertips hovered over the nasty black bruise stamped across Elias's jaw before falling limply in his lap. "Oh gods. What did I…"

"You didn't."

"I *did*. I could've killed you." Kallias ground the heel of his hand into his eye, his chest surging with a racking heave. "Why did you…I could've *killed* you."

When Kallias's head dropped against Elias's shoulder with a heavy *thump*, Elias did not let him fall.

"You couldn't have. Promise." The dark-haired Nyxian warrior put his head down on Kallias's shoulder, too, his tears soaking into the prince's sleeve. Steam drifted off his cheeks in ghostly ribbons.

"I'm sorry," Kallias moaned. "I saw him hurting you, I tried…I was so far away—"

"Stop."

"I was almost too late—"

"*Stop*."

For several minutes after that, Kallias wept in painful hacks, like each sob ripped something out of him, like a wound gushing blood. And Elias wept with him, surge for surge, a sparring of sorrow finally set free.

That lull allowed him to finally sit back on his seat and skim the room, pressure packing his head like someone had stuffed cotton in his skull. His thoughts thrummed like a held pianoforte note as he took in the changes: his parents each had one arm around each other and one arm around Soren, all three of them crumpled on the floor; Soren's eyes were closed, one hand over Ramses's wrist and the other over Adriata's. His parents leaned into each other, temple to temple, their gazes taking turns assessing him and his brother.

He didn't see Cassi. And when knuckles delicately skimmed down his spine, trailing tingles through his skin, he figured out why.

"That," she whispered in his ear, "was *extremely* foolish."

"Mm." He turned and kissed the tip of her nose. "Always a fool when I'm around you."

He'd spend all the gold in the palace coffers just to keep her gilded gaze on him a second longer. Especially when she looked at him like *that*, like no one had really looked at him before.

"My fool," she murmured, running her thumb over his chin. "Don't frighten me like that again."

Finnick Atlas had never belonged to anyone. The idea of being owned, bought or blackmailed or beguiled, had once been his worst nightmare.

Regrettably, he feared those terrors had finally come true. And the most frightening part of all was how very little he minded.

But thoughts of belonging and beguiling brought his gaze back around, prodding every corner of the room just to be sure—and just as he'd thought, one body had vanished entirely from their little gathering of grievers.

He had done as she asked; had done his *best*. And instead of thanking him or throttling him or taking her own turn telling Kallias what an idiot he was…

Raquel had left without a word.

CHAPTER 70

KALLIAS

The morning after those he loved fished him out of a grave of his own digging, Elias Loch broke into his new room without knocking.

"Get up," he said, followed shortly by a flighted shadow hurtling for Kallias's head.

Old battle reflexes tugged his arm up just in time to bat the projectile down; when he sat up and scrubbed the sleep out of his eyes, he found a wrinkled pair of swimming shorts crumpled sadly on the floor. "What're those for?"

Elias narrowed his eyes, amusement shifting to concern like sand trickling from one half of an hourglass to the other. "Are you joking, or do you actually not know?"

Kallias squinted at his friend. Something was off about him, but between the blur of sleep and the artificial dusk preserved by a thick curtain drawn over the window, he couldn't put his finger on it. "No, I know what they're *for*, but why—"

"Just get up and follow me. There's something you need to see."

A second round of scrubbing cleared his vision enough to realize what, exactly, was wrong with the picture in front of him. And it wasn't the golden eyes—he'd spotted those yesterday. "Are...are you wearing *swimclothes?*"

Elias crossed his arms with a discomfited roll of his shoulders. He still wore a shirt, but his black pants cut off just above the knees, and his feet...were those *sandals?* "I'm not the thing you need to see. Quit ogling and get up."

He obeyed the second order, at least. "I have to be dreaming."

"If you dream about me in these ridiculous pants, I'd keep that information to yourself around your sister."

"Ha, ha. I didn't even know you knew how to put sandals on."

Elias grunted.

Kallias squinted again. "...Oh."

"I've never worn them before."

"You didn't do too badly, the straps are just—"

"Mock all you want. I just spent the last month traveling with Everin Arden—you can't touch me."

The urge to laugh died immediately.

You can't touch me.

The bruises beaten into him suggested otherwise.

Elias's gaze softened. "Hey. Don't."

"I just..." Kallias shook his head, helpless to mend it, helpless to find the right words. What apology could put this right? What words could halt a blow already thrown, already taken? "You should have let him have me."

Kallias didn't know where it came from. But one moment, he was standing before his friend, trying to find the right words—the next, Elias had cut straight into his breathing space, seizing him by a fistful of his shirt and pushing him back. "*What* did you just say to me?"

The mattress springs shrieked in protest as Kallias landed hard on his backside, eyes widening. "*Hey!*"

"If you think I *ever* would have...that I would trade..." Elias dragged in a slow breath through his nose; he smoothed his hands down his face, then dropped to his seat beside Kallias. Snagged his shirt just below the collar, forcing Kallias to look him in the eye.

Dammed-up tears gleamed in the light shed by Elias's tattoos, glossing his dark eyes in a fiery glaze.

"Two favors," he said.

Kallias blinked. Anger to sadness to pleading—the rapid shifts were making him dizzy. But he didn't have to think about his answer. "Name them."

"Firstly, never say that to me again. If you're waiting for all of us to apologize for loving you too much to let you die, you'll be waiting a gods-damned long time. And secondly…would you help me undo this?"

Elias held out his necklace, the one he'd worn since Artem…the one that used to carry Soren's ring. And the battlemate braid he'd done for her.

That braid was gone. But another had taken its place.

Kallias stared mutely at that twist of ragged navy cloth. Cloth cut from a stolen shirt—the one Raquel had stolen back in Artem. One she'd never returned. One he'd never really tried to get her to return.

"Eli," he whispered hoarsely.

Elias bent to catch his gaze, jaw clenched, fire burning away the tears he hadn't shed.

"I was never going to let him have you," he rasped. "That was never going to happen."

Kallias cursed, dashing away his own tears; he lurched across the bed and embraced Elias once more, knocking his own breath out of his chest with the force of it.

"Thank you," Kallias muttered. "For not letting me give up."

"As if I was going to let you leave me all alone with your insane family." Elias pulled back, gripping the back of his neck and giving him a gentle shake. "And speaking of…a third favor?"

Kallias frowned. "As many as you need."

"Stop asking questions, stop saying stupid things, and go get changed." Elias pulled him back to his feet. "I'm too tired for patience, and I don't know how much time we have."

"Fine." Kallias started to go, then stopped. "Wait, did you say you were traveling with *Everin Arden*? Elias, what happened while I was—"

"Sounds like a question to me!"

Kallias dropped it and went to change. But he couldn't help smirking when he came back to a famous Elias scowl…and adjusted sandal straps.

When his toes sank into the sand, his knees very nearly followed suit.

It wasn't *the* beach—not *his* beach. Not home.

But it was close. Just close enough.

Especially when he counted four other redheads already in the water.

Well, three and a half. His parents and Soren were far enough out that he might not have recognized them at all without the sun bouncing off their hair, lighting each head like a fiery beacon. Finn's feet dangled off his picnic blanket, just enough for the waves to nip at his heels, but the rest of him was safely sequestered on the spread of cotton. He lay with his arms crossed under his head, wearing a shirt and swim shorts, a pair of sun-shielding glasses layered over his usual pair.

As if that wasn't enough, the sight of a blue-tinted braid bobbing in the choppy gray water, drifting well past even where his parents would comfortably go, almost shamed him right back into his shoes.

He hadn't had a chance to speak to any of them before the healers had arrived, shooing everyone but him out of the room so they could assess his condition.

He owed them all some kind of *sorry*. But more than all the others, he owed Raquel one incredible depths-damned apology.

The kind that would see him breaking his promises to her one more time, because he planned to drop to his knees before her and tell her all the reasons he didn't deserve her—and all the reasons he hoped she would show him mercy anyway. And then, if she let him live, maybe he'd find out what had happened to make her comfortable with doing a dead man's float so close to his mother, who'd taught him every technique he knew for killing in the water.

"It's not going to bite, you know," Elias said from behind him.

"Is that so, Eli Dorian?" Kallias tapped his chin. "I seem to recall you almost falling on your ass the first time a wave came after you."

Elias's chuckle sweetened some of the shame weighing his bones down like sopping-wet sand. "Well, once you've nearly drowned in the belly of a sentient mountain, this isn't quite so intimidating."

So far, remarkes like that were the worst part of this daunting, dreamlike aftermath: realizing exactly how much he'd missed. And exactly how much those events had changed the most important people in his life.

He'd closed his eyes on the Sirena shore. With the exception of fleeting glints of consciousness here and there, he remembered nothing between then and hearing Finn beg him to *remember*. To follow him home.

Let me save you.

He had—not realizing what the consequences could have been for Finn. And when he'd realized how close Finn had come to losing himself in the void swallowing what little remained of his mind, when he'd realized how many of those mottled bruises and cauterized scars on Elias's body matched the indents of his knuckles, when he'd realized how much Raquel had risked to honor the request of a dead man…

Guilt dug into him like a broken shell stuck in his sandal.

He'd been furious. Worse than. And the guilt…he hadn't felt shame like this in months.

Not since he'd committed to staying sober.

That thought only hammered another layer of humiliation over his conscience. During the transition between his sickroom and a homier space that hadn't been sanitized half to death, he'd snuck away just long enough to track down his cousins' liquor cabinet…and had stared at it, mouth dry as sunbaked bone, for ten torturous minutes.

Withdrawing from alcohol had been torture. Withdrawing from magic…

Like his worst hangover times ten. He'd needed something to take the edge off. *Anything.*

His fist had just closed around the neck of a half-drunk cognac bottle when the hairs on the back of his neck stood on end, tingling with static.

"So eager to dig a new grave already, are we?" Tempest had asked.

Kallias hadn't turned around. Hadn't been able to. The God of Nature's challenge clanged through his head, his skin buzzing, his feet frosted to the floor.

"You can try again, I suppose," the god had mused. *"Find another way to see yourself out, so to speak. But from what I know of that woman…I wouldn't test it."*

Anger—and something a little uglier, a little greener—had thawed him out enough to make his escape. He'd slammed the liquor cabinet door hard enough that something shattered inside, a cataclysm of glass and amber rain dribbling from under the door's lip, and then he'd just…walked away.

He owed his aunt a new bottle of something. He'd find out later. Not a good idea to risk going back to check.

He'd been lucky Tempest had been there to snap him to his senses. Chances were he wouldn't get lucky if he gave in to temptation a second time.

"Come on." Elias clapped him on the shoulder, knocking those thoughts away. "I could use a lesson or two."

Kallias frowned at him. This couldn't be the same Elias who'd refused to wade any deeper than his ankles. Definitely not the one who'd cursed like a sailor when a flicker-fish had nibbled his toes. "You want to learn how to swim?"

"I need to learn how to swim," Elias corrected, a story lurking behind his sunlit gaze. "And I at least trust you not to shove my head under. Soren…"

He hid a smile. "I'd give it five minutes."

Elias rolled his eyes. "Thirty seconds at the absolute longest. Trust me."

He trusted very few people more—and no one more when it came to his sister.

The sand cushioned his steps as he trailed behind Elias, walking toward Finn and…

Wait.

Kallias stopped, the sand swallowing him up the ankles. His jaw loosened, about to drop entirely off its hinges.

Finn wasn't alone on that blanket.

A curly-haired young woman was propped up on her elbows beside him, her eyes shut, freckled face basking in the sun; her swimclothes were a sunny shade of yellow, reflecting the leaves clinging for their lives to the few deciduous trees huddled in the shadows of their darkwood neighbors.

He'd seen her before, briefly, helping Vaughn—whose presence was another shock he had yet to confront face to face—after Finn had come to consciousness in his sickroom. But he hadn't paid her much attention. He'd assumed she was an off-duty healer who'd been caught in the halls and called to help, but now that he was getting a better look…

That face was more familiar than a fleeting encounter in the aftermath of a miracle. Mind-bendingly so. But he couldn't stare at her long enough to place her without either coming off as rude or accidentally getting his brother's attention, so—

"Occassio," Elias murmured in his ear.

Kallias snapped around, searching the lip of foliage where forest gradually sifted into sand; but Elias's simmering glare was locked elsewhere.

On Finn.

On the girl beside him.

Oh, he had to be kidding. That couldn't be…surely no one was *actually* allowing…

He blinked at Elias, patiently waiting for his friend to break, to admit Soren had put him up to some poorly timed prank—but Elias merely blinked back, his lip curled at the corner.

His hip itched. Gods, he needed his sword back. "Why in the depths is no one *doing any*—"

"Finn's insisting it's his choice."

Of course he was. Kallias dragged his hands down his face, and Elias nodded. "I know."

"And you all believe him?"

"*I* do." Kallias knew that hunch to his shoulders; it was the closest Elias got to sulking. "No one else does. You want to take that fight, be my guest, but Soren's gotten in the ring twice already. Hasn't made a difference."

Twenty-four hours. He'd been back for less than twenty-four hours. "I'm going to go ask if Tempest wants my body back."

Elias's face spasmed; a smirk, almost, then a forced scowl. He scratched at his beard. "That's not funny."

Well, he wasn't entirely joking. "Do you really want me to teach you how to swim?"

"If you're up to it." Elias held a hand out—then swatted Kallias's hand when he reached back.

"Ow!" Kallias snatched his hand back, rubbing his stinging knuckles. "What in the depths was that for?"

"I'm offering to take your *shoes*, not trying to hold your hand!"

"Well, then, say that next time!"

Elias grumbled under his breath, but took Kallias's sandals when offered; he marched over to the blanket, shucking off his own shoes and dropping both pairs in front of Finn's feet.

Finn promptly kicked them straight into the water.

Elias scowled down at him. "Seriously?"

"Can't hear you," Finn said, sticking his little finger in his ear and pretending to clean it out. "Sleeping."

"I'm not even going to dignify—"

Finn covered his ears with a guttural snore; Occassio giggled, tipping her head back to catch a little more sun. It was hard to tell, since he was avoiding looking directly at Finn like his life depended on it, but he thought his brother's hand might've shifted over hers.

His head snapped toward Elias, who put his hands up, enough disgust on his face to sicken a seasoned sailor.

"We're really just letting this go?" he muttered as Elias reluctantly shuffled toward the water, catching his friend by the elbow when he stumbled in the sand. Three times.

"Don't get me involved," Elias grumbled. "I'm keeping five feet between me and her at all times."

Kallias glanced back over his shoulder. "Are her eyebrows sparkling?"

Elias patted his jaw firmly, forcing him to turn back around. "I wouldn't make direct eye contact."

"Did you get more superstitious while I was…absent?"

"I'd call it *reasonably cautious.*"

His throat tightened. "Gods, I missed you."

Elias wrapped an arm around his shoulders, an awkward squeeze he might have laughed at if he wasn't worried it would hurt Elias's feelings. "Yeah," he mumbled gruffly. "You too."

Foam tickled Kallias's toes as he paused at the edge of the water.

He took a deep breath through his nose. Saltwater had a certain scent nothing could mimic; and though Arborian beaches borrowed a sinus-clearing sniff of evergreen needles and crushed bark and fresh growth trampled under trail-hardy boots, the sea always smelled the same.

Like home.

The muck of loamy sand glommed onto his feet as he waded in, trying to suck him in deeper every time he took a step. The chilly water lapped eagerly at his legs, bumping against his knees like a hound begging for scratches behind its ears, nibbling at his fingertips to search for treats.

He let his fingertips trail over the surface, only the pads of his fingers submerged.

No dangerous purr in his chest. No hair-raising current of energy. No frost lumped in his veins.

Good. He thumbed sea spray from his eyes, relishing the salted sting. *That's good.*

He hadn't been cold in so, so long. And when one of the waves reared back to soak his middle, an icy shock splashing up to his chest, a strange hunger clenched in his stomach.

His lungs hadn't forgotten what to do. When he summoned a breath, they expanded without complaint.

He dove headfirst into the ocean's embrace, arms open, ready for whatever it threw at him.

Compared to Atlas's crystalline sea, even Arborius's ocean fancied itself a forest; thick clumps of kelp warded off the massive boar-sharks that floated in the murky tides around the island, their mottled brown flesh the perfect camouflage in waters often clouded by dirt and forest debris and storm-stirred sand. The kelp forests provided a natural deterrent; they weren't fully effective, but they did the job well enough without venturing into less humane solutions. Arborians had a vested interest in protecting the wellbeing of wildlife…even when that wildlife made its home beyond the island's borders.

The kelp forests also gave him goosebumps in a bad way. The way it caressed his legs always felt like some slimy creature winding itself around him, testing whether it could make a piece of prey out of him.

Still. Better than a shark infestation.

"…And we didn't have the faintest idea who each other was, not even me and Elias," Soren was saying as he waded out, her back facing him. His parents both seemed engrossed in her tale; his father watched her with rapt attention, his mouth poised in an almost-smile, ready to chuckle when appropriate; his mother, however, seemed content with her intent frown. "Didn't even know each other's names."

"That must have been frightening," his father sympathized.

Soren shrugged her burn-scarred shoulder, rubbing it absently. "Not as frightening as thinking I was engaged to Everin Arden for almost an hour. Besides, it wasn't my first time forgetting, you know? It's funny looking back."

"No, your father's right," Elias interrupted, coming up behind her and wrapping his arms around her waist from behind. "It was awful. She called me names."

Soren gasped. "Could it be? Elias Loch? In the *ocean*?"

"Your cousin told me my horizons could use some expansion."

"I am *so* proud of you."

"Well, I can't take all the credit." Elias nuzzled into her temple, his voice lost in her hair; Kallias couldn't tell what he said, but Soren gripped him by his wrists and shoved him off, putting enough force into the blow that Elias yelped, flailing his arms like a seagull forgetting how to take flight as he tried to keep himself from falling on his ass in the water.

Kallias didn't have a chance to get a word out before his sister barreled into him, her arms locked around his waist, her sunburned face warm against his shoulder. He couldn't tell if the layer of damp between her skin and his came from tears or sea spray.

"Shut up," she sniffled.

"I didn't even say anything yet!"

"You were about to, I felt you breathe in."

Well, she wouldn't be feeling it again if she squeezed him any harder. But he couldn't bring himself to pry her loose. Instead, he gathered her closer and gave her the biggest hug of his gods-damned life.

Her fire-eaten shoulder shook under his hand; he tightened his hold there, forcing himself to map each ridge of scarring and the warmth buried underneath.

Healed. Warm. *Alive.*

"Elias?" Soren called, voice muffled in his shoulder. "Did you kick his ass for me?"

"Thoroughly," Elias assured her.

"Good. I'll skip it, then. I wasted all my spite on Finn for *his* stupid stunt."

"Like you're one to talk." Now he pried himself away, putting on his best big-brother scowl. It'd never done much for Finn, but maybe she'd be different. "What's this I hear about Everin Arden and a god-killer?"

Soren and Elias even didn't look at each other, but somehow, he could have sworn he saw a shared story settle in their golden eyes—another new development. A silent agreement on which details they were willing to share.

"Our little field trip is not even in the same sparring circle as you and Finn giving yourselves up to gods." Soren spun her ring around her fourth finger, the trapped sunlight sparkling in its facets nothing compared to the blazing ire in her eyes. Her scowl could've ended armies in one fell swoop. "And you'd better thank anything you're mad enough to pray to that I'm in a forgiving mood, because *gods* Kallias, I could just *kill* you for it!"

"Don't look at me," Elias said, flashing his palms when Kallias shot him a pleading look. "I fight beside her, first and always."

"No murdering each other on your aunt's shore," his father warned— tears dripped from his chin, but his smile said everything as he waded forward and tugged Kallias into another hug, thumping him on the back with one hand, cradling the back of his head with the other.

His eyes burned like he'd splashed them with saltwater. "Hi, Papa."

"My boy," was his father's only reply, a raspy prayer just broken enough to resurrect a memory he'd tried to murder in its sleep: the King of Atlas on his knees the first night after Soleil's funeral, brow bent against her headstone, singing a seaside lullaby to his sister's shallow, symbolic grave. "My boy."

His father kissed him on both cheeks, then turned him gently outward…and before he was ready, it had already happened.

Kallias and Adriata Atlas stood barely a foot apart, gazes locked, chins raised.

His neck ached to bend. His knees begged to touch the ground. But his back refused to bow.

"Whatever you have to say," he rasped, "say it. I'm ready."

He had borne her wrath for a thousand sins great and small. He could bear this too.

His mother's throat bobbed. Her chin rose another notch.

"Do not make me bury another child," his mother said, her iron glare ruined by the quaver in her voice, the tremble in her chin. "Do you hear me? I have endured…so much. I cannot endure that. Do not make me bury you."

All the righteous anger that had sustained him since he'd laid his title at her feet, slammed her office door behind him, and strode off to steal a spy from their drowning dungeon vanished with a blink of her damp eyes. The feeling in his knees followed when her next blink freed a tear.

He couldn't *stand* seeing his mother cry.

Her sob reached straight into his chest and strangled his heart, squeezing until bitterness suffocated. Until it ached like a broken bone with every beat. "I'm sorry. I'm so sorry, Mama—"

"Stop." She shielded her eyes as if staring into a beam of summer sun. "I will not hear an apology from you when the blame is entirely mine. *I* am sorry."

Sorry. The word came out in tatters, like she'd had to drag it out with her teeth, but…

He'd never heard his mother apologize. Not to anyone. *Never.*

She grabbed him by his wrists, tugging him closer; she held him by his face next, her palms damp and shriveled from soaking in the sea. But he couldn't have torn himself away if her hands were coated in acid.

"I am so sorry, love," his mother whispered. "I am so sorry I didn't hear you…I am so sorry I didn't *listen.*"

Not a single word came to mind. Not one that could capture the depth of what churned inside him, waters whipped into a whirlpool by his mother's *sorry.*

Instead, he hugged her again, laughing through tears as Soren and his father joined—and laughing harder when Soren tugged Elias in after them, ignoring his halfhearted protests.

But he didn't miss that Finn stayed on the sand, hand in hand with the goddess who'd dismantled his mind piece by piece...and that Raquel allowed herself to drift further and further away, allowing the sea to hold her the way he desperately longed to.

The way he didn't deserve to.

CHAPTER 71

RAQUEL

She waited until Kallias seemed fully distracted by keeping Elias from drowning before she struck out for shore.

"Coward," Finn called after her when she retrieved her towel and stormed past him; she flipped him off over her shoulder, but didn't dare slow down to engage properly.

The wind blasted sand at her back, scolding her for her rudeness as she trudged onto the path that led back to Elderwood proper. Twigs and rocks nipped her heels as she went, but she didn't slow, not even to put on her boots.

She knew how quickly Kallias could move through water and sand; if she didn't want to get caught, she had to hurry.

"Raquel!"

Gods damn it.

"Raquel, wait!" Branches broke, leaves rustled; the timid creatures who scurried from shadow to shadow fled for their lives as Kallias stumbled through the brush after her, swearing softly, shaking leaves out of his hair and swatting at invisible insects. "Gods, I forgot how much I hate the woods. Just—listen, if you're angry, fine. Be angry. If you never want to speak to me again, say so. But you have to at least *say so.*"

"Oh?" Fury buzzed over her bones; she didn't stop walking, afraid they'd catch fire. "Last I knew, you seemed to believe goodbyes were optional."

"That's not fair."

"You don't want to talk to me about what's not fair."

Kallias cursed again. "I know. I know, that was stupid, just—ow! Raquel, will you just *wait*, please?"

"Depends on what I'm waiting for." She stood her ground at the edge of the boardwalk, forcing him to stand just below her eyeline. "If you're going to tell me all the reasons you *had* to do what you did, I won't hear them."

"No, you won't." The defeat in his gaze wasn't gratifying. She almost shouted herself, almost told him to stop looking at her like a kicked hound—but that seemed hypocritical. And counterintuitive. "I'm sorry. I hate that I had to do that."

So did she. "I thought you were dead."

"I did too."

"You lied to me," she said, choking on a shard of her broken heart.

He folded both hands behind his neck, staring up at the sky. "I know."

"I love you."

The buzzing tension building in her chest burst; snow-bright light lashed the sky, thunder applauding her foolishness. Or bravery. No, foolishness.

A storm had rolled in with remarkable speed, blotting out the sun, silencing the birds. She could find no blue to give her hope, nothing but soot-limned hulks of pewter and charcoal, rain rumbling in their bellies.

Kallias's whole body hitched like that lightning had whipped across his back. His hands fell to his sides.

He stared.

Raquel Angelov was not easily frightened. But that silence, that uncomprehending stare…that terrified her.

She hadn't planned on saying it. Had planned against saying it, actually.

But the thing was, she *hadn't* said it—not when he'd needed it, not when it mattered. She had tried to reason with herself, to hammer it back into hate or at least *indifference*, to drive it out of the well-guarded trove in her haggard heart.

She had never been good at loving kindly—and Kallias, more than anything else, more than *anyone* else, deserved kindness.

But she loved like a drake defending its hoard. And gods, she was absolutely *ravenous* for him tonight.

Tonight and tomorrow and gods-knew how long after. As long as he'd let her keep him. As long as she could call him hers.

Only hers.

She had not held her silence out of anger. She had held it out of fear.

But fear would not serve her here. If Kallias sensed fear, he'd let her run.

She didn't want to run.

So she rolled her shoulders, forcing out fear, calling in courage the way she called stormclouds and cyclones.

I am the Eye of the Storm, the Riptide, the Skybreaker, she said. *I am going to war, and you are going with me.*

And with the fondest touch of wind against her cheek, courage answered her call.

"I love you," she said again, and it wasn't a confession that time. It was the sword she held to his heart. "But I will *not* do this again. I will not fight for you if you won't fight with me. I will not make you promises if you will not keep yours. I will not spend the rest of my life wondering if I'll wake up next to you or another gods-damned letter. I love you—now you need to decide if you're going to let me."

Perhaps a dusting of chronomancy had infected her power, too. She could have sworn time stood still for those few seconds or hours or years that she waited, watching an ocean of thought churn behind fathomless eyes, seaglass and stardust just enchanting enough to sway a soldier into sacrificing her death-claim on his soul.

A harsh swallow. His lips parted.

And the sky followed suit.

With a rip like rent fabric, the storm broke free. A torrent of pelting rain and wind that smelled of homesickness and thunder that shook the massive darkwoods to their very roots.

This storm was neither his nor hers. But it seemed like an answer, regardless...and not the answer she needed.

"You should go find your family," she said as she turned aside, jumping off the path and shouldering past him, clenching all her emotion into her jaw. If all that heat gathered in her bones, it couldn't find its way into her eye. *No more damned tears.*

Another rush of rain dumped itself over the forest, and she picked up her pace—then stopped when the wind blew a strand of hair away from her ear, whispering urgently beneath the bellowing storm.

Letting her know Kallias hadn't followed her.

When she turned around, she found him standing with his head tipped back, eyes closed, fingers splayed upward…catching the rain. Letting it soak his suit, his skin. Letting it wash away the tears she wouldn't have noticed if the wind hadn't tattled, swearing it could tell the difference between clouds and princes and the ways they wept.

"Kallias?"

"It's cold," he said, hoarse and brittle, cracked through like ancient porcelain pulled from a dust-coated shelf.

"Cold—?"

"The rain." When that porcelain met damp air, it crumbled to pieces—and he crumbled to his knees, hands still outstretched, gathering raindrops as if counting every precious tear shed by the sky. "Gods, I can actually *feel* it, I couldn't feel anything when he was…and when the magic started, too, everything stopped feeling cold, and I just…" He shook his head. Sobbed. Laughed. "I can feel it again."

Her throat burned. She had to swallow to say his name without sobbing, too. "Kallias."

He opened his eyes. Seaglass and stardust and a storm of grief. A smile fissured with a thousand fault lines, one blow away from breaking.

"I want to stay." He gripped his knees like he was trying to hold himself in his own skin. "Gods, I want to *stay*."

She dropped down next to him, knee to knee. Set her hands over his. Imagined spectral claws sinking in, refusing to let him go.

Mine.

She did not know if a certain storm god could still hear her prayers. But if he could, she hoped he knew it would be the last one she offered him—and one she would answer herself.

Not a plea from devotee to divine. A promise of retribution from a relentless riptide.

All that she touched, she would take. And if anyone reached for what she had not offered again…

Mine.

They would learn why no one braved the beaches when riptides claimed the current.

She rested her head against his, closing her eyes, breathing in wintermint and petrichor and sea salt. "So *stay*."

His lip trembled as he reached out, thumbing a drop of rain away from her cheek.

"I love you," Kallias said. "*Gods* do I love you."

Thunder rolled through her chest, a powerful peal of feral need. "Prove it."

Finally, *finally*, he gave her the smile she'd been waiting for—the eye-crinkling kind that cleaned years of sadness out of the creases. "As you order, Officer Angelov."

No. Not an order this time—a prayer of its own kind.

She needed proof not penned with parchment and pain. Proof that once upon a time, Raquel Angelov had been loved—and now that it had come back to her, it would never abandon her again.

And he did not let her down.

When he surged forward and kissed her, she anchored herself in him with a curl of fingers in his hair, ignoring how the ends bristled in unfamiliar ways against her fingertips. She traced her fingers from his nape to the curve of his shoulders, between his shoulder blades…reacquainting herself with the raised scars that spelled out his goodness, his sacrifice, in a language only they could read.

The scars they both bore on behalf of the other.

"Stay," she whispered when he let her up for air, holding him by the hair, eyes locked on his.

"I will."

"Swear it."

"I swear."

This time, she stole the proof herself. And neither of them particularly cared when the sky began to fall above their heads, unleashing droves of rain the likes of which hadn't been seen in Arborius in centuries.

The eye of the storm was the most peaceful place one could be, after all.

CHAPTER 72

FINN

Finn was trying very hard not to figure out what the remarkably fast onset of bad weather implied about how Kal and Raquel's conversation had gone.

At least the rain had given him a great excuse to escape the beach. He wasn't strictly against a sunbathe and a soak, but Arborian weather wasn't half as hospitable as Atlas's. Even dry and safe on the sand with his shirt still on, he'd been one strong breeze away from a shiver. Not his favorite swimming weather.

Now, taking shelter from the sudden storm in a bakery in the heart of Elderwood? *That* he could get behind.

Especially when that bakery was named *Knead to Know*.

One of the few structures in Elderwood *not* constructed within a tree—which already made them smarter than the majority of their peers—the bakery had not only surprised him with its brick-and-ivy walls, but with its size. Most bakeries he'd patronized in the past were shoved into a row of similarly squished-in shops, narrow and long on the inside like the building was sucking its breath in to fit into the gap.

Not *Knead to Know*. It had caught his attention in the first place because it proudly conquered the center of Elderwood's city square; moss-laden pavers circled it without challenge thirty feet around, allowing space for employees to roll out sample-laden vendor carts and tempt passersby with bite-sized portions of their wares. And if that didn't persuade the milling masses to change course, the sirenlike smells singing to them from the bakery's propped-open door would have done the job. Molten chocolate, sourdough, cinnamon, pastry sugar…and a powerful punch of peanut butter that had grabbed him by the lapels and dragged him in against his will.

Or at least, that was the story he and Cassi invented in case anyone caught an attitude about them going missing for a few hours. But between former gods fuming over losing their edge and flagrant royals flaunting new titles, everyone really had better things to be worrying about.

The truth was, the two of them had raced each other through that circle of samples—her clockwise, him counter—until they met up at the other side armed with two samples each, both having pled for an extra for their absent partner.

Unfortunately, the samples were divine. Delicious enough to make two lifelong scammers feel good, honest guilt for something as silly as stealing an extra bite.

Enough to make two pickpockets take coin from their own purses and—gods help them—*wait their turn* in line.

"It's really not that funny," Cassi sighed as she sat down on one of the plush jewel-toned armchairs playing barstool beside a low glass table, setting her mug of hot cocoa on one of the painted darkwood coasters. She kept her brown paper bag of goodies firmly clutched in her hand, the top folded over four times. Absolutely pickpocket-proof.

He could have stopped chuckling to pout about not being able to steal any of her sweets instead, but that would mean she'd won, and he couldn't have that. These little games of theirs were no less important now that they'd both forfeited their first. He slid onto the wooden bench across from her seat, setting his own cocoa down. It wouldn't taste as good coming out of a mug, but he'd make do. "Oh, come on. Give 'em some credit. It's a clever name."

"I could come up with five better puns right now."

Finn held up five fingers, waiting.

"Well, not *right* now." Cassi rolled her eyes, crossing her arms under her frilled shawl—a hand-knit thing in a shade of dusty blue that kept distracting him for some reason. "I need sugar first."

"I've never seen you in blue," he said.

She lit up like a brand-new birthday candle. "You noticed."

"I notice everything."

"Not everything." She held out her hand and popped her fingers out, revealing a marble-bright chocolate nestled in a corrugated wax wrapper. Brulee-brown. One of the dozen peanut butter truffle he'd purchased seconds ago.

He blinked, then opened his back and peeked in at the confectionary box inside. Untouched to the estimation of his naked eye.

He set the bag down and propped his chin on his hand, gazing at her the way he'd always wrinkled his nose at when his siblings did it. An open, sappy sort of staring that he was only now beginning to understand.

He wasn't searching for weaknesses or tells or traces of potential betrayal. He just liked looking at her.

Gross.

"I hate this," he mumbled.

"Oh, relax," she groaned, swinging out of her seat to join him on the bench instead, her hip bumping his. "I'll give it back."

"Not that." He pointed at his face. "Look what you've done to me."

She studied him for a moment, then stretched across the table, leaning in closer. And closer. And closer.

Only when their noses brushed did she say, "I give up. What am I looking at?"

"You *ruined* me," he complained. "I should be figuring out how to steal that candy back, not to mention plotting my revenge—which will be bloody and brutal, by the way—and instead I'm sitting here thinking about how pretty you look in blue. It's pathetic!"

A slow, nearly shy smile. "You think I'm pretty?"

"Don't change the subject." He was already distracted enough.

She clasped the rhinestone-capped button holding the shawl closed between her fingers. "I could take it off?"

Revealing the lemonade-sugar silk corset underneath. No sleeves. Acrobat arms on full, wanton display.

He hemmed. Hawed. "Ummm…maybe don't."

Gods, what a disaster. That was the longest *um* he'd ever uttered in his life.

The giggle fit didn't help, either. She abandoned her armchair and slid onto the bench beside him, kissing his cheek. "I think I might enjoy ruining you."

He flinched away, mock-gagging as he rubbed the kiss off. "Stop! You're making it worse!"

"Mm." She flicked a sprinkle of sugar-glaze off his mouth with her thumbnail. "You don't look ruined to me. Maybe a little tired."

Rude. He put on his best pout, letting his head loll back toward her; then promptly fumbled it when he came face-to-face with her double-dimpled smirk.

Who needed chronomancy when her smile stopped time all on its own?

"And by tired, you mean handsome, right?"

"Sure." She carded her fingers through his hair without a care, like she'd done it a thousand times. He surprised himself by leaning into her touch, letting her support his head while he yawned; she cupped his cheek, laughing. "What, is it past your bedtime?"

"Yes," he moaned. Ever since they'd split their magic down the middle, he'd started getting tired again. His body hadn't yet found the balance between wide awake and about to pass out.

"Poor thing." She patted his cheek. "Want to take these cocoas back to Astrid's?"

"I can't believe I'm saying this, but I'd like to avoid stealing from these artists if we can help it."

"You really like that pun."

"It's not often you see ordinary people come up with something clever. I try to honor it when I find it."

"We could bring the mugs back tomorrow."

Now *that* was an idea. "And get breakfast?"

"It would save me from watching you yawn for an hour. And…whatever you want to call this." She wrinkled her nose at the clamor in the middle of the room, where a cluster of rowdier clientele were dancing to the fiddle music being played in some other part of the bakery; while the main space was open to accommodate the serpentine line of people that never seemed to shorten, the building broke off into several other nooks and crannies for people to make themselves comfortable while they enjoyed their treats. Unfortunately, the one they'd chosen had turned into what appeared to be an attempt by a younger couple to teach their horde of friends some kind of line dance they'd learned on their honeymoon to Tallis. Lots of kicking and shuffling. Lots of potential for cups to get knocked over and shattered. Lots of obnoxious shouting and laughter at each other's expense. "This is atrocious."

"My thoughts exactly." He stole her other hand and kissed her fingertip before lacing his fingers through hers. "Should we show them how it's done?"

"Sure." She squinted at the lofted rafters. "Think we can get a tightrope up there?"

He'd do just about anything if it'd win him another second to bask in her smile. "I'll see what I can do."

One dimple disappeared; then the second. The opposite of what he'd wanted. She looked askance, her hand slipping from his cheek to rest over his heart instead. "They're acting like we won a war, not a battle."

"Yeah. I've heard victory's quite the high." Even if the victory didn't really belong to them. People would take any reason to act like fools.

"This isn't victory. It's *a* victory."

"I know."

"Tenebrae's not going to—"

"I know, Cass." He sat up, shaking off her hand; he set his to her cheek instead, and she breathed out through her nose, closing her eyes. Letting her wrinkled brow relax. "And so does everyone with any skin in this game. They're just taking a breath. We can all take a breath tonight, yeah?"

She nodded, opening her mouth…but nothing came out.

He frowned. "What? Do I have something on my face?"

Silence. She just stared at him—no, past him, through him—lips parted, pupils blown. Her fingers slackened, releasing their grip on his shirt.

She tipped back. Started to fall.

Terror broke every bone in his body, and he lunged, catching her by her shoulders; when she failed to rouse, bent bonelessly against his hands, he scooped her up as swiftly as he could, glancing once over his shoulder to make sure no one had seen before he drew her arm over his shoulders and pulled the hood of her shawl over her head, half-carrying her out. He put on a one-man show all the way down three hallways, hoping everyone would see only a couple exhausted by all the commotion, until he found a door toward the back of the building labeled *Employees Only.*

Signs only stopped people who believed paper and ink held some kind of authority. He pushed through the door into the small, sparsely furnished room beyond. Empty. *Good.*

"Cassi," he hissed as he stumbled inside, kicking the door shut, holding her closer to try and feel her breathing—gods, he couldn't feel if she was breathing. He hadn't checked her pulse. Why hadn't he checked her pulse? "Hey, you have to wake up, you can't just make fun of me for needing a nap and then beat me to—"

The power found him before the pain did.

It started like always: a flood of pink, a painful tension stretched across the front of his skull, a loss of all feeling everywhere else in his body. But this…

This was not his usual vision.

This pink was not rose petals and cotton candy and gemstones. This was a vivid pink, a *dark* pink, a pink that flushed darker, and darker, and brighter and brighter until—

Until it wasn't pink at all.

Until he swam headfirst through a sea of blood.

He surfaced with a hacking cough, spitting; the salt-and-metal taste made him want to vomit, but he shook it off, forcing himself to tread as he craned his neck, searching…

Oh, gods.

Blood. Bloody waves lapping at the sand; bloody clumps of sand scattered along the shore, some in the shape of footprints, some much larger, darker, the imprints sickeningly close to being body-shaped. But there were no bodies. Only blood.

The world spun, a zoetrope flung by a lazy caretaker who didn't care if the thing fell apart; when it steadied, red returned, so searingly bright it dizzied him nearly to death.

No sand, no sea—ice and snow and brick buildings, blood sliding down to wet the cobblestones, watering long-dead patches of grass under their shimmering white blanket.

Another nauseating spin.

A palace of crystal and glass and so many shades of red he couldn't name them all— a thousand facets of ruby and garnet and worse.

Three more shifts of scenery. A castle of stone. A fiery mountain and the city inside. And last of all…

An evergreen forest, its roots drinking greedily from the puddles of red that watered them.

"There is more than one way to sow chaos."

The song of a thousand blades pulled from their sheaths. The din of bodies covered in armor colliding with each other. He shoved his hands against his ears, but nothing helped—the clamor grew and grew until it roared, until it hurt, until his skull began to collapse on itself—

"My first vision showed me your death."

Bloody Atlas blue. Bloodless freckled skin. A mouth still parted, still painted in blood, still posed in the shape of its last words.

"How many graves does it take to bury a kingdom?"

"Only one, if you fill it wisely."

No. He clawed through the bloodied sand—or grass, or cobblestones, or glass, or stone—crawled on his hands and knees, reaching for that death-touched blue. Who—he had to see who—

"Finn, wake up!"

Not until he saw their face—not until he knew—

"Finn!"

A slap slammed into his cheekbone like a sucker punch, pain ringing from ear to ear; he flinched from it with a gasp, his lungs spasming like he'd been holding his breath for minutes on end.

Cassi hovered over him, brows ground together, lips thin—utterly grim. Her eyes glimmered, reflecting his own dread.

He sat up, getting his bearings—the bakery, a break room, no one around to catch them. "Did you see..."

She nodded. "I saw."

He swallowed. Wiped the sticky trail of blood from under his nose. Tried not to flinch at all the red. "Should we..."

They both looked toward the shut door together. Toward the muffled music of laughter, of stamping feet, of dancing people happy to make fools of themselves for the sake of fun.

Trying, just for one night, to pretend they had won something that mattered.

He scraped his teeth over his tongue, still tasting blood. His hands ached. The smell of iron turned his stomach.

"Tomorrow," Cassi whispered at last. "You...you're right. We all need to take a breath."

He took her hand. "Did you see who..."

She stayed fixed on his fingers, intent on wiping the blood from them. She wouldn't look him in the face.

He let the question die.

"Tomorrow," he agreed instead.

The darkness knew them, this thief and this fool—the spooks and shades they loved so much huddled in close, spreading protective wings over their two favorite tricksters. If anyone happened to look inside, they would see nothing but a pair of shadows joined by pickpocket hands and haunted gazes.

So perfectly mirrored, one couldn't tell where the thief ended and the fool began.

EPILOGUE

KALLIAS

It took three days for him to track down the traitor in their midst.

Well, *one of* the traitors in their midst. Depending on whose finger was doing the pointing, far more than one lurked in the dappled forest and sun-pocked paths of Elderwood.

But only one he cared to corner today. Only one whose actions had to be answered for face-to-face.

When he opened the door to the old card room he and his siblings and cousins had once taken over each time they made their biannual visit to this island, Vaughn Drakos-Atlas was seated on the chaise, elbows on knees, hands splayed before the fire.

He hadn't been sure if a summons sent by way of tree-palace page would be enough. But there his brother-in-law sat, fingers twined in a praying pose, foot tapping nervously against the rug Soren and Sparrow used to claim as their own after their older relations claimed the proper seats.

Gods, he looked…awful.

Kallias's heart sank as he took in Vaughn's countenance: his skin sapped of color, nearly gray; his black hair overgrown, badly in need of a cut; his gray eyes red-rimmed, soaked through with misery.

Misery that only deepened when he lifted his gaze and found Kallias in the doorway.

"Before you start," Vaughn said, "please, I need to tell you how…I do not have the *words* for—"

Kallias held up his hand. "Stop."

Vaughn's mouth snapped shut. He bowed his head like a man awaiting punishment. A man waiting for the whip to fall.

Old scars smarted across Kallias's back. He shrugged his shoulders until the sensation ceased, then slid into the seat across from Vaughn, covering his brother's folded hands with his own.

"I'm not here to hear your apologies," he said.

Vaughn closed his eyes, chin lowering, sorrowful acceptance washing over his face. "I under—"

"I'm here to ask you if you are willing to hear *mine*."

Vaughn's eyes flew open so quickly he almost expected them to pop out of socket, rolling across the table like the world's most macabre marbles. "I…I misheard you."

"You did not." Kallias held both his gaze and his hands as steadily as he could, despite the emotion making it nearly impossible to speak. "I should have pushed harder for answers from and for you. I knew things were off with Jericho, and I was too caught up in my own chaos—" poor choice of words, "—to get to the bottom of it. I take responsibility for that. But I have to know…gods, Vaughn, why didn't you *tell* me?"

Vaughn stared at him for one heartbeat. Two.

On the third, his head fell to their clasped hands, and he wept.

Gods, even his tears were cold.

"You owe me *nothing*," Vaughn rasped, his confession falling from his lips like crumbling temple stone. "Not kindness, not mercy—let alone an *apology*. I am the reason our people have suffered so long. I am the reason we lost Atlas. I am the reason Jericho…"

Jericho.

His heart strained for the door, afraid for his elder sibling in an entirely dissimilar way to how he feared for his younger ones.

One shattered soul at a time. He could not carry more than that.

"And I am the reason you have been forced to hold Tenebrae at bay alone all these months. I am the reason Finn's mind nearly melted out of his ears," which would have been an improvement, in Elias's opinion, a comment Kallias had dunked him underwater for, "and I am the reason Elias wears bruises in the shape of *my* fists. None of us are innocent in this."

"Actually, I didn't do a damned thing," Finn announced, appearing in the armchair like a ghost settling in for a night of fireside reading, a book already open in his hand. Kallias's bones tried to jump straight out of his legs, but Vaughn actually stopped weeping, coughing on his last sob until it came out as a chuckle instead. "Except saving pretty much everyone and looking unspeakably handsome while doing it."

"How do you *do* that?" Kallias demanded.

Finn smoothed a hand over the side of his head with a modest shrug. "A little saltwater spray, a serum I purchased from a perfectly ordinary and un-hag-like old woman about two hundred years back, a good tailoress—"

Kallias let go of Vaughn to mime out strangling his younger brother. Finn grabbed onto his own throat, mock-gagging and flailing one arm out as if trying to escape. "You know what I *mean*."

"I'd say you get used to it," Vaughn sighed, "but I've done enough lying for one lifetime."

Finn, never one to let a joke die prematurely, played it out until he slumped over the chair's arm, tongue out, effectively strangled; then, once Kallias had kicked him in the shin enough times, he finally revived with a squeaky gasp and one hand slapped over his chest. "I'm telling Mama you threatened violence against my person."

"Can you stay serious?" *And visible, preferably?* "I didn't invite you here to show off."

Finn's eyes widened in distress—just a little *too* wide to be earnest. "Was I showing off? I didn't mean to, but being better than everyone else just comes so naturally…"

He'd feared things were forever altered between them after what Finn had done to drag him back from the brink, that his brother might never joke or smile or fool around the same way again.

He should've known better, honestly. The ocean would evaporate to sand and shark bones before Finnick Atlas lost his ill-timed sense of humor.

"I brought you here because we need to have a gods-damned *talk*. Just us." Siblings to siblings, family to family. "Us before all."

Tension swept humor straight under the doorjamb, ushering it into the hallway. Finn and Vaughn traded side-eyed looks; Vaughn leaned in while Finn leaned back, both folding their arms. Waiting. Letting him say his piece.

Once, that would have scared him witless.

For so many years, he'd kept his tongue collared and leashed and caged, only allowed to step out of line when strong drink loosened its bonds. And when he'd set it free at last, he'd still feared it, fled from it, so certain he could not wield it properly he'd given it up to someone else. Someone better. Stronger.

Tempest had used the power he'd given away to hurt those he loved. And thanks to his fear, his shame, he had not been there to stop it.

He would *never* let it happen again.

"We all kept secrets. We all made mistakes. We all broke promises." He looked to Finn, then Vaughn, then folded his own hands on the table. "Including the one we made to each other. And it stops now."

Maybe if they'd all leaned on each other the way they'd needed, the way they'd promised, none of this would have gone the way it had.

"I couldn't agree more," said Soren, her head popping in right beside his.

Kallias swore, stopping short of slapping her like a gnat that had just landed in his ear. "*Gods,* Soren!"

"What? I knocked!"

"She didn't," said Elias, holding the door open for Raquel before letting it shut behind them. Even in the tranquil, sputtering candlelight from his aunt's desk, pearls of amber wax clinging to their crowns, the Godkiller glowed; a light that only shone so brightly in Soren's presence.

A new marriage, Soren had told him smugly just the day before, would do that to you.

Even so, Kallias couldn't imagine the feeling measured up to what coursed through his veins when Raquel took the seat beside him, hand sliding leisurely up his spine and coming to rest at the nape of his neck. Her charcoal-black hair, stripped entirely of its dye, wore the telltale frizz and fragrance that came after a seawater soak. A knit tunic hung loosely from her strong shoulders, softening her in a way he couldn't have imagined. A yarnspun garment dyed a rich, sea-blooded blue.

The color suited her entirely too well. Distractingly well. Devastatingly well.

"I *meant to* knock," Soren corrected herself.

"What is this?" Apprehension rewound the tension strung through Vaughn until his jaw flexed, looking wearier and warier as each new arrival made themselves at home at this table.

"It's an intervention." Soren stole the seat next to Finn and kicked her feet up on the table beside his, their heads tilting at nearly the same angle. "Not just for you, either, so don't go pulling any puppet strings. I have an offer I'd like to put on the table...for all of us."

"Again," Finn said, "I really didn't do—"

"If you finish that sentence," Raquel interrupted, idly teasing the hair at Kallias's nape like it wasn't on the verge of impairing his ability to finish a sentence himself, "I'll zap you so hard your hair will stand on end for a month."

Kallias closed his eyes, hauling in a deep breath like his life depended on it.

That color. That smell. That *touch*.

It suddenly occurred to him that he might be in danger.

"Let's hear it," he managed. Gods, even his tongue tingled with the metallic buzz of lightning.

"No more secrets." Soren's glare tapped Vaughn first, then Finn and Raquel. Then it swung to Kallias. "No more sacrifices. I need you to promise—I need *all of you* to promise." When she looked to Elias, her entire self shifting in his direction, that commanding countenance softened. "If we're in this, we're in this together...or not at all."

"Together," Elias agreed without hesitation. Onyx fire scorched into Kallias's soul as his friend leveled a look in his direction, waiting.

Vaughn shifted once more in his seat. Finn rolled one shoulder, tipping the opposite way of Soren now. Raquel's hand stilled, fingertips lingering in his hair, turning until he could meet her sighted eye.

With a start, he realized they were all looking at *him*.

No more secrets. No more sacrifices.

No more *shame*.

"Together," he promised, reaching back and taking Raquel's hand, guiding it over his head to rest in the center of the table.

Soren shared a look with Elias, then a smirk with Finn—then she set her hand on top of his and Raquel's. Elias's followed, their wedding bands clacking together. Elias had picked one out just yesterday, with Kallias's help—the Nyxian's way of making up for the two of them getting married while he'd been elsewhere.

He hadn't decided yet if he was going to forgive them for it. But yesterday had been a strong start.

"Switch," said Finn, looking at the pile of hands in marked distaste.

Soren blinked at him. "What?"

"You and Elias switch. I'm not holding his hand."

"You're not actually going to be that ridiculous."

"Switch or I'll go off and do this alone. I was doing just fine until you all—"

"You had a wall's worth of glass held over your head before Tempest and I got there," Raquel reminded him.

Kallias's turn to blink. "Wait, what?"

Finn shooed him off. "Nothing. Look, I'm happy to go back to what I was doing. I like my secrets, so…"

Soren groaned to the ceiling, but she snatched her hand out from under Elias's like a stage magician pulling a cloth out from under a full glass. The same trick he'd seen a thousand times at the cheap magic shows Finn begged to go watch at the lower city theater as a boy.

"There." She slapped her hand down on Elias's. "Better?"

"Much, thank you." Finn set his hand over hers, his smirk tightening into a grim smile. "Together."

Which left Vaughn. With whom all of this had begun. Thanks to whom they had a fighting chance at ending it.

His fingers flexed, curling over his bicep as he tightened the cross of his arms. As he stared at their joined hands, hooded gaze heavy with an exhaustion so profound Kallias's own bones ached with the weight of weariness.

"I know how it feels," he told his brother. "To have nothing left. To wish the fight could be over. All of us do." Soren was nodding when he leaned in, locking eyes with Vaughn, refusing to let him look away. Refusing to let him slip the way he had. "But you are not fighting alone anymore. And I still need my brothers fighting beside me…all of them."

Vaughn nodded, a slow, contemplative dip of his chin; and when he set his hand at the very top of the pile, he gazed back at Kallias with a fervor that made him almost, almost believe they were going to make it out of this alive.

"Together."

THE END

ACKNOWLEDGMENTS

Listen. I just released two books in a year, so if I keep these brief…forgive me. You all know the drill. If I forgot you, I still love you. My brain is a colander, my thoughts are the water, and obscure Disney references are the pasta. I don't pick what stays and what goes.

To Renee, who always answers "It's too bad I can't do this completely unhinged and/or evil and/or plot-ruining thing" with sensible statements like "WHY NOT?" and "DO IT RIGHT NOW." And "IF YOU DON'T DO IT, I'LL NEVER SPEAK TO YOU AGAIN." and various Palpatine/Kermit/Shia LaBeouf gifs. You can direct all Godkiller and Tightrope Scene complaints her way. Thanks for enabling me in my feral plot goblin ways, bestie. Let's pilot a Jaeger together sometime.

To my Indiana writing tribe: thanks for letting me crash the party. You remind me there are phases to both life and creativity, and it's important to honor whatever phase we're in, even if we wish it was different. (And to remember that phases are temporary, and change will come, and humans are wildly adaptable, and all the things nobody likes hearing when they're in a "I don't think I'll ever write again" phase.) You're awesome.

To the Intrepid 2025 crew: you put up with me at the most spite-driven point of my author career. Here's to smashing security tags off legally purchased sweatpants, Derry Girls, and hot girl PJs. (Also, if you're here, tell me which Muppets my characters would be + who would be the one human.)

To the Foster crew: you ALSO put up with me at the most spite-driven point of my author career. Thanks for welcoming me onto the team, putting up with my silly goose moments, and showing me what a community really looks like. (And also for the free coffee. That helped a lot.) Here's to another decade of the best coffee (and the best baristas) in Michigan.

To my family: you know what you did. You always show up, always go above and beyond, and always make the worst jokes at the best times. Sorry I keep writing ginormous books. The next one will probably not be shorter.

And lastly, thanks to my nephew, Callen Jay, who tried very hard to help proofread this book even though it is too heavy for him to lift. Also he can't read. DeeDee loves you too, Bug.

ABOUT THE AUTHOR

Cassidy Clarke is a proud Michigander, barista, and Hallmark movie expert who loves all things fantasy, from Disney movies to Dungeons & Dragons. Her debut series THE BLOOD AND WATER SAGA is a high fantasy love letter to the lost princess daydreams of her childhood and an attempt to put her experience growing up with three younger siblings (all of whom are cooler than her) to good use. She spends her days writing like she's running out of time, binging Critical Role campaigns, hoarding pretty dice like a dragon, and baking the world's best chocolate chip cookies.